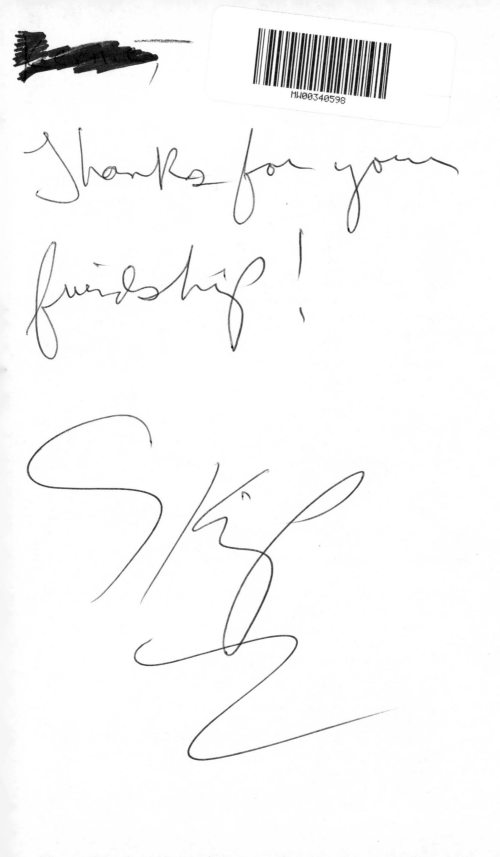

Thanks for your
friendship!

For Sara, my dear wife,
whom I love and fight for.

And to my children.

Writing *The God Virus* series has been a long journey for me. I began writing it in the year 2012 and it went pretty fast. I was a stay-at-home dad at the time, while my wife worked as an electrical engineer. The three kids were all 6 years old and younger, so I just let them play around me as I wrote. I began with the premise: "What would happen if there was a terrorist attack on the power grid and all the power went out across the world for ... a long, long time?"

Originally, I thought it would be just one book, but ... art and story, it seems, has a mind of its own. So I listened to the story, and it told me to write a second book. That book was *The Shadow Militia*, where Uncle Rodney came into his own and became a hero without equal. I think my favorite character in that story is Harold Steffens, the crop-dusting pilot who gave his life to save the town from being overrun by The Horde. I wrote *The Shadow Militia* in less than a year. This one just seemed to reveal itself to me very quickly. I hate it when stories make me wait. Most of this book I wrote while we lived in Hamilton, Michigan, and I used D's Cafe and the Allegan State Game Area as my office of choice.

Again, I listened to the story, and it told me to write a third book, and that gave rise to *The Saracen Tide*, which I wrote in 2014 and 2015. This one was tougher for me, because I thought I was going to end it at three books. Plus, how was Uncle Rodney going to stop an army of 30,000 jihadists? Frankly, I didn't know, so I had to wait for the story to tell me, and she took her sweet time. I think one of my favorite scenes in the entire series is Captain John Darkfoote sailing the SS Badger toward the Mackinaw Bridge. (And I love that Gordon Lightfoot song!)

I took some time off from *The God Virus* series after that and wrote a non-fiction book called *Civilian Combat: The Concealed Carry Book*. I needed time to think about how in the world Uncle Rodney could possibly defeat the Blind Man, who had him hopelessly outnumbered and outgunned. By then we'd moved back to my home town, and I did a large portion of the writing in Oak Hill cemetery in beautiful downtown Orangeville, Michigan. (It's just a bar, a few churches and a gas station.) I would sit in my car, surrounded by all my dead relatives and write in the peace and solitude of history. I found it very relaxing, but it took me two years to finish *The Blind Man's Rage*. In retrospect, I think I just didn't want to say good bye to all the characters I'd grown to know and love. I miss them even now as I write this introduction.

The first 100 pages came slow and hard, because I still didn't know how to defeat the Blind Man, but, after that, it was like drinking through a fire hose. I think I wrote the final 100 pages in two months time.

I wrote the epilogue grudgingly, hanging on to my friends as long as I could, but ... in the end, we all have to say good bye. So, it is with a sense of accomplishment, but also with an even deeper feeling of sadness and loss, that I bid Uncle Rodney and his family and all the rest of the shadow militia a fond farewell. I will return to you now and then just to say hello. This story has made my life richer, so I thank God for giving me this story and all the wonderful characters that I now call my friends.

Thank you for reading *The God Virus* series. Please don't forget to leave a positive comment on Amazon. It really does help. Okay, now I'm off to find another story. I can only hope that it will be as interesting and satisfying as Uncle Rodney, but ... let's face it ... there's only one Uncle Rodney!

Skip Coryell

The God Virus

Skip Coryell

CHAPTER I

S TEVEN MAXWELL WAS A CYBER TERRORISM SPECIALIST FOR the United States Department of Homeland Security. To put it plainly, he was a government geek. To be even more specific, he was assigned to the National Cyber Security Division. His job was to simulate attacks on the private sector power grid and then develop procedures for defending against any cyber weaknesses he discovered.

And Steven Maxwell was very good at his job.

Despite that, he had grown unhappy with his position and with his meager pay. If that had been his only complaint, he would have simply gone to the private sector and gotten a raise. But the roots of his discontent ran deeper, much, much deeper. And that's why he was sitting in a coffee shop, waiting for a man he'd never met, contemplating a terrorist act, the same kind he worked so patriotically to guard against every single day. He looked around him now. It was an open room, with tables all around him, and he felt hemmed in by people. It's not that he hated people. He liked them as everyone else did, on a case-by-case basis. The woman to his left was typing on a laptop. It was cheap hardware and Steven turned his nose up. She was cute though.

He looked back down at the walnut-veneered table top beneath his folded hands, sitting calmly beside his Blackberry. The question nagging him right now was this: Was he a traitor? Was he capable of selling out his country?

Steven pushed the self-indictment aside. No, he could never betray his nation. But still…he was here wasn't he? The man had left a message and Steven had responded. He hadn't said no. On the other hand, he hadn't said yes either. Besides, it wasn't all black and white. The country was already lost. The government deficit was closing in on thirty trillion dollars, and hyperinflation was beginning to set in. If the Chinese ever called in their loans, the game would be over. He mused about it for a second. And then there was the proposed government take-over of the internet. Not just regulation, but an actual iron-fisted, jack-booted cyber-shackled software tyranny. From what he'd been seeing around the office, the higher ups had been preparing for it for years, and now they were ready to erase the final vestige of American freedom. Maybe he was doing the country a favor by bringing down the house of cards now before the commies took the first shot. Yes, maybe he wasn't a traitor? Perhaps he was America's first cyber savior? Interesting thought. He had to admit that the hacker part of him would revel in laying low the powerful.

The blonde waitress walked over and placed a napkin down in front of him and then his glass of Mountain Dew on top. She was shapely, with a face that merited a second glance. He smiled weakly without looking up.

"Thank you."

The waitress walked away silently. Steven stared at her butt as it moved out across the room. He had always been polite. He looked down at the green liquid, watching the fizzy bubbles break free one at a time from the side of the glass and float quickly up to the surface beside the crushed ice. He smiled nervously. Yes, he'd always been polite ... not very confident though, especially with the ladies. He wondered why they never asked him out?

He ran his fingers through his greasy, long hair and took a sip of his Dew before glancing down nervously at the time on his Blackberry. The man was late. He put his drink back down on the table, and that's when he saw the writing on the already-dampening napkin in front of him. He picked it up. It was written in black ink, a barely-readable scribble of characters. He squinted his eyes to read it.

> "Go out the back door.
> Turn left down the alley
> Wait by the dumpster."

Steven looked up nervously, placing his palm over the napkin so no one could read it. He glanced around the café, wondering if they could see him right now. He was scared, but it was a thrilling fear, one that gave him chills and made him feel more alive than usual. He got up and pretended to walk to the restroom, but then he kept going down the dark hallway and out into the shadowed alley. The wooden door slammed shut behind him like a vault, and he cursed himself at his lack of stealth. The warm, muggy air hit his face and he breathed in the late summer humidity. His asthma didn't like it. He looked to his left and then to his right. No one was there, so he walked over to the dumpster, barely discernible ten yards away. He got the feeling someone was watching him, and he caught himself wondering if anyone was hiding inside the trash. He laughed nervously at his paranoia. That was silly. He was just going to talk to a gentleman about a business deal. It's not like they were spies or anything.

That's when he felt the barrel of the gun press against the back of his left ear. He froze, and all he could think was, *I knew it! He was hiding in the trash!*

"Don't move, Mr. Maxwell. I'd hate to blow your head off before we have a chance to hire you."

The man had a chilling voice, like Anthony Hopkins in *Silence of the Lambs*. The adrenalin surge hit him hard and unexpectedly, and that's when Steven felt the wetness run down his legs and soak into his socks. Right now he felt like more geek than spy. Finally he found his voice. It wavered when he spoke.

"Why the gun?"

The man laughed, but ignored his question.

"In ten seconds a van will pull up at the end of the alley. You and I will walk slowly over and get in the back. You will cooperate. You will not cry out. Do you understand?"

When Steven nodded, the gun barrel rubbed softly against the hair on his scalp. It almost tickled. He heard the van's engine before he saw it. The gun pushed him forward and Steven walked. A few seconds later he was pushed inside and the door slid shut. He didn't resist as a pillow case pulled down over his head. It seemed odd to him, but as the van sped away, all he could think was *I hope I don't get in trouble for not paying for my drink.*

"WE'VE BEEN WATCHING YOU CLOSELY, MR. MAXWELL."

The man paused but Steven didn't answer. He wasn't sure it was a question. Besides, on the ride over they'd already hit him twice for speaking, and he wasn't about to risk it again. In the past twenty minutes he'd been kidnapped at gunpoint, bagged, beaten, and now he was duct-taped to a chair. His first thought was *I've decided not to be the cyber savior of the world. I like my boring, government-geek job with low pay. In fact, I can't wait to get back to my small, cramped cubicle and churn out work that will be unappreciated by my boss and my peers.*

"I spoke to you, Mr. Maxwell and you didn't respond. That is very rude."

"Uh..." Steven hesitated, unsure what he could say to avoid another beating.

"Take the bag off his head so I can understand him, please."

The voice of this man was different than the Hannibal Lecter who'd abducted him. It was soft and measured, almost seductive in nature. He felt the bag being ripped off his face and the bright light hit him full in the eyes. He blinked several times until his pupils adjusted. The man across from him was sitting in the dark, just a shadowed form. Steven glanced up and the light overhead seemed to shine down on only him, blinding him, laying him bare, illuminating every shadow of his wrinkled soul.

"Now, Mr. Maxwell. Let's try this again, shall we? You would like to have a civil discussion with me, wouldn't you?"

Steven nodded his head up and down.

"I asked you a question, Mr. Maxwell, and if you don't answer me, then I'll take it as a rude gesture on your part."

Then Steven heard the Hannibal Lecter voice speak for the first time since the alley, this time in a hushed whisper.

"He nodded *yes*."

His inquisitor smiled.

"I can't hear your head rattle when you nod, Mr. Maxwell. I'm blind."

This time Steven found his voice.

"Oh, I'm sorry. I didn't know."

The man in the chair leaned forward as he spoke.

"Good, human compassion. I like that. No need to pity me though. I hate pity. It's only deserving of the weak, and I am anything but that."

He leaned back in his chair again before continuing.

"As I said before, Mr. Maxwell. We've been watching you closely, and we know that you are less than thrilled with your job, your boss, your pay, and, most importantly, the U.S. government."

The man paused.

"Mr. Maxwell, please be kind enough to wait for my pause, and then respond. Things will go much smoother if we have a conversational protocol. Do you agree?"

Steven started to nod his head, but caught himself.

"Yes, sir."

"Oh my! You are so polite! I like that."

"Thank you, sir."

"Now we're getting somewhere. You should respond now to my previous statement, Mr. Maxwell."

Steven thought for a moment, then spoke.

"Yes, all that's true. But how do you know all that?"

The man just smiled but ignored the question.

"We are here to help you, Mr. Maxwell. You've spent your whole life working hard and excelling at what you do, but no one has rewarded you. You graduated valedictorian of your high school then on to MIT where you graduated early, Magna Cum Laude. You spent ten years at Microsoft before being recruited by Homeland Security, and you've been there for six years without a single promotion."

The man paused.

"Steven?"

"Uh, yes sir. That is all correct."

"Good. You never married. You don't even date, although you do surf pornographic websites when your urges get too much to bear."

He paused. Steven lowered his head slightly.

"Yes sir."

"Nothing to be ashamed of, Mr. Maxwell, everyone looks at porn." He laughed out loud. "Well, not everyone. I'm blind, and braille just leaves way too much for the imagination, if you know what I mean."

He paused again.

"Yes sir."

"Now what I want to do, Mr. Maxwell, is to compensate you for the wrongs perpetrated against you by society. I'd like to place the sum of ten million dollars in a numbered Swiss account in your name. In return, all I need from you is a favor. A simple favor, really, only five minutes of your time. Are you interested, Mr. Maxwell? Shall I continue?"

Steven looked back up and thought for a moment. He remembered his boss at work, how he watched his every move, how he timed his breaks and lunch hours, how his peers laughed at him behind his back, and how the women never looked at him the way he looked at them. He weighed the morality of what he was certain they were going to ask him to do, because, in truth, he'd thought of it on his own many times. Getting back. Getting revenge. Getting rich. Bringing them all down to size. Then he spoke.

"Yes. Please go on."

The blind man smiled like a cat with a mouse between his paws.

"You have to understand that once I share this with you, that you must go through with it. If you don't, if you back out, if you turn on us, then my associates will visit you again, and they will do so with less subtlety than today. Understood?"

Steven nodded out of habit but quickly followed up with words.

"I understand."

"Good!" The blind man nodded to the person with Hannibal Lecter's voice, who then stepped forward into the light. Steven looked up and saw the black balaclava over his face, but cringed when he met the man's gaze. His eyes were cold, distant and hard. He never wanted to see this man again. Steven was reminded of the cold, wet urine on his pant legs which contrasted with the hot sweat on his brow and chest.

The man reached into his jacket pocket. He remembered the gun and Steven stiffened in fear. He pulled out a small memory stick and placed it in Steven's front, shirt pocket. The man's eyes smiled like ice, then he backed away and resumed his place beside the blind man who started talking again.

"On that memory device is a piece of software we'd like you to load into the proper computer system. We have chosen you because you have intimate knowledge of all power grid vulnerabilities. You know when, where and how to overcome all failsafes and defenses. Do you understand, Mr. Maxwell?"

Steven looked around nervously. "You want me to take down the grid."

For the first time, the man nodded before he spoke.

"Yes, Mr. Maxwell. Will you do that for us, please?"

Steven didn't need to think about it for too long. He hated the government. He hated his job. He hated his life. And here was a chance to change it. This was his shot at happiness. He could be important. On the flipside, he comprehended that if he refused, they would kill him right there in the dark room. His body would be dumped somewhere cold and lonely and perhaps it would be eaten by fish or crabs. He considered both options and chose piña coladas on the beach in a warm, sunny island over sleeping with the fishes. Not only was he polite, but he'd also graduated Magna Cum Laude. He was no dummy.

"Of course, sir. I wouldn't want to be rude."

The blind man laughed out loud.

"I like you, Mr. Maxwell. I like you a lot. My associates will see you get home safely now."

The man stood.

"Oh, this must be done tomorrow at 4PM Eastern Standard Time. Is that good for you?"

This time Steven smiled.

"Yes sir. Nice meeting you, sir."

The blind man laughed as Hannibal Lecter led him away into the darkness.

"He's a polite man, such a polite man."

CHAPTER 2

Menomonie, Wisconsin - September 7

D AN BRANCH RAISED THE BINOCULARS TO HIS EYES AND what he saw broke his heart. Oddly enough, it also made his blood boil. He loved his wife, and he was going to kill her with his bare hands.

He watched as she leaned across the table at the local Applebee's and kissed the other man full on the mouth. Dan ground his teeth but couldn't bring himself to pry the binoculars away from his eyes. In a fit of anger, the only question on his mind was "Which one of them do I torture first?"

Dan took a deep breath and lowered the binoculars. In his heart of hearts, he knew it would be foolish and wrong to do anything right now. He needed to calm down. He needed to get some distance. After all, this wasn't her first affair. Dan thought about that for a moment. *Affair*, it was such a harmless, such a benign word to affix to an act that almost always resulted in the destruction of a family, in the pain and loss of divorce, and in the heart-wrenching confusion that kids would feel for a lifetime. Instead of *affair*, maybe they should call it *treachery*. But somehow he just couldn't imagine his wife saying, "Hi honey. I'm having a *treachery* and I'm going to divorce you, break your heart and warp our children for life. You don't' mind do you?"

He reached down into the cup holder and picked up the mocha Frappuccino. He liked the glass bottle. It just seemed cool to him. He took a sip of his all-time-favorite drink, but the liquid had somehow lost its flavor.

Dan took the binoculars off from around his neck and laid them beside him on the seat of his old Ford, F-150 pickup truck. The body was rusted out, the frame was a bit bent, the windows sometimes rolled down but wouldn't go back up unless you pulled with one hand and rolled with another. But the radio worked very well.

A mighty sigh left Dan's tortured lips, and a tear rolled down his right cheek. He wiped it away, but another quickly took its place. He had to divorce her. He knew that. He had forgiven the first fling, but how could he let it go this time, assuming she even wanted to stay married to him, which he doubted. The woman had always confused him. She was so nice when she wasn't drinking too much and sleeping with other men.

It was 8 o'clock at night in early September with a heat wave hanging on like Velcro, so he had both windows open to keep the heat from killing him. The truck had an air conditioner, but it didn't work. He had married Debbie 6 years ago in a park just outside of town. It had been a beautiful wedding, but Debbie had gotten drunk at the reception and passed out on their way to the motel. The marriage had gone downhill from there.

He raised the binoculars up again and saw them holding hands atop the table. Suddenly, he felt very stupid and ashamed. She was making a fool of him for the whole town to see. Other people had to know. He could tell by the sympathetic looks they gave him at church and at work. He hated the pity. He put the binoculars down again and turned the ignition key. The truck turned over a few times and then clicked like the staccato of a machine gun.

"Darn it, you lousy piece of crap!"

He popped the hood latch, hopped out of his truck and slammed the door behind him in anger. The battery was old, and this would keep happening until he could afford to buy a new one. He opened the hood and looked down at the battery cables again. They were a little loose. Dan got a Crescent wrench from the toolbox in the truck bed and tightened them down. Just as he was finishing, he heard a voice behind him.

"Hey Dan. You need a hand?"

He turned around and saw Chris Flanders, his friend from work. He forced a smile onto his face. He didn't want Chris to know what he was doing here or that his wife was cheating on him.

"Hi Chris. Just have a loose cable. It should start up once I tighten it down. Just finished up."

Chris put his truck in park and shut off the engine. Dan's heart sank. *Great.*

"Well, I'll just stick around until I know everything's okay. What are friends for, right?"

Dan nodded. "Yeah, right. Thanks." He quickly hopped back into the cab and turned the ignition, but nothing happened. He slapped the steering wheel with his hand and then bounced his forehead off it for good measure.

"Ouch! Man that hurts!"

Outside he saw his friend shaking his head. Chris walked up to the open window. He was a big man, 28 years old, and always seemed too happy. Chris had that sympathetic look in his eyes, and Dan felt his stomach sink.

"Dan, I just came from inside the restaurant, and I saw Debbie in there sucking face with that no-good McKinley fella from Eau Claire." He reached through the window and placed his big, meaty hand on Dan's left shoulder and squeezed firmly. "You don't gotta take that crap from her. You need to do something, man!"

Dan looked up, and the tears were welling in his eyes again. But he shrugged his shoulders helplessly.

"What can I do, Chris? I'm at the end of my rope here."

Chris smiled. "That's his truck over there. The fancy, new, midnight blue four-wheel-drive with the custom flaming eagle paint job on the hood."

Dan turned his face to look at it. "Yeah, okay. So he's got a nice truck. So what."

Chris shook his head impatiently. "Give me a break, Dan. Don't you have any self respect at all?" He turned away as if controlling his frustration. Then a moment later he turned back again. "Okay, here's the deal. I'll show you what to do the first time, but after this you're on your own. Agreed?"

Dan cocked his head to one side but finally nodded his head. "Okay, I guess."

Chris smiled. "Just watch and learn, my friend." He reached in through Dan's window and picked up the 12-inch Crescent wrench off the dash and walked over to the truck of Debbie's lover.

Dan sat inside his beat-up truck and watched in awe as his friend began to abuse the man's shiny, brand, new truck. First, Chris worked over the front end, breaking the headlights and the turn signals. With his free hand he pulled out a jackknife and slit all four tires. Dan watched as the truck suddenly became about 8 inches shorter. Crack! The windshield was gone. Then as a final coup de grace, he scraped his knife several times across the flaming eagle on the hood. It sounded like fingernails on a chalkboard. The 3,000-dollar custom paint job was ruined.

Chris backed away and then nodded in satisfaction before walking back over to Dan. He reached in and set the wrench back on the dash.

"Ya see, Dan, none of what I just did will keep your wife from cheating on you, because she's a worthless, conniving bitch. But when people treat you like that and you do nothing, it leaves you damaged on the inside. You can't bury the anger. It's toxic man. Like a cancer it'll eat you alive." He paused as if forming his thoughts. "You have to dump her. It's the only way she'll respect you. And respect is a lot more important than love."

Chris turned to walk away, but then stopped and canted his head back toward him. "Stop by the house if you need to get drunk at a safe place. I'll buy the beer."

And then he got into his truck and drove away. Dan looked back over at the demolished truck and shuddered. All he could say was "Wow!".

DHS National Cyber Security Division - September 8
The next day Steven Maxwell glanced down into the lower-right-hand corner of his computer screen. The time was 3:52PM EST. He reached down into his jacket pocket and his fingers closed over the thumb drive. Thumb drives were restricted here at DHS, so he'd been forced to smuggle it in. In truth, he liked the fear, even though the risk was great. Late last night he'd looked at the contents of the drive. There was the promised piece of software, which he immediately tried to open. It was locked. Then he saw a README FILE which he opened. It came up in MS Wordpad. In big, black characters it said:

4PM EST
You know what to do.
We are watching you!

Steven looked up and scanned the other cubicles around him. Where are they? Can they really get inside here?

"Steven! Did you finish debugging that tracer module yet!"

Steven jumped forward in his seat, almost falling off onto the floor. He pulled his hand out of his pocket to catch himself from falling. As he did so, the thumb drive fell to the carpet. He quickly placed his foot over it, hoping his boss hadn't seen it.

"I asked you a question, Steven! Did you finish the module or not!"

Steven knew it wasn't really a question, but a command. He lowered his head into his best bottom-of-the-pecking-order fashion and nodded his head slowly. He was very careful not to make eye contact.

"Yes, sir. I was just getting ready to send it on to you for review."

His boss smiled triumphantly.

"Good! I need it by 4:30 so I can run a test on the full tracer tool. Make sure I get it by then."

Steven nodded meekly.

"Yes sir. I will."

His boss walked away. Steven watched him go and glanced back down at his computer clock. It read 3:57 PM. He looked around to make sure no one was watching.

Then he picked up a pen and clumsily dropped it to the floor. He slowly reached down to retrieve it and scooped up the thumb drive as well. The clock changed to 3:58PM.

He took the cap off the drive and inserted it into the USB port on his computer. He looked around again, trying not to look nervous. Of course, to anyone watching, he simply looked like a man who was nervous, but trying not to look nervous. The MS Explorer window came up and he looked at the two files. One said README. The other said THEGODVIRUS.EXE. The clock clicked over to 3:59PM.

What did the God Virus mean? What would it do? Would it bring down the whole power grid? If so, for how long? He'd been thinking about it half the night. He wanted so much to be able to explore the code. Apparently, the only way to find out was to double click.

A stubborn, cold sweat formed on his brow and he quickly wiped it away with his polyester shirt sleeve. He placed his right hand on his mouse and moved the pointer over the file. He hesitated, the small, black arrow poised like an electronic dagger, ready to stab. The digits on his computer clock rolled over to 4:00PM with a deafening crash. Time was up.

His right forefinger moved down and rested on the mouse button. He waited. He thought. He contemplated. He mused. But there was no answer. It was what it was, and the only way to find out was to...

Steven thought of his boss and double clicked.

Menomonie, Wisconsin

The next night Dan walked into his house and heard loud music coming from his 14-year-old step son's bedroom. He walked to the door and knocked politely, but there was no answer. He knocked again.

"Jeremy! Can you turn that down please?" There was still no answer, so he opened the door. On the bed, in a tangle of naked arms and legs was his step son with the 12-year-old neighbor girl in the height of adolescent ecstasy.

"Jeremy!"

The boy looked up and immediately became angry.

"Get out of my room! Now!"

Dan's jaw dropped open, and he backed out and closed the door. Inside the room, he could hear the squeaking of springs over the chorus of some really angry music. Normally he would walk away, but this time the image of Chris Flanders came to mind. He saw the Crescent wrench come down on first one headlight and then the other. He heard the knife scraping over the paint job, and a newfound resolution steeled itself inside him. He hesitated, took a deep breath and opened the door.

"Get outta my room, old man!"

Slowly and ever so calmly, Dan walked over to the corner of the messy room and picked up the ball bat. He smiled and looked Jeremy full in the eyes. The boy's face took on a confused look. Dan took a full swing at the stereo and the music suddenly stopped. Dan swung again and again and again.

"What are you doing to my stuff! Are you crazy?"

Dan looked up.

"Tonya, it's time for you to go home now."

The young girl clutched the blanket over herself as she picked up her clothes and hurriedly put them back on. The look of terror was ever so present, and Dan had a feeling she would never come back.

Jeremy stood up, totally naked. He was a big kid for fourteen, muscular, and broad-shouldered. He took a step toward Dan and raised his fists. Dan dropped the bat and punched his step-son in the face three times before the boy went down in a heap, clutching his hands over the blood.

Tonya skirted past him out the door.

"Have a nice day, Tonya. Tell your parents hello."

Then he looked down at Jeremy, naked and writhing on the floor. "I'm sorry, son, but you've had that one coming for a long time. Sorry to make you wait so long."

Jeremy pulled his hands away from his face and screamed as blood poured out his nose and mouth.

"I'm going to tell my mom, and she'll call the police! She'll take pictures of this and you're going to jail!"

Dan nodded resolutely.

"Yes, I suppose so. But the thing is, Jeremy. I really don't care what she does. I don't care if I go to prison for a few years, so long as I respect myself. But I do care if my step son is screwing the neighbor girl in my house, which is against the law by the way, so you'll be joining me in prison. I also care if my wife stays out all night with other men. I care if she yells at me. I care if a young boy disrespects me in my own home. I care about all those things. However, I no longer care what the police might do to me if you call them."

Dan crossed his arms over his massive chest and smiled.

"So, I suggest you get dressed and clean up your room. It's a pig sty in here."

Dan turned and closed the door behind him. He went to the kitchen, opened the refrigerator door and pulled out an ice-cold mocha Frappuccino. He tore away the cellophane, twisted off the cap and took a long swallow.

"Smooth!"

And the drink never tasted so sweet.

Arlington, Virginia

Steven was home now, lying in bed, waiting for something to happen. The blue, cotton sheet was pulled up tightly over his face, exposing only the red-streaked orbs he called eyes. His head pressed anxiously into the down-filled pillow until his neck muscles ached. The night was muggy and hot, and he had the air conditioner on full blast, but it still only brought the temperature down to 75 degrees. He needed to buy a new one. He just wanted this to be over.

Steven sat up in bed, swung his legs over the side and walked over to his computer desk. The only light in the room came from his computer screen. He pressed the "refresh" button, hoping to see new email. Nothing. He reached over and picked up his Blackberry. No text messages. No phone messages. Nothing! He was in the dark.

As he stood there, hovering nervously over the desk, his computer suddenly switched to battery power. Steven seemed confused by it. He knelt down and checked the power cord only to find everything in place. Then he picked up his Blackberry and tried to call his office phone. The phone was dead. A rush of adrenaline coursed through his bloodstream as he walked hurriedly over to the window. He looked out into the city and saw...only blackness.

Along with the adrenaline came uncontrollable anxiety. He got up. He sat down. He got up again, only to seat himself once more. Steven tried his computer, then his Blackberry. Nothing. Oddly, he felt a growing sense of accomplishment. He didn't know what he had done, nor the extent of it. Steven only knew that he'd done something. He'd affected the world and the people around him for the first time in his life. For a moment, he thought he felt something akin to pride. It was a new experience for him. But the feeling was short-lived. As Steven stood there in the dark, he heard a click at his door, then the slow creak as it opened.

In a final moment of enlightenment, he knew they had come for him. The sense of pride faded, and was replaced with terror as he watched the blacker-than-night shadow walk slowly toward him. Steven felt like a kid in his room at night who was having a nightmare. He knew the only way to end the terror was to move, but he was paralyzed into stasis.

Steven felt the black balaclava move toward him. He sensed the presence of the gun. His eyes saw the flash of light. Then another. And another. He stood there for a full 10 seconds, then, slowly, ever so slowly, his head filled with dizziness and he collapsed to the floor.

His last sensory experience was the feeling of the gun barrel pressed against his left eye. There was a final blast, a shock, and then total, ethereal darkness.

The man with Hannibal Lecter's voice smiled beneath the mask and then turned and walked away into the thousand-year night.

The White House

"Mr. President, sir."

President Bob Taylor looked up from the chair and grunted at his aide without speaking, all the while thinking *Why are you bothering me?*

"We have a situation, sir."

The President looked at him impatiently. Yes, and..."

The aide spoke with a nervous edge to his voice, afraid that delivering bad news of this magnitude might not be conducive to a long and happy career in politics.

"The country is under attack, sir."

"Excuse me?"

"Yes, sir, under cyber attack."

Bob Taylor was about to demand more details when the lights in the oval office flickered, died, and then came back on again as emergency power kicked in. A worried look came over his face.

"It's the power grid, sir. The Joint Chiefs and some of the cabinet are meeting you in the situation room in 15 minutes. It doesn't look good, sir."

The President thought for a moment, then braced his hands on the desk as he stood. The President was a tall man, handsome, and many thought, too young to be President, especially during a crisis. He walked around the desk and hurried out of the room with the aide following him. The two Secret Service men were waiting outside the door and escorted him down to the Situation Room.

BACK IN MENOMONIE, WISCONSIN, DAN BRANCH WAITED ON THE SOFA IN his underwear for the police to come and arrest him for a crime he hadn't committed. While it was true he hadn't destroyed his wife's boyfriend's truck, he had beaten up her son. He was pretty sure that was still a crime.

The remote control was in one hand and a mocha Frappuccino in the other. Dan was utterly convinced this would be his last Frappuccino for the next few years, as he was certain they didn't serve Frappuccino in prison. Despite that, there was a smile on his face, and he felt pretty darn good. He wondered to himself *Can I go to hell for thinking like this?* He stopped channel surfing at the local Fox News station and listened to the talking head.

"The blackout appeared to begin on the eastern seaboard and has slowly spread inland. Experts say it's still too soon to tell how far the power outage will spread and how long the power will be out on the East Coast."

The announcer was a beautiful blonde, the one that Dan had always enjoyed watching. He instantly forgot about his own troubles and was absorbed in the news of a major power outage.

"We go now to our Fox News affiliate WPGH in Pittsburgh to Professor Roy Percy. The professor is the foremost expert on power grid modeling and simulation."

Professor Percy showed up on the split screen. He wore a grey cardigan sweater and sported a bald head and black-rimmed glasses. Professor Percy was extremely overweight and had a very serious look on his face.

"Professor Percy, thanks for joining us today."

The professor nodded but said nothing.

"What can you tell us about the nature of this power outage that seems to be hitting the entire eastern seaboard?"

The professor shifted in his seat uncomfortably and pursed his lips tightly before speaking.

"This is widespread. It's serious. I would say that it's a matter of extreme national security."

The blonde reporter seemed confused by his statement.

"National security? This is a power grid problem. Isn't it?"

Professor Percy turned away from the camera for a second in order to form his thoughts.

"Yes, Eileen, it is a power grid problem. But the Capitol of our nation is without power, so the continuity of government is of major concern right now. We have no idea when the power will be restored, what caused the power loss, or even if it can be contained."

"So are you saying that this outage could actually spread to other parts of the United States?"

"Absolutely! For all we know this could be a cyber terrorist attack by another nation. The East Coast could be just the beginning of a very long, dark night for America."

The reporter hesitated and looked skeptical.

"Professor, assuming this was a terrorist attack, what country is capable of doing something like this?"

"The most likely candidate is China as we've long known they've been developing a cyber-attack scenario for several years now. Many times in the past two years the Department of Homeland Security has linked smaller cyber-forays into our power grid as originating from inside China. Kind of like a testing of their software and capabilities. They've been feeling us out, getting to know our weaknesses and vulnerabilities. I'm not the least bit surprised by this outage. Whether it's attributable to cyber terrorism or not, there are just way too many vulnerabilities in our power grid, and ..."

Suddenly, the professor's voice stopped in mid sentence and the split window turned blank. The blonde reporter seemed surprised and looked around the room for confirmation of what had happened. None came.

"I'm sorry folks, but we seem to have lost our connection with WPGH in Pittsburgh. We'll try to re-establish our connection. Stay tuned for more news when we come back."

The blonde reporter was replaced by a commercial featuring a singing, animated greensaver light bulb. Dan put the remote down on the coffee table and leaned forward. He thought to himself, *What in the world is going on?*

Just then his cell phone vibrated on the glass table top in front of him, making it move almost an inch with each pulsing vibration. His heart skipped a beat. Only one person sent him text messages, and that was Debbie, usually when she was going to be out all night, but didn't want to tell him with a phone call where he could ask questions. He picked up the cell phone and read the terse, unexpected message.

Alas Babylon!
Uncle Rodney

Dan's heart leaped into his throat. He hadn't spoken to his uncle in six months. More importantly, he knew the meaning of the message. It was a code that his uncle had set up with him long ago.

And it was not good.

CHAPTER 3

Menomonie, Wisconsin - September 9

I T WAS 2AM AS DAN PUSHED HIS OVERFLOWING CART TOwards the checkout lane at the local Wal*Mart. The store was usually empty at this late hour, but tonight things were different. The store had become packed within the last 10 minutes, with people frantically moving from aisle to aisle, loading up carts with food, flashlights, batteries and other supplies. Dan could see the fear in their eyes and feel the tension in the air. People had been watching the news about the power outages. They knew it was moving westward like an unstoppable wave and were stocking up just in case. Dan was suddenly happy that he'd come here so quickly. By morning the merchandise in this place was likely to be cleaned out.

As he moved to the checkout lane, he took one last look inside his cart. Among other things he had a case of Spam, two cases of pork and beans, ten 4-pound bags of rice, a camp stove, fuel, one hundred rounds of 12 gauge shotgun ammo (a mixture of buckshot, slugs, and field loads) fifty rounds of number 3 buckshot in four-ten gauge as well as fifty rounds of four-ten slugs, and one hundred rounds of nine millimeter pistol ammo. He also had an axe, a large Buck hunting knife, two sleeping bags, a machete, and last, but not least, one heavy duty truck battery.

The cashier's eyes looked tired as he rolled up to the checkout counter and began loading the supplies onto the conveyor belt. Right about now Dan was appreciative of his Uncle Rodney for keeping him fifteen minutes ahead of the shopping horde. He glanced discreetly over at the cashier, and she was staring at him out of the corner of her eyes as she worked quickly to scan each item. Dan shook his head from side to side as he unloaded the cart. His checking account was already overdrawn, and now he was about to compound the problem by maxing out his Visa card.

He thought to himself *Alas Babylon.*

The cryptic message still echoed in his head. Dan knew his old uncle was different than most people, but still … Uncle Rodney had never been one to panic. Dan groaned as he picked up the multi-fuel campstove. In a pinch it could also burn unleaded gasoline as well as the traditional Coleman fuel.

"Aren't you Debbie Branch's husband?"

The beeping scanner had suddenly stopped and the middle-aged cashier was looking over, trying to make eye contact with him. Dan avoided her gaze by continuing to load a large, blue poly tarp onto the belt.

"Ah, yeah, Debbie's my wife."

The lady nodded and started scanning again.

"Yep. I thought so. I cut her hair yesterday. I got a second job over at the "Clip Joint", but it's only part-time ya know. At least for now. As soon as business picks up there I can quit this midnight shift job and do hair full time."

Dan didn't say anything. He looked behind him at the crowds of people filling up their carts. They would be lining up behind him soon. He didn't want to encourage her, but despite his silence she just kept on talking.

"So what did you think of her new hair-do?"

Dan nearly dropped the bag of rice he was lifting. He hesitated a moment. The truth was she hadn't been home in three days, so he hadn't seen her hair close up, but he certainly didn't want to explain that to a total stranger.

"She was real excited about it, almost like a silly school girl going on a first date or something."

Dan shuddered at the cashier's words and blood raced to his cheeks. He thought to himself, *Yes, it was a date, but certainly not the first or the last.* He smiled before speaking.

"You did a great job. Best ever I think."

The cashier smiled. "Yeah! That's what she told me too! She said she wanted something sexy, something that would light up the bedroom when she pulled up the covers, if ya know what I mean." She winked at Dan, and he was hating the woman more than ever now. He picked up the twenty-four inch long machete and gazed at it before finally placing it on the belt.

"So what you gonna do with all this stuff? Goin' campin' er something?"

Dan's frustration mounted as he lifted a case of Spam and then a one-hundred round box of shotgun shells onto the belt. The cart was empty now, and he was about to say something rude when someone spoke behind him.

"Excuse me, sir."

Dan turned and looked at the Menomonie Police Officer who was standing in line behind him with a bottle of Mountain Dew. Dan redoubled his patience and forced a disarming smile.

"Yes, officer. Did you want to go ahead of me?"

The man looked into Dan's eyes as if trying to read his mind. The officer shook his head. "No, I was just wondering why someone would need all that ammunition. Hunting season's a ways off yet."

Dan continued to smile and didn't miss a beat with his reply. "Oh, yeah I suppose it does look unusual. But you see I'm leaving for Montana in a few weeks for a big hunting, fishing and camping trip. It's a once in a lifetime deal."

The officer almost smiled. "Yes, I go there every year with my two oldest sons. It's a good time."

Dan nodded and started to turn away.

"But that shotgun ammo you've got isn't the best choice. You might be better off with a high-powered rifle out there." He looked at Dan skeptically, but Dan didn't return his gaze.

"That'll be eight hundred sixty two dollars and seventy-three cents."

Dan turned around and pulled out his wallet. When he swiped the Visa card he prayed to himself, *Please, God, let the card clear just this once.* He had no idea what his wife had already charged with it. For all he knew she'd already sucked the credit cupboard bare. Dan waited a few seconds, but the cashier just stood there. The card reader screen in front of him seemed to be stuck on "Please Slide Card". Sweat beaded up on his forehead. The cashier reached over and held out her hand. "Let me see that card for a second."

Dan hesitated, looked over at the cop, then let her have the card. "What's wrong?"

The woman looked at the card, turned it over in her hand a few times, then smiled. "Yeah, just what I thought. The magnetic strip is all dirty and it's not reading it."

Dan relaxed a bit. "Can you punch the numbers in by hand?"

The woman laughed. "Men! You're all alike! I could punch in the numbers by hand, but then you'd still have this problem the next time you bought something! I got a better idea." She raised the card up to her mouth and slobbered out a gob of spit onto the magnetic strip. Dan grimaced and turned away. Then she used her shirt tail to scrub off the dirt. "There! Try it now!"

Dan reached out and reluctantly grabbed the card, being careful not to touch the magnetic strip as he swiped it through the reader.

"Waiting for Approval..."

"Waiting for Approval..."

"Waiting for Approval..."

Dan began sweating again as the police officer moved closer. Finally, the screen gave him mercy.

"APPROVED!"

The cashier laughed out loud.

"Man you were really sweating on that one weren't you."

Dan faked a smile, but inside his head he picked up the machete and hacked off her head, then laughed as it rolled around on the tile floor.

"Yes, you really had me going on that one."

Dan took his receipt, placed all the bags into the cart and nodded back to the police officer before walking away.

When he got to the parking lot he picked up his pace, hoping to get out of there before the cop made it out. After everything was loaded into the back of the pickup, he got in and drove away, leaving the obnoxious hairdresser and the nosy cop behind him.

Three blocks from the Wal*Mart Dan saw the police strobe light up the night behind him. He slammed his fist on the dash and cursed out loud before pulling over. He kept his hands on the steering wheel as the policeman walked up to the driver's side window.

"License, registration, proof of insurance please."

Dan looked over and recognized the cop from Wal*Mart. He was smiling. Dan reached back with his right hand to get his wallet, all the while noticing that the officer had his own right hand on the butt of his pistol. Dan moved slowly, but didn't say a word.

The officer looked down at the documents briefly.

"Please stay inside your vehicle. I'll run these and be right back."

Inside, Dan was fuming. *How could it get any worse?* His wife was screwing another man; his son was screwing the neighbor girl; but the only one screwing Dan was the Wal*Mart cop. To top it all off, his Uncle Rodney, the man who'd raised him after his father's death, had just told him to come on home, because the world was about to end. Immediately he winced. He knew better than to ask what more could go wrong. In Dan's world, it could always get worse.

Dan looked up and the police officer was standing outside the window again. It startled him and he jumped, all the while wondering, *How do they sneak up like that. It's like they take a class in sneakiness.*

"Mr. Branch, you don't mind if I take a look inside your truck, do you. I'm sure you have nothing to hide."

Immediately a red flag came up inside Dan's head. His Uncle Rodney had home schooled him, and he knew his rights.

"Actually, sir, I'm very tired, and I'd like to get home to bed."

The officer's jaw tightened, and Dan could tell he wasn't used to being refused.

"If you have nothing to hide, sir, then I see no reason why you wouldn't allow me to search your vehicle."

Dan sighed deeply. He knew this wasn't going to end well.

"Officer, with all due respect to your position and to you as an individual, you do not have permission to search my vehicle."

A determined look spread over the officer's face, and then he frowned.

"Keep your hands where I can see them and step out of the vehicle, sir."

Dan thought about asking him why, but he knew better. The best way to handle this was to comply with all his commands, even though his civil rights were being violated. Then he could file a complaint later on with the man's superiors.

"Of course, officer. I'll step out now."

Just then the entire city went dark. The only light came from the spotlight of the police cruiser behind him.

"What was that?"

Dan didn't answer the policeman. The officer glanced down at Dan and ordered him not to move. Dan kept his hands on the steering wheel in plain sight. The officer hesitated, then he reached up to his right shoulder and keyed his mike.

"Dispatch, this is Unit 17. "

There was nothing but static in response. He keyed the mike again.

"Dispatch, this is Unit 17. Is anyone there?"

Inside, Dan smiled. His Uncle Rodney had been right. There was a moment of indecision on the officer's part, then police sirens broke the silence further back inside the city limits.

Just then his microphone came back to life.

"Attention all units! Attention all units! We are now on auxiliary power. Return to base. I say again. Return to base immediately!"

The police officer threw Dan's driver's license and documents through the window and ran back to his cruiser. Dan listened as the tires squealed on the pavement and the siren started up.

A few seconds later, Dan was all alone on the side of the road. He let his hands drop off the steering wheel, and then he leaned his head out the window into the warm, humid, early September air. Looking up into the sky, he was awed at the sight of thousands of stars. He thought of his wife lying beside another man, and he knew he should be sad about it, maybe even crushed, but … right now, all he could think about were the stars. They were beautiful.

He reached down and turned the ignition, but all he heard in response was the staccato clicking of a dead battery. He let his head drop down onto the top of the steering wheel and laughed out loud. Dan reached down onto the floor on the passenger side and grabbed the Crescent wrench. Thank God he'd just bought a new battery with money he didn't have.

He stepped out of the car, looked up into the night sky and smiled. Yes, it could always get worse.

The White House - September 9

The situation room was buried deep beneath the White House. It was soundproof, bugproof, and electronically secure in every facet. The President sat at the head and each chair around the big table was already occupied. The meeting had been going on for fifteen minutes.

"So, Terrence, does the NSA agree with the FBI's assessment of the situation?"

The President leaned back in his big, leather chair to listen to the response. Irene Sebastion was a lean woman with ever-whitening hair. Five years ago, before taking this job, it had been jet black.

"Yes, Mr. President. We agree that this is an act of cyber terrorism. But we just don't know who is responsible. It could take weeks to figure that out."

President Taylor looked over to his Department of Energy. "Frank, how far is this likely to spread?"

The head of the Department of Energy was a bald man with a large, bulbous nose. He took out a handkerchief and blew before answering his Commander-In-Chief.

"I don't know, sir. I don't have a clue. This has never happened before."

The President looked displeased. He glanced over to his CIA Director, Anthony Hooker. "Tony?"

"Sir?"

"Who did this to us?"

He squirmed a bit in his chair but maintained eye contact with the president, which was no mean task at the moment.

"We're not sure, sir. But we do have a list of candidates. We're checking them out right now."

The President tried to maintain his patience, but it was failing.

"And the candidates are?"

"China is the most obvious choice, sir, with Russia close behind. We have a lot of other enemies, but none as sophisticated as the Chinese. It's possible that some of the richer oil-producing countries in the Mid-East could have purchased the technology, but not likely. My best bet is China."

The President moved his gaze over to his immediate right at the Director of Homeland Security.

"Eleanor, is there any chance this was domestic terror?"

Eleanor Freeland was in her mid-sixties with gray hair and a slender frame for her age. Her face was creviced with wrinkles and stress marks, and her piercing blue eyes lit up when the President talked to her.

"No, Mr. President."

"And how can you say that which such surety. You didn't even think about it."

She smiled dangerously.

"Because, Mr. President, in order for it to be domestic, it would had to have originated from inside my Cyber Security Division, and those people have been vetted with extreme prejudice. We run a very tight ship over there. I would say there's hardly any chance of this being an inside job. I agree with the FBI and the CIA. I think it's China."

The President threw up his hands in exasperation.

"What proof do we have? I can't attack China without proof? And if they are responsible and I don't do something, then they could follow up with a nuclear strike to finish us off while we're crippled."

The Commander of the Joint Chiefs thought this the right time to pipe in.

"Mr. President, if I may."

The President nodded curtly.

"Mr. President, we have time to think about this. The blackout is contained to the East Coast, and most of our nuclear assets are located either deep inside the heartland or out to sea in submarines. We can wait a while and still order a counterattack if need be. There's only one problem."

"Continue."

"What if it is the Chinese? What if the blackout spreads to our missile silos, to NORAD, to command and control all across the country. If it was the Chinese, I'd bet my money they're getting ready to follow up with a first strike as soon as the blackout reaches the plains states. And the first place they're going to hit, Mr. President, is right where we're sitting. Washington DC will be toast, and from a military standpoint, there's not a thing we can do to stop it."

For the first time in his presidency, Bob Taylor showed his fear. He didn't answer the Joint Chiefs. He didn't know what to say, and he certainly couldn't say what he was thinking at the moment. Namely, *I'm scared and I don't know what to do.*

Off to his left he heard whispering. He turned and saw Eleanor Freeland speaking with a short, unassuming man who sat behind her. The President waited a few seconds before interrupting.

"Okay, Eleanor, what's so secret you have to keep it from the President of the United States?"

Eleanor nodded to the man behind her then waved her hand to shut him up. He immediately silenced, and she turned back to face the table before speaking.

"It's nothing, Mr. President, just a suggestion that I believe is untenable and premature."

The President didn't like that answer.

"Hmm, well the problem I have, Eleanor, is that I seem to have zero options right now, so I'd really like to hear anything that might give me a handle on this thing."

He pointed to the man behind her.

"So who's your little friend who likes to whisper while I'm talking?"

Director Freeland tried to regain her composure before speaking.

"This is Sam Hollister, he's the Assistant Director of our Cyber Security Division."

The President interrupted her.

"Why isn't the Director here? Shouldn't he be?"

She nodded.

"Yes sir, but he's in Los Angeles on an inspection tour. Sam has been with the division since it began and is fully briefed on all the division's activity."

The President narrowed his eyes.

"Okay Sam, what do I need to know?"

Director Freeland started to speak, but the President cut her off with a wave of his hand.

"Let the man speak, Eleanor. I want the benefit of his opinion. Lord knows, no one else in here can give me anything else to work with."

Sam Hollister glanced at his boss and she answered him by lowering her head. He turned to face the President. His voice wavering as he spoke.

"Mr. President. I was just reminding Director Freeland about a counter-cyber-terrorism tool we've been developing over the past 3 years."

He hesitated, but the President prodded him on with a look.

"It's not a defensive tool, sir. It was developed to operate in a first-strike scenario."

Bob Taylor leaned back in his chair again,

"You're talking about the Ludlow Virus?"

Sam raised his eyebrows in surprise. The President smiled.

"Don't be shocked, Mr. Hollister, I am the President of the United States, and contrary to the mainstream press, I'm not a complete idiot. I read every report that crosses my desk, including ones written by you. So, tell me. How can this "tool" help us with our potential dilemma with the Chinese?"

Sam looked over at his boss again, but she looked away as if washing her hands of the whole affair. He sighed and plunged forward.

"Since the Ludlow Virus was designed as a first-strike option that is virtually untraceable, it allows us to attack without the recipient nation knowing exactly who is responsible."

The President interrupted him.

"How is that possible?"

Sam threw up his hands.

"Just look around you, Mr. President. We have been attacked and no one in this room, not the greatest minds in America, knows for sure where it came from. When delivered discreetly, no one need ever know it came from us. And it would shut down whatever country we send it to, just like this foreign virus is shutting us down."

Eleanor Freeland noticed the look in her President's eyes and she didn't like it. She'd seen it before and she knew that he was seriously contemplating use of the Ludlow Virus. She quickly spoke, trying to head him off from a hasty conclusion.

"Mr. President, I need to remind you that so far we've contained the power failure to the East Coast. If it stops there, we'd be sending a nation with 1.3 billion people back into the stone age. Many of them would die from disease and famine."

Just then, as if on cue, a Secret Service agent walked in and handed a note to the Secretary of the Department of Energy. All eyes moved to him as he unfolded the paper and read it silently. His face grew ashen. The President was the first to break the silence.

"Frank? Talk to me."

Frank looked up and spoke in a solemn voice.

"I'm sorry, Mr. President, but we've just lost all power east of the Mississippi River and south on down to the gulf. And it's still spreading."

President Taylor leaned forward with his elbows on the table. No one spoke. They just watched as he gazed ahead at nothing in something akin to a thousand-yard stare. Finally, Eleanor prodded him.

"Mr. President? Are you okay?"

He jumped as if startled. Then he looked over at Sam Hollister.

"Mr. Hollister. Tell me more about this Ludlow Virus. How does it work? How fast is it? How would we get it loaded? In layman's terms please."

Sam Hollister began to talk, but Eleanor Freeland couldn't hear him. She was too busy thinking about the severity of what they were contemplating. And then from somewhere deep in the recesses of her mind, she heard the voice of long-dead Jim Morrison. The DOORS song *The End* kept playing to her over and over and over.

This is the end Beautiful friend
This is the end My only friend,
the end of our elaborate plans,
The end of everything that stands,
the end

CHAPTER 4

Menomonie, Wisconsin - September 9, 4AM

DAN BRANCH SAT ALONE IN THE DARK EATING A LARGE BAG of Buffalo Ranch style Doritos and drinking Mountain Dew. He never mixed Frappuccino and Doritos. It just wasn't right. It had been two hours since his incident with the Wal*Mart cop. After changing the truck battery, it had started right up, and he'd driven straight home. Thankfully he'd already filled up his gas tank along with four other five-gallon cans. He knew that no one would be buying gas anytime soon now that there was no electricity to work the pumps. He'd listened to the news on a Minnesota station on the truck radio which confirmed that all power was out east of the Mississippi river, and no one knew the cause or when it would come back on.

In the back room he could hear his stepson snoring. Jeremy had left hours ago after their skirmish, but then returned while Dan had been at Wal*Mart. Dan assumed he was drunk and would be sleeping until morning. Just thinking about his stepson and their altercation made him sad. Over six years ago when they'd first met, Dan and Jeremy had gotten along well, very well, and Dan had found himself excited at the prospect of raising Jeremy as his own son. That had lasted until about two years ago when the boy had fallen into the wrong crowd and started up on drinking and drugs. Dan had never really thought of Jeremy as a stepson, and he felt pretty guilty right about now for punching him, even though he'd had it coming in a major way. In truth, Dan still loved the boy ... and his mother.

His thoughts returned now to his Uncle Rodney and the ciphered message. He knew his uncle was sincere, and that he wouldn't joke about a thing like this. And the fact that half the country was sitting in the dark right now supported the idea that this was indeed a true crisis. But ... *Alas Babylon*... Could it really be that bad?

From age twelve Dan had been raised by his uncle in northern Michigan after his father had died of cancer. Dan had never known his mother or any of her relatives. As a child he'd accepted that without question, but since then, he'd realized how odd that was. His mother had just up and left him. To this day, that very thought was a mood-altering experience for him.

As he sat alone in the dark, he thought to himself, *Am I being left again by the woman I love?* The answer rang back painful and obvious. *It's 4AM. Do you know where your wife is?*

On one occasion he'd asked his father about his mom, but only once. That was the only time he'd ever seen his father cry. He suspected that Uncle Rodney knew the inside story, but he'd never had the guts to bring it up after that. Besides, the past was the past, and he'd best leave it there. Nothing but pain in the wake of that ship.

He heard the creak of Jeremy's door as it opened. Dan waited a moment, then turned on the big flashlight sitting on his lap. The room lit up and Jeremy covered his eyes and turned his head away.

"What the hell are you doing? My head is killing me! Turn off the light!"

Dan left the light on, but did lower it away from Jeremy's face.

"You okay, son?"

Jeremy stopped and turned back toward him. Dan could see the black eye and the swollen face even in the dimness.

"Of course I'm not okay! My dad just beat the crap out of me, and my head is killing me!"

Dan sighed.

"Yeah, well, sorry about that, son. But you should know better than to come at me while I'm holding a ball bat. That was really stupid. I could have killed you with that bat."

Jeremy didn't say anything. He just stood there. Dan got up and moved over to the wall where he stood. He was surprised to hear whimpering.

"What's the matter?"

"Just leave me alone!"

He reached out and touched Jeremy's shoulder, but the boy pulled away and pressed himself up against the wall.

"Don't touch me!"

Dan nodded. "Yeah, okay, fine. I can understand that." He paused and then continued. "But I think we need to talk about something."

"I got nothing to say to you, old man!"

Dan smiled sympathetically and he shook his head, more in pity than anything else. "So you're admitting that you just got your butt kicked by an old man?"

Jeremy said nothing, so Dan continued.

"Listen, Jeremy, we've got some real problems here. This blackout isn't only here in Menomonie. I was listening on the news until the outage, and it's happening all over the country."

Dan waited a few seconds. Finally, Jeremy lowered his hands from his face and glanced over at his stepfather.

"You serious?"

"Yes, I'm afraid so."

"How could that even happen? I mean, it's never happened before, right?"

Dan nodded and placed his hand on Jeremy's shoulder again. This time the boy shrugged, but didn't move away. Dan's hand remained on the boy's shirt.

"Jeremy, this could be really bad."

His son looked back toward his room.

"I got some candles."

Dan sat on the couch again, and a few minutes later Jeremy returned with two lit candles. He set them on the coffee table and they cast eerie shadows all across the room. It reminded Dan of times when he was a kid when the power would go out in Michigan during a thunder storm. Back then it had been exciting. But not today. This was different.

"Do you think it was an EMP burst?"

Dan had been trained in the basics of NBC warfare years ago in the Marine Corps, so he knew a little about EMP, but he was surprised by Jeremy's question.

"How do you know about EMP? Do they teach that in school?"

Jeremy shook his head. "No, I saw a TV show about it called *Jericho*. It was about a nuclear missile going off over the United States, and it fried every circuit board in the country. Nothing worked anymore. Not Facebook, not Twitter, YouTube. Nothin'!"

Dan nodded his head. "That's the Compton effect."

Jeremy looked over at Dan.

"Yeah, how'd you know that?"

"I learned all about nuclear, biological and chemical warfare when I was in the Marine Corps."

Even in the dim light Dan could see Jeremy's facial expression change.

"Oh...yeah. I forgot you were a Marine." He paused. "No wonder I can't whip you."

Dan smiled involuntarily. Then he chuckled.

"Don't worry. Time is on your side. Soon you'll be kicking my butt every day and twice on Sundays."

Jeremy smiled as well.

"Don't try to be nice to me. I'm still mad at you. You beat me up pretty bad."

Dan shifted his butt on the couch so he was facing the boy straight away. He let out a long sigh.

"I was wrong to hit you. But I was mad, and you were way out of line. You've got no business taking advantage of that girl. It was immature selfishness on your part. What if you've gotten her pregnant?"

This time it was Jeremy's turn to laugh.

"She's not pregnant. I was wearing a rubber."

Dan narrowed his eyes. "Where did you get them?"

A stupid grin spread across Jeremy's face, causing him to wince out loud when it reached his battered cheek.

"I took them out of your sock drawer."

Dan shook his head from side to side.

"I hate to break this to you, sport, but those rubbers are five years old and full of holes."

Jeremy's smile began to fade.

"I don't believe you."

"You don't have to believe me. We'll just wait a few months and find out for ourselves. Are you ready to be a father, get a job, settle down?"

Jeremy didn't answer for almost a minute, and Dan decided to let him squirm for a while. He still loved the boy, but he needed a good scare for his own good.

"I guess I screwed up." He shook his head as he spoke. "I just really like sex. I didn't know it was going to be so nice."

Dan nodded. "Yeah, I know. But sex at the wrong time can really screw up your life, not to mention the girl you're with."

The boy moved his right hand up to his chin and held it there in thought.

"We can talk about that later, Jeremy, but right now we need to figure out what to do about the power."

Jeremy still didn't answer, so Dan kept talking.

"Can we call a truce right now until this crisis is over?"

Dan extended his right hand outward and held it there, waiting for the boy to take it. Jeremy hesitated, looked at it, then he thought about the darkness. He would never admit it, but he was deathly afraid of the dark. He reached out his hand and squeezed as hard as he could. Dan squeezed back, matching him pound for pound. In the end, Jeremy relaxed his grip and let his hand drop. It was all crimped together from the pissing match he'd just lost.

"Okay, but just until Mom gets back. Then all bets are off."

Dan smiled and offered him some Doritos.

THE NEXT DAY DAN WOKE UP AT 1PM TO THE SOUND OF GUNFIRE IN THE distance. He propped himself up in bed on one elbow and was immediately awake. He'd expected this to happen, but not so soon. If it had been only him, Dan would have loaded up and left town last night, but Jeremy had refused to leave without his mother. The sun was high in the sky and shining in on his face through the window. He looked over and saw the empty space beside him.

She hadn't come home last night ... again.

Dan thought about what that meant. *She slept with the man from Eau Claire and is probably nursing a hangover this morning.* His mind drifted back eight years to when they'd first met. Dan had been visiting the local Baptist Church and he'd seen the most gorgeous, slender blonde woman at the end of the pew where he was sitting. She'd looked back at him and smiled.

Three hours later Debbie had showed up at his door wearing a mini skirt, stiletto heels and black, fishnet stockings. Apparently she'd copied his name and address off the hospitality book they'd passed down the row. Everyone signed it, but Dan had never imagined signing the church book would result in the wildest time of his life. It had given him a whole, new outlook on church hospitality.

He had been twenty-six years old at the time, and was taking night classes from the local University. He was accepted into the Engineering Technology program, but never really got around to taking any actual engineering classes. Oddly enough, he was more interested in the humanities, and kept taking history and literature electives, making him wiser, but bringing him little closer to graduation. Prior to his college days he'd spent four years in the Marine Corps as a grunt. Now, at age thirty-four, he was at a dead-end factory job, with a shattered marriage, and the world was about to end, not with a bang, but a whimper.

One day, after 3 months of incredible bedroom passion, Debbie had announced she was pregnant. The next week he'd married her. Dan was old-fashioned at heart and known it was the right thing to do. He looked back on that now and shook his head in disgust. He'd also known the right thing to do was to wait for marriage to have sex, but that idea had gone out the window when she'd kicked off her stiletto heels and wrapped her long, slim legs around him.

In retrospect, any person who viewed church as a pick-up bar probably wasn't marrying material. Debbie had been twenty-one at the time and her son, Jeremy, had been six years old. Dan punched his pillow several times in frustration. *I was such an idiot!*

Just then he heard police sirens downtown, and looked up as Jeremy walked in his bedroom through the open door.

"Can you hear that? I just went over to Jason Mather's place and he said the college kids were looting downtown. The police are running out of places to put them."

Dan nodded his head. They were renting a small house on the Red Cedar River about a mile out of town. He knew that would buy them a little time, but he also knew that within a few days downtown Menomonie would be gutted, and the police would no longer be able to control all the hungry and terrified people. Once the population realized the lights weren't coming back on anytime soon, law of the jungle would take over, and the Golden Horde would spread out across the countryside. Thank God they were in northern Wisconsin and not closer to Chicago. His Uncle Rodney had taught him that The Golden Horde referred to the Mongolian conqueror, Batu, who had spread out across Russia during the thirteenth century. His Uncle had said that after the collapse, it would be an American horde that spread out across the land like locusts, consuming and destroying everything in their path. Dan knew their only hope of making it to Michigan was to stay ahead of the horde.

"We have to get out of here, Jeremy. In a few days Menomonie is going to be a war zone and we don't want to get caught up in it."

Jeremy glanced over at the empty half of Dan's bed. Dan lowered his head.

"She didn't come home last night did she."

Jeremy looked out the window.

"I guess I didn't expect her to, but...I was just hoping, ya know."

Dan nodded. "Yeah, I know. I've been hoping for a long time."

Jeremy's eyes misted over, and it was hard for Dan to believe this was the same kid he'd punched out just yesterday. He sat up in bed and swung his feet out onto the floor before finding his pants and pulling them on.

"We'll spend the rest of the afternoon packing up the truck and getting things we need, then slip out of town after dark. We'll take back roads all the way. They should be less dangerous than the interstate."

Jeremy plopped himself down on the chair beside the bed. He had a faraway look in his eyes.

"I'm staying here."

"Excuse me?"

Jeremy looked over at him.

"You know I can't leave mom here by herself."

Dan stood to his feet and zipped up his trousers. Then he slipped on his boots and began lacing them up.

"It's a mistake, Jeremy. She may never come home, and even if she does, she won't be here long. She's a wanderlust, son, and she's just not the settling-down kind."

"Then why did you marry her?"

Dan flinched as if stung by a bee.

"Because I was stupid. I thought with my Johnson instead of my brain."

"That must be old people talk, because I don't even know what that means."

Dan finished lacing his boots and walked over to the dresser. He pulled out a grey t-shirt and pulled it over his head.

"It means that the weakest part of a man is just below the waist."

Jeremy cocked his head to one side.

"You mean you were screwing my mom?"

Dan turned his head away in shame and embarrassment.

"Don't rub it in! I feel stupid enough as it is right now."

Jeremy looked down at the floor.

"So, let me guess, my mom faked a pregnancy, and you felt obligated to marry her. Am I right?"

Dan tucked his shirt in and put on a belt.

"Something like that."

Jeremy laughed softly.

" That's the oldest trick in the book. And you had the nerve to lecture me about Tonya."

"I'm running into town to check things out. When I get back I'll start packing up the truck. It would be nice to have your help if you're still here."

Dan walked out the door, and Jeremy called after him.

"Can you pick up some more milk? Everything in the frig is all warm."

Dan shook his head from side to side and muttered to himself. "Warm milk. That's the least of our worries."

CHAPTER 5

The City - September 9

MENOMONIE, WISCONSIN WAS FIRST SETTLED IN 1830 when James H. Lockwood and Joseph Rolette built a lumber mill near the confluence of Wilson Creek and the Red Cedar River. Over the years, Menomonie had been claimed by Spain, France, England, and the United States. The latter finally won out, and the city had now grown to a population of over

14,000 people. Up until twelve hours ago, for the most part, those 14,000 residents got along pretty well, but once the lights went out, about 6,000 of them went nuts!

When Dan turned right off river road on the outskirts of town, he knew he was going to have trouble. Black, billowing smoke rose up from the heart of town. There was a conspicuous absence of sirens that bothered him. He could hear plenty of screaming though, and then a few more gun shots. He wondered to himself, *How could it break down so quickly?*

Then off to his right he saw a police car with its strobe lights still blinking. There was an officer lying face down on the side of the road, and he wasn't moving. Dan's first instinct was to stop, and he did so. Before getting out of the car he looked around carefully. His nerves were tighter than a gnat's butt stretched over a barrel. When he walked up closer, he saw the dark liquid drying in the hot sun beside the cop's head. On closer inspection, Dan could see half the man's face had been blown away, probably by a shotgun. Flies buzzed around the officer's head, landing, then taking off, then landing once again, only to repeat the deadly dance over and over as heat radiated up off the black pavement. It was then he recognized the corpse of the Police Officer who'd pulled him over last night after shopping at Wal*Mart.

At that moment, Dan took back all the skepticism he'd ever given his Uncle Rodney. All the while Dan was growing up, he'd seen the way people had responded to his uncle's eccentricities. Some had even laughed behind his back, saying it was some kind of neurosis he'd picked up in Vietnam. He doubted they were laughing at him now. Before, he'd never taken the man seriously, but now, only twelve hours into a world without electricity, he suddenly believed. With the conviction of Noah, building an ark in the desert, he believed with all his heart.

Dan looked over at the police car. It was filled with bullet holes and steam rose up from the hood. Things were scattered out onto the pavement, and he knew it had been ransacked of anything valuable or dangerous. The cop's jacket was crumpled in a heap a few feet away, and Dan walked over to it. He picked it up and brought it back to the body, where he laid it over his mangled head. Dan read the man's name tag: Sergeant Jim Miller.

Yesterday Sergeant Miller would have called for back up and a SWAT team and 50 officers would have saved him. Today, it was a different world, and any person with a gun and enough savvy to stage an ambush could kill a cop with impunity. Dan realized that if the police weren't safe here, then neither was he. He'd seen enough. Dan jumped back into his truck and came to a decision. He fired up the truck and did an illegal U-turn … because everything was legal now. Without the rule of law, all things were legal to those who had the power.

"SOMEBODY KILLED A COP?"

Dan nodded his head without speaking. He was sitting in the living room on the couch with his head down almost between his knees, trying to get over what he'd just seen. Jeremy sat across from him in the recliner, leaning forward, trying to get his father to talk about it. He would never admit it, but his young heart was excited by all that had happened, even though he knew it was wrong to think so.

"How did it happen?"

Dan shook his head back and forth. "I don't know. It just did, okay, and I don't want to talk about it anymore." He got up slowly. "We should be packing our stuff and loading up the truck right now, because we're leaving by day's end."

Jeremy popped up beside him. "But my mom! What about her? We can't leave my mom here by herself!"

Dan turned on him with more vehemence than he knew was in him. "She's not alone, Jeremy, remember? She's with another man, and she may or may not be back." Dan took his head in both hands and squeezed his temples in an attempt to make the throbbing go away. Jeremy grabbed his wrist.

"Please, Dad. Please. She's my mom. I know she's been bad to you, but … I still love her."

Dan stared out over Jeremy's head into the blue painted wall behind him. His body was in the room, but his mind was somewhere else. "I can't, Jeremy. Even if I wanted to get her, I have no idea where this guy lives in Eau Claire. We'd never find her."

Jeremy let Dan's wrist drop. "I know where she is, Dad. I can take you there."

Adrenaline surged into Dan's blood, and his muscles tightened up like knotted rope. "How? How could you know where he lives?"

Jeremy looked down at the floor and spoke to the dirty, yellow, shag carpet in a hushed voice. "I've been there before, several times."

Dan tightened his jaw. "So you knew all along about her affair?"

"The whole town knew, Dad! Mom's been cheating on you for years. How could you not know that?"

In his heart, Dan had known all along, but it's one thing to know, and quite another to accept what you know. "It's too dangerous in Eau Claire. If people are berserk in Menomonie, can you imagine how crazy things are in a bigger city? We have to assume the worst."

Dan started to walk away, but Jeremy's next words stopped him cold. "He lives four miles outside of town in the country. We can take back roads all the way, and we should be safe."

Dan turned around and stared back at his son, but Jeremy wouldn't make eye contact.

"Please, Dad, just try and if she won't come or we can't find her, then I'll go to Michigan with you."

Dan heaved out a sigh and rubbed his eyes with his left hand. Suddenly he felt very alone … and very betrayed. He looked back up and choked back his emotions.

"All right, son. Let's load up the truck first. Then we'll get going, but if we can't find her, then we head north to the upper peninsula."

His son nodded, and without saying another word they both went off to pack.

It took them six hours to get everything loaded up. Dan drained the hot water heater in order to fill up all the plastic bottles he could find, then he drained the gas out of the old Buick that had been sitting in the front yard for over a year. Before loading everything into the truck bed, they lifted the cap onto the back and bolted it securely in place.

As the sun was getting low in the sky, Dan made his final check around the house.

He walked back to the bedroom and looked at the bed where he'd slept with Debbie. The covers were all messed up, and he didn't bother to fix them. Dan knew if he drug this out he would cry in front of his son, so he slowly backed his way out of the room. He closed and locked all the windows, and turned off the main breaker switch just in case power came back on while they were gone.

As he walked out of the kitchen, the Bible on the counter caught his eye. He stopped and reached down to stroke its leather. He thought, *Why not?* and picked it up on the way out. It couldn't hurt to take God along on the trip.

Once inside the truck, he fired up the engine and didn't look back. Jeremy glanced down at the large pistol on Dan's waist. "You're not going to shoot anyone are you?"

Dan didn't answer. He just gripped the steering wheel as hard as he could and took the back way out of town. He was painfully aware this was a new world with new rules. The old law said "No Guns Allowed", but the new law said, "No Guns - No Survival!" And Dan chose to survive.

As Dan drove through the back roads of Dunn County, he did so with reservations. On the one hand, he knew that if he left his wife here in Wisconsin, he would always feel guilty about it, would always wonder what happened to her and if one more try might have made the difference. Despite the fact she was with another man, and had, in effect, already broken their marriage vows many times before, he still felt conflicted. On the other hand, he had no desire to see her with this man again. It had killed him in the Applebee's parking lot to see them kissing. A big part of him wanted to drive north and forget he'd ever seen her, to leave her cheating heart and all the chaos that followed her behind him forever. Nonetheless, he did still love her. Love was a funny thing. He loved her and wanted to kill her simultaneously. He wondered if that was normal.

"So why did you grab that Bible?"

Dan was snapped out of his thoughts. He didn't want to talk right now.

"I don't know. I saw it on the counter and something just came over me all of a sudden and I wanted it with us on this trip. Like maybe if we had it that God might help us out a little bit."

His son shook his head back and forth and laughed out loud. His response annoyed Dan.

"What's wrong? Why is that so funny?"

Jeremy looked down at the Bible on the seat between them. "I don't know. It just seems funny that you packed up six guns and a thousand rounds of ammo, but decided at the last minute to bring a Bible."

Dan grunted out loud. "Nothing odd about that. Christians need guns to protect themselves from bad people just like the atheists do I suppose."

Jeremy turned his head and hung his right arm out the window as they passed a field of corn that was over seven feet high and beginning to yellow. There was a distinct smell of cow manure in the air.

"Are you going to shoot Pete when you see him?"

"The man's name is Pete? I didn't know that?"

"Yeah, his name's Pete. He's a tool and die maker."

Dan glanced over for a second, then quickly back to the road. "Is he a nice guy?"

His son turned his head, and the shiner on his eye showed up pretty good in the fading sunlight. "Well, he's pretty nice. At least he hasn't beat me up yet."

Dan forced a playful smile on his lips. "Well, he doesn't know you yet. Give it some time."

"That's not funny, Dad!"

He laughed nonetheless. "Yeah, I know. Sometimes I make light of things to keep from crying."

Jeremy brought his arm back inside the window. "You cry sometimes? I didn't think old people did that."

"Stop calling me old! I'm only 34. And yes, I've been crying a lot lately. Seeing the woman you love with another man will do that to you."

Jeremy shrugged. "I suppose. I don't really know much about love. It seems over-rated from what I've seen between you and mom."

Dan was quiet for the rest of the drive. Ten minutes later Jeremy pointed at a gravel driveway. "Turn left here." Dan pulled in, drove about 50 yards before coming to a stop on the grass. A run-down, double-wide trailer was off to their right. "There's mom's car. I don't see Pete's truck."

Dan answered with a grimace. "It's probably in the auto-body shop."

"Why would it be in the shop?"

But Dan ignored him.

"Maybe you should stay out here, Dad. They might not like seeing you, and I think mom might act better if it's just me."

Dan nodded but said nothing. He was completely happy staying out in the truck. The last thing he needed was to see the two of them together again. Jeremy got out and slammed the truck door. He walked a few steps then turned back.

"Don't come in with that gun, okay. I don't want you shooting anyone."

Dan nodded. "Be careful, son. If she doesn't want to come, just back on out and we'll get out of here."

Jeremy walked away without looking back. When he reached the porch, he opened the door and walked in as if he'd been living there for years. Dan thought to himself, *Yeah, Pete must be a real nice guy. All adulterers are like that. Real sweethearts!* Dan sighed out loud, as if every cubic inch of air was leaving him in one mighty gasp. He looked down at the Bible on the seat. He touched it with the fingers of his right hand. Then his hand brushed against the holstered pistol on his right hip. It was a Taurus Judge, a five-shot revolver chambered in four-ten shotgun shells or 45 long Colt. It was large and bulky, but packed quite a punch at close range. The first three chambers he had loaded with number three buckshot. The last two were slugs. Jeremy was right; it did look odd to him, the huge gun on his hip only inches away from the word of God. Bibles and bullets. He wondered, *Was he a hypocrite?* Then he laughed to himself. Of course he was a hypocrite. Wasn't everyone?

"BOOM!"

The gunshot rang out, breaking the silence of the sunset behind him. Then he heard screams. Without thinking he jumped out of the truck and ran toward the house. When he reached the trailer door, he was surprised to see the big pistol already in his right hand. He hesitated, more screams, then he threw open the door and jumped inside not knowing what to expect. The living room was empty; it was a pig sty with pizza boxes and beer cans all over the floor. "BOOM!" Part of the wall to his left exploded, showering his face with powdered dry wall. It came from the next room over.

"Mom! No! Please!"

Dan moved to the doorway. He had the gun tight in both hands out in front of him and peeked carefully around the corner. He saw Debbie swing the gun over in his direction. "BOOM!" He jumped back just in time, but dry wall and wood splinters smashed against the left side of his face, blinding him for several seconds. He worked quickly to wipe the blood and dust from his eyes. He could hear Jeremy pleading with her.

"Mom, please. We're going to Michigan where it's safe. We want to take you with us. We still love you mom!"

"Shut up you little puke! I don't want to hear it from you! Now get out of here before I shoot you both."

Dan crawled slowly back over to the door. He had seen her up on the bed. Pete was lying next to her with his eyes closed. By the color of his skin, Dan was sure he'd been dead for quite a while. His son and his wife were both crying inside the room.

"Why did you bring him here! I didn't want him to see me like this! Now he won't love me anymore!"

Dan wasn't sure she was talking to him or to Jeremy. She always talked crazy like this when she was drunk, but she'd never used guns before. She didn't even like them.

"Don't shoot me momma!"

"I want you outta here, boy! You just go back home and wait for me there."

Dan peeked around the corner and saw Jeremy nodding his head. Tears were running down his cheeks and his blonde hair was covered in dry wall dust. A huge, gaping hole was above him, letting in light from the outside. Dan thought quickly. If he rushed her, she'd shoot him for sure. If he did nothing, she might shoot Jeremy. She was crazy when she was drunk. A thought came to him quickly, *Had she killed Pete?*

"I'll leave momma. Okay? Just don't shoot me. I'll go home and wait for you."

Debbie lowered the shotgun.

"Yeah, and don't forget to feed the cat."

"We don't have a cat, Momma."

The gun came back up.

"Don't argue with me, son! Now get home and feed the cat! And cook me up one of those TV dinners with macaroni and cheese and fried chicken. The dark meat, not the white!"

He watched as Jeremy got up slowly and walked toward the door. The gun followed him as he went.

"Okay. Bye Momma. See you when you get home. Don't be late."

Jeremy reached the door and walked past Dan, who was already crawling backwards. Once outside, they walked back to the truck. He held his son as he heaved sob after sob upon his father's shoulder.

"She was gonna kill me, daddy!"

Dan stroked the back of his head. "Shhh, hush now. It's going to be okay." Jeremy hadn't called him daddy in years. "We're just going to wait out here until she passes out, then we'll sneak back in and carry her out. Okay?"

Jeremy nodded with his face pressed tightly against his father's muscular shoulder. For the longest time neither man moved. They just stood there hugging each other in the fading sunlight, waiting for the drunkard to sleep it off.

Two hours later, Dan walked back into the house alone. Five minutes later he came out carrying his wife's body. She was already dead.

CHAPTER 6

The Exodus - September 9

DAN DROVE NORTH THROUGH COLFAX, HOPPED ON COUNTY Road M to Sandy Creek, then cut over to New Auburn. From there he took 40 up to Island Lake and then Ladysmith. He figured so long as he stayed off the big highways, they would be okay. Actually, Dan was quite versed at getting out of Dodge in time of crisis. After all, he'd been raised by a Vietnam vet and a hard-core prepper. To be truthful, he hadn't heard the term "prepper" until a few years back. A prepper was someone who prepared religiously for a breakdown in society where food would be in short supply, police and emergency services would be nonexistent, and the law of the jungle reigned supreme. For the past ten years, hardly a month had gone by when he hadn't received something in the mail from his Uncle Rodney. Once it was a book called *How to Survive the End of the World as we Know it*"; another time it was a DVD on home canning and food dehydrating; once he'd even received a small bag of junk silver coins. At the time, he hadn't known what junk silver was. Apparently the U.S. government used to make coins out of ninety percent silver, but ceased doing that in 1965.

Dan glanced down at Jeremy who had finally cried himself to sleep, and then down to the Taurus four-ten gauge revolver on his right hip. He remembered the day Uncle Rodney had mailed him the gun. Debbie had opened the box and freaked out upon seeing it. She hated guns and had given him a ton of grief for it. It wasn't just that the gun was unregistered or that it was illegal to send it through the mail, but his Uncle Rodney had shipped it fully loaded. The next day Dan had called to scold him for his foolishness, but his Uncle, the king of overkill, had laughed at his concerns and simply said, "Now why in the world, son, would I mail you an unloaded gun? It's no good without the bullets! And the last thing I'm gonna do is register it, because then the government will know I have it! Think, boy, think! I don't need any ATF thugs sniffing around my door!"

That was his Uncle Rodney in a nutshell, no pun intended.

Everytime Dan went through a small town, he kept a very watchful eye and didn't stop or slow down. Most of the people in rural northern Wisconsin were different than in Menomonie. They probably knew what was going on in a general way, but were less effected by it. Northern country folk were more independent and less prone to over-reacting. But Dan knew that in a few days, these small towns would be visited by refugees from St. Paul and from Milwaukee, maybe even Chicago, and unless the people got organized, they would be picked clean like vultures on roadkill. The thought just occurred to him that his Uncle Rodney would be having the same problem with refugees fleeing Grand Rapids and Detroit. He needed to get there quickly.

His wife's body was in the back, rolled up in sheets and blankets, and he knew she would start to bloat, smell and draw flies in a few more hours. Jeremy had pleaded with him to take her along, so despite the impracticality, he'd carefully laid her in back under the watchful eye of his son. It was about a nine-hour drive to his uncle's house, then they could give her a decent burial and a ceremony. Dan figured they could bury her on the hill overlooking the house. She would like it there under the oaks. For a moment he pondered the absurdity of his last thought. *How could she like it there? She was dead.*

The reality sunk in like lead in the pit of his stomach. A few days ago he'd been willing to fight to get her back, but now ... if the truth be known ... deep down inside, a part of him felt relieved to be rid of her. Sure, he was sad, and he still loved her, but ... she was an incredible burden and a heartache he'd been suffering through for years. Despite that, the feeling of relief carried along with it a flipside of guilt. In fact, he was feeling so many conflicting emotions right now, that he couldn't sort it all out. Guilt, pain, sadness, relief, and even a bit of anger. It was all lumped in there like a recipe for peach jam that just wouldn't gel.

He glanced down at Jeremy again. He saw the tear tracks running down the boy's cheeks; they were still drying. Maybe he would sleep through the whole trip. It would be good for him. Had it really only been a little over 24 hours since he'd caught him in bed with the neighbor girl? It seemed like a lifetime ago.

He was headed east now on highway 8. His plan was to take it all the way into the Michigan Upper Peninsula and then hook up on U.S. 2.

A pick-up truck passed him coming the other way. It was loaded down with supplies and had a man and a boy perched on top with shotguns pointed over the cab. Dan was surprised at the lack of police officers out here in the sticks. True, there weren't that many to begin with, but he expected the rule of law to still be in force out here in the country, at least in the form of the County Sheriffs. But he hadn't seen a single law enforcement officer since leaving the edge of Menomonie. The last policeman he'd seen was missing half his head.

Dan looked down at his gas gauge. It read three-quarters full. Along with the gas he had in back, he would have no problem making it home to northern Michigan. His plan was to drive straight through until morning.

It was after midnight now and pitch dark outside. His eyelids were starting to droop a bit so he reached into the console and pulled out one of the Mocha Frappuccinos. He'd purchased a twelve pack last night at Wal*Mart, and he had a strong suspicion that once these were gone, it would be a very long time before he drank another one.

He peeled away the cellophane, twisted the top and took a sip of the warm fluid. It was like magical, life-giving nectar.

Dan tilted his head back to take a deeper drink, and when he lowered his head back down the White-tailed deer was already full in his headlights. He slammed on the brakes, throwing Jeremy into the dashboard. The big doe bounced off his grill, got back up again and bounded off into the alfalfa field to his left.

"What are you doing?"

Dan saw steam already rising up from the hood of his truck. He let out an exasperated sigh and his forehead came down hard on the steering wheel. All he could think was *At least the radio still works.*

"Calm down, Jeremy, I told you to stop swearing!"

Jeremy was holding his head in his hands. Blood poured out from between his fingers from the new gash in his forehead. Dan slammed the shifter into park and reached over to his son. "Let me take a look at that cut." Jeremy pulled his hand away, but all Dan could see was blood in the dimness of the truck cab. He turned on the dome light and then wiped away the blood with an old, fast-food napkin. "This cut's pretty deep. You're going to need stitches, son. Here, hold this napkin over it. Press down hard until it stops bleeding."

Jeremy complied with a painful moan.

"What happened to the truck?"

Dan opened the door and stepped out to take a look at it. "I hit a deer." He moved to the front and looked down at the steam rising from beneath the hood. It was either a broken hose or the grill was shoved through the radiator. In the present situation, neither prospect was a good one. Up ahead he saw a driveway surrounded by pine trees. He didn't see any buildings, so he hopped back in and slowly nursed the truck forward. As the truck turned left onto the gravel drive, the headlights revealed a hundred plus marble and granite headstones. He thought to himself, *How apropo.*

"Dad, this is a graveyard! We can't stop here."

Dan looked over at his son impatiently. "We don't have a choice. We've lost our water, and if we keep going we'll over heat and burn up the engine."

"Is Mom okay?"

Dan parked the truck behind a row of bushy spruce trees. No sense in bringing undo attention to their presence. He then looked in the rear-view mirror and saw his wife's body had been slammed forward by the sudden stop and was now scrunched up against the truck cap window.

"Yeah, your mom's fine."

The bleeding had stopped now, so Jeremy took the bloody napkin away from his head. "What are we going to do?"

Dan thought about it for a second. He glanced down and saw the remains of his Frappuccino soaking into the floor carpet. "I don't know, son. Let me take another look under the hood."

Fifteen minutes later he determined that a plastic grill shard had sliced through the radiator hose. He repaired it temporarily with a liberal amount of heavy duty duct tape.

"What now? Will it still run?"

Dan shrugged. "I don't know. Probably."

He looked up into the darkness and saw a million stars. It was peaceful here among the graves. "We'll get a few hours sleep, then at first light we'll drive a bit and see what happens."

Dan moved to the back of the truck and spent fifteen minutes laying the air mattresses and sleeping bags on the soft grass underneath the pine trees. He then got out two MREs and an electric lantern. Dan opened his plastic bag of food and started to squeeze a thick stream of "Spaghetti with Meat Sauce" onto his tongue.

"What the hell is this stuff?"

"I thought I told you to stop swearing. Why do you do that?"

"I just want to know what I'm eating, that's all."

Dan lowered the tin foil pouch of tomato, pasta and meat mush before answering.

"Well, I think you can ask questions without swearing. If you don't learn to talk respectable then you'll never get a decent job in life and succeed."

Jeremy looked at him in disbelief. "You've got to be kidding me! First you tell me it's the end of the world, then you tell me I have to stop swearing or I won't succeed. Make up your mind! Which one is it?"

Dan thought for a moment. "Oh. Right. I guess you can go ahead and swear now." Then he added. "But you don't have to be so grumpy, and you could be a little more grateful for what you have. It could be worse. These could be those old C-rations my Uncle used to feed me when I was growing up."

"So, what's a C-ration?"

Dan finished swallowing his food before answering. "It's food that came in olive drab tin cans left over from the Vietnam War. Instead of spaghetti and meat sauce it had names like *Turkey and Turkey Parts*."

Jeremy looked at him blankly in the dim light.

"Turkey parts?"

Dan smiled and nodded. "Exactly what I used to think. It could have been beaks, talons and gums all ground up in a can for all I knew."

"Damn! That's some nasty stuff!"

"Will you stop swearing!"

Jeremy cocked his head to one side in disbelief. "Dad, you're kidding, right? In the last 24 hours my hometown has become a war zone; my Dad beat me up; my mom killed her boyfriend, then overdosed on drugs; I'm sitting in a cemetery eating liquid food surrounded by dead people, and the truck is broke down."

Dan thought again and conceded his point. "Okay, so you've had a bad day. No one denies you that. But you have to look on the bright side. I gave you the cheese tortellini. You should eat it up and get some sleep. Tomorrow's a big day."

Jeremy threw the MRE down onto the grass and screamed as loud as he could. "I HATE YOU! You are so stupid! You don't care about me! You are the worst dad in the whole world, and I hate you!"

With that, his son turned his back and crawled deep into his sleeping bag and pulled it up over his head. Dan sat there dumbfounded, holding the half-eaten spaghetti pouch in his limp hand. He looked up at the stars, then at the pine boughs. He could smell them in the humid night air. Dan thought to himself, *Yes, it can always get worse.*

He put away all the food except the spaghetti he was eating to keep it away from wild animals, then climbed into his sleeping bag. There was an owl hooting a ways off, and tree frogs singing close by. A few weeks ago he'd heard Cicadas buzzing in the tree tops, but they were gone now. A part of him wanted back the past, but another part, a deeper part, felt more contented than he'd ever felt in his entire life. He didn't understand that. Dan finished sucking down the spaghetti, all the while wondering, *Why do I feel so at peace in this graveyard?*

Dan crawled down into his sleeping bag. He rolled onto his right side like he usually would, but the bulk of his pistol revolted against him. He thought about taking it off, but then rolled over onto his other side. The gun gave him comfort.

He listened to his son whimper for a half hour, then it was replaced by his deep, steady breathing. Only then could Dan's mind drift off into the night.

CHAPTER 7

The Men - September 10, 2AM

DAN WOKE UP IN THE MIDDLE OF THE NIGHT TO THE SOUND of screams. At first he thought they were his own, but when he sat up in the sleeping bag and touched his mouth, he knew it wasn't so. He looked over to his left and saw Jeremy still sleeping in his bag. The scream came to him again. It was blood curdling and it was close by. With the hairs standing up on his arms and neck, he jerked out of his sleeping back, and put on his shoes. He hesitated a bit, then walked over to his truck cab and quietly opened the door. The scream sounded again. This time he could tell it was from the far side of the cemetery. He looked over and saw a dim light. From behind the seat he pulled out the scoped, Winchester Model 1800 shotgun and quickly slipped off into the night in search of the unknown terror.

෧ ෧

The woman's back was pressed down on the bed of the pick-up truck by four men. Two kneeled up by her head, pinning her wrists down on the plastic bed liner while two others were stationed at her legs trying desperately to pry them apart. A fifth man, the one in charge, threw the woman's skirt up onto her writhing belly and began to unbuckle his belt.

"Hold the witch still!"

The woman screamed again as she thrashed on the truck bed. The man unzipped his pants and let them drop to his ankles. He laughed out loud. "Man I love it when they scream and fight like this. It just turns me on!"

He moved closer to the truck bed. "Slide her in closer, boys." The man smiled as he leaned down near the woman's face. She was tear-stained and bloody. "Don't worry, little lady, this will only take a few seconds. I'll try to be gentle." The other four men laughed with him and the lady screamed again.

Dan's first shot took off the leader's head at the base of the skull. It seemed to explode in the dimness of the night, and then his silly, bare legs collapsed, followed quickly by his torso. Two seconds later the man holding her right leg was hit in the back. The 12-gauge slug passed cleanly through his heart, then slammed into the shoulder of the man still holding her right wrist. Both men fell, one squirming on the truck bed, the other on the grass beside his leader. The man on her left wrist jumped up and out of the truck bed. The one who remained standing was hit high in the leg and went down to the grass. The truck engine revved to life and sped off into the graveyard, knocking down headstones and bouncing radically up and down. Dan fired his two remaining shots into the driver's side of the cab, but it was difficult hitting a moving target with a scope in the darkness. The truck reached the paved road and accelerated into the night. A few seconds later, the truck engine began to wind down, and the truck coasted to a stop.

"Dad! What's going on?"

When Jeremy ran up behind him, Dan reached out to grab his son and pulled him down behind the large, granite headstone beside him. "Stay down, son. Two of them are still alive."

Dan gazed out into the darkness. Only the truck's headlights almost 100 yards away lit up the night.

"I'll get a flashlight!" Jeremy jumped up and ran off before Dan could stop him. As his son's footsteps faded, Dan started to hear other sounds. One of the men was in his death rattle; he was gasping for air, as the muscles around his airway began to relax. It was a pitiful sound that Dan had heard several times before on deer he'd shot. But this time it was different. These were men, and he had killed them.

Off in the distance the truck's engine purred lightly. Then it stopped altogether. Dan knew that inside the cab, the man was either dead or dying. The adrenaline surge that had hit Dan's body just one, short minute ago began to make his hands shake as the realization of what he'd done began to set in.

The death rattle stopped, and quiet recaptured the night. Dan lay on the ground dumbfounded that it had all happened in just a few seconds. Suddenly, fear for his own life took over and he fell apart and sobbed on an unknown grave. Off in the distance, he heard Jeremy rummaging through the truck cab for the flashlight. About two minutes later, Dan heard his son's footsteps coming up behind him. He reached up to wipe away his tears, then he gathered his wits and grit his teeth so his son wouldn't see him crying.

"I got two of them, Dad."

Dan said nothing, but reached over and accepted the big Maglight from his son. Leaving the shotgun on the ground, Dan got up and moved to the cover of a tree three feet away.

"Stay down, son. I need to make sure."

Safely behind the thickness of the Maple tree, Dan turned on the flashlight and lit up the darkness around him. He wasn't prepared for what he saw. Three bodies were stacked twenty yards away, almost on top of one another. Dan searched for movement, but saw nothing. He looked over at his son. "Jeremy, I need you to watch for movement, if you see anything, yell to me and tell me where it's coming from, relative to my position." He saw his son nod and his flashlight turn on. Jeremy's eyes were as big as saucers.

Dan stepped out from the tree and ran twenty feet to the next Maple. They were all about 10 inches in diameter, and had been planted in a line. They were perfect for his purpose. After three more movements, Dan was within 10 feet of the bodies. He shined the light all around, but couldn't find the fourth man. By now his hands had stopped shaking, and an eerie calm overtook him. He shined the light on the three bodies. A cold front had moved in, and a billow of steam was now rising above the death. He could smell the blood in the cool, night air, and it threatened to close up his nostrils. Dan moved the flashlight to his left hand, loosened the thumb break on his holster and eased out the big, Taurus Judge revolver. He walked over to the pile, and saw two shotguns and a rifle lying on the ground beside them. Two of the men also wore sidearms. The whole thing had happened so quickly, they hadn't been able to draw their guns and return fire. Dan thought about what he'd learned in the Marines. *The element of surprise can overcome superior numbers and superior firepower.* Until now, all his learning had just been book knowledge and hear-say.

That's when he saw movement 20 yards away. The man was on the ground, crawling slowly. Dan looked at the grass and saw the thick trail of blood. He was surprised that human blood shown in the light just the same as deer blood. Dan slowly closed the distance to only six feet, keeping straight behind the man as he moved. That's when he saw the gun in the man's right hand slowly raise up and point in his direction. On reflex alone, Dan moved to his left while shooting. The four-ten buckshot tore into the man's upper body. Five shots later, Dan heard the hammer clicking on empty cylinders. He forced himself to stop pulling the trigger and lowered the gun. The man was no longer moving, and the Glock pistol lay on the grass beside him. Dan holstered his Taurus and picked up the Glock. He felt the sticky blood on the grips. As he knelt beside the dead man, Jeremy walked up and stood beside him.

"Dad, you killed four guys, man!"

Dan nodded. "Yes, but there were five of them. I need you to stay here behind that headstone while I go up and check out the truck."

Jeremy looked down at the dead man, and obeyed his father without question. Dan walked away, then he stopped and turned back around. "If you see a woman, don't hurt her. They were raping her, and I think she's still here hiding somewhere. We need to find her and help her."

It took Dan about two minutes to reach the stalled truck. The headlights were still on, so he approached from the rear. There was no sign of the woman. Suddenly, he was reminded of the Menomonie police officer who had snuck up behind his car the night of the blackout. Things had changed so much in so short a time - as if the hand of God had reached down and flicked a switch.

Dan shined the light into the back of the cab window and saw the man slouched over the wheel. He moved carefully up to the driver's side door and pulled on the handle. It opened easily. When he shined the light on the driver, he could see the gaping wound on the left side of his neck. The shotgun slug had done its job.

Dan looked around the truck and off into the darkness on the side of the road. He called out, but found no trace of the woman. He reached in and turned off the truck's headlights. That's when he heard his son yell to him. Dan sprinted back to the cemetery. When he shined the light down on his son, he saw Jeremy holding the shoulders of a woman close to him. She was sobbing, and Jeremy hushed her gently.

"It's okay, lady. My dad's the good guy. He saved you."

Dan shoved the Glock into his belt at the small of his back and dropped down beside the two. He felt like a clumsy cowboy when he spoke to her for the first time.

"It's okay, Ma'am. They're all gone now."

CHAPTER 8

The Woman - September 10

AFTER TAKING THE WOMAN BACK TO HIS TRUCK, DAN RE-turned to the road and drove the other pick-up back to the cemetery and parked it behind the trees beside his own. The truck was new and shiny, still boasting dealer plates from Milwaukee. Without a doubt, it was stolen.

It was a grisly job in the eerie darkness of the graveyard, but he then piled all the corpses together. With that task done, he washed his hands and face using a hand pump by one of the graves. Then he brought the lady a rag and a pan of water. She had stopped crying now.

Dan and Jeremy waited a few yards away on top of their sleeping bags for her to finish. Jeremy tried to ask questions, but Dan shushed him into silence. The moon was high in the sky by now, and lit up the grave stones all around them. Dan quietly reassessed the events of the past hour. He thought it odd, that he was replaying the shootout in his mind, analyzing it, and picking out things he should have done differently. He felt a strange numbness, akin to the feeling he'd experienced the first time he saw his wife kiss another man. Inside him, a door had opened with a rusty scrape and then a thud, unleashing something, a part of him that he'd kept penned up inside his whole life. But now it was out. Just for a moment, he wondered if life was still worth living.

The woman finished washing and walked back to the sleeping bags where she sat down on the grass. Dan moved off his sleeping bag and offered it to her, but she just stared straight ahead as if she'd seen or heard nothing. Jeremy looked over at his dad, wondering what to do next. Dan nodded to him.

"Just go ahead and get some sleep, son. We've got a long drive tomorrow." By now the last vestige of adrenaline had worn off and Dan felt exhausted. Despite that, he took the time to reload first the shotgun and then the Taurus pistol. After reholstering, Dan brought the woman an MRE and a mocha Frappuccino. He laid them at her feet like a gift, and then backed away. "Go ahead. We have plenty." She looked down at the food. Her hand ran silently over the glass Frappuccino bottle, but still she said nothing.

"I'm Dan, and this is my son, Jeremy."

She looked out over the graveyard and directly up into the moon, staring at it like a coyote.

"Are you okay, ma'am?"

Dan noticed in the dim light how frail the woman looked. She was slender with a light complexion, and he couldn't help but notice how attractive she was, even after the ordeal she'd been through. Dan thought to himself, *I've just killed five men, and my dead wife is bloating up in the back of my truck, but for some reason I still notice attractive women. I'm going to hell for sure.* He looked away, ashamed of himself.

"Well, okay. I can see you don't want to talk right now and I don't blame you." He pulled up a blade of healthy, green grass and began to tear it up with his fingers. "I've had a rough day myself." He threw the grass bits onto the ground. "Listen, I'll just sleep inside the cab tonight, and you can use my sleeping bag when you're feeling up to it." Dan glanced up at the moon. "We can talk in the morning when we all have some sleep under our belts." He hesitated. "Sound like a plan?" She didn't answer, so Dan got up and walked over to the truck. He piled in the front seat and stretched himself out as best he could. It was then he noticed the smell of decay, and realized his wife would never make it back to Michigan. In the morning he'd tell Jeremy they had to bury her here in the cemetery. Dan wondered why he didn't feel sad about that. Truthfully, he wasn't feeling much of anything right now. His feelings felt all blurry, like he knew they were there, but couldn't quite make out the details.

He thought to himself again, *Am I going to hell for all this? Did I do wrong?* Dan had never been as religious as he should, but still, he was no moral vacuum. Yes, he'd made mistakes, like anyone else, but he usually tried to do the right thing. After a few minutes contemplation, he concluded that killing the five men was less wrong than watching the poor woman get raped. He'd acted almost solely in accordance with his instinct and his personality. It worried Dan that his response had been instant, without thought, and totally merciless in its execution. He thought again about books he'd read over the years: *Lord of the Flies* by William Golding and *Heart of Darkness* by Joseph Conrad, and even the *Bible* for that matter. All of them proclaimed that man was inherently evil, and when left to his own devices, without accountability and the rule of law, that society would break down and the human heart would become evil and desperately wicked. Lying in the cramped cab, with the stench of his rotting wife behind him, and the five bodies piled up outside … Dan wondered.

WHEN DAN FINALLY WOKE UP, THE SUN WAS ALREADY HIGH IN THE SKY. He jerked himself up and a savage pain shot through his neck where he'd been laying it against the door. His left leg was asleep, forcing him to wait a few minutes for the frozen numbness to thaw out and then for the tingling to go away. He heard a car drive by on the road, then voices.

"So what happened after your car broke down?"

Jeremy's voice was clear and easy to understand, but the woman's reply seemed muted and sad.

"Scott left me alone in the car to walk to the next town for help, but he hadn't gone two hundred yards when those people stopped and got out of their truck. Scott started running back to me, not knowing what they wanted, whether they were friends or not." She hesitated. "At first they were smiling, so I rolled the window down an inch to talk. I told them we'd run out of gas and that was my husband running back toward us."

From inside the cab, Dan thought her voice sounded tired and stressed simultaneously, like a balloon blown to the point of bursting.

"But once Scott got back to the car, their smiles went away. They stepped in front of Scott when he tried to open the car door and get inside with me. That's when I noticed the guns on their hips, and I knew for sure we were in trouble. That man with the black hair, the leader, he nodded to the others and Scott was immediately attacked and thrown to the pavement. I started honking the horn, hoping someone would hear and come help or that it would scare them away. But it was useless. While I watched, they … well …" She started to cry again, regained control and finished the sentence. "Well, Scott is dead. They beat him to death on the pavement."

The woman broke down entirely and cried on the grass beside Jeremy. Dan felt guilty for listening and sat up in the cab. He cleared his throat to let them know he was awake and stepped out onto the grass and walked over to them. Jeremy looked up at his father. "Her name is Kate." And then he added without tact; "They killed her husband, beat him to death about ten miles up the road. She wants us to bring him back here and help her bury him."

Dan thought for a moment. *He had a shovel in the truck, and they had to bury Debbie anyways, and this was the perfect spot.* Dan took a few steps and then kneeled down beside the crying woman. He thrust out his right hand awkwardly. "I'm Dan Branch, from Menomonie. This is my son, Jeremy." But Kate didn't accept his hand. She didn't even look up from her crying. Dan sighed and stood back up.

"We'll take the new truck there and back. That way we save twenty miles worth of gas."

Jeremy looked surprised. "Dad, why don't we just take that brand, new truck all the way to Michigan?"

Dan shook his head. "No. It doesn't belong to us." Then he walked back over to the dead men's truck and hopped inside. "What kind of car was it?" Dan heard Kate softly say, "A blue Ford Taurus."

Dan slammed the door and yelled to Jeremy as he started up the engine. "Come on, son. You can help me, and we need to talk anyways." Jeremy got up slowly and then hesitated. "But what about Kate? Maybe I should stay and make sure she's okay." Dan replied by shaking his head resolutely. Jeremy got in the truck. Dan called out before driving off. "We'll be about thirty minutes, Kate. If anyone bothers you, there's a loaded shotgun behind the seat in the cab." Dan saw Kate's head nodding in reply. He revved the engine once and pulled out onto the road.

"Dad, I don't think we should leave her alone. She's not doing very good."

Dan gripped the steering wheel firmly. There was blood all over the upholstery. Dan wondered how the shotgun slug had missed the windshield. "She just needs some time alone, son. Besides, I wanted to talk to you about something."

Jeremy went silent and turned to his right to gaze out the window. Dan let out another huge sigh. "Come on, Jeremy, don't make this any harder than it has to be!" He fixed his eyes on the road straight ahead. Jeremy snapped his head around as if on fire. The shiner on his eye was in full bloom now, not to mention the swollen gash on his forehead.

"I'm not going to let you bury my mom out here where I can't visit her! I want her coming with us to Michigan!"

Dan gritted his teeth and squeezed the steering wheel until his knuckles turned white. "Son, I'm telling you we don't have a choice anymore. Didn't you notice the smell back there? It's been two days and her stomachs all bloated up to near bursting! We need to get her in the cool ground. It's the only dignified thing to do."

Jeremy didn't answer at first. Dan looked over and saw the tears streaming down his face. "Why is this happening to us, Dad?" Dan reached over with his right hand and placed it around his neck. When the truck slowed to a stop, Dan threw the shifter lever in park and slid over next to him.

"It's not just us, son. It's everyone. I think the whole world is like this now, and it's going to get worse, much. much worse. We need to get on the road and back to Michigan where we can survive. Getting caught on the road like this is sure death. You saw what happened to Kate. The longer we wait, the more dangerous it's going to get. People from the city will be out here soon, looking for food and a place to live. We have to bury your mom and get over to my Uncle Rodney's house. He's prepared. Trust me when I say he's probably the most prepared man on this planet."

Jeremy kept crying, and Dan just held him for a minute or two. A car passed by. It slowed as it did and the two men inside craned their necks as they rolled by. Dan's eyes met their hard gaze until they were gone. "We gotta go, son. It's too dangerous here." He released his son and slid back over on the seat, put the truck in drive and sped off.

A few minutes later Dan saw a blue, mid-sized car parked on the side of the road up ahead. Jeremy stopped crying and looked up as Dan brought the truck to a halt behind it.

"You better stay here, son. Let me see what the deal is. This might not be very pretty." Dan jumped out of the truck and walked slowly up to the car. His right hand rested heavily on the grip of his big revolver. There was no one in the car. No broken windows. No blood. No body. No sign of a struggle. Dan was confused. Then he saw the paper shoved under the driver's side windshield wiper. He took it off and opened it up. The note read:

Hank, I ran out of gas. Don't worry though. The Thompsons picked up me and the kids and we're at their house waiting for you. All is fine.

Love, Christie

Dan got that hollow feeling in the pit of his stomach again. He felt a sudden need to get back to the cemetery. He dropped the note, got back in the truck, and drove ten miles back as fast as he could. But he was too late. The woman and his truck were already gone.

CHAPTER 9

The Betrayal - September 10, 10AM

"**WELL, DAD, YOU WERE RIGHT. THINGS ARE GETTING** worse. Now we've lost our truck, all our supplies, and she's stolen my mom. We have to get her back."

Jeremy shook his head from side to side as he spoke. "Boy, she just didn't seem the type to me. I'm surprised."

Dan looked out the truck window, his eyes scanning every inch of the cemetery, but for what, he didn't know. "Listen, son, just because someone is in trouble, doesn't mean they have character. She was a stranger and we helped her. But, as it turns out, she was one of the bad guys too."

Jeremy looked over at his father. "I don't want to believe that, Dad. I talked to her for a long time while you were sleeping. She was a really nice lady."

Dan didn't answer. He just kept scanning the graveyard while he tried to think of what to do. She had all their equipment, food, gas, and an arsenal of guns and ammunition.

"I'm serious, Dad. Did you know she was a nurse at a hospital in Milwaukee. She was heading to her cabin in the Upper Peninsula to wait until the power comes back on."

Dan looked back over at his son with a frown on his face. "Jeremy, do you remember that time you had a girlfriend on Facebook? You said she was sixteen years old and beautiful, and you wanted to meet her so bad. Do you remember that?"

Jeremy winced but didn't answer.

"So, how did that date work out for you, son?"

"That's different, Dad. That was online. I met Kate in person, and I know she wouldn't lie to me."

Dan rolled his eyes in disbelief. "Son, she already lied to us! We went to her car, but it wasn't hers. There was no dead husband! She's a liar! She's a thief! She stole everything we own along with your mother's dead body! Wake up! That woman, whoever she is, has yet to tell us a thread of truth!"

The boy looked out the window again. A light breeze blew on his face, gently moving a few locks of his blonde hair. Dan started up the truck and drove out of the cemetery driveway.

"Dad, you're going the wrong way. Michigan's east of here."

Dan growled out loud. "You don't think I'd leave Wisconsin without giving your mother a proper burial do you?"

His son's eyes smiled ever so slightly. Then Dan gunned the engine and squealed the tires on the pavement, throwing Jeremy's head back into the seat.

"Besides, all our gas was in that old truck, and this one only has a quarter of a tank. Without that truck, we're screwed."

Rodney Branch sat up on the side of the hill overlooking his compound through the scope of his .308 caliber hunting rifle. He called it a compound just to make himself feel better, but, in reality, it was just a house, built into the side of a hill with a chicken coop, goat yard, and a pig pen. But, regardless of whether you called it a compound, a dump, or a rolling estate, it still belonged to Rodney Branch, and he was willing to die defending it. That's just the way he was, with no apologies or hesitation. Some people called him dedicated; some called him eccentric; but most people called him just plain, crazy.

But Rodney didn't mind at all. In fact, he found it rather liberating, because society expected so little from insanity. For years, the normal people had been laughing at him as he prepared for the end of the world as we know it. Rodney smiled, his yellow teeth almost visible beneath his beard and moustache in the sunlight. Then he said out loud, just barely audible to himself and to no one else.

"I don't hear anybody laughing anymore. The goose is cooked. The deal is done. The lights are out. We're having fun."

Rodney's old mind drifted off to the only person on the planet he cared for. He'd raised his brother's son from a pup, but now he was in Wisconsin, hopefully, making his way back home. The old man prayed for his safety, not just for Dan, but also for himself. Because Rodney knew that a lone wolf would not survive this hunt. It would be too long, too hard, and too fierce. The lights were out for good, and this was just the beginning of a very long and brutal thousand-year night. He whispered to God almighty, wanting a reply, but not really expecting it. "Hey God. I know you're up there. I can hear ya breathing." Then he laughed softly to himself. "Just get the kid home safe, okay? We got a deal. old man?"

There was sudden movement down below, about fifty yards from the house, and Rodney swung the scope around slowly to check it out. He saw the man carefully making his way through the trees. He carried a light backpack with a shotgun in his hands. Rodney laughed out loud. "He's dressed like a peacock! How's he supposed to sneak up on me like that?" The man was dressed in bright green dress pants with a red, short-sleeved shirt and tie. Rodney shook his head back and forth in disgust. These morons had been flooding out of the city for a day now, driving until they ran out of gas, then walking, trying to take advantage of the first people they came upon. The old man felt sorry for them. He knew they wouldn't survive, realizing that most of them would die on the road, or, worse yet, would survive only by killing and taking what belonged to someone else. It was a new world with only two options: Kill or be killed.

Rodney Branch had no intention of being killed. He brought his right eye down to the scope and sighted the target. It was a hundred-yard, slam-dunk shot but he didn't have the heart to take it. It didn't matter. This guy was clueless, and he was destined to die, if not today, then tomorrow. If not here, then twenty miles down the road. But Rodney just didn't feel like shooting anyone today, especially some weak, ignorant city slicker who didn't know which end of the barrel the round came out of.

But, despite that, he couldn't let the man ransack his house. Rodney pursed his lips together and made a light kissing sound. Within seconds the hundred-pound German Shepherd was panting at his side. The old man smiled and scratched the dog's huge head. Rodney pointed down the hill, and the big dog's ears perked up. He growled softly. Rodney whispered in the dog's right ear, "Go down, Moses!"

The big dog took off racing down the hill straight for the intruder. By time the man saw him coming, it was too late. He raised his shotgun, but Moses lunged forward and parted the man's scalp with one savage bite, sending a sea of red blood spilling out onto the ground. The man screamed and dropped his shotgun. Moses backed up and lunged forward again, but the man had recovered and was already running back into the woods.

Rodney smiled up on the hillside. He let Moses play with the man for a while, then he whistled and the big dog came running through the woods and then back up the hill.

"Good boy, Moses! Good boy! Did you get the nasty man? Did you get him good?" Moses licked his master's face, and they both walked back down the hill to the house. Rodney stopped long enough to pick up the man's shotgun and examine it. It was a Benelli.

"Holy Moses! Can you believe this gun! I've always wanted one of these!"

Rodney unloaded it and then walked toward the house. He laughed out loud. "We'll just hold on to it until the gentleman comes back for it. Wouldn't be right to steal it." He spoke directly to his dog now. "Thou shalt not steal! Right Moses?"

The old man and his dog plodded up onto the big porch. Rodney leaned the Benelli against the house and then sat down in the rocker with his rifle atop his lap. Moses took his place at the right hand of the master. Rodney started to rock slowly back and forth, back and forth, back and forth, scanning the tree line, waiting for the prodigal son to come home.

FIVE MILES DOWN THE ROAD, DAN AND JEREMY CAME UPON THEIR TRUCK, abandoned beside a corn field. The cap was open along with both cab doors, and much of their belongings were scattered on the pavement and in the ditch. Steam still rose up from underneath the hood where the damaged radiator hose had broken once again.

"Looks like that duct tape didn't hold. Dad."

Dan slowed to a stop about 30 yards away. He looked around cautiously, down the road and out into the corn fields on both sides. "Stay inside, Jeremy." When he got out of the truck and walked closer, the smell of gas was obvious. Dan unholstered his revolver, and then looked underneath the truck. He saw the wet spot on the pavement where they'd punched a hole in his gas tank and drained it dry. He looked into the back and saw the extra gas cans were gone as well.

"Can I come on up now, Dad?"

Dan holstered his pistol and motioned with his hand, and a few seconds later his son stood beside him. They walked to the front of the truck, and that's when they discovered Kate in the tall grass off the front bumper. Quickly, Dan ran to her and kneeled down in the grass. "Stay back, son." The woman was naked from the waist down, and it was obvious she'd been raped and abused before finally dying. Dan stripped off his t-shirt and spread it over her nakedness. Only then would he allow Jeremy to come forward.

His son fell down to his knees, vomiting out his stomach onto the Queen Anne's Lace and the Chicory weeds in the road ditch. A car pulled up, slowing as it drove by as all the occupants gawked in dismay. The driver saw the dead body and accelerated in a cloud of blue smoke. Traffic from down south had picked up the last few hours, and Dan knew the people were starting to leave the city in droves now. The need to get out ahead of them was urgent, because with more people would come even more bloodshed.

Dan's mind began racing, compiling a list of all the things they needed to do before the people who'd killed Kate or others like them came back. That's when he saw his wife's bloated and rotting body a few rows into the corn. He could hear the flies swarming around her. A breeze picked up and blew the stench over to the road where he kneeled beside Kate's dead body. The numbness set in with a renewed vigor.

While Jeremy remained on his hands and knees in the ditch, Dan walked over and wrapped his wife back up in the blankets. The stench was almost unbearable, and he fought against the spasms in his stomach and throat muscles. Dan walked over to his son and held him. As Jeremy cried in his arms, Dan kept a watchful eye. Five minutes later, he picked his son up and carried him back to the new truck and laid him inside the cab. For the next thirty minutes, Dan loaded what was left of their supplies into the bed of the new truck, then he carefully laid Kate and Debbie on top and slowly drove back to the cemetery.

CHAPTER 10

The Funeral - September 10, 8PM

DAN AND **J**EREMY BOWED THEIR HEADS OVER THE MOUND OF dirt in front of them. The ground was hard, and it had taken them the rest of the day to dig three holes: one for Debbie, one for Kate, and a larger hole for the five rapists. Amazingly, only one person had stopped in to ask what they were doing. He was an old man named Joe who had been visiting his wife's grave every day for the past seven years. Dan hadn't known how to explain the seven bodies on the ground in front of them, so he'd just told the old man the truth. Joe had just nodded his head and made the sign of the cross on his chest. He'd even helped them dig, and now he stood beside them as they prepared to pay their final respects.

It was a cloudy day, looking like rain, so Dan wasted no time with his eulogy.

"Okay, God, we've got seven dead people here. One we loved. One we wrongly trusted. And five we killed." Dan felt a few drops of rain and continued on. "We don't really know what's going on in the world right now or why people are all of a sudden acting so mean but I assume you do."He hesitated and looked over at his son, who'd been crying the whole afternoon."I suppose people have always been like this, and it just took one little nudge to push civilization over the brink of civilized behavior. My wife, Debbie, that was Jeremy's mom, she kind of went astray there at the end, but we know she was sorry, and we'd like you to cut her some slack." He paused and looked up. Jeremy nodded to him."The other lady, Kate, she stole our truck, but I suspect she got more punishment than she deserved at the end. We ask that you give both Kate and Debbie special consideration on judgement day. After all, none of us are perfect." The fingers of his left hand were interlaced with the fingers on his right, and they tightened involuntarily when he prayed for the five rapists. "These other five strangers, well, we caught them raping an innocent woman, and I shot them all dead. If that's a sin, then I apologize, but please bear in mind these are hard times, and that I didn't enjoy it."

A long line of cars began passing by on the road, so Dan wrapped it up. "Okay, God, I guess that's about it, except we need to ask for your help getting to Michigan. We need gas and we should've been there by now, but things keep going wrong. We could use a break, so please protect us and keep us from evil. Thanks God. Amen."

Jeremy and Joe echoed with amens of their own. Dan reached over the mound and shook Joe's hand. "We gotta get heading east again, Joe, or we'll never make it." He looked down again, weighing his yet unspoken offer. "Are you sure you don't want to come with us? We've got room, and I really don't think things are going to be real safe here alone in a few days."

The old man smiled and looked over at his wife's grave thirty yards to the left. He didn't speak, but Dan understood and smiled in return. Joe reached out his hand to Jeremy, but the boy ignored it and rushed forward, embracing the frail, old man in a hug. "Thanks for helping me bury my Mom. I appreciate it." Joe hugged him back, then looked him straight in the eye. "You get on now with yer papa. He's a good man. And you do what he says." Jeremy nodded and Joe glanced over at Dan and added, "Why didn't you tell me you needed gas?" Dan just shrugged. As Joe walked away he called over his shoulder, "Go east a mile, and the third house on the left is mine. There's a five-gallon can of gas in my garage. Take the gas and the can. You're going to need it." Then the old man walked over to his wife's grave as if they'd already left, not bothering to wait for a response. The old man sat down on the grass and looked out into the alfalfa field across the way. It would need cutting again, soon, but he doubted his neighbor would bother. There were just too many things happening right now.

Dan walked over and got inside their new truck. He waited as Jeremy dropped to his knees and said his own private prayer. Amazing as it was, in the midst of all this death and hate, Dan was starting to like his son again. Jeremy finished up and walked over to the truck, all the while glancing over his shoulder every few steps. As far as he knew, he would never come this way again, and he knew this good bye was forever.

By the time Jeremy was on the seat beside him, Dan had already started the engine. He waved to Joe, but the old man wasn't looking, was just talking to his dead wife in the breeze as the rain started to come down harder. The truck pulled out onto the pavement, leaving the man and the cemetery to the grace of God.

"WHAT ARE YOU DOING UP THERE, RODNEY?"

Rodney Branch was halfway up a wooden light pole, standing on the steel screen platform of his climbing tree stand just off the county road. There was a socket wrench in his left hand, and he almost dropped it when Sheriff Joe Leif called up to him from the ground. He'd been so focused on loosening the solar panel off the pole that he hadn't heard the patrol car pull up and stop.

"Hey, Joe, how's it going?"

The Sheriff was young in comparison to Rodney, middle-aged, well over six feet tall with a muscular build and black hair, just starting to grey at the temples.

Joe nodded as he spoke. "Fine, Rod, just fine, but you didn't answer my question."

The old man went back to loosening the nut that clamped the medium-sized solar panel to the pole. "Sheriff, I'm kind of busy right now, and this is dangerous work. Do you mind if we talk about this later?"

Sheriff Leif looked around uncomfortably to see if anyone was watching. "Rod I've got to tell you that martial law has been declared and my men have orders to shoot any looters on sight."

Rodney stopped turning the wrench. "Orders from who?" The Sheriff shook his head in exasperation. "From the Governor and the State Police that's who. I've got to maintain some semblance of law and order in this county until things get back to normal."

Rodney laughed out loud. "Joe, you know as well as I do that things aren't getting back to normal for a long, long time." Sheriff Leif lowered his head. He was getting a kink in his neck from looking almost straight up at the pole. In his gut, he knew the old man was right. Things were bad, real bad, and he was worried. The State Police had abandoned all the rural counties and moved closer to Lansing, Detroit and the other big cities in the state. Joe had communication with the Capitol, but not much information was filtering down to him. Right now, only three days after the blackout, his little county was an island and Lansing felt five million miles away. Most of his deputies were home with their families, trying to take care of them, and even if they'd been willing to patrol the roads, there was a severe shortage of gas for his vehicles, as shipments of everything, including gas, food, and parts, had ceased to flow into town, or anywhere for that matter.

The Sheriff came to a silent decision and moved off a few feet before sitting down on the grass in the ditch. He thought for a moment, then spoke. "Okay, Rodney Branch. You and I need to talk. I know darn well that you've been preparing for this thing ever since I was a kid, but now I need your help trying to salvage what I can and maintain some peace around here."

The old man responded by laughing again. He finished loosening the last nut and the solar panel dropped down and swung from the rope attached to Rodney's platform. He bent down, untied one end and started to lower the panel down to the ground. Joe stood up and walked over to catch it before it hit the dirt. "Thanks Sheriff." Rodney smiled. "I guess this makes you an accomplice."

Rodney came down a foot at a time in his climbing platform, and soon he was standing on the ground again. The Sheriff looked him straight in the eye. "I'm serious, Rod. I need some help. I was on my way to your house to talk."

Rodney loaded the solar panel into the back of his pickup truck, then sat down on the tailgate. "What kind of help?" Sheriff Leif sat on the tailgate beside him.

"To start with can you tell me what you're hearing on your short wave radio? You're the only one around here I know of who's got one."

Rodney reached into his shirt pocket and took out a pack of Camel unfiltered cigarettes. He shook one out and offered it to the Sheriff who quickly shook his head no. "Suit yerself." Rodney lit it up and took a long draw before exhaling the smoke above his head. "Seems to me a man has to die of something, may as well be cancer." The Sheriff didn't push him into answering. It would do no good. Rodney just sat there, smoking his cigarette in silence. When he was finished, he finally said something of substance.

"I'm hearing that Detroit is a dangerous place. People are dying left and right. The bad apples have taken over the barrel. Half the cops are either dead or AWOL and anyone who ventures out of their house is taking their life into their own hands." He crushed the cigarette butt out on the heel of his boot and stuck it inside his shirt pocket. "Yeah, right. You think Detroit was rough a week ago, it's downright lawless now. Lots of gunshots, law of the jungle taking over. Rape, pillage, plunder, you know, the usual, just lots more of it. Anyone still there in a month will be dead most likely."

He glanced over to make sure the Sheriff was still listening and to get an indication of his state of mind. "Flint and Saginaw are pretty much the same. The only place on the east side of the state that has any semblance of law and order is Dearborn."

That last statement caused Joe to perk up. "Dearborn? Why Dearborn?"

Rodney frowned. "Think about it, Joe. It's the biggest concentration of Muslims in the Midwest. Once law and order broke down, the Mullahs took over and declared Sharia Law. They were already organized before this chaos came down. This is an opportunity for them, and they won't waste it." Rodney hesitated, and looked over at his friend. "I expect they'll be coming this way sooner or later."

The Sheriff reached up and scratched his left cheek. "What for? There's nothing up here this far north?"

Rodney smiled and took out another cigarette. "That don't matter none. Nature abhors a vacuum, and anyplace that isn't organized and strong will suck them up like smoke in a chimney."

Joe shook his head back and forth. "I don't believe it. You never liked Muslims, but I just don't believe they'll leave the east side."

The sound of Rodney's laughter echoed out across the road. "Suit yourself, Sheriff." Then he looked him full in the eyes. "But what if I'm right?" Then he added. "You can even forget about the Muslims. maybe you're right. Maybe they won't come. But can you sit there and tell me the hordes in Grand Rapids, Lansing, and Detroit are going to stay bottled up while they starve and die of disease?" Rodney blew a cloud of smoke above his head to keep it out of Joe's face. "No way, Sheriff. Even those peace-loving, God-fearing Christians will spread out once they get hungry and people start shooting at them. There's a lot of people with guns in Michigan, and not all of them are as nice as you."

The Sheriff lowered his head and thought for a moment. "Yeah, I know. I've been thinking the same thing myself." He looked over at Rodney just in time to see him finish off the second cigarette. "So what do you think we can do about it?"

Rodney laughed again. "We? You're the Sheriff, not me." The younger man hopped down off the tail gate and turned and smiled. "You were born and raised in this county, and you fought for your country. No matter what other people say about you, I know you wouldn't let your neighbors die without putting up a fight."

Sheriff Leif reached into his front pants pocket and pulled out a gold-colored Deputy badge in the shape of a star. "Now raise your right hand and repeat after me, old man! I, Rodney Branch, do solemnly swear that I will support and defend the Constitution of the United States against all enemies, foreign and domestic; that I will …"

Rodney clenched down on his teeth hard, grinding them together as he swore to himself. He didn't hear the rest of the oath, but he'd had it memorized for years. The Sheriff paused, waiting for Rodney to speak. Finally, the old man unclenched his jaw. "Why are you doing this to me, Joe? I'm an old man, and I just want to be left alone long enough for the kid to come home so I can die of old age."

The Sheriff smiled. He knew he had him.

CHAPTER 11

The Silence - September 11, 7PM

THEY WERE ALMOST DUE WEST OF IRON MOUNTAIN NOW, and Dan figured they had just enough gas to make it into Michigan and halfway to the Mackinac Bridge. But, after that, it was up to God.

It was about 2 hours before dark now, and they had pulled off the road onto a two-track deep inside the Nicolet National Forest. Jeremy sat on the bank of the small stream with his feet dangling down into the water while Dan slowly sipped on his creek-cooled Mocha Frappuccino. Several of them had broken, and, after this one, only three bottles remained. He felt a strange calm as the silence of the woods was broken only by singing birds and the wind blowing in the tops of the tall pine trees. Dan had always loved the thick, heavy smell of pine.

"Can I build a fire, Dad?"

Dan looked over at Jeremy and nodded. "Sure, don't see why not. We're so far back I don't think anyone will see it from the road."

Jeremy smiled and walked off into the woods looking for dead sticks and kindling, being careful not to hurt his bare feet. Dan had taught him how to build a fire way back when the boy was still Cub Scout age. Debbie had been furious, accusing him of teaching him how to "play" with fire. But, on this one occasion, Dan had defied her and taught him anyways. The next week Jeremy had burned down the neighbor's tool shed. There had always been so much he'd wanted to teach Jeremy, whom he'd always considered his son, how to shoot, hunt, fish, survive in the wild, but Debbie just didn't want him learning outdoor skills for some strange reason. He sipped his cold mocha and looked out into the pine boughs. It was odd and almost scary how quickly life could change. Three days ago Jeremy was screwing the neighbor girl and cussing out his father. Now, he was asking permission to build a campfire. The boy was scared, and he needed Dan more than ever. But what the boy didn't know, was that Dan needed Jeremy as well. This was no time to be alone.

A memory of his father stirred, and Dan remembered fishing with him as a boy. After all these years, he still missed him, almost to the point of tears. Dan brushed the memory aside. He assumed there were black bears over here on this side of the state, but didn't really know for sure. The fire was probably a good idea. It might scare them off.

He considered listening to the truck radio while Jeremy gathered wood, but decided not to. Although he was desperate for information, radio broadcasts were few and far between, and none of the big-city stations were even on the air. Once in a while he could pick up a small-town station operating on low power with a gas generator, but he expected this would last only until they ran out of fuel. Then the radio would go strangely silent. He suspected that television was a similar situation. In the end it didn't matter. The news these days was reduced to rumor, and if the rumors were true, then America was in deep trouble. Chicago was rioting and burning; there was no food; no clean water; no police to stop the killing and no firemen to put out the blaze. Civility, like a thin veneer, had been stripped away, leaving humanity at its basest level. Dan wondered *Is it law of the jungle now, kill or be killed, don't get involved in other people's business, protect what is mine at all costs? Is God still there, or did He turn out the lights on his way out of the galaxy?* It was as if America had traveled back in time two hundred years, and each passing day was pushing them further back into the dark ages.

Dan listened to the sounds of the woods now. There was no noise, no clutter, no honking, no engines, no jets overhead, no voices, no radio.

The voice of man had been silenced, and only the God-made sounds had survived.

Silence was a new way of life for Dan, and he found himself thinking more and more about life and God and existence. Before the collapse there just hadn't been time to think about where he'd been, where he was going, or even how to get there, much less reflect on morality or the question of right and wrong. But now … he had all the time in the world.

Dan put the bottle down on the bank beside him and picked up the Bible again, letting it fall open randomly on his lap. He closed his eyes the way he'd done as a child and pointed to a verse on the page and read it out loud, half expecting it to solve all his problems or give his stressed out life some peace and direction. The verse read:

"If a man has sexual relations with a woman during her monthly period, he has exposed the source of her flow, and she has also un- covered it. Both of them are to be cut off from their people."

Dan surprised himself by laughing out loud. Then he thought to himself, *Okay, thanks God, important hygiene tip.*

"What's so funny, Dad?"

Dan turned around surprised and the Bible slipped from his fingers and slid down the bank toward the stream. He quickly reached out and grabbed it before it hit the water. Jeremy dropped the wood in a pile and then sat down beside his father. Dan smiled.

"Well, son, I was just thinking about how I've always wanted to teach you things. You know, stuff about outdoor survival, shooting, hunting, cooking over a campfire, all the things your mother hated so much."

At the mention of his mother, Jeremy's face shadowed over, but then, just for an unexpected moment, he smiled.

"Do you remember that time I burned down the neighbor's shed?"

Dan laughed again. "Oh yeah. Boy did your mother ever ream me out for that one! And what about the time you tried to make gun powder and launched that home-made rocket through the living room window."

Jeremy nodded sheepishly. "Well, I wasn't aiming for the window. It just kind of popped up out of nowhere." He thought for a moment, reliving the past. "Mom sure was pissed off at that one."

The smile on Dan's face grew bigger. "Yup. I remember that day. I couldn't tell you this, because your mom would have killed me, but I was really proud of you for that."

Jeremy looked confused. "You were proud of me for launching a rocket through the window of our house?"

Dan shook his head as he talked. "No, son. I was proud of your ingenuity. You saw something you wanted and you went for it. You didn't know how to make a rocket, but you went on the internet and you read up and you figured it out all by yourself." Dan's eyes clouded over. "It was partly my fault anyways. I should have been there teaching you how to do it."

Jeremy lowered his head. "So why weren't you?"

Dan looked over and Jeremy raised his head. They locked eyes for a crucial moment in time. Dan pursed his lips. "Because I was stupid and selfish, son. All I could feel was my own pain and my own loneliness." He tossed the Bible down to his left. "If I'd been a real father, a better man, then I would have risen above my problems and focused on things I could change and good I could do. Instead, I just wallowed and you suffered for it. I'm sorry about that, and I wish I could take it back."

His son gazed out into the pines ahead. "Yeah, well, mom was a handful, wasn't she?"

Father and son laughed together. "No kidding, you can say that again. More than a handful. Your mom always reminded me of that Billy Joel song, *She's always a Woman.*

Jeremy asked innocently. "*Who's Billy Joel?*"

"Oh, just some old fart from the seventies who sang songs at a bar and played piano. He probably lived in LA, so he's most likely dead by now."

"Sing it to me."

Dan looked over skeptically. "Excuse me?"

"Just sing to me, Dad. Like you did when I was a kid."

The man thought about it for a moment, trying to remember the words. His Uncle

Rodney had sang along with the cassette tape player while hoeing the garden. The memory came back and Dan started to sing slowly.

She can kill with a smile,
She can wound with her eyes.
She can ruin your faith with her casual lies
And she only reveals what she wants you to see
She hides like a child,
But she's always a woman to me.

Dan hesitated and glanced over at his son to see how it was being received. Jeremy seemed transfixed, so he sang some more. He couldn't remember the whole song or the right order, so he just closed his eyes and sang what he knew.

She is frequently kind
And she's suddenly cruel
She can do as she pleases
She's nobody's fool
And she can't be convicted
She's earned her degree
And the most she will do
Is throw shadows at you
But she's always a woman to me.

Dan stopped singing. He couldn't remember the rest. He thought of his wife, and his eyes misted over.

"You got a good voice, Dad. I remember it when you used to sing to me at bed time. I liked it."

Dan looked up, surprised. "Really?"

Jeremy nodded. "Yeah, especially that song about the bright, golden haze on the meadow."

Dan smiled a bit. "Yeah, Rogers and Hammerstein, I like that one. My father used to sing that to me at bed time. Heck, he used to sing it all the time, He'd sing it and whistle it. He was happy when he wasn't thinking about my mom."

Jeremy lowered his head and dug at the ground with a small stick, throwing up black dirt between his legs. "She died when you were little, right?"

Dan nodded.

"And now my mom's dead too." He hesitated. "Does that mean we have something in common?"

Dan looked over and smiled. "It's more than that, son. We have a lot in common. I'm your father. You're my son."

Dan let the words sink in. There was a moment of clumsy silence. Then Dan stood up and walked over to the pile of sticks. "Okay, son, and now I'm going to teach you how to build a proper fire."

That broke the awkwardness of the moment, and Jeremy stood up as well, brushing the dirt and leaves off the back of his shorts.

"Forget it, Dad. You just watch the master, and I'll show you a fire to end all fires!"

Dan folded his muscled arms across his chest firmly. "So you think you can teach the old man how to build a fire?"

Jeremy copied his father, folding his arms across his chest as well. When the boy spoke, his voice was playful and almost happy.

"Think about it Dad. Who burned down the neighbor's shed? It was me, wasn't it? Not you. I say that makes me uniquely qualified to build a campfire, don't you?"

Dan let his arms drop, and for a moment the heaviness of the apocalypse melted from his shoulders.

"I got a better idea. Let's race. First person to get a fire going two feet high wins."

Jeremy mocked him. "Bring it old man!"

Dan yelled "Go!" and both of them set about scurrying for tinder and kindling, running, laughing, for a moment forgetting the chaos of the cities, the death, the loss, the mayhem.

And for a moment, the silence of the forest was filled.

CHAPTER 12

Great With Child - September 12, 2AM

S OME TIME BEFORE DAWN, DAN WAS AWAKENED BY blood-curdling screams. He stirred inside the nether world that exists only between sleep and reality. At first he thought it was part of a dream, then it was real, then dream. The screams came again, and his eyes popped open wide.

"Dad, can you hear that?"

"Yeah, son. I hear it. Probably just a coyote. There's lots of them up here."

The scream came again, sounding more humanlike than before. "That's not a coyote, Dad. That sounds like a woman."

Dan pulled his knees up and rushed out of his sleeping bag. He laced up his boots and double-checked his pistol. "Stay here, son. I'm going to check it out." And then he stood up and raced off into the woods toward the eerie sound. The scream sounded again, sending chills up Dan's back, and he adjusted course slightly. As he got closer, he slowed his pace and tried to make less noise. When he got even closer, he could hear voices.

"Please, no!"

It was a woman's voice, and Dan was reminded of the five men he'd killed just a short time ago. He unsnapped the thumb break on his holster and slowly drew out the big, Taurus revolver. The next voice he heard was a man's.

"Hold her down!"

And then another man, this one deeper and huskier. "Ouch! She bit me!"

Dan was startled at the sound of brush crashing behind him. He turned and pointed the gun just as Jeremy stumbled and fell at his feet. "Hi Dad."

Dan held his finger to his lips to quiet him. The two men kept talking.

"Hey! Did you hear that?"

"Yeah, it's just a deer. These woods are full of them. I used to hunt them when I was a kid. Just tie her hands back up so we can get her back to the cabin."

The woman screamed again, and was rewarded with a fist to the side of her head. She didn't scream again.

"Careful, Mike. Don't damage the merchandise."

Dan and Jeremy remained hidden in the bushes as the two men began dragging the unconscious woman off through the woods. They made a terrible racket. Jeremy spoke now in a whisper. "Dad, what should we do?"

Dan reholstered his pistol and thought for a moment. On the one hand, he was sure this type of thing was happening all over the country, so was it really a big deal that it was happening here too? After all, they couldn't save every woman. On the other hand … Then Jeremy broke his concentration. "We have to help her, Dad!"

Dan shot back a reply, surprised to hear himself say the words. "Yeah, right! Just like the last woman! The one who stole our truck and everything we own?" The hurt look on Jeremy's face caused Dan to feel ashamed. He softened a bit. "Cone on, Jeremy, we can't save everyone who's in trouble."

Jeremy nodded his head in the dimness of the coming dawn. "I know, Dad. I know we can't help them all." Then he looked his father full in the eyes. "But we can help this one." Dan's shame intensified as he looked down at the ground for a moment. The sound of the men dragging her away was slowly fading into the distance. Another moment passed, another, and then another. "Dad?"

Dan looked over at his son and frowned. "Go back to the truck and wait for me there." Then he moved slowly off into the woods, following the sound of rustling leaves.

TWO HOURS LATER DAN CREPT QUIETLY BACK INTO CAMP. JEREMY LOOKED up and saw the face of his father, smeared with black mud, like he was wearing a mask. His eyes were dark, opened wide, with a stare that scared him. He seemed like a different version of the same person. He looked like a Teddy Bear on crack.

"Put out that campfire!"

Jeremy immediately doused it with water. It hissed as smoke and steam rose up into the air and was lost in the treetops above. "What happened, Dad?"

Dan sat down on the bank with a heavy sigh. He felt so much older than he had three days ago.

"They have her in a cabin about a half mile from here. She's duct-taped to a chair now right beside another man. She looks very pregnant to me. I think she's in labor."

Jeremy's eyes opened wider. "Wow! Cool!"

Dan's eyes snapped back at him. "No! It's not cool! She's being held by three men, all heavily armed. Two of them are the same guys who stole the stuff from our truck and killed Kate. They've got my shotgun and my AR-15."

Jeremy squirmed on the bank beside him.

"What's an AR-15?"

But Dan ignored him. He was already deep in thought, making a plan, trying to figure out how to save the two strangers without getting himself killed. Jeremy sat there quietly. This man was different than the father he'd grown up with. He'd been somehow transformed into this Marine fighting machine, and it scared and awed him simultaneously.

AT THE BREAK OF DAWN, DAN WAS LYING ON THE GROUND, COVERED IN brush and leaves on a small hill overlooking the cabin. Out in front of him on the ground rested his fifty caliber inline ignition muzzle loader. He would have preferred his AR-15 with a thirty-round magazine, but they had stolen it from him. Now, he was reduced to relying on two hundred year old technology, albeit, significantly enhanced. With the fifty caliber Power Belt round and a double load of Pyrodex, Dan was deadly accurate out to two hundred yards. The big problem was reloading time and the huge amount of smoke the rifle gave off. He would get off only one shot. After that they'd know where he was, and it would take him almost a minute to reload.

As he lay in wait he thought about his son. It was time to teach him how to shoot, not just for his own protection, but for Dan's as well. It would have been helpful to have some flank security in this ambush, but without the proper training and equipment, Jeremy was more a liability than an asset. If he lived through this day, Dan planned on changing that.

Down below, Dan saw the front door of the cabin swing open and two men stepped outside. One of them carried Dan's shotgun, and the other clasped his AR-15. At a distance of one-hundred-fifty yards, Dan could hear their voices, but not make out the words. They both lit up cigarettes and stood on the porch laughing and talking. One of them leaned against the vertical support log on the wraparound porch. They were looking right toward Dan, but he knew they couldn't see him. Dan took some time to slow down his breathing and his heart rate. Then he slowly raised his eye up to the scope and settled in for the shot. The taller of the two men leaned the AR-15 against the cabin wall and took a leak off the porch. Dan took his time, just the way Uncle Rodney had taught him, and two minutes later he began taking up slack in the trigger. The crosshairs rested squarely on the man's solar plexus. Oddly enough, when the blast rang out, Dan felt no remorse, no guilt, no sense of regret - only recoil. The smoke cloud rose up, obscuring the porch from Dan's view. When it cleared away, Dan saw one man standing and one collapsed on the wooden planking. That's when he noticed small pieces of bark flying off the trees around him. Dan moved behind the tree beside him as the man emptied all thirty rounds blindly into the hill side. Quickly, Dan began to reload. When the man ejected the empty magazine, Dan raised the muzzleloader and fired, this time hastily. The big lead slug hit the man low in the abdomen, knocking him to the floor of the plank porch. Dan reloaded again. By now the man was screaming for help as he bled out in the morning sunshine. Dan centered the crosshairs on the wooden door, waiting for the last man to come out. But no one came. He scoped the windows and saw the shades move off to the right. Raising the scope to his eye, he let the expensive Leupold optics gather in light and focus the shape of a man's head as he peered out the glass. Dan took careful aim, and slowly and gently pressed the trigger straight to the rear. The shot boomed out. The smoke rose up. The man fell down.

Dan remained on the ground another ten minutes, waiting for the man on the porch to bleed out and die. His screams died down, lessened and eventually silenced. It reminded Dan of times he'd been deer hunting and had accidently wounded animals. He always hated those times and suffered with the animal as they lay bleeding. But this time … the ambivalence was gone. This was a different Dan Branch.

CHAPTER 13

Unto Us … A child - September 12, 7AM

FOR THE PAST FOUR HOURS JACKIE HAD BEEN FEELING CONtractions, but they were irregular and not real strong. She knew it was the stress that had caused her baby to come two weeks early. She also knew that unless she could get herself free from the duct tape and the chair that her baby would die; her husband would bleed to death; and she would die, not necessarily in that order.

She heard her husband moaning behind her and she pressed her head back trying to touch his own, but he'd slumped forward and was out of her reach. A week ago they'd been in the Dominican Republic giving aid and shelter to hurricane victims, and she'd been appalled at their living conditions and the corruption. Now … she wondered … was America any better off than Haiti? Had the only difference between America and third-world countries simply been money and power?

"Don! Stay with me honey!" She called over her shoulder several times, but he didn't respond. The gunfire on the porch had ceased, and she could hear birds chirping away outside. The man called Hector was laying on the wooden floor about six feet away. She knew he was dead because most of his head was gone. Jackie wondered what had happened. The other two men hadn't come back in from their cigarette, and she'd heard Hosea's screams start out loud and panicked, then listened as they'd dissipated into whimpers, and then quiet moans. She guessed he was dead now.

Hector was the one who'd beaten her husband over and over again without asking a single question. Over and over he'd punched Don until he'd lapsed into unconsciousness, and then he'd laughed and talked about raping Jackie and then killing her baby. All through the night the men had sniffed more and more drugs. It was like they didn't even need sleep.

A contraction came on again, starting slow, like a wave moving toward the beach, then it rose up as it hit the shallows, then cresting as it pounded onto the shoreline. Jackie heard someone screaming, then realized it was her and forced herself to close her mouth. The pain subsided and she could hear nothing but the birds outside, her own rapid breathing, and the slow, steady dripping of her husband's blood down onto the wooden floorboards. He would die soon. She struggled again at the duct tape, but it held her fast.

Jackie slumped her head forward onto her chest and prayed. "Dear God! Aren't going to get us out of this? Aren't' you going to save us? We dedicated our lives to you, and you reward us with torture, pain and death? Can't you at least kill us quickly?"

As if in answer, there was a scuffle on the wooden planking outside. Jackie looked up and saw a man peering carefully through the window. She couldn't make out his face, because it was all blacked over with something. She quickly thanked God that the man wasn't Frank, and then apologized for calling him a doubting him. Perhaps, this man was different. Perhaps, he would kill them all quickly. Her mind, her faith, her hope, in just a few short days, had been reduced to this thinking: that the best life had to offer was a quick and painless death.

Jackie looked up again and the man's face was gone from the window. The dripping of Don's blood continued. A small field mouse scurried along the wall until it came to the brains spilled out and splattered on the floor. The little mouse stopped and sniffed. Jackie was surprised at the absurdity of her own thoughts. *I need to get some mouse traps. I can't have a mouse running loose in my cabin.*

Just then she heard a hand touch the doorknob, and Jackie watched as it turned. The mouse scurried away and disappeared through a small hole in the wall that she'd never noticed before. The door opened slowly, letting in light from the rising sun behind; it cascaded in swiftly, in streaks of light, making the blood on the floor shine bright red. The door swung open, and the man stood there outlined in brightness, his pistol pointed in, searching out the room for someone to kill. Jackie waited for the loud boom and the flash of the muzzle, but it didn't come. The man lowered his gun and took another step into the room.

The smell of death and blood and brains was all around her. The man walked in and stood over her, looking down. She wondered why he didn't say anything, why she didn't say anything. The man looked over at the dead body on the floor, then at her husband, then back at her. Finally, after what seemed like hours, he spoke.

"You okay, ma'am?"

Jackie started to weep. He was polite. He must be one of the good guys.

And then she felt the next wave moving toward the beach, surging, building, coming closer, and bringing with it pain, and suffering, and the inevitable promise of life or death.

THREE HOURS LATER DAN PLACED HIS KNEES ON THE EDGE OF THE BED AS he leaned over the woman with her skirt hiked up to her waist. The water had broken two hours ago, making the contractions stronger and eventually settling in at a steady once every five minutes. Now they were coming much closer together. Dan reached his hand in to feel the progress of the baby. The head was right there, ready to come out.

"Oh, Dad, that is so gross! How can you do that?"

"Just shut up, son, and get me that towel over there."

Dan moved his fingers around and tried to spread out the opening as best he could.

He looked up into Jackie's eyes and smiled weakly.

"How's it going, Jackie?"

For some unknown reason, his smile infuriated her, and his sense of calm was driving her crazy. He'd been doing it for almost an hour now and she just wanted to reach up, grab him by the ears and scream into his face. *"How do I look like I'm doing? Do I look okay to you? No! I'm trying to shoot a bowling ball out my vagina! So just shut up, wipe that grin off your face and let's get it done!"*

But she didn't say anything.

"Okay, on this next one we're going to push, not real hard, just enough to get the baby's head so I can see it."

Jackie felt the next wave, and it was bigger and stronger than anything so far.

"Okay, Jackie. Go ahead and take a deep breath and push like you're having a bowel movement."

Jackie pushed. Jeremy peered over Dan's shoulder.

"Wow! Cool Dad. Look at that."

Jackie wanted to slap the boy. Instead, she pushed again and then stopped as the pain subsided.

"Okay, I can see the top of his head now. We're making good progress. Tell me when the next one starts and we'll try to get his head out."

Jeremy moved in closer.

"How did you learn to do this, Dad."

Jackie felt like she was on display at a museum.

"I saw it on The Learning Channel just last week."

Jackie's heart sunk. *The Learning Channel? My baby's life is in the hands of a one-hour TV special!* She opened her mouth to say something derogative, but pain wisely cut her words short.

"Okay, Jackie. Go ahead and push when you're ready."

But she was already gritting her teeth and bearing down.

"Whoa! Not so fast. You're going to tear! Softer, Jackie, keep control." Jackie let off just a hair, but the urge to push was just too strong."

Then the head came out just as the wave crashed on the beach.

"Okay! Stop now, Jackie!"

Dan held the baby's head in his left hand and reached down with his right to wipe away the fluid.

"Now give me the turkey baster, Jeremy! Now! Quickly, I have to have it!"

Jeremy fumbled with the rubber and plastic bulb, and dropped it on the floor. Dan reached down and got it himself. He quickly sucked the mucus and fluid out of the baby's nose. Almost immediately the little thing began to cry.

"Jackie, you have to push again. Just get one of his shoulders out."

Jackie felt her spirits lift with the sound of her baby's cry. "But I don't have a contraction."

"It doesn't matter, just see if you can push her out."

Jackie pushed, but nothing happened. She felt very weak, like she was ready to pass out. Then another contraction started to build.

"Okay, you need to push now."

The baby was screaming.

"I got the towel ready, Dad."

"You have to push, Jackie!"

Jackie ignored them both, waiting just a few seconds longer until the wave began to crest. She screamed and pushed. The baby slid out and Dan grabbed her with one hand on the head and the other on her back. She was wet and slippery and he almost dropped her to the floor.

"Don't drop my baby you idiot!"

"I need the towel now, Jeremy."

But Jeremy was watching in awe with his mouth dropped open.

"Give me the towel, son!"

Jeremy put the towel on the bed and Dan laid the baby inside it.

"She's the wrong color, Dad."

Dan didn't say anything. He quickly rubbed the baby's skin, getting off the wet, sticky slime. When he was done, he wrapped the baby in the towel and raised her up to Jackie's chest. She cradled her and wept softly to herself.

Dan returned to the woman's legs, hesitated, then quickly went to work. With a piece of monofilament fishing line, he tied off the umbilical cord and then with a pair of hair-cutting sheers, lopped it off.

"Dad, that baby's black!"

Jackie didn't say anything. She was too busy holding her little girl, kissing her and crying.

"Son, go outside and get the canteen out of my backpack."

"What for, Dad? We got water right over there."

Dan snapped back at him.

"Just do as I say, son!"

Jeremy grudgingly left the cabin.

When the door closed behind him, Dan stood up and looked down on her.

"Listen, Jackie, you have a tear down there that I need to sew up, and I've never done it before. I'm thinking it's going to hurt a lot."

Jackie looked up at him with disbelief and laughed for the first time in days.

"So how many babies have you delivered before this one?"

"None. I helped deliver a calf once though."

She went back to loving her child.

"Then do your worst, farm boy. I'll try not to flinch."

Dan smiled, but she no longer wanted to slap him. Instead, she looked over to her husband, on the floor across the room. He was on blankets with a hole in his side put there by the man who'd just saved her life and the life of her child. She didn't know which would kill her husband quicker: the bullet in his side, or the color of her baby's skin.

CHAPTER 14

A time to kill - September 12, 2PM

"DAD, YOU NEED TO STOP SHOOTING PEOPLE ALL THE time. At least until the ground softens up a bit." Jeremy stabbed his shovel into the hard dirt one more time and hit a root. The shovel's blade glanced off it, and the boy cursed under his breath. "Is one big hole good for these guys, or do we have to do three smaller ones?"

Dan sat off to the side with his feet hanging down in the newly dug hole. He couldn't tell if his son was serious or trying to be funny, so he gave him the benefit of the doubt. "Just the one hole today, son. These are all bad guys."

Jeremy picked up the hatchet and knelt down to chop away at the root. "So the rule is we bury good guys in good graves, and we pray over them, but the bad guys get one hole and no prayer?"

Dan grunted. "Yeah. I guess that's it."

Jeremy stood up and pushed hair away from his eyes. Dan noticed the boy needed a haircut. "So why do we have to bury these guys at all? They're pretty bad people, right?"

Dan stood and picked up his shovel again to dig. It was a good question in light of all that had happened in the past few days. "I think it's important to maintain a sense of dignity and respect for the dead, even if the dead are evil."

Jeremy went back to hacking at the root. "Sorry, Dad. I just don't get it. Why don't we just dump their bodies a few miles down the road and let the animals eat them? After all, they were torturing Jackie and her husband."

Dan pushed the shovel into the ground and then drove it deep into the hard dirt with his right boot. "We don't bury them for their sake. We bury them to keep ourselves from becoming like them, son. Rules of decency are more important now than ever, because ... well, because there's so much evil out there and it's important that good wins over evil."

Jeremy threw the root out of the hole and picked up his shovel again. "My Social Studies teacher, Ms. Maynard, would call that altruistic." He hesitated. "But, I guess it don't really matter all that much anymore. She lived in Eau Claire, so I'm guessing she's dead by now."

Dan kept shoveling, but thought his son's statement was sad. Even after all that had happened, he still couldn't believe that society was over. It had collapsed and now it was every man for himself. Three dead men were piled up not 10 feet away, and he and his 14-year-old son were having a conversation on ethics. Life had changed so fundamentally, so radically, and so quickly. He felt like he was just riding along on a river, out of control, just hanging on to a log in whitewater, and reacting to everything that was happening along the journey. But he had a feeling that every decision he made, to shoot or not to shoot, to kill or let live, to help or to hinder – each decision would contribute to either make him a better or a worse person. Dan knew that instinctively and wanted to teach it to his son, if at all possible. But the thing was, he really didn't know if it was possible, or wise, or even practical in a day and age where lawlessness was the law of the land. He stuck his shovel in the dirt and leaned on it.

"Jeremy. Look at me, son."

Jeremy stopped digging and looked his father full in the eyes. "Son, we may not survive the trip to Michigan. Or, if we do survive, then we could die soon after getting there. Life is pretty uncertain right now, and that makes everything we do today all the more important. Because, well, because we may not have a tomorrow." He reached over and touched his son's shoulder. "Jeremy, it was always true before, but we had life so easy that we didn't realize it. Now, more than ever, it's important that we do good in the eyes of God. Because we could be meeting Him face to face at any moment."

Jeremy nodded, but didn't have the words to respond. He looked down, then back up again. "Is that why you've been reading that Bible so much?"

Dan smiled softly and nodded. "I suppose so. Nothing like death to get a man thinking about life. And I suspect I haven't killed my last."

Jeremy bowed his head again, avoiding his father's gaze. "Dad, will I have to kill too?"

Dan wanted to lie to him. He wanted to scoop him up and bring him close. He wanted to tell him over and over again that everything would be alright and he'd protect him from the bad guys like when Jeremy had been younger. But this time he moved his right hand out and lifted his son's chin up so he could see his eyes. "Listen, son. Do you remember when you were younger and you kept telling me at bedtime there was a monster in your closet?" Jeremy nodded, his chin pressing down slightly on his Dad's fingers.

"Well, back then I told you the monsters weren't real, but now I can't say that. Because now they are real, and we're burying three of them right now. There are more monsters out there, maybe lots of them, and there's a pretty fair chance that some of them will need killing."

Jeremy turned away. A tear formed at the corner of his left eye,and he quickly wiped it away. "So I will have to kill someone?"

Dan went back to digging. "Tomorrow I teach you how to shoot. My life depends on it, and so does yours. But I promise that I'll get you back to Uncle Rodney's where things are safer and we have some friends to help look after us. That's the best I can do, son."

Jeremy nodded and went back to digging.

JACKIE OVERTON SAT ON THE BED BESIDE HER HUSBAND, HOLDING HIS hand and cradling their newborn daughter in her free arm. He was sleeping, and his hand felt hot. She let go of his fingers long enough to touch his forehead. It was burning, but not sweating anymore, and she didn't know what that meant. Her own head still hurt where the men had beaten her, and she was tired and sore from birthing, but all in all she was in pretty good shape, considering what she'd been through.

Jackie's hair was down now and properly brushed. It was long, straight and as black as midnight. Her eyes were dark and deep as well, a gift from her Lebanese mother.

Jackie had spent the first years of her childhood in Beirut, living with a Muslim mother and a Christian father. The fact her parents had married was nothing short of miraculous, but that single act had taught Jackie more about unconditional love than anything else. Her father had been willing to die to consummate his love for her mother. Indeed, he had died for her mother, one night when their apartment was stormed by Islamist, who were infuriated that her mother had defied Islamic law by marrying an infidel and then spawning a Christian child. The other kids had called her an abomination that needed to be purged. The men had killed her father that night, beat him and cut off his head in the alley beside the apartment.

That same night other Christians had whisked her and her mother away to temporary safety. Within a year they were in America and living with her paternal grand parents. Jackie had grown to not only hate the Muslims who'd robbed her of a father, but all of Islam.

And now … she looked down at her baby, her black baby, and then to her husband, her white husband. She had cheated on a man who loved without bounds, and her guilt was worse than death itself. Of course, Don knew nothing. She had been discreet, and it had been a short-lived affair.

Her husband looked terrible. She looked over at the blood stains on the floor, then down at her daughter, suckling on her breast in complete comfort and calm. The baby was oblivious to the death and horror going on around her. That was the nature of babies, and they survived only by the grace and discretion of their parents.

Jackie had a terrible feeling her husband was dying. The man called, Dan Branch, had said he was gut shot. Such a cold and callus way to say it. He had attacked three men, killed them, and saved the life of her and her daughter, but one of the bullets had accidently hit Don in the process. The stranger had saved him and killed him all in one shot.

And now, as Jackie sat on the bed, waiting for her husband to die of infection, she wondered which would be worse: for her husband to die in his sleep before seeing his daughter, or for him to die after realizing his wife was a whore.

Either way, she also knew she was waiting for her own death. And it would be terrible. Once the man and boy were done burying the bodies, they would ransack the cabin, taking what they wanted and leave. But at least they would leave without harming her and her daughter. They were good enough people for that. Then … Don would die, and she would be alone again, helpless in a brutal world of evil men, unable to protect her daughter. But then again, what reason was there to grow up?

Her and Don had realized the nation's course. That's why they'd bought the cabin last year and why they'd fled Chicago when they had. The lights weren't coming back on. She knew that. And what made it worse, everyone else knew it too. Every person inclined to do evil was no longer restrained by the rule of law, leaving them free to rape, pillage and plunder as they saw fit. It was only a matter of time before they were found, just as they'd been found by these three men. And then … her and her daughter would die. Of course, that was the worst-case scenario, and if no one found them, they could starve or freeze to death here in the cabin, at peace with God in beautiful surroundings.

And then she could be with her parents again. She would show them her husband

and her beautiful new baby, and they would smile, and laugh, and they would be happy again. Yes, happy again. Jackie found herself smiling. Then she looked back down at her dying husband. Yes, happy again, if he forgave her. But first … but first … not so happy. Her smile went away as she held her daughter and waited for her husband to die.

CHAPTER 15

Mr. Lechter and the Blind Man - September 12, 4PM

ACCORDING TO THOSE DOING BUSINESS WITH HIM, JARED Thompson was known as the Blind Man who kept Hannibal Lechter on a leash. Of course, *all that glitters is not gold and skim milk masquerades as cream.*

And Jared had made a living at masquerades - a very good living.

Jared was a very secretive man, and he had remade himself so many times that he sometimes woke up in the morning having to remind himself of who he really was, at least on that particular day. But most days he was just a blind man employing a very ruthless and competent assistant who just happened to think and sound like Hannibal Lechter. His assistant's real name of course was Sammy Thurmond, but no one feared and respected a man named Sammy Thurmond. So people just called him the Blind Man's Assistant.

Jared sat at the table now with Sammy off to his left standing slightly behind him. Two more of his men were in the background, just in case. But they didn't have names; they were simply mindless muscle, waiting to kill someone on his command. Sammy was the important one. He was devious, strong, and ruthless, just sort of evil; but the most important aspect of his character, at least to Jared, Sammy Thurmond was insanely loyal and protective. They were a good team. Jared made the plans, and Sammy carried them out - no questions asked. For Jared, it was a match made in heaven.

The door on the wall across from them opened up and three men in black suits walked through. They all carried submachine guns at the low-ready position. None of this bothered Jared; it was pretty standard in his line of work. Every day was a risk, and every second a gamble. He could die at any moment, but the important thing, at least to him, was knowing that should he die all his enemies would be captured and tortured before their deaths. He had paid a lot of money to arrange that deal. And he'd also hired someone else to supervise the torture and subsequent execution - just to make sure.

Jared Thompson was a stickler for redundancy.

Once the three machine guns were in place, a fourth man walked in and sat down across from Jared. This man was different than the others. He wore Arab garb, had a large nose and plenty of black and grey facial hair.

Jared didn't like the man, but he loved his money.

"You have achieved a great victory for Allah, may he be exalted."

Jared didn't say anything. He just nodded mutely, staring ahead blankly through his sunglasses, feigning humility to the Sheik across the table.

"The infidels have been humiliated and rendered impotent. We are grateful for your services."

Jared bowed slightly with his head. He knew this man couldn't be trusted, that the Sheik was a lunatic and considered Jared to be an infidel, deserving only of death or complete submission to Allah. But Jared didn't like Allah either - or his prophet Mohammed, or anyone else named Mohammed, Ahmed, Abdul, or any other ridiculous name of Middle Eastern concoction. Come to think of it, Jared didn't like anyone. He didn't even like himself, and a part of him, the innermost part, the part that only came out at night and in his dreams, was simply waiting impatiently to die. What no one else knew or understood was that all Jared's money, all his power, all his plans and schemes, were just a distraction from his own despair, simply a means to keep himself from self destructing for one more day.

"We have need of you again."

Jared thought to himself, *Of that I have no doubt. By yourself you are incapable of doing anything, even the most basic of things like taking a leak or making love to a woman. Everything has to be arranged for you, bought and paid for. You are a helpless man, kept alive only by the protection your money buys you. And it's not even your money. You stole it from your people, sold their oil and forced them to serve you. You are a despicable man.*

But on the outside, Jared nodded like a snake.

The Sheik motioned with his hand, and the man behind him produced a file folder. The Sheik slid it across the table. Jared opened it and studied it a moment. Jared ran his fingertips across the braille, quickly reading every detail. He smiled inside. They were so predictable. The dollar sign with a number followed by seven zeros made him laugh to himself. He wasn't doing this for the money. He had his own agenda. Besides, money was just paper now, in any currency.

But on the outside, Jared remained the nodding snake.

"None of this is a concern for you?"

Jared spoke for the first time.

"It's not a problem, sir. It will be done as you require."

The Sheik smiled and nodded triumphantly. In his mind, Jared was a traitorous infidel, willing to sell his own people into bondage, willing to rape, pillage and betray not only his country, but his heritage and remove all freedom from the land.

But Jared knew better. It was true that he'd brought on the thousand-year night with the help of his Muslim allies; it was true that anarchy was now loosed not only upon America, but upon the world; but what the Sheik didn't know, was that deep down inside, Jared Thompson had twenty-twenty vision.

Jared slowly and ceremoniously removed his sunglasses and looked deep into the Sheik's dark eyes. Then he looked into the face of the Sheik's three bodyguards, one at a time, registering the surprised look on their faces as the Blind Man met their gaze.

Jared nodded and Sammy Thurmond pressed a remote button in his coat pocket. The bullet-proof glass popped up, shielding Jared from the gunfire that erupted soon after. When it subsided, Sammy pressed another button and the bullet-proof glass lowered. The Sheik was slumped down over the table with a bullet wound to the left shoulder and the right arm. All of his body guards were dead, as were two of Jared's.

Jared looked into the man's eyes and smiled.

"I - I thought you were blind?"

Jared laughed.

"That's okay, I thought you were stupid. That's the difference between you and me. I was right, and you were wrong."

The Sheik's eyes filled with terror and confusion.

"But why? Why would you do such a thing? We made you rich!"

Jared stood up and produced a pearl-handled nine millimeter pistol from his coat pocket. He aimed it across the table straight into the Sheik's face.

"Because you're impolite. And I don't like you."

Jared pulled the trigger. The Sheik's head jerked back and then slumped forward again.

"Besides, I'm a patriot, and I won't let foreigners come into my own country and take it over."

He glanced back at Sammy who immediately stepped forward. Jared placed the pistol in his hand and walked out of the room, stepping over dead bodies all the way to the door. He stopped at the exit and glanced over his shoulder.

"Bury the Muslims at the pig farm outside of town. Have our men cremated. It's only right."

Sammy remained expressionless as he nodded compliance.

"I never liked that man. He is so impolite!"

Jared left the room.

CHAPTER 16

A Slice of American Pie - September 12, 8PM

"HE'S DYING FROM INFECTION, AND THERE'S NOTHING I can do to stop it. He needs a hospital."

Tears welled up in Jackie's eyes, but she refused to let them fall in front of Dan Branch. She would wait and cry alone later on. But what he asked next surprised her.

"Where's the nearest hospital from here? How far away is it?"

She looked up at him...puzzled. "Why do you ask?"

Dan leaned back and made eye contact with her. He knew she hated him; it was obvious by the way she glared at him; but to ask a question like that she must think him a heartless brute. He sighed and maintained his calm demeanor. "Because we need to get him to a hospital or he'll die for sure. They have to operate and clean out the infected organs and then pump him full of antibiotics. There's still a bullet in there too that has to come out."

Jackie thought to herself, *Yes, a bullet that you shot into him.* But she didn't say it aloud. She knew it was irrational, that Dan Branch had saved them, but he hated him for it and would never forgive him. She mumbled softly. "Eagle River has a hospital. It's a 40-minute drive from here."

Dan looked down for a moment. Forty minutes worth of fuel, 80 minutes for the trip, not to mention the added danger of traveling to a city in this chaos. And most important of all…Eagle River was in the wrong direction. Dan looked over and saw Jeremy studying him. He was reminded of his talk with his son earlier in the day. He recalled his words vividly and painfully. *Now, more than ever, it's important that we do good in the eyes of God. Because we could be meeting Him face to face at any moment.* He cursed himself inside for hesitating to do the decent thing.

"We'd better get going then. He won't make it until morning." Dan stood up beside the bed and walked toward the door. "I'll make room in the truck bed for him. I'll have to drive easy but fast. Time is important."

Jackie's mouth dropped open and she looked at him in disbelief. *Why was he doing this?*

"Jeremy, I need your help."

They both walked out the door to the truck. Once out of hearing, Dan turned and faced his son. Jeremy was the first to speak.

"Are you sure this is a good idea, Dad?"

Dan didn't answer right away. "No, I'm not sure, but I do know it's the right thing to do. I shot that man, so I need to try and save him. It's cut and dried."

Jeremy lowered his head. "I thought you said the cities weren't safe?"

Dan reassured him. "Eagle River is small. It should be okay." Then he started walking to the truck. "I want you to stay here with Jackie and the baby. They're going to need a man to protect them."

Jeremy opened his mouth to argue, but Dan held up his hand to cut him off. "It's decided. The baby is newborn and Jackie will have all she can do just to keep the baby alive. She's going to need help. I can make the drive alone, but you're needed here."

Dan stopped at the truck and opened the door. He reached behind the seat and pulled out the Winchester Model 1800 shotgun. He quickly showed him how to operate it before handing the firearm to his son.

"Never point it at anyone you don't mean to kill. And anyone who tries to hurt you, Jackie or the baby has to die. Understand?"

Jeremy swallowed hard before answering. "Yes, sir. I'll do my best."

Dan forced a smile then moved to the back of the truck to drop down the tailgate. Ten minutes later, the wounded man was loaded into the truck bed and Dan was ready to roll.

Jackie walked out onto the porch and stood there holding the baby. She wanted to cry, but she would do it later. Dan walked over to Jeremy and hugged him tightly against his chest. "Protect the women and children. That's your job now."

Jeremy squeezed him back, and nodded his head. He was trying to be brave.

"Just hurry back, Dad. We need to get to Michigan."

Dan glanced over to Jackie and nodded his head. "I'll do my best, ma'am. Watch my son, please."

Jackie lowered her head, but didn't answer. Dan turned and hopped into the pick-up truck and drove off down the two-track to the main road.

Jeremy stood and listened until the sound of the truck's engine was faded and gone.

He wondered if he'd ever see his father again.

THIRTY MINUTES INTO THE DRIVE, DAN NOTICED MORE AND MORE HOUSES, so he knew he was getting close. He'd have to stop and ask directions, and that thought unnerved him. He knew strangers would not be taken too kindly. He reached down and hit the "search" button on the radio, looking for a station that might give him some intel, but no such luck. There were very few cars on the road and the few people he did see outside were armed to the teeth.

Suddenly, the radio came alive with a tired, slow voice.

"This is Danny Dixon, the voice of Eagle River's classic rock. We'll be broadcasting for five minutes every hour on the hour as long as the fuel lasts. Sorry folks, no music today. In the immortal words of Don McClean *I went down to the sacred store, Where I'd heard the music years before, But the man there said the music wouldn't play.*

The man's voice quivered a bit before going on. "Now ain't that the saddest words you ever heard?"

There was silence for a moment. Dan remembered the lyrics to the classic rock song *American Pie*. He had never understood them, but they had intrigued him nonetheless.

"So the music won't play today, but maybe tomorrow, the good Lord willing. But for today, I have a list of do's and don't's from the Eagle River Community Emergency Response Team."

The DJ then rattled off a list of precautionary instructions on boiling water, on eating spoiled food, how to go to the bathroom without polluting the city, and the list went on. Dan half listened. He had *American Pie* stuck in his head now and it wouldn't go away.

He was singing, "bye-bye, miss American pie.
Drove my chevy to the levee, But the levee was dry.

Dan started humming at first, then he broke into song. It was crazy, and he knew it, but for some reason he just couldn't stop.

Them good old boys were drinkin' whiskey and rye And singin',
"this'll be the day that I die.

"And now for the news."

Dan immediately stopped singing and listened to Danny Dixon.

"There is no contact at all from Madison. It is rumored that the Capitol building burned to the ground last night, but it can't be confirmed. Martial law was declared, but no one knows if the Governor is even alive. Citizens with Ham radios have reported that all the major cities are being looted and burned by hungry and angry mobs. The Eagle River Chief of Police has asked that anyone with prior military or law enforcement experience report to the city hall as a volunteer. You will be briefed and trained for duty.

"The Eagle River Fire Chief has imposed a ban on indoor cooking as many cities have already burned down, and the Chief has no way to put out the fire.

"As to the rumors of foreign invasion on the West Coast, well, those are just rumors and no one knows what to believe anymore. Just be careful with those firearms and conserve your ammo just in case.

"Okay, well that's all the time I have. I'll fire up again in 55 minutes for an update. Have a good night, and God bless Eagle River."

The voice cut off and was replaced with static, leaving Dan more lonely than before. The song flashed into his head again.

I met a girl who sang the blues
And I asked her for some happy news,
But she just smiled and turned away.

Up ahead Dan saw the flashing strobes of a city police cruiser and a fire engine, so he slowed down. As he drew near, he saw a dozen men behind cars with shotguns and rifles all aimed at him.

And in the streets: the children screamed,
The lovers cried, and the poets dreamed.
But not a word was spoken;
The church bells all were broken.

Dan kept his hands on the steering wheel and let the truck roll to a stop, all the while wondering, was this the last train to the coast?

JEREMY WATCHED AS THE LITTLE BABY SUCKED ON HIS MOTHER'S BREAST. A week ago he would have been embarrassed or even chuckled and made a derogatory comment at the sight of a woman's bare breast, but in light of all that happened, Jeremy no longer felt trite. The sight of a mother feeding her baby seemed as natural to him as anything he'd ever seen.

"How come your baby's a different color?"

Jackie flinched inside at the question. This boy was so blunt, not in a rude way, because she sensed that he wasn't trying to hurt her, just that he was curious and really wanted to know. The boy's only fault was lack of boundaries and no sense of social appropriety. She measured her words before speaking.

"I made a terrible mistake."

Jeremy nodded. "Yeah, that's what I figured." He shrugged his shoulders. "It had to be that. What else could it be, right?"

Jackie looked at him and halfway smiled. *On the other hand, his raw honesty was somewhat refreshing when juxtapposed to the verbal games that most adults played. If this boy was thinking it, then he was saying it.*

She just nodded her head and looked back down at her baby.

"My mom made lots of mistakes like that too. It killed my dad, hurt him real bad." He hesitated and looked down at the floor. "I guess it killed her too, in the end that is."

Jackie looked up again. "Your mother is dead?"

Jeremy nodded. "Yes, she died three days ago of a drug overdose."

She shifted the baby in her arms, allowing the child to get a better grasp on the nipple. "I'm sorry to hear that, Jeremy."

"We buried her yesterday in a cemetery a ways back." He rubbed his eyes briefly. "It was the best we could do."

Jackie smiled softly. "At least you still have your father."

Jeremy smiled. "Yeah. I do. If you have to have a dad, then I guess he's the one I would choose. He's saved my life twice already since this all started."

Jackie shifted her gaze. She seemed suddenly more interested. "Yes, I guess we have that in common then. He saved my life too, and the life of my baby. How did he save your life?"

Jeremy shrugged his shoulders. He was holding the shotgun in his left hand with the stock end resting on the floor. He leaned it up against the wall in the corner. "He's just always there for me, even before all this happened. I knew I could count on him, even when I cussed at him, abused him, you know, all the things that kids my age do to parents just cuz we're screwed up and angry."

Jackie remembered her teen years and nodded in agreement.

"And then he shot those five guys the other night who were raping a woman in the cemetery."

Jackie's eyes got big. "He shot five men? I mean five men plus the three men he shot today?"

Jeremy nodded. "Yeah, it's really weird. We keep running across people that are being hurt, and the only way to save them is for Dad to shoot somebody."

Jackie's brow furled and she couldn't help but think, *What manner of man is this who kills eight men in three days? And is he going to kill me too?*

"But they were really bad dudes, and they needed killing. Dad saved that woman, then she stole our truck and all our supplies, so we had to chase her down, then we found her dead on the side of the road along with mom's body. We took them back to the cemetery and buried them. An old man helped us and then gave us 5 gallons of gas to make it here. He was a good man, but he stayed there and prayed over his wife's grave. He was a nice old man and I hope he's okay."

The boy shrugged again. "We're trying to make it to Dad's Uncle Rodney's house in Michigan. Dad says he's more prepared for this than anyone else in the world. He raised my dad after his parents died. We have that in common, because both my parents are dead too. Dan is really my step-dad, but he feels more like a real dad than anyone I ever known."

Jackie was looking up now and they locked eyes for a moment.

"He's one of the good guys, Jackie."

Jackie nodded and then looked back down again. She fumbled with the baby as she changed breasts and then continued the feeding.

Jeremy kept talking, and Jackie just listened. He talked about his mom cheating on his dad, not once, but many times. He talked about shooting a rocket through the kitchen window, about a girl named Tonya, and a dog he'd had named Elijah that had been run over by a car. A few times she thought he would cry, but he quickly changed the subject and ended up smiling and even laughing in some places.

After a half an hour, she started to like him. And then an unusual thing happened. Jackie talked too, not just a little, but a lot. She shared about her husband, her childhood, the murder of her father and even about her affair with the Haitian refugee.

An hour later, when they were both all talked out, Jackie laid the sleeping baby on the bed and cooked some food. It was nothing fancy, just a can of Dinty Moore stew and some bread and butter. They both ate in silence, but it was now a graceful silence. In her mind she wondered, *Where is my husband? Is he alive? Will he forgive me? Will my baby live?*

They both finished eating. The boy walked out onto the porch and stared into the night, waiting for his father to return.

Jackie went back to the bed and lay beside her new baby. Now that she was finally alone, she held the baby and she cried.

"I WANT YOU TO KEEP YOU HANDS WHERE I CAN SEE THEM, AND VERY slowly exit the truck."

Dan assumed it was a police officer talking to him, but he couldn't see anyone because the blinding search light from the police cruiser was in his eyes. Before getting out of the truck, Dan unholstered his big pistol and put it on the front seat beside him. Then he opened the door and raised his hands above his head. His heart was pounding in his chest beyond his control.

"He's got a gun, George!"

Dan heard the accusation, but was quick to correct them."

"No, my holster is empty. I left my pistol on the seat in the truck. I don't want any trouble. See, look at it."

Dan turned to the side so they could get a good look at his empty holster.

"Easy, men. The holster's empty."

A big man in a police uniform stepped out from behind the car and walked slowly toward him. He stopped six feet away before speaking again.

"State your business, stranger."

Dan squinted in the bright light and tried to shade his eyes with his left hand.

"I got a man in the truck bed. He's hurt real bad, and he needs a doctor. I just want to get him to the hospital here."

For a moment there was no answer. Dan felt naked in the light with so many guns pointing at him, but he had no choice but to endure their skepticism, at least for now.

"What's your name and where are you from?"

"I'm Dan Branch. I live in Menomonie over near Eau Claire, but I'm headed to my home town in Northern Michigan to ride this out where I've got friends and family."

The police officer took a step closer. The man's head blocked the light so Dan could finally get a good look at him. His hair was black and grey, but it was all messed up and his face was streaked with blood and dirt. He had a feeling that something bad had happened here.

"What kind of injury?"

Dan hesitated.

"He's been gut shot. Him and his pregnant wife were attacked about 40 minutes from here. She's okay, but he needs surgery and antibiotics."

The man was quiet for a moment, and when he spoke again, his voice was cold and emotionless.

"You need to turn around and head back out of town. No one can enter. It's for our own safety. Orders of the Mayor."

Dan looked at him in disbelief. How could this happen in only four days time?

"But…he'll die."

The policeman's voice wavered a bit now, but his face remained stern.

"Sorry. I got my orders. No one gets into town for any reason. No exceptions."

Dan took a step forward.

"Stop!"

The police officer drew something from his waist. Dan assumed it was a gun, so he froze in place.

"What's wrong with you guys? Are you just going to let a good man die when you have the means to help him? I'll leave him with you and I'll wait here if you want. Just help my friend. Please."

Dan watched the inner struggle move like a spasm across the cop's face.

"Listen, friend, I don't like this any more than you do. But this is a dire situation. We've already shot and killed a dozen men in the last two days, and every last one of them claimed to be the good guys. But they weren't. We let them in, and they murdered and raped the Mayor's wife and daughter. We're not trusting anyone again, so you need to turn around and leave while you still can."

A sudden wave of anger filled Dan as he took another step forward. The Taser darts sprang out and lodged in his chest sending 50,000 volts pulsing through his body. Dan collapsed immediately, writhing in pain on the pavement.

"Daniel, go check the bed of his truck and tell me what you see."

The cop was standing over him now, and every time Dan tried to get up, he pushed the Taser button again. After three times, Dan stayed down."

"He was telling the truth, George. The man back here's been gut shot. Don't look none too good, either."

"Check his pulse."

There was silence for about thirty seconds. Dan just lay there unmoving. Finally, Daniel yelled out.

"He's dead, George. No pulse and no breathing. He's still warm though and hasn't stiffened up. Must be pretty recent."

"Okay then. Open his cab door and unload his pistol. Then bring me the bullets and help me get him back inside his truck."

The man did as he was told, and soon handed 5 four-ten shotgun shells to the cop. The cop smiled and placed them in his pocket.

"Must be carrying a Taurus Judge. That's a mean gun."

He looked down at Dan, then latched on to his right arm and lifted him to his feet. Dan was surprised at how powerful the man was. The other man, Daniel, lifted him by the other arm and they both drug him to the cab.

The police officer pinned Dan up against the truck door and looked him straight in the eye from just six inches away.

"Can I trust that you'll never come back here again?"

Dan was weak and wobbly, so he didn't answer right away. The cop stepped back and hit the Taser trigger again. Dan spasmed and fell to his knees. But this time he was mad. He reached up and ripped out one of the darts and lunged forward, falling down around the man's ankles. He felt a kick to the groin and doubled up on the ground, but still reached out to the cop's pant leg. Now both men were kicking him. He felt the officer's baton crash against his head and face several times. Finally, he covered up with his hands, absorbing the blows, hoping just to survive.

And the three men I admire most:
The father, son, and the holy ghost,
They caught the last train for the coast
The day the music died.

As he lapsed into unconsciousness, the sound of Don McClean's singing laughed inside his head without remorse or mercy.

They tossed Dan's body into the truck bed and drove him out ten miles before stopping by a hayfield. They parked the truck and the cop took one last look at Dan and the dead man before shaking his head. In his mind, he couldn't help but think, *So this is what we do with good people now. How did it come to this?*

Then he reached into his pocket, pulled out the five loose four-ten shells and threw them on the floor of the truck bed. He said out loud. "Don't come back, Dan Branch from Menomonie. You may be one of the good guys, but if you do, we'll have to kill you. And we're the good guys too."

The officer turned and walked back to his cruiser where Daniel was waiting.

"Get out of the driver's seat, Daniel. This is my car."

Daniel moved over and the cop got inside and drove away, leaving Dan Branch to the night.

CHAPTER 17

A Time to Heal - September 13, 10AM

JEREMY HAD MOVED TWO CHAIRS OUT ONTO THE PORCH, and he and Jackie were waiting there when Dan's truck lumbered back in and coasted to a stop. He was slumped over the steering wheel with his face down. Jackie held the baby close while Jeremy ran forward to the truck.

"Dad! Are you okay? I waited up almost all night long!"

The boy reached the cab and looked in just as Dan raised his head and turned. What Jeremy saw caused an adrenaline dump into his bloodstream and his heart to pump faster.

"Oh my God! Dad, what happened to you?"

Jackie stood up and walked over still clutching her baby. When she saw Dan's swollen and bloody face, she ran back into the cabin. A moment later she returned with a wet rag. Jeremy already had the truck door open, and Dan had fallen out onto the dirt driveway.

"Roll him over on his back, Jeremy."

Jeremy complied while she checked his pulse and his breathing. She noticed his left eye was swollen totally closed and the right eye was open just a slit. Jackie shook her head, wondering how he'd even managed to drive back.

"Get me a bowl of water and another towel from inside. We have to clean him up and see how bad it is."

It took ten minutes to wash up Dan's face and to get him inside on the bed. Jackie removed Dan's shirt and saw the mass of bruises there. She thought to herself, *It will be a miracle if no ribs are broken.*

She disinfected the cuts on his face with iodine and Dan came to briefly. He looked up through one eye and saw Jackie hovering over him. When he spoke his voice was raspy and labored.

"I'm ... sorry."

A clouded look came over Jackie's face, and she jumped up and ran back out to the truck. When she reached it, she looked into the truck bed and saw the stiffened, discolored body of her husband. His eyes were open and lifeless, staring out at nothing.

Back in the cabin, Jeremy heard her scream again and again. The baby awoke and she cried too. Dan coughed and some blood ran down his chin. Jeremy wiped it away with the rag as he cried along with Jackie and her baby.

But to Dan, it was all a foggy haze except for the pain in his face and his chest. He passed out again, leaving his son ill-equipped to deal with the chaos and pain around him.

Jeremy, who only five days before, had been worried about acne, Twitter, Facebook, and Hotmail, stared out blankly, trying desperately to cope with this harsh, new world.

JEREMY'S SHOVEL HIT THE DRY, PACKED EARTH AND GLANCED OFF A STONE, landing harmlessly to one side. Jackie had asked him to bury her husband beneath the oak tree to the left of the cabin. To the boy that meant only one thing: lots of roots. But he didn't have the heart to refuse her. She was already in enough pain, so Jeremy dug and hacked his way through the roots and dirt while she stayed inside to take care of the baby and his father. It was a wise division of labor.

The blisters on Jeremy's hands had popped several days ago and were already turning into calluses. He sat down on the edge of the hole with his feet hanging down inside. From experience, Jeremy knew that most of the roots would be at the surface, so once he got down a foot or so into the yellow sand, the ground would get softer and the digging would become easier.

Jeremy didn't like this new life of his. It seemed stressful. But the more he thought about it, the more he had to admit that the old life hadn't been that great either. He'd gone from a drunken, carousing mother with an overbearing stepfather to a dead mother and a stepfather who kept shooting people. And the worst part was, Jeremy had to bury all the bodies.

He took a long drink of water from the milk jug beside the hole. Fortunately, there was a hand pump well beside the cabin that gave them fresh water. Apparently Jackie and her husband, Don, had purchased this cabin for the sole purpose of living without electricity. Jeremy couldn't help but wonder what type of person would do something like that.

He looked over at Don, wrapped in a blanket beside him, and nodded his thanks. Jeremy wondered, *Why don't I feel weird sitting next to a dead guy?* He put the jug of water down and pulled his Blackberry out of his front breast pocket. He turned it on and waited for it to power up. There was no signal - again. Then he pushed the button on the right side to view his pictures and videos stored inside. He pulled up and played the video of him and his mother. On the screen, he watched as his mother hugged him, and he tried to pull away. He remembered that night explicitly. She'd been a little drunk and was trying to hug him in front of other people. Jeremy had stopped liking that about four years ago. But now…he would do anything to have her embarrass him just one more time.

He thought about his stepdad, laying inside on the bed, swollen and bleeding, wondering *Is my dad going to die as well?* He didn't know. Jeremy just knew that five days ago was a million miles away, and that he didn't even feel like the same person. He felt older.

He listened to his mother's voice over and over on the Blackberry as tears welled up in his eyes but refused to flow. Finally, the video stopped playing and his Blackberry shut down for good. It was useless with dead batteries. The boy felt like crying, but then he looked over at the dead body beside him and laughed out loud. What good would it do to cry? In the face of all the death and change, crying seemed like a senseless act.

He jumped back down into the hole and started digging again, and two hours later he was done. As carefully as possible, he drug the body down into the hole. He winced as it crashed down and landed headfirst. He heard the neckbones crack. As quickly as he could, he straightened out the body and tucked the blanket edges back in where they belonged. He was glad that Jackie hadn't seen that.

Five minutes later Jackie came out holding the baby in her arms. She stood over the hole, not crying, not talking, just standing.

"I'm sorry, Jackie. I wish we had a box or something." That was all that Jeremy knew to say. He wanted to console her, but he was a teenage boy with limited social skills and life experience. The truth was, Jeremy was growing emotionally numb. What he didn't know was that Jackie was growing numb as well. The two of them stood over the hole looking down at the blanketed body.

"Dad says good people should get words said over them and a prayer. Do you want to say something?"

Jackie kissed her tiny baby girl. "I'd like to be alone with him for a minute, please."

Jeremy nodded. Inside he was relieved, and quickly went back in the cabin to check on his father. Jackie stood over the grave alone now. She allowed herself to cry for a minute or so, then shut off the tears as if on command, as if they flowed from a spicket deep down inside her.

"I don't know what to say, honey. I wasn't counting on all this. I just want you to know that I love you, despite what I did. I know you must realize by now I cheated on you, and I feel terrible about it. I deserve to be in the hole instead of you. I know that, and I'm so sorry. Please forgive me, honey. It was the only time I did anything like that. I don't understand why I did it, but I'm going to have to figure it out. I wish so much I could get your forgiveness, but I guess I'll just have to live with the guilt. Lord knows I deserve it."

She looked down at her baby, the black-skinned, Haitian little girl baby, and allowed the tears to flow once more, and she spoke through sobs.

"I wanted to share parenthood with you, Don. I wanted to have *your* baby. Instead, I had to pretend, all through the pregnancy, that my baby was yours, when I knew in my heart she wasn't. It doesn't make me love her any less, it's just…I wish she was yours so I could have a part of you to hold and love forever. But, instead, I have the baby of a man I never knew and met only once. I deserve this."

She bent down carefully and scooped up a handful of yellow dirt and tossed it onto the blanket. Then she walked back inside the cabin.

A few minutes later Jeremy came out and filled in the hole.

Northern Michigan - September 14, 8PM

It had been a week now with no word from his nephew, and Rodney was beginning to worry about him. The plan had always been clear. When he sent the message, Dan was to beat it back here to Michigan as fast as he could. Something must have gone wrong. And that's why Rodney was loading up his Ford F-250 and heading out just before nightfall.

He knew it was dangerous, perhaps even foolhardy, but…he felt he had no choice. Everything around him, all the preparations, he hadn't done for himself, but for the kid. So, even though his chances of success were slim to none, he figured a slim chance was worth taking. Besides, a slim chance was a million times better than no chance.

"Where in God's name did you get a Thompson submachine gun?"

Rodney was jolted out of his thoughts by Sheriff Leif's question. He just smiled and threw the cigarette butt onto the ground.

"Do you really want to know, Sheriff?"

Joe Leif gave him his best "why-do-you-do-this-to-me look" before sighing. He changed the subject.

"So what's in this black case here?"

"A fifty caliber BMG hunting rifle."

"A hunting rifle? What can you hunt with a fifty caliber?"

"Anything within fifteen hundred yards."

Joe shook his head in despair. "God help us all. You are such a felon! I'll never be re-elected if this gets out."

The old man lit another cigarette and took a heavy pull on it. "I wouldn't worry about that if I was you. Don't think they'll be many elections going on for quite some time now. But, tell ya what. If there is, I'll vote for you a hundred times if you like."

Joe shook his head back and forth in exasperation. "God help us all!"

They finished loading up, and then got in and drove off just before dark. If all went well, they'd reach Menomonie by morning, and then they'd know his nephew's fate. Rodney had welded steel pipes on the front bumper and steel plates around the cab, bed and tailgate. The extra weight would ruin his gas mileage, but Rodney had installed an underground diesel tank years ago and had filled it up over a week before the blackout. This mission would not fail for lack of fuel.

Rodney looked in his rear-view mirror and saw Moses standing on the porch, watching them drive away. He felt a sense of excitement, knowing he was driving into a world of unknown danger, knowing that he might die on the roadside from a stranger's bullet. So many unknowns, so much had changed. There was nothing he could be sure of save one thing: *I'll bring my boy back or die trying!*

When the truck faded from view, Moses lay down on the porch and placed his head on his paws, nestling in for the long haul.

THAT NIGHT, JACKIE AND JEREMY ATE TOGETHER IN SILENCE. JEREMY DIDN'T know what to say, and Jackie had no intention of talking. Dan and the baby slept quietly in the background.

After a dinner of canned stew and bread, Jeremy washed the dishes without being asked. The dishwater was cold, but he put in extra soap to ward off the germs.

When he was done, he walked over and sat down beside his father. He stayed there looking at him for a half hour, then went out onto the porch where he sat on the wooden planking with his legs dangling off and his forearms and chin resting on the railing. He recalled the fire-building contest he'd had with his father and smiled involuntarily.

"What could you possibly have to smile about, Jeremy?"

Jackie had come outside without him knowing it. Jeremy looked over his shoulder and the smile went away. "You're a real glass-half-empty kind of girl aren't you?"

"What?" She looked at him in amazement. "Did you just refer to me as a girl?"

The boy smirked to himself. "You heard me. Did I stutter?"

Jackie walked up to the railing and looked down on him. "Anyone ever tell you that you can be a real snot sometimes?"

Jeremy made an adolescent farting sound by pursing his lips together and pushing out air and spit. Jackie ignored the gesture and forced herself to focus. A few seconds later she spoke again.

"I just wanted to tell you thank you."

Jeremy looked up surprised.

"What for?"

She sat down on the porch beside him.

"For burying my husband."

Jeremy turned back to look into the woods.

"No big deal. I bury a lot of people now."

She looked into the woods too.

"Well, it was a big deal to me. So, thanks. I owe you one."

The boy reached up and scratched the peach fuzz on his face. "Is my dad going to make it?"

She looked over at him as if surprised. "Well, yes, of course he is. All the wounds are superficial, no broken ribs that I can tell, no internal damage. Unless he gets an infection, then he should heal up just fine. I'll keep bathing him with soap and disinfecting the wounds to make them heal faster."

A half smile came to Jeremy's lips.

"Okay, then, guess we're even."

The woman looked off to the left of the cabin at the mound of dirt.

"Can you make a wooden cross for Don tomorrow?"

Jeremy thought about it for a moment and then nodded.

"Yeah, sure, no problem." Dad taught me how to lash sticks together with rope. I can do it."

Jackie's curiosity got the best of her despite all she'd been through the past week.

"So what is your dad like?"

Jeremy shrugged.

"I don't know. I used to think he was just a normal, pain-in-the-butt dad until a week ago."

Then he told her all about the ball bat and how Dan had smashed his stereo and punched him in the face. She laughed spontaneously.

"Hey! It wasn't funny!"

Jackie covered her mouth to stifle it.

"I'm sorry, I just got this image and I couldn't help myself. You know you had it coming, right?"

Jeremy turned his face away so she couldn't see him smiling.

"Maybe." Then he added. "I used to be a bit of a jerk, back when I was a kid."

Jackie suddenly saw the sadness in his statement. *Back seven days ago when he was still a kid.*

"Did your dad really kill all those people?"

Jeremy nodded, but was quick to defend him. "He had to. It was kill or be killed. I never knew he could do things like that. He was a Marine ya know." Then he looked thoughtful for a moment. "I was lucky he didn't kill me that day in my bedroom."

Jackie listened and fifteen minutes later he was still talking. Finally, when he paused, she interjected.

"Your dad sounds like a good man, a capable man." She went silent. Jeremy noticed. "What's wrong?"

Jackie shook her head. "I was just wondering...what do you think he's going to do to me and the baby?"

Jeremy frowned and started to answer just as the baby began to cry inside the cabin. Jackie hopped up quickly and called out over her shoulder as she walked back inside.

"There's some rope in the tool shed along with a bunch of other stuff that Don put in there. You should check out all those boxes in there. He stocked up on all kinds of things. We should inventory them."

Jeremy nodded and then she was gone. He thought for a moment. His dad was right.

Women don't make any sense. He called them an enigma. He stood up and walked out to the tool shed to take a look. It was good to know that his Dad would be okay.

Menomonie, Wisconsin - September 15, 4AM

"Are you sure this is the right place, Rodney?"

The Sheriff pointed his flashlight on the door knob as Rodney wiggled it and then moved off to check the windows and then the back door.

"Hush up, Sheriff. We wake the neighbors and we're liable to eat some buckshot!"

They had driven straight through without stopping. The reserve fuel tank had served them well, and they'd eaten MREs while driving and relieved themselves in Coke bottles. Once, near Eagle River, they'd run into a road block, but quick thinking had taken them down a side road and around the town. Everything else was quiet. Now they both stood outside Dan's house. It was locked up tight with no sign of life inside.

Rodney let out a deep sigh as he unzipped his pants and urinated on the lawn. Sheriff Leif walked over to see what he was doing.

"What are you doing, Rodney?"

He finished up and shook it off. The Sheriff heard the zipper come up and shook his head in disgust. "Can't you at least go behind a tree?"

The old man ignored him and walked over to the sliding glass doors off the side deck. He stepped up onto the wooden planking and pushed the gas grill to one side. After grabbing the door handle firmly, he lifted up hard and muscled the glass door out of the track and carefully set it on the deck leaning against the vinyl siding.

"Rodney that's breaking and entering."

Rodney laughed. "Only if I get caught."

Joe Leif followed reluctantly, all the while thinking, _If he gets caught, then I get caught too._

Once inside the house, Rodney went straight to the basement stairs and walked on down. "Shine that flashlight over here, Joe." The beam lit up a wooden book case on the cement block wall. Rodney felt around the edge until he found the latch. He swung the book case out, revealing a row of four olive-drab, metal wall lockers. The doors were unlocked. He opened them and found all the lockers empty.

Rodney smiled.

"He made it out of town."

Joe stepped up beside him.

"How do you know?"

He pointed at the empty lockers.

"He took all the gear with him."

"How do you know it wasn't stolen?"

Rodney shook his head from side to side. "And you call yourself a cop. There were no signs of forced entry, Joe. Looters tend to break things when they're in a hurry."

The Sheriff nodded. "Yes, I suppose you're right. So what was inside the lockers?"

Rodney turned and headed back up the stairs, talking as he went. "Oh, nothing much. Just the essentials."

For the first time since leaving Michigan, Joe Leif laughed out loud. "For you that could mean an Abrams Tank and a dozen Stinger missiles."

"Absolutely! The right of the people to keep and bear arms shall not be infringed."

When they reached the top of the stairs, Joe hesitated. Rodney stopped and turned around. "What's wrong, Sheriff?"

"You don't actually have a tank back at your place do you?"

Rodney smiled and toyed with the lawman just for fun. "Of course I do, Joe. I bought the M1 Abrams Tank do-it-yourself-kit off Ebay three years ago, but I just haven't gotten around to putting it together yet."

Sheriff Leif laughed nervously. "You don't really have a tank ... do you?"

Rodney picked up his pace and walked out the side door. He put the door back in its track and walked over to the truck with Joe close on his heels.

"Let's turn some miles, Sheriff. I want to find some place to hide out before daylight. We'll get some sleep and then make the mad dash back when it's dark again."

They both crawled up into the cab of the F-250, fired up the diesel engine and headed back for Michigan. All the while, Rodney wondered *Where are you kid. Why didn't you get home?*

The Cabin - September 15, 8AM

Dan woke up that morning and immediately tried to get out of bed. He rolled out onto the floor and screamed with excruciating pain. Jeremy and Jackie rushed over from the breakfast table and helped him back onto the bed.

"Dad, you can't be getting up yet. You're all broken up inside."

Dan tried to talk, but the pain was too great. His chest was a mass of bruises and his face felt like it was on fire. He lay there unmoving, hoping to die just so the pain would stop. It was then he realized he was breathing too fast, so he purposefully slowed it down, taking longer, slower, steadier breaths.

Dan closed his eyes for a moment, and when he opened them Jackie was over his face, her long, midnight hair cascading over her shoulders and hanging down on his chest. He looked at her with his one, good eye, and couldn't help but notice how attractive she was. Inside, he winced. Here he was, on his deathbed for all he knew, recently widowed, stranded away from home during the apocalypse, and he was still noticing good-looking women. His Uncle Rodney had told him it was the Branch family curse. Dan couldn't argue with him.

"Just relax, Dan. You're hurt pretty bad, but you'll heal up if you just stay relaxed and let your body do its job."

Her voice was soft and soothing. Jackie lifted his head up, placed two capsules in his mouth and poured water down his throat. He took as much as he could but then choked.

Jeremy looked at his Dad's swollen and bruised face, trying to smile, but couldn't. "It's okay, Dad. We're going to take care of you. Just go back to sleep."

Dan closed his eyes, and the world became fuzzy and dark. He could hear their voices, but had no idea what they were saying. Then the voices faded away, and his world went once more black.

"Is he okay, Jackie?"

She nodded and then walked back to the table. Jeremy followed her. "Yes, he'll be fine. I've been giving him Tylenol with Codeine."

"What are those?"

Jackie smiled. "Something that will make him feel a lot better than you and I do at this moment."

Jeremy nodded his understanding. "Oh, you're giving my dad drugs."

She sat back down at the table and picked up her spoon again. "No sense in letting him feel all that pain. Nothing gained there."

Jeremy watched as she took a bite of her ground wheat cereal. Don had stocked three hundred pounds of Red Wheat in the pantry along with a grain grinder and a host of other food. No matter what else happened to them, they would have plenty to eat. But, already, Jeremy missed ice-cold Mountain Dew and pizza. Wheat just wasn't quite the same. He felt like he was at a health food camp for senior citizens. Most of all, Jeremy missed junk food: good old fashioned refined sugar, BHA, BHT, Monosodium Glutamate, and partially hydrogenated vegetable oil. They were the building blocks of every growing teenager.

"I thought you didn't like my dad?"

Jackie stopped her spoon right before her next bite, then placed it back in the bowl. "What gave you that idea?"

Jeremy looked over at his dad as he talked. "I saw the way you looked at him after we buried Don. You hate him. You think it was his fault that your husband died. But I don't see it that way. He almost died trying to save your husband's life."

Jackie considered denying it, but then shrugged. "Since when did you become so astute?"

"I'm not astute. I don't even know what that word means."

Jackie couldn't help but smile. "In this case it means you can see inside people, know what they're thinking and feeling."

"So I was right? Cool. I'm not used to that."

It was still too close after her husband's death, the birth of her illegitimate child, and the end of the world as she knew it to tell for sure, but she saw all the signs that she might someday like this young boy.

"I'm sorry, Jeremy. I know what the facts are, but my feelings don't always agree with reality."

Jeremy nodded. "Yeah, I know how women can be. Dad says they don't make much sense and they can drive a man insane."

She looked at Jeremy, then over to Dan, then back to Jeremy again. "Your dad said that about women?"

The boy nodded.

She took another bite of her wheat, placed her elbows on either side of her bowl atop the table and grimaced.

"No more Tylenol with Codeine for him then."

Jeremy smiled and took another bite of his wheat.

"I hate your cooking, Jackie."

She nodded. "I know. Me too."

The baby cried. She got up and brought her over to the table to nurse her. Jeremy watched as she bared her breast and the baby latched on.

"I'm supposed to turn my head away and complain how gross that is, but…I don't know, things like that just don't seem important anymore."

Jackie nodded. "I know what you mean. Things like wholesale death and destruction just have a way of cutting through all the superficial crap and reminding people what's important in life."

Jeremy nodded. "Well, I don't know what superficial is, but you might be right about the crap part. Life is pretty crappy right now. But, if my dad gets better and we make it back to Michigan, then…I just might have a shot at figuring out what life is all about."

She looked up from her nursing and smiled slightly. "Keep it up, kid, and you just might grow into a man."

He ate the rest of his cereal without talking. His spoon clanked into the glass bowl. Jeremy looked at her, then down at her baby. "You mind if I ask a personal question?"

Jackie's face began to cloud over. "I don't know. What's the question and I'll tell you?"

"How come your baby's black?"

Jackie turned her head away and frowned, considering the question for a moment. "My baby's black because I cheated on my husband and lived to regret it. I screwed up. I hurt him, and I feel pretty bad about it. I should be dead in that hole outside, not him."

Jeremy leaned back in his chair and shrugged. "I don't know. Maybe we should all be dead in that hole. I screwed the neighbor girl and she was only twelve years old. I didn't love her or anything. I just wanted to use her. That's worse than what you did, because I'm only fourteen. You're old and it took you thirty years to get this bad. I got bad in half the time it took you."

Jackie looked over at him, not knowing what to say. She could see he was serious and it saddened her.

"What can I say. We're all bad. We've all sinned."

Jeremy nodded in agreement.

"Yeah. We've sinned. But, I wonder, about God, what's He going to do to us. Can He forgive us?"

Jackie thought about it for a moment, finally realizing there was more depth to this boy than she'd first realized. "Yes, I think God can forgive us. He's a pretty big guy." She paused. "But I wonder. I think God will forgive us, but can we forgive ourselves?"

Jeremy brushed the hair out of his eyes and then met her gaze. For a moment, he was silent.

"Maybe all this world falling apart stuff is God's way of cleaning us up and giving us a second chance."

Jackie looked up. "You think so? I'd like that."

He stood up and took both their bowls to the sink.

"Well, I forgive you, Jackie."

Suddenly, she wanted to cry, but she held it in.

"I forgive you too, Jeremy."

There was silence save the sound of dishes being laid in the sink.

"I'll do the dishes. You just keep feeding the baby."

And that was the last time they talked about sin.

CHAPTER 18

Uncle Rodney goes Commando - September 16, 2AM

RODNEY WAS DRIVING EAST ABOUT TWENTY MILES FROM Eagle River when the large, White-tailed buck jumped out in front of his truck.

"Watch out, Rod. Got a deer up there."

The old man responded by stepping on the gas pedal, and the truck lurched forward, pushing Sheriff Leif back in the seat. He reached forward and dug his fingernails into the dash board.

"What are you doing, Rodney?"

The deer turned its neck and looked into the big truck's headlights. It was the last thing he ever saw. There was a big thump, and the truck lurched a bit. The deer careened off to the side and landed thirty feet off the road unmoving.

"Just testing the integrity of my new steel bumper system."

Joe let go of the dashboard. The imprints of his fingernails were still there.

"You ruined my dashboard, Sheriff."

Joe tried to smile.

"If you keep that up I might lose control and soil your leather upholstery as well."

Uncle Rodney laughed out loud. "That's good, Joe. You're starting to loosen up and get a sense of humor. You take life way too seriously."

The Sheriff moved his head over to the left to look at the speedometer.

"How fast are you going?"

Rodney was still grinning.

"We're making good time. I want to get back into Michigan before daybreak."

Joe frowned. "The speedometer says we're going ninety-eight."

"Oh, that. Well, the speedometer's busted."

"Really?"

"Yeah. It broke when I hit that deer back there."

Now Joe was smiling. He was silent for a moment.

"So, what do you think happened to your nephew?"

The smile on Rodney's face faded away. He thought a bit before answering. "My gut tells me he's okay."

Joe looked over at him. Rodney's face looked dangerous in the dimness of the truck's console lights.

"I don't know, my friend. It doesn't look good."

Rodney nodded to himself.

"Don't worry. He's okay. I can feel it in my gut."

Joe didn't agree with him, but he relaxed back into his seat in silence. Several minutes later they saw flashing strobe lights up ahead as they come upon the outskirts of Eagle River. Joe leaned forward in his seat.

"That's the first law and order we've seen since we started. It's encouraging."

Rodney cast him a sideways glance.

"Maybe."

The Sheriff didn't like Rodney's tone, but he let it go. "Better let me do the talking on this one, Rod."

He slowed the truck down and coasted to a stop about twenty yards in front of the police cruiser. The big searchlight turned on and lit up every crevice of the truck cab blinding them.

"I say we put pedal to metal and blow clean through. We'll make the U.P. before dawn."

But Sheriff Leif was already halfway out the door.

"Just stay put, Rodney. I'll have us out of here in no time flat."

As Rodney watched from inside the cab, he saw Joe walk forward, then stop, then raise his arms above his head and turn around. Two men came out and removed his pistol from his side, then put him down on the pavement. As the Sheriff was being handcuffed and led away, Rodney quickly formed a plan.

Two more men came out from behind the barricade with pistols drawn. They approached Rodney's truck from the driver's side. He waited until they got within fifteen feet before hitting the accelerator. As he drove by the old man quickly opened the door, knocking them both to the pavement. He spun the wheel and the truck slid around pointing him back west. Gunfire erupted from behind him, and he heard the clanks of lead on steel plates. Two minutes later the strobe lights were no longer visible.

Rodney glanced down at the speedometer and let up on the accelerator. Five miles out of town he pulled the truck into a cornfield. He drove down the fence row, then pulled into the corn. The stalks fell down by the hundreds as he hid the truck deep inside the field. He shut down the truck and listened to the engine cool.

He thought about the Marine Corps, about his time in Vietnam. The smart thing to do was get on the road and beat it back to Michigan. But…one thing kept coming back to him, haunting him, reminding him of deeds long gone. He said it out loud, as if the saying gave it blood and bone and flesh.

"No man left behind."

Uncle Rodney was already forming a plan.

Eagle River - September 16, 10AM

Sheriff Leif paced back and forth in his jail cell like a caged animal. He couldn't believe they were treating him this way. After all, he was part of the brotherhood. He was a county Sheriff for pete's sake. What happened to professional courtesy? When he'd first seen the strobe lights of the roadblock, Joe's first thought had been *I'll just show them my badge, talk to them, and they'll escort us through town.*

But that hadn't happened. Not even close. He'd been handcuffed and thrown into the back of the cruiser. Then after Rodney had taken off, they'd hauled him out and beaten him with batons before taking him here. He told them he was a Sheriff from

Michigan but they laughed and took his badge, his wallet, everything. And now he was waiting for the Chief of Police to come in and question him. Normally, he'd be confident about his outcome, but Rodney's hasty retreat had lessened his chances of talking his way out of this mess. *I can't believe Rodney just left me like that!*

He heard footsteps coming down the hall and two people laughing. When he saw the Chief of Police, his heart fell. The man's eyes had that look, like Barney Fife on steroids.

Sheriff Leif smiled and reached his right hand through the bars in an attempt to shake the Chief's hand. The Chief just stood there, looking at him with a penetrating gaze. Inside, Joe was a little confused. He'd never been treated this way before, certainly not by law enforcement. He'd always been afforded the respect of his badge and his office. But this man...he could tell...this man respected no one.

"My name is Sheriff Joe Leif from Northern Michigan. My friend and I were on our way back home when your people stopped us."

The Chief said nothing.

"You've no doubt seen my badge, my ID, my Glock 22. I'd be appreciative if you'd just drive me to the state line so I can hitch a ride home."

The Chief's icy face broke into full-out laughter.

"Why, sure, Mr. Leif, we'll take you all the way to the bridge if you like. I'm sure this is a big misunderstanding, and we'll have you home in your warm, safe bed by nightfall."

Joe's smile dropped to the floor and bounced around on the concrete until lying lifeless and still.

"Why are you doing this, Chief?"

"Because I can." He turned away for a moment, and when his face came back around, his eyes were full of hate and rage. "I'm doing this because I have no proof of who you are! I'm doing this because people from Chicago and Milwaukee have been invading this town for days now, stripping us bare and even killing some of us! Eagle River is a closed town. Nobody gets in and nobody gets out."

Joe pursed his lips together but said nothing.

"It's my job to protect the good people of Eagle River. I owe nothing to you or anyone else who visits. You should have drove around us. We're an island in a war zone, and we have to protect ourselves."

Joe involuntarily took a step back. He thought for a moment. "I'd like to do that now, Chief. I understand your concern, and I'd just like to get back home so I can protect the good people of my county as well."

The Chief's eyes appeared to soften, just a bit.

"You don't have to give me back my badge or even my gun. My partner's probably waiting for me a few miles down the road. Please, just let me walk out of town and you'll never see either of us again. Please."

The Chief moved his left hand up to his chin and stroked it gently in thought.

"As a County Sheriff and fellow Law Enforcement Officer, you are deserving of professional courtesy. I'll let you go, and I'll even give you back your gun and badge. But first I need to verify who you are. When communications are restored, and your story checks out, then I'll send you on your way."

A rush of adrenaline surged through the Sheriff's bloodstream. First he was afraid, then the fear was quickly followed by anger.

"You can't hold me here! The communications may never come back on. It could be years! I haven't done anything! If you keep me here then I want a lawyer! I want to be charged!"

The Chief's face began to turn red, and it didn't stop turning. Joe could see the man's jaw clench and his teeth grind together. When Joe stopped talking, the Chief very calmly said.

"As far as I'm concerned, martial law has been declared. Your civil rights are on hold. The Constitution no longer exists. For the foreseeable future, I am the law. I make the rules. You will stay in that cell until I say you leave. And if you cause any trouble, I'll personally take you to a secluded woods and put a bullet in your head."

He hesitated and then smiled.

"You're not in Kansas anymore, Sheriff. This is my town. Get used to it." And then he turned and walked away.

Joe felt dizzy and light-headed and had to sit down on the bed to keep from falling over. Suddenly, he had the distinct feeling that he would never leave this place alive. He'd made fun of Rodney for believing that society wouldn't recover, that law of the jungle reigned. But now…he wished he'd never gotten out of the truck, Rodney should have run the roadblock. But how could he have known there was a crazy man in charge of an entire town? Ten days ago the Chief would have been committed to a mental hospital, but now he was in charge.

Joe lay down on the bed and curled into the fetal position.

Eagle River - September 17, 2AM

The city jail was easy to find. It was the only building for blocks around with lights. Rodney had already checked out the big, diesel generator in back. It wasn't guarded. In fact, he didn't think anything was guarded. These people were so confident and sure, they had become very lax in their security. Arrogance was a flaw which he had every intention of exploiting.

Several hours ago, just after dark, Rodney had started his long hike in from the cornfield. There were few lights on so finding the lit-up jail had been easy. There was a police cruiser parked in front. He knew it was functioning,because he'd watched it pull up and the police officer walk inside. Rodney crouched down and ran up to the car. He peered inside and saw the keys still dangling in the ignition. He shook his head from side to side in disgust. *Man, these people were stupid.* He opened the door and took the keys and gave them a toss into the bushes nearby. Then he crept around the edge of the building to where the diesel generator blared away. He pulled out his big Leatherman and opened the wire cutters. With one snip the wires were cut and the night became deathly quiet.

Rodney pulled the night vision goggles down over his eyes and lit up the night. He moved right up to the front door and walked in. Once inside, he could hear voices.

"Damn it, Jerry, I thought I told you to refill the diesel generator out there!"

Another man answered. "I did. I think I did anyways. Where's the flashlight? I can't even see my hand in front of my face."

The first man bumped his shin on a desk and yelled in pain.

"There's one out in the cruiser. Let's go fetch it and get the lights back on."

It took both men the better part of a minute to find the door and leave Rodney alone. He stood pressed against the wall as they walked right past him within arm's reach. The old man couldn't help but smile. It would be so easy to kill them both. He quickly moved down the hall all the way to the back. There were only three jail cells, and Joe was sleeping in the last one. Reaching down into the right cargo pocket of his camos, Rodney pulled out the CTS-M-14 thermite grenade and placed it on top of the door lock. Without waking Joe, he lifted up his night vision goggles, pulled the pin and stepped back to a safe distance. Rodney knew from experience that it would reach four thousand degrees Fahrenheit and burn through over a half inch of steel in less than twenty seconds. The show was about to begin.

SHERIFF LEIF WAS DEEP IN THE BOWELS OF A SADISTIC NIGHTMARE, DREAMing that he'd been captured by an evil feudal lord and imprisoned below the keep in his rank dungeon. He was chained to the wall, and festering sores covered his body, oozing out puss and blood. In the dream he had a long beard, suggesting that he'd been there for many years. He was skinny and naked and covered with filth. The stench was unbearable.

As he sat there with his bare back against the stone wall of his cell, the jailer came forward with a torch burning pine pitch. The light was bright and hurt his eyes. They quickly adjusted and he watched as tiny drops of flaming pitch fell to the dirt floor and extinguished. In the light of the licking flames, he saw the face of his tormentor.

"I am the law. You have no rights. Now you will die. I have decreed it."

The Eagle River Chief of Police threw the torch inside his cell onto a pile of blankets and rags. Rats scurried into the corners as the blaze burned higher. The light blinded Joe's eyes, and the heat grew intense. He screamed in his dream, over and over again, all the while pushing himself up against the wall in an effort to escape the heat.

When Sheriff Leif woke up, he heard a man scream, but quickly realized the voice was his own. The moment he opened his eyes, he saw the intense light flashing off the brick wall in front of him. He felt the heat on his back. Then the light quickly ceased and he heard the cell door come open with a metal clank.

"Let's get out of here, Joe."

He turned and saw a man dressed in camo with big goggles over his face. He smiled, knowing that it could only be one man in the world. He quickly jumped up and hugged the old man.

"You came back for me!"

"Shhh, be quiet. They probably already heard you screaming. We got to beat feet out of here before they block the front door. Here, put on these goggles and these black cover-alls. Joe worked fast and soon both men were walking for the front door. Just as they reached it the door burst open and the flashlight beam poured in blinding them both.

"Don't move or we'll shoot!"

Rodney pulled Joe to the side just as bullets sprayed into the space they'd just occupied. They were on the floor now and Rodney reached into his left cargo pants pocket and pulled out two M67 fragmentation grenades.

"It's time to make a new door. Get behind this steel desk. Push over that filing cabinet in front of us."

Joe complied and Rodney tossed the first grenade out the front door. "Better close your eyes and plug your ears." The grenade landed and rolled down the steps before exploding, sending shrapnel across the face of the building. The second M67 landed near the far wall. After exploding, Joe felt the night air come inside and looked over at what used to be a far wall. Rodney unholstered his Colt 1911 and fired several rounds through the front doorway as they jumped up and ran through the hole in the wall.

They were outside now, running to the bushes. It was pitch black again but with night vision they could see like it was high-noon. They heard voices behind them and the night was filled with a dozen gunshots as the captors fired blindly into their own building. Joe was terrified, but Rodney laughed as he ran. They reached the drainage ditch where the gear was stored, and both of them fell down in a clump. Rodney was breathing in gasps like he'd just finished a marathon run.

"I need a cigarette really bad."

Joe looked back but could no longer see the jail cell. The gunshots were still ringing out in the night.

"Here, put on this backpack and carry this rifle."

Joe looked down at it. "Is this an AR15?"

Rodney scoffed. "Not a chance. What would I do with a sissy gun like that? This here's a full auto M16A1. You got ten thirty-round mags in your pack there."

Joe pushed the goggles back on his head but could see nothing, so he put them back down again.

"Where in the world did you get a Vietnam-era M16? And don't tell me on Ebay because I know better."

Rodney smiled. "I got it in Vietnam of course. I was a supply sergeant my last six months in-country. I got a lot of stuff like this. Yup, it's old, but I took good care of it. It fires almost every time."

Rodney jumped up and started moving again.

All Joe could think was *Almost every time?*

Four hours later they were back inside the F-250 and touring down the road at ninety-five miles an hour. Sheriff Leif looked over at the speedometer and frowned.

"Can't this thing go any faster than this?"

Rodney pushed down on the gas pedal. They stopped for nothing, and four hours later they rolled to a stop in Rodney's driveway.

Moses jumped up and ran out to greet them, barking all the way. Joe looked over to Rodney and said.

"Okay, that trip was educational."

Rodney smiled and lit up a cigarette. He looked up at the clear, blue sky before releasing the smoke from his lungs.

"Yes, I found it...invigorating."

Joe looked at him with questioning eyes.

"Doesn't it bother you in the least that we may have killed or injured some police officers back there?"

Rodney took a puff off his cigarette and then flicked off the ashes. "Well, if you're asking me if I feel any remorse, then, yes, sure. I feel bad about it." He thought for a moment, then knelt down to pet Moses. "But I'll tell you what bothers me more. We drove into Wisconsin to help my nephew, and you were beaten, arrested, and thrown in jail without due process. Your God-given rights were taken away, not by thugs, or gang members or bullies, but by people who used to uphold the law."

Rodney threw his cigarette down and ground it into the dirt with his boot. "I like you, Joe, but you best reach around and pull yer head outta yer ass and smell what's going on in the world. Things are different. Things have changed. This is a whole, new world, and yer gonna have to choose sides. Yer gonna have to ante up and take a stand for what's right."

Rodney started to walk away, but then stopped and turned around again. He pointed his finger at Joe and started to shake it fiercely. "When cops turn bad, their life is forfeit. And that's the way it should be. This is not anything new. The rule of law has collapsed before. Sometimes the good guys turn bad. Sometimes the strong oppress the weak. There's nothing new here. The only big question to answer isn't how I *feel* about it, but what am I going to *do* about it!"

Sheriff Leif let him walk away. He stood there stunned. He couldn't believe he was hearing these words from his friend. But then he thought about it as he walked to his car and started to drive away. He remembered the hateful look on the face of the Eagle River Chief of Police. He'd seen that look before, but it had always been on the face of a crackhead or a drunk or an armed robber...one of the bad guys. But he'd never seen that much hate and arrogance in a law enforcement officer. It was like the world had gone collective crazy, like the thin veneer of civilization had been stripped away leaving the basest traits that humanity had to offer.

As Joe drove home to his wife and kids. he couldn't help but wonder. *What is going to happen to us? What life have we left my kids?* The Sheriff thought about it long and hard, but in his heart, he knew that Rodney was right, at least most of what he'd said. And the one thing kept coming back to him over and over and over again.

The only big question to answer isn't how I *feel* about it, but what am I going to *do* about it!

He thought about it all the way home, trying desperately to form an answer to the impossible question.

CHAPTER 19

The Great White Invasion - October 25, 6PM

IT HAD BEEN OVER A MONTH SINCE **D**AN HAD COASTED BACK into the cabin driveway, beaten, bruised and battered. Jackie had nursed him back to health, but they hadn't really formed a friendship. Dan avoided talking to her whenever he could. Neither Jeremy nor Jackie understood the way he ignored her. They had even discussed it once while Dan was out taking a walk, but came to no conclusions.

"Okay, Dad, I got the last of it loaded into the truck. Anything else you want me to do?"

Dan walked past him and continued on into the cabin. "I'll get that heavy nylon tarp, then we can cover everything up. No sense taking any chances with the weather. Looks like it might rain tonight."

Despite the rocky start at the cabin, with Dan killing three men, then Jackie's husband's death and Dan's injuries, they had neither heard nor seen another human in over a month. Apparently, Jackie's dead husband had chosen the hideaway site well. They were a long way's off the road, and more than fifty miles away from a town of any size. Just to be sure, Dan had instructed Jeremy to camouflage the end of the drive with brush and to cut down the mail box. Dan came back with the tarp, and the father and son spread it out over the truck bed and tied it down.

Jackie watched the two men from inside the cabin, holding her little baby, wondering whether she was doing the right thing. They had invited her to come along, and Jeremy had insisted when she'd balked. The boy was turning out to be quite a sweetheart, and they had become good friends. He was very good with baby Donna as well, changing her diapers, holding her so she could rest, and whatever else was needed. From what he'd told her of his past, Jeremy had become a much better person after the lights went out.

But his father...she didn't know about him. He was such a stoic, always frowning at her, seldom talking at all. For some strange reason, Dan Branch both aggravated and intrigued her.

She looked down at the baby and smiled, then looked back out the window. She caught Jeremy grinning at her as he waved.

Once the truck was all set, they came in and sat down at the table for a dinner of canned beef, canned green beans and biscuits. As usual, Dan said nothing.

"Good biscuits, Jackie."

Jackie smiled, then looked over at Dan. He saw her staring as if she expected him to say something. Dan just grunted and went back to his meal. He thought about her as he ate. *That woman is always looking at me. She hates me. I know she does. I don't blame her either. I killed her husband. One night she'll slit my throat while I sleep.* That's what he was thinking, but he said something completely different. "Yes, the biscuits are good. Thank you."

She nodded and took a bite of her food. The fading light from outside filtered in through the window, lending an elegant shine to her jet-black Lebanese hair. Dan noticed how it cascaded over her petite shoulders and on down to her chest. He didn't hate the woman, but everytime he looked at her, he was reminded of her dead husband, the man he'd wrongly shot. Jackie made him cringe, and filled him with guilt.

"What's that stuff on your hair, Jackie?"

She smiled and looked over to Jeremy. It's scented olive oil. Don had it imported from Lebanon. I like it because it reminds me of my homeland"

Jeremy nodded while he shoveled on another fork-full of beef. "Cool. I like it. It smells nice." He looked over at Dan. "It sure smells nice. Right Dad?"

Dan looked up from his food, and hesitated before responding. "Yes. It smells nice."

Jackie narrowed her eyes, wondering to herself, *why does this man hate me so? I've done nothing wrong to him.* The baby started to cry, so she pushed her chair back and went to the other side of the room to feed her. Dan turned his head away as she bared her breast, and the baby latched on.

"That's pretty cool the way you do that, Jackie. Without your breasts Donna would probably die."

Jackie smiled. "It's the old-fashioned way, but I suspect all babies will be breast-fed from now on or not at all." She looked over and saw that Dan had turned his chair slightly to face the other wall. She thought for a moment before speaking with a waver in her voice. "Is there anything else I need to get ready before we go to bed tonight, Dan?"

Dan answered without looking over in her direction. For some reason, he always felt very uncomfortable when she fed the baby. He didn't understand it, because it seemed like the most natural thing in the world. "No. I think we've got it all covered. We should probably get to bed early though, so we get good sleep and an early start at first light."

Jackie reached down and softly stroked Donna's black hair as she nursed. Her hair was black and coarse, but not kinky. The baby's skin was dark, but had an olive hue to it.

Everyone finished eating, then Jackie and Jeremy did the dishes while Dan cleaned his gun. For the past week, ever since Dan had been able to move around, he'd been teaching Jeremy how to shoot a long gun and a pistol. Fortunately, the boy turned out to have a natural talent for it. Once the dishes were done, Dan spread his sleeping bag out on the couch and crawled down inside it. Jeremy spread his bedding out on the floor a few feet away, while Jackie took the bed with the baby inside a box beside her.

The cabin was all one, big room, and Dan hated the close proximity to Jackie and her baby. Dan pulled the sleeping bag over his head and rolled over away from her direction.

No, he didn't hate her, but he didn't like her either. In fact, just looking at her made him furious. That fact aggravated him, because he didn't understand it and couldn't control it.

Once snuggled in bed, Jackie opened up her Bible and read to herself Psalms chapter 46 by the light of an oil lamp. Then she contemplated the first few verses.

1 God is our refuge and strength,
A very present help in trouble.
2 Therefore we will not fear, though the earth should change And though the mountains slip into the heart of the sea;
3 Though its waters roar and foam, Though the mountains quake at its swelling pride.

It had long been one of her favorite passages. It calmed her, reassured her, reminded her that no matter what happened to her, God would be there, even in the face of oppression, pain of loss and hopeless odds. God would be there, and she would claim any promise He was willing to offer her. Ever since Don had died, she'd spent more time reading the Bible and praying. She'd even read some with Jeremy, and the boy seemed genuinely interested in God.

Jackie didn't realize it, but she looked stunningly beautiful in the faint lamp light. She slowly closed the Bible, followed by her eyes, as she prayed softly to herself so no one else could hear.

"Dear God. You are my refuge and my strength. Please protect me and protect my baby." Then she blew out the oil lamp and rolled over in the cold, lonely bed.

A few yards away, Dan Branch peeked out from beneath the sleeping bag, watching her every move. And he wondered to himself, *Why do I hate her?* And then, *Why ...* But he never finished the thought.

He rolled over and fell asleep, cursing all women under his breath, and cursing himself for what he was feeling.

DAN WOKE UP FIRST AT 6AM AND DRESSED HIMSELF QUIETLY IN THE DARK, pulling on his boots last of all and then walking outside. He was shocked to see nothing but white. The wind was howling through the trees with the snow blowing almost parallel to the ground. It was coming down so hard and fast that he couldn't even see the truck parked thirty feet from the porch. He stepped off the wooden planking and sunk to his knees in cold, wet snow. He cursed out loud. Then he stepped back up on the porch and waited there for five minutes, getting a feel for the storm and calming himself down. He thought to himself, *Even if we make it out to the main road, we'll never make it home.*

With stooped shoulders weighted down like lead, he opened the door and walked back inside, leaving the cold and wind to do its worst.

"BUT THIS WON'T LAST FOR VERY LONG, WILL IT, DAD?"

Dan moved the oatmeal around in his bowl without looking up. He didn't answer.

"Dad?"

Dan glanced up as if hearing his voice for the first time that morning. "What?"

Jeremy looked over at Jackie and then back to his father again. "I said, this isn't going to last for very long is it?"

Dan grunted. "I don't know, son. Probably not. This is a pretty early snow, even for this far north. We'll need a warm front to melt it off though, since there won't be any snowplows to clear off the roads."

Jackie broke her silence for the first time that evening. "But what if it doesn't melt? What if we're stuck here all winter long? We don't have enough food to eat, and we don't have enough wood to burn for heat. Winters are real long up here."

Dan was quiet as Jeremy looked over expectantly to his father, waiting for an answer. Finally Dan folded his hands together and placed them under his chin before responding.

"Well, I guess we have to plan for the worst. I wasn't expecting this to happen, but now we have to deal with it." He ran his fingers through his greasy, blonde hair before finishing. With no hot and cold running water, he only washed his hair and bathed every other day. The Branch family had always been gifted with greasy skin and hair.

"Let's wait a few days to see what happens. If it warms up and thaws off, then we'll plan on heading back to Michigan before the next storm hits. If it stays cold, then Jeremy and I will cut wood with that old handsaw and axe in the shed out back. It'll be hard work, but it has to be done or we'll freeze to death."

Jeremy interrupted him. "What about food, Dad?"

Dan nodded. "Not a big problem. There's that stream a ways off where you and I first camped. It leads to a pond where we can fish. There's also plenty of game here, rabbit, deer, and whatever else we can shoot. A couple of deer, and we should be set for food until spring. We can supplement it with the grain and the canned goods and all the other food that…" Dan hesitated a moment before continuing. He swallowed hard. "With all the other food that Don and Jackie stockpiled here. We'll be a lot better off than most people this winter."

Jackie nodded and looked down at her baby and chanted her silent mantra *God is our refuge and strength, a very present help in time of trouble.* She repeated it over and over and over again, as if the words held power and could save her and her baby.

Inside, she cried, but she swore that no one would ever know her tears.

A Day of Risks - November 18, 6PM

It had taken almost four weeks of back-breaking, bone-chilling work, but the wood was cut, split and stacked all around the cabin. There was a large, White-tailed doe hanging in the pine tree beside the cabin as well. Dan had put it up twenty feet to keep it away from any wildlife that might take an interest. The snow had not stopped, in fact, it had intensified, and, after a few days, Dan realized that winter was here to stay.

"I'm going to attack Madagascar from South Africa, and I'll be rolling three dice."

Dan looked up and his mouth fell open. "Are you nuts, son. I outnumber you four to one! You're going to lose!"

Jackie looked over at the "Risk" board game of military conquest and smiled. She loved watching them both play. She enjoyed witnessing their tantrums, their testosterone-fogged displays of manliness that served only to jade their tactical decisions. Jeremy was extremely aggressive, attacking in a kamikaze-like rage that sometimes worked, but always left his father frustrated and sometimes angry at his wanton display of foolish aggression. Dan's style of play was more calculating, like a chess player he thought out every move, always having a mission, an objective, always attacking at the right time and defending when needed. He was a very good tactician. But he had one weakness. Dan was predictable.

"I think he can take you, Dan."

Dan ignored her, but Jackie continued. "Let's face it, Dan. You're a lousy roller and Jeremy is lucky. You don't have a chance."

Dan looked over at her. She was nursing the baby again, right there in front of him. The baby's eyes looked over at him, mocking him as she suckled. All Dan could think was *Breast feeding really sucks!* He had begun to talk to Jackie a little more over the last few weeks as if he'd become desensitized to her presence. Because, let's face it, the cabin was small and it was cold outside. She was always there, every place he turned, so he had been forced to deal with her and his own feelings.

"I suppose you think you could beat me too?"

Jackie smiled tauntingly. "In a heartbeat, old man!"

Dan grated his teeth together and pursed his lips tightly. "I'm not an old man. I'm only 34."Jackie and Jeremy both laughed out loud. "Well, you're the oldest man for miles around as far as we know." Jeremy agreed by nodding his head up and down.

Dan thought for a moment, trying to regain his composure. *Why did he hate this woman?*

"Okay, Jeremy, let's clear the board and start over, and we'll see if General Jackie is all talk or whether or not she can run with the big dogs."

Jackie smiled and whispered softly. "Woof! Woof! Bring it on, farmboy."

They quickly set up the game and began to play as the wind and snow raged on all around them. The fireplace glowed with red-hot coals and gave off extra light to help out the two oil lamps on the table beside them. Dan quickly conquered Australia and began collecting two extra armies per turn. He then used Australia as a launching pad for his military offensive. But something strange happened. Jackie fell back, absorbing his attacks, slowing his offensive, and then Jeremy countered with his usual and customary kamikaze attacks to his flank. Dan destroyed his son's armies, leaving him all but defenseless. He planned on finishing him off the next turn, but Jackie handed in a match and used the extra armies to drive him back into Australia. Dan, who had never lost at "Risk" before, was now fighting for his life.

And every time Jackie attacked him…she smiled.

Two hours later, Jackie made her final roll and won the game. Dan was both shocked and impressed.

"How did you do that? I've never lost before."

Jackie smiled slyly. "What a coincidence, neither have I."

"I can't believe that, Dad. You got beat by a girl!"

Dan's eyes flashed angrily. "Oh shut up, son. She beat you first."

"Yeah, well, she beat you second. This girl is good!"

Then Dan looked over at her, his face taking on a grave look. "Seriously, Jackie, how did you do that?"

She thought for a moment. She so much wanted to bring him down to size, but figured he'd already suffered enough.

"I'm from the Mideast. War is in our blood, in our genes. It just comes natural to me."

Dan accepted her explanation with a nod of his head. "Okay, makes sense. I'm really impressed."

But Jeremy wouldn't let it go as he howled out loudly. "My Dad, the mighty Marine, vanquished by a Lebanese, breast-feeding Mommy!"

Dan's face clouded over again, as he slid back his chair with a screech on the wooden planking. "I need to get some fresh air."

As he walked out the door, Dan pulled on a wool coat. He didn't like wearing it, but

Jackie had offered it to him. Since he'd brought no winter clothing, he'd had no real choice but to accept it. Dan wore the same size as her now-dead husband, but he didn't feel right wearing the clothes of a man he'd killed.

As the door shut behind him, he walked over to the edge of the porch and leaned against the four-by-four column and looked up at the full moon. His breath steamed out, billowed, and then was carried away by the icy-cold breeze. The snow had stopped and the wind had died down right after night fall as it often did. Dan felt the ice seep down into his eyes and his bones. He thought about his Uncle Rodney, wondering if he would ever make it back there. He thought about everything that had happened in the last three months, amazed that his life could turn so quickly and so radically. Dan sucked in the ice-cold air and held it in his lungs for a moment before letting it out. Closing his eyes, he tried desperately to get a handle on all his conflicting emotions, but he just couldn't sort them all out.

Just then the door swung open with a creak and Jackie walked over to him, the snow screeching underneath her boots. She stopped beside him and looked up at the moon.

"It's pretty tonight."

Dan nodded uneasily.

"I needed some fresh air too. I love Donna, but sometimes I just need to get out of the room. It's like I'm on duty with her twenty-four seven and it wears me out."

Dan said nothing and, as usual, it drove Jackie crazy. She glanced over at her husband's grave. There was a four-feet high wooden cross jutting up through the snow. She knew his body was down there in the frozen ground. *How long had it been? Only two months? It seemed like years.*

"Jeremy told me about his mother, Debbie, your wife. I'm sorry it all happened the way it did." Dan looked up into the moon, but said nothing. "It must be painful…and confusing for you."

Dan nodded. "It is what it is."

Jackie laughed softly and pulled the lapels of her coat together to block out the cold. "What's so funny?"

"It's you, Dan. It's you. You're so stoic, so tough all the time, never letting anything out. Never talking. Always pretending like nothing phases you, like you're superman or something."

A hint of a smile turned up on the left side of his mouth. "No, I'm not superman."

"No?"

"Of course not. Superman would've kicked your butt in Risk."

Jackie smiled.

"Dan Branch, was that humor coming out of your mouth?"

But Dan didn't answer, so she quickly changed the subject. She pointed out to the woods as she talked. "So, what do you think is happening out there, beyond the woods, in the big cities I mean?"

Dan thought for a moment. He looked down at his boot and kicked some packed snow off the porch and into a drift. "Millions of people are dying. They're starving. They're freezing. They're dying of sicknesses that used to be cured with a doctor's appointment."

Jackie nodded. "I know you're right. How many do you think will die?"

Dan shrugged his woolen-covered shoulders. "I don't know, maybe seventy percent the first winter."

Jackie's eyes narrowed. "That many?"

"It's not just the cold and hunger and sickness. There's also people being murdered out there wholesale. The weak are being slaughtered by the strong to acquire what they have. The strong will survive and the weak will die. Our society has always been an artificial one, unsustainable over the long haul. Sooner or later it had to come to this."

Jackie looked over at the side of his face. "Why do you say it was inevitable?"

Dan looked back at her and their eyes met. "Because people are selfish, and they can always be counted on to do what's in their own best interest. I don't know how the lights went out, and maybe we never will know, but I can bet you one thing: it probably had something to do with greed and power."

For a moment, Jackie could say nothing, then she surprised him. "You've just talked more to me in the last two minutes than you have since we met."

Dan shifted his feet uncomfortably on the snow-covered wooden planking. "I - I don't know what to say to that."

Jackie laughed, her eyes shining like obsidian in the moonlight. "That's because you're a man, Dan Branch. And real men don't *talk* - they *do*."

Dan looked off over to the right, away from her. She felt him slipping away, so she talked fast before he left completely.

"I want you to know that I don't blame you for my husband's death. Sure, yeah, I did at first, but I'm over that now and we have to move on without it. You and I are going to be trapped together in that little cabin for the next four months, so we need to talk to each other or I'll go stir crazy." She paused. "So…can you please tell me…why do you hate me so much?"

Dan shifted his legs so the left was now over the right as he leaned against the column. He wasn't expecting the direct approach. "I didn't know you could tell."

She smiled softly. "Dan, I'm a woman. Of course I can tell."

The moon looked down on them both, wondering how long it would take them to get it all out in the open. He was in no hurry. The moon had all night.

"I don't hate you. I don't think. But I don't like being around you. Makes me feel uncomfortable. You remind me of my wife." He kicked the toe of his boot into the porch again.

She seemed surprised. "Really? May I ask why?"

Dan hesitated, unsure of himself. "Because you cheated on your husband, so I identify with him."

Blood rushed up to fill Jackie's face and she slumped over the railing as her head filled with dizziness.

"I - I." But she couldn't finish her words. Tears filled her eyes and ran down her cheeks unopposed. Then her nose began to run. She turned off to the side, so he wouldn't see the unladylike display.

Suddenly, Dan felt like a jerk.

She sniffed a few times and then wiped her nose on her sleeve. Dan turned away to give her privacy.

"I suppose I deserved that…and more."

Dan said nothing. He just let her talk.

"Don was a good husband. He provided well, and he was very kind to everyone. He deserved better than me."

The anger that welled up in Dan confused him, but he seemed helpless to stop it.

"So if he didn't deserve it, then why did you do it to him? What would possess a woman to do that to a man who was good to her?"

Jackie said nothing at first. She'd been asking herself the same question for almost a year now. *Why did I do it? Why did I betray the only man who ever loved me?* When she answered him, she surprised even herself with the sudden clarity of her response.

"Because in a moment of passion, I acted out of the weakest part of my character." She continued to sob, but quieter now.

"So what does that exactly mean? You only did it once? It surprised you? The devil made you do it?"

Jackie steeled her resolve and turned off her tears. Dan noticed the change and was intrigued by it.

"No one made me do it. *I* did it. I'm responsible for it. I hurt the man I love. He was good to me, and I betrayed him. I have no defense, and I accept full responsibility."

She started to cry again. "There! I'm a bad person! Are you happy now? I deserve to be disrespected and abused. I know that and … I welcome the pain."

Dan's eyes squinted together as he looked at her in wonder. "Are you serious? You really feel this way?"

Jackie nodded, but couldn't speak through the tears. Dan grunted and kicked some snow off the porch into the drift.

"Heck, I guess you're nothing like my wife then. She laid with lots of men, and never felt bad about it. I don't think guilt was in her." Dan looked out at the blowing snow. "No, you're not like her. Truth is, if she'd been more like you, I would have forgiven her and we could've moved on and made a happy family."

Dan's voice wavered in the cold. "But she wasn't like you. She felt no remorse."

Suddenly, Jackie stopped feeling sorry for herself and focused on the man beside her.

"I'm sorry, Dan. I know you're a good man. I can tell by watching you, and by things that Jeremy says. You didn't deserve what she did, and I hope you know it wasn't your fault." She stopped for a moment to think, then went on. "Sometimes people just do bad things. I did a bad thing. I take responsibility for it, and now I have to live with what I've done."

Dan looked over at her, but his attitude had suddenly changed. His anger had faded, and been replaced with a small measure of respect.

"God will forgive you for it. He always does." He hesitated for a moment. "All of us need a little forgiveness right about now. At least you didn't kill anyone."

Jackie raised her head up and looked over at him. Their eyes met. Dan pointed to her nose and said. "You're dripping." She turned away to clean it off, then turned back again.

"It wasn't personal, Dan, what your wife did. She was broken inside."

Dan nodded. "I know that. Doesn't make it any easier though. I'll get over it."

Suddenly, she wanted to rush over and hold him, like she was holding a child just fallen and skinned on the playground. But…she couldn't. So she just nodded. Then he surprised her.

"I want you to know that I respect you for being honest with me, and for your heart. You have a pretty heart. Our God is a God of second chances."

The twinkle began to come back in her eyes.

"Thank you, Dan."

"You're welcome. Like you said, we've got to get along in the cabin all winter long, so we best be honest with each other from the get-go."

Jackie looked out at the snow. "Isn't it odd how you can start a conversation, or a day, or anything, really, with one perception, like, *this day sure sucks*, and then, in a flash, with just a few words, the whole thing can go from blackness to light, from sadness to something so much better."

Dan hacked up some phlegm and spit off to one side. Jackie grimaced.

"Oh, I don't know. You're making me nervous now."

A soft smile traced Jackie's lips. "Nervous? Why? I'm the one who just went to confessional."

Dan smiled softly himself.

"All women make me nervous. Especially…women that look like you do."

Jackie thought for a moment, trying to decipher his words. And then it dawned on her, and she was surprised. "Dan Branch, do you think I'm attractive?"

Dan turned and looked at her angrily. "No, of course not! You shouldn't say stuff like that."

She smiled again. "Then what kind of woman do I look like that makes you so nervous?"

Dan turned and spit again to his right into a bank of snow. "You're not entirely ugly."

Jackie looked over at her husband's grave and then back at Dan. *This is too weird for me.* Dan seemed to read her mind.

"Anyways, we shouldn't be talking about it since my wife just died and your husband too, and he's lying right over there underneath that tree, probably listening to every word we're saying."

Jackie nodded. "Yeah. I suppose you're right. It's still grieving time for me and for you too. But…" She looked out at the pure, white snow, sparkling like diamonds in the night. "If I don't have some adult conversation for the next four months I'll go totally crazy. I'll make a deal with you."

Dan looked over uncomfortably. "What deal?"

"If you promise to try and talk to me more, then I'll promise to start looking less attractive."

Dan looked down at the snow, trying and failing to stifle a smile. "Well, now, I guess that's an offer I just can't refuse."

The baby started crying, and Jackie turned and walked back inside without saying another word. Dan was getting cold, but he didn't want to go back in yet. He still had some analyzing to do. Inside, the baby quieted down, and he could hear Jeremy talking to her. He wondered what they were saying. He thought about his dead wife, how she'd cheated on him so consistently, how she'd killed herself. He thought about the nine men he'd killed, knowing that he might be required to kill again. Dan thought about the condition of his heart. He knew, deep down inside that he was changing, that things like that couldn't happen to a man and not change him, either for the better or for the worse. And he wondered...*what is happening to me. Am I getting better, or am I getting worse?* And then it occurred to him. *Maybe I'll ask Jackie.*

The man part of Dan was confused. *Why do I feel so close to her now? Where did my anger go?*

After one, last look at the moon, he whispered out loud to no one in particular. "And I'm not getting old!"

Dan Branch trudged clumsily back inside the warm cabin. But outside on the porch, the moon kept glowing down on the new-fallen snow, making it shine, making it glisten. In the cities, hundreds of miles away, the snow covered the corpses while a different moon shown down. But here...out here ...away from it all, the night was beautiful and pure.

CHAPTER 20

Christmas - December 25, 8AM

"**I** DON'T KNOW, JOE, AREN'T MOST PEOPLE ALONE THESE days?" Rodney crushed out the cigarette on the snowy porch with his boot before blowing the cloud of smoke up and away from the Sheriff who stood beside him.

"I suppose so, but I wanted to stop by and invite you over for Christmas dinner anyways. I know Marge and the kids would like seeing you. This is a holy day, ya know."

Rodney gazed out at the treeline as if looking for something. Joe Leif saw him staring and followed his gaze on out to the woods. "Still no word from the boy?"

The old man shook his head from side to side. "No way he'd let himself get caught out in this winter, especially if he had the young one with him. He's still comin' though. He'll make his move after the thaw."

Joe nodded. "So you think he went north or south?"

Rodney laughed. "That boy's too smart to go anywhere near Chicago right now. He went through the U.P. Probably still holed up somewhere." He spit off to one side into the deep snowbank. "He'll be here in Spring."

The Sheriff no longer wore his uniform, except on official business, and he only drove his police cruiser when he had to. Today he was dressed in insulated coveralls and riding a snowmobile to conserve gasoline. He always pulled a small sled for hauling things and people through the snow as well. In the Spring he would be on a quad or a horse, depending on the petroleum situation. Joe hesitated for a moment before attending to official Iroquois County business. Then he just spit it out.

"So, what kind of talk are you hearing on the Ham Radio?"

Rodney chuckled to himself. "I wondered how long it'd take you to ask that."

Joe smiled. "Just doing my job. Well, and I can't help but be curious myself about it. You hear anything from the major cities?"

The old man brushed a six-inch layer of snow off the porch railing and then leaned his forearms down on top of it. "Not a word, Joe. I gotta tell you though, only an idiot would be broadcasting from inside the cities right now. Anyone with a Ham radio would have to have one big-assed antennae, and that's a dead giveaway. Most Hams were smart enough to get out the first few days."

"So you've heard nothing?"

Rodney pulled a Marlboro red hard pack out of his breast pocket and shook out another cigarette. He offered another one to Joe, but the Sheriff shook his head. "I didn't say that."

Joe waited patiently as the old man took out his Zippo and lit up. Then he asked again. "So, what'd you hear?"

"Talked to a guy near Jackson a few days ago. He saw about two hundred inmates moving down I-94 west towards Kazoo. They were raping, killing and eating everything in their path. They were organized and extremely effective."

Upon hearing this, Joe brushed away more snow off the railing and leaned down closer to the old man. "So, do you think we have enough posse to take them out?"

Rodney looked over at him and laughed. "Why in the world do you keep calling them the posse? Ya know darn well they're the militia! We've organized and trained four hundred citizens to defend this county and you insist on calling them posse."

Joe smiled. "Well, technically they are posse. I swore them all in as deputies just like I did with you. What difference does it make?"

"Well, none, I suppose, at least on a practical level. I just think you still got that political correct bug up yer ass that says the word "militia" is a bad thing."

Joe couldn't deny it, so he redirected the conversation. "You never answered my question. Can we take them?"

More smoke exhaled and was carried away on the sub-zero breeze. "Yer darn right we can take 'em. We can take on a thousand guys like that."

Joe smiled, reassured by the assessment.

"But those inmates from Jackson Prison are the least of our worries, Sheriff. I doubt they'll even make it this far north. It's too hard to keep that many scum in line for more than a few months. I doubt they'll go any farther than Grand Rapids. Then they'll run into some rival gang, maybe bigger and meaner, then they'll fall apart or mutate into something else altogether."

The old man stopped talking, and Joe was forced to wait while Rodney took his sweet time organizing his thoughts. A bright, red Cardinal landed on a tree branch a few yards away. Joe watched it for a moment until Rodney continued.

"Remember when I told you about Dearborn last fall?"

"Joe nodded.

"Well, word on the airwaves is they got organized. They were pretty smart about it too. They got themselves armed to the teeth, then they took over all the warehouses in the Detroit area. They got supplies up the wing wong, and they're giving food to anyone who converts to Islam."

The Cardinal hopped off the branch down to a rock where Rodney had spread some seed and began feeding.

"So why is that such a bad thing? No more anarchy, and people who need food are getting it in an organized fashion. I got no problem with that. It could be a lot worse you know."

Rodney took one last drag off his cigarette and then threw it down on the porch before grinding it out with his boot. "You need to read up some on Islam, my friend. It's not the religion of peace that the old media used to tout. Islam in its truest form has always been a religion of conquest, almost from its inception."

Joe questioned him further. "How so?"

"Read the history. It's in their own book. You don't understand radical Islam. It was founded by one man, a man with self-serving interests, and he spread his power and influence by conquering others. Muhammad claimed to be God's prophet, therefore, anything he said was considered equal to that of God. Did you know that Muhammad had 23 wives and concubines? One time he wanted to marry the wife of his step-son, something that was forbidden by Islamic law, so he simply claimed to have received a revelation from Allah that it was now lawful for him to take her as his wife. His step-son, who was a good Muslim, wanted to please the prophet, so he immediately divorced his wife so Muhammad could bed her. On another time, Muhammad, the great prophet of Allah, married a 6-year old girl, then consummated that marriage when she was only 9 years old. Joe, you need to understand Islam for what it really is. Allah is not the god of Judaism and Christianity. He is not the god of love and tolerance."

Rodney looked out at the treeline again, scanning it for any movement. "Nope, he ain't full of love. He ain't Santa Claus. But he sure is comin' to town."

Joe didn't speak for almost a full minute. He just soaked it all in, not wanting to believe it. "But what about the government? They can't do anything once the state or the feds get up and running again."

Rodney laughed out loud. "Pie in the sky thinking, my friend. Pie in the sky."

The Sheriff zipped up his coveralls to ward off the chill he was feeling. "God almighty, I hope you're wrong about this."

The old man nodded his head. "Yeah, me too. I got a bad feelin' though that I ain't." Then he looked over at Joe and their eyes met. "We need to meet with the other Sheriff's around us and form an alliance. It's the only way we can be strong enough to fight them all off. Right now we're a lone wolf, and a wolf all by himself can't survive. He needs the pack to hunt and thrive."

Joe shoved his hands down into his pockets and let them warm for a few seconds. "This is a heck of a thing to be talking about on Christmas."

Rodney smiled and then burst out laughing altogether.

"Hey, I almost forgot. I got presents for you."

Joe smiled and shook his head. "I didn't get anything for you, Rodney. To tell you the truth, I didn't even think about it."

Rodney stepped inside the door and then walked back out with an olive drab ammo can. There was a red bow tied around the handle. "It's 500 rounds for your Glock."

Joe laughed and his eyes got moist. Rodney stepped back in the house and reappeared with a case of MREs with a smaller gift-wrapped box on top of it.

"The MRE's are for your whole family. There's a lot of good stuff in there. This here box is a thousand rounds of 22 caliber for your son."

He stepped back inside and reappeared one more time with a duffel bag. He dropped it down on the porch with a thud. "It's full of canvas, denim, and cotton for Marge. I know she sews, and this stuff will make some pretty sturdy clothes for all of you." Then he laughed. "And from what I can see you lost a bunch of weight and need some new trousers."

The Sheriff stepped over and hugged the old man. Rodney's arms remained at his side for several seconds, then he reached up and grudgingly returned his friend's hug. Finally, he said. "Hey, Sheriff. Break it up. I don't want the neighbors to get the wrong idea."

Joe laughed and stepped back. "You don't have any neighbors, Rodney." They both loaded the presents onto the snowmobile sled, and then Joe put on his helmet and waved as he fired it up and drove away through the snow.

Rodney stood in the snow, with the ice-cold wind blowing straight through his old bones. He raised his hand and gave a slight wave. He mouthed the words "Merry Christmas" before walking back inside to sit by the fire and finish cleaning his shotgun.

Christmas - December 25, 9AM

"Merry Christmas, Jackie."

Dan Branch led the beautiful, Lebanese woman by the hand out to the porch. She was blindfolded, and when they stopped on the snow-covered planking, Dan reached behind her to remove the dish towel from her eyes.

When she looked out at the bright snow, it took several seconds for her eyes to adjust to the brightness. Then she saw it, and gasped out loud, reaching up with her hands and covering her mouth. "Oh Dan! It's beautiful!"

There, in the snow in front of her was a shoveled path that led from the front porch all the way out to her dead husband's grave. The walls of the path had been carved through five-feet-high drifts. Jackie stepped down off the porch and into the path. She could barely see over the top of it.

"Dan, it must have taken you hours to do this!" Dan stepped down beside her and was surprised when she threw her arms around him, hugging his chest. Her face brushed against his cheek, and he shivered when he felt her skin and smelled the scented oil in her hair.

"So you like it?"

She smiled and he could see tears running down her cheeks. "Like it? I love it! It's the best gift I could ever have." She brushed the tears away. "Sorry, I didn't mean to do that in front of you."

Dan cocked his head to one side and took a step back away from her closeness. Still, even after a month of talking to each other about personal things, she made Dan shiver whenever they were close. Deep down inside, he wished she felt the same way.

He thought it odd that he could feel that way just over three months after his wife's death. He still loved Debbie, and he knew Jackie still loved Don, but…their love was different. Jackie had so many fond memories of Don, and she talked about them often. Dan listened to her almost every day. Sometimes she cried; other times she managed to hold it back. But there was always a twinkle in her eyes when she spoke of her husband. It wasn't that way for Dan. When he thought of Debbie, there was always pain, regret, and remorse, always thoughts of her other lovers, and the image of her kissing the man from Eau Claire, and sleeping in his bed. It was different, much different, and Dan envied Jackie the feelings and memories she treasured. Yes, he envied her pain.

"Come walk with me."

Dan seemed surprised when she reached back her mittened hand and grabbed onto his own. He hesitated, so she pulled him along as they walked out to the grave. Dan stumbled along behind her, feeling like he was intruding into another man's bedroom. It felt awkward.

" I so much wanted to come out here and visit him, but the drifts just got too big for me. It must have taken you forever to dig this out."

In truth, Dan had been digging all night long as she slept. It was the only way he could surprise her. After all, the four of them lived together in a small cube, so there were no secrets.

"Did Jeremy help you?"

"No. He was sleeping."

She stopped and turned around. Dan almost bumped into her. "You were out here all night long digging in the dark? For me?"

Dan smiled and the shivers started to overwhelm him. "It's only because I feel sorry for you. It's your ugliness. I did it out of pity."

She immediately pushed him down in the snow, then jumped on top of him, smearing a handful of cold powder in his face. Dan screamed and then laughed. He rolled over and pinned her down in the snow in a perfect wrestling reversal. Their faces moved closer together; their breath came out in steamy puffs, mingling, rising, and rolling away as one.

Dan looked into her dark eyes. She looked back. Their smiles faded, slowly at first, then abruptly. Her hair had fallen out of her stocking hat and cascaded out onto the white snow, lending the perfect black and white contrast. Dan felt his heart beating like the engine of a race car. Then he saw her lips form into a frown.

Dan mouthed the words "I'm sorry. I didn't mean to…" He rolled off of her and onto his back in the snow. She remained there beside him, looking up at the white overcast of the winter sky. Jackie reached over and grabbed his hand again. This time her mitten was gone, and she removed his leather glove, gripping her fingers into his palm and squeezing tight.

"I mean it, Dan. This is special to me."

Dan nodded his head in the snow.

"I know. That's why I did it. I feel like I know you now."

Jackie rolled over onto her side, placing her right hand onto Dan's chest. She gazed down into his eyes. He loved her perfect olive skin. "What are we going to do, Dan?"

He lifted his head and rolled over to face her.

"I don't know, Jackie. But it's ten below zero out here and I feel like I'm burning up inside."

Jackie moved closer and kissed him lightly on the lips. It was a brief kiss, a loving kiss, but he could still feel the heat of her passion through it. "I'm burning up too, Dan."

She repeated the question. "What are we going to do?"

He thought for a moment, then he blurted out the craziest idea that came to his mind. "Let's go ask Don."

Jackie's eyes narrowed for a moment, then they brightened. "That's crazy!"

She jumped up and pulled him to his feet, then dragged him stumbling behind her all the way to her husband's grave. When they both stopped, Jackie looked over at him and beckoned for Dan to start.

"No way! I'm not going to start. He's your husband!"

She smiled back. "Yes, but you're the one who shot him."

Dan's face screwed into a frown. A few seconds later he relented. "Okay, fine. I'll do it."

He looked back to the cross in front of him. It was made of Red Cedar, and the bark was beginning to peel off about halfway down the main beam.

"Okay…okay. Yes, I can do this."

Dan cleared his throat. "Hi Don. Merry Christmas to you." Don didn't answer. He just lay there quietly, taking it all in. Jackie nudged him to continue. "Tell him how you feel, Dan."

Dan looked over at her like a puppy waiting in line to be drowned in a bucket of water. "Jackie this is crazy." She responded with a frown and shoved out her lower lip. Dan looked at the grave, then back at her, then back at the cross again.

"Okay, here it is, the thing is, Don. I fell in love with your wife. I didn't mean to, but we got stranded here in this cabin together, and then you died…well, technically, I killed you, but that's what happened, and there's nothing I can do about that now, so it's water under the bridge. But the thing is I love her and there's nothing I can do about it and it's driving me crazy, so…I was wondering …would you mind terribly too much if I married your wife?"

Dan saw Jackie collapse to the ground out of the corner of his eye. He reached over and caught her while she was still on her knees. Then he knelt down beside her.

"Are you okay?"

She was crying now, with full-blown tears and wailing like a siren. "That's the most romantic thing I've ever heard. You just asked my husband for my hand in marriage."

Dan looked over at the cross, then back to Jackie and nodded. "Yeah, okay, I guess that's true." For a moment the silence was broken by the sound of Don rolling over in his grave, but neither Dan nor Jackie could hear it. They were too busy staring into each other's eyes.

"I love you, Dan."

"I love you, too, Jackie."

Then Jackie looked over at the cross and asked her husband point blank. "Don, is it okay with you if I marry Dan?"

There was no answer, save the howling of the winter wind.

"I'll take that as a yes."

Jackie turned back to Dan and fell into his arms. They embraced on their knees before the cross, then kissed in the polar wind, feeling only warmth and love. Hand in hand, Dan and Jackie rose up and walked back to the cabin.

Mercifully unaware, Don's dead corpse remained frozen under the ground.

One Hour Later

"Dad, this is crazy! Are you sure you want to do this?"

Dan nodded enthusiastically. "Of course I'm sure, son. I thought you liked Jackie."

"Well I do. Of course I do. She's fantastic! And I love the baby too, but, this just seems too weird for me."

Dan scoffed at him and waved with his hand. "Are you kidding me, son. This is nothing compared to what I did an hour ago."

"Do I want to know, Dad?"

"What?"

"Do I want to know what happened an hour ago?"

His father smiled. "Ask me again when you're eighteen."

Jeremy bent his head down and placed it in both palms.

"Dad! I don't want to hear any of this! What are you wanting me to do?"

"We just want to get married, son. There's nothing wrong with that. We're both consenting adults. We love each other, and we're both available. This is cut and dried."

Jeremy raised his head and yelled back the most obvious thing he could think of. "But we're in the middle of the wilderness and there's not a pastor for miles around!"

Dan smiled. Jeremy took a step back and started to shake his head from side to side in protest. "No way, Dad. No way!"

Fifteen Minutes Later

"Do you, Jackie Lynn Overton, take this man, Daniel Edward Branch, to be your lawfully wedded husband, to have and to hold, from this day forward, for better, for worse, for richer, for poorer, in sickness and in health, until death do us part? If so, please say, 'I do'."

Jackie looked into Dan's eyes and said "I do."

The fourteen-year-old boy turned from Jackie over to Dan and repeated the same phrase for his father. Dan immediately said "I do".

"You have declared your consent before the church. May the Lord in his goodness strengthen your consent and fill you both with his blessings. What God has joined together, let no man tear apart. Amen. You may kiss the bride. But try not to gross me out."

Dan and Jackie stood in front of the cross once more, turned toward one another and fell into a warm embrace. They kissed long and hard until they were interrupted by the sound of a baby's cry.

"Dad, I think the baby's hungry. We better get back inside and feed her. Besides, it's cold out here."

Dan turned and gave his son a hug. "Thank you, Pastor."

Jeremy shrugged his shoulders and threw a handful of rice as they walked back toward the cabin. He followed them, complaining all the way. "Please, God, don't send me to hell for this. My Dad made me do it."

CHAPTER 21

The Honeymoon - January

THAT SAME NIGHT, **D**AN MOVED OFF THE COUCH AND INTO Jackie's bed, where they consummated their new marriage all night long. Jeremy, who had moved up from the floor to the couch, was forced to plug his ears and press the pillow tightly over his face with the covers pulled way up like a shield.

Finally, after several hours of nonstop intimacy, They paused and listened to the sound of Jeremy snoring just a few yards away.

"He's really being a good sport about this don't you think?"

Dan smiled. "Yeah. He's growing into a pretty, good kid." Then he rolled onto his right side and propped his head up with his right hand. The moon reflected off the snow and came into the small window over their bed, shining through the frosted pane. Dan reached over with his left hand and caressed Jackie's skin softly. "I feel like we've been stranded on this desert island with no hope of being rescued. But, truth is, I don't want to be rescued anymore."

Jackie moved closer to him, placing her right hand on his side. "Neither do I, be rescued I mean. I just have a feeling that we're better off here than most others. It's got to be really bad out there. I almost feel guilty. I mean, here we are with enough food, with warmth, with family. We're safe here while others are dying."

Dan thought for a moment. "True enough, all of it. But I have to tell you, honey. Next year may not be this easy. If we stay here, our food will run out, and we have no way of replenishing it. But if we make it back to Michigan, then we have a whole community of friends to help us out. Uncle Rodney has been stocking up for decades, because he saw all this coming."

Jackie's brow furled slightly. "But…how do you know he's still there?"

Dan laughed out loud, but she quickly shushed him.

"You'll wake the baby!"

He placed his hand over his mouth in an attempt to stifle his laughter. "I'm sorry, Jackie, it's just that you don't know Uncle Rodney. The man's too tough and too mean to die. I guarantee you when the last man falls to the ground on this green earth, then Uncle Rodney will be there to dig the grave. He's a stubborn, old coot."

Jackie's frown gradually turned into a smile. "You really love him, don't you?"

Dan nodded. :After my dad died, Uncle Rodney took over. He raised me and made me who I am. I owe it all to him."

"Is that part of the reason you're so set on going back there?"

Dan smiled. "Just a part of it, honey. I wouldn't drag you and the baby all the way through hostile, strange territory if I didn't believe it was worth the risk."

She moved her hand off his side and down onto his stomach where she ran her fingers through the hair on his abdomen. "But...what if he doesn't like me?"

Choking back more laughter, Dan answered her right away. "Of course he won't like you! He doesn't like anyone! But he will feel sorry for you and take you in, if for no other reason, than you're so butt ugly!"

Jackie started to beat on his chest and Dan rolled over and laughed out loud. "You beast! Why do you say such things?"

"I'm sorry, but I was a Boy Scout, and I cannot tell a lie."

She stopped hitting him and he pulled her close. Jackie reached up and kissed his throat while she whispered. "I was a girl scout you know."

Dan feigned disinterest. "That's nice."

"You should have seen me in that short, little uniform skirt."

"Really? I loved those skirts. Do you still have it?"

Jackie reached down and caressed the inside of his thigh. Dan immediately rose to her expectations. She smiled. "Oh my! Is your little boy scout saluting me?"

Dan grabbed her and pulled her closer. "I hope you understand I won't be able to walk in the morning."

She opened her mouth and kissed him fiercely, then bit his lower lip tenderly. "Join the club. Now shut up and do your worst, farm boy."

And he did.

January 7, The Long Winter

"But I want to know more about your Uncle Rodney. Tell me about him."

Dan smiled first, then his face grew tense as he thought about it. Finally, he sighed out loud. Both of them were on the couch. The baby lay on the bare, wood floor on a blanket, playing with a spoon. Jeremy was outside, splitting wood, his intermittent blows of the axe to oak could be heard as tiny thunderclaps inside the warmth of the cabin.

Jackie played with the ends of her black hair and pulled both legs up on the seat cushion underneath her bottom. She remained silent, intrigued by his facial expressions, wondering what could be so complex about Uncle Rodney that would cause Dan to react this way.

"Uncle Rodney's not easy. I don't know that I ever understood him."

"Well, that's okay. I didn't ask you to explain him. Just paint me a word picture. Start with his physical appearance, and then just expand from there."

Dan's smile slowly returned. This was one of the things he liked about Jackie. She could open him up, look down inside him, see all the screwed up things, and still find something useful.

"I suppose I could do that." He paused and his eyes looked up to the bare rafters as if he was seeing a picture not inside the room. "I haven't seen him for years, but even back then he seemed old. Probably in his seventies by now. His hair was grey and white last time I saw him; it was long, down past his collar. It was usually greasy but combed back out of the way. Uncle Rodney always wore flannel and denim. Always.

Even in the heat of summer. The man knows what he likes. He has a purpose about him that I envy, because I wish I had a handle on my life, my purpose, what I'm supposed to be doing."

Jackie's eyes perked up and she listened to his monologue more closely.

"But ... at the same time ... that man scares me."

Jackie cocked her head to one side.

"Really? How so?"

"Well, he's just so cock sure of himself all the time, so capable. Just watching him walk, even though he's old, you get the feeling like you don't want to mess with him. You can tell by looking at him that he's the top of the pecking order. And that's confusing too, because by so many other world standards, he's at the bottom rung of life."

Jackie reached over and softly scratched Dan's neck, just below the hairline. She'd been cutting it for him since they'd been here.

"He's a poor man, lives in an old house built into the side of a hill. There's a swamp on one side and the hill in back and to the east. His house is cluttered, but everything else about his personality is highly organized. Once he makes his mind up to do something, then nothing can stop him. He never gives up. He's resilient, indomitable, stubborn, and above all ... tenacious."

He stopped for a moment as if to let the last word sink in. *Tenacious.*

"Those sound like pretty admirable qualities, honey. Is there anything you don't like about him?"

Dan laughed out loud. "Yeah, sure. There's lots I don't like about him. He's resilient, indomitable, stubborn ... tenacious."

Jackie smiled with him. "Okay then, so your Uncle Rodney is complicated?"

Dan nodded.

"Well, then it looks to me like the apple didn't fall that far from the tree."

Dan gave her a confused look. "You think I'm complicated?"

Jackie moved closer to him, letting her feet swing back out and onto the floor again until they came to rest again on the edge of the blue, baby blanket. "Honey, I *know* you're complicated. It's your defining characteristic." She kissed him on the mouth, with her right hand behind his head, scratching his neck like she would the fur on a puppy dog.

After a few seconds, their lips separated. Dan looked uncertain. "Okay, so, is that good?"

She nodded enthusiastically. "Oh yeah. I like my men stubborn, and resilient and most of all ... tenacious!"

She released him and bent down to pick up the baby. They both looked at Donna's face, into her deep, black eyes, and Dan touched her cheek with his callused, thick fore finger.

"I feel like I could stay here forever."

Jackie nodded her head in agreement. "Okay, then, let's do it."

Dan got up and threw another piece of oak onto the fire. Sparks popped up and rose into the chimney. He stirred it with the poker, looking into the red and yellow-hot coals as if being consumed by them. Jackie broke the silence again.

"Okay, so what's bothering you now?"

He smiled and looked off to one side so she couldn't see his face.

"Come on, farmboy! Tell me what' you're thinking! I married you so now I own you. You have to tell me everything. No secrets!"

Dan tried to change the subject. "Why do you always call me farm boy? I was born and raised in the north woods."

Jackie narrowed her eyes at him. "Are you trying to dodge my question?"

She knew him so well after just a few short months. It was unnerving. He played with her some more.

"Okay, lady. You tell me why you call me farm boy, and I'll tell you what I'm thinking."

She smiled. "Okay, but you have to promise to tell me what you're thinking. And not just this one time, but every time I ask you. Agreed?"

Dan pondered her proposition for a moment, and thought to himself, *If I go along with it, then I'll have to tell her anything and everything I ever think. On the other hand ... it could lead to some really nice "snuggle time" later on. But, of course, he couldn't tell her that.* It was an easy answer.

"Yeah, sure. Agreed. So why do you call me farm boy?"

Jackie leaned in closer before answering. "Have you ever seen the movie *The Princess Bride*?"

Dan nodded. Yeah, sure. Who hasn't?"

"Well, do you remember at the beginning when Buttercup was harassing Westley by constantly asking him to fetch her water, or fetch me that cup, things that she could have gotten herself?"

Dan nodded. "Yeah, I remember. I only saw it once. I liked the swordfighting scenes."

"Well, then the grandfather, played by Peter Falk said this. I've got it memorized:

That day, she was amazed to discover that when he was saying "As you wish", what he meant was, "I love you." And even more amazing was the day she realized she truly loved him back."

Dan thought for a moment, trying to remember the first time she'd called him farmboy. And then it came to him.

"I remember the first time you called me farmboy."

As she pulled her baby closer to her, she smiled. "Oh really? I'm flattered. I don't remember. When was it?"

Dan reached over and brushed the baby's black hair on the right side of her head. He'd never seen a baby with so much hair before.

"It was just before we delivered this little baby. You were screaming in pain, and not very appreciative I might add."

Jackie's eyes softened as her whole face lit up. "You remembered the first time. You really do love me don't you?"

Dan didn't answer her. He just stared into her eyes. Jackie reached over and placed her free hand behind his head and pulled him closer. "Kiss me, farmboy!"

Dan answered her quietly as he moved closer.

"As you wish."

CHAPTER 22

The Winter of Our Content- February

AFTER THEIR DUBIOUS, NONTRADITIONAL WEDDING, **D**AN and Jackie, fell into a winter lull filled with routine and work. They woke up everyday at dawn, usually via baby Donna who now served as their alarm clock. Dan would build up the fire, while Jackie nursed the baby. Then both Jeremy and Dan would grind enough wheat for the day. Jeremy used an old mortar and pestle, which was cumbersome and slow, while Dan fashioned a larger, more efficient grinder from two grinding wheels he'd found out in the shed. Every morning, their breakfast consisted of wheat porridge, leftover venison from the night before and unleavened wheat bread toasted over the fireplace.

After breakfast, Jackie cleaned up while Dan and Jeremy either split wood or hunted wild game. Dan showed his son how to fish from the fast-flowing stream that ran past the cabin using grubs and insects found inside rotting logs. The hardest part was breaking through the ice, which was usually achieved by smashing logs over the surface. They found if they broke the ice every day, it remained thin in one spot. The fish they caught were small, either Dace, Trout, or Shiners, but they were tasty, nonetheless, and were a welcome change from a steady diet of grain and red meat.

Jeremy soon discovered he had a natural talent for hunting, once Dan taught him the basics, and soon Dan left most of the hunting and fishing to his son.

For lunch they had meat sandwiches, supplemented with a can of beans or corn for variety. Afterwards they played with the baby, talked, and sometimes napped.

Dinner was always cooked in the large, cast iron kettle that hung in the fireplace. Jackie surrounded the kettle with small, hand-shaped loaves of baking bread. Inside the kettle, she added whatever the hunters provided for her. As a result, the cabin was always filled with a mouth-watering aroma of cooking meat, sauce and vegetables. It wasn't unusual for the kettle to contain a mixture of fish, squirrel, rabbit, and deer simultaneously. To the kettle, they added dried beans, sometimes rice, even cat-tail roots that Dan and Jeremy dug up from around the shallow pond. As long as there was ample salt, Jackie remained confident she could scare up a meal that filled their bellies and had a semblance of flavor.

After the first month, even Jeremy admitted her cooking talents were improving.

The last of the candles and kerosene soon were used up, but Dan discovered that deer contained a waxy tallow of fat beneath their hide that would burn just fine, even though it didn't smell the best.

At night, they played Risk, and Jackie usually won. Throughout the long, winter weeks, Jeremy became less aggressive in his playing style, while Dan became more adventurous. By the end of February, Jackie was still winning, but the games were much, much closer.

Some nights, Dan taught Jeremy about infantry tactics and basic strategy. Jackie listened closely as Dan talked about the proper way to set up an ambush, how to move silently through the leaves, and demonstrated fire team hand signals. Using the old, Army Ranger Manual that Uncle Rodney had sent to Dan many years ago, all three of them became proficient in a myriad of outdoor survival skills as well as battlefield tactics like flanking maneuvers and how to dig in and hold the high ground.

All three of them read the manual from cover to cover several times during the winter, and Dan quizzed them weekly on what they were learning.

Through it all, Jackie gained a new understanding and appreciation for Dan's mindset. He was a very careful and calculating man, not afraid to take a calculated risk, but neither would he take a foolish gamble with human life. He was a capable military man with an indomitability and resilience that just wouldn't quit. Jackie grew to feel safe under his wing and worked hard to gain his respect and to please him.

Dan was diligent about watching his new soldiers, examining their choices, analyzing their personalities, and finding out exactly what they were likely to do in any given situation.

To round it all out, Dan taught Jackie how to shoot a pistol and a long gun. She turned out to be an excellent shot, especially at long ranges. Most of their shooting was dry fire, so as not to give away their location. But Dan believed that some measure of live fire was necessary for sighting in and for confidence building.

Always, at night, just after dinner, Dan would read from the Bible. Then, Jackie, who had graduated from Bible College, would then explain what she believed the scriptures meant. She was impressed that Dan was able to relinquish the leadership role to her during that time. But the bare truth was, Dan didn't know much about the Bible, and Jackie did. Dan caught on fast and asked probing and insightful questions. He was an impressive student. She was especially happy with Dan's prayers. They were lacking in pretense and very down to earth, as if God was really there listening to them, and He was a real person. More than ever before, her faith came alive during the dead of this winter.

Jeremy and Dan fell in love with baby Donna, and spent many hours playing with her. During these times, Jackie enjoyed fading to the background and just watching the two men play with her child. By the month of March they had become a cohesive, intimate family and military unit, ready to fight and die for each other on a moment's notice.

By winter's end, they were prepared for the newly formed tooth, fang and claw world that featured a world without lights. Oddly enough, all three of them were happier than they'd ever been.

March 6, The Second Power Failure

"Jeremy! Why did you do it?"

Jeremy looked down at the ground but said nothing.

"Do you realize what you've done? We can't get home now!"

Every day for the past four months, Dan had started up the truck and let it idle for five minutes just to keep the battery charged up. He wasn't a mechanic, but he knew that harsh, cold was rough on a car battery, and that it would likely go dead if he didn't.

If that happened, they would likely never make it back to Michigan. So he was furious when he saw Jeremy's cell phone plugged into the power inverter and the ignition switch turned on. That morning, he turned the key, but nothing happened. The battery was drained.

"I want an answer, Jeremy! Why were you even bothering to charge up your cell phone when there's no service anyways? That's the stupidest thing I've ever heard of!"

Tears welled up in Jeremy's eyes and his face turned red as he stomped off the porch and ran into the woods through the snow.

"Get back here, son! Don't you ..."

Dan felt Jackie's grip on his sleeve.

"Don't Dan. Let him go."

Dan looked at his wife like she was crazy. "Don't you understand what he's done? We can't leave now. We're stranded."

Jackie nodded. "Yes, I understand, but the cell phone was important to him."

Dan looked perplexed. "Why? It doesn't even work."

Jackie moved closer, cradling the baby in her left arm and putting her other around Dan's shoulder.

"The camera in his phone works, and all the pictures of his mother are in the memory. It's the only thing he has left of her. He watches them everyday when he thinks no one is looking."

Dan took a moment to let it all sink in. "But ... why didn't he tell me? He could have plugged it in while I run the truck everyday?"

Jackie cocked her head to one side. "Really, Dan, come on now. He's a man, and men just don't do well with tender feelings. Anger, yes, a man can do anger, but not remorse, not sadness and a sense of loss." She hesitated. "Your son is grieving, and it embarrasses him."

Suddenly, Dan felt like a jerk. His head slumped down, and he moved off the porch and into the snow after his son. The snow drifts had been melting, and Dan was getting anxious to head back home. Now, it appeared, that was all in jeopardy, unless he could think of something to recharge the battery.

But first ... his son.

He found Jeremy sitting on a large shale rock by the pond.

"Hi son."

Dan moved up behind him.

"Can I sit down with you?"

He could hear the boy's sobs over the steady peal of the north wind.

Jeremy didn't answer, but he hadn't expected him to, so he just spoke his peace.

"I'm sorry, son. I screwed up back there. I shouldn't have yelled."

No response from his son.

"Jackie told me about the pictures of your mom on the cell phone. I didn't know or I would have offered to recharge your phone every day while I started up the truck."

Dan reached into his pocket and pulled out the phone and handed it to Jeremy. Jeremy reached his hand out and took it without turning his head.

"I didn't know you had those pictures. I'd like to look at them myself."

Jeremy spoke for the first time.

"Yeah, right. You don't even think about my Mom anymore. You're too happy with Jackie."

Dan thought for a second before talking.

"I think about your Mom everyday, son. I still love her, and I miss her. I miss her smile, her laugh, and the way she used to hold me." He paused, as if thinking. "And I miss her smell too."

Jeremy turned back to him. "You mean the Jasmine scent she always wore?"

Dan nodded. "Yep. And even the Ivory soap she washed with. It always had a very clean smell, and it reminds me of her."

Jeremy nodded. "Yes, I remember that soap. She always tried to get me to use it, but after I turned eleven, I just wouldn't do it anymore. It was baby soap." Jeremy tightened his lips together as a tear ran down his cheek. "I wish I had used the soap now. It was important to her."

Dan nodded. "Yeah, she tried to get me to use it too. I told her it wasn't manly enough for me." Dan put his hands into his coat pocket to ward off the cold. :There are a lot of things I regret, Jeremy. Those are things I have to live with."

Jeremy looked over to him. "But how could you still love her even after all the things she did to you?"

Dan turned out into the cold, facing the wind as he pondered the question. "Hmm, that's a good question. I've had a lot of time to think about it these past few months. I have to admit, that I was really mad at your Mom for a long time, but…after a while, anger just loses its draw on a man, ya know what I mean?"

Jeremy nodded.

"She did some pretty bad things though, Dad. I mean, she's my Mom and I'm still mad at her myself. So how could you possibly not be mad at her?"

Looking out over the frozen pond, Dan tightened his arms around his torso in an effort to hold in the warmth.

"I think the trick is to understand nature. Nature abhors a vacuum, and you can't just not hate someone. You have to put something in its place. So, in order to not hate your Mom, I have to love her instead. Every day I pray to God that He will forgive her and give her a second chance. I think the only way to stop hating someone is to start loving them."

Jeremy thought about it for a moment.

That sounds like a pretty good way to handle it. I might try that too. So, do you think God will do it, give her a second chance I mean?"

Dan shrugged his shoulders. "I don't know, son. I would never presume to know the mind of God. He pretty much does what He wants to all the time. And I don't begrudge Him that. He did create us all, so I suppose that gives Him the right. But the way I figure it, there's no harm in me asking for the favor. God gives people second chances all the time, so why not your Mom too?"

A tiny smile moved onto Jeremy's face. It went away suddenly. "So, are you still mad at me?"

Dan laughed out loud. "I sure am, but I won't stay mad for long. You know I love you."

Dan reached over and hugged his son. Jeremy hesitated, but then returned the gentle gesture.

"Are you going to punish me?"

Dan was surprised to hear the question. It seemed so absurd after all that had happened in the past 6 months that his son still worried about a little thing like that. It was almost as if he wanted a consequence for his action. So Dan gave it to him.

"Absolutely. You're grounded from television for a week."

Jeremy laughed out loud now too, and soon they were both laughing together.

"Let's take a look at those pictures on your phone. I would love to get a gander at your Mom again."

Jeremy powered it up and both men began viewing the photos and the video clips of their old family. When they were done, Jeremy asked the obvious question.

"So, Dad, how are we going to get home now?"

Dan looked into his son's eyes before answering, as if measuring the boy's mettle.

"Well, son. I have a few ideas, but I'm going to need your help. It might be dangerous."

Jeremy didn't hesitate. "That's okay. Everything we do now is dangerous. I know that. But you can count on me. I'll do whatever it takes. I won't let you down, Dad."

Dan turned to face his son. "Okay then, son. Here's my idea, and you can tell me what you think."

The two men talked on the rock for thirty minutes. The wind died down a bit as the sun came out briefly from behind a cloud. When they were finished, they walked back to the cabin as one.

CHAPTER 23

The Plan Comes Together

DAN AND **J**EREMY STARTED BY REMOVING THE BATTERY AND bringing it inside the cabin to warm up. Then they cleaned off the cables to make sure they were getting a good connection. Once the battery was warm, they hooked it back up and turned the key. The engine turned once, but wouldn't start up. In the end it just clicked as if mocking them.

"Dan, honey, wouldn't there be a few abandoned cars on the main road? We could take batteries out of them until we found one that worked."

His hand moved up to his chin as he thought.

"Maybe, but any car on the road right now has been there since the first snow. That means it's been sitting idle for months and is deader than the battery we have here."

Jeremy piped in. "So how do we usually handle this?"

Dan was quick to answer. "We go to the store and buy a new battery or we get a jump start from someone else. Or we could plug in a battery charger to recharge this one."

"None of that's going to work, Dan."

Dan grunted at his wife, still deep in thought. The baby started to cry and Jackie rushed over to get her off the floor. She was rolling over now and even crawling a bit. The baby was quick to laugh and smile, and was fast becoming the most popular entertainment in the cabin.

Dan turned to face the window. Just then the sun broke from behind a cloud and streamed into the cabin. The days were getting longer now, so things were warming up, and they were seeing the sun more and more, which was a welcome change.

Suddenly, Dan smiled.

"What are you thinking, Dad?" Jeremy smiled too. "Jackie, Dad's got an idea!"

Jackie rushed over with the baby in her arms. "What is it, sweetheart?"

He looked at her and reached his hand out to the window, The sunlight landed on his skin.

"We use the sun, Jackie. It's simple."

Jackie looked perplexed. "Dan, we don't have any solar panels or anything to build them or even know how to build them if we did."

Dan reached out and grabbed her by the shoulders. He turned his wife to look him full in the face. "Sweetheart, you and I may not have solar panels, but the Wisconsin Department of Transportation has thousands of them."

Dan and Jeremy looked up at the wooden pole. The lone solar panel was hanging above them twenty feet off the ground. It was small, but big enough to trickle charge the truck battery. They'd walked through the snow for five miles before finding this one, always giving houses a wide berth, not willing to take the chance on a hostile resident, determined to protect his home.

"How we gonna get up there, Dad?"

Dan looked around. Both of them were wearing snow camo made from bed sheets, and were barely visible against the backdrop of snow. "We need us a ladder."

"But we don't have a ladder, dad. All we got is a few tools and this twine."

There was a sound off in the distance. Dan took the hat off his ears so he could hear better.

"That's a snowmobile! Quick, get off the road. We need to hide in the swamp!"

"But, Dad, we could flag them down and get help."

Dan ran for the swamp, yelling over his shoulder as he went. "Follow my orders! Now!"

Thirty seconds later the snowmobile raced by on the highways, kicking up a plume of white snow in its wake. The man was dressed in a snowmobile suit and helmet with some type of long gun strapped over his back. Neither of the men spoke until the machine was long out of sight and the engine's drone faded away.

"Why didn't we get his help, Dad?"

Dan turned toward his son. "We'd better talk."

They both sat down on a log. Dan unslung the AR-15 from his shoulder and leaned up it against the log. Jeremy did the same with the Winchester shotgun.

"We don't know who that guy was, Jeremy. He could have shot us, then followed our tracks back to the cabin and then killed Jackie and Donna."

Jeremy's face clouded over. "Why would he do that, Dad?"

"To get the things that we have, son. That's the way things work now. Yeah, sure, a year ago we would've flagged down the first person to pass us and they would have helped. But this is a whole, new world we have now, and you know how dangerous it is, right? I mean, you saw the last guys we met. We had to kill them before they killed us. That's the way it is now."

He could tell that Jeremy didn't want to believe him, so he continued. "Listen, son. I know this is tough to take, but think of it this way. Do you know why we didn't stop at that house back there to ask for help?"

Jeremy shook his head from side to side, then took off his white stocking hat to run his fingers through his hair.

"Not really, Dad. I would've stopped for help. Not all people are bad now, just like all people weren't bad before the lights went out. Some people are still good. Look at us - we're still good. Right?"

On the one hand, Dan admired his son's ability to look for the best in people. On the other hand, it might get them all killed.

"We no longer have the luxury of trusting strangers, son. We can't do it. If we trust the right people, they'll maybe help us, but … if we trust a bad guy … we could all die. From now on, we trust no one except each other until we have evidence to trust another."

Jeremy looked disappointed, but nodded his head in compliance. "Okay, Dad. I trust you."

Dan smiled. "Okay then, here's what we do."

After explaining it to him, Jeremy used a small bow saw to cut down three saplings about four inches in diameter. It took a full hour, but he was finally able to cut ten cross pieces which Dan quickly lashed onto the other two saplings to form rungs. Within two hours they had a fairly sturdy ladder which they promptly leaned up against the power pole.

Before making his way up, Dan gave his son final directions. "Your job, son, is to steady the ladder. Don't let me fall. If I get hurt, we won't make it back before dark and we'll freeze out here. If the snowmobile comes back, hide in the swamp again until he leaves."

A look of concern came over Jeremy's face. "But what if he doesn't leave, dad?"

Dan's face grew stern. "Under no circumstances are you to come out of the swamp. If something happens to me, get back to Jackie and the baby and protect them. Do you understand?"

Jeremy didn't answer.

"I said - Do you understand!"

Reluctantly, his son nodded in response.

Leaning his AR-15 up against the pole, Dan began making his way up the ladder, slowly, and very carefully. Jeremy did his best to hold it steady, but the ladder wiggled back and forth against the pole. It would have been hard enough with an aluminum ladder, but it was especially dangerous with lashed-together sticks.

Finally, Dan made it to the top. He tied the rope around his waist and then around the pole. Next, he took off his gloves and pulled the Crescent wrench out of his front pocket. He closed up the wrench to about half and inch diameter, then placed it on the nut for final adjustments. At first, the nut wouldn't break free. It was on tight. The wrench slipped off twice, threatening to strip the head, but on the third try, the nut finally broke free.

"How's it going up there, Dad?"

Dan looked down and smiled.

"Good son, just three more nuts and I can lower it down to you."

Dan removed the next nut with no problem. Then he tied another rope around the ladder rung and onto the metal bracket of the solar panel. Just as he started to loosen the third nut, Jeremy yelled up to him.

"Hey, dad, can you hear that?"

Dan's pulse quickened. It was the high-pitched whine of snowmobile engines approaching.

"Get in the swamp, son!"

Dan started to untie the rope, but his fingers were numb from working the cold, metal Crescent wrench. He looked down and Jeremy was still there.

"Hurry, dad!"

"Get in the swamp, son!"

Dan looked out and saw the two snowmobiles approaching from the west, each was pulling a sled. He tried to stay calm as he worked the knots loose, but it was no use. His hands were just too cold. The snowmobiles stopped below him and both men dismounted. Dan looked down for Jeremy, but he was no where in sight.

"What are you doing up there, stranger?"

Both men had removed their helmets and were smiling up at Dan who had no choice but to cling helplessly to the ladder.

"Oh, just hanging around I guess."

One of the men laughed out loud. "Well, looks to me like you're stealing county property."

Dan hesitated. He didn't trust the man's tone of voice, or the look on his face.

"Well, actually, I think I'm stealing state property, but I reckon they won't be using it for a while so it's okay."

The man's smile went away.

"Well, partner, you reckoned wrong. Ya see, my friend and I are planning on taking every solar panel off this stretch of road for fifty miles in both directions. It's a business venture you might say."

Dan glanced out into the swamp hoping that Jeremy was running away to safety. He thought to himself *how am I going to get out of this mess.*

"Listen guys, I can appreciate a good business deal, so let's strike a deal right now."

The taller man appeared to be in charge, and his smile grew even bigger until it spanned the full width of his face. Then he laughed out loud.

"Now, son, what could you possibly have that we want?"

Dan pointed down at the AR-15 leaning against the power pole. "Take my rifle in return for this one solar panel and leave me unharmed. That's all I ask."

The two men looked at each other. Finally they both burst out laughing.

"Get the man's rifle, John. I'll take care of this guy."

The other man picked up Dan's AR and walked it over to his snowmobile. He placed the rifle inside the sled began to lash in down with a bungee cord.

"Thanks for the rifle, partner. But we can't let you have the solar panel. It just wouldn't be good business."

Dan looked around, thinking desperately, wondering how to get out of this mess. He was tied to a pole, twenty feet off the ground, hanging by a rickety ladder. Dan realized that he was about to die.

"Out here, my friend, possession is nine-tenths of the law. And the way I see it, we possess the rifle, the solar panel and we possess you."

He walked up to the ladder, placed his right hand on a rung and started to shake. Caught by surprise, Dan fell off the ladder and the rope around his waist hiked up under his armpits, before quickly cinching tight around his lungs and cutting off his air supply. Dan hung there while both men laughed below.

After thirty seconds without air, Dan began to gasp and choke. The men laughed even harder.

"Look at him up there, John, swinging off that rope like a monkey."

The man directly below the pole lifted up his coat and drew a 45 caliber 1911 pistol from his holster before aiming it at Dan, swinging helplessly on the rope.

"I feel merciful today, stranger. We can't just leave you up there to die a slow and agonizing death." The man's trigger finger eased back as he centered the front sight on Dan's head. He timed his trigger pull with the swaying motion of Dan's body.

BAM! The man dropped his forty-five into the snow as the shotgun slug tore into his chest. Red blood sprayed out onto the white snow as the other man looked on in shock. Jeremy's shotgun barked out again, this time shredding the rope tied to the pole, releasing his father for the 15-foot drop into the snow. The other man ran towards the snowmobile and the engine quickly fired up. Just as he began to speed away, several shots rang out, sending the man sprawling into the snow. One shot to the man's head with Dan's Taurus revolver had quickly done the job.

Dan turned in the snow and pointed his revolver at the first man down, who was now bleeding out in the snow just a few feet away. As Jeremy walked out of the swamp, Dan took the rope off his torso and caught his breath.

By time they reached the man, he was almost dead. A red, bubbly froth was coming out his mouth, and he coughed it out onto the snow. Jeremy looked down and tears welled up in his eyes.

"I'm sorry, mister, I didn't want to do that."

The man looked up at him, and the crow's feet around his blue eyes wrinkled as he squinted up at Jeremy. He uttered his final words through his bloody gasp.

"You're … a … boy?"

Then the life in his blue eyes went out like the flame of a candle. Jeremy's shot had gone under his right armpit, through both lungs, then partially blowing off his left arm at the elbow as it left his body.

Dan was proud of his son's shot, and relieved at his survival, but he didn't say anything at first. Then he heard whimpers and looked up at his son. Tears flowed freely down Jeremy's cheeks. He walked over and hugged him with his left arm.

"He was going to kill you, dad. He would shoot you for a gun you were going to let him have for free."

Jeremy looked into Dan's eyes. "Why?"

Dan shook his head. "There's evil in some folks. It just happens."

He squeezed his son hard.

"But you saved my life. That's what matters."

He turned his body and they both hugged as the snow began to drift lazily down.

An hour later they made their way back to the cabin in the snowmobiles. The new snow covered their tracks behind them.

CHAPTER 24

Decision Point

JACKIE HAD BEEN SHOCKED TO SEE TWO MEN DRIVE UP ON snowmobiles. In fact, she'd met them at the door with a pistol aimed at their heads. Only when Dan saw the gun pointed at him did he think to take off his helmet.

"Oh, Dan! You're back!" She let the pistol come down and rushed off the porch where he scooped her up. They held each other for several seconds while Jeremy looked on clumsily.

"Let's get inside honey. The snow's coming down pretty hard now."

"Where did you get these snowmobiles?"

Dan pointed back to Jeremy as he spoke. "Son, go ahead and throw a tarp over the sleds to keep the snow off the new gear. Then come on inside and we'll talk."

Once inside, Dan told her everything that had happened. She was relieved that Dan was okay, but her first concern was for Jeremy.

"That's going to mark him, Dan. It will change him."

Dan nodded. "I know. It's sad, but he's strong. He'll be okay. Besides, he'll have to just reason out that he had no choice." Dan looked over at the door, expecting his son to walk through at any moment. "These are hard times, and hard times make for hard men. But it is what it is. We're going to be seeing a lot of things we wouldn't normally see from now on." He shook his head sadly. "Normally I wouldn't be driving a stolen truck, and I certainly wouldn't take two snowmobiles that didn't belong to me. But ... I don't know, Jackie. The rules are all screwed up now. I have to figure out what's right and wrong, and I have to do it in the context of keeping my family alive. I feel like ... well, like I want to know what's right and what's wrong, so I can do right, but the lines are blurred now."

Dan looked like he wanted to cry, so Jackie leaned over and pulled his head into her shoulder. The baby was playing on the blanket by the fireplace. Outside, they could hear Jeremy moving things around in the bed of the pick-up truck, looking for the tarp.

"I know, Dan. But I have confidence in you, in your judgement and in your sense of right and wrong. We'll figure it out together, but in the meantime we need to pray about it, and maybe God will help us decide some new rules that keep us on the right path." She hesitated. "What do you think?"

He pulled his head up and smiled at her. "I think I married the right woman."

Just then Jeremy stomped the snow off his boots and walked through the door. As soon as he walked in, Jackie got up and walked over to hold him. Jeremy just stood there, like a rock, not sure how to respond to her.

"It's okay, Jeremy. You did the right thing. You shot a bad person, and you saved your dad's life in the process. You had no choice." She put her palms on either side of his face and moved his head down so his eyes met hers. "I would have done the same thing, Jeremy. I would have killed those men to save your father. They were bad people, and they needed killing. Think of how many other people they would have killed and hurt before someone else stood up to them and put an end to it."

Tears ran down his cheeks. Jackie wiped them away and smiled softly. "In bad times like this, Jeremy, people either get better, or they get worse. You are becoming a better person. You were forced to defend the people you love against a bad man. You did good, son."

The tightness in Jeremy's face lessoned. She'd never called him "son" before, and it made him feel good.

Dan walked over and the three of them embraced for a few seconds more. Then they sat down for bread and venison stew.

"First, let's look at the pros and cons of both ideas. We'll list them out on paper, then analyze them before we decide what choice to make. Sound good?"

Jeremy and Jackie both agreed. Jackie held baby Donna over the table toward Jeremy.

"Here, Jeremy, hold Donna so I can take notes."

Dan sat at the head of the wooden table with Jeremy on his left and Jackie on his right.

"But first, I want to read you both something. It's from Ecclesiastes chapter 4, verse 12. It very simply says '*Though one may be overpowered, two can defend themselves. A cord of three strands is not quickly broken.*'"

Jeremy looked down at the wood as he held the baby. His father looked over at him. "Son, without you today, I would have been over-powered. I want to publicly thank you for saving my life."

Dan hesitated while Jeremy just nodded his head softly. Then Dan continued. "We are the three strands, and we are bonded together through our love of God and our love of each other. No one is going to stop us from getting back home. This family stands together as one cord, strong, loyal, and, if need be, fierce."

Dan held his right hand out onto the oak wood table top in front of them and kept it there. Jackie looked him in the eye and smiled before placing her own hand atop her husband's. Jeremy looked at them both, one at a time. Then he reached out slowly with his right hand and completed the cord.

For the rest of the meeting they talked freely about the pros and cons of two plans: Do they wait for the thaw and drive back in the truck? or, Do they go now in the snowmobiles? It was a tough decision, because there was so much risk involved in both methods.

Jeremy argued for waiting and taking the truck.

"It will be warmer, and more comfortable for the baby and Jackie. We'll be able to haul more food and equipment too. We've already got it started back up by jump starting it with the snowmobile battery. It's a brand, new truck and not likely to break down. With the roads dry of snow, it will take less time as well. And what happens if we take the snowmobiles and a warm front moves in and melts the snow? We'd be dead in our tracks."

Jackie countered quickly with an argument of her own. "But the same thing could happen with the truck. A blizzard could come and snow us in. We'd be stranded for days in the cold."

Jeremy interrupted her. "Yes, but only for a few days. With snow-mobiles we'd be stranded until next winter when the snow comes again."

Dan nodded. "That's a good point."

But Jackie wasn't done yet.

"The snowmobiles are smaller, they're all-terrain vehicles and we won't be restricted to roads. With the truck we'll have to drive through dozens of towns, and some of them are likely to be hostile. The snowmobiles can drive through the woods, open fields, across frozen swamps, you name it."

Dan reached up to scratch the beard on his chin. He'd let it grow out the past few months. His hair was blonde, but his whiskers had a red-dish tint. It made for an interesting face. He chimed in.

"What happens if we get to the Mackinac Bridge and it's blocked with stalled cars? With snowmobiles we could snake our way through, even zip across on the ice in the straits if it's still cold enough."

Jackie made one, last point. "And what about gas? The truck gets less than 20 miles per gallon, and a snowmobile gets more than double that. Truth is we only have enough gas to make it halfway back with the truck. Where would we get the rest of the gas? We can make it all the way with the snowmobiles."

Jeremy shook his head back and forth. He clutched the baby tighter to his chest. "It's too cold for the baby."

Dan nodded. "That's a good point, son." He paused for a moment. "On the other hand, if we run out of gas halfway there, we're stranded in the cold as well."

He glanced over at Jackie. "Honey, make a list with two columns detailing the benefits and disadvantages of each. Then we'll look at it and decide."

It took Jackie only five minutes, and when she was done, the list looked like this:

Truck	
Benefits	**Disadvantages**
Provides warmth & shelter	Gets us only halfway
Transports more food & supplies	Confined to roads
Doesn't rely on snow.	May not be able to cross bridge
Will travel faster.	May get stranded in blizzard

Snowmobile	
Benefits	**Disadvantages**
Gets us all the way	Will be cold for baby
off-road to avoid trouble	Carries less supplies
Can't get snowed in	Must have cold & snow
Will cross bridge & other roadblocks	Travels slower than truck

When she was done, all three of them poured over the list together.

"I don't know, Dan. They look like the exact opposites of each other."

Jeremy agreed with Jackie. Dan nodded his head. "Yes, it certainly does. But…"

Jeremy slid the baby over to Jackie across the table. "What? What are you thinking, dad?"

Dan pointed to the list. "Some of these items carry more weight than others. For example, speed isn't as important as distance. If we can only make it halfway, then we may be better off staying where we are. At least here we have shelter, security, and all our supplies. If we can't make it all the way, I don't want to go at all." He moved his finger down to another item. "On the other hand, if a blizzard comes up and we freeze to death ..."

Jackie threw up her hands. "It's six of one and half a dozen of the other! The problem is we don't know for sure what we face out there."

Dan shook his head. "That's not entirely true. We know from experience that security is going to be a big issue. There are people out there who will kill us just to take our gear."

Jeremy interrupted him. "But what about the weather, Dad? We have no way of knowing if we'll have snow or not. For all we know we could be driving into a tropical heat wave."

Dan and Jackie both nodded. "That's true, son. But we shouldn't make a decision based on variables we have no control over. With conditions as they are, we'll make it home faster with the snowmobiles. We can make the trip in two days, and it would take one heck of a heat wave to melt all the snow, especially this far north."

"Are the two machines dependable?"

Dan answered Jackie's question. "Yes, I've looked them over, and they're pretty new and seem in good shape."

Jeremy shook his head. "I don't know, dad."

Dan smiled. "No one knows but God, son. Especially when we're talking about the weather. But we have to go with what we know, not by what we fear might happen. If no one can argue with my logic, then we'll leave day after tomorrow as soon as this storm lets up."

There was nothing but silence around the table. Then Jeremy looked him in the eyes. "I think we should pray about it, dad."

Dan smiled. "Agreed. You go ahead, son."

All of them bowed their heads as Jeremy talked to God.

"Okay, God. Here we are, wondering what to do. We need to get home, and we need your help. Please give us enough snow to get us home safely. It's all up to you, God." And then he added. "And please forgive us for killing those two guys today. We didn't want to do it."

Jeremy said "Amen" and the others repeated it in agreement.

They opened their eyes, all smiling at one another, as if relieved that a decision had been made. The wind and snow blew outside, hammering itself mercilessly against the cabin walls, but the walls held. They spent the next hour creating a list of the food and supplies they could take with them, giving special weight to security and shelter.

When they finally went to bed, Dan lay awake for several hours just thinking, wondering about the decision they'd made, wondering if he was leading them all out to their deaths. He felt bad about the lives taken today, so he went over every detail of the skirmish over and over again. But, still… he could find no way around it, even with the calm and wisdom of retrospect. In the end, he fell asleep after 2AM. His chest rose and fell with steady breathing. Jackie's arm came around him as he slept and squeezed reassuringly. She nuzzled her face up to his neck, taking in the sureness of his smell and the solidity of his touch.

A few feet away, Jeremy lay awake, knowing instinctively that he'd crossed a line he couldn't take back ever again. His Social Studies teacher would call it the Rubicon, but… it didn't matter what she thought. She lived in Eau Claire, and was probably already dead.

The wind continued to howl outside, but, even in the warmth of the cabin, with the fire glowing in the hearth, Jeremy pulled the sleeping bag up over his neck, but … he still felt cold.

CHAPTER 25

Moonshadow Recon

"**M**OONSHADOW, THIS IS EAGLE RANGER. SAY AGAIN YOUR last, over."

The man keyed the SINCGARS radio again before speaking. "Eagle Ranger, I say again. I'm requesting a priority 1 recon patrol in your sector. I'm looking for two white males and one female, traveling together across the border into your sector. They should be heading towards my location."

"Roger that, Moonshadow. Please relay names and descriptions of each."

Moonshadow leaned back in his rocking chair, deep inside his underground bunker. Very few people in the Shadow Militia knew his real name, but that was by design. It had always been imperative that he remain anonymous, but the day was fast approaching when he'd shed his anonymity and go into full military battle mode. At that time, there would be no turning back. He keyed the mike again and gave Eagle Ranger the description of all three people, along with any other details he could think of.

The SINCGARS was a satellite-based radio using 25 kHz channels in the VHF FM band, from 30 to 87.875 MHz range, using single-frequency and frequency-hopping modes. The frequency-hopping mode hopped 111 times a second making it very secure. Despite that, Moonshadow and Eagle Ranger were careful to follow protocol, using no names or exact locations. Everything they said would have been considered cryptic at best by any outside listener. Moonshadow was always amazed at the new technology. The comm gear they used now was nothing like the AN/PRC-77s they had used back in Nam.

And the Shadow Militia needed the security to protect them from the United States Government. The FBI and ATF had long made it a matter of routine to try and infiltrate and fragment all state militias, and that's why the Shadow Militia had been formed. They operated under the surface, in the shadow of the public militia. In fact, they were so secretive, that not even the Commanding Generals of the state militias knew of its existence. Their numbers were small, but they were all highly trained and well equipped, mostly special ops types, former Army Rangers, Marines, Green Berets, and a few Seals. They made Rambo look like a Cub Scout.

And Moonshadow was their unassuming leader.

"Roger that, Moonshadow. Is that all?"

Moonshadow hesitated, then keyed the mike one last time. "Affirmative, Eagle Ranger. Please advise when contact is made. Roger, over and out."

The old man placed the radio down on the steel barrel filled with red wheat. Off to the side was an entire pallet of 5.56mm NATO rounds in olive drab steel cans. Beside that was a pallet of Stinger missiles, one of fragmentation grenades, and still another of 7.62mm rounds. Just to be safe, Moonshadow never smoked down here.

Instead, he leaned back in the chair, placed his hands on the arms of the rocker and slowly moved back and forth, back and forth, back and forth. The movement and rhythm cleared his head and helped him think. But no amount of thinking and rocking could create the security he yearned for. He wanted the reassurance they were okay, but it just wouldn't come.

Departure day

The sun was shining on the day they left the cabin and headed east toward the Upper Peninsula. Jackie was seated inside the lead sled, facing the back, with Donna in her arms, wrapped inside blankets. She was set up to keep her daughter warm, out of the wind, and she could even breastfeed her while the snowmobiles were on the move.

Jackie found it a bit disconcerting they had to leave many of their supplies behind. There simply wasn't enough room in the sleds. But most disturbing to her was leaving the gravesite of her first husband. She glanced over at the wooden cross jutting out of the snow. This was the cabin she'd bought with Don to live in when everything else went bad. But the collapse had taken his life as well as many others, and things had changed.

She left a note on the table inside which said:

To whom it may concern:

This is my home. Please use it to keep warm and safe from danger. You may live here as long as you need shelter. Please take care of it as if it were your own. Leave it in good order for the next person in need.

My husband, Don, is buried beneath the cross. Please respect his grave.

May God bless and keep your family.

Jackie Branch
The Owner

Dan and Jeremy came over to her now and kneeled down beside her and the baby.

"Are you ready sweetheart?"

Jackie looked into Dan's eyes and nodded, but said nothing. She didn't want to cry in front of him, afraid he would misinterpret her tears. She loved Dan and would follow him anywhere. She would even die for him, but … this cabin had given them safety and refuge and peace in the eye of the storm. Now they were leaving it behind never to return.

Dan held his right hand out. Jackie covered it with her own, quickly followed by Jeremy's.

"Dear God. We ask you for easy travel, for moderate weather, and for a safe passage all the way home. We praise you and lift you up. Amen"

Jeremy bent down and kissed the baby on the forehead. "Keep her warm, mom."

"I will, son. Drive safe."

Dan took one final walk around the cabin before placing the helmet on his head and mounting the snowmobile. He was anxious to get back, but this moment sobered him, and he couldn't help but remember last September, the day after the collapse, when he'd left his home in Menomonie.

So far, the nine-hour drive had taken him over six months. And he was only halfway home.

Dan fired up his machine, followed quickly by Jeremy's. They moved out over the snow toward the main road, leaving their place of refuge behind, not knowing what dangers lie ahead of them.

Building an Army

"You don't need a police force. You need an army."

Sheriff Leif looked over at his friend, trying hard to hide his exasperation and impatience. Rodney had been pushing him into this for months now, but he was resisting every step of the way.

"I don't need an army, Rodney! I'm not a General, I'm a Sheriff."

Rodney smiled and pulled a pack of Camels out of his front right pocket.

"There's no smoking in the building, you know that, Rodney."

His Zippo popped open and torched the end of the cigarette. "It's okay, Joe. This is medicinal tobacco and I have a prescription from my doctor."

The Sheriff gritted his teeth together and tried hard not to grind his jaw back and forth.

"You are really starting to get on my nerves, old man."

Rodney blew smoke out the left side of his mouth so as not to envelop his friend in the cloud.

"I understand. I get that a lot these days. It's amazing. I don't even like myself anymore. But that doesn't diminish the validity of what I just said." He took another drag off the Camel and let the smoke sit in his lungs for a few seconds. "You need to train your posse in basic battlefield tactics. They need to know about flanking maneuvers, how to set up an ambush, basic recon, hand signals, battlefield first aid." Smoke came out of his mouth as he talked.

"Where are you getting all those cigarettes? Everyone else has been out for months now."

Rodney smiled. "Ebay, but don't change the subject. All I'm asking is that you let me train them in the basics. It's not like I'm going to form them up and have them parading around town like soldiers."

Joe looked away and focused on the picture on his desk of his wife and kid. His son was holding up a ten-inch Blue Gill and his wife was smiling at him. Vandalism had increased over the past month, probably stemming from the hundred or so refugees camped out in the state game area five miles down the road. Some of the residents had openly suggested they go and burn them out and force them to move on. Joe had come down hard against it, threatening to throw anyone in jail who took the law into their own hands. To top it all off, rumors had been circulating about bands of thieves roaming the countryside, in the counties to the south of them.

"Let's come back to that in a minute, Rodney."

The old man crushed out his cigarette on the heel of his boot and placed the butt in his left, front shirt pocket.

"Sure. You're the Sheriff." And he smiled when he said it, like it was the barb on the end of a fish hook.

Joe squirmed in his chair before speaking. "So, Rodney, what are you hearing on the short wave these days?"

Rodney gave him a cold, blank stare.

Joe pursued it further.

"Come on, Rodney, you're a patriot!"

His hard stare got colder.

Joe exhaled as if in defeat.

"Okay, Rodney, here's what I'll let you do."

Rodney smiled slightly.

"Go ahead and start training the military vets. But this is just a pilot program to see how it's received by them and by the community."

Joe leaned forward in his chair.

"Agreed?"

Rodney's face broke into a full smile now.

"Sure thing, Joe. After all, you're the Sheriff. if that's what you want, then I'll start right away."

He got up to leave, but Joe stopped him.

"Hold on there, not so fast. Tell me what you're hearing on the short wave. Are all those rumors true?"

Rodney hesitated before sitting down and lighting up another cigarette. He ceremoniously blew out smoke, knowing the Sheriff was waiting impatiently for him to speak. "Well, some of the rumors are true, and some are false. Which ones are you worried about most?"

Joe tried to steady his breathing before he spoke. "The rumors about two hundred murdering rapists heading our way. Is it true or not?"

Rodney paused for dramatic effect, and took another puff off the Camel before answering.

"It's true. But I would put their numbers more at 300, not 200. If they come here we can take them, provided we play it smart."

A faraway look settled in the Sheriff's eyes. He glanced back down at his wife and son in the picture. It had been taken at Lake Piqua right before the collapse on their last family vacation. It was quite possibly the last vacation they would ever take. Now, every waking moment was spent just trying to eat and survive.

"If you were in charge, how would you handle it?"

Inside the privacy of his mind, Rodney's aging body did a cartwheel and topped it off with a handstand. But on the outside, he remained stoic.

"Well, I suppose … if it were me, I would …"

And then he told him everything, holding nothing back. Joe's eyes opened wide and his pulse quickened.

CHAPTER 26

A Perilous Journey

THERE IT WAS, STRAIGHT AHEAD AND TO THE RIGHT. LAKE Michigan. It had taken them four hours to reach the Michigan border, but now, Dan's heart leaped upon seeing it.

There was ice still on the lake out to about 100 yards offshore. but it was breaking up around the beach. He wanted to head for the bridge on the frozen lake, but didn't dare. March ice was seldom stable, even this far north.

He came to a stop on the beach, and Jeremy's snow machine came up beside him. Both engines died down, until all they could hear was wind.

"Is this Michigan, Dad?"

"Sure is, son. Can't you tell?"

Jeremy took off his helmet and scratched his head. "Not really. Looks a lot like Wisconsin to me. I've never been to Michigan before."

Just then the baby started to cry.

"Dan, I need to change her diaper. Can the two of you form a windbreak around me so she doesn't get so cold?"

Dan nodded, then reached into the back of the sled and pulled out a small, blue tarp.

"Come on, Jeremy. Let's wrap this around the sled so they stay warm."

A few minutes later, the baby was changed and Jackie began nursing her. Dan and Jeremy drove the snowmobiles up into a small copse behind a dune where the wind was blocked and built a campfire.

"We won't be able to do this very much once we get to more populated areas, but this stretch south of Ford River on M-35 is pretty secure. Hardly any people at all around here. But the closer we get to Escanaba, the more dangerous it might get."

Dan spread out the paper map of Michigan on the back of Jeremy's sled, but the wind kept blowing it closed.

"Sure wish we had a GPS. But I guess those days are long gone."

Jeremy walked up behind him. "Why don't we just use the GPS on my cell phone?"

Dan and Jackie looked at each other, and then over at Jeremy. "You mean it still works?"

"I don't know. I haven't tried it. Trying to save the battery."

He reached into his front pocket and pulled it out. A few seconds later he smiled. "We can only get three satellites, but it's working."

Dan folded up the map and stuck it back in the sled. "Let me take a look."

Dan took the Blackberry from his son and smiled. "Will you look at this, Jackie. I can't believe it still works. Apparently the collapse didn't affect the satellites. We should be able to navigate around Escanaba without running into too much trouble."

The three of them huddled around Jackie's sled as they made plans. "See, we can go just past Ford River, then veer north until we get above Escanaba, then turn back east.

That way we don't have to follow the lakeshore where all the towns are."

Jeremy clapped his father on the back. "Sounds like a plan, Dad."

Dan looked his son in the eyes. "Makes me wish I hadn't thrown my cell phone away so quickly. Thank you, son."

Jeremy caught himself blushing and turned away smiling. "No problem, Dad."

"Let's keep moving, honey. The baby's pretty restless and I want to get this done as quickly as possible."

Dan nodded and passed out some water, bread and dried meat. They all ate hurriedly and then Dan put out the fire. Five minutes later they were running northeast straight down M-35. There were very few houses near the beach, but when they came to one, they quickly skirted around it, giving it a wide berth for added safety.

A few miles from Ford River, Dan turned north away from the beach. Once inland, they saw more trees and swamps and Dan used them for cover as much as he could. They were making good time when all of a sudden Dan's snowmobile hit a large rock and bounced high into the air. Dan was thrown clear, but the snowmobile came down with a crash, overturning the sled with Jackie and the baby inside.

Jeremy swerved to the right, missing the rock and the crash. He came to a stop just a few feet away from the overturned sled.

Dan landed in a snowbank unharmed, but Jackie's body was half out of the sled, pinched between the frozen ground with the sled lying on top of her.

By time he reached Jackie, Jeremy was already there lifting her head up off the snow.

"Mom! Mom!"

Jackie didn't move. Her eyes were closed and her face and forehead were bleeding.

"Don't move her, son until we know her spine is okay."

Dan looked around on the ground. "Where's the baby?"

Jeremy ran around the sled frantically, looking for Donna, but couldn't find her. Suddenly, they heard crying and traced it to a snowbank about twenty feet away. The baby was still wrapped in its blankets with her face down into the cold snow. She screamed as loud as she could until Jeremy scooped her up and cuddled her close. He talked to her all the way back to the sled where his father kneeled beside Jackie.

"Please God, let her be okay! Please God!"

Dan checked Jackie's legs and quickly saw the blood seeping through her snow pants. He carefully tipped the sled back onto the runners, then he pulled out his knife and cut away the cloth from her ankle. He shuddered upon seeing the white bone sticking out through her skin. A compound fracture.

The baby started crying again, but Jeremy couldn't silence her. "What do we do, Dad?"

Dan shook his head from side to side. "I can't believe I didn't see that rock. We should have stayed on the road."

He moved away from her leg on up to her head. He checked her pulse by feeling the carotid artery. It seemed weak and slow to him, but he didn't know for sure as his medical training was limited at best. He lifted up on her left eyelid and watched the pupil. It didn't seem to be responding to the light.

"I think she has a concussion. Nothing we can do about that. We'll know more when she wakes up. Right now I have to make a splint for that leg. Thank God she didn't cut an artery."

"Dad, I can't make the baby stop crying. I don't know what to do. Is she going to die, Dad? What's going on! What should I do?"

Dan looked up with fear and fire in his eyes. "Just shut up for a second and let me think!"

Dan's fingers pressed against his helmet. He quickly ripped it off and threw it to the ground. The icy, cold wind blew his greasy, blonde hair, making it slap against his bearded face.

"First, I'll keep your Mom warm with blankets, then build a fire. After that I'll cut the wood I need for a splint. Hopefully by then she'll be awake and can tell us more."

Jeremy looked desperate. "But what about the baby? What should I do?"

Dan spoke as he moved to get the blankets. "Unwrap her and check out every inch of her body for wounds. If you find nothing wrong, then wrap her back up and keep her warm. Try to distract her by playing with her and feeding her some of that applesauce in the MRE packets."

Dan glanced over at his snowmobile. It had crashed into a tree when it landed and looked ruined. The afternoon sun would soon be going down, and with it, temperatures would fall. They both went to work, quickly, efficiently and desperately.

"Dad, she's waking up!"

Dan hurried over to Jackie just in time to keep her from choking on her own vomit. He carefully moved her head to one side and rolled her over slightly. Her splint was in place to lessen the chance of further injury to the leg, and the shelter was up as well, protecting her and the baby from the wind.

"Jackie! Sweetheart! Can you hear me?"

Her lips moved and Dan leaned down to hear her whispered reply.

"Stop yelling. My head hurts."

Dan smiled and kissed her on the cheek. "Don't worry, honey. You're going to be okay. You just have a concussion." And then, almost as an afterthought he added. "And don't move your legs. One of them has a compound fracture and you don't want to make it worse."

She smiled weakly. "Oh, is that all."

Then the baby started crying again, and Jackie tried to get up. "No, honey. Stay down. The baby's okay."

"I want to see her. Bring her here or I'm getting up."

Jeremy, just a few feet away by the fire, heard her words and came over with baby Donna. They propped up Jackie's head and then placed the baby in her waiting arms. "I have to nurse her."

Once she started to suckle, the baby quieted and Jackie smiled. "My head hurts, Dan."

"I know honey. I have the Tylenol ready." She took the pills with water.

"The light hurts my eyes."

Dan nodded. "Yes, I know. But just keep your eyes closed and rest until we get ready to move again. Are you warm enough?"

She nodded her head. "Ouch!"

"Don't move your head, honey. Just whisper. Just use words."

"I feel like I'm going to die."

Dan's heart-rate skyrocketed. "No, you're going to be okay. As soon as you're done nursing, we're going to load you up and get you some help."

But Jackie didn't answer. She was already drifting off to sleep.

CHAPTER 27

Moving out

THE SNOWMOBILE MOVED SLOWLY, PULLING THE SLED BEHIND it. Every time it bounced, even slightly in the snow, Jackie winced in pain. Jeremy was driving while Dan walked beside the sled, cradling the baby in his arms. It was slow going, and the sun was setting. The wind was picking up now as it usually did at sunset, and the temperature began to plummet.

"Stop, Jeremy!"

Jeremy came to a halt in the snow, and his father walked up to him.

"Let's take a look at the GPS again."

Jeremy pulled it out of his front pocket and looked at it. "It says no signal, Dad."

A frown moved across Dan's face, but he said nothing.

"So what do we do now, Dad?"

Dan was getting sick of people asking him that question. He was tired of having to pretend like he knew what was going on. "No problem, son. We just keep heading east until we reach Lake Michigan. Then we turn left and follow it up the coast until we reach Escanaba. They have a hospital there."

Jeremy nodded. "Okay." Then he quickly added. "So which way's east?"

Normally, Dan would take this opportunity to smile and teach his son, but not today. "Just keep the sunset on your back and we'll be fine."

Jeremy's brow tightened up inside his helmet. He was thinking *What happens when we can't see the sun anymore?* But he didn't voice his thoughts. He was too afraid his father had no good answer. So he started the snow machine up and moved forward again, being careful to keep the sun on his back and trying to take the smoothest terrain.

Dan dropped back again, walking along the sled, trying to stay strong for the others, clinging desperately to the baby and what little faith remained inside him. He looked down at his wife's ashen face, then down at the baby. Dan was surprised to see her eyes open. Donna looked up at him and laughed. Dan smiled too. His heart took a step up, and he began to sing softly to his child.

"Oh there's a bright golden haze on the meadow. There's a bright golden haze on the meadow. The corn is as high as an elephant's eye. And it won't be long till it reaches the sky."

Jeremy heard the singing and glanced back over his shoulder briefly. He whispered a prayer to God. *Please help us, Lord.* Then he started singing too, doing the best he could to keep from jostling his mother, all the while thinking, *If my Dad can do it, then so can I.*

Rodney sat beside his short wave radio listening. The dog was at his feet, and the fire crackled beside him. He was warm. He was safe. He was frustrated.

He so much wanted to be up in the U.P. out in that late-winter storm, searching for the kid and his family, but it wasn't possible or wise. So he continued to sit in his rocking chair, forcing himself to monitor broadcasts, listening for any clues that might tell him three people had been found and rescued.

But no word came, and the silence was deafening.

Dan huddled over his wife, trying to keep her warm. The baby was between them, and she was crying now. Jackie had lost consciousness again a few hours ago, and Dan had been unable to wake her. Jeremy sat over by the fire, but it was hard to get the wet wood to burn hot enough to make a difference.

As the wind howled all around them, Jeremy thought to himself *And I was worried about a spring thaw?* He took off his gloves and held them closer to the flames. After a few more minutes of shivering by the fire, he walked over to his Dad.

"Dad, is she going to be okay?"

Dan looked up and raised the visor on his helmet so he could be heard. He shook his head in frustration.

"I don't know, son. At first I thought she was going to be okay, but now I can't even get her to wake up."

Jeremy looked down at the baby. "What about baby Donna?"

"So long as she stays warm she'll be okay. She's eating enough. I've been chewing up the crackers and putting them in her mouth and she eats them okay. We have the canned milk, but I can't figure out how to make the nursing process work without Jackie's help, and we don't have a baby bottle."

Dan reached down and checked Jackie's pulse again. It was still weak.

"Maybe one of us should go for help, Dad."

His father looked up at him and shook his head from side to side. "It's too risky, son. We have no guarantee we'd find anyone in time, and no idea what kind of person we'd find. We could end up making things worse."

His son looked out into the wind. "How could things possibly get any worse?"

Dan's brow furled as he winced at the question. "It can always get worse, son. Always."

Jeremy shrugged. "So what's the plan, Dad?"

Dan thought about it for a second. His reply was terse and unsure.

"I guess we just try to stay warm until the snowstorm lets up … and we pray."

That answer frustrated Jeremy. He wanted to do something. He looked down at Jackie. The baby was still crying and it broke his heart to hear her cries. Everything inside him wanted to do something - anything.

"Okay, Dad. I'll pray."

"EAGLE RANGER, THIS IS MOONSHADOW, OVER."

There was nothing but silence coming from the radio. Eagle Ranger, this is Moonshadow. Please acknowledge, over."

Rodney put the radio down with a heavy sigh on the barrel beside him. It could be the weather. He knew it was pretty bad up there right now. It wasn't like Eagle Ranger to not respond. Maybe he was out looking for them right now. *No,* he thought, *Eagle Ranger would have his radio with him at all times.*

He turned back to his notebook and continued to jot down notes. He was in the process of writing up a draft training plan for Sheriff Leif. He didn't want to, but Joe had insisted he put it all down on paper before he started training his men.

Rodney was disgusted by paperwork. He liked the Sheriff, but was convinced the man was living a year in the past. Now was the time to cut through all the red tape. Now was the time to rise up and press on full speed ahead instead of forming committees and having brainstorming sessions and writing mission statements.

Nonetheless, he wrote down a few more words, then tried to organize them into something cohesive. Then he smiled to himself and thought to himself, *How's this for a Mission Statement. We train hard. We fight hard. We kill anyone who tries to hurt us.*

He shrugged and said out loud. "I don't think that one will fly, at least not yet. But Rodney knew from experience and from his study of history that his time would come. He was not a peacetime leader. He was more of a take-names-and-kick-ass kind of guy. He was reminded of Winston Churchill's famous quote about war and peace.

Those who can win a war well can rarely make a good peace and those who could make a good peace would never have won the war.

Sheriff Leif was a good man, but he was still stuck in the peace of yesterday. Rodney couldn't help but wonder, *Will he be able to make the transition into war, because war was undoubtedly coming; it was coming like a freight train, straight at them, and it would not stop to wait for good men to get the stomach for killing.*

On the contrary, Rodney had the stomach for killing. He'd done it before and would do it again. He wouldn't enjoy it, but, nonetheless, he would do it without flinching and without hesitation.

He reached over and picked up the radio again.

"Eagle Ranger, this is Moonshadow, over."

Silence. "Eagle Ranger, this is Moonshadow, over." More silence.

Rodney spoke out loud to no one. "Where are you, Dan. Why aren't you here? I need you, son."

CHAPTER 28

The Impetuosity of the Young

DAN AWOKE TO THE SOUND OF HIS SNOWMOBILE DRIVING away. He quickly threw off the blue tarp, which was covered with a full foot of snow. It showered down on him, blinding his eyes for a moment, but by the time he was up and moving, the snowmobile was already out of sight.

He looked around quickly, taking everything in. The sun was up and shining, the fire was a weak smolder, the wind and snow had stopped, and his son, Jeremy, was no where to be seen.

He looked down again at his wife and child, sleeping soundly. They both looked so vulnerable and frail. And, as the drone of the snowmobile's engine faded into the east, Dan whispered a prayer before setting out to rebuild the fire.

JEREMY DROVE AS FAST AS HE COULD THROUGH THE SNOW. THE STORM had lifted, so he was able to make good time. He remembered what his dad had said about direction, and headed straight into the sunrise. As he drove through the knee-deep fresh, powdery snow, he contemplated the ramifications of what he was doing. He knew his father would be upset with him, but he saw no other way to save Jackie's life. They needed help, and his father wouldn't do it, so that left only him. Besides, he'd learned from experience that it was sometimes better to ask for forgiveness than for permission.

After fifteen minutes he drove down into a cedar swamp, snaking through it, always looking for the high ground. He'd never been in a cedar swamp before. By time he was deep inside it, he realized how lost he was. He pulled up onto a mound and stopped his machine before pulling his cell phone out of his pocket. He had a signal now, and checked his location. He smiled. Not too much further and he'd be there.

THE BABY WAS CRYING AGAIN, AND DAN HELD HER, ROCKING HER GENTLY, talking to her in a soothing voice, but nothing he could say or do seemed to make her feel better. He looked down at his wife, lying in the sled. She was still alive, but she should be awake by now, and that bothered him.

He walked over to the fire and kept singing to baby Donna.

> *"He was singing, "bye-bye, miss American pie.*
> *Drove my chevy to the levee, But the levee was dry."*

Dan stopped in mid-verse. When was it he'd sang that song last? Then it came to him. It was the night he'd been beaten nearly to death in Eagle River. Perhaps he should choose another song.

Amazing grace! How sweet the sound
That saved a wretch like me. I once was lost, but now am found,
Was blind but now I see.

Baby Donna stopped crying and looked up at him. She reached her little hand up out of the blanket and grabbed onto his shaggy, dirty, blonde beard. Dan smiled and then took her tiny fingers in his own. He'd never held a black baby before Donna. Perhaps it was odd he'd expected them to be different from white babies, but they weren't. The only difference appeared to be the color of her skin. He found himself wondering why blacks and whites didn't get along better. Personally, he didn't know any blacks in Menomonie. There just weren't that many. From his experience in the Marine Corps, he knew that most of them lived in the big cities. He recalled that in boot camp, the color of a man's skin didn't really account for much. Black and white pulled together or everyone failed. He thought about it for a moment and realized that it was probably that way all over the country now, whether in the city or country, whether black or white. People who pulled together would survive, and those who tried to go it alone would likely die.

Then his thoughts shifted to his son, traveling alone in the frozen north woods of the upper peninsula, and he shivered. Deep down, in his heart, he knew that Jeremy was right to go for help. There was no other way, but … who could they trust? How would Jeremy know the good from the bad? He closed his eyes and whispered another prayer. When he opened them, baby Donna was smiling at him.

Dan smiled and began to sing again, this time softly and ever so tenderly.

When we've been there ten thousand years,
Bright shining as the sun,
We've no less days to sing God's praise,
Than when we first begun.

The little baby slowly closed her eyes and drifted off to sleep.

"Eagle Ranger, this is Eagle Recon 3, over."
There was silence for a moment, and then a voice came over the radio. "Eagle Recon 3, this is Eagle Ranger, go ahead, with your sit-rep, over."

Donny Brewster hesitated before keying the mike and speaking. "Dis is Eagle Recon 3, I finished da search a sector seven, but need ta head ta town fer food and get rested up a bit, eh. I go ta Ford River to da cafe and get warm, then head ta Escanaba by da river just ta see what I can see, eh?"

"Roger that, Eagle Recon 3." There was silence for a few seconds, then another transmission. "Also, be advised to cut the accent, Eagle recon 3. It gives away your location. Besides, you're from Detroit and we all know it. You're just another troll like me."

Donny heard someone laughing just as the transmission cut out. He spit at the ground in exasperation. He hated that disparaging troll label. Up here in the U.P. there were only two kinds of people: yoopers and trolls. Most of the others up here were either of Finnish, Canadian or Native American descent. And even though the locals had accepted him, he knew that in their minds, he would always be a troll, someone from under the bridge, someone who'd come up to escape the rat race and get a little peace in God's country.

He'd joined the Shadow Militia by invitation, because that's the only way it happened. Truth is he'd gotten out of the Marine Corps six years ago and hadn't been able to get a job. But then again, what kind of job could he get as a retired Marine Corps sniper? There just wasn't a whole lot of legitimate work out there for a man is his line of work. *"Hi, my name is Donny Brewster. I'm looking for a job. Is there anyone you'd like killed today? I specialize in 1,000-yard headshots."*

The more he thought about it, the more he realized that the reason he'd been accepted into the Yooper community was his affinity for firearms. Some people up here were great drinkers, others good at cutting trees or moving ore. Donny Brewster was just a guy from Detroit with good eyes and a steady aim.

He put the radio back in his pack and slung his M1 Garand over his shoulder and began the long trek back into town. He loved the Garand. He'd gotten it through the Civilian Marksmanship Program, and enjoyed shooting it. Sure, there were lots of other rifles that surpassed it in various ways, but Donny was nostalgic. His father had carried the M1 in Korea, and his grandfather in World War II. Somehow, when he carried it, he felt closer to them, even though they'd been dead for many years now.

The M1 was designed by John Garand and fired an eight-round clip of 30-06 cartridges. The rifle had plenty of knock-down power, and Donny was good with it out to 600 yards, even with the stock open sights. The rifle was a good shooter, and his was decked out with a few extra goodies, making him better able to reach out and touch someone using long distance. General George S. Patton had called the M1 "the greatest implement ever devised for battle".

Donny dug his ski poles into the snow and pushed off down the little hill. He was almost to the river when he heard the whine of a snowmobile engine.

AT THE TOP OF THE RIVER EMBANKMENT, JEREMY HESITATED. HE WONdered if the ice could hold him, but then he saw a group of people out on the ice. It looked like they were fishing, so he nosed the machine down the slope and out onto the frozen river. He was relieved to reach the first two men who were watching his approach. When he pulled up, he killed the engine, hopped off the snowmobile and ran toward them, ripping off his helmet as he went.

""Hey! I need help! My mom is hurt and she needs a hospital!"

The two men held fishing poles in their hands and continued to fish as he talked. One man jerked his pole up and pulled in a Blue Gill about 8 inches long. His friend came over to look.

"What bait ya got, eh? I ain't got no bites yet."

"I use da mousies eh. Dey pretty good ya know."

Jeremy stood in front of them, wondering why they wouldn't respond to him.

"Hey guys I need your help. My mom is hurt really bad. She's got a compound fracture and a concussion. We've got a little baby, and my Dad is back there with them until I can get help.

Both men looked over at him and smiled.

DONNY WAS NEAR THE RIVER'S EDGE NOW IN A CLUMP OF TREES. HE SET-tled down in the snow and took his spotting scope out of his back pack. He trained it on the group of men now surrounding the snowmobile and its rider. They appeared to be circling him like a pack of wolves. He noticed five of them as rough, local characters of disrepute he wouldn't trust alone with a goat, let alone a teen-aged boy.

And then he wondered, *Is this the father's son I'm looking for?* He pulled the radio out of his pack and called Eagle Ranger.

"BUT MY MOM IS DYING, AND ALL YOU CARE ABOUT IS STEALING MY SNOW-mobile? I can't believe this!"

The other men looked around each other and laughed out loud. There were eight of them now with more coming over.

"It ain't just the machine, boy, though that would be enough. You also got a good shotgun there."

Jeremy looked the man in the eyes, noting his lack of yooper accent. He must be from the lower peninsula or Wisconsin. It didn't matter though. Jeremy recognized the look in his eyes and the tone of his voice. The man he'd killed had the same look and sound. He wanted to cry, but he held it in. It would only encourage them, like blood in a shark tank. And then he thought to himself, *There has to be someone good here. Not everyone can be this bad. There must be someone good enough to help me.*

The man who spoke last took a step forward and held out his hand. "Give me the gun, kid, and we'll let you walk away, minus the snow machine, of course."

A determined look came over Jeremy's face, and he clenched his jaw and hard-ened his gaze. Oddly enough, he was more angry than afraid. Slowly, he unslung the Winchester shotgun from his back and pointed it at the man in front of him.

"I've got five rounds of double-aught buckshot that says the gun and the machine are mine."

DONNY PUT HIS RADIO BACK IN HIS PACK AND LAUGHED OUT LOUD WHILE he watched through the spotting scope as the boy drew the shotgun down on eight men. "I like this boy. He's got spunk!"

His M1 was already out on the snow in front of him as he lay in the prone position readying himself for the shot. He tucked the stock into his shoulder firmly and put down the spotting scope. Then he nestled his cheek on down into his favorite spot and started to breathe slowly. He guessed the distance at two hundred yards with a four-mile-per-hour west wind. An easy chip shot to the green. Slowly, he breathed, just barely. Gradually, he took up slack on the trigger. For now, he just watched and waited to see what would happen.

THE MAN LAUGHED OUT LOUD. "NICE BLUFF, KID. BUT YOU JUST TOLD US you only got 5 rounds. And there's eight of us. Now, I'm no accountant, but …"

The words never left the man's mouth, because suddenly … his mouth was gone.

Jeremy hadn't consciously fired his gun, but somehow it had come up to his shoulder and fired directly into the man's face. And just as mysteriously, Jeremy pivoted to take a bead on the next man who was moving toward him.

Just as he was about to pull the trigger, the man's head exploded in a misty cloud of crimson. Two of the eight men now lay fifteen feet away on the snow, painting the ice red. The boy quickly switched targets, but the man he was aiming at quickly turned and ran. Jeremy let him go and brought another man's head into his sights. But this man turned and ran as well.

Then, almost as if they all shared the same brain, the other men turned and ran off the ice, leaving their fishing gear and their foolish pride behind.

Suddenly, Jeremy was standing on the ice alone. There were other onlookers, but they stayed back. His hands started to shake, and he felt his throat constrict as the bile rose up into his mouth. The boy bent over and heaved his stomach out onto the ice. As he kneeled there alone, he heard someone coming up behind him and turned. He tried to bring the gun up and aim, but the adrenaline dump had left his muscles weak and his nerves frayed.

"You okay, boy?"

Jeremy started to cry now and let his butt drop down onto the snow. The man moved his skis across the ice and was soon kneeling beside him. "What's your name, boy?"

Jeremy caught his breath in mid sob. "I'm … I'm … My name is Jeremy Branch."

Donny Brewster smiled. "That was good shootin', son." He put his arm around the boy. "and those guys needed killin'."

Suddenly, Jeremy was reminded of his father. "My dad and mom and my baby sister need help."

Donny nodded but didn't say anything. He took his pack off his back and pulled out the radio.

"Eagle Ranger, this is Eagle Recon 3, over."

"This is Eagle Ranger, go ahead, over."

Donny smiled at the boy while he talked.

"I have Jeremy Branch and need extraction, over."

"Roger that, Eagle Recon 3. Any news on the other priority ones?"

Donny looked down at Jeremy.

"Where's your dad, son? Can you take me to them?"

Jeremy nodded as he pulled his cellphone out of his pocket and handed it to his rescuer.

"They're at waypoint A."

Donny laughed out loud. "You are good, son. Who trained you?"

Jeremy tried to smile. "I'm my father's son."

Donny nodded. "I bet you are."

He keyed the mike again.

"Eagle Ranger, this is Eagle Recon 3. That's affirmative. Stand by for grid coordinates, over."

Donny read off the coordinates from the GPS before signing off. Then he put the radio back in his pack and slung it over his shoulders again.

"Let's go get your family, kid."

Jeremy looked up with awe in his eyes.

"Who are you?"

Donny laughed out loud. "A year ago I was Donny Brewster from Detroit. But today, I'm Eagle Recon 3."

Then he helped Jeremy up to his feet and over to the Snowmobile. "Let's go, kid. We got clicks to turn."

CHAPTER 29

The Shadow Militia

F OR THE NEXT TWO WEEKS JACKIE AND BABY DONNA RESIDED at St Francis Hospital in Escanaba. Jeremy and Dan stayed at the home of Colonel Roger "Ranger" McPherson who lived just outside town.

The rescue had come just in time to save Jackie's life. She'd lost a lot of blood and suffered from exposure. The doctor said the concussion would heal in time. With the help of an operating room and modern instruments, her leg was quickly set and the wound sewed shut.

Dan was amazed to see that Escanaba was an island of civilization surrounded by anarchy and violence. One night at dinner, Dan asked Colonel McPherson how they'd managed to maintain law and order.

"It's really quite simple. We saw it coming, and we made a plan. We set out the rules and we hold firm to them."

Dan lifted a fork full of canned corn to his mouth and questioned him further. "So what are the rules?"

The Colonel's eyes grew stern. "You steal - you die. You murder - you die. You rape - you die."

Dan stopped chewing his corn. "How do you enforce that? I mean, by what authority?"

Jeremy was interested and he stopped eating as well.

"We enforce it with steel resolve and the help of God. We try to be fair, but the days of impunity are over. We worked it out with the Delta County Sheriff soon after the fall."

Dan nodded. "The Fall? That's what they're calling it now?"

Colonel McPherson set his fork onto the table. "Yes, The Fall, the collapse. They both mean the same thing. Society has broken down and chaos and evil are loosed upon the earth."

Dan took another bite of corn, and Jeremy chimed in. "Is that why people can walk on the streets without dying here?"

The Colonel laughed out loud. "You have a blunt way about you, kid. I see why Donny took a shine to you."

He moved his hands up onto the clean, white tablecloth and interlaced his fingers beside the white china plate of food. "Edmund Burke said, "All evil needs to triumph is for good men to do nothing." He paused. "We organized the good men, and we did something. We defeated the evil. And we continue to do it everyday."

Jeremy looked over at his father. "Dad, can we stay here?"

Dan smiled and shook his head. "Sorry, son. We have to get back to Uncle Rodney. He's an old man and he needs us."

Colonel McPherson looked over at him and started laughing so hard the table shook. Dan and Jeremy stared at him with no idea of what to say. Finally, Dan spoke. "Why is that funny?"

"I'm sorry." It was all the Colonel could do to stifle his laughter. "I'm sorry, Dan, but your Uncle Rodney is the last person on this planet who needs your help." Then his face grew serious again. "Don't you have any idea who your Uncle Rodney is?"

Dan looked offended. "Of course I do! He raised me when my father died. I know everything there is to know about him."

The Colonel shook his head from side to side.

"Negative, son. Not everything." He thought for a moment, placing his clasped hands beneath his chin and resting them there while he decided what to say. At last, he pulled his hands down and smiled.

"I may as well tell you both now. You'll find out soon enough as it is."

He pulled the white, linen napkin from his lap and wiped his mouth before speaking. "People call me Colonel because I'm the commanding officer of the Upper Peninsula Shadow Militia."

It sounded ominous and impressive, but neither Dan nor Jeremy had any idea what he was talking about. The Colonel could tell they were confused, so he pressed on.

"The Shadow Militia was formed decades ago in the event society collapsed, or, God forbid, our government needed major realignment." He let that sink in before continuing on. "We are a small, but well funded and equipped group of highly trained, elite individuals, dedicated to the continuity of a constitutional society."

Jeremy raised his hand, and the Colonel laughed again. "You don't have to raise your hand, Jeremy. What do you want?"

"Colonel, I'm only fifteen, and I have no idea what that means."

The Colonel looked over at Dan and nodded. Dan smiled and looked over at his son. "It means, Jeremy, that the Shadow Militia is the good guys. And they can really kick ass!"

The Colonel clapped his hands together once, and a servant came into the room. "Well said, Dan." He looked over at the servant. "Felicia, we're ready for our cherry pie now."

Dan turned away from the servant and back to their host. "But … what does the Shadow Militia have to do with my Uncle Rodney?"

Jeremy laughed now. "Don't you get it, Dad? Your uncle is in the Shadow Militia." He looked across the table at the Colonel as if asking for confirmation.

"Well done, Jeremy. But it's even bigger than that."

He turned and looked Dan square in the eyes. "Your uncle isn't *in* the Shadow Militia. He *is* the Shadow Militia."

Dan's face clouded over. A million thoughts ran through his head, connecting dots, memories, conflicts that now seemed to make sense to him after years of hiding in the dark.

"Why do you think we went looking for you? The General ordered it. Priority one."

Felicia came in with the pie and placed it at each setting. Dan looked down at it with disbelief. So many people out there starving, dying, suffering, and he was here surrounded by clean linen, eating roast beef, corn and cherry pie. He took a bite and it exploded with flavor inside his mouth. Dan closed his eyes and almost cried. The Colonel smiled at his response.

"General Branch has ordered you transported out of here back to his location at 1300 hours tomorrow. Your wife and baby are fit to fly, and I'll see that everything is in order. I'm taking you home myself."

Jeremy's jaw dropped open and he looked over at his father in shock. Finally, he spoke. "General Branch?"

Dan smiled to himself all the while enjoying the cherry pie. He loved his Uncle Rodney. Then he looked over at the Colonel.

"Colonel McPherson, there is one thing we have to do before leaving."

The Colonel nodded. "Anything. Just ask and you'll have it. You're priority one."

Dan smiled. "Can you have an ordained minister of some type meet us at the hospital tomorrow morning?" He placed his left hand on his son's shoulder. "We have some unfinished business to attend to."

Jeremy breathed a sigh of relief. "Thank God! It's about time!"

THE WEDDING CEREMONY TOOK PLACE BESIDE THE HOSPITAL LAWN ON THE freshly shoveled sidewalk. Jeremy was the best man and Colonel McPherson and Donny Brewster signed as witnesses. Baby Donna was the Maid of Honor. The ceremony was presided over by Father Francis Connors. The sun shown during the whole wedding, and then quickly slipped behind a cloud when Father Connors announced, "I now pronounce you husband and wife. You may kiss the bride."

And he did.

RODNEY BRANCH STOOD ON THE COURTHOUSE LAWN BESIDE SHERIFF LEIF. The weather had turned mild the night before and the snow was thawing quickly.

Rain was coming, and soon the roads would be clear again.

"Why did you want to meet me out here, Rodney?"

Rodney pulled out a pack of Camel nonfiltered and placed one white tube between his chapped lips.

"There's some things I have to tell you before they get here. I've been keeping some things from you, and I don't want you to be blind-sided."

Joe Leif grimaced. "What have you done now, old man? Whatever it is, I bet you a million bucks it's going to get me in trouble isn't it?"

Rodney shook his head and smiled as he pulled out his Zippo and lit up. "No, it won't get you in trouble. To the contrary. It's good news. They found my nephew, Dan."

The Sheriff's face changed from a grimace to a beam in a second's time. He reached over and hugged his friend in a rare embrace. "Oh, thank God, Rodney! Thank God! I can't wait to see him again. It's been years. Is he here now? Can I see him?"

Rodney's face clouded over just a bit. "Well, yes, he'll be here any minute now. But that's what I wanted to talk to you about."

Joe cocked his head to one side and looked up into the northern sky. "Can you hear that?"

Rodney looked down and sighed. "Yup. Sure can. Sounds like a helicopter. Just a wild guess, but I'd say it's an Apache AH64 attack helicopter by the sounds of it."

Joe looked back down and over at his friend. "Rodney? There's more than one. What's going on?"

The sounds came closer now, getting louder by the second. "Oops, here comes a different one. That's two Apaches and what's that other sound? Hmm, sounds like a Bell UH-1 Iroquois. You know … a Huey."

As Sheriff Leif looked on in surprise three helicopters circled above the courthouse lawn. The two gunships continued to circle, providing security, as the Huey touched down gently on the snow-covered lawn. Joe covered his face as the wind whipped snow up all around him.

As the engine was cut and began to wind down, a tall man in olive drab fatigues stepped off and strode quickly over to them with his head down low. Upon reaching them, he stood stiffly at attention.

"Colonel McPherson reporting as ordered, sir!"

Joe looked at the soldier, not quite knowing what to do or what to make of it. He glanced over at Rodney and saw him smile. Rodney snapped to attention and smartly returned the Colonel's salute.

"At ease, Colonel. Thanks for coming."

Then he turned to Joe and made introductions.

"Colonel McPherson, this is the Sheriff of Iroquois County, Joe Leif. Sheriff, this is Colonel Roger McPherson of the Shadow Militia. He's the commanding officer for the Upper Peninsula."

The Colonel reached out his hand, and Joe reacted by extending his own weakly. The Colonel pumped it heartily up and down. "Pleasure to meet you, Sheriff." Then he turned back to Rodney. "General, we have your priority one personnel on board as ordered, sir."

Sheriff Leif turned away from the Colonel as his mouth dropped open in confusion. "Rodney, why is this man calling you a General? And what is the Shadow Militia?"

The Huey's rotors had almost stopped turning now, and Dan Branch hopped down, followed by Jeremy who was holding baby Donna, and his new wife, Jackie, who hobbled on crutches. Dan raced over to them and threw his arms around his uncle. "Uncle Rodney! Thanks so much for saving us! It's so good to be back home!"

Joe moved his hand up to his chin and stroked it gently, all the while wondering, *Okay, Rodney, what have you done now?*

"Dan, you remember Sheriff Leif?"

Dan smiled and shook his hand. "Of course, hi Sheriff. Good to see you again. You've put on a little weight."

Rodney laughed out loud, and Joe frowned at him.

By now the others had reached the sidewalk. "Uncle Rodney, allow me to introduce my wife, Jackie, my son, Jeremy, and my daughter, Donna."

Rodney put out his cigarette, field stripped it and stuffed the butt inside his front, shirt pocket. He bowed slightly.

"Pleasure to meet you, ma'am. I suspect there's a long story to all this. I trust you're helping my vagabond nephew grow up a bit?"

Jackie smiled. "Yes, General. I'm doing the best I can, but you have to understand that he's quite a handful."

Rodney laughed. "Of course he's a handful! He's a Branch! We were born to be wild!"

Joe looked on in amazement. "Rodney, why are they calling you General? Where did you get three helicopters?"

But before he could answer, the Colonel interrupted.

"General, we did the flyover south of here you ordered."

Rodney's face grew more serious. "And?"

The Colonel looked him straight in the eyes.

It's not good, sir. It's as you suspected. A large force heading northwest in your direction."

Rodney's eyes took on a faraway gaze and he reached up to stroke his cheek. "How many?"

"About one thousand strong, sir, gaining strength as they go."

"Armaments?"

"A few armored personnel carriers, a dozen Humvees, but mostly civilian transportation. Mostly light arms with some fifty cals. We were fired upon."

Rodney nodded. "Estimated Time of Arrival?"

The Colonel's face took on a grave look when he answered. "Not long, sir. Maybe a week. maybe a bit longer."

Rodney nodded. Then he turned to Joe. "Sheriff, we have strategy to discuss. May we use your conference room?"

Joe looked at him, all of a sudden feeling a hundred years older. He hung his head down and stared at the sidewalk.

"Okay, let me get this straight. He's a Colonel?"

Rodney nodded.

"You're a General?"

Rodney's head moved up and down again.

"There are one thousand bad guys heading this way?"

"Yup."

Joe nodded. "Okay, so far so good. Now here's the most important question." He pointed to the Apaches circling over the town. "Those helicopter gunships? They belong to you?"

Rodney smiled. "Well, not exactly. I don't own them. I just command them."

The Sheriff smiled. "Okay, Yeah. Sure. You can use my conference room."

As they all walked down the sidewalk to the courthouse, Joe couldn't help but ask. "So, tell me. Where does a guy get military attack helicopters?"

Rodney laughed. "You know. Same place I got my Abrams Tank. On Ebay!"

Jackie looked over at Dan as she struggled to keep up on crutches. "Your uncle has a tank?" Dan shrugged. "I don't know." And then his mind switched over to the horde of one thousand men heading this way, raping, destroying and killing everything in their path. He'd seen them himself on the flyover. As he'd looked on from the relative safety of the helicopter, he'd watched as a man raped a little girl in broad daylight. Bodies had been strewn everywhere, and, while he flew over, men, women,and children had been lined up and shot in the streets.

It was the Golden Horde that his Uncle Rodney had taught him about. And it was coming here. Coming here to kill his family.

Book 2 in The God Virus Series

The Shadow Militia

Skip Coryell

CHAPTER 1

The Golden Horde Advances

DAN BRANCH SAT NERVOUSLY AROUND THE BIG CONFERENCE table at the old, red brick courthouse that he'd passed thousands of times before in his youth. The old world, the one with electricity, now seemed like a million miles ago. So much had happened since those innocent days of his youth, but, if he was honest about it, even then, there'd been nothing innocent or carefree about growing up with his Uncle Rodney.

And now he knew why.

Way back then he'd always known there was something different about his uncle, something strange, something vague, maybe even something special, but ... General Branch? His own uncle, the leader of the Shadow Militia? He mulled it over in his mind as Uncle Rodney pulled out a pack of Camel nonfiltereds from his front breast pocket. Rodney reached in his jeans to pull out his trusty Zippo, but Colonel MacPherson already had a Bic lighter out in front of him, suspended over the table, its flame reaching up toward the dead, fluorescent lighting in the ceiling above.

The big window curtains on both walls of the corner room were wide open, letting in the rare March sunshine. Dan gazed out at the courthouse lawn. A small crowd had gathered around the two Apache attack helicopters resting there, flanked on all four sides by Shadow Militia soldiers in full battle gear bearing M4 carbines. The Huey had already been dispatched to take Jeremy and Jackie to the Sheriff's house to be with his wife, Marge, until this meeting was over. Then, they'd be picked up again for the final move to Uncle Rodney's house in the woods a few miles outside of town.

Dan had no idea what would happen then. Things had changed. No, everything had changed. His anticipation of a tedious, difficult life of survival had been dashed when they'd flown over the small city of Greenville, Michigan, a few hours ago. The carnage he'd seen there still made him shiver inside.

"Why do you smoke in here, Rodney? You know I don't like it."

General Branch looked over at his friend and smiled. "God came to me in a dream, Sheriff, and he told me it was my purpose in life to teach you patience."

Sheriff Leif cocked his head and raised his left eyebrow.

"Yeah, right. To teach me patience." He mumbled under his breath. "Those things are going to kill you."

Rodney ignored the comment and looked over at Dan and his face grew serious.

"Dan, I feel I need to apologize to you. I kept a lot of things from you while you were growing up. I led a bit of a double life, but there were things I just couldn't tell you. I wanted to spare you the complication, and we just couldn't risk the security compromise."

The General then glanced over at Joe Leif. "You too, Sheriff. I just couldn't tell you everything back then. It would've put you in an awkward position as the head law enforcement officer of the county, because I was doing things in violation of federal and state laws."

Sheriff Leif watched the thick, blue smoke drift up from the cigarette until it stopped at the ceiling and billowed out toward the walls.

"I think I understand. You didn't want to be arrested for illegal arms trafficking." He nodded out the window at the lawn and the growing crowd. "You know, little things like a fleet of attack helicopters, battle tanks, and only God knows what else." The Sheriff gritted his teeth and ground them slightly. "For all I know you could have a bunch of ICBMs buried in your back yard!"

The Sheriff noticed his voice was rising, so he clamped his mouth shut and looked away. Rodney smiled sympathetically. "Don't be silly, Joe." And then he grinned. "I would never stockpile nuclear weapons on my own property. I'd put them in the state forest where they couldn't be traced back to me."

The two men locked eyes like bulls in an arena. Then, the Sheriff's eyes softened, and he looked down at the table top. When he finally spoke again, it was with a great sense of reluctance in his voice.

"So, are you going to help me save my people or not?"

General Branch glanced over at the Colonel where their eyes met briefly. From across the table, Dan sensed the two men had communicated in that single, short glance in ways he'd never known possible. He thought to himself, *They have a long history.*

Rodney leaned back in his chair and snuffed out his half-smoked cigarette by rolling the burning ash between his fingers. He put the butt into his breast pocket.

Colonel MacPherson was speaking now. "Sheriff Leif. The Shadow Militia has the highest respect for the office of Sheriff. The office of Sheriff is the one remaining constitutionally mandated and elected office in this county, perhaps even in the whole state for all we know." He paused.

"You are in charge of Iroquois County. We are here simply to advise and assist."

Sheriff Leif looked up from the table. He met eyes with the Colonel and then with Rodney Branch.

"Are you serious, Colonel?"

Colonel MacPherson nodded. "We are at your service, sir."

The hint of a smile moved across Sheriff Joe's lips. "Okay then. I'd like you to take ten of those attack helicopters and annihilate the mob heading toward us."

The Colonel didn't answer. His lips pursed tightly together.

General Branch leaned forward again, placing his elbows on the table with both fists on either side of his chin.

"We can't do that, Joe."

Sheriff Leif's chair slid backward into the wall as he stood. "What! You can't? What does that mean? You said you commanded them. What's going on here, Rodney?"

Suddenly, Rodney felt the need for the other half of his cigarette, but he denied himself the urge. He let his hands fall down onto the table. Dan Branch watched as his uncle's eyes grew frozen-stone cold before speaking. Dan shivered at the change.

"There are certain things we know, but cannot divulge. The things we know demand we not tip our hand. We cannot deploy our forces in mass. It would jeopardize not just Iroquois County, but the entire Midwest."

Moving both arms up to his chest, Sheriff Leif folded them together and looked down at the two military men.

"What kind of a cock and bull story is that?"

Rodney looked down at the table top, and when he spoke, his voice carried an apologetic tone. "I can't tell you, Joe, and you're just going to have to trust me."

"What!" The Sheriff slammed his right fist down on the table top as he screamed. Then he made an effort to regain his composure before he spoke again. Sheriff Leif bit down on his lip, and Dan thought for sure it was going to bleed. Against his better judgment, he decided to get involved.

"Uncle Rodney, please. We have a thousand murderers heading this way to rape our women and kill our children. Don't keep us guessing. Exactly what *are* you allowed to do? How *can* you help us?"

General Branch glanced over at the Colonel as if they were mind melding again. Dan thought he saw his uncle give a slight nod, but he couldn't be sure. Finally, Colonel MacPherson turned back to the Sheriff and spoke.

"We can help arm you. We can train you."

Sheriff Leif looked over at him in disbelief. "How are you going to do that when they'll be here in just over a week?"

The Colonel's eyes locked onto the Sheriff like a laser. "We can also slow them down."

Joe Leif leaned his shoulders against the wall behind him as he thought. Finally, he sat back down in his chair and scooted it back up to the table.

"Okay. You can slow them down. How much? How much time can you give us?"

Slowly, a smile spread across the Colonel's face. When his grin reached full bloom, he exclaimed, "A month. We can give you thirty days."

✯ ✯ ✯ ✯

They were all back at Uncle Rodney's house now, seated on the front porch and no one was talking. The Colonel had flown away with his three helicopters, purportedly to make some arrangements and prepare for the county's defense. Jackie felt more vulnerable now that he and his soldiers were gone. She wondered, *Perhaps we should have stayed in Escanaba where it's safe?*

She held baby Donna on her lap now. The pain in her broken leg had subsided, but her skin underneath the cast was starting to itch like crazy. Dan's Uncle Rodney had relinquished his old rocking chair to her with a gentlemanly smile. Jeremy sat a few feet away with his right elbow propped up on the wooden railing. The big German Shepherd named Moses was lying beside him as the boy stroked his massive head.

"So shouldn't we be doing something right now? Like training, practicing, shooting our guns or something? I mean, hey, we've got a thousand screaming bad guys coming straight at us, and they want to kill us all."

Uncle Rodney laughed out loud. "I like your son, Dan. He's a straight shooter. He doesn't mince words, and I respect that in a man." Rodney glanced over and nodded at Jackie a few feet away before adding, "And from a woman as well."

Jackie smiled back nervously. She just didn't quite know what to think of Uncle Rodney. He seemed like the kind of man who could open the door for a lady with one hand while shooting a man in the back with the other. But at the same time, she had a feeling that he would die for Dan, and even for her and Jeremy and baby Donna, simply because Dan loved them, and that trait alone made him one of the good guys.

"I'm interested to hear everything that happened to you after leaving Menomonie, but you must be tired from all the travel …"

Rodney let the sentence trail off into the breeze around them. Dan smiled, knowing it was his invitation, that the General wanted to hear a full debriefing of his exploits. Dan thought to himself, *I have a few questions of my own, old man.* Dan stood up abruptly, and ran his left hand through his lengthening, blonde hair from forehead to neck. He glanced over at Jackie, all the while, smiling with his eyes.

"Honey, do you mind if I walk with my uncle for a while? We have a lot to talk about."

The concerned look was still on her face, but Jackie forced a smile and a nod.

"Can I come too, Dad?"

"Better not, Son. We need a man here to watch after the place. We won't be far though. Just fire a shot if you need help."

The two men walked off the porch and down the drive. When they reached the dirt road in front of the house, they turned left and walked away. Jackie watched them until they disappeared, all the while wondering what kind of fate was about to fall on her and her baby.

"So what happened to your other wife, Debbie?"

Uncle Rodney's voice was emotionless as they both walked down the dirt side trail through the woods. Dan answered him curtly.

"She killed herself with a drug overdose."

Rodney thought for a moment and nodded.

"No offense on the dead, but that doesn't surprise me a bit. I never liked that woman."

Dan didn't say anything at first. Then he answered shortly. "You were right about her."

His uncle took a pack of cigarettes out of his pocket and started to shake one out, but he hesitated and then replaced them in his pocket. Dan gave him a quizzical look.

"You're not smoking?"

The old man shook his head. "Nope. I'm cutting back. I have to stay alive for now."

Then he continued his questioning. "The boy seems like good stock. Has he proven himself yet?"

Dan nodded. "Unfortunately, yes." And then he recounted the story of how Jeremy had shot and killed the man on the snowmobile and after that the man on the river.

Rodney grunted and reached up to his lips to remove the cigarette that wasn't there. "And you? How many did you have to kill to make it here?"

"Nine."

Rodney stopped walking. He stared directly into his nephew's eyes. Then he nodded and started walking again. "I recognized the look. I knew you were different. I trust they all needed killing." It wasn't a question, but more a statement of fact.

"And the woman. If she's going to live with us I need to know it all."

This time it was Dan who stopped walking. He looked deeply into his uncle's eyes before talking.

"She's the best. I place my life in her hands. I would die for her."

Uncle Rodney contemplated his answer and finally nodded. "She looks Muslim to me. I don't trust Muslims. You know that."

Dan nodded. "Yes, I know. Her father was a Christian. Her mother was a Muslim who converted to Christianity when they both fell in love. The Muslims murdered Jackie's father, and she grew up with her paternal grandparents here in America after that. She went to a Christian college, married a missionary. They were together when I ran across them."

Rodney looked down at the sand and then back up again. "So where is her husband now?"

"He's dead. I shot him."

Uncle Rodney reached back up to his shirt pocket for a cigarette but caught himself halfway.

"You killed Jackie's husband and then married her?"

Dan nodded briefly.

"How exactly does that work, young Daniel?"

A big sigh escaped Dan's lips. He didn't want to go into this, but he knew he had to satisfy his uncle.

"They were both strapped to chairs in their cabin. She was pregnant and due. The man was torturing them. He needed killing and I obliged him. The bullet passed through and hit her husband. I tried to save him, but he was gut shot."

The old man looked over to his left and off through the bare trees. It would be another month before leaves started to take limb.

"So you delivered her baby and holed up in the cabin until March?"

Dan nodded.

"And she forgave you?"

Dan nodded again.

"That's not the Muslim way."

Then he looked back at his nephew with frankness in his eyes. "Listen, Daniel, I've never been married. Don't know the way of men and women, so I won't presume to pass judgment on the two of you. So just tell me straight out. Does she love You?"

The right side of Dan's lips turned up as he nodded.

"Would she die for you?"

"I believe she would."

Dan watched as the wheels and gears twisted and turned inside his uncle's head. He'd expected this, all the while knowing his uncle wasn't equipped to live with a woman in the house much less children. Dan added the clincher.

"If she goes - I go."

The face of the old man tightened into a grimace, his wrinkles coming together like the confluence of a million dry creek beds. Finally he nodded his head and slumped his shoulders.

"All right then. It's settled. But you're responsible for her. The little baby too. I don't want her crying at night. No getting into my stuff. And everybody pulls their weight. I'm not running a homeless shelter here."

Dan hesitated. Then his next words surprised even him.

"Uncle Rodney, listen to me. We'll agree to stay and help you out here. But you have to understand that we're a family, and we want you to be part of that family too. Jeremy is my son, Donna is my daughter, and Jackie is my wife. That's a sacred thing of God."

Rodney raised his left hand up to scratch his chin in thought. Dan went on.

"And you're going to have to be a good grampa to the kids. No cussing in front of them, church once a week and no smoking in the house."

Rodney's left eyebrow raised up involuntarily in a reflex action at the last statement, as if to say, *Oh really? You're going to tell me what to do in my own house?* But the old man didn't say that. He thought silently to himself for a full minute, scratching the stubble on his chin, his eyes wandering off into the woods. The longer he waited, the more nervous Dan became.

Finally, a smile spread across his uncle's face. His left hand moved over to his breast pocket and pulled out the pack of Camel unfiltereds. He started to shake one out, but then he abruptly stopped. The cigarettes suddenly crushed and crumpled as Rodney's hand squeezed shut. Then he tossed the crumpled-up pack to the side of the trail.

The old man placed his hand on Dan's shoulders and turned him around to face the way they'd come.

"Welcome home, Daniel."

They walked away down the trail, not saying another word until they reached the house.

CHAPTER 2

The Sniper

"**T**HAT'S HIM? THAT'S THE GUY WHO'S GOING TO GIVE US AN extra month to prepare?" Sheriff Leif looked over at Rodney in disbelief. "One guy? That's all you can spare for us?"

Rodney, wearing a heavy, green wool shirt and flannel-lined jeans, just smiled.

"He's not *just* one guy. He's a highly trained Marine Corps sniper. That man is a force of one, capable of head shots almost a mile out."

The Sheriff nodded. "Okay, that's fine. But we've got a thousand bad guys headed our way. How many of them can he kill?"

Rodney smirked. "As many as we let him. But who he kills is more important than how many. That simple, unassuming man is here to cut the head off the snake."

Donny Brewster was wearing a tattered pair of faded, black jeans and a green T-shirt that read *Jesus Saves*. He walked straight up to Rodney, snapped to attention and saluted crisply. Rodney reached out his right hand.

"No more saluting, son. We're in a war zone now."

Donny Brewster accepted his general's handshake.

"It's an honor, sir."

Rodney pointed at Joe Leif. "Thanks for coming, Sergeant. This is Joe Leif, Sheriff of Iroquois County. We are here at his discretion."

Donny turned and offered his hand. Joe accepted it, feeling firsthand the strength in the man's grip. That was when he noticed the power in the man's upper body. Even though the T-shirt was large and loose, it was obvious Donny Brewster worked out.

"Thank you for coming, Mr. Brewster."

Donny smiled broadly. "It's my pleasure, sir, and I mean that in every sense of the word."

Joe thought to himself, *What does he mean by that?* But he said nothing. Just then Dan Branch walked up behind them. Joe was surprised when the two men embraced.

"Good to see you again, Donny! Jeremy knows you're coming and he's excited about it."

Donny smiled. "Roger that, Marine. Maybe we can get together before I head out." The sniper glanced quickly over at his general, who nodded slightly.

"Dinner at my place tonight at 1800 hours, Sergeant. You can have some down time, then we'll brief you tomorrow and get you on your way."

Just then the crew chief from the Blackhawk helicopter walked up carrying a duffle bag. He threw it down at Donny's feet. "You still have those two footlockers in there, Donny, but I know better than to touch a sniper's gear."

Donny laughed out loud. "Good call. I'll get them myself."

"I'll help." Dan stepped forward and walked with Donny over to the Blackhawk where they began unloading the two, large, plastic footlockers.

"This one's pretty light. What's in it?"

Donny smiled. "Just my Ghillie, and some clothes."

Dan nodded at the one Donny was now unloading. "And what ya got in there?"

The sergeant's face became more serious. "These are my babies. No one touches my babies."

Dan laughed out loud. "You snipers are such stoics."

As the two men walked back to the General, towing the footlockers behind them, Joe Leif looked on thoughtfully, all the while wondering. *How could things change so fast? Six months ago I'd probably be arresting this man, but now he's our greatest hope?* He looked down at the ground and sighed. These days he was just holding on for the ride, never knowing what the new day would bring.

"Ma'am, I gotta tell ya. This is for sure the best damn food I've had in ages." Donny Brewster shoveled another spoonful of food into his mouth. A piece of venison fell off his lips and onto the table, but Donny seemed not to notice.

Across from the table, Dan smiled quietly as his wife winced at the sniper's lack of table manners. Jackie thought to herself, *If he's around for very long, I'll have to do something about that.*

Jeremy sat beside his new idol, smiling broadly, secretly wanting to go into battle with his new friend. Uncle Rodney looked on from the head of the table and thought to himself, *I have to order Sergeant Brewster not to cuss in front of women and children.* General Branch was a man of few words, thinking multitudes, but saying very little. For him, Stoicism was a serious religion. He'd learned long ago that the only words regretted were the ones spoken.

"Thank you, Sergeant Brewster. It's just goulash." She couldn't stop herself from glancing over at Dan's uncle as she spoke. "We seem to have an amazing supply of food here."

Dan laughed out loud. "Didn't I tell you, honey? My Uncle Rodney is a prepper par excellence! He's been preparing for this since Noah stepped off the boat."

Jackie nodded. "I can see that. And we have electricity, hot and cold running water, even toilets that flush." She glanced over at Uncle Rodney suspiciously. "I haven't seen that in over six months."

Uncle Rodney locked eyes with her, his whole face taking on the countenance of granite. Jackie couldn't help but think, *He's sizing me up. Give him something to think about.* Jackie and Rodney's eyes remained locked for a full ten seconds. No one spoke. Dan looked up and felt his chest tighten, all the while thinking to himself, *Don't challenge him, honey. Back down.* But he couldn't say it out loud, so he had to helplessly watch the silent battle. Slowly, he reached his hand over and placed it on her knee. He squeezed softly, and was surprised when she pulled her leg away.

Finally, Jackie ended the confrontation with an almost imperceptible wink of her left eye before turning away. Uncle Rodney picked up his fork again and smiled deep inside, all the while thinking, *She's an alpha. How interesting.*

Jeremy, oblivious to the tension, shattered it with his next question. "Donny, can I go with you on your mission? I want to help."

Dan looked up abruptly, his eyes immediately turning to steel. "No!" Then he faltered, realizing how loud and abrupt his objection had been. Donny stopped eating and glanced up at Dan. Finally, he smiled.

"Not this time, champ. This one is a solo run." He looked over at his general as if to glean direction, but received none. "But as soon as I get back, I'll teach you some sniper secrets." Donny paused. "We got a deal?"

Jeremy's face broke into a grin as he reached his hand over. Donny gave him a firm handshake to seal the new covenant. Dan relaxed and slouched his shoulders down a bit. The relief was etched all over his face.

Jackie bent down to pick up baby Donna who'd been crawling under her chair. She scooped her up and drew her close to her face. All this testosterone was getting on her nerves. *Why can't men just relax?*

General Branch placed his fork beside his plate and pushed it away as if signaling the meal was over. Sergeant Brewster saw this out of the corner of his eye, and took two big gulps of food before doing the same. Jackie looked on, amazed at how clearly the pecking order was established. She wondered to herself how Donny, a strong, capable man in his prime, could so completely give himself over to Rodney's will.

General Branch reached into the front breast pocket of his flannel shirt and pulled out three sheets of paper. He handed one to Dan and another to Jeremy. He kept the last for himself.

"This is the standard duty roster. It outlines all the daily tasks that must be done here at the base, how they are to be done and at what time they are to be accomplished." Rodney's voice had suddenly taken on a commanding tone. He was in commanding officer mode now.

Dan looked over at Jackie and saw her face flushed red with anger. The look scared him, and he was surprised he'd never seen her like this before. Then he thought for a moment. *Yes, Uncle Rodney has a polarizing effect on everyone he meets. Why would Jackie be any different?*

"You forgot to give me a copy."

Rodney ignored her statement.

"Jeremy, you'll take the first watch from twenty-two-hundred hours to zero-one-hundred hours. I'll take the second watch, and Dan, you get the third. Reveille is always at zero-seven-hundred hours, no excuses, no exceptions."

Jackie cleared her throat, but Uncle Rodney continued to ignore her. She spoke anyway. "General, doesn't it make sense for me to take a shift too? That way everyone pulls a two-hour shift instead of three."

They locked eyes again. Rodney tried to stare her down, but she wouldn't budge.

"Don't you need a good night's sleep so you can take care of the baby all day, cook the meals and clean the house? I would think you'd welcome a full night's sleep."

Jeremy looked across the table and watched his new mother smile. It frightened him. Jackie shook her head defiantly. "I can do the job of any man here, and I'm not a slacker. If I'm going to stay here, then I want equal work and responsibility."

Uncle Rodney smiled back, but his smile contained something secret, no malice, no fear, just the simple statement, *I'm in charge and I know things you don't.* He pushed back his chair and got up. Slowly, he walked toward the front door. When he reached it, he opened the door and motioned with his left hand. "After you, me lady ."

Jeremy looked nervously at his father. Dan looked nervously at Donny. Donny looked up at Jackie and smiled.

She pushed her chair back and it tipped over behind her onto the floor. Jackie thrust the baby into her husband's arms. "Take care of the baby! I'll be right back!"

She picked up her crutches leaning against the wall and headed for the door. When the door closed behind Rodney and Jackie, the air pressure in the room seemed to lesson. Jeremy was the first to speak. "Dad? Is he going to kill her?"

Dan looked over at Donny imploringly, who just laughed out loud.

"What are you looking at me for? He's *your* uncle!"

Dan nodded, "Yes, but he's *your* general." He looked longingly at the door. "Besides, I don't really know who's out there right now. Is it the General, or my Uncle Rodney?"

Donny shrugged. "Doesn't matter. There's a couple storms a brewin' and one's a typhoon and the other's a tornado."

Then he turned back and started shoveling more goulash onto his plate. "Besides, nothing we can do about it. Gives me a chance to eat more carbs."

Dan looked over at his son and then back at Sergeant Brewster. "My wife is out there with a tornado, and all you care about is food?"

Donny laughed again. "I never been married, but why is it that most men underestimate their women?" He waited, but Dan said nothing. Jeremy looked over at his father, then started to scoop out more food onto his own plate.

"Yeah, Dad. Why do you do that?"

Then Jeremy and Donny laughed, giving each other a high five. Dan's face turned red and he slammed his palm down hard on the table.

"Donny! My wife's out there with a mad man and he's angry!"

Donny calmly took a bite and chewed fully before swallowing. "Hey, listen, man. You don't understand. When I said one of them's a tornado and the other's a typhoon, I was talking about your wife too." He paused, giving Dan time to cool down. "General Branch would never hit a lady. And, besides, she'd probably kick his butt anyway."

He went back to eating.

"That woman's tough! I can tell. She's got that look."

☆ ☆ ☆ ☆

Once outside, Jackie followed Rodney as best she could on crutches down a trail to the left of the house. They passed a small swamp and then walked up a hill. Jackie found herself out of breath and struggling, but her pride drove her on. Every few minutes Rodney would get way ahead of her and have to stop and wait. A half mile later, Rodney stopped and turned to face her. He could see that the time and distance hadn't ebbed her resolve in the least.

Rodney sat down on the ground and leaned his back up against the trunk of a Jack Pine. He let out a deep breath.

"Man I'm gettin' old." He looked up at Jackie and she just stood there, towering above him, leaning forward on her crutches. "Please, Jackie, please sit down with me."

Jackie became suspicious of his change in demeanor, but felt stupid standing over him. She plopped herself down six feet away with her back to a scrub oak. They both looked out towards the woods in front of them. There was silence for several minutes. All of a sudden, Jackie could hear the wind in the trees as night began to set in around them. The snow was still a foot deep inside the trees, with patches of bare ground where the sun shone in and reached the ground. She felt the cold and wet soaking through her jeans and wondered why it didn't seem to bother the old man.

A bright, red Cardinal landed on a branch a few feet from Rodney's head. Jackie watched and was surprised to see him smile at the little bird. He reached out his right arm with his forefinger extended, but the bird flitted away. The old man's smile faded and disappeared. His face turned stone cold as he turned his head toward Jackie.

"So, young lady. What's it going to take to move you from the liability column to the asset column?"

She answered his question with a question.

"Have you always been this arrogant?"

Rodney turned his head away, thought for a moment and then turned back again. "Okay, I could have worded that better. Let's try it again." He paused. "Jackie, why do you want to sit up watching the darkness for two hours in the dead of night when you could be sleeping in a nice, warm bed?"

She looked at him blankly, afraid to show any emotion in front of him, but she answered him nonetheless.

"Because it's my duty to my family to pull my weight. As a mother and wife, it's my job to help protect my family. I am honor bound to protect the weak and to defend the helpless. My daughter is helpless. She needs me strong, not lying in a safe, warm bed while others sacrifice on our behalf."

The old man cocked his head to one side and smiled softly. He thought for a moment. "And what taught you this deep sense of honor?"

Jackie pursed her lips tightly together, and then she moved her long, black hair off her neck so it flowed down around her. "Six months in the wilderness watching two men risk their lives and shed their blood and sweat for the safety of my daughter, myself and my husband. We were strangers, but they took us in. They would have died for us. And now ... I'll die for them."

Uncle Rodney nodded in confirmation and smiled broadly. "Now you're talking my language." He groaned as he got up stiffly and stood before her. "But let's hope it doesn't come to that." Then he changed the subject abruptly, as if it was the most natural transition in the world. "Can you shoot a pistol?"

Three-quarters of a mile away Dan and Jeremy heard the gun shots. Dan flinched, then stood up and headed for the door at a run, but Donny's commanding voice halted him in his tracks.

"Dan! Stop! Think!"

Dan turned around at the door and looked back at him. "Didn't you just hear those shots?"

Donny nodded. He walked up to Dan and put his hand on his shoulder and squeezed tightly. "If you and I are going into battle together, we have to trust each other. I trust General Branch and I trust your wife. C'mon, Marine. You have to do the same. Step up. Control your emotions."

Dan hesitated, then walked slowly back to the table and sat down. Donny joined him there in his chair beside Jeremy. Then, out of the blue, he asked an unrelated question.

"So, what do you guys miss most about the good old days before the end of the world?"

Jeremy laughed and spoke right away. "I miss Tonya, the girl from next door."

His father shot him a deadly stare, and Jeremy quickly backtracked. "It's her smile. I miss her smile and her white teeth. They were very straight. It was amazing really."

Donny laughed again. "Okay, must be a story there, but I won't ask. What about you, Dan?"

Dan sighed and slumped down in his chair with his arms on the table.

"Ice, cold, Mocha Frappuccino. And man could I ever use one about now."

"I think if you tighten up your grip with your weak hand, it'll give you a more stable shooting platform and you'll be able to hold a tighter group."

Jackie smiled and nodded. "Yeah, that's a good point. I'll try that. Thanks."

Rodney slowed his pace as they reached the driveway, and Jackie followed his lead. "So can you shoot an AR like that, too? You're a pretty good shot with a pistol."

Jackie shook her head. "No, I wish I could, but Jeremy and Dan seem to be the snipers in the family."

The old man stopped in the sandy driveway. He reached out and touched Jackie's shoulder with the finger tips of his left hand. His command voice returned, but this time without the sharp edges. "Don't worry about it. I have some videos you can watch, and we'll take you out for some private instruction. You'll be a long-distance marksman in no time."

Jackie bowed her head down as she remembered the old man reaching his fingertips out to the little bird. She thought to herself, *That's how I'll choose to see him from now on.*

"Listen, General Branch, I'm sorry for acting the way I did. It's not my normal way."

The old man nodded. "I know. These are tough times. But do me a favor, please."

She nodded apprehensively. "Okay, what is it?"

"When Sergeant Brewster or any other soldier is present, please treat me with respect and don't question my orders. But when we're alone or just family, please call me Uncle Rodney. Then you can speak your mind in any tone you like."

Jackie nodded and smiled. "Of course, Uncle Rodney. I understand. There's a war on. Command presence prevails."

Rodney smiled. "So is there anything else we need to discuss privately before we go back inside with the others?"

She took a step closer before answering. "Just one other thing. I need to thank you for raising my husband and for taking us all in. I appreciate your kindness." And with that, she reached out and hugged the grizzled, old soldier. Rodney's back straightened as he came to attention, not quite knowing how to respond. He couldn't remember the last time he'd been hugged. So much had changed. And more change was coming. Nervously, he moved his right hand up to pat her back. After a few seconds, they separated and walked up the drive, onto the steps and back into the house as darkness fell all around them.

CHAPTER 3

Taking Action

THE ALARM WENT OFF BESIDE RODNEY'S BED, BUT HE COULD
barely hear it. He slept on a cot with a thin mattress on top and a sleeping bag. There was a small, pot-bellied stove that he fired up each night before turning in that kept the small room warm. His bedroom was only ten-feet square with a low ceiling. Even before the power grid crash, he'd kept the room dark and simple. There was a metal, olive drab, military locker against one wall with an old, wooden foot locker beside it. A clean change of olive drab utilities along with his boots rested neatly on top, waiting impatiently for the start of a new day. On this particular morning, a full battle pack and M16 rifle sat off to one side next to the locker.

The night before, he'd shaved and asked Jackie to cut his hair close to his scalp with a razor. He looked more military now, and he felt tighter and more in control of himself.

The alarm kept ringing, and Rodney reached over clumsily to tap the button on top. It was an old, wind-up alarm clock he'd had since just after boot camp. That made the clock over fifty years old. It was an antique, but, like him, it was still simple and very dependable.

Rodney threw open his sleeping bag and swung his feet out and onto the bare, cement floor. Somewhere around fifty years old he'd noticed his feet still hurt even after a full night's sleep. The older he got, the tougher it was to find enough reason to get out of bed in the morning. Then around sixty he'd begun to understand the lure of death's appeal. The old man had long considered it cruel that finally, after all these decades, when he knew enough to merit his existence, his body was falling apart around him. Here he was, getting ready to lead and fight the greatest battles of his time, but only after he'd grown old and nearly useless.

He turned the small lamp on beside his bed, and it lit up the room with little more than a dimness. It was connected to a car battery beneath the cot and would last for days, since he spent very little time inside the room. Over the years he'd collected dozens of car batteries which he constantly trickle charged off a solar panel array on the sunny side of the hill. Two walls of the house were surrounded by dirt banks all the way up and onto the roof. It looked a little like one of Tolkien's Hobbit houses from *The Lord of the Rings*. The main part of the house, with the dining room, kitchen, living room and bathroom were on the main circuit powered by much larger batteries. There were three other bedrooms branching off the main house that relied on car batteries for light just like his own. By last year's standards, his energy set-up was archaic, but now, after the power crash, he was one of a select few with electricity, and he was very careful not to advertise that fact.

But the real purpose of Rodney's bedroom was not to sleep, but to guard the below-ground level of the house. The solid, steel door to the left of his cot was protected by three heavy padlocks. The door frame was reinforced and solidly anchored into the cement wall behind his cot. It was clearly a custom addition that Rodney had built himself. No one knew of it save himself and Daniel.

He grabbed the clothes off the footlocker and hurriedly dressed in the same way, in the same sequence that he had for the last fifty years. The last thing to strap on was his nylon duty belt with his 45 caliber 1911 pistol and two extra magazines. He was truly neat, meticulous, and a creature of habit. Normally he would have lit up a cigarette by now, but, not today, not anymore. Never again.

With his boots laced up, he stood and donned the pack, grabbed the M16 and the handheld field radio and took the padlock off the door leading to the rest of the house. Others would no doubt think it strange that he padlocked himself into his bedroom each night, but that's the way he'd done it for years, and he wasn't about to change now. It was a security issue, and he never compromised on security. To say he'd never really been one to care what others thought of him was a gross understatement. Besides, everyone who'd been calling him a kook for decades now relied on him for protection.

Quietly, he stepped out of his bedroom and into the living room where he quickly padlocked the door from the outside. Everyone else was sleeping except Daniel who should be on the roof with a radio, his rifle, binoculars and night vision.

The phlegm in his chest was nagging at him now, but he held the coughing at bay until he opened the door and walked outside into the pre-dawn blackness. Daniel would have heard the door open, so he called him now on the radio.

"Hawks Nest this is HQ Actual, over."

The response was almost immediate, and Rodney smiled with satisfaction at his nephew.

"HQ Actual, this is Hawks Nest, go ahead, over."

"Hawks Nest, be advised I'm exiting through the front and you should hold fire, over."

"Roger that, HQ Actual. Will comply."

Rodney wanted to chat with him, just because he hadn't gotten much of a chance since his return. Everything had been moving at light speed, and would continue to do so. But, even though the radios were encrypted, he couldn't break procedure and condone personal chatter on the airwaves. No exceptions. But, for some reason, he just wanted to hear his boy's voice.

"Thanks, Hawks Nest. Sit Rep, please."

"All is quiet, HQ Actual. No incidents to report. It was a good night. Over."

The old man smiled and keyed his mic one last time.

"Roger that, Hawks Nest. Will return by noon chow. Over."

"Roger that, HQ Actual. This is Hawks Nest, out."

Rodney fastened the radio inside a pocket on his packstrap and headed for the road. His upper body was still in pretty good shape, for a man of his advancing years, but his lungs were going to need some work. He'd been smoking for decades, and hadn't really done a lot of hiking. Today would be the first of many pre-dawn, solitary force marches.

A mile into the woods, when he was sure Hawks Nest could no longer hear him, he knelt down and coughed out all the phlegm from his lungs onto the dried oak leaves. He should have stopped smoking years ago, but he hadn't. And now, when the world needed him most, he was less than his best.

Slowly, he stood up and wiped the slobber from his mouth and chin. With his rifle in his left hand, he looked up at the hill in front of him like it was Mount Everest and began the long climb.

☆ ☆ ☆ ☆

"Dan, I want you set up on that hilltop over there with your AR15 and your binoculars. Make sure your radio is on the right frequency, and don't transmit unless you see
a security risk. Understood?"

Dan Branch nodded and smiled. "Am I supposed to salute you now, Uncle Rodney?"

The old man laughed out loud. He was wearing a quilted, green, flannel shirt and
blue jeans to ward off the mid march northern Michigan chill. It was almost dark now,
and they were expecting the Huey at any moment."

"Just get up there and do your job, Marine."

Dan turned to Sergeant Donny Brewster and held out his right hand. The two men
shook firmly and locked eyes for a moment.

"You stay cool out there, Donny." Donny nodded but didn't say anything. "I want
you to know that I appreciate what you're doing for my family and for my home. I
really do."

Donny smiled. "Semper Fi, Marine. You take care of the wife and kids, cuz I want
a hot, home-cooked meal when I get back from the boonies."

"You got it, Donny." Dan looked at him one last time, wondering if he'd ever see
him again. Then he turned and strode up the hill to set up the lookout post.

"Don't take any unnecessary chances, Sergeant. Give us as much information and
time as you can, but don't get killed in the process." He hesitated. "And that's an
order."

Donny was wearing RealTree camo with a wool sweater underneath. He reached up
and pulled his boonie hat down over his eyes just a tad. His pack lay on the ground beside him, and his rifle was still encased. A 9mm Glock was strapped to his right thigh,
and his suppressed M4 leaned against Rodney's truck. Rodney had insisted on driving
twenty miles away from town to the most secluded area in the county. He didn't want
anyone to associate military helos with his home town.

"General, that's one order I plan to follow to the letter."

Off in the distance, they heard the heavy blades of the Huey in the dense air getting
closer. General Branch reached out his hand and the two men shook in silence. As the
helicopter touched down, Rodney backed away. Donny grabbed his gear and walked
over to the Huey with his head down. The blades lowered the wind chill, but Donny
was acclimated from the long, hard winters of the Upper Peninsula. In a few seconds,
the helicopter took off again and headed east ten miles and then turned to the south.

A few minutes later Dan climbed into the truck beside his uncle.

"Did you see anything, son?"

Dan shook his head.

"Good. At least we got off to a positive start."

Uncle Rodney fired up the diesel engine and drove out of the small field and onto
the two-track logging road back into the safety of the trees.

With all the nonchalance of a Sunday drive, Uncle Rodney asked, "So what is that
wife of yours serving us for chow tonight?"

A smile spread across Dan's face as he answered.

"It's a surprise. You're going to love it."

General Branch frowned. "I don't like surprises. It's not healthy in my line of work."

The two men grew silent, both contemplating the future and the tasks at hand. So much was riding on Donny Brewster's shoulders.

CHAPTER 4

A State of Flux - State Forest Refugee Camp

"YOU FOLKS GATHER ROUND ME, NOW, YA HEAR?"
Sheriff Leif dropped the mic down a bit with his left hand as he waited for people to pull in closer around his police cruiser. Rodney Branch stood behind the open door on the passenger side. Joe looked out across the sea of tents spread out before him. The refugees kept coming up from the south, trying to stay ahead of the horde of looters and murderers. Last week there had been only one hundred people here at the campgrounds, but now, he guessed the number had tripled. "Keep coming in, folks. I need you all to hear what I have to say."

Once they were all in, the Sheriff felt a little intimidated. He glanced over at Rodney for support. For some reason, he just felt safer when the old man was around. He cleared his throat, clicked the mic on and began his rehearsed speech.

"We had another break-in back near town last night. That's the third one this week. I'm here to ask if any of you have any information about it."

The crowd murmured among themselves, but no one spoke to him. "I'm not accusing anyone, I just need to know if any of you can help me out with information."

A man near the front snickered. "Sure sounds like an accusation to me, Sheriff."

Sheriff Leif made eye contact with him, trying to stare the man down, but it didn't work. The crowd took a step closer. They looked at him like he was the bad guy, and he just couldn't believe what he was seeing. A year ago these were probably all good folks, but now … anything was possible.

"We didn't do anything wrong, and we have a right to be here. This is state land, and you don't have any jurisdiction in the game area."

This time it was a different man than the one who'd first spoken out. There were four rough-looking men flanking him. All of them were armed with rifles and shotguns.

Joe held up his hand in a calming gesture. "Yes, I know you have a right to be here. But you have to understand my first loyalty is to the citizens of Iroquois County. They elected me, and I answer to them and them alone."

He stared into the man's eyes for a few seconds, then moved from man to man. He thought to himself, *Don't let them smell your fear. Command presence. Sell it or you're dead meat.*

"Martial law was declared long ago, so I *do* have jurisdiction here. But let's not argue that. I'm just here to tell you that my men have orders to shoot any looters on sight with no questions asked. So please be careful when you wander off state land here and onto private property. The people are getting pretty nervous and they might do something less than prudent."

Five men stepped forward and another six filled in the gap behind them. They came to within fifteen feet of the cruiser before stopping.

"We don't like your tone, Sheriff. And we don't answer to you or anyone else." The man was a head taller than six feet with massive shoulders and chest muscles. Apparently the food shortage hadn't effected his diet. The men behind him wore confident smiles.

"Listen folks, we don't want any trouble. I'm just trying to do my job here."

The big man folded his muscled arms across his chest.

"Neither do we, Sheriff. But unless you're here to bring us food or medicine or extra blankets, then … well, we just got no use for you here."

The Sheriff glanced over at Rodney for moral support, but the General was already easing himself back into the cruiser.

Joe looked back over at the crowd and pasted his best relax-and-have-a-nice-day smile on his face. But the men pressed in closer, moving to within ten feet of the car.

Just as Joe was about to speak, something came flying out the passenger side window of his cruiser. It landed on the ground in front of the advancing men. He glanced over at Rodney just in time to hear a deafening explosion. The shock wave pressed up against him, and he felt sand and gravel hit him full in the face.

Someone yelled "Grenade!" and the men stopped advancing and started to retreat back as fast as they could. Several more grenades came out Rodney's window as Joe quickly jumped into the cruiser and closed the door behind him.

As more explosions went off in front of the car, Joe fired up the engine and backed out as fast as he could. Uncle Rodney was still pitching grenades out the window as they turned around and pulled away. Joe looked in the rear-view mirror but all he saw was thick, white smoke billowing out and up totally obscuring the campgrounds. They heard gunshots, but nothing hit the car as they sped away.

Once they were on the main road again, Joe looked over at Rodney. "What did you just do? You just killed dozens of innocent people back there!"

Uncle Rodney just smiled. "No, I don't think so. Those were just flash-bangs. Just enough bang and noise to disorient them long enough for us to get the hell out of there before you got us both killed with all your flowery speech. The last two were smoke grenades. I got 'em on eBay."

Rodney slammed on the brakes and the car skidded to a halt on the pavement. Uncle Rodney took his hands off the dash and stopped smiling.

"Why do you always get so emotional about things, Joe. I thought you did pretty good, considering those folks are starving, homeless and afraid for their wives and children. You walked into a no-win situation. What did you expect?"

Joe pursed his lips together but didn't answer.

"Did you actually expect them to hand over the bad guys to you on a silver platter? Right now the line between good and bad is a little blurry."

Joe thought about it for a second, but he couldn't fight off the anger he still felt about what Rodney had just done.

"I can't believe you just did that. They could've been hurt back there."

Rodney folded his arms across his chest. "Did it occur to you at all that we were outmanned and outgunned, not to mention outflanked, and those men weren't coming in closer to shake your hand, Sheriff. You and I were about to die, and I saved your sorry ass!"

Joe pressed down on the accelerator again. "Maybe. We'd better get out of here in case they're following us." Joe shook his head back and forth. "I just … nobody ever did that to me before. It's like nobody respects the law anymore."

Rodney looked at the road ahead, and, after he'd calmed down a bit, he began to feel sorry for his friend.

"Joe, it's not that people have lost respect for the law, it's that the law has changed. People aren't sure what it is anymore. The law is in a state of flux. Right now anything that doesn't help people survive is meaningless to them."

The Sheriff looked over at him with a confused look on his face. "What do you mean? It's always been against the law to attack a law enforcement officer. That hasn't changed."

Rodney shrugged his shoulders. "Yeah, well, maybe. But you have to start looking at it from their perspective if you want to understand it. Most of those men have a wife and kids who got ran out of their homes. They lost their jobs, lost their way of life, and now they can't even put a roof over their heads and feed them a decent meal. That takes away a man's self respect and replaces it with something more dangerous, something more violent."

Rodney looked out the window at the passing trees. "You just handled it wrong, that's all. You set them off like flames in a powder magazine."

For the next mile Joe didn't say anything. Finally, he gripped the wheel tighter, making his knuckles turn white.

"Okay, so my way didn't work out. I can see that. I'm not too proud to admit when I'm wrong."

Rodney nodded and snickered to himself. "Did you see the look on that big guy's face when he saw that grenade land between his legs?"

The Sheriff thought for a moment and then smiled slightly. "I think his life was flashing before his eyes, and it wasn't pretty."

The old man laughed before reaching into his breast pocket for a cigarette. He quickly realized they weren't there, and dropped his hand back down again.

"So, how many deputies do we have now to defend the county?"

The Sheriff's smile faded away. "I deputized three hundred men, but last week when I mustered them, only seventy-nine showed up."

"That's a problem."

"No kidding."

Uncle Rodney thought for a few seconds. Then he looked over at Joe and smiled. "I think I know how we can get us some more fighters."

A concerned look came over Joe's face.

"Okay, I'm listening."

The next day they returned to the state campgrounds with three truckloads of food, blankets and basic medicine. They were quickly surrounded by armed men, but very calmly got out of their cabs and started throwing cases of MREs out onto the ground in front of them.

The people pounced on the boxes of food like a swarm of locust.

Once all the trucks were unloaded, the big man from the day before walked up. Rodney met him with an extended right hand. The man hesitated, then met Rodney eye for eye before gripping his hand firmly.

"We have extra, at least for now, and it just didn't seem right to keep it all to ourselves while good people went hungry."

The man's stone face finally relaxed. "Okay, that's nice, and we appreciate it. But what's the catch?"

Rodney smiled knowingly. This guy was more than big and strong. He was also very smart.

"Is there a place where you and I can talk?"

The man nodded and turned to leave. Rodney fell in behind him. They came to a large tent with the flaps tied open. A campfire burned about ten feet away from the entrance. The whole scene reminded Rodney of old black and white tintype photos he'd seen of Civil War campsites.

"C'mon inside and sit down."

Rodney followed him in and soon both men were sitting across from each other at a small, folding card table.

"My name is Rodney Branch. I got a place a few miles west of Iroquois City."

The big man nodded. "Jason Little. Grand Rapids."

And then the two men talked.

Thirty minutes later Rodney walked away with the promise of one hundred fighting men to help defend the county. In return, he'd promised sanctuary and permanent homes for a select number of families from the campsite.

Over the next few days people formally applied for permanent residency to Iroquois County. There were already fifty homes in the area where the owners had either died or were unaccounted for since the collapse. These houses would be turned over to refugees who could demonstrate a key skill or resource critical to the defense and well being of the county. In many cases simply a willing fighter with a good firearm and extra ammo was enough to foot the bill.

Once the new residents had been chosen, Rodney and the Sheriff held a formal swearing in ceremony at the camp. Each man, woman and child raised their right hand and swore the following oath:

> *"I hereby declare, on oath, that I absolutely and entirely will support and defend the Constitution of the United States of America and the laws of Iroquois County against all enemies, foreign and domestic; that I will bear true faith and allegiance to the same; that I will bear arms on behalf of Iroquois County and that I take this obligation freely without any mental reservation or purpose of evasion; so help me God."*

In that way, the camp was nearly emptied out in three days time. The rash of burglaries stopped.

CHAPTER 5

Bad Moon on the Rise

SERGEANT DONNY BREWSTER PEERED DOWN THE HILL JUST north of Greenville. He couldn't believe what he was seeing. He estimated the camp at twelve hundred, most of them able-bodied men. And their numbers seemed to be growing as he watched. At this rate, by the time they reached Iroquois, General Branch would be fighting against an army of three thousand men.

The large parking lot surrounding the warehouse was filled with a hodge-podge of vehicles with everything from military HumVees to snow plows and semi trucks and trailers. Off to one side there appeared to be a group of twenty quads. The pavement of the parking lot was bare of snow, and fires now burned in dozens of places interspersed across the landscape. Wooden pallets from inside the warehouse had been dragged outside and set on fire to keep the rank and file soldiers warm.

Donny had thrown a white, vinyl tarp over himself and his gear, allowing only his face to show. He also wore white gloves and a white ski mask. Beyond thirty yards, he was nearly invisible, even from the air. After being dropped off by the helo, he'd hiked in the last ten miles and dug into the top of this hill. Now, he was ready to lay perfectly still at a distance of seven hundred yards for the next ten hours, watching, taking notes, analyzing, probing for weakness. Donny Brewster was on the hunt.

That night, just after sundown, Donny quietly broke camp. After moving back into the trees and stretching his tired muscles, he packed up a few choice supplies and walked around the encampment to the far side of the warehouse. He'd already mapped out the camp's security, complete with the location of each guard. From a military standpoint it was pretty relaxed, so he easily slipped into the front parking lot and from there into the back lot where all the troops were staged. Once inside their perimeter, it was easy to move from campfire to campfire, listening intently to anything he wanted so long as he didn't bring attention to himself.

As Donny sat just outside the light of the fire and listened, he heard a mixture of sounds: diesel generators, men talking, laughter, anger, the screams of a woman, and the unmistakable sound of his favorite band, Credence Clearwater Revival. He just sat there for a few minutes enjoying the words.

Don't go around tonight,
Well, it's bound to take your life,
There's a bad moon on the rise.

"So when we pullin' outta this place, Mikey?"
Donny's ears perked up as he listened to the two men talk just a few yards away

from him.

"Boss says tomorrow. He wants to keep headin' north fer some reason."

"Why we keep headin' north for? It's cold up there and most the people are south. I don't get it."

Donny heard the man hack up some phlegm and spit before answering. "Yeah, you don't get it cuz yer so stupid! The reason we left Grand Rapids is cuz we had no choice!"

There was a pause. "What? Ya mean cuz of that other gang? We could of taken 'em." Donny leaned in closer.

"Maybe. Maybe not. Boss said it weren't worth the risk. GR was bout tapped out anyway. Sides, the others got most of the military hardware. Boss says we need more of our own and the smaller cities north got plenty of stuff. If ya wanna live high on the hog like this, ya gotta keep movin' on."

The other man nodded in the darkness. Donny moved away from the fire and walked slowly toward the warehouse. He was wearing a green poncho that hung down to his knees. It helped hide his tactical vest laden with his suppressed M4 on a 3-point sling in front of him, his 9mm suppressed Glock, and a variety of other ordinance including smoke grenades, thermite, C4 and fragmentation grenades.

Donny didn't like coming in close like this, but he knew that after tonight security would tighten up and things would have to be done from longer distances. This was his one best shot at inflicting massive damage and chaos.

He worked his way up slowly, but then stopped and waited outside the fire closest to the warehouse. Security seemed to tighten up around the entrances to the building. He knew from his daytime surveillance that each door leading in was guarded by two men. And up on the roof, there was a man with a rifle stationed at each wall. He would assume they had night vision.

Donny sat down with his back leaning up against the big tires of a semi trailer to wait for everyone in camp to fall asleep. Just then the back door of the trailer opened wide and something was thrown out onto the ground. It landed just a few feet away from Donny. He looked down at the young woman, naked and unmoving. Her face was battered, bruised and bleeding.

"How many more guys we got? Raise your hand if you haven't gone yet."

Thirteen men clustered by the fire raised their hands. "Okay, Jim. Bring us another one. Should be the last of it for tonight. I need some sleep."

Donny looked down at the woman lying beside him on the ground. She wasn't moving. As discreetly as possible, he reached his hand over and placed his fingers on her carotid artery. There was no pulse.

"Next in line."

Harold Steffens stepped up slowly to the table on the courthouse lawn. He was a tall, thin man, nothing but skin and bones, frail and old, wearing an ancient United States Army uniform. Over his right shoulder, on a sling, draped a large rifle that was older than most of the men who'd already volunteered for the Iroquois County Home Guard. Harold stood proudly at attention in front of the Sheriff who looked at him and shook his head.

"Harold, what are you doing?"

The old man looked him straight in the eye with a fierceness that belied his age. "I'm here to serve my county."

Joe Leif placed his elbows up on the white, plastic table and rested his chin on his folded hands. "How old are you, Harold?"

Harold slumped his shoulders slightly but didn't give in. "I wasn't aware there was an age requirement, Sheriff. But I have ID and can prove I'm at least eighteen."

The Sheriff stood up and walked around in front of the table. He gently placed his hand on the man's shoulder and leaned in closer.

"Harold, does Myra know you're doing this?"

The man's lips pursed together, and the deep wrinkles around his eyes tightened with anger. "Myra's been dead for two months, Joe. She caught pneumonia just after Christmas."

Joe nodded and lowered his head in sadness. "I'm sorry, Harold. I didn't know."

"That doesn't matter. I'm here to serve. I'll fight and die if I have to. I'm healthy and I still got my eyes. I can shoot as good as any man you got standing here."

General Rodney Branch had been watching from twenty feet away, waiting to see how the Sheriff would handle this. Finally, he walked up and stood in front of Harold Steffens. The old man saw Rodney's uniform and suddenly stiffened to attention and immediately saluted. General Branch returned the salute smartly and crisply.

"At ease, soldier."

Rodney looked the old man up and down. "That's a nice M1 Garand you have there, Sergeant. Where'd you get it?"

The old man's wrinkled lips smiled slightly.

"At a small beach in France, sir."

Rodney nodded. "I see you were with the 3rd Armored Division. That means you saw a lot of action."

The old man nodded resolutely. "Yes, sir. We called ourselves The Third Herd. We lost a lot of good men on that continent."

The General's mouth frowned, but his eyes continued to sparkle. He looked over to Sheriff Leif. "Sheriff, can you spare this man? I need to assign him to a special unit. We're short noncoms, and this man has the training and experience I need for an important mission."

Joe Leif looked off to the left. A stiff, cool breeze picked up from the north, causing a chill to run through his bones. Finally, he stuck his arm out and shook hands with Harold Steffens. "Welcome to the Home Guard, Sergeant Steffens."

The old man smiled, and a thousand wrinkles smiled with him.

"May I speak with you privately, General Branch?"

Rodney motioned for Harold to sit down and wait for him in the chair beside the table. As soon as the two men were out of earshot, Joe cut loose on Rodney.

"What the hell do you think you're doing? That man is eighty-some years old! He won't last a day on the battlefield!"

General Branch nodded. "I expect you're right, Sheriff."

"Well, then ..."

Rodney interrupted him.

"You're right when you say he won't last a day on the battlefield, but this battle will be over in less than a day. So, maybe, just maybe, he might have a fighting chance. Besides, if we lose this battle, he'll be dead anyway. At least this way we give him a reason to live."

Sheriff Leif stood there unmoving, trying desperately to figure out what Rodney had planned for the old man.

"Let me put it to you another way, Sheriff Leif. This man fought his way from Normandy all the way through France, into Belgium and Nazi Germany." Rodney paused to let it sink in. "Did you see those medals on his chest? The Purple Heart? The Silver Star? That man shed his blood for both of us. They don't give those medals away. You have to earn them."

Joe Leif looked down at the ground. "Yes, Rodney, I know. It's just ... that man was my grandfather's best friend. I just don't want to see him get hurt."

Rodney's eyes softened a bit, but he didn't let up. "From now on, anyone you deem too old for combat, just send them to me. Sergeant Steffens will lead them into battle. And he'll make us proud. And the very worst that can happen is he dies with honor instead of wheezing helplessly sick in a bed all alone."

General Branch turned and walked back over to the old man. The man stood up and snapped back to attention.

"Do you have a few minutes, Sergeant Steffens? I have a few ideas I'd like to discuss. We have a battle to plan."

✯ ✯ ✯ ✯

It was 4:00 a,m, and Donny Brewster was flat against the east wall of the warehouse, standing at the base of a ladder leading up to the roof. After taking one final look around, he moved up the ladder and climbed thirty feet to the rooftop. Just before peering over the top, he flipped down his night vision and turned it on.

When he peeked over the rooftop, he saw the first sentry leaning up against the three-foot ledge with his back turned. Donny had already removed his poncho, so he quietly swung up onto the rooftop, rotated his M4 up to his chest and took aim. A few seconds later he heard the sound of the rifle action opening and closing, then a thud as the guard hit the tar and gravel-covered rooftop.

He quickly moved to the south wall and dispatched the second sentry who was carelessly smoking a cigarette. The west sentry was just as simple. But when he closed in on the north wall, something wasn't right. He couldn't find the guard. He waited five minutes, but still - no movement. He picked up a small stone and threw it forty feet out towards the wall. Still - no sign of the sentry.

After another five minutes of scanning and waiting, Donny flipped back his night vision and pulled a small infrared monocular from a pocket in his tactical vest. He looked through it, scanning first the far end of the wall, working his way back. Only then did he see the small, red blotch sticking out from behind the upraised ceiling vent. Now that he knew where to look, Donny put away the IR and flipped his generation 4 NVIS back down over his eyes. It was obvious now. There was a boot-covered foot about twenty feet away from him. He rotated his M4 around behind him and unholstered his 9mm Glock. As he walked slowly and carefully over the gravel, his footsteps sounded to him much louder than they really were, so he moved slowly. Upon reaching the foot, he peeked around the vent and saw the man asleep on the job. He calculated the angle and quickly put one round through the man's left eye socket. Donny thought to himself, *You'll sleep much better now.*

With all four sentries dispatched, Donny descended quickly down the hatch and into the heart of the building. From there, he moved from the warehouse portion into the front offices. He holstered his nine millimeter and drew his suppressed 22 caliber pistol from the front of his tactical vest. With stealth derived from practice, he moved from office to office, almost noiselessly dispatching every man he found. Most of them were lying on mattresses or cots, and a few of them had naked women beside them. The sound of the smaller action on his 22 caliber pistol was much quieter, allowing him to leave the women alive. He presumed most of them were unwilling participants.

After eliminating fourteen men, he moved past a conference room with papers rolled out onto a big table. He looked down at the map and saw a large, red, felt pen circle around Traverse City. Donny smiled, pulled out his cell phone and snapped a picture. After finishing his sweep of the building, he climbed back up onto the roof and exited the camp the way he'd come.

Before first light, he was back on the hill, totally concealed in his hidey hole, ready to watch all hell break loose with the coming dawn.

CHAPTER 6

The Blind Man and Hannibal Lecter

THE BLIND MAN SAT AT THE HEAD OF THE LARGE, RECTANGU-lar mahogany table. His high-backed chair was plush leather that seemed to rise up and envelop him. Also at the table were six other men. They were seated rigidly and uncomfortably in small, metal folding chairs. Behind each regional leader was his second in command, and behind him was his personal bodyguard. So the room was a bit crowded.

At that moment, several women came in and cleared away the remnants of the gourmet meal they'd just consumed. Within thirty seconds the table was empty and wiped clean except for a small paper cup of wine in front of each leader.

Behind the blind man was his assistant, Sammy Thurmond, but no one knew his real name save the blind man, and the blind man's real name was Jared Thompson. But no one knew that either, except for a few hand-picked dead people.

Jared was wearing dark sun glasses and a black suit with white shirt and tie as was his assistant. Sammy touched his boss on the shoulder signifying all was ready then looked straight ahead.

"I trust all of you had a good meal?"

No one answered, though a few glanced around the table nervously. By now all of them knew it was the blind man who'd created the thousand-year night. They also knew the demise of the rich, Arab Sheik who'd hired him to bring down the power grid. Most of them were prepared to swear allegiance in order to share in Jared's power and to avoid the Sheik's fate. But there was one holdout.

"And now, I propose a toast."

Jared picked up his own long-stemmed crystal goblet and raised it up. The other six men hesitated, but then, one by one, as if falling to an unseen pressure, each man slowly raised the paper cup of wine in front of him. Jared smiled and thought to himself, *As if they have a choice."*

"By drinking this wine you signify your allegiance to me and only me. You will serve me like slaves, unwavering and unfailing. You will obey me and only me. If you succeed I will reward you. If you fail, I will kill you."

The blind man raised his glass.

"To loyalty and unity."

At first, no one moved. Then Jared drank and put his glass back on the table. Finally, the man to his left drank as well. Then, one by one, all capitulated to Jared's will … save one man.

Walter Herwath was from Los Angeles, and he now ruled all of southern California with an iron fist. The once beautiful and depraved paradise was in a shambles. After the fall, it had become disease-ridden, looted, and burning. But Walter had risen to the top of the herd, destroyed his competitors and restored cosmos from all the chaos. Walter Herwath was proud, and he never shared power.

"Wonderful! I'm happy that we're all on the same page. And now …"

But Jared stopped in mid sentence as Sammy reached down and tapped him gently on the shoulder then leaned down and whispered in his ear. Jared frowned.

"I see."

And then he laughed out loud.

"I made a joke. Don't you get it? I said 'I see'. I'm blind!" He kept laughing as he spoke. "I see said the blind man."

But no one else laughed. They just looked around nervously. Finally, when the room was quiet again Walter spoke out.

"You're just a weak blind man who can't read the writing on the wall. Southern California is mine because I earned it. And no one is coming in just because they think they can." He looked around the room at each man and then straight over at Sammy. "You can have southern California, over my dead body!"

Jared smiled.

"Please count down for me."

Sammy raised up his wrist and lifted his sleeve revealing his watch. Then, in his Hannibal Lecter voice, he began to count down. "Seven. Six. Five."

The men around the table began to squirm in their cheap, metal folding chairs. But Walter jumped up from his chair in anger.

"Four. Three. Two."

Walter yelled as loud as he could while drawing his pistol from his shoulder rig. "This is bull!"

"One."

Walter's gun slipped from his hand and fell onto the expensive mahogany table top. He clutched at his chest and began to cough. Blood and foam bubbled out his mouth and spilled on the table in a crimson pool. Walter's eyes rolled up into his head as he came down hard on the table. They didn't re-open.

Jared heard the thud and smiled. "Oh, I'm sorry. I'm not being a good host. It would be rude of me not to explain."

He folded his hands on the table in front of him. "You see, I took the liberty of lacing the chicken and the prime rib with a deadly toxin. I needed to know who would be loyal to me, so I put the antidote in the glass of wine Walter just refused to drink. The rest of you will live though since you toasted to our loyalty and unity."

Jared then looked in the direction of Walter's second in command. "And what about you, Carlos? It would seem with the death of Walter you've just inherited a regional empire. Would you like to relinquish your independence and pledge your obedience to a mere blind man?"

Carlos looked down at Walter's dead body and shook his head in disbelief. "You are a crazy man."

Jared made a clicking sound with his tongue against the roof of his mouth. "Oh my. Now that's not very polite."

Carlos was large for a Mexican, standing six feet five inches in height. He had dark hair and eyes with a neatly trimmed beard and moustache.

"Southern California will stand against you, and my brothers from the south will rise up and join me."

Jared glanced over his shoulder and nodded. Just then a TV screen began to drop slowly down through the white-painted ceiling. "I want you to see something, Mr. Ramirez."

The television turned on, showing a panoramic view of the Los Angeles skyline. Jared laughed. "So Carlos, how can you stand *against* me when there's nothing left for you to stand *for*?"

The camera view panned out to a distance of about twenty miles. There was an explosion, a very large explosion. The mushroom cloud rose up and then billowed out as all of Los Angeles melted and burned in the uranium-induced heat wave.

Carlos' mouth dropped open in shock. Sammy Thurmond pulled out his pistol in one smooth motion and put one shot into Carlos' brain. The second in command's lifeless body dropped down onto that of his boss.

Jared smiled again.

"Well ... okay. That was an interesting development." He hesitated before going on. "It would appear there is no one to lead southern California. But ..." The blind man threw up his hands. "That doesn't really matter since Los Angeles no longer exists."

He waited a few seconds, allowing everyone to look at the malignant cloud filling the big screen. Jared knew, that they knew, Los Angeles could just as easily be the fate of Chicago, or New York or Miami ... Jared let that realization sink in.

"And, now that we're all on the same page, my staff will pass out some information and fill you in on the details of what you will be doing over the next few months."

Jared stood and Sammy pulled away his chair. "So, if there are no further disagreements, I'll be on my way."

The blind man walked slowly out of the conference room with one hand on Sammy's elbow to lead him. As he left, the blood of Walter and Carlos joined together, mingled and became one before pouring off onto the floor. In the background, the sound of uranium thunder filled the room as what was left of Los Angeles melted and burned.

CHAPTER 7

The Warehouse of Death

"**H**OW DID THIS HAPPEN?" MANNY LOOKED DOWN AT HIS fallen leader. There was a tiny bullet hole in his left temple and no exit wound. He covered his nose with his sleeve. It was already starting to stink inside.

"We don't know. I guess somebody broke in and shot him."

Manny looked up and over at his next in command. He was a moron, but he was a loyal moron. "So you're telling me that one man broke in here and killed forty-three men without being seen or heard?"

Buster Bancroft squirmed under the scrutiny of his new boss. "Ah, well, I guess it's really forty-eight if ya count the four guys on the roof." The two men behind him snickered under their breath. Buster was loyal and big, huge actually and very strong, but not the sharpest tool in the shed. His father had told him repeatedly as a child, "Son, you couldn't think your way out of a wet, paper bag!"

But he'd killed his father with his bare hands, so that no longer mattered and Buster had forgiven him since then. He looked down sheepishly when he heard everyone snicker. "It's forty-seven, ain't it, Manny."

Manny smiled. "Doesn't matter, Buster. Those men are just jealous of your physical attributes."

Buster smiled. "Yeah, it's always been big like that."

Manny looked down at the swollen body of his dead boss and thought for a moment. This was unfortunate and a bit disconcerting, but … it also saved him the trouble of doing it himself. Ever since they'd left Grand Rapids he'd been forming a plan to kill his boss and take over, but now … someone else had done it for him.

But the million-dollar question was … who? And was he coming back?

Manny spent the next two hours going from room to room, studying the carnage, trying to glean clues and figure out exactly how this had happened. At one point, he'd even pulled out his knife and dug into a man's brain to retrieve the bullet. He'd read somewhere that the best assassins used 22 caliber to maintain silence.

Perhaps the rival gang in Grand Rapids had sent someone after them? Manny shook his head. No, he didn't think so. This was something else.

He cleaned the blood off his hands and sat down to think. *What should he do? More importantly, what was in his best interest?* Manny wasn't like most of the others in this encampment. The majority of them were just hoodlums, punks, gangbangers, druggies, sex fiends, while a few were certifiably crazy or just plain evil. But Manny was different. Sure, he could kill with the best of them. He could rape, sodomize, kill, steal and destroy … but those were just tools of the trade. These other guys did it for enjoyment, or worse yet because they had to obey the voices inside their heads. With Manny, it was just business, a means to an end. So he killed often, and with purpose and discretion. But, more importantly, he always made a plan and stuck to it so long as it advanced the cause of Manny. Selfish ambition was Manny's sole, defining characteristic.

He sat down at a small desk out at the loading dock and quickly drew up a list of everyone he knew and trusted. His entire chain of command would have to be set up all over again. Of course, most of it was already in his head anyway, since he'd been planning for this day, but he'd never suspected that everyone would be killed. In fact, the only reason Manny had survived was just dumb luck. The boss had sent him on a raiding party to get more women and supplies. Anyone could have done it, and he hadn't really been necessary for the menial task. But … the dead and bloating gang leader had trusted only Manny. And that trust had been Manny's salvation.

Manny gave the list to Buster. "Go get these people and bring them to me right now."

Buster nodded and started to walk away. "Buster!" The big man turned around and stared at his boss. "And get somebody to haul all these bodies out of here. Put them in the back of a semi and dump them two miles from here in that gravel pit we passed on the way in. No need to bury them. I just don't want the guys to see."

Buster nodded again and walked out to follow his orders. Buster Bancroft may not have been very smart, but he was loyal, and smart enough to know when to ask questions and when to do as he was told.

Iroquois City - A Town in Training

"No! In this situation you hold the knife like this and let the man come to you. He'll be out of control, hyped up on adrenalin, but you have to keep your cool."

General Rodney Branch was wearing newly pressed and starched olive-drab fatigues. They were the same fatigues he'd worn in Vietnam, and he looked like General Patton on steroids. Rodney rotated the small bayonet in his right hand like a drum major twirling a baton. The knife's balance was off, but Rodney held on to it like a pro. He put up his fists in a classic fighting stance with the knife pointing down at the ground.

"And when the man comes forward, you punch at his face. He'll try to block you with his arms. And that's when you slice through the arteries in his wrist. Once he starts bleeding out, you follow up with a punch to his throat, taking out the carotid and his windpipe." Rodney went through the motions fluidly, defined into muscle memory through a lifetime of mindful practice. "And then you quickly move on to the next enemy soldier." He handed the knife back to Jason Little. Jason smiled.

"You've done this before. Are you really a general?" Jason Little stood towering over Rodney, but somehow, despite the man's obvious hugeness, Rodney was not diminished, and Jason knew it. Jason smiled. "Are you always the toughest man in the room?"

Rodney's face looked grim and determined, as if the pending battle were happening in fifteen minutes instead of several weeks. He didn't answer either of Jason's questions.

"Jason, what did you do for a living back before The Day?"

The big man tried rolling the knife around in his palm the way Rodney had done, but it fumbled to the ground and stuck in the dirt. He bent down sheepishly to pick it up. "I was an accountant for a bakery. We made mostly cereal, Pop-Tarts, Toaster Strudels, all kinds of breakfast foods." He hesitated. "Why does it matter?"

Rodney met his gaze. He'd been working out hard now for almost two weeks and much of his former toughness and bearing had returned. "Because we don't need any accountants in Iroquois County. We need warriors. We need leaders. We need you to learn how to kill like it's second nature, like you've been doing it your whole life. And you have to make it look effortless."

There were eighty-five men and a few of the tougher women surrounding him in a circle as he spoke with their leader, teaching them all how to kill. He looked around at the motley crew seated on the grass. They'd already been through hell just getting this far north, and their old lives and ways were shattered, replaced by something brutal and riddled with chaos. General Branch thought to himself at breakneck speed. *What could he offer them? What did they need most at this particular moment in time?*

"Are there really a thousand people coming to kill us?"

Rodney looked over toward a woman seated on the ground with her legs crossed Indian style. She was slight of frame, with long, blonde hair that reached down to the middle of her back. He recognized her eyes. He'd seen the likes of them before many times in the dark of night, just before a battle. She had the look of a woman who knew she was going to die.

"Stand up!"

She obeyed his command; because he was at the top of the pecking order; because it was law of the jungle, and because he could kill her with a simple twist of his hands.

"Step forward!"

She once again complied. Rodney could see her shaking almost uncontrollably. He reached his right hand out to Jason Little and motioned with a twitch of his fingertips.

"Give me the knife."

Jason looked at him with a single unspoken question in his eyes. *What are you going to do to her?*

General Branch swiveled his head on his shoulders quicker than a hawk looking for prey. "The knife!"

Jason reluctantly handed Rodney the small bayonet. He held it in his hand like an old friend come home to visit. Rodney turned to the woman.

"What is your name?"

She looked down, avoiding the intensity of his gaze, but Rodney quickly admonished her. "Stand like a man! Look me in the eye!"

The woman looked around at her peers, but no one moved. She felt all alone in the vise-like talons of a mad man. Then she looked into Rodney's eyes, and what she saw there made her blood turn to ice. It was the coldness. It was the enigmatic maelstrom in his eyes that caused her to shudder in fear and revulsion.

"What did you do before The Day?"

Rodney caused his eyes to soften, knowing she needed his prompting to speak. He asked her again. "What did you do before The Day?"

Finally, she found her voice. "I was a mom to my daughter and a wife to my husband."

Rodney smiled and nodded. "That's a noble profession and worthy of all your attention." He hesitated. "But today, you are a warrior. You are here to kill or be killed."

She said nothing, and Rodney looked deep into her eyes, sizing her up, testing her mettle, wondering what she was capable of. "Where is your daughter now?"

She looked up quickly and immediately met his gaze as if being challenged. "She's safe with a friend." She went quiet again, but Rodney sensed she had more to say.

"Speak your mind, soldier."

Her words were short and crisp.

"I don't know if I can kill anyone."

Out of the corner of his eye, Rodney saw several others nodding their heads slightly. He looked up and they quickly stopped. Then he met the woman's gaze once more.

"What is your name?"

"My name is Lisa."

"And your daughter?"

"She's five years old. Her name is Sam."

The General nodded. "Yes, good. Now here's what I want you to do. I want you to close your eyes. I'm going to paint a picture for you. Let the picture play out in your mind. Can you do that, Lisa?"

Lisa looked at him with questions in her mind, but finally nodded and closed her blue eyes.

"You're at your house here in Iroquois. In the middle of the night you hear a scream. You run to your daughter's bedroom and see a man. He has Sam on the bed. She is screaming and struggling, but the man is too strong for her. She is pinned down and he begins to rip off her pajamas. Sam is screaming as loud as she can, 'Mommy! Mommy! Help me!' But you are too scared to help, and you don't have the training necessary to kill him. You are too decent and pure to take another human life, so you let the man rape your daughter. And while your daughter dies in pain, terror and torment, you look on, because you don't have the will or the courage to stop him."

Lisa looked up. There were tears in her eyes, but the sheep-like countenance was gone, replaced with a mixture of both fear and anger. Rodney thought to himself, *It's a start*. And then he handed Lisa the knife. She hesitated, then reached out and accepted it from his open palm. Lisa looked at it and rolled it in her hand, then hefted it from first one hand and then back to the other.

"Lisa, the man in your daughter's bedroom is coming to town. He's coming for Sam. What are you going to do? Are you going to learn to fight him? Or, are you going to cower and die while her helpless screams echo in your ears for eternity?"

The door to a secret room in Lisa's mind swung open with a creak. It was a part of her she'd never felt before. She looked up and the fear was gone. She replied coldly with two words.

"Teach me."

Then Lisa fell down to her knees in front of him, not in worship, but in voluntary submission. She held the knife out to him with both palms facing up.

The General nodded and took the knife. He stepped quietly behind her and grasped her long, beautiful,blonde hair in his left hand. He squeezed and pulled it out behind her.

"Lisa, I do this now as a symbol of your loyalty and commitment. You are now a mother … and a warrior."

The razor-sharp knife came down and severed her hair with one, quick slice. Lisa stood to her feet and turned to face the old man. Rodney let the hair fall to the ground, before handing her the knife.

She turned and walked over to the other seven women in the crowd. They all stood, as if on some unspoken command, and turned, dropping to their knees. One by one, Lisa cut their hair, letting it fall to the ground before being carried away on the breeze.

"You are a warrior."

The hair separated and fell.

"You are a warrior."

Step to the next woman.

"You are a warrior."

Again.

"You are a warrior."

Seven times the knife came down.

Seven times a warrior rose up.

Seven women.

Seven warriors.

Lisa turned and walked back to the General with all seven trailing in her wake. They stood at attention before him, and only then did Rodney sigh in relief.

Jason Little looked on in awe.

"How did you do that? I can't even get my wife to cook me dinner."

General Branch ignored his question.

"Jason, for the next two hours I want you to review and practice the proper use of rifle and bayonet with the men. Pay particular attention to the horizontal butt stroke, the diagonal slash, and the basic jab."

The big man nodded. "Ah, okay."

General Branch turned and walked away. Eight warriors followed him to begin their special training.

CHAPTER 8

Domestic Drudgery

"**B**UT I DON'T UNDERSTAND WHY HE WON'T LET ME FIGHT! He's letting other women work right alongside the men, and those eight he chose out last week are being trained like some kind of Special Forces team or something."

Dan Branch looked at his wife helplessly. She was strong willed, and this was one of those arguments he knew would never go well for either of them. As far as Dan was concerned, it was a lose-lose.

"I don't know, honey. You'll have to ask Uncle Rodney. I just don't know why he does all the things he does." He shrugged his shoulders. "Does anybody?"

But that wasn't good enough for Jackie Branch. "But you know more about him than anyone does. He raised you! He's your blood! He shares more with you than with anyone else."

But in his heart, Dan knew her last statement wasn't accurate. His Uncle Rodney was in commanding general mode now, and there were many aspects of him Dan was learning for the first time, despite the thirty-some years they'd known each other.

"Honey, I love you, but you know I've gotta get going. Uncle Rodney wants me to find all those supplies by the end of the week."

Jackie folded her arms across her chest and stuck out her lower lip in defiance. Dan smiled. "Did I ever tell you how sexy Lebanese women look when they're angry?"

They were outside the house, and the weather had turned mild, so the baby was playing on a blanket beside the porch with some pine cones and sticks. She was at the stage now where everything went into her mouth. The dog, Moses, was lying on the wooden decking of the porch on an old rug. Jackie turned her back on Dan before speaking.

"Don't sweet talk me Dan Branch. You haven't heard the last of me on this one."

Of that Dan was sure. He placed his hands on her shoulders and kissed the back of her head. His only reward was a mouthful of coarse, black hair. He lingered behind her long enough to smell the scented olive oil she combed into it each morning. She was quite the woman, and he was madly in love with her, despite, or maybe because of, her fiery ways. His wife was not a woman to be trifled with. He shuddered to think what might happen if she ever found out the real reason she didn't train with the others.

In the end, Jackie watched as he walked off down the path toward town. Most everyone walked to town these days as gas had become scarce. Most people had a small supply, but were hoarding it in case of emergency, whatever that might entail. Of course, Uncle Rodney had more than most, as was the case with just about everything else. But, for some reason, he insisted they lead the same lifestyle as everyone else.

Jackie looked down at baby Donna and frowned. She loved her daughter, but ... for some reason, she still wanted to contribute, to pull her own weight, not just by cooking and cleaning and doing laundry and watching babies, but by preparing to fight like everyone else.

Dan had moved the old ringer washing machine out onto the front deck for her as he did every week. She sighed and dropped down onto the blanket to play with the baby.

"Hi honey. Do you love me even if I can't fight like everybody else?"

Baby Donna laughed and bit down on a pine cone. She was teething again. Jackie played with her a few more minutes before walking up the deck steps to the old ringer washing machine. They were lucky to have it as most people were without electricity and had to wash their clothes on a rock down by a river or stream. Because of Rodney's foresight and hard work, they were one of the few families to have any considerable amount of electricity to work with.

Jackie was lucky, no, more than that; she was blessed. By all rights her and her daughter should have been tortured and killed in that isolated Wisconsin cabin last fall. Instead, Dan Branch and his son, Jeremy, had rescued them. Then Dan had fallen in love with her, and her with him.

For some reason, no one in town asked her why her baby was black. Maybe they thought she was adopted, or maybe that her first husband had been black. But, as far as she knew, none of the townspeople knew the truth: that she'd cheated on her first husband on a mission trip to Haiti. But Dan knew, and Jeremy knew. And probably by now Uncle Rodney as well. He suspected the men were protecting her reputation as best they could. And she loved all three of them for it.

She turned on the garden hose and heard the water pump kick on as the small electric motor worked to suck up water from thirty feet below the surface. Jackie measured out a cup of lye soap flakes that she'd cut up from a bar last night and dumped it into the water. Once the tub was full, she pushed in the clothes and turned on the agitator. It moved slower than her Maytag back home, so it took longer for the clothes to get clean, but time was something she had more of now. Life was slower, and that was one part of her new world that she liked.

While the machine worked, she watched her baby play. Then she glanced over at the sentry post at three o'clock about thirty yards into the woods. She could see him high up in the tree, but only because she already knew he was there. Uncle Rodney seemed to have a knack for camouflage. She guessed he could make just about anything, big or small, seem near invisible.

The sentry post was manned twenty-four seven. At night by Dan, Jeremy, herself and Uncle Rodney, but by a Shadow Militia member during the day when the men went off to train for war. She had more questions than answers about the Shadow Militia. To her they seemed like the Masons on steroids. So secretive, so strong, always so disciplined and ready to follow any order Rodney gave them. She had no doubt any of its members would run into a hail of gunfire upon their general's command. She wondered now, *How had he gained that much loyalty?*

For the rest of the morning she did laundry, but her mind was free to analyze and plot, *How do I get past Uncle Rodney? How do I persuade him to let me train with the others?*

All the while, it never occurred to her that most people wouldn't want to fight, that they'd be thankful for the domestic drudgery she was now living through. But, for some reason, to Jackie, it felt like a life sentence with no chance of parole.

Donny Brewster - Master Sniper

Donny lay there in the prone position with the butt of his Crusader Broadsword rifle tucked firmly into his shoulder. The trigger came back ever so slowly and gently. Finally, Donny felt the recoil, and took one quick peek through the ACOG 4x scope.

The man was lying on the ground, motionless, with the top half of his head no longer intact. Donny thought to himself, *It's true, snipers do get more head!*

He quickly packed up, and started moving to his fallback position. Out on the road he heard the quads fire up and begin the chase. This was Donny's third week in the bush, and he'd grown quite a beard and become a bit gamey smelling.

It had taken the mob almost a week to re-organize enough to get moving again, and they were now traveling at a snail's pace about twenty miles north of Big Rapids. Their present course and rate of speed would put them just south of Iroquois within two weeks. That said, Donny had accomplished his mission. He only hoped it was enough.

The first week Donny had been able to kill dozens of men each day, but they'd begun to adapt to his guerilla tactics, taking good advantage of the speed and all-terrain mobility of the quads. The longer he kept this up, the more dangerous it would become. Eventually, if they got lucky, Donny would be captured or killed. But Donny had no intention of letting that happen.

As the sound of the quads came near, Donny scrambled into the river and grabbed onto the rope he'd pre-positioned for his getaway. Most of his gear was on the other bank, and the nearest bridge was miles away. Even if they knew where to look, he'd be far away setting up the next ambush by the time they got across the deep river. By strapping his rifle onto his back, he was able to pull himself hand over hand within a few minutes.

Thirty minutes later he was four miles away down inside a trench with branches on top of him. He had claymores set up all around him just in case they stumbled onto him. In the confusion of the mine going off, shooting out its load of deadly buckshot, Donny would be able to melt slowly again back into the ever-thickening north woods of Michigan. He'd stay there until dark, sleeping in dry clothes and a down-filled mummy bag, recharging his batteries, staying warm, gathering up as much sanity as he could muster, and, more importantly, planning his next ambush.

Yes, Donny Brewster was a Master Sniper. And he was the best.

Manny Makes a Plan

"You say he does it this way every time? Just shoots one guy and then falls back?"

Manny looked over at the little man before him and nodded his head. "Yes, just like this every day, usually in the morning when the sun is at his back. We can't see him because the sun blinds us, and by time we get the quads up there he's long gone. He's really starting to piss me off!"

The little man laughed. "If I was you, Mr. Manny, I'd be more than pissed. I'd be afraid."

Manny grit his teeth and ground them slowly back and forth to keep from swearing. He needed this man and his talents. Finally, after gaining his composure, he was able to talk again. "Just tell me straight out. Can you kill him?"

Robbie looked up at the hillside where the sun was now well over the treeline. He could easily pick out the best spot for the sniper to strike. Robbie pointed to a little indentation in the hillside about six hundred yards away.

"Leave me here with a week's supplies, and I'll do the rest."

Manny looked over at the little man like he was crazy. "Leave you here? In the middle of nowhere? Don't you want a quad or some more men?"

Robbie laughed again, and the laugh infuriated Manny. But the gang leader kept his cool this time. "I work alone. Just get me some MREs and I'll be fine." He started to walk up the hill, then hesitated and turned back around. "Just leave the food here in the ditch. I'll pick them up after I'm done scouting around up there." Then he added, almost as an afterthought. "This man's good, but he's on foot. Instead of stopping at every little town to rape and pillage, you should go as fast as you can today without stopping. He'll have to march all night long to catch up. By morning he'll be exhausted and in a hurry, more likely to make mistakes. I can exploit that."

And then Robbie turned and walked up the hill without looking back.

That day, Manny tried to do as Robbie suggested, but his men were undisciplined and it was tough to sell. The men were used to stopping at every house they saw along the highway and killing the men and raping the women. He didn't begrudge them their fun as it didn't really hurt anything, and it kept them happy and compliant. So long as Manny led them where they wanted to go, he knew they would follow. That was an immutable gang law he knew he couldn't break. So instead of fifty miles, they made only twenty miles by nightfall. He hoped to himself, *Maybe it will be enough.* But he knew, even as he thought it, that it was a hope in vain.

That morning, just as they were pulling out, the lead truck blew a front tire. When the driver got out to examine it, Manny was watching safely from one-hundred yards to the rear. He shook his head from side to side in disgust. *Don't they know by now?* The second shot came down off the hillside and the driver was knocked to the ground. The .308 match-grade bullet went through the heart and then the spine. Everyone else scrambled for cover, and soon the annoying whine of the quads drowned out all else as they raced up the hill.

Robbie had positioned himself perfectly higher up the hill and further down by only two hundred yards. Usually he didn't like getting this close; it was just too risky. But after examining and studying the sniper's ambush site yesterday morning, he knew the best shot he'd get was probably a sniper on the run. And moving targets required less recoil and a higher rate of fire. Not to mention the fact he was working under less than ideal circumstances with sub-par equipment. When Manny had come to him with the job, he'd been hesitant to accept it. Unfortunately, it had been made clear there were only two choices: kill the sniper and be richly rewarded, or turn the job down and receive a bullet for his impudence. Robbie had lost all three of his sniper rifles in the chaos following The Day, so the best he could scrounge up for this job was a stock AR-15 with a nice Leupold scope. It was better than nothing, and, along with the element of surprise, he would be able to kill his opponent.

Without the second shot into the driver, Robbie never would have seen Donny Brewster's location. It was that well hidden. As soon as he saw the tiny flash of movement, he brought up his rifle scope and cursed to himself for not being faster. The man was already on the move. Robbie tucked in his 5.56 mm semi-automatic rifle and unloaded the thirty-round magazine into the fleeing sniper.

Donny Brewster was surprised when he felt the bullet thud against his left arm, and even more surprised when another bullet came through his left ear, leaving a ragged hole. He stumbled, then ran again. Another bullet hit him in the butt, but he kept moving as bullets kicked up in the dirt all around him. After fifty yards of running into the thick woods, the bullets stopped. But Donny continued on, checking the seriousness of his wounds as he ran. He knew distance and cover was his friend at this point. If he was to survive, he'd have to put as much distance between himself and the shooter as possible.

Robbie smiled as he quickly ejected the empty magazine and shoved in another full one. By the time he'd reloaded, the target was nowhere to be seen. He was certain he'd hit the man at least once, and he struggled to maintain control as he felt his pulse quicken with anticipation. He spoke softly to himself out loud. "Don't blunder down there quickly. Stay calm. Focus. Take your time. Be smart."

He forced himself to wait thirty minutes before going down to check for blood, giving the other sniper time to bleed out. He knew instinctively that a mortally wounded man with no chance of flight was even more dangerous than one unharmed.

Finally, he slowly picked his way down the hill to the spot where Donny had been lying in wait. He saw the empty 3.08 caliber brass cartridges, and frantically searched the ground. A broad smile invaded his face when he saw the blood glistening on the leaves below. He kneeled down and looked off in the trees just to make sure he was still alone. Robbie picked up the leaf and looked at the blood from close up. He let loose with a torrent of swear words under his breath. *No bubbles. No bone!*

He hated tracking wounded game. The sniper looked down at his mediocre rifle and spit on the ground off to one side. If only his rifle was the worst of it. He could deal with that, but, more crucial, was his lack of premium match-grade ammo. All Manny's people could give him had been NATO green tip rounds, and they just zipped on through flesh without causing massive tissue damage and blood loss.

He looked at the blood trail winding off toward the woods. It was ample blood, and, if his opponent kept bleeding like that, he'd be able to track him down within a few hours. But … there was a danger. The wounded sniper had a long-range rifle, had already proven his deadly accuracy, and would be able to set up an ambush or booby traps or a series of both.

He was beginning to wish he'd taken Manny up on his offer of men and quads. Robbie could let them blunder ahead and take the first few bullets for him, while he maneuvered into position for a good, killing shot. Unfortunately, he had no radio and no time even if he did.

It was man against man, and Robbie knew he was the best.

CHAPTER 9

The Hunter becomes the Hunted

GENERAL **B**RANCH PUT THE RADIO MICROPHONE DOWN, AND walked out of his secure, private room, through the kitchen and out onto the front porch. Dan and Jeremy were already there, sitting in the rockers.

"The trick is keeping a consistent angle while you move the stone across the blade." Jeremy watched with interest as his father showed him how to sharpen a knife.

"It would be better if we had a beveled block to fasten the stone to, but we can do it this way too. Just takes longer."

Jeremy nodded, and they both looked up when Rodney walked onto the porch. Moses raised his head, but only for a moment before plopping it back down on his paws. Dan saw right away that something was wrong, but he knew better than to pry. Jeremy didn't.

"What's wrong, Uncle Rodney?"

The old general said nothing, just looked off into the woods as if they weren't there. Jeremy looked over at his father with curious eyes. Dan discreetly furled his brow and shook his head no. He carefully put the knife back into its sheath and handed it back to his son with the sharpening stone.

"Why don't you take this inside where you can work in the kitchen on a flat, stable surface? When you can wet your forearm and shave hair with it, then come on back out here and show me."

His son nodded and looked over his shoulder as he walked back into the house. As Jeremy was walking away, Dan called out after him. "And be careful! Don't cut yourself!"

Jeremy knew he was being left out of something interesting, and he didn't much like it. Once they were alone, Dan got up from his rocking chair and walked to the railing to stand next to his uncle.

"Is it something I need to know about?"

Rodney's eyes looked over at his nephew. Dan met his gaze and thought to himself, *He looks older than he did a few hours ago.* Rodney looked back out into the trees.

"Maybe. Not sure we can do anything about it though."

"Is it Donny?"

Uncle Rodney turned toward him. "How did you know?"

Dan shrugged. "Just a feeling. I've had it ever since he left. A bad feeling. Like something isn't going right for him."

The General nodded his head. "Me too. He's really good, but not the luckiest man in the world. This mission needed some luck. It's unpredictable, tough to control. Too many unknowns."

Dan frowned. "How bad is it?"

"Bad. He's hit multiple times. Not life-threatening with proper treatment. But he's being hunted."

Dan looked at him quizzically. "Hunted? By a gang?"

The old man's shoulders sagged as he leaned onto the railing. "They got them a sniper."

Dan turned away from the woods and leaned the middle of his back against the wooden porch railing. He hadn't shaved in a week, so he stroked the stubble on his cheeks thoughtfully.

"We have to go get him."

Rodney shook his head from side to side.

"Can't. Too risky in the daylight to fly the choppers down there. We need to keep a low profile. And if we drive down it'll take hours and be too late, assuming we make it at all."

He leaned his elbows up on the railing and sighed.

"No, Donny knew the risks going in."

Dan couldn't believe what he was hearing. He moved off the railing and assumed a stiff posture.

"What the hell are you talking about? That man saved my life and the lives of my family when we were dying in the snow in the Upper Peninsula!"

Uncle Rodney didn't answer right away. He turned to face his nephew, and was surprised at the determination he saw in Dan's eyes. He shrugged.

"There are larger considerations. Things more important than one man's life to worry about."

Dan had always been stocky and strong, but the hard life after The Day had strengthened and hardened him even further, on the inside as well as the outside.

"I don't care about that. He saved my life. I owe him mine. He's a Marine. I'm a Marine. There's a million reasons to go after him, and you can't give me one good reason not to, other than some obscure, unnamed story about jeopardizing the entire Midwest. I don't care about all that stuff. We got a man out there bleeding and dying while we sit back here safe and sound. That don't wash with me."

Inside Rodney smiled. *Yes, his boy was a Branch and a true leader. He had the right stuff for the times.* The old man was reminded of all those years after his brother's death when he'd been trying to raise Dan on his own. He'd always wondered if the boy was internalizing any of the lessons he'd tried to teach him. Now he knew that Dan had learned it all and then some. Parenting took faith, but standing before him now was the final product of his hard work and belief.

"Well, there might be one way we can help him …"

Dan unfolded his arms from his chest. "Okay, I'm all ears."

Running on Empty

Sergeant Donny Brewster put the radio back inside one of the many pockets of his backpack. When he'd first called, the General had been vague on whether he could get him out, but then he'd called back only fifteen minutes later with a plan. If he could elude or defeat his pursuer for the rest of the day, they could extract him by nightfall. It was an offer he was in no position to refuse.

Donny rolled over onto his side to finish cleaning out the bullet wound in his back side. Fortunately for him, the round had gone in the thick of his muscle and come out cleanly with no ripping or tearing. He shoved more alcohol-soaked gauze into the entry and exit wounds in an attempt to stem the bleeding, but the gauze was quickly saturated with blood.

Thankfully, the wound on his upper arm was more superficial than he'd first thought, and the bleeding had stopped. Donny could even use the arm so long as he was willing to endure the pain associated with movement. The hole in his ear had already clotted over for the most part, and was just a slow drip every ten seconds or so. He quickly shoved two more Tampons into the holes in his backside and taped over them.

He had to keep moving, but he also had to form a plan. Donny thought about the attack on him, and formed a quick opinion on his adversary. He was definitely ex-military, maybe even Special Forces, and not just some gang banger who'd cross-trained into marksmanship. Donny wondered to himself, *Why is this guy shooting target rounds instead of ammo that will do more damage? It doesn't make sense. He obviously knows his tactics, since he's already ambushed me so skillfully, and evaded disclosure long enough to execute the attack. His positioning was textbook perfect.*

Donny opened up a plastic bag and swallowed two more wide-spectrum antibiotic pills. No need to take chances on infection out here in the boonies, especially with wounds as serious as his own. And then Donny thought again, *His attacker's positioning had been textbook perfect.* The wounded sniper thought about that for a few seconds as he quickly packed up and moved out again. *Maybe he could exploit that?*

As he limped along through the heavy woods, Donny wondered how soon General Branch would arrive, wondered if he would arrive at all. He quickly shook his doubt away like nasty swamp water running down into his eyes. The General would come. Of course he would come. He wouldn't abandon him, wouldn't leave one of his own behind. The Shadow Militia was a brotherhood. Donny pressed on, ignoring the pain.

The Pursuer Closes in

Robbie looked up ahead and saw the empty plastic bag resting lightly on top of the dead, brown bracken fern leaves. He moved back instinctively into the shadow of the oak tree beside him. He thought to himself, *It's almost as if he placed it there so I could find it on purpose.* Like a paranoid cat, Robbie moved out slowly, turning his neck from side to side in slow motion, scanning the forest for any sign of his prey.

When he reached the plastic bag, he plainly saw the twelve-inch wide circle of blood on the dead leaf floor. A quick scan saw the leaves had been misplaced all around the area. Robbie thought to himself, *So this is where the enemy sniper had stopped to bandage his wounds and tried to halt the bleeding.* His eyes followed the trail of misplaced leaves another twenty feet through the woods, but he saw no more blood. Then his eyes rested upon the empty round cardboard tubes on the ground beside the blood. *Tampon tubes? To stop the bleeding?* Robbie remembered his battlefield first aid training and smiled. There would be less of a blood trail now, but ... still ... there would be a trail.

Robbie forced himself to move slowly through the woods, making as little noise as possible. It was very difficult to be silent while walking through the thick layer of dead, brown leaves. They were so thick and old they felt spongy beneath his feet. It had been an hour since his last respectable spot of blood, but the wounded man's movement through the early spring north woods was obvious. His prey appeared to be dragging one foot behind him as he struggled across the terrain. There were more hills now, not big ones, just small, gradual rises, but, nonetheless, they seemed to be taking their toll on the wounded sniper somewhere out in front of him. It was only a matter of time now.

Donny stopped for a moment to rest. The weight of the pack on his back, and the Crusader Broadsword rifle attached to the sling on his chest were beginning to take their toll on his stamina. He looked behind him at the trail he'd left, then he reached up and squeezed his left ear lobe to make it start bleeding again. A few drops came down onto the dried leaves.

Two hours ago, when his bleeding had halted, it had occurred to him he should simply fade noiselessly off into the woods and disappear. The General would pick him up after dark, and this episode of his life would be over. But ... there was a part of Donny that just didn't like that idea. It was the sniper part, the part of him that loved the thrill of the hunt, the part of him that had killed strangers in and out of combat, had stalked and hunted and preyed. No, there was a big part of Donny Brewster that wanted to prove he was the better man, the better soldier, and the better sniper. Something told him, something instinctive, that he *needed* to kill this person in order to stay the man he'd worked so hard to become.

Yes, fading away would be the smart, safe thing to do. Donny squeezed his earlobe again and watched the blood drip down to the leaf-covered floor. But, if Donny wanted a safe life, he could have married that pretty cheerleader, had babies and lived in the suburbs. No, Sergeant Donny Brewster didn't want to be safe. He wanted to be dangerous, indeed, thrived on it.

Sometimes he caught himself wondering what General Branch felt like, being so old, being, well, not in his prime anymore. He was reminded of that Toby Keith song, "I'm not as good as I once was, but I'm as good once as I ever was." Donny shook his head from side to side. This was as good as he would ever be, and he'd milk his abilities for all they were worth or die trying. Right now, all Donny could think of was fighting the man who'd shot him. If the man hunting him turned out to be better than him, then, so be it. Donny would die in a hail of gunfire. Better that than sitting alone in a rocking chair.

This was Donny's day, and he would prevail. He reached into his pocket and took out another 1200 milligrams of aspirin and popped them into his mouth. He quickly chewed them up and swallowed. Aspirin was a blood thinner, and he desperately needed to bleed more if his plan was going to work. He reached into his pocket and pulled out another blood-soaked gauze pad. Donny threw it onto the ground and then moved on up the hill. It was a big one. The last one.

General Branch gunned the engine of his quad and took off in a burst of speed over the field stretching out before him. Daniel was close on his heels pulling a small trailer behind his own quad. They had chosen an isolated stretch of national forest as their route down to rescue Donny Brewster. The roads were undoubtedly faster, but there was no sense in taking any chances on being spotted. Besides, once they left Iroquois County, their friends would be few and far between. In general, people had grown mighty leery of strangers in the past six months, and were more likely than not to shoot first and ask questions later.

Rodney looked down at the screen of the locator hanging from a rope around his neck. As long as Donny was still moving, they knew he was okay. All Shadow Militia, even Rodney, had a surgically implanted transponder in their back which allowed anyone with the know-how and technology to track them to within a few yards. And Donny was definitely on the move.

The old man pushed his quad even faster. The sun was well past noon, and they still had many miles to turn.

Robbie looked down at the bloody gauze pad, then up the hill. It was a steep and steady slope. He wondered how the man was still even on his feet, much less heading up that hill.

Something inside Robbie caused him to shudder. Something wasn't quite right. He looked up the hill again. The trail was clear. It was more than clear. It was obvious. That bothered him.

What if … Robbie let the thought trail on off into the setting sun. He'd been tracking this man for most of the day now. The initial blood had been profuse, but then had dried up within five hundred yards of the ambush. And it had all been dark red muscle blood. No bubbles and no bone. The drag marks were getting more serious and pronounced now, indicative of someone on their last leg, someone beginning to weaken and stiffen up, someone who had gone as far as they possibly could on the sheer strength of a powerful will. But still … *What if …*

Robbie looked up the hill and saw the pile of brush just before the peak. He stared closely, thought he saw the slightest of movement, then brought his rifle scope up to his right eye. It was confirmed. There was something moving inside that brush pile. He quickly dropped down to the woods floor and thought. Either the man was too weak to continue and was either dying or making his last stand here, or, this was a trap. Either way, the wounded man was in the brush, and Robbie had to somehow confirm his death or move in to finish him off should he still be alive and dangerous. He didn't dare go back to Manny without a confirmed kill. He knew better. Slowly, Robbie raised up his rifle and looked through the scope again. After five minutes of patient spotting, he thought he saw the bill of a baseball cap. He watched for fifteen more minutes, then he thought he made out a single dark eye socket.

Donny was in place now, lying silently, waiting, noiseless, in perfect calm, for the storm to follow. What would the other man do? Would he come up the hill? Would he shoot from there. Would he try to flank the brush pile by traversing the hill from the left or right? Donny didn't know. But … still … he waited. Why? Because that's what snipers do. They wait … and they kill.

"We have to hump the rest of the way in."

Both quads were silent now. Rodney moved off a few yards and started collecting brush to cover up his ride. Dan followed his lead and started covering up his own quad and trailer.

"How far away is he?"

Rodney answered without halting his work. "Just a few miles."

Dan nodded. "Good. We should have him safe and sound by daybreak." He placed another branch on his quad. They had to collect a lot, since the trees were still void of leaves. Dan continued. "So which way is he heading now?"

Rodney looked down at the locator hanging from his neck. Dan thought he saw a slight stutter in his uncle's movements. It wasn't pronounced, just subtle, something one would expect from anyone other than Rodney Branch. Then his movements continued as quickly as they'd halted.

"He's not moving anywhere."

"What?" Dan held the bare branch over his quad trailer as his uncle kept moving.

"You heard me. He's not moving anymore."

Dan let the branch drop, then walked over closer to his uncle. "Is he dead?"

As if in answer to Dan's question, ten shots rattled off in quick succession a few miles away. There was a pause, and then another ten shots rang out.

Dan and Rodney's eyes locked for just a moment. They both gathered up their packs and their rifles. Rodney moved into the lead, and then marched quickly down the hill with Dan close behind.

Robbie ejected his empty magazine and quickly moved to reload, but, before he could do so, he heard the gentle sound of a man laughing behind him. Robbie froze.

Rodney looked down at the locator and adjusted his course slightly to the left. They were going up a hill now, trying to be quiet, but failing miserably. Rodney cursed the dead leaves with each step. The sun was low in the sky now, causing shadows to lengthen and spread out across the woods floor, lending an eerie gloom to the panic. There had been no more gunshots, but they were almost there. According to the transponder, Donny still had not moved.

When they reached the top of the hill, Rodney held up his right hand and both men halted and dropped to the ground as if they were one person. Rodney pointed to the ground about twenty feet ahead. Dan's eyes popped open wide in disbelief. There, dangling from a rope about twelve inches off the ground was a rabbit hanging by its back legs. The rope which held him fast was draped over a tree branch. Dan's eyes followed the rope over twenty feet closer to the hill peak to a pile of brush. Every time the rabbit struggled, the brush moved.

Dan looked over at his Uncle Rodney and saw the wide smile on his face. Both men crawled up to the peak and then looked down to the bottom. They saw two men. One was on the ground on his stomach with his hands zip-tied behind his back. The other, was standing over him. Dan watched through his rifle scope as the man unzipped his fly and urinated on the helpless man's back.

Rodney laughed out loud when he heard the unmistakable voice of Sergeant Donny Brewster. "And that's for shooting me in the ass!"

CHAPTER 10

Final Preparations

SOMETIMES FRIENDSHIP CAME FROM THE MOST UNLIKELY places. Jackie smiled inside as she securely strapped baby Donna into the olive drab, military-style backpack. Such had been the case with her and Uncle Rodney. After their initial friction, he had warmed to her, at least in private, and he'd even taken a liking to her baby, bouncing the little girl on his knee, and holding her. Once, she'd even caught him making silly baby voices to her child when he thought no one was listening. He even fulfilled his promise of teaching her rifle marksmanship, and they practiced almost every day.

She crossed her arms in front of her the way Uncle Rodney had taught her, and quickly hoisted the pack up and onto her back. She adjusted the waist strap and walked over to the waiting quad. No one was allowed to use the quads without special permission from the General, but Jackie had one allocated for her private use. Why? Because she was on special assignment, by order of General Branch. And no one, not even Dan, was allowed to know what she was doing. She'd been working at it for over a week now, and it was driving her husband crazy. But that was okay. Jackie believed one of the keys to keeping a man happy was keeping him guessing. Never let him figure you out lest he take you for granted, and, above all else, every once in a while throw your man a curve ball.

But that's not why Jackie was doing this. She just wanted to help, and her personality wouldn't allow her to be shoved off onto the sidelines while the men had all the fun planning and preparing and fighting. Jackie Branch was a woman of action!

Jackie slowly mounted the quad and started it up. She reached down and massaged her mending leg. Back before The Day, she'd undoubtedly still be in a cast and on crutches. But times were different now; the need was urgent. Everyone had to pull their own weight regardless of personal sacrifice. For the first time in her life, Jackie felt beholden to the community around her, and an obligation to serve something greater than herself. Jackie had never been in the military, so she didn't realize what she was feeling was a sense of duty and honor. But even though she didn't know the right words, she knew it made her feel good.

She dropped off baby Donna at Marge Leif's house, and was quickly on her way again. Within five minutes she reached her destination. Sergeant Harold Steffens was waiting for her in his pole barn behind his house with the garage door open. She drove the quad in and turned off the engine. It took all their strength for her and the old man to pull the rope and close the door, shutting out the world to the secrets they were doing inside.

The Interrogation

"I've been trained in interrogation techniques. I should be the one who questions him."

Robbie Mankowski was now strapped to a chair in a barred cell at the county jail. On the outside, he remained defiant, but on the inside, he was trembling. He knew there would be no cavalry for him. Manny wouldn't be riding in on a white horse, and there was no hope of rescue. He was at their mercy. He looked into the eyes of Sheriff Joe Leif and saw compassion and civilization. Then he looked over at the cold, stone stare of General Branch. He didn't dare say it, but he wanted to be questioned by Joe Leif, the civilized one.

Rodney Branch walked out of the cell, and Joe Leif followed him into the outer office out of ear shot. When the General spoke, his voice was devoid of emotion. "How long will it take you?"

"Just a few days."

"That's too long. We need to know all we can about their new leader, about how they operate, about what they plan to do and how they plan to do it."

Sheriff Leif was almost pleading. He wasn't stupid. Rodney was an old friend, but he wasn't the friend he'd known all these years. For the first time in his life he wondered, *Who is Rodney Branch? What is he capable of?*

"Listen, Rodney, let's be blunt. I know darn well what will happen to this man if you question him. I know all about military style enhanced interrogation techniques, and I won't let it happen in my county on my watch."

General Branch remained stoic.

"Rodney, you told me you are here simply to advise and assist, that you respect the Constitution and my authority as the chief law enforcement officer of this county. If that's true, then you have no choice but to do it my way."

Rodney turned his eyes toward the Sheriff and smiled. "Of course, Joe. The prisoner is yours. Please call me on the radio with any information you get, so I can incorporate the intel into our defense plan."

Joe suddenly felt relieved.

"Really?"

Rodney laughed out loud.

"Of course, Joe. I'm not a barbarian. You've known me your whole life."

He paused. "The prisoner is yours. Just let me get my satchel. I left it in the cell. Then you can get busy. Please hurry though. We need to know what he knows as quickly as possible."

Rodney started to walk back to the cell. "I'll be back at my place for the rest of the day."

General Branch disappeared from view, leaving the Sheriff alone with his thoughts. *Wow! He really does respect my authority.* And then he felt guilty about doubting his friend's fidelity, his character, and his sense of right and wrong. Joe Leif bowed his head in his hands and wiped the sweat off his brow, he hadn't even realized was there. After wiping his hands on his pants, he sat down at his desk and started writing down questions. He'd interviewed dozens of criminals in his career, and he knew just how to do it. Two days tops and he'd have this man broken.

"BAM!"

Joe Leif jumped in his chair at the sound of the gun shot. It was loud, like the 45 caliber that Rodney always carried. Quickly, adrenaline shot into his bloodstream, paralyzing him in his chair for several seconds. Then he heard a scream. Not a yell, not a shout, but a primitive animal sound that caused Joe's hands to turn to ice. He jumped up and fell down onto the floor as he scrambled around his desk. The scream came again and again and again.

Finally, Joe rounded the corner and raced down the hallway to the cell. He fumbled with his sidearm, not really thinking ahead about what he might do with it. Rodney was just holstering his pistol as Joe arrived. There was sheer terror etched all over Joe's face, but General Branch radiated an eerie calm. He smiled.

"Like I said, Joe. The prisoner is all yours."

And then he walked away. Joe didn't try to stop him. He didn't dare. He looked over at the prisoner, still fastened to the chair. Robbie Mankowski was crying now, weeping like a small child. His left foot was bleeding from a large hole, the blood seeping out of his boot, forming a pool beneath him. The hilt of a three-inch folding jack knife stuck straight up from his right thigh. The blood had soaked into his pants and was now dripping onto the floor.

Joe was stunned and suddenly felt very weak. Robbie lifted up his head and began to plead with the Sheriff. And there, the worst horror revealed itself. Carved into the man's forehead was the letter "M". Blood seeped down into the man's eyes and down to his mouth as he tried to talk without sputtering.

"Please, I, have to ... talk."

Joe didn't know what to do.

"I have to get you to the doctor. Quickly or you'll bleed to death."

"NO!"

The force of the man's voice startled Joe into stasis.

"But why?"

The pain in Robbie's eyes held Joe steady like a vice.

"Please ... ask me anything. He's coming back."

And Robbie Mankowski talked for hours, even while being treated by the doctor. The Sheriff, feeling terrified, angry and a little grateful at Rodney, wrote it all down.

Making Soldiers

Dan Branch walked up and down the firing line like a sentry, barking out orders, making adjustments and suggestions on how to tighten a bullet group or operate the action of a particular weapon more efficiently. There was nothing typical about these people or their weapons. Their arsenal was more like something you'd see at a pawn shop instead of an army base. Of the twenty or so people on the line, there was a variety of AK-47 types in 7.62 millimeter and AR-15s in 223 caliber. Several people didn't own rifles or carbines, so they were shooting their deer hunting shotguns. As shotgun slugs and most other ammo types were at a premium these days, most of their practice was restricted to dry fire and lecture. He looked down on the end and saw a father and son practicing with .50 caliber muzzle loaders. Under General Branch's orders, no person was turned away regardless of training, race, gender or physical handicap. The best prepared mentally and physically would be placed on the front lines, while the rest would be held in reserve and in support positions. The latest reports now numbered the advancing horde at fifteen-hundred strong and still growing.

The horde was now in the Grayling area getting ready to make their westward turn to Traverse City. According to Donny Brewster, and the info extracted from Robbie Mankowski, the new leader of the horde was planning to set up permanent house in the rich and trendy Lake Michigan port city. Unfortunately for Dan, Iroquois was on a direct line between Grayling and Traverse City. The big port town had everything an unruly mob of cut-throats and villains could ever ask for: rich tourists with expensive toys and plush houses. Most of TC's summer residents had fled Chicago shortly after The Day in their sailboats and yachts, thinking they would be safe and comfortable in their second homes on Michigan's golden coast. This was not a good day to be wrong. They were a soft target, an isolated plum just waiting to be picked. Uncle Rodney estimated they had just one more week to train, and then their troops would have to be deployed throughout the county in accordance with the General Branch defense plan.

Dan continued with his standard lecture on firearms accuracy.

"And the sixth and most important element of marksmanship is trigger press. Indeed, according to the great Masaad Ayoob, the trigger is the heart of the beast. Master that and your group will stay small and inside the bulls-eye. The trick is to maintain a soft and gentle touch while pressing the trigger slowly and steadily directly to the rear."

The people on the line were on the ground in the prone position, dry-firing as he spoke. The intermittent sound of clicking firing pins filled the afternoon air. A mild spell in the weather had set upon them, much to Dan's delight, with temperatures nearing sixty. It wouldn't last long, but he'd take it while he could get it for sure.

"If you can squeeze the trigger without moving the front sight, while maintaining perfect sight alignment and sight picture, then you'll be inside the bull every time."

Dan looked at the plethora of people he had before him, wondering, *A week from now, which of you will still be alive?* Of course, if they failed to stop the advancing horde, then only the lucky ones would be dead. His thoughts drifted momentarily to Jackie and Jeremy and little baby Donna. What would happen to them if … he let the thought trail off into the sinking sun. He wouldn't let that happen. Marine Corps. The mission. Whatever it takes.

Dan renewed his speech with heightened vigor. Whatever happened, these people wouldn't die because he'd taught them to shoot incorrectly.

An Old Man Prepares

Harold Steffen's back was bent with age. Some mornings he could barely walk, while on others he didn't bother getting out of bed at all. After Myra's death, he'd contemplated following her quickly, indeed, had even held the revolver to his right temple and teased the trigger with a little pressure. But since he'd joined the Shadow Militia, he'd been up every morning at dawn.

The mid-morning sun streaked into the pole barn as he worked, slowly, ever so slowly. There were times when, if anyone by chance had been watching, he could have been mistaken for a store-front manikin. Harold moved the wrench slowly, tightening the bolt down as much as he could. He sighed and whispered softly to no one in particular. "The woman can finish it."

Jackie was with him almost every day now. Harold was the brains. He knew how to fix it, but he no longer had the strength. But Jackie was a strong woman, and easy to work with. She rarely talked, and Harold found that comforting. He'd never liked a woman who talked a lot. Myra had talked out of control, but his love for her had been such that he'd tolerated it for sixty-five years. Sixty-seven if you counted the courtship.

In a few days they could fire up the engine, and a few days after that would be the test flight. It was cutting it close. The horde was almost here, and Harold hadn't flown a plane in almost twelve years. Undoubtedly he would die on the runway, but … if he could … if it flew …

Harold smiled.

CHAPTER 11

The Horde Approaches

MANNY GOT OUT OF HIS BIG **H**UMMER AND STRODE CONFI-dently up to the front gate of the Grayling National Guard base. There were olive-drab-clad bodies strewn all over the tarmac, rotting in the cool northern Michigan breeze. In a few more days the smell would be overwhelming.

Major Danskill was waiting for him at the position of parade rest with his body stiff and his arms behind him, hands clasped in a military manner one over the other. There were several HumVees strategically located around the guard shack with their fifty caliber machine guns lowered, manned and ready to shoot at the first sign of betrayal.

Manny looked around at all the military hardware and drooled inside. He estimated they had about one hundred men, all heavily armed with M-16s, Squad Automatic Weapons (SAWs), frag grenades, and rocket launchers. And this was the light stuff.

If he played his cards right, he'd walk out of here armed to the teeth as the mother of all warlords. If he screwed up, well, he'd be carried out in pieces. *Note to self. Don't screw up.*

Manny was aware of the general story of what had happened here just a few days ago. Mostly because he'd been in on it from the start. Major Danskill had been a Chief of Police back before The Day and the commander of a Military Police unit here at Graying. He was a weekend warrior with two deployments in Iraq and another to Afghanistan. He'd been the unwavering servant of the United States Army for twenty years, but Manny knew something the army did not. Major Danskill had a secret vice. Well, two vices, actually. The soldier was addicted to heroin, and he had a taste for small boys, which was hardly regulation. Both hungers were insatiable and becoming increasingly difficult to feed.

Manny was here to fill that need.

★ ★ ★ ★

Corporal Mike Stanton was perched near the top of the tall Norway Pine in his Ghillie suit peering through his spotting scope at the front gate of the Grayling National Guard base. Colonel MacPherson had sent him here over a week ago to observe and report. A few days ago he'd witnessed a fire-fight, more like a massacre, as one group of National Guardsmen had slaughtered about fifty of their unsuspecting comrades. After that, it had been fairly quiet until a few minutes ago when the yellow Hummer had arrived with an entourage of Suburbans and well-armed bodyguards.

Mike watched as the leader stepped out of the Hummer and approached the gate. He spoke to the Major briefly, then was let inside. His bodyguards remained outside the gate. Corporal Stanton took as many pictures as he could with the camera attached to his spotting scope.

There was silence for thirty minutes, then three deuce and a halves pulled up to the gate and quickly drove out. A few minutes later three Bradley fighting vehicles approached the gate and were let out as well. Mike kept snapping pictures. He would send them via satellite link to the Colonel as soon as this was over.

Then he heard a rumble.

The sound got closer, then, finally, the Abrams tank came into view. The horde now had heavy armor.

Donny Brewster - Intolerable Patient

Even though she was a Registered Nurse, Lisa Vanderboeg didn't appreciate being relegated to nurse maid duties, but she did so out of loyalty to General Branch. And ... well, she had to admit ... out of curiosity as well.

The sniper man was in bed now resting, but he'd fought her all the way, wanting to get up and move around. He'd demanded to know where his rifles were, until, finally, the General had visited and calmed him down. It had been almost two weeks now, and while the other women were training, she was cleaning his wounds while watching her daughter. Although the duty was tolerable, and, some would say, even choice, Lisa didn't like waiting by idly as the horde advanced on her daughter.

She looked over into the corner where Sam was playing. Samantha was a miniature copy of herself, or so people told her, with her long, flowing blonde hair, but sporting the curls of her father. The thought of Lisa's husband caused her to wince. Jim had died shortly after The Day at their home in Grand Rapids. But prior to that Jim had been forced to watch as the men had raped his wife. But, for Lisa, the rape had been nothing compared to the pain in her husband's eyes as he was forced to look on help-lessly while two men violated her. At least Sam had been spared.

That same night, after her rape, while the two fiends slept in the other room, Lisa was able to loosen the rope around her wrists. She'd quickly untied Jim, who went into the next room with a busted chair leg. The first man was beaten to a pulp, and Jim had just started in on the second intruder when a shot rang out. The bullet hit him in the hip, breaking the pelvic bone. Jim had gone down instantly. He tried desperately to get up, but couldn't. The man raised his gun to fire again, but Lisa had picked up the chair leg and slammed it into his head. The lag bolt, still fastened to the wood, had pierced the man's eye and driven itself into his brain. He'd died quickly. Jim, on the other hand, had taken three days to pass on, forcing Lisa to watch helplessly. None of her medical training could be brought to bear, simply for lack of supplies and equipment. Lisa and Samantha had cried over his dead body, then held a funeral in their back yard. Sam had taken a lock of her father's hair. They'd left the next day, trying to make it out of Grand Rapids to the north where Jim had relatives.

If not for Jason Little and his family, they would have died for sure. They'd never made it to Jim's relatives, but now, thanks to General Branch, Iroquois was now their home. General Branch had given them sanctuary and a place for her to raise her daughter. Lisa was beholden, and she would pay her debt, whatever the cost, so long as her child could have a shot at a happy future.

"So what's on your pretty mind today, ma'am?"

Lisa came out of her thoughts and looked over at Donny Brewster's perpetual grin. She just wanted to slap him. In another life she might have found him attractive, perhaps even welcomed his flirting, but not today.

"How are you feeling?"

Samantha heard his voice and came over to the bed.

"We've been waiting for you to wake up Mr. Donny."

Donny smiled at five-year old little Samantha. She'd become his special friend and near-constant companion over the past few weeks, much to the displeasure of her mother.

"Well, I'm feeling pretty good today, especially now that you're here."

Samantha smiled. "Are you ready to fight bad guys again?"

Donny laughed and reached back to rub his wound. Then he nodded. "I think I'm getting pretty close. If it's okay with your mommy I'd like to move around a bit and maybe even try to walk." Donny looked out of the corner of his eye to Lisa, but she was stone-cold sober as ever. Donny thought to himself, *If I could just get her to smile ... she would be so attractive. I wonder what happened to her?* Donny hadn't admitted it yet, but he was indeed truly smitten by his young nurse. Despite her melancholy demeanor, Lisa Vanderboeg was a sharp woman, and putting Donny in the same room with her for two weeks was a recipe for romance.

But she didn't seem interested. In fact, she'd rebuffed every subtle advance he'd made. "Nurse Lisa? What do you think? Can I try walking today?"

Lisa thought to herself, *Sure, go ahead. Let's start with a long walk off a short pier.* But out loud she said, "Sure. I think you're ready." In truth, Lisa wanted him up and around as quickly as possible for two reasons: the first being she wanted him to fight the horde to help save her child. Whatever else Donny might be, she knew he was a great warrior. She'd heard from the other girls that he'd killed over fifty men on his latest mission. That intrigued the warrior part of her that had taken root and grown steadily over the past few weeks. Lisa had been changing. The rape of herself, and the murder of her husband had fractured her, and she felt like two people. There was the warrior Lisa, and there was the mother Lisa. She didn't like feeling diametrically opposed to herself.

So, with Samantha's help, Donny sat up and swung his feet out onto the floor. Lisa watched the initial pain ebb across the man's face. Then, as if he had the power to turn it off, the look of pain went away. Donny smiled. "It feels great." Little Sam placed her tiny hand in his own as Sergeant Brewster raised himself up, placing his full weight on his legs. Lisa thought she saw the look of pain again, but it went away as quickly as it had come. The perpetual smile stayed there.

Donny slowly walked around the room with the five-year-old girl leading him. Then he stopped and looked down at Samantha. "Would you like to dance, Miss Sam?"

The little girl's eyes lit up like sparkling blue water. She politely nodded and gave a little curtsy. "Why yes, Sergeant Brewster. May I lead?"

Donny laughed and extended both his hands downward. "Of course. After you, my lady."

Lisa watched in awe as her little daughter danced around the room with a deadly sniper. Both of them laughed as they danced. Suddenly, Lisa smiled, and then she cried. Donny looked over and saw the tears streaming down the woman's face. He quickly bent down to his dance partner. "My lady, I've enjoyed the dance, but I'm afraid I have to rest now. Would you mind if I spoke with your mother alone about my medical condition. Just for a few minutes."

Samantha took a step back and curtsied. She looked over at her mother, saw the tears and ran to her arms. "What's wrong Mommy?" The two girls embraced and held each other for several seconds. Donny watched on, feeling like he was invading their personal space.

"I'm fine, honey. Why don't you go downstairs and play with the Legos. Build me something good, and I'll be down in a few minutes to check it out."

Sam kissed her mother, then ran to Donny and kissed him on the cheek as well. "You are a splendid dancer Mr. Donny."

Donny laughed out loud. "As are you, my lady."

The little girl backed away and pranced out of the room leaving the two adults to talk about things she neither understood nor cared about. When she was gone, Lisa wiped the tears away and looked coldly at Sergeant Brewster.

"I want you to stay away from my daughter."

Donny's smile quickly faded.

"Excuse me?"

Lisa turned her head toward the window. "You heard me. I don't want her getting close to you."

Donny's shoulders sagged, and he moved back over to the bed. The look of pain returned to his face, and this time it stayed.

"Why are you saying this? I like your daughter. She's a wonderful person, and you could be too, if you let yourself."

Lisa stared out at the bare branches on the oak tree in her new front yard. They were swaying mildly in the breeze.

"She's been through enough already. I don't want her bonding to a man who will probably be dead inside a week. She doesn't need that."

Another smile slowly reached his lips, then like the tide, it pushed in until it conquered his face. "You don't want *her* to bond with me, or you're afraid *you* will bond with me?"

Donny got up off the bed again and walked over to Lisa. He was wearing grey, cotton sweatpants and a blue T-shirt. On the front it said, "If God wanted us to be vegetarians, broccoli would be more fun to shoot." Donny stopped a mere twelve inches away from her face. *She has the most beautiful, blue eyes.*

"You know you like me."

Lisa turned back, but now her blue eyes had turned to fire and rage. Her hand flashed out and slapped him across the face, leaving the red imprint of her fingertips on his cheek.

"I want you out of here as quickly as possible. You obviously are feeling much better. Just get out there and kill people. It's obviously what you enjoy most. It's who you are!"

The pain in Donny's eyes was apparent. Even while she was saying the words, Lisa regretted it. But she couldn't stop herself. Nonetheless, she felt guilty and softened just a bit. "Will you just get out there and save us from the horde?"

Donny's smile suddenly returned, as if it had never left. He slowly got down on one knee, reached up and took her hand in his own. Lisa stiffened as Donny gently kissed the hand that had struck him.

"As you wish, my lady."

Then Donny stood. He backed away, never taking his eyes off Lisa's face. He reached the bed and sat down while putting on his shoes. When he was done, he stood back up and walked out of the room.

CHAPTER 12

Battle Plans

THEY WERE BACK AT THE COURTHOUSE CONFERENCE ROOM, and Colonel MacPherson stood ramrod straight as he clicked the remote, advancing the PowerPoint presentation one more slide. The electric cord came down off the projector into a power inverter which in turn ran cables to a car battery on the tile floor. The Colonel was wearing heavily starched, olive-drab fatigues. A Colt forty-five caliber 1911 pistol was snapped securely in his strong-side retention holster.

"The Horde is advancing now from Grayling at an alarming pace. If nothing is done to slow the march, they'll reach the outskirts of Iroquois City in two days time."

The picture of a long convoy was being projected onto the wall in front of them. Someone had pinned a sheet over the conference room window to darken the room. The convoy stretched out over a mile. It contained military HumVees, deuce and a half trucks, civilian semi-trailers, U-haul trailers, a couple of gas tankers, and Dan thought he even saw a Toyota Prius near the back.

Colonel MacPherson advanced the slide and Dan could hear the audible rush as everyone in the room caught their breath. Further back in the column were three Bradley Fighting vehicles and an Abrams M1 tank weighing over sixty tons.

"But that's not the biggest problem."

The Colonel paused for effect. "The Horde now has heavy armor as well as three Bradley Fighting Vehicles. The forward armor on an M1 of this kind is 600 millimeters thick. It has a laser-guided targeting system, accurate out to 8,000 meters. It's only real vulnerability is from the air, but that involves capabilities that Iroquois County forces do not currently possess."

He looked around at all present, but no one spoke. They appeared to be stunned into silence.

"Now the Bradleys are a different matter. They have sufficient armor to ward off any attack by small arms, and their strength lies in their speed. They can traverse open terrain at a speed of well over forty miles per hour. They could be used as cavalry to outflank any traditional attack or defense, followed up quickly by more infantry to mop up."

General Branch looked around the table, quickly assessing their mood. Dan appeared stone-faced. Sergeant Brewster was smiling. Sheriff Leif looked like a deer in the headlights of a Peterbilt. Rodney smiled in satisfaction. He already knew they could do it, but he wanted Joe to squirm a bit after all the crap he'd been given for torturing his prisoner.

Rodney put on his poker face and looked over at Sheriff Leif. "What do you think we should do, Joe?"

Sheriff Leif looked surprised. He glanced down at the Formica table top in front of him. "I still say we should use your helicopter gunships to take them all out. That would be so much easier."

General Branch nodded. "Yes, it would be easier. We could complete the operation in a few hours time and neutralize The Horde forever."

Joe's brow tightened. "But you're not going to do that, are you, Rodney."

Uncle Rodney shook his head from side to side. "I already told you, Joe. We can't do it. And even if I could, there are down sides. This is an excellent opportunity for Iroquois County to cut her teeth in battle."

The Sheriff scoffed out loud. "Cut our teeth! Are you crazy? That's an M1 tank! We can't stand up to that thing! It'll drive straight into town and tear us apart!"

Rodney leaned back in his chair. He let out a heavy sigh. Sometimes Joe discouraged him beyond repair.

"Joe, it's only one tank. Now if there were two squadrons of them, then maybe you'd have reason to gripe. But I can teach Jeremy how to take out one lone tank."

Colonel MacPherson nodded. "Absolutely. One tank is nothing. Sure, we'll have to deal with it, but we can give you a plan and the know-how. You just need the courage to execute it. I'm more concerned with the Bradleys than I am the tank."

General Branch stood up and stretched the muscles in his back. Every once in a while, out of habit, he still reached into his breast pocket for a cigarette. He guessed he'd be doing that for the rest of his life, however long or short that might be.

"The way I see it, Joe, we have three phases in our defense to plan. The first two are strictly offensive in nature. One, take out the tank and the Bradleys. Two, wound as many of their infantry as possible. And three, prepare the city for attack."

The Sheriff's head came up in a questioning glance. "Wound them? Why are we wounding them? Shouldn't we be killing them?"

Colonel MacPherson cut in. "Negative, sheriff. Wounding is desirable in this situation. Our tactic is to slow their advance. If we kill a man, he drops and is left behind. If he's wounded, the others are forced to stop and deal with him. Our strategy has always been one of attrition. Buy time, harass their column, depress their morale, make them nervous as hell. All these things when put into a coordinated action will seriously degrade the ability of The Horde."

Dan had been intent on every word from the others in the room. Now he looked up. "But these guys are ruthless. What makes you think they'll stop to render medical attention to their fallen comrades?"

General Branch answered his question. "They won't help them, Dan. They'll shoot them and leave them behind. But that's one more bullet they can't use against us."

The Colonel smiled. "And when done over the course of two days, shooting their own people will degrade morale. That's what we want; to lessen their capability as a fighting unit. They're already a rabble of undisciplined men, and that's a good thing for us. But if we can strike fear and cause desertions, that helps us even more."

Uncle Rodney sat back down again. "I won't blow pretty colored smoke up your ass, Joe. This is going to be tough, and if even a few hundred of The Horde gets through ... well, it won't be pretty on the population of the town."

Dan broke in. "So, basically, we have to stop them all. We have to kill almost two thousand cut-throats and murderers in order to save our women and children."

Rodney looked over at Colonel MacPherson, who then looked over at Sheriff Leif. Joe Leif hung his head.

"I don't know if we can do it." His fear hung in the air like the stench of infection.

Donny Brewster had been silent until now. He'd been thinking about Lisa and little Samantha, and Jackie and baby Donna. Finally, he stood to his feet.

"Permission to speak candidly, General?"

Rodney nodded his consent. "I expect no less from you, Sergeant."

Donny pointed at the tank on the screen. "I'll take out the tank and the Bradleys sometime in the next twenty-four hours. I'll just need a lightly armed fire team and a few more goodies."

Colonel MacPherson looked over at General Branch. Dan could tell they were doing their military mind-meld thing again. Finally, the Colonel nodded his consent. "Very well, Sergeant Brewster. Have the plan written out for me in four hours, and I'll see you have the men and materiel you need for the mission."

Donny laughed out loud. "Begging the Colonel's pardon, sir. I don't need men. I need women."

This comment raised even the General's eyebrow. Joe Leif opened his mouth to speak, but quickly shut it again. He knew better than to call Donny Brewster, their sniper messiah, into question. If it hadn't been for Donny Brewster, The Horde would have reached them weeks ago.

The Colonel smiled too. "This should be interesting."

Sheriff Leif broke the silence. "That leaves the second phase, wounding as many of The Horde as possible." He hesitated. "I want to do it."

Dan looked up with surprise in his eyes. He hadn't expected that one. But General Branch was not caught off guard. He immediately countered.

"You can't, Joe. We need you here to coordinate and lead the defense of the town, phase three. People here know you and respect you. I'm afraid they still see me as a bit of a lunatic. You are the man they feel comfortable with. They'll follow you. You have to rise to the occasion and inspire them to fight."

Joe looked over, not knowing exactly what to say. He thought to himself, *Am I being insulted or praised?* Dan rescued him from his internal dilemma.

"I want to lead phase two. Donny can help me set up a plan. But I've been helping to train most of the recruits, and I know their abilities. I can pick the right people for the right job."

Colonel MacPherson looked over at the General, who let out a heavy sigh and looked down at the table top. He'd had every intention of leaving Dan behind to help coordinate the town's defense. But the moment Dan had spoken the words, he'd known it was the right thing to do. Dan had the training. He had the courage and he'd already proven himself in battle. Donny Brewster was undoubtedly the best qualified to handle it, but he'd have his hands full taking out the armor. Rodney looked over and met the Colonel's gaze. The General nodded and only then did the Colonel speak.

"It's decided then. In four hours time we'll meet back here. The three of you will have written plans describing your intentions in every detail. I want logistical needs, manpower requirements, time schedules, the whole shebang."

The Colonel stood to his feet. He cast an imposing shadow across the dimly lit room. "Any questions?"

The men looked at each other, realizing they now stood on the cusp of history. They would either live or die tomorrow based on decisions they made today. It was a sobering thought.

Donny Brewster was the only one smiling.

Four hours later they all met again. Rodney and the Colonel went over the plans privately, then met with each one individually. They asked questions, pointed out flaws, and played devil's advocate. The end result was the initial battle plans became much stronger.

Joe's plan needed the most help as he had no military experience. In the end, General Branch assigned Colonel MacPherson to work with Joe one on one to hone the plan and make it better. They worked well into the wee hours of the morning. But in the end, even the Colonel was happy with Joe's plan.

While everyone else scattered about to prepare for their phases of the operation, Rodney went back to his house and talked to Jackie. They left baby Donna in Jeremy's care and both hopped on quads. Jeremy looked after them, listening to the sounds of their fading engines, jealous, almost angry at being left out of the action.

When they both reached Harold Steffen's pole barn, Uncle Rodney shook his head in disappointment.

"It's not ready yet?"

Harold looked tired. He'd been working twelve hours a day on the plane, and it was taking its toll on his eighty-some year-old body. Jackie stood nervously off to one side.

"I'm not the man I used to be, General. I just can't move fast enough."

General Branch smiled while standing stiff and proud beside him. He would never let on his disappointment. He thought for a moment.

"You just need an experienced mechanic to help finish the delivery system? Someone with youth and strength?"

Harold smiled. "Well, I suppose so. But youth and strength is a lot when you don't have much of either."

The General forced himself to laugh out loud. "No worries, Sergeant Steffens. Colonel MacPherson's helicopter pilot is still here. I'll send him over right away. He's a captain, but I'm giving you tactical command of this mission. It's all going to rest on your shoulders, Sergeant."

Harold smiled. Then he nodded. "Yes, sir. You can count on me, sir."

Rodney made a call on his radio, then he left Jackie and Harold behind to finish their work. If they failed, there was still a chance to defeat The Horde. But if they succeeded? So many lives would be saved.

CHAPTER 13

Donny's Crazy Plan

SERGEANT DONNY BREWSTER STOOD AT THE HEAD OF THE courthouse conference room as he gave his briefing. Eight women were seated around the table, while Sheriff Leif and General Branch were seated against the wall behind them as observers.

"The Bradley Fighting Vehicle's main armament is a 25 mm cannon. It fires up to 200 rounds per minute and is accurate up to 2500 meters. To compliment that are twin missiles capable of destroying tanks at a range of over two miles. The Bradley also has a 7.62 mm machine gun, just to the right of the M242 25 mm chain gun."

Donny pressed the remote button and the PowerPoint slide advanced to show a different view of the Bradley Fighting Vehicle. He pressed the button again and again, each time showing close-ups of the equipment he was describing.

"The Bradley is also equipped with a TOW missile system for use against tanks and other armored vehicles."

One of the girls raised her hand, so Donny stopped talking and pointed to her.

"What exactly does TOW mean?"

"TOW stands for Tube-launched, Optically-tracked, Wire command data link, guided missile, not that it matters."

The girl shrugged and added sheepishly, "I'm so glad I asked."

Donny continued without further interruption.

"The Bradley weighs approximately 30 tons and is protected with explosive reactive armor, which means anything we have to shoot at it will bounce off like eggs on brick."

He looked around the table and smiled.

"And those are the easy targets. The real challenge is going to be destroying an M1 Abrams tank. It's long been the main battle tank of the United States for good reason. Here are the specs."

Donny pushed the remote button again and another slide came up showing all the details of the Abrams.

"The Abrams weighs just over sixty tons, give or take a few. In combat it has a four-man crew, though I expect The Horde is still trying to figure out how to train enough men to operate it. The hull and turret armor is about six hundred millimeters thick, too tough for anything we have."

Lisa was sitting near the front. Her initial reunion with Donny had been clumsy, but professional. Much to her surprise, he had requested her for this mission.

"The primary armament is a 105 mm rifled cannon. For support it has three machine guns, one in fifty cal and two in 7.62 millimeter. So, as you can see, it's pretty tough to take out while operating in battle mode.

"The M1 is powered by a Honeywell AGT1500C multi fuel turbine engine with fifteen hundred horsepower. The tank can travel at a maximum speed of thirty-five miles per hour on tarmac and twenty-five off road."

Sergeant Brewster looked around the room. No one spoke. Several women had their heads down. One had tears in her eyes. Lisa broke the silence.

"So how are we going to kill these things? They sound indestructible."

Donny smiled, showing all his bright, white teeth.

"And that's the million-dollar question isn't it? How do we defeat an enemy with heavy armor when all we have are small arms and a few grenades?"

Donny advanced to the next slide. It showed a four-man tank crew in full battle dress standing atop the Abrams.

"The answer to your question is simple. We hit them in their weakest spot, which, for a man, is located directly below the waist."

Donny used the red dot of the laser pointer until it rested on the groin area. He moved it slowly from one man to the next. When he looked up, Lisa was staring at him in horror. When she spoke her anger was obvious.

"You are using us as sex objects? You want us to have sex with these animals to give you long enough to disable these things?"

Donny's smile faded.

"Well, it sounds unreasonable when you word it like that. I just want you to create a diversion. I need only ten minutes. The sex is optional."

Lisa ground her teeth together. General Branch looked on from the back, trying to gauge the wisest response. Sheriff Leif squirmed uncomfortably in his chair beside Rodney. He'd voted against the mission altogether. Rodney decided now was the time to intervene. He stood up and strode confidently to the front.

"Sit down, Sergeant Brewster."

Donny was more than happy to comply. Rodney took a deep breath and then launched into his speech.

"Listen, Ladies, I know this isn't what you were expecting, and none of you have to go through with this. I realize we're asking a lot. If things go bad all of you could be raped or tortured or killed outright. I understand that. But we're desperate here and we need to use all weapons at our disposal, even if that weapon happens to be sexist, dangerous or politically incorrect." He paused. "You've all heard the phrase, 'All's fair in love and war?' Well, sometimes love and war intersect, and that's where you beautiful ladies come in. If I could use men I would, but … I just don't think it'll work as well."

He stopped talking, not knowing what more to say. Like so many other battle plans of his past, it had all made so much sense on paper. But then you add the human element, and things break down.

A slender, well-built brunette was the first to speak. "So, are these guys cute or are they dogs?"

The question caught General Branch off guard. "I'm not sure. We don't have that level of intelligence on the tank crew."

Lisa looked at him and shook her head from side to side. Finally, she spoke up again. "I hate to admit it, but it's a good plan, all things considered."

Another girl, this one a redhead sounded appalled when she responded. "What? Are you crazy? Lisa, they want us to have sex with these lunatics!"

The good-looking blonde laughed out loud. "Get off your self-righteous high horse, Emma. I know darn well you've had plenty of sex before, probably even the rough stuff."

The redhead seemed offended, but clamped her mouth shut without responding. The General continued.

"Ladies, we've been giving you special training for a reason. All those hand-to-hand moves we've been teaching you, and the knife-fighting techniques; they were for this purpose. Each of you is uniquely qualified to accomplish this mission. And if it works, you'll have saved thousands of lives. Men, women, children. All innocent people will live because you did this." He hesitated. "But it's strictly voluntary. Any one or all of you can say no, and none of us will think the lesser of you. We won't tell a soul."

Another woman, middle-aged, attractive, a little on the chubby side asked one last question. "What happens if we don't do this?"

General Branch hesitated, as if finding the words to use, but then he just blurted it out. "If you say no, then we send thirty men to take the armor crews out by force. It will be bloody on both sides, and the chances for success go down exponentially. Plus, there will be no way to get the men out after the armor is destroyed."

"So they'll all die?"

Rodney met Lisa's gaze. He nodded silently. Lisa swallowed the lump in her throat. It went down hard. The General spoke again.

"We're going to leave the room now. You ladies go ahead and talk it over amongst yourselves. We'll be waiting outside when you're ready to give us your answer."

With that, the three men got up and walked out the door. It closed behind them with an echo that pierced Lisa to her core.

☆ ☆ ☆ ☆

"So why did you choose me? Why am I part of the Bradley crew?" Lisa added sarcastically. "Aren't I attractive enough to make the cheerleading squad?"

Sergeant Brewster ignored her question. "Please focus, Miss Vanderboeg. You have just a few hours to learn to operate an M242 Chain gun and an M240C 7.62 millimeter machine gun. It's not easy."

She snapped back at him. "Don't ever call me 'Miss'! It's Mrs. Vanderboeg to you!" She paused, but Donny said nothing. "Now tell me, why did you choose me for this? I want to know."

Donny turned back toward her and placed the remote on the table beside him. He wanted to get through this. He wanted her to learn and prepare for the mission. Yeah, sure, he had some hormones ablaze for her, but this was a mission where people were going to die, and many more would die if they failed. He calmly began his explanation.

"*Mrs* Vanderboeg, you were chosen because the testing we gave you revealed you best qualified to serve as crew for the Bradley Fighting vehicle we're going to use in the attack. You have the night vision of an owl, and your eyes adjust quickly to night flash. Both are good characteristics in a night-time firefight, especially with a high-caliber machine gun."

Donny wondered if he should tell her the rest. She settled the question for him.

"What else. That's not all. I can tell you're holding something back."

Donny smiled impatiently. Then he nodded. "Sure. There are two other things: First, you have a little girl and she needs you. The other girls are single and never been married, so if they die, they won't be leaving anyone behind. I'm not saying being on the Bradley crew ensures your safety, quite to the contrary. This is a very dangerous mission with a high chance of failure. However, you will stand a better chance if you're on the Bradley. Second, we know of your history. You've already been raped once before, and I doubt your psyche could handle it again."

Lisa sat stunned into silence. She squirmed back and forth in her chair. Finally, she spewed her next sentence haltingly. "So … the other girls are … going to… die?"

Sergeant Brewster looked down at the ground and said nothing. What could he possibly say to make her feel better? He felt like they were using these women, and that went against the grain of manhood for him. They should be protecting the women, not sending them into battle. He'd only mentioned the idea to General Branch because he believed for sure it would be thrown out. But the General had latched onto it enthusiastically. "No free rides," he'd said. "The women have to pull their weight, and this plan is tactically sound. They'll never see it coming. It will save lives."

Lisa's eyes started to mist over, but then Donny watched as something else happened to her. Within a few seconds her face turned to granite, and the mist was instantly gone. He watched her grit her teeth with a mighty resolve.

"Show me the training film again. I want to watch it a hundred times if I have to."

Donny nodded and suddenly felt a new respect for her. Lisa watched the film over and over and over again, until, finally, operating the gun, loading it and clearing a jam became almost second nature to her.

After two hours straight, Donny was starting to believe his plan had a chance for success.

CHAPTER 14

Dan Readies his Team

"DAN I WANT YOU TO BE EXTRA CAREFUL. YOU'RE GOING to be very vulnerable out there for a few days or even more, depending on how successful you are. And you're going to be all alone. We won't be able to get help to you, at least not very quickly."

Dan smiled and flashed his uncle a snappy Marine Corps salute. His Uncle Rodney scoffed at him. "I told you, son, we're in a war zone! Stop saluting me!"

Dan and the hundred men behind him were all dressed in various brands and patterns of hunting camo. They all carried different weapons ranging from high-powered sniper rifles to primitive bows and arrows. The newly commissioned Major Branch had organized them into fire teams, squads and platoons. They were a hodge-podge group to be sure, poorly armed, and not quite ready for prime time battle, but Dan didn't question their resolve. He'd picked them not for their age and fitness, but for their skills and their fighting spirit. Dan wanted people he knew wouldn't turn tail and run, and he didn't much care about their gender or their age. Many of them, and he didn't know exactly how many, would fight bravely and die.

He'd said goodbye to his family a few hours ago, and it hadn't gone well. Jackie had been furious that he'd volunteered, and Jeremy had been angry that he was being left behind. In the end, Dan knew the only way to improve his relationship with his wife was to come home alive, and he fully intended to make his wife happy.

"Godspeed, Daniel. You'd better come back here in one piece. Don't you dare leave me at home with all that youth and estrogen, because I just can't handle that."

Major Branch smiled and gave his uncle and commanding general a manly embrace. "Roger that, general. I'll try not to disappoint you."

With that, Dan turned and addressed his soldiers.

"All right, let's head on out. We've got clicks to turn and Horde to kill."

They force-marched down the road at a furious pace. The lead platoon carried a Gadsden flag with the words "Live free or die" at the bottom. It blew in the slight breeze, rippling as the force went on their way, with nothing but the dissonant sound of boots on gravel taking the place of a professional cadence.

✮ ✮ ✮ ✮

That night, after taking a full day to get his fire team in place, Sergeant Brewster peered down at The Horde's encampment. The sun was setting low and they were already settling in for the night. Donny couldn't help but notice the differences in the opposing force. Somehow, they'd become more disciplined, more regimented and effective. He couldn't help but wonder if Manny, this new leader, was even more dangerous than the one he'd killed weeks before.

He brushed the worry aside. It didn't matter. He was a Marine, and all that concerned him was the mission. He looked over at Lisa lying on the ground beside him, while the other three women provided flank security. She was a beautiful woman in a lot of different ways. He chastised himself for thinking about it. *I'm on a mission. Focus! The mission! Focus!*

"What does it look like?"

Donny said nothing. He simply handed her the binoculars and pointed five hundred yards down the hill at their objective. Lisa sucked in her breath. "Wow! That's a big tank."

Donny chuckled to himself. "No kidding. And the Bradleys aren't small either."

Lisa lowered the binoculars. She had camo grease all over her face. So did Donny, and when he smiled, all she could see was white in the fading light. They talked as they waited for the sun to go down.

"So, are you scared?"

Donny couldn't help but think to himself, *I love a beautiful woman in camo and face paint. It doesn't get any sexier than that.* Lisa thought for a moment before answering him.

"I don't know. Guess I just feel kind of numb inside right now. The only real fear I have is not making it back to Sam."

Donny nodded, and a slight sadness moved over his face. She sensed the change. "What's wrong?"

Donny pasted the grin back onto his face, but Lisa saw right through it. "Tell me what's wrong. I want to know."

The smile faded like the setting sun. Finally, Donny let his head drop down. "I don't know. I guess I envy you."

Lisa cocked her head to one side. "Excuse me?"

Donny nodded. "Yeah. I've been on so many missions, been shot at so many times, that I never stop to think about what I have waiting for me at home."

Lisa raised the binoculars again. She scanned the encampment, then lowered them again. "So, who do you have waiting for you at home. And where exactly is home?"

Donny raised his head up again and took the binoculars from her. "No one's ever waiting for me. And home is where my rifle is."

Lisa tried to look into his eyes, but he turned away. "That is so sad, Donny."

"Call me Sergeant Brewster."

Lisa laughed a little bit too loud.

"A little comic relief. I like that in a man."

For the next half hour they watched the camp set up. Donny took note where the sentries were posted outside the camp. He'd already taught the girls how to crawl quietly, and he knew from his last visit that a mixture of rock and country music would be playing loud enough to drown out the sound of their movements. And, if that wasn't enough, the gas and diesel generators were sure to help.

Finally, the sun was down, and they formed up and began the long, slow crawl into position. Donny couldn't help but wonder, *Are we crazy? Is there any real possibility this plan will work?* He didn't know it, but Lisa was thinking the same thing.

☆ ☆ ☆ ☆

Two miles further west, Major Branch and his three platoons of Iroquois County militia had just reached their ambush site. He set his men to work digging in. A man walked up to Dan, started to salute, but quickly recovered.

"Sorry, Dan. Force of habit, I guess."

It was completely dark now, but they'd gathered on the edge of a swamp, surrounded on three sides by high ground where they could use small amounts of artificial light without being seen.

"Did you get them all planted, Larry?"

Captain Larry Jackson was an old man by Dan's standards, but he was knowledgeable on the ways and skills of battle, more specifically, demolitions and guerilla warfare.

"You got that right, Danny boy. They come through here after us and they'll be in for one helluva surprise!"

Dan nodded. "Good. What about the roads?"

Larry nodded, but Dan couldn't see him in the darkness.

"All covered. They'll get through it, but they'll do so slowly, and we'll take a few out in the process."

Dan nodded up the hill. "Larry, you oversee the defenses while I head up that hill to get a gander."

Larry nodded. "Yes sir, Major Branch."

Dan chuckled at the way his old friend said it. When Dan had grown up, Larry had already been an adult. Now, Dan was leading him into battle as his superior. But Dan wasn't the kind to let it go to his head.

"Hey, Dan. You'd better take someone with you for flank security. We shouldn't take any chances tonight."

Dan smiled in the darkness. Then he thought to himself, *Yes, I'm the Major, but this guy has more experience. A wise man would do well to listen to him.*

"Roger that. Send me two quiet men."

A few minutes later the three soldiers moved as quietly up the hill as possible. Dan was amazed at how hard it was to move through the brush without making noise. Even after seven months without civilization, most of them still hadn't rediscovered the primitive art of moving through the woods.

When they reached the top, Dan dropped down onto his belly and looked out at the bonfires and lights. His two guards spread out to his left and right. He could faintly hear the generators and what appeared to be the sound of ZZ Top singing *Sharp-dressed Man*. It seemed so out of place to him. Then he realized how long it had been since he'd heard music. It had been that night on his way to Eagle River in Wisconsin.

He sang the song softly, just barely audible now. "Bye, bye Miss American Pie, drove my Chevy to the levy but the levy was dry. Them good ole boys was drinkin' whiskey and rye, singin' this'll be the day that I die. This'll be the day that I die."

He'd almost died that night. It seemed so long ago and far away. The wind changed directions and picked up speed, carrying the song to him on the wings of the night. "Every girl's crazy 'bout a sharp-dressed man."

Suddenly, the old world seemed so shallow to him. Dan looked off to his right where the paved road led up the hill. To the right of that is where Donny and his girls would be coming, assuming any of them lived through the battle.

Major Branch closed his eyes for a moment and imagined himself snuggling in bed with his wife. He always liked to press his stomach up to Jackie's back and drape his right arm over her side until his hand rested on her stomach. *He couldn't help but wonder, Will I ever do that again?*

He heard someone issue a command down below. He watched for a few more minutes, then gathered his guards and moved down the hill to quiet them down. It was going to be a very long night.

✮ ✮ ✮ ✮

Back at Iroquois City, Sheriff Joe Leif and General Branch sat at the county jail monitoring the radio, hoping for information on how the mission was progressing. But the radio was silent.

"Why aren't they talking to us, Rodney? Don't they know we're sitting back here wanting to know what's going on?"

Rodney involuntarily reached for his left breast pocket for the cigarettes that were no longer there. He hated the waiting.

"They were ordered to maintain radio silence. We have to assume The Horde is monitoring radio traffic now that they have sophisticated comm gear inside the Bradleys and the Abrams. It's not worth the risk just to make the commanders feel good."

The Sheriff nodded his understanding, but he didn't much like it. Joe was staring down at the floor, then he got that eerie feeling that comes only when one feels he's being watched. He looked up quickly and saw Rodney's eyes fixed on him with a grimness that made him shudder. Joe squirmed.

"What?"

Rodney shrugged it off and turned away.

"It's nothing."

Joe cocked his head to one side.

"It is too, something. Now what are you thinking about?"

The General sat up straight in the cheap folding chair and crossed one leg over the other.

"I was just thinking about Robbie, the sniper we interrogated."

The Sheriff nodded. "And?"

Rodney dropped his crossed leg down onto the floor again before speaking. "And, I was just wondering why you didn't give me more grief about it. I expected you to try to arrest me or something. But you did your best at chewing me out, and then you let it go."

Sheriff Leif smiled. "Why is it always the same with you military guys born for greatness?"

Rodney cocked his left eyebrow in curiosity. "Excuse me?"

"You know what I mean, Rodney, so don't be faking humility on me now. I've known you my whole life, and deep down inside, even though you lived right here in this podunk little town, I knew you were different than the rest of us. I knew darn well you were going to do something great or crazy. I didn't know what, and, quite frankly, just between you and me I expected it to be against the law."

Joe shook his head from side to side. "And I guess, according to the old rules, it is against the law, but ..." He let the sentence trail off.

"Are you telling me you thought I was a madman? A lunatic?"

Sheriff Leif laughed to himself. "Hell, Rodney, I still think you're a lunatic. After you shot that guy and cut him and stabbed him? I think you removed all doubt on that one. Right about now crazy and reckless is your defining characteristic."

Rodney didn't say anything. He just waited for Joe to finish speaking his mind.

"But I gotta tell ya, Rodney, even though the things you do are against everything I was trained for, and everything I'm emotionally prepared for ..."

Joe looked down at the floor. "You get results." He hesitated, almost ashamed of himself. "You're the man who should be leading this county, not me. You're the man who can make the tough decisions under stress. I can't do it, but it's like you do it without even blinking."

The General sat unmoving, listening, gathering intel, wanting his friend to go on.

"The way you took charge at the campsite a while back, throwing that flash bang into the crowd, then coming back with supplies and recruiting them. It fixed everything." He paused long enough to make eye contact. "And when you stabbed that guy in my own jail, I was furious. But not at you - at myself."

The General locked eyes with the Sheriff.

"But after I slept on it that night, I realized I wasn't mad at you. I was mad at me, for not having the guts to do what needed doing. I had to rely on you. My way, my inability to act decisively would have ended up killing more civilians, the ones I'm sworn to protect." The Sheriff lowered his head. "I'm ashamed of myself."

For a few seconds, General Branch remained silent, assessing what his friend *wanted* to hear as opposed to what he *needed* to hear. In the end, he did what he always did. Rodney spoke his mind.

"Listen, Sheriff, I hear what you're saying, and I agree with it all, so far as you went. I've always known that good peacetime leaders seldom make good wartime leaders. But the opposite is also true. During peacetime I feel like a fish out of water. Maybe that's why I've spent my whole life either fighting or preparing for a fight. But the truth is this war won't last forever, and when it's done and the smoke clears, Iroquois is going to need someone like you to help them rebuild. That's where you shine."

The Sheriff looked up hopefully. Then he smiled. "So, you make the mess and I'm stuck cleaning it up?"

Rodney laughed out loud. "You got that right, Joe!"

The two men laughed together for a bit, then somehow got on the subject of fishing before The Day. Fishing had changed after the lights went out. Sport fishing was nonexistent, but instead, people now fished for survival.

The radio stayed silent, but Rodney and Joe just kept talking into the night, waiting, reacquainting, reassuring each other they were both the same friends they'd been before The Day.

As the door closed behind him, and she heard his footsteps fade down the hall, Lisa cried in front of the window. Suddenly, she felt very fragile and very much alone.

CHAPTER 15

Night time Assault

"**S**O IS IT TRUE?"
 Lisa was huddled on the ground beside Donny, listening to the music and voices coming out of the camp. They were only twenty yards away now, hiding in the shadows being thrown by the lights of the camp, waiting for the moment when they would attack and most assuredly be killed.

"Is what true?"

Donny looked over at her, and the light from the camp hit him in the side of the cheek. "You know. Is every girl crazy about a sharp-dressed man?"

Lisa was amazed at Donny's ability to stay calm and even make jokes in a deadly force situation. She moved closer to his ear before whispering. "Will you please shut up? Aren't you the least bit afraid we might die tonight?" Lisa couldn't see his face, but she assumed he was grinning.

"Only if it enhances my chance of survival."

Donny looked over at the other three members of his fire team: Tara, Brenda and Lynne. All three were dressed in _Victoria's Secret_ negligees. The women had taken the time to fix their hair, make-up, even their nails before moving into this jump-off position. Donny watched them, and could tell they were nervous. If he told the truth, he was nervous too. Donny didn't want them to die, but he saw little chance for them. He'd gotten to know them better the past few days, and he was starting to hate himself for coming up with this plan.

"Stay here until the men are busy with the girls. Then sneak up to the troop compartment door and join me inside the Bradley. It's the one farthest from the bonfire. It's the only one with the troop door in the DOWN position."

Lisa followed Donny's gaze and nodded. She looked over at the other girls, and swallowed the lump in her throat. She was feeling guilty about her comparatively safe role in this plan. While the other three girls were being repeatedly raped, she'd be deep inside the safety of an armored fighting vehicle. Lisa thought about returning to her daughter, Samantha, fighting the ambivalence of feeling good about her role and bad about her guilt. She'd heard Donny use the term "survivor's guilt", and she knew she was feeling it now, well before the mission's end. She shook her head and told herself, _Don't count your chickens before they hatch, girl. First you have to survive_ *long enough to feel guilty.*

She looked over at Donny, but he was already gone, now kneeling beside the other girls. She couldn't make out what he was saying, but she did hear Tara reply, "Can't we just get this thing over with. I'm freezing in this skimpy little outfit."

Lisa watched from her vantage point as her comrades moved into position on the far side of the camp. She lost them from view, and the next time she saw them they had left the safety of the bushes and were marching up to one of the Bradley Fighting Vehicles.

"Hey guys. Manny sent me over here with these three girls. Said it's a special treat to celebrate the addition of armor to our group."

The three women were trailing in his wake, strung together with a rope with wrists tied up. All eight of them saw the girls and stood up in unison, as if they all had the same thought. At first, The Horde members didn't say anything. Finally, one of them spoke.

"Manny said that? These women are for us?"

Just as Donny had predicted, the men were so excited about the girls they didn't even ask who he was. He played along with the ruse as best he could.

Donny nodded. "Yeah, that's what he said. He said to let the armor guys get first crack at these girls. Said you could have them all the way till morning."

The men crowded around the girls, moving in like wolves ready to attack. Donny remembered his last time inside The Horde's camp as the lifeless body of the woman had been thrown out of the semi trailer. She'd been raped to death. He prayed the girls would catch a break.

The dominant male of the pack reached out and grabbed Tara by the wrist. "I want this one first!" Then he cut the rope tethering her to the others and drug her to the back of the closest Bradley. Tara resisted but didn't scream and was no match for his strength. Donny listened to the whirring of the electric motor as the troop compartment door came down. Finally, the man stepped inside and dragged Tara behind him. Three more men grabbed Brenda and took her to the second Bradley. "You two can hold her while I go. Then we can trade off until we're done." Lynne was hauled away by three more men and ended up in the Bradley closest to the woods, the one Lisa and Donny were going to use to complete the mission.

That left Donny standing alone beside the bonfire with the remaining Horde soldier. The man turned toward him, and Donny's heart caught in his throat as the man called him by name. "Hello Donny."

Lisa was just about to sneak closer to her assigned Bradley when she saw Donny begin to talk excitedly to The Horde member beside the fire. The man was big, much bigger than Donny, and held himself straight and proud. His hair was cut short, but he had a good week's growth on his face. Lisa got a sinking feeling in her stomach when she saw The Horde soldier pull a bayonet out of its sheath from his belt. She wanted to cry out, *Donny, watch out! He's got a knife!* But there just wasn't time and she was too far away. She raised her M4 instinctively and was about to aim in when both men separated. Donny went to the Bradley closest to Lisa, and the other man hurried over to where Tara had disappeared.

Lisa's heart was pounding now, wondering what was going on and what she should do. Then Donny's words came back to her, *Just follow the plan*. But even that confused her, because even Donny wasn't following the plan, and the plan belonged to him!

In the end, she made her way over to the back of the Bradley and peered in just in time to watch Donny holster the suppressed nine millimeter pistol. Three men were crumpled on the floor, and Lynne was retrieving her negligee from the bench seat.

Donny barked to Lisa in a low voice. "Get her some clothes. Then man the twenty-five millimeter chain gun." He walked out the back and into the night.

Adam Cervantes came in low behind the big man, and raised up with his bayonet ready to strike. He plunged the big knife into the man's back between the vertebrae, severing his spinal column. The man dropped to the floor like a bag of wheat, banging his head on a stowage compartment on the way down. Tara looked up at him with terror in her eyes. Adam smiled as he raised one forefinger to his lips and made a shushing sound.

"Hurry up and get your clothes on, then go to Donny's vehicle. I'll meet you there."

Then he turned and strode out the Bradley where Donny was waiting. Together, they moved quietly to the remaining Bradley. They were surprised to see the compartment door was still up, and Brenda was pinned to the dirt while the other man came down on top of her. Donny shot the man on the left with his suppressed Glock in the back of the head while Adam came in unannounced on the right slashing the other man's throat as he moved.

The man on top of Brenda gave out a surprised cry just before Donny's knife slit his windpipe. The dying man fell down on top of Brenda, gurgling blood into her face and on the ground around her. Brenda turned her head to one side and wretched out the contents of her stomach, all the while trying to wipe the blood from her eyes.

Adam looked over at Donny. "It's good to work with you again, brother."

Donny looked at him grim-faced. "Let's get out of this place while we still can."

Adam Cervantes smiled. "Fine, but I get to drive."

Dan Branch watched from two miles away as Donny and Lisa opened up with the armaments of the Bradley. Lisa targeted the other two Bradley's with the twenty-five millimeter chain gun while Donny loaded up the TOW and sent a rocket into the Abrams Tank across the field. Lisa had expected an explosion and a column of flames reaching up to the sky, but the death of the tank was less dramatic than she'd anticipated.

Adam already had the six hundred horsepower engine running, and, as he began to drive away, Donny targeted the two shot-up Bradleys just to make sure they never moved again. Once they were away, Donny manned the 7.62 M240 machine gun and took out as many of The Horde as he could. He focused his efforts on the bonfires, while Lisa lit up as many vehicles as she could with the chain gun.

As they drove away into the night, The Horde's camp site was alive and burning. Dan Branch lowered his binoculars and nodded his head as he smiled. "Impressive."

Larry Jackson stood beside him laughing. "We'd best get in place, Major. This night isn't over by a long shot."

Dan nodded and both men moved off into the darkness, barking out orders as they went.

"Over there! Up that hill! I see the flare." Adam Cervantes pointed up at the flare now on its downward plunge to the earth below. His head was jutting up out of the Driver's Vision Port. Lisa was still manning the chain gun while Dan reloaded the machine gun to her right. The rest of his female fire team was in the troop compartment getting back in their camo, preparing to engage anyone who pursued.

Lisa looked back at The Horde encampment, amazed at the burning and chaos they'd caused. At present, there was nothing for her to do, so she focused on listening through her helmet as Adam and Donny talked back and forth.

"We need to get off this road, Donny. They'll be coming for us soon. We're only going thirty miles per hour and they'll catch us in no time."

She heard Sergeant Brewster laughing in her ears.

"All we have to do is make it over that hill and we'll be safe. We just have to make sure they catch us on the downhill side."

Adam didn't answer right away. "What do you have cooking, Donny? What's going on?'

Donny laughed again. "You'll see. It'll be fun."

Lisa was now convinced that Donny Brewster was crazy. But still ... she found him interesting. She saw lights moving now, coming out of the camp, more than she could easily count.

"Donny, we have lights coming toward us from the camp. Lots of them, maybe twenty or more."

"Thanks, Lisa. I see them. Start shooting at them."

Lisa thought for a moment. *That didn't make any sense.*

"Dan, I can barely aim this thing, much less hit a moving target while bouncing up and down on this road."

Once again, the laugh came that was starting to grate on her nerves. "Just start shooting. I want them to know where we are. They have to follow us."

Lisa fired away, aiming as best she could at the light down the hill. They heard and saw the big twenty-five millimeter gun, and all the lights began to focus on their location. They steadily came closer.

Lisa kept thinking to herself, even as she fired with little effect down the hill. *He's crazy. We're going to die. I know he's crazy. Please, God, let him be sane.*

They crested the hill just before the quads caught up with them. There were over twenty of the little vehicles, lit up in the night like fireflies,closing on them, cresting the hill, then swarming around them. They began to spout fire. Lisa heard the bullets helplessly clanking against the Bradley's armor and she cringed at the sound.

"Stop it right here, Adam. This is where we make our stand."

Lisa couldn't believe what she was hearing. Apparently Adam had a problem with it as well.

"Donny Brewster have you gone mad!? We should be heading off through the boonies right now before those HumVees catch up with us. They've got TOWs mounted to a few of their vehicles. If they can figure out how to use them, we're dead if we stay here for very long."

Donny laughed again, this time almost hysterically. That's when the first quad ran into the trench that Dan Branch and his men had dug. The driver flew over the handlebars and landed in a heap. Another quad met the same fate, then another and another. The quads slowed but didn't stop.

"That's impressive, Donny, but how are we going to stop the TOW missiles? They're almost up the hill."

Donny's answer confused him.

"Viper Actual this is Viper Mobile, do you copy, over?"

There was silence. No response. Donny repeated the transmission. "Viper actual this is Viper Mobile, come in, over?"

There was another pause. The HumVees were almost up the hill. "Viper Actual this is Viper Mobile, if you can hear me, 'Fire for effect!' I say again fire the FPF!"

Parachute flares began falling from the sky, and Lisa cringed down into the gunner's seat as the night lit up all around her. She watched as tracer bullets streaked through the darkness, seeking out the quads. And wherever the tracers landed, the lesser guns focused. There was such a massive hail of gunfire she was happy to be inside the Bradley where it was safe. She watched as one of the HumVees lit up in flames. She thought she saw a lone soldier running away from it and jumping down into a hole. Then, just as quickly, another militia man jumped up and ran to the burning vehicle adding another Mason jar of gasoline to the fire.

As Lisa watched, a dozen men jumped out of the trench to throw Molotov cocktails against the sides of the three remaining HumVees. Six of the men were cut down instantly by fifty caliber machine guns mounted on top of the vehicles, but the rest got through and two more HumVees started burning in the night. Lisa heard screams as men on fire ran out into the darkness before falling to the ground as the life burned from them.

The remaining HumVee turned around and vanished over the hill and into the night. As quickly as it had started, the battle was over. The troop compartment door came down slowly and all of Donny's team exited the back. Lisa looked around at the carnage illuminated by the three burning vehicles. As she watched, almost a hundred men rose up out of the trenches and walked toward her.

Two men approached the Bradley and Donny Brewster snapped to attention, saluting crisply.

"Darn it, Donny, will you please stop that. You're twice the soldier I am."

Donny laughed. "Doesn't matter, Dan, cuz you're the Major and I'm just the sergeant."

Major Branch paced forward and threw his arms in a bear hug around his friend. He looked over and nodded to Adam Cervantes. "And you must be Adam."

Army National Guard Staff Sergeant Cervantes stiffened and gave Dan a salute. Dan hesitated, then straightened and returned Adam's salute. "Guess I'm going to have to get used to that."

Then he lowered his right hand and extended it to Adam. "Thanks for your help,

Adam."

Staff Sergeant Cervantes clasped his handshake.

"It was my pleasure, Major." He then nodded at the dead bodies all around. "Nice ambush. You do good work."

A grim look overcame Dan. "Not good enough. We lost some men."

The Major nodded and then turned away. As he walked off, Donny turned and smiled back at the four women behind him. "Nice work, girls. You did great!"

But none of the women were smiling back. To the contrary, they wore the faces of women scorned.

Lisa turned to Brenda. "I say we shoot him for keeping us in the dark like that."

Brenda nodded. "Yeah, and then we castrate him for allowing us to think we'd be raped and murdered."

Donny started to back away. "Now girls, let's not over-react. Don't get all emotional on me. You did great!" Donny kept backing away, but the four women kept converging.

"Hey Dan! I need to talk to you about our plans." Donny ran off after the Major, leaving the women alone with Staff Sergeant Cervantes. The girls turned their attention to him.

Tara came forward, her short, blonde hair shining in the firelight. "I want to thank you for saving my life." She moved to him and wrapped her petite arms around the big soldier. Adam bristled, not knowing how to respond. Brenda and Lynne followed suit, followed by Lisa.

Donny Brewster had reached Dan thirty yards away and they both watched through the firelight.

"Dan, I don't get it. I saved their lives, and look how they repay me. They threatened to castrate me and Adam gets a group hug? I don't get it!"

Dan chuckled and shook his head. "I told you to tell them the whole truth, but you wouldn't listen to me."

Dan turned away, leaving Donny to catch up. Both men walked off into the night, surrounded by carnage, heading off to plan the next round of death.

CHAPTER 16

Eastern Iroquois County Boonies

DONNY BREWSTER WAS LYING FACE DOWN ON THE DECK IN the back of the Bradley Fighting Vehicle with his pants pulled down to his ankles when General Branch marched up and looked in.

"Sergeant Brewster, I hope I'm not interrupting anything."

Lisa maintained her focus on Donny's bare behind as she poured on more rubbing alcohol and cleaned out the wound. Donny screamed in pain. "Why are you rubbing it so hard!?"

The General chuckled to himself. "Now, Sergeant, we all told you it was best to tell your fire team the full details of the mission. Maybe next time you'll obey the orders of your commanding officer." General Branch nodded to Lisa.

"Thanks for your service, Miss Vanderboeg. I hear you did great back there in combat last night."

Lisa smiled up at him. "You're welcome, General Branch. I'm just anxious to get home to my little girl."

The General nodded. "You can take one of the quads to your home. I'll send someone by to pick it up later."

Donny turned his head and tried to look behind him. "Don't call her 'Miss' or she'll bite your head off, general."

General Branch looked over at the woman with a question in his eyes. She looked back with a mischievous smile on her face. "The General can call me Miss Vanderboeg anytime he likes. And do you know why?" Lisa poured more rubbing alcohol into the wound where Donny's stitches had ripped. He screamed in pain.

"General, you have to save me from this woman! She's going to kill me."

The General ignored him and so did Lisa. "I'll tell you why, Sergeant Brewster, because, unlike you, the General is a gentleman. He tells a lady when she'll be in danger and when she's safe. Not like a scoundrel who lets her unnecessarily worry about being raped and murdered."

She stuffed a gauze pad into the once-healing bullet wound and twisted it. "Now hold still! I have to get out all the infection or we'll have to amputate your buttock."

It took all Rodney's self control to hold in his laughter. He winked at Lisa. "Nurse Vanderboeg, I think I see more infection down deeper. Make sure you get it all out. The Sergeant is important, and we'll need him to fight on the front lines very soon."

Donny's forehead hit the floor with a thunk. "It's too late, general. I'll be dead long before The Horde arrives." Donny screamed again.

"Shut up, soldier! I haven't even touched you yet!"

The General regained his composure before speaking again, this time in his command voice.

"Nurse Vanderboeg, when your patient regains consciousness, please tell him we have a meeting at my command post in fifteen minutes. It's mandatory."

Lisa nodded and smiled before returning to Donny's bare behind. There were some days when she just loved being a nurse.

☆ ☆ ☆ ☆

Colonel Roger "Ranger" MacPherson stood before the gathering of officers and noncoms inside the CP tent. He was ramrod straight, muscular and taut with military bearing. Every fiber of his body screamed out the command, *Obey me! I'm in charge here!* He looked out at the thirty or so leaders within the Iroquois County Militia seated in front of him. He studied them now, just as he had studied men for decades of his Army career. Some of them were terrified and others were eager; while the remainder occupied every spot in between along the continuum.

"Sergeant Brewster of The Shadow Militia will now give you a briefing on last night's engagement."

The Colonel watched as Sergeant Brewster walked slowly up to the front. He couldn't tell for sure, but the Colonel thought he detected a slight limp in the Sergeant's gait. He noted it for future reference as he walked to his seat in front and took his place at the right hand of General Branch.

The sides of the tent were rolled down, and a small pot-bellied stove was burning in the center. A storm had moved in this morning, bringing a mass of arctic air down from the Upper Peninsula. Even though it was early April, a blizzard was expected that night.

"Last night we attacked The Horde encampment with a four-woman fire team, effectively destroying one Abrams tank and two Bradley Fighting Vehicles." Donny paused for effect. He noticed the men looking around at each other at his mention of four women attacking The Horde. He thought to himself, *Perhaps that will shame them into bravery.* "The third Bradley was captured and is now in our possession, and will be used for defense of Iroquois County."

Sheriff Leif stood near the back of the tent, just listening, soaking it all in. He was the acting commander of the Home Guard, and it was his plan they'd be putting into effect when The Horde finally rolled into Iroquois City. He was amazed at what The Shadow Militia had done the past month to train the county militia. He looked at Donny Brewster and recalled how he'd first mocked Rodney for sending just one man to hold off The Horde for an additional three weeks. He would never ridicule The Shadow Militia again. They were a force to be reckoned with. They'd trained the county, equipped them, and imbued his people with hope and courage. His only reservation was of his own character. His own self doubt nagged at the corners of his mind with every waking moment.

Am I good enough? Will I fight or will I freeze?

Donny Brewster continued speaking.

"In our escape, we attacked The Horde, killing dozens as we fled. Major Branch and his militia company were entrenched in a pre-arranged ambush site. They attacked and destroyed three HumVees and twenty-two quads. Total enemy casualties is estimated at ninety-seven dead and twenty-eight wounded." He paused for a moment as the militia soldiers smiled and looked around at one another. A happy murmur rose up from the crowd. "Unfortunately, it was not without a cost. Eight militia were killed and seven more wounded."

Donny looked over at Colonel MacPherson, signifying he was done. Then he walked stiffly back to his seat.

The Colonel stood and walked back up to the front of the room.

"And now, General Branch will address the meeting."

As he walked back to his seat, Rodney got up and placed himself where Colonel MacPherson had been standing just a few moments before. He looked out at the crowd and smiled grimly. Just a few weeks ago some of these people had been homeless in the state game area, others had been living lives of quiet discontent, just fighting to put food on the table for their families. Today, it all had changed. Now, they were fighters. They were reluctant warriors. He looked into the third row back at eighty-some year-old Harold Steffens. Jackie Branch, his own daughter-in-law, sat beside the old soldier. He wondered if their role would change the outcome. It was still a secret what they planned to do.

"Aerial reconnaissance supplied to us by Sergeant Harold Steffens has given us the following intelligence." He looked over at Harold and smiled slightly in thanks. "After last night's attack, The Horde is now bogged down and regrouping fifty miles east of Iroquois City. Major Branch and his company of Militia Rangers have been hampering their movements using guerilla tactics all morning and afternoon. So far they report another fifty-three enemy dead and one-hundred and twenty-five wounded. That's an estimate, but I have confidence in the numbers."

He paused and tried to read the crowd.

"The Rangers will continue to harass and slow The Horde as long as they can, thereby giving Sheriff Leif enough time to prepare and harden Iroquois City defenses. Major Branch has already lost ten more men since last night."

A grumble went up from the crowd.

"All men who fall will be returned to Iroquois. They will receive a funeral with full military honors, with their families present. They are forever to be considered heroes. All who fall in defense of the weak will be celebrated in song and reverence for decades to come. Their families will be taken care of, and they will not be forgotten."

The grumbling lessened, but did not stop completely.

"Sheriff Leif will be coordinating the defense of the town. He will now outline his plan and give final assignments and logistical orders for preparation."

The General stepped back to his seat. While Sheriff Leif walked up, he did so slowly, wondering all the while, *Will I be brave? Will I run? Will I freeze? Or will I fight with honor?* But, through all the thinking, the most obvious possibility, that he would die, never crossed his mind.

The Militia Rangers

Dan Branch pulled out his satellite phone and let it hover in his hand in front of him. He waited for the lead truck to reach the Improvised Explosive Device (IED) before pressing the button. The small explosion rocked the truck as the engine block was compromised with armor piercing rounds shooting up from below. The long line of trucks and cars stopped, forming a bottleneck and a perfect ambush site. The militia opened fire from heavy cover as The Horde scrambled to leave their vehicles one hundred yards down the hill. Dan had planned his ambush well. The Horde would have to charge up the hill through a hail of gunfire to counterattack and drive them off. But by then, Dan and his militia would be miles away.

Major Branch let his men fire several rounds each until all the easy targets had been wounded. Men of The Horde screamed below in agony from shots to the groin and legs. They would eventually die, but not until slowing the advance and striking fear into the hearts of their comrades.

It was over in thirty seconds. Dan gave the order to fall back, and all twenty-five of his soldiers quietly withdrew. An hour later they would be set up a few miles down the road for another attack.

Manny Takes Charge

Down below, Manny cursed at the ineptitude of his soldiers as they cowered behind the engine blocks of their vehicles. The shooting had been silent for two minutes now, but still no one was moving to counterattack. Fueled by anger, Manny broke from cover and raced to the front of the column.

"Get up you fools! They're gone already! How many times do they have to do this before you figure it out?"

Manny stood out in the middle of the road, totally exposed. "See! Look at me! Grow some balls and push this truck off the road so we can get going again. None of this will end until we reach Traverse City."

Manny had been analyzing the militia's tactics all morning. It was a battle of attrition and he was losing it. Manny had studied military history, and it reminded him of the April 19th, 1775 battle of Lexington Concord. The British with a far superior force were followed and hounded all the way back to Boston by peasants and farmers shooting from behind rock walls and trees.

A man was screaming on the ground off to his left as he lay in agony clutching his now-shattered and bleeding private parts. Manny regained his sense of calm as he walked up to the screaming man, unholstered his pistol and shot the man in the head. The screaming stopped. One by one, The Horde stood up, more afraid of Manny than the militia. One of them organized a clean-up, and soon the truck was pushed off the road.

During the process, three more people were wounded by toe poppers. Manny shot two of them, but the last man quickly stood up and limped off to bandage his wound. Manny let him go. He'd already examined this new technique of the militia. The booby trap was planted in the ground along the side of the road at every ambush site. It was simply a short piece of PVC pipe affixed to a small square of board with a nail jutting up into the pipe. The militia placed a .223 caliber round into the pipe with the primer resting lightly on the nail. When stepped on, the bullet was pushed against the primer, exploding the primer which fired off the round. The bullet went through the man's shoe, sometimes exiting and hitting him in other places as well. Manny remembered reading about this as he'd studied the Vietnam War.

As he stood thinking, waiting for the truck to be removed, another man screamed to his left and fell down into a small hole in the ditch. Manny walked over to confirm what he already knew. The man clutched at his foot in pain. A penny spike pounded through a board was sticking out the bottom of his boot. "Shut up or I'll shoot you!"

The man instantly quieted. Manny reached down and yanked the board and nail off the man's boot. The man screamed once but quickly regained his composure. Lifting the nail to his nose, Manny smelled the distinct odor of feces. He tossed the nail back into the hole and walked away.

These people were very good at their jobs, and Manny wanted to know why. More importantly, he was going to need help. At this rate he'd never make it to Iroquois City, much less his final destination.

Manny yelled out to his assistant. "Buster! Get me my radio!" Within a few minutes he was arguing with someone. Buster sat by listening, all the while thinking to himself, *Things aren't going as planned.* Already several people had snuck off into the woods, and more would follow if something wasn't done. Worst of all, Buster would have to tell Manny the bad news.

Finally, Manny dropped the radio handset and smiled. The alliance had been formed.

Many miles away, back at the Grayling National Guard base, Major Danskill put down the radio and yelled at the Sergeant. "Send in Captain Foster. Now!"

While the Sergeant carried out his orders, Major Danskill opened the wall safe and took out the Sat Phone. It was only to be used when talking to his superior.

As he waited for his boss to answer the phone, he smiled and shook his head in amusement. How long had it taken? Just a few days for Manny to lose his tank and his Bradleys? As a military leader, the man was incompetent. And now he wanted more. More tanks, more men, more ammunition. Major Danskill laughed at Manny's insatiable thirst for power. Every man had his vice, his weakness, his own personal lust to be either conquered or fed.

"Yes, sir. This is Major Danskill with a situation report."

The man on the other end simply said, "Go ahead."

"As you suspected, we have movement in northwest Michigan. It's organized in a military fashion."

Danskill listened to the response before replying. "Yes, sir. Right away, sir. We'll leave within the hour."

A thousand miles away, deep inside a fortified bunker, the man disconnected from the Sat Phone. The call disturbed him. Civilians organized into military units, making coordinated and military-style attacks. That could be a problem as he preferred unorganized and terrified resistance. Who could be leading these people? He wondered.

He set the Sat Phone on the coffee table beside him. It was a special coffee table, stolen from the estate of a Columbian drug lord, hand-carved out of some rare jungle tree. He didn't know the name of it. Most importantly, the drug lord and his entire family was dead now. He'd seen to that personally, and he viewed the table as just a souvenir from another exotic country. His life was full of souvenirs, and they were ornately displayed about him in his sprawling bungalow: lamps, couches, paintings, even a few statues. He liked the finer things in life, and his living area looked more like a Manhattan penthouse than a huge complex of underground bunkers.

The man glanced over at his assistant, who stood there almost at the position of attention. "I like military officers. They're so competent, so efficient, so meticulous in planning and detail." He paused, "But, most importantly ... they're polite."

Sammy Thurmond nodded, his blank eyes staring out at the wall on the far side of the room.

CHAPTER 17

The Next Day

MAJOR DANSKILL FOCUSED ON THE **GPS** SCREEN INTENTLY. His XO, Captain Foster, stood beside him like an obedient pitbull eager to serve his master. After receiving the urgent distress call from Manny, he'd left Grayling ASAP. Manny was an incompetent. Danskill had always known that, and he planned on exploiting that trait when the time was right. But for now he'd just play along like a good little rent-a-soldier.

"Captain, we should hit them here. They'll be expecting the same counter-attack from Manny and his men, so it should be a rout. We want to capture a few alive for intel, but the rest need to die. Understood?"

Captain Foster smiled. "I'll draw up the plans immediately, sir."

✯ ✯ ✯ ✯

Dan Branch looked down at the advancing column of vehicles coming toward him and his men. They were now just inside Iroquois County only thirty miles from his family. Most of his seventy remaining militia rangers were feeling the same sense of urgency as Dan was. They'd killed a few hundred of the Horde, but they kept coming, gaining in strength, and every time they passed through a town they picked up more recruits. Dan had learned from a refugee how the Horde was able to enlist the service of so many men. Upon reaching a town, they would line up all the residents, then separate the men from their families. Through a bullhorn, the Horde leader would issue the ultimatum: either enlist and serve in his army, or watch your wives and children be raped and killed. Most men complied to save their families. And that's how the Horde continued to grow despite the losses inflicted by Dan Branch and his Militia Rangers. It also explained why some of the Horde soldiers were deserting.

"On my command, Captain Jackson." Dan lifted his binoculars and peered down at the center of the enemy column. He didn't want them getting used to the same old tactics and refining their counterattack, so he was hitting them in the rear this time just to mix it up and keep them guessing. Dan had noticed the Horde was getting better at reacting to his ambushes.

"Blow it, Larry."

Captain Larry Jackson pressed the button and a second later there was a huge explosion down on the road. A deuce and a half truck was thrown up twenty feet in the air; it traveled backwards as it flew and landed on a Toyota Prius two vehicles to the rear. Two other SUVs were blown off to the side, leaving a huge crater where the road had once been.

"Holy ... Larry, what was in that one?"

Larry Jackson smiled. "I told you these fertilizer bombs worked."

"Fire!"

In accordance with the plan, all his men picked out targets of opportunity. They shot men in the groin. They shot vehicle tires. Most importantly, anyone down below who looked like they were taking command, those people were given top priority. This time Dan let them shoot a bit longer than before. He figured the size of the blast would leave the Horde more disoriented than usual, and he knew from past experience the enemy quads would all be massed in the center front of the column waiting to react to their attack.

"Cease fire! Move! Move! Move!"

All seventy of Dan's men moved as one unit to the rear of the enemy column. They made their way down the hill and crossed the road to their prearranged rally point. They'd never done this before, and the Horde wouldn't expect it. Once on the other side, Dan and his men moved a mile off the road and formed a group. Off in the distance they could hear the quads buzzing angrily up the hill where they'd launched their ambush. There was a muffled explosion and Larry Jackson smiled at the success of his booby trap. *One more quad bites the dust.*

"Okay men, third platoon set up perimeter security. All the staff NCOs come with me to debrief and plan the next attack. We move out again in twenty mikes!"

Third platoon followed orders while the rest of the rangers sat down to take a break. Most of them were military veterans of one sort or another, but the average age was forty-five years old. Dan had been amazed how quickly these old men had hardened in the past few days of battle. They were old, but they were tough and grizzly north woods men, and, most importantly, they were fighting for their homes and their families. So far they'd made a very good accounting of themselves, and Dan had grown proud to lead them.

He huddled off to one side of the left flank now with his leaders and pulled out the plastic laminated topographical map of Iroquois County. Captain Jackson was still smiling. But then, without warning, Dan raised his hand, and a look of concern spread across his face like a malignant infection.

"Can you hear that?"

The small group of staff noncoms froze in place, none wanting to admit what they all knew was true. "Everyone, get down behind cover! Incoming!"

And while the Militia Rangers hid in the brush, the steady womp, womp, womp of turning rotors came closer.

★ ★ ★ ★

"Eagle Leader, this is Sparrowhawk. I have infrared confirmation of company size unit one click east of your location. What are your orders?"

There was a moment of silence as the Apache attack helicopter circled the Militia Rangers from above.

"Sparrowhawk, this is Eagle Leader. Engage and destroy enemy ground units, over."

The Apache helicopter pilot hadn't always been evil; it was just something that had happened to him a little bit at a time. A bad decision here, a mean action there, and then, finally, the day when he'd made the move to follow Major Danskill. His wife and family were probably dead, so nothing else really mattered. What he'd discovered, is once he'd started down the road ... there was no turning back. One sin just seemed to lead to another, and another, and another. Until, finally, opening fire on seventy men defending their home just didn't seem like that big a deal anymore.

The pilot looked though the Integrated Helmet and Display Sighting System which was already slaved to the aircraft's 30 mm automatic M230 Chain Gun. Wherever he looked with his helmet, the chain gun followed. In the first pass, he lit up the woods and tore the rangers to shreds. Then he started to bank around for his second pass.

Down on the ground, third platoon was firing frantically at the Apache but with no effect. Major Branch looked on helplessly from forty yards away. In five seconds thirty-five soldiers were torn apart, and the helicopter was banking for a second pass. Dan heard Captain Jackson yelling beside him, then realized he was being shaken violently.

"Dan! They've got infrared! We've got to retreat!"

The Apache had completed his bank now, and Dan finally reacted and took command.

"Retreat to rally point! Retreat to rally point! Retreat! Retreat!"

And with that Larry Jackson threw Dan behind a large oak tree as the Apache made his second pass. More body parts, dirt and wood chips flew up and out through the brush. The noise of the gun was deafening and the small arms fire died down as people fell to the ground and as others scattered through the woods.

Dan looked down at his feet and saw he was running now. Captain Jackson was pushing him along from the rear yelling at him to run faster. Four hundred yards down the embankment they came to a river. By now Dan had recovered his composure and dived head first into the water. The icy cold closed over him and shocked his system to its core. Larry Jackson dived in after him as did several of his other non coms. The current was strong and moved them quickly downstream. They swam for the far bank, but all their gear and clothing weighed them down. Just when they were about to drown, Dan's feet hit the surface of a sand bar and he wearily brought his feet underneath him and raised up to a standing position.

Off in the distance, the sound of the chain gun ceased, leaving an eerie calm to the woods. Then they heard the Bradley fighting vehicles moving in to mop up whatever resistance was left. Dan's head was swimming in a frozen fog. *My men are dead. The Horde is advancing. They have attack helicopters. They now own the sky.*

"Larry, see if your radio still works. We need to get this intel to General Branch and Iroquois City."

They trudged on over to the far bank of the river where Captain Jackson fired up his radio and relayed the information back to base.

✫ ✫ ✫ ✫

Major Danskill stepped out the back of the Bradley and looked at the ground, littered with blood and flesh and bone. He smiled.

"Captain Foster! Bring the survivors to me for interrogation."

His Executive Officer looked over with a frown on his face. "I'm sorry, sir. There are no survivors."

Danskill looked over at him perplexed and raised his right eyebrow in question. "Really?"

"Yes, sir. They refused to be captured. They fought to the last man."

The Major raised his left hand up to his chin and continued to peruse the carnage. He felt ambivalent about this. The soldier part of him was impressed. They fought to the last man. That was praiseworthy. But without prisoners there was no intel, and they'd be going into Iroquois City blind. And he wondered, what kind of force am I up against? These aren't just farmers. He shrugged. It didn't matter. Whoever they were they'd be killed - to the last man if need be. He had Bradleys and tanks and Apache helicopters. Whoever they were; they didn't have a prayer. He walked over and kicked a dead body just to make sure.

☆ ☆ ☆ ☆

General Branch set down the radio and plopped himself heavily in the folding chair beside him. His eyes looked off in the distance, seeing nothing but a blur. Finally, Sheriff Leif spoke to him.

"What does that mean, Rodney? Are all of them dead?"

General Branch looked up and met Joe's gaze. He shook his head from side to side, wearily, as if it took every last ounce of energy he had left. Suddenly, Joe saw a tiny glimpse of Rodney for what he was deep inside: weak, old, just an ancient old man who'd outlived his prime and wanted nothing more than to die and sleep through the ages. "No, Sheriff, there are seven of them left, maybe a few others, but they're all scattered or dead."

"But the Horde has more Bradleys and now an attack helicopter?" Joe paused. "How did that happen?"

Uncle Rodney looked down at the floor. "They must have come from Grayling. I pulled the surveillance too soon. I guess that was a mistake. I'm sorry."

Sheriff Leif moved over to the cement block wall and leaned heavily against it. Then he looked back over at the General, and his next words were more of an indictment than a statement of fact. "But you have attack helicopters. You have equipment we don't even know about yet. You could have stopped this!"

Rodney Branch slumped his shoulders and looked down at the floor. Inside, he knew it was true. Yes, he could have stopped them. He could have supported them, but … at what future price … at what unintended consequences?

"Don't just sit there! Say something! We trusted you! We followed you!" The Sheriff, all six and a half feet of him walked over and grabbed Rodney Branch by the shoulders and shook him hard. "Now what are you going to do about this?"

Something inside the General snapped loose like an iron lock, and he jumped up, grabbed Joe's hand and rotated it behind the man's back with the quickness of a cat. In less than a second big Joe Leif was on his knees with a 45 pistol placed on the back of his head.

"Just shut up. I have a plan. Of course I have a plan. But don't touch me! I don't like it!" Rodney holstered his firearm and walked away. "Now come on, Joe. We've got work to do."

The Sheriff, still stunned and on his knees, looked after the old man as the door opened and closed behind him. *How had he done that?* He kneeled a few seconds longer, and then got up and followed.

CHAPTER 18

Iroquois City

THE YOUNG BOY STUMBLED UP THE CONCRETE STEPS OF THE courthouse, opened the door and fell inside. He'd been beaten and slashed with knives across his face, chest and back. The boy crawled to the conference room leaving a bloody trail in his wake. He reached up his broken hand and scratched on the wooden door.

From inside, Sheriff Leif heard the scratching and opened the door. He gasped when he saw the bloody boy at his feet. Colonel MacPherson rushed over and scooped the twelve-year-old boy up and placed him on the conference table in the center of the room. The boy was mumbling the same thing over and over again. "They're here! They're here! They're here."

Joe's face hardened and he stepped over and placed his hand in the boy's open palm. "Joshua, is that you?" The boy's face was cut so badly it was hard to tell. "Is that you, Joshua?"

The boy went silent. Colonel MacPherson reached up to the boy's throat but could find no pulse. "He's gone, Sheriff." Joe Leif threw his head down on the boy and cried on his dead body. Colonel MacPherson stood ramrod stiff. He waited a few seconds, then grabbed Joe by the shoulders and lifted him up straight. He rotated the Sheriff around until they looked eye to eye. "Where did this boy live, Joe? I need to know how close they are." Joe didn't answer, so the Colonel shook him. "Where are they Joe?"

Joe Leif looked up with terror and despair in his eyes. "His family lives right here in town."

2 Hours later - Iroquois City Courthouse

"We sent a squad to the boy's house. His father was murdered along with their little girl and a newborn baby." Colonel MacPherson's voice broke as if the saying of it was too much to bear. "Looks like the mother was abducted. The two Home Guard who were stationed in front of the courthouse for security appear to have deserted. We don't know if they were in on it or not."

Joe Leif sat at the conference table with his head in his hands near despair. General Branch listened from the head of the table. His eyes were stone-cold when he spoke. "We have to assume The Horde knows all about our defenses." He looked over to the Sheriff. "You'll have to make some changes Joe, some big changes." Then he looked over to Sergeant Harold Steffens. The old man looked tired, but very much alive. "What did you see from the air, Sergeant?"

The ancient man locked eyes with the General and smiled. "They've made camp seven miles east of town in the state forest. Looked like about two thousand strong with hundreds of vehicles of all types. They weren't making any attempt to hide themselves. I think they feel indestructible right about now."

The General nodded. "I agree. They're pretty confident. But what about the Bradley fighting vehicles and the Apache helicopters?"

"I saw none of them, Not even tracks in the snow. And if I'd seen an Apache they would have blown my little crop duster out of the sky. I can't out fly them and I have no armaments."

Sheriff Leif moved his hands away from his face and looked over at General Branch like a wounded animal about to die. "We have to evacuate the city, Rodney. It's our only hope of survival."

Rodney Branch said nothing. He simply shook his head signifying disagreement. Joe Leif stood up at the table towering over the shorter man in a last-ditch attempt to posture him into submission, but General Branch would have none of it. He glanced over at Colonel MacPherson. "Take charge of the city's defenses and make the necessary changes. Try not to embarrass the Sheriff in how you do it. Invoke his name as if he's still in charge."

Sheriff Leif's face turned red. He tried to speak, but nothing came out. Finally, without saying a word, he stormed out the door. General Branch watched the man leave, then looked over to Sergeant Steffens. "When can you fly again?"

The Sergeant answered calmly. Rodney noticed the old man looked ten years younger since the day they'd met. "I can be up again in two hours."

The General nodded. "Thanks Harold. I need to know where they are at nightfall. I don't think they'll attack until tomorrow. They've covered a long distance and they'll need time to rest and regroup. And they are cocky, so they'll feel no need to hurry. In the meantime they'll be stripping the countryside of food and supplies. I expect they'll be partying tonight. Then they'll sleep in and be moving against us about noon tomorrow. In the meantime we'll bring as many people as we can inside the city and arm all who will fight." He looked over at Colonel MacPherson. "Colonel? Are you seeing anything I'm not?"

Colonel MacPherson shook his head. "No, I don't think so. But I would like some more intel. Permission to send in Sergeant Brewster?'

"Good idea, Colonel." He looked down at the map spread out on the table before them. "So where is the Sergeant right now? How long will it take to get him in play?"

The Colonel smiled. "He's been observing The Horde all day sir. All I have to do is make the call."

General Branch returned his smile. There were times when he depended on Ranger MacPherson more than anyone knew. Sometimes it got lonely at the top.

"Then this meeting is adjourned. We'll meet back at nightfall to make final plans to defend the city."

As General Branch walked out, Colonel MacPherson and Sergeant Steffens looked after him.

"Where do you think he's going, Colonel?"

The grizzled, old army ranger stared at the still-closing door. "Beats the hell out of me. But wherever he's going, it can't be good for The Horde."

Sergeant Steffens almost laughed out loud. He was amazed at the confidence these two men inspired in him. Here he was eighty-four years old and flying into battle. He thought to himself, *Are you watching me from up there, Myra? Are you proud of this old man?*

He smiled to himself, confident that he'd soon be joining his wife. The thought gave him a great measure of courage and peace.

Dan Branch comes home

Jackie Branch saw her husband coming and ran out to meet him at the end of the drive. Dan killed the quad's engine and braked before he ran over her. She tackled him just as he stepped off the vehicle, and both of them almost fell to the ground. Dan looked over and saw Jeremy looking out from the porch.

"Don't you ever leave me again!"

Dan hadn't had time to clean up, and he was still wet and muddy from the all-night trek back to Iroquois City. Her husband was smiling, but it was a weary look, one filled with internal suffering and shame. Jackie saw the look on his face and frowned. "Aren't you happy to see me?"

Dan nodded. "Of course I am, honey. It's just been a long week," Then he hesitated, wondering how much to hold back. "I've killed a lot of men. And most of my rangers are dead."

His wife held him close. She reached up with her clean, soft hands and stroked his face. "It's okay, baby. Uncle Rodney filled me in. It wasn't your fault. There was no way you could have known. Not even your uncle knew."

In his mind, Dan knew she was right, but in his heart, he wasn't so quick to dismiss his responsibility. He knew it was a burden he would carry for the rest of his life. Dan held her quietly for several seconds, soaking in the reassuring smell of her long, black hair. The snow was a few inches deep and there was a chill in the air. With all his adrenaline used up, Dan began to shiver.

"Oh, honey. Please come inside by the fire and get warm. I'll get you out of those wet clothes and give you a bath."

The two of them walked to the house, leaving the quad where it was. Dan hugged his son blankly. He felt all used up, like a dirty dish rag all wrung out and lying draped over the sink.

After a bath, fresh clothes and a hot meal, Dan, Jeremy and Jackie were seated around the table as baby Donna played on the floor.

"What was it like, Dad?"

The stern look on Jackie's face gave her son a voiceless rebuke. Dan didn't answer at first. Jackie thought he looked lost inside himself, and she wondered if she would ever get him back again. Finally he answered his son.

"We killed them for several days, as many as we could. And then they attacked with an Apache and killed most of my company. Only seven of us survived that I know of."

"Oh." That's all Jeremy could muster. His romantic, boyhood picture of war had just been shattered. Jackie broke the silence.

"Is Larry Jackson okay?"

Dan nodded. "Yes, he made it plus most of my noncoms. We were off to the side when the attack happened. That's the only reason we survived."

Jackie hesitated before asking the next question. "What's going to happen now, Dan? What does it look like?"

Her husband looked down at the baby smiling on the floor and chewing on a rubber spatula. He seemed to be gaining strength from the little girl's innocence. "I have to be back in an hour. Colonel MacPherson is leading the Home Guard now."

Jackie looked perplexed. "I thought Joe Leif was doing that?"

Dan shook his head. He seemed to be recovering as he talked to his family. "No, not anymore. I guess he had a bit of a falling out with Uncle Rodney. We don't know where he is right now. The Horde is about seven miles east of town in the state forest. They're getting ready to attack tomorrow. I'm supposed to gather up all the refugees and arm them as best I can and organize a new company by morning."

Surprisingly, he got off his chair and sat down on the floor beside baby Donna. He began to play with her as if no one else was in the room and The Horde was a million miles away. Jackie looked over at Jeremy, but saw he was already looking at her. Their eyes met and she nodded to him.

"Dad, I think I should be part of your new company. I want to fight."

Dan stopped playing and lay down onto his back. The baby crawled up and rested on his chest. After a few seconds, she closed her eyes and quickly fell asleep. Jackie looked down, and, in better times would have been the happiest woman in the world. But not today. She got up and took the baby off his chest and moved her to their bedroom. When she came back out Dan was seated at the table again. He looked different, somehow rejuvenated back to the old Dan, but also a little bit like his Uncle Rodney.

"I think that's a good idea, son. I don't want you to have to fight, but quite frankly you have the training and the experience. And if The Horde breaks through, well … I think the lucky ones will be dead."

Jackie was surprised at her husband's candor, but certainly saw his reasoning. "And what about me, Dan? Do I fight?"

Dan shook his head. "Not this time, honey. Uncle Rodney has something special you can do that will keep you and the baby safe while still helping the cause. He said he'll stop by tonight and brief you on it. He didn't tell me the details. He said I didn't need to know."

Jackie chewed on that for a bit. A month ago she would have disbelieved it, but not now. Since their talk in the woods and her special assignment with Sergeant Steffens, she'd gained a great measure of respect and trust for Uncle Rodney's abilities and his intentions.

She nodded her head silently and helped Dan and Jeremy get ready to go. Within a half hour they were packed and loaded on the quad to head back into town. Jackie stood on the porch and waved as the quad fired up and raced away. She watched until the quad was completely out of sight and she could no longer hear the engine. Then she walked back inside to watch her baby sleep.

CHAPTER 19

The Horde Encampment

MANNY STOOD IN FRONT OF THE BIG, LOG CABIN LODGE AT the state forest campgrounds and surveyed the expanse of his domain. He was reminded of the words about Alexander the Great: *"And when Alexander looked out over the breadth of his domain, he wept for there were no more worlds left to conquer."*

Manny hoped that someday he would be able to weep just as Alexander had before him. He'd studied all the great military leaders, Genghis Khan, Atilla the Hun, and Adolf Hitler, and what he lacked in practical experience, he made up for with ruthlessness and focused study. But he didn't like this campground, and he couldn't wait to move out tomorrow morning for the final attack on Iroquois City. This campground had them hemmed in by woods, and it would be just too easy for someone to sneak in close and attack or infiltrate. And then his mind turned to more serious matters.

Major Danskill, *What was he going to do with him once he'd served Manny's purpose?* More importantly, what would Danskill do once Manny had outlived his usefulness? He was smart enough to know it was a marriage of convenience, and the divorce rate among scoundrels was one-hundred percent.

Once Traverse City was taken, Major Danskill would have to die. That was a given. But how to achieve it; that was the only remaining question. He'd have to be careful as the Major had proved himself a worthy adversary with plenty of resources.

Beyond that, Manny was already planning out the invasion of Grand Rapids. He hadn't liked being tossed out of the city, but he'd had no choice, and he fully intended to return as the conquering hero just like General Mac Arthur to the Philippines. Could he launch a two-pronged invasion by attacking with a land force from the north and an amphibious assault from Lake Michigan? He suspected there were hundreds of sailboats at TC he could use for just such a purpose. How many new recruits would he gain in Traverse City? Probably thousands more. It was a big town.

A group of six men walked up to Manny and stood before him. Manny's three bodyguards made no move to stop them, though they remained vigilant with M4s at the ready.

"You sent for us, Manny?"

Manny smiled. He liked Albert, the way he obeyed so readily. He hated the name though. "Albert" was just too nerdy. "Yes, Al. Sit down please."

Albert looked around for chairs, but finally just plopped himself on the cold concrete. The five men with him looked around reluctantly before following suit. Manny remained standing, all five-feet, eight inches towering over them.

"I need some more intel."

Albert cursed Manny but only on the inside. They'd already been up half the night taking prisoners from inside the city, and he'd been hoping for a rest before the attack. If not for the drugs in his bloodstream he'd be dead on his feet. Manny was a slave driver to say the least.

"I need you to scout an area to the north of the city at these grid coordinates." Manny pulled a piece of paper out of his pocket and handed it down to his lieutenant. Albert looked at it and nodded his head.

"Is there anything special you want us to look for?"

Manny smiled. Albert's name may be nerdy, but he was undoubtedly perceptive. "Yes, I want you to spy on Major Danskill. Just watch for a few hours, then take a prisoner, as high a rank as you can safely get, and bring him back to me for interrogation." Manny also pulled a stack of cards out of his pocket and handed them down to Albert. "These are non-picture documents that identify you as citizens of Iroquois City, just in case you get caught. I don't want you traced back to me."

Albert looked at the top document. It was an Iroquois County library card for a man named Lenny Switzer. He didn't like this job. It sounded dangerous. But the million-dollar question was: What is more dangerous? This mission or defying Manny?

"Yes, Manny. We'll get right on it."

Manny smiled and nodded. "I need it done before daybreak, so hurry." Manny turned to walk away but stopped and turned back abruptly. "Oh, and … you and your men will be richly rewarded." The other men smiled, but Albert just nodded as Manny turned and walked away. It was going to be a very long night.

☆ ☆ ☆ ☆

Donny Brewster watched through high-powered binoculars from underneath the snow-covered brush pile as Manny walked back inside the lodge. As near as he could tell these six men had just been given a job to do, and Donny planned on being there to supervise while they carried it out. He watched as the six men got up and followed their leader back through the camp and into one of the smaller cabins. Fifteen minutes later they emerged carrying M-16s and full backpacks. Wherever it was they were going, they were humping it at least part of the way. The six men walked over to quads and threw their gear into a trailer before mounting up and driving away. As the little caravan snaked their way through the campsite, Donny slowly and carefully left the cover of the brush and faded back into the woods. As he headed back to his own quad a half mile away, he pulled out his radio and talked as he ran.

"Tango two this is Tango one, over."

The response was almost immediate.

"This is Tango two, go ahead, over."

"Do you have a visual on the midget caravan heading out of camp?"

"Roger that, Tango one. They are nearing the entrance."

"Please maintain surveillance as long as possible. Let me know which way they go. I'm shadowing them on quadback."

"Roger that, Tango two."

Donny didn't bother to sign out. He broke into a full sprint and was soon on his quad heading to cut them off.

Ten Miles North of Iroquois City

Major Danskill put the radio back down on the elegant, oak dining room table and called for his second in command.

"Captain Foster!"

Within seconds the Captain entered the room and stood at attention. "Yes, sir."

"I just received word that Manny is sending six men to our location to take a prisoner for interrogation. They should arrive on quads from the east. Please double the guard tonight and extend the listening posts out to a mile."

Captain Foster saluted and strode out of the room. Major Danskill looked down at the map on the table. Manny was no problem. He could handle the gangbanger turned General Wannabe, but there was something else bothering him. He studied the map and the layout of the Iroquois City defenses. They were just too perfect, too precise, too … military.

He couldn't help but ask himself, *Who is their leader?* The question vexed him to his military bearing core. He had to find out. Danskill had long studied military science, and the words of Sun Tzu called out to him now. *"If you know the enemy and know yourself, you need not fear the result of a hundred battles. If you know yourself but not the enemy, for every victory gained you will also suffer a defeat. If you know neither the enemy nor yourself, you will succumb in every battle"*

The ancient warning bothered him. Know the enemy or succumb. He knew they weren't mere farmers, but ... *who are you?* The ambushes and heavy losses inflicted on Manny's column was not just text book perfect; it was also peppered with creativity and improvisation. Without the Apache helicopter and its infrared sensors and chain gun, he never would have found the attacking force to destroy it.

Manny had over two-thousand soldiers, but, however well-supplied, they were un-disciplined and untrained. The thought hit the Major like a sledge hammer. *They might be beaten.*

Major Danskill looked down at the map again. He would use Manny to draw them out, and if Manny was destroyed, so much the better. But Manny could weaken them, making it easier for his own force to take the town. But first, he needed a plan. He needed to find their weakness. He looked to the west and smiled.

Five Miles East of The Horde

Donny Brewster let out half his breath and pulled the trigger slowly and gently to the rear. He felt the recoil and then looked through the scope to see the quad pull to the left and lurch to a stop. The quads behind them stopped as if on command. All six of the men got off their quads and stood near the flat tire, just staring down at it helplessly.

Donny keyed his radio, "Tango two this is Tango one. Fire for effect." Then he raised his own rifle scope to his right eye and began firing again.

Albert was looking straight at his second in command when his head seemed to explode before his eyes. He hesitated, paralyzed in shock, as two more of his men went down almost in unison. As Albert ran to his quad, the remaining two men in his command slumped to the ground. One of them, shot in the pelvis, continued to scream and writhe on the ground in agony. A merciful follow-up shot to the head silenced him.

Albert jumped on the quad and reached down to turn the key. The next shot went into his quad's engine block. Then he heard an engine roar to life and watched as someone raced toward him. He jumped down behind the engine and unslung his M16 off his back as he moved. Just as he raised it to fire, a bullet hit him in the left ear, tearing it completely off. Albert dropped the rifle and fell to the ground, clutching at the bloody mess. A few seconds later he was looking up at the muzzle of a 9mm Glock pistol.

Adam Cervantes spoke in a hushed, almost soothing tone. "Hello Albert. Do you have a few minutes? We need to talk."

CHAPTER 20

The Defense of Iroquois City

MAJOR BRANCH LOOKED OUT OVER THE EIGHTY-SEVEN PEO-ple huddled in a mass in front of the courthouse steps. They were an odd bunch, some were just kids no more than twelve years old while others were in their seventies. Almost a quarter of them were women. On the inside, he sighed, knowing he'd been given an impossible task. On the outside, his face beamed with pride at his new command. And when he spoke, his voice was loud and steady, exuding the permanence of bedrock, imbuing his new troops with his own strength.

"The Horde is camped seven miles east of town. They have two-thousand men and will attack the city in the morning. If they succeed, then most of us will be dead. Refugees tell us The Horde always rape the women and children before killing them. Then they devour the town and all its resources like locusts before moving on." Dan studied the haggard faces in front of him. They'd already been through so much. It seemed unfair to ask more of them. But these were desperate times.

"But this is our town. We live here. Most of you were born here, and we're not going to let that happen to our families. Let there be no mistake: we are fighting for our homes and our very existence. The Horde wants your wives and children, to devour them, to torture them, to take from them their very souls." Dan hesitated as he looked out across the crowd, wondering if his words were having any impact. "But here's what I say. I was born here. I was raised here. I was in Wisconsin hundreds of miles away when all this happened, but I didn't stay there. I fought my way back. I came home. And now I'll fight to protect that home. I have a wife and two kids, and if The Horde wants them, then I have only one thing to say to The Horde. Molon Labe." Dan pronounced the ancient Greek phrase 'Ma-lown Lah-vey'.

"My Uncle Rodney taught that to me as a kid. It means 'Come and get them'. It was first uttered by the Spartans at the Battle of Thermopylae in 480 BC when King Xerxes of Persia asked them to lay down their arms and surrender their freedom."

Out of the corner of his eye Dan saw a middle-aged man reach his arm around a fourteen-year-old boy and squeeze. "But now, almost twenty-five-hundred years after the Spartans refused to surrender, I stand here before my friends and my home town, and I ask you to fight. And I would never ask you to do anything I wouldn't do myself." Dan placed his hand on Jeremy's shoulder and squeezed. "My own son will be fighting beside me. If we fail - we die. But if we win - our children live on."

Dan looked down and saw a determined look on his son's face. "But we will never surrender! We will never give up! We will never yield! We will fight until our very last breath so that our children and their children can live on. But I need to know … who will fight beside me?"

And then there was silence. It was deafening. And Dan couldn't help but wonder, *Are they going to leave, or will they stand and fight?*

Finally, an old man and his wife in the front row stepped forward. The man was carrying a double-barreled shotgun in his left hand. Without warning he raised it up over his head and screamed in a grizzled and throaty voice "Molon Labe!" His wife repeated his words. There was more silence, and then another man near the back cried out as well. "Molon Labe." Dan raised his own AR15 above his head and answered their cries "Molon Labe"! Then Jeremy did the same beside him. Like the ripple on a quiescent calm, just waiting for the wind to disturb it, the crowd rose up and lifted their weapons above their heads and cried out in one voice "Molon Labe"! Over and over the crowd chanted the battle cry "Molon Labe! Molon Labe! Molon Labe!"

Almost a block away Sheriff Leif heard the war cries of his own people and huddled in shame behind a dumpster.

Five Miles East of The Horde

Donny Brewster and Adam Cervantes stood outside the small pole barn with their prisoner tied up inside propped up against a bale of hay. As it turned out, Albert had allergies and they could hear him sneezing incessantly like a machine gun.

"I say we torture him until he tells us everything."

Sergeant Brewster shook his head at his friend and laughed. "Are you kidding me? He's already soiled himself and he's dying of allergies. All we have to do is ask him straight out and he'll sing like a canary."

Adam turned away. "Yeah, I know. I've never tortured anyone though, and I was hoping to expand my resume."

Donny reached over and put his right hand on Adam's left shoulder. "Well, at least your heart is in the right place. You're dedicated. I like that." Inside there was a pause in the sneezing, and they heard Albert yelling as loud as he could. "There are grid coordinates in my pocket written on a piece of paper!" He sneezed several more times. "Major Danskill and all his forces are there. He's got six Bradleys and three tanks. The attack helicopters are there too!"

Donny looked over at Adam and cocked his head to one side. "This man's loyalty to The Horde is truly awe-inspiring. Should we let him live?"

Adam smiled and looked out across the field and into the woods. "So we're not going to torture him? I've always wanted to water-board someone."

Donny reared back his head and laughed. "I like you, Adam. You're pretty cool for a National Guard guy. I was water-boarded once, just for fun. It takes a lot of water. We don't have any."

Adam's eyes sparkled in the light of fading day. "Hey! I could've been a Special Forces guy too." He paused. "I just lacked the physical stamina, mental acuity, and the advanced training."

Donny smiled again and turned to walk back into the pole barn. "Let's go get some more intel."

Adam opened the door and let Donny go first. "So are we going to torture him or not?"

Two-thousand Feet Above The Horde

Harold Steffens had been an infantry soldier during World War II with the Third Armored Division, but after the war he'd learned to fly bi-planes. After the excitement and trauma of world war, he'd been anxious to get home and marry his childhood sweetheart, Myra. He'd gotten a stable job at a nearby factory and they'd started a family, bought a house outside Iroquois and had lived there all their lives. Flying his bi-plane had supplied the thrill he'd needed to escape the boredom of small-town life. World War II had changed him forever.

Then in 1964 he'd quit his job at the factory and bought a Grumman Super Ag-Cat. For decades he dusted the fields of Iroquois with fertilizers, weed killer and seeds, whatever the farmers wanted. Even though his Super Ag-Cat was old, it still responded well, and that was more than he could say about his own, tired, old body. Nonetheless, today he felt up to the task of saving the world.

The basic Grumman Ag Cat had been the first airplane specifically built and produced by a major aircraft company for agricultural aviation. The first Ag-Cat flew its maiden flight on May 27, 1957, and had been in the air ever since.

Harold's Super Ag-Cat had a 600 horsepower engine, a length of 23 feet and a wing span of 35 feet. But the most important aspect of Harold's plane was the 300-gallon spray tank and all the supporting nozzles. But for Harold's final mission, 300 gallons wouldn't be enough. That's why he'd been working so hard the past weeks retrofitting it with a 500-gallon tank. If he was honest with himself, he didn't even know if it would get off the ground fully loaded. But the stakes were high, so he was willing to take the chance. It wasn't that big a deal since he planned on dying tomorrow anyway. He made a mental note to have someone cut down the trees at the end of his runway; it would do no one any good if he crashed and burned on take-off.

Harold flew over The Horde encampment taking pictures with the digital camera the way General Branch had instructed him. As long as he stayed up high he'd be safe from small-arms fire. After ten minutes he had all the pictures he needed, banked the plane and headed home.

Ten Miles North of Iroquois City

The sun had already set, and Adam and Donny surveyed the old farmhouse two-hundred yards away through Night Vision binoculars. On the outside it looked like any other farm, with the exception of the Abrams tanks, Bradley Fighting Vehicles and Apache helicopters. They tried to count the tents and soldiers, but there were just too many of them. Donny finally settled with an estimate of two-hundred.

"Should we try to get closer?"

Donny shook his head. "Why? You got a death wish?"

Adam smiled in the darkness. "No, just wanted to add recon to my resume." Donny lowered his binoculars.

"Does it look like they're getting ready to move out to you?"

Adam nodded. "Yup. Tents are starting to come up. Stuff being stowed into the Bradleys and the trucks."

Just then one of the Abrams tanks started their engine. The sound dominated the night and drowned out the voices of the soldiers. "Looks like they're running through the Abrams start-up checklist to me. That JP8 hybrid diesel fuel has to warm up for 20 minutes, according to the book that is."

Donny nodded in agreement. "Let's fall back to the quads and get this called in. The General needs to know about this."

They quietly withdrew and made their way back to the quads over a mile away.

In The Bunker

General Branch had just left the house with his squad of Shadow Militia security detail. They were an impressive bunch of soldiers. Baby Donna was asleep now beside

Jackie in a wooden crate filled with blankets. Uncle Rodney had taken her and the baby into his bedroom. She'd been shocked at the austerity of the little room. It was barren except for a wooden footlocker, a cot, a pot-bellied stove and a metal, olive-drab wall locker. But Rodney hadn't stopped there. He'd also taken her through another locked door and down a manhole using a ladder leading below the house. It was like a fallout shelter, only much more advanced.

She looked around her now in awe at the stacks of crates and boxes. Now she knew why they had so much food. But it was more than that. On a wooden box beside her was written "TOW 2A/B". The box she was using as a chair said "M72A2". Jackie had no idea what that meant, but Uncle Rodney had left explicit orders not to touch anything.

He'd given her a sleeping bag, a cot, a portable bucket latrine, and there were several pallets of MREs and bottles of distilled water off to her left. She could probably survive down here for months if she had to.

But the main reason she was here was the fancy radio in front of her. She didn't know what it was or how it worked, but Uncle Rodney had given her written instructions on how to monitor the broadcasts and what to listen for. She'd taped the list of frequencies to the desk she was sitting at. Some were for aviation; some for armor; and others for ground troops. She surmised the aviation frequency was for talking to the Apache helicopters, wherever they were. But to her knowledge not even Uncle Rodney had any tanks.

Out of curiosity she opened the file drawer on the left side of the desk to see what was inside. She reached down and picked up the hand grenade. It seemed heavy for its size, and it was shaped wrong. In the movies she'd seen grenades were always shaped like pineapples, but this one was round. She saw the pin and was careful not to touch it.

Baby Donna started to cry, so she picked her up and rocked her back and forth. Under no circumstances was she to leave the bunker. In fact, even if she wanted to she couldn't, since Uncle Rodney has locked it from the outside.

Her instructions were clear and simple. Monitor all three of the radio frequencies and listen for one phrase: "Fire the Golden FPF ." If she heard that phrase, she was to relay the message over a different radio that was off to the right. It was bigger and more complicated, but it was already set up for her. She just had to turn it on, depress the handset and transmit.

Just then she heard someone talking; it was on the ground forces frequency. She recognized the voice as Donny Brewster. "Tango Actual, this is Tango one, over."

Uncle Rodney's voice came back almost immediately. "Tango one this is Tango Actual, go ahead, over."

"This is Tango one, we have confirmed sighting of the following: two-hundred enemy soldiers, four Abrams tanks, two Apache attack helicopters and four Bradley fighting Vehicles. Please confirm receipt of transmission, over."

"Roger that, Tango One. Message is received. Please send coordinates, over."

"This is Tango One with figures to follow:" There was a slight pause. "4 - 4 - 1 - 1 - 7 -5 - 0 - 5. I say again 4 - 4 - 1 - 1 - 7 -5 - 0 - 5. Please confirm, over."

"This is Tango Actual, I confirm as follows, 4 - 4 - 1 - 1 - 7 -5 - 0 - 5, over."

Donny's voice came back right away. "This is Tango one, the enemy force appears to be bugging out. What are your orders?"

There were several seconds of silence before Uncle Rodney came back. "Tango One this is Tango Actual, your orders are to observe and report. Do not engage without authorization."

"Roger that, Tango Actual. Out."

Jackie looked down and spoke to baby Donna. "Wow! We're listening to the whole war in the comfort of our own home! This might be cool!"

CHAPTER 21

Iroquois City HQ

COLONEL MACPHERSON SAT DOWN AT THE TABLE ACROSS from his commanding general. Rodney was impressed with the man. For the decades he'd known Ranger MacPherson, he'd always seemed unflappable. He never got tired, never got discouraged, never wavered in his duties or made poor judgments. The two of them were alone now for the first time in days.

"Why the hell do you continue to follow me after all these years, Mac?"

The Colonel smiled slightly. "It's because I have no life of my own to speak of, sir. No wife, no kids. My prostate's the size of Texas, so sex hasn't been an option for over ten years now."

Rodney laughed out loud and then took a sip of his coffee. He liked it thick and black, especially the night before battle. When the laughter died down the Colonel spoke again. "Actually, sir, if I may be so candid, the reason I follow you is because you're one of the few men who are worthy of my service."

General Branch cocked his head off to one side but remained smiling. "I'm not even sure how to take that, Mac. Care to expand?"

The grizzled, old soldier across from him locked eyes with his general. "I follow you because when I served under you in combat you exemplified what it means to be an Army Ranger. Honor, duty, integrity, courage. They're not just words to me. I would die for those words, and so would you. I follow you because you've earned my service through your personal sacrifice and bravery, and because you were the first to see the need for The Shadow Militia."

Colonel MacPherson paused and turned away to look at the wall. "I follow you because no one else leads me where I want to go the way you do. You've got more brains and balls than anyone else out there. And then …" He paused again and smiled just a tad. "There is the matter of my prostate."

Rodney Branch reared back in his chair and laughed as hard as he could until the whole table shook. About a minute later the room was quiet again. The General stood up from his chair and walked over to the window. He looked out into the darkness. Neither man said anything for a time.

Slowly, the General turned and spoke. "We have four Bradleys, four Abrams tanks

and two Apache attack helicopters moving quickly to our rear flank. They're supported by two-hundred professional infantry."

The Colonel nodded. "Yes, I know. I heard Sergeant Brewster's transmission"

Rodney looked over at his second in command to meet his gaze. "That doesn't
concern you?"

"Of course it concerns me. And we have to deal with it. The big question is how?"

The General nodded and moved back to the table where a plastic-laminated map
was spread out before them.

"Sergeant Brewster has them here and moving in this direction. They'll be in position to attack within a few hours. But I don't think they'll attack until The Horde
has done its worst damage. And that won't be until tomorrow, maybe later if I have
anything to say about it. But when they do attack; it's going to be tough. The citizens
of Iroquois have no weapons capable of taking out an Abrams."

Colonel MacPherson interrupted his thoughts. "You know we can't help them beyond our charter?"

Rodney nodded with genuine sadness. "I know, but there must be something we can
do to help, to give them a fighting chance. They've been brave and they deserve that
much."

The other soldier looked down at the floor. "I know,sir. But I have to remind you
of our rules of engagement. We can't tip our hand. If we do, well, then it's not just
Iroquois that will suffer. Let's face it, sir, we're only here because this is your home
town. There are cities like this all over the country being raped and pillaged. This is
but one, small town among thousands."

Rodney turned his back on the Colonel and stared out the window again. "Are you
saying it was a mistake for me to intervene here?"

The Colonel smiled to himself. "Of course not, sir. You and I both know generals
don't make mistakes. Let's just call it a calculated risk with avenues for both success
as well as failure."

Colonel MacPherson was watching the General's reflection in the window and
thought he saw the hint of a smile.

"Colonel, you said one of the reasons you follow me was my sense of honor. My
honor tells me we can't give these people hope and then abandon them. We have to
find a way to help them within the bounds of our charter."

He turned back around and a smile spread across his face as he spoke. We are fight-
ing a battle with a militia army of farmers and factory workers." He paused for effect.
"So tell me, Colonel, what do farmers and factory workers have that can take out an
Abrams tank?"

At first the Colonel seemed confused, but then, little by little, a smile of his own took
root and bloomed across his military face. "You're a genius, sir. A military genius!"

Rodney Branch scoffed at his friend. "Yeah, right. But you and I both know we're
just two old men on the downhill side of life with nothing to lose and nothing left to
live for. The General smiled. "And then there's the matter of your prostate. I'm going
to requisition you a new one after this battle is over."

The Army Ranger snapped to attention and gave the General a crisp, military salute.
General Branch snapped to attention and returned the salute.

"I'll make it happen, sir."

And with that the Colonel rushed out the door in search of the right materials in the proper proportions.

Restoring the Sheriff

"How did you find me?"

Colonel MacPherson remained stoic in front of Sheriff Leif. "Your wife told us you might be here at the church. I think it's a good place to be right now. I've always been a praying man myself, especially on the night before battle."

The Sheriff was sitting all slumped down in a wooden pew near the front of the auditorium. A large wooden cross filled the center of the podium up against the wall. "You must think I'm a real coward to walk out the way I did, to leave the fight and demand we retreat in order to survive."

The Colonel stood ram-rod straight before him. As usual, every muscle in his body was taut in readiness. "I don't get paid to think, Sheriff Leif, I get paid to follow orders."

The Sheriff tried unsuccessfully to lighten the atmosphere with his next remark, but failed miserably. "The Shadow Militia gets paid? By who?"

His remark went unanswered.

"I don't pretend to understand civilians, sir. They don't compute to me. I'm a simple man with black and white thinking. My selector switch has only two modes: FIGHT and DIE. Anything beyond that seems irrelevant to me."

The Sheriff stood up and stretched his back, then he ran his right palm through his greasy, unwashed hair. "What do you want with me, colonel?"

"The General needs your help with a project."

"A project?"

"Yes, sir. The General would like you to build a series of bombs to help defend the city against an armored attack from our western flank, sir."

"What?"

The Sheriff collapsed back down in the church pew and began praying again while Colonel MacPherson filled him in on the details.

The Horde Encampment

Manny called it making love, but, in reality, it took only about forty-five seconds before it was over. The woman left his bed in silence, and Manny would never see her again. That's the way he liked it, and he never slept with the same woman twice. Relationships were just too time-consuming and complicated. Manny noted that few of the other great conquerors allowed themselves to get tied down or mixed up in constraining female relationships. In Manny's mind, women were good only for cooking and breeding. It was simple, straight forward, and it made sense to him.

Outside his lodge, he could hear the music and voices of the party in full swing. The debauchery would continue until about 2 a.m. when it would begin to subside and eventually fade away altogether by three o'clock. It was predictable.

That bothered him from a security standpoint, but he knew there was little he could do about it. His soldiers weren't really soldiers at all, and therein laid both their greatest strength and their greatest weakness. Manny knew so long as he kept the men fed, laid and drugged, they would follow him to the ends of the earth. But if he wavered on even one of the three, they would turn on him like jackals on a carcass. He had learned the secret to being a great leader; *People will only follow you so long as you're taking them where they already want to go.*

Manny got out of bed and walked over to the log-made table. He loved the smell of pine. He looked down at the map and smiled. It was a good plan. Estimates showed less than five-hundred townspeople in arms against his twenty-five hundred. He knew they'd captured one of his Bradley fighting vehicles, but that would have to be deployed against Major Danskill and his forces as they attacked the town from the western flank. He called it Operation Hammer and Anvil. Danskill was the anvil, cutting off any escape, and The Horde was the giant hammer that would smash down on the farmers and townspeople futiley trying to protect the town. That was assuming they were still there to fight. Some of the towns they had already rolled through, the smart ones, had been abandoned long before their arrival, and all they had to do was collect up the supplies before partying and moving on.

But another thing weighed heavy on his mind. Albert was yet to check in. He'd sent him to spy on Major Danskill and capture a prisoner for interrogation. But Albert had fallen off the face of the earth. Had he been captured? If so, he was surely dead by now. Had he deserted? Not likely, but if so, Manny could get ten more people like him in a matter of hours. Albert was easily replaced.

The music was blaring away outside his window, but he wanted to sleep. Lovemaking always did that to him. He recognized the song now, and started humming along with the lyrics.

I've paid my dues - Time after time
I've done my sentence - But committed no crime

Yes, *Queen* was a good group.

And bad mistakes - I've made a few
I've had my share of sand kicked in my face
But I've come through

Manny could relate to that. People had kicked him before, but he'd gotten the best of them.

We are the champions - my friends
And we'll keep on fighting - till the end

The song blared on and soon Manny was singing as loud as he could, so loud that he never heard Buster walk up the stairs and into his bedroom.

We are the champions
We are the champions
No time for losers
'Cause we are the champions - of the world

Manny looked up in anger, embarrassed by the situation and that Buster had heard his terrible singing voice.

"Who said you could come up here?"

Buster looked confused. "Ahh, you did."

Manny was naked, so he walked over to the dresser and put his clothes on. Buster waited patiently by the door.

"So are you going to tell me what the hell you want or just stand there all night?"

Buster's face flushed red. He didn't like being yelled at. "Ah, well, I just thought you wanted to know when we're bein' attacked, that's all."

"Attacked!"

Manny jumped on the bed and landed on the other side where his boots lay on the floor. "Well why didn't you say so? Where are they? What's happening? Talk to me!"

Buster seemed confused by all the questions, so it took a moment to sort them out.

"Answer me! Now!"

"A bunch of quads and trucks raced up to the campground entrance and killed our guards. Then they set the ticket booth on fire along with a couple trucks we had up there."

Manny finished lacing up his boots and jumped up, grabbing his M4 as he went. "Let's get down there and find out what the hell's happening."

Manny stormed down the stairs followed closely by his assistant. Manny heard gunshots, but *Queen* was still playing loudly in the background.

The Horde would not sleep tonight.

CHAPTER 22

Preparing the Iroquois Air Force

IT WAS LATE AND SERGEANT STEFFENS WAS EXHAUSTED. BUT for some reason he just couldn't sleep. The Captain had left two hours ago and everything was as ready as it ever would be. The larger tank was fitted; the spray rack had been modified to increase the flow, and the Super Ag Cat was fueled and ready for its final mission. The big question weighing heavy on his mind was this: Could he even get the thing off the ground? He knew it was too heavy, much heavier than the specs called out, but he felt the added payload was worth the risk in the toll it would take. Harold didn't mind dying tomorrow. He didn't mind going home to Myra. He looked forward to it, actually. In fact, if truth be told, and if by some remote chance he survived, Harold knew he would be disappointed.

He held the flare gun in his hand, and looked down at it now. He seemed amazed at the wrinkles and gnarls that had overtaken both his hands. Old age had a way of sneaking up on a man. One day he was young and strong and handsome, and the next … well, in the next, his life was almost over now. He recalled a sermon he'd heard from decades ago on the fleeting nature of life. Harold had memorized the verse to keep death from sneaking up on him.

"Yet you do not know what your life will be like tomorrow. You are just a vapor that appears for a little while and then vanishes."

Harold sat in the wooden chair in his pole barn beside the airplane, moving in closer to the pot-bellied stove. It gave off just enough heat to keep him from freezing to death. He was the entirety of the Iroquois County Air Force. Harold knew the General and his Shadow Militia had more than enough firepower to destroy The Horde and Major Danskill's puny forces, and Harold had always wondered why he didn't just do it and be done with it. Why should so many townspeople have to fight and die without reason? All the death seemed in vain. But the General had revealed to him the secret reason, and Harold had agreed. It was far better for one old man to die, and Harold didn't mind dying to save others. Self sacrifice was how he'd won the Silver Star so many years ago in France, and that's how he'd lived the remainder of his life. To change now would seem to disrespect everything he'd lived to date.

No, Harold Steffens would finish strong. He moved his left hand up to his collar and fingered the silver bar General Branch had pinned on his uniform. He recalled the General's words of just a few hours before.

"Pilots are officers, and you, sir, have exemplified in every fashion that you are an officer and a gentleman."

Harold smiled. He spoke out loud to his plane. "Better late than never." And he wondered if Myra would be impressed. Lieutenant Steffens pulled the green, wool blanket up around his torso and closed his eyes, waiting, just waiting for the dawn, waiting for the final vapor to rise up and fade away.

The Iroquois Welcome Wagon Visits The Horde

Chain saws fired up all across the state forest campgrounds, and trees began to fall everywhere. Twelve oaks fell across the camp's access road, effectively trapping Manny and his men on the wrong side of the camp, thereby rendering them unable to head back in. Manny fumed helplessly as he watched his trucks at the main entrance burn out of control.

Back inside the camp Major Dan Branch and his company of men and women wreaked wholesale havoc in the darkness. Manny had taken all the alert guards to the camp entrance with him, leaving only the drunk and sleeping to protect his encampment. Most of The Horde slept through the devastation that was now ensuing.

General Branch's orders had been clear. "Reduce The Horde's ability to transport soldiers." Major Branch accomplished this by throwing dozens of Molotov cocktails, nothing more than Mason jars filled with gasoline, on most of the vehicles. That gave the militia plenty of light to work by. Meanwhile, sharpshooters hidden in the brush cut down any of The Horde members who were alert enough to pop out of their tents. The fire and confusion allowed Dan's soldiers to work unopposed for almost five minutes. Chain saws felled trees onto the roads and trucks. All of the cabins were set on fire, and most of the occupants died mercifully in their sleep from smoke inhalation. Five dedicated men shot out the tires of any trucks escaping fire or the trees.

By the time The Horde was able to organize any real resistance, Major Branch and his militia faded back into the trees and began the seven-mile walk back to Iroquois City.

Protecting the Iroquois Rear Flank

Colonel MacPherson's original idea had been to place a series of truck bombs beside the road leading into town from the west. But, to his credit, Sheriff Leif had improved the idea. "If we place the bombs in plain sight they may cause suspicion and be easy to evade. Let's make it harder for them."

And so Joe Leif had enlisted the service of Mark Englerth who owned a local excavation company to dig a long trench using two back hoes. They worked through the night, but by 4 a.m. the task was finished. The local farm bureau had donated fifteen-thousand pounds of Ammonium Nitrate fertilizer, while the plating plant across town gave them enough Nitromethane solvent to create a trench bomb over one-hundred-twenty yards long. They linked it together with a series of blasting caps and wires then covered up the fresh dirt by using the city's snowblower. As if signifying His divine approval, it snowed an inch from 4 a.m. to 6 a.m., and by daybreak the mother of all bombs looked like just another stretch of road.

To give them more options, Colonel MacPherson also had four mobile bombs made. Two old clunkers plus a Yugo and a Toyota Prius. Both of the latter were requisitioned in the dead of night from the local car dealership. All four of them could be detonated remotely. General Branch had personally organized the defenses for the east side of town where The Horde was expected to make a frontal attack. But, just in case, he also stationed one-hundred defenders to the north and also to the south of town, They could be used as a ready reserve and to prevent The Horde from flanking the town. The mobile fertilizer bombs were spread out across the city as part of a rapid reactionary force.

By 6 a.m. General Branch gave final orders to the Home Guard leaders. They were huddled around a large bonfire near the center of town as he spoke.

"You soldiers did a great job. Because of all your hard work this town now has a fighting chance. I want to thank the Sheriff for his leadership and his ingenuity at covering our rear flank." He glanced over at Joe Leif who was now in his Sheriff's uniform. It was clean and sharply pressed thanks to his wife, Marge. The Sheriff just nodded and looked down at the ground sheepishly. He knew the truth, how he'd walked out only hours before, and he was humbled and thankful for this second chance.

"I want to thank Major Branch and his men and women from the newly formed Militia Rangers who attacked The Horde camp just a few hours ago. Because of their bravery and military creativity, we'll have several more hours to prepare."

He held his hands out in front of him to soak in some warmth. The snow had stopped now, but it had left a thin blanket of pure whiteness all around them.

"Before I give you your final orders, I'd like to have Father Fish and Pastor Bowman say a few words to God on our behalf."

Both men came forward and stood side by side in front of the fire. They were wearing Car-Hart insulated coveralls with home-made snow camo made from white bed sheets. Father Fish was holding an over and under twelve gauge trap shotgun in his left hand with the hand-carved, mahogany stock planted in the snow. Pastor Bowman wore a holstered Springfield XD in 9mm but also held a 30.06 hunting rifle with a Bushmaster scope. Father Fish spoke first.

"Dear God. We come before you with praise that we have survived for so long. We are deeply grateful for your steadfast love and mercy. Please be with us in the coming battle. Focus our minds, embolden our hearts. Fill us with courage and resolve for what we are forced now to do. Amen."

Pastor Bowman stepped forward and took a more direct approach to God. "Dear God. The Philistines are marching on our city. We need to kill them. To the last man they need to die. They are evil and don't believe in you. We must purge the land of their lust for power. So come to us in the time of our need. Help us kill them all. Amen"

General Branch smiled. "Now those were mighty fine prayers, men. Thanks and keep talking to God for us. We need all the help we can get."

Then he turned to the others as they stood around the bonfire. They moved in closer to hear their leader's every word, and to somehow, if it was possible, soak in any leftover strength he might be giving off.

"Okay, we've got our work cut out for us on this one. I won't BS you about it. Lots of us are going to die in the next eight hours." He looked around from man to man, meeting eyes whenever he could. "But if we fail, if even a hundred of these butchers make it into town, you can kiss your families goodbye, because they'll leave no survivors. It will be a slow and painful death for the people you love and hold dear."

Then he hesitated. He needed to embolden them, leave them with strength and hope.

"But if you follow my orders; if your hearts remain true and strong, you will prevail and your children will be saved." The General rubbed his hands together in front of the fire.

"Now ... here's what we're going to do."

CHAPTER 23

Meanwhile Back at the Horde

B USTER STAYED OFF TO ONE SIDE AS HIS BOSS ROAMED BACK and forth like a caged animal. The sun had just come up and the extent of the damage done by the Iroquois Rangers was becoming more and more apparent. Most of The Horde's vehicles had been destroyed or rendered useless, but several of them could be salvaged just by changing the tires.

"Get me a hundred chain saws and start cutting these trees up and get them out of the road! I want to be moving into that town in two hours."

No one moved so Manny unholstered his pistol and fired it three times into the air. "Did you people hear me?" Buster backed away, putting a standing tree between himself and his boss. Others, most of them still hung over from the night before, simply stood and stared blankly at their leader.

"I said move!" And to emphasize his point, Manny walked up to the biggest man around him and fired one shot to the head. The man went down instantly in a heap.

"I said move! Now!"

The encampment instantly fell into a frenzy of people now miraculously sober.

They searched out chain saws and began clearing the road. Within the hour, two of the deuce and a half trucks were drivable and began hooking up ropes to the logs and pulling them out as well.

For the next two hours Manny stood by with his body guards, all with weapons drawn, watching intently to make sure no one slowed down. After that work was completed, Manny called his remaining leaders together for a talk. Many of the others had died the night before, burned to death in the cabins.

"We're going to walk seven miles into Iroquois City. And when we get there, anyone who opposes us is going to die. Anyone who surrenders is going to be raped, tortured and killed. When we catch the leader, I want him taken alive. I have a special brand of pain to inflict on him. Do you all understand?"

The twenty-three men nodded, almost in unison. "And another thing, if any of your men balk, if they hesitate, if they run, you are to shoot them immediately."

Some of the men smiled, others were terrified, while others simply stared back at him blankly. These men were the soul-less, the damned, and they had abandoned long ago any shred of human compassion or dignity. They would do as ordered so long as it kept them alive, gave them power and brought them pleasure.

At 11 a.m. The Horde was assembled on the road leading out of the state campgrounds. They were a rabbled-looking bunch, but still numbering almost two-thousand strong. Manny extended his left palm out to Buster who was standing beside him. Immediately Buster handed over the megaphone, and Manny moved it up to his mouth.

"We stand poised on the cusp of our greatest battle." Buster thought to himself, *What's a cusp?* "But we will move ahead and we will crush them like no other enemy we've faced. Last night they attacked in a cowardly fashion, in the dead of night as we slept. But now we are awake and we are not happy! We will attack in force and kill every living creature. We'll kill the men, the women, the children, even their dogs and cats must die."

Manny paused to gauge their response, but no one said anything. "And when we are done, after they've been sufficiently raped, tortured and killed, we will take everything of value and then burn the town to the ground. No stone will remain on top of another." Still no one said anything. There were no cheers as Manny had expected. So he went on.

"And then we march on to Traverse City, the jewel of the Michigan west coast, plush with million-dollar homes, ripe for the picking. We will conquer it and live there like kings, lacking nothing, and all our dreams will come true."

The crowd finally erupted in cheers and Manny smiled and raised up his M16 and fired into the air. The crowd reacted by raising their own firearms and firing as well. A few minutes later the crowd quieted, but not before three of them slumped to the ground dead from accidental gunshot wounds.

They dragged the bodies off the road, and Manny gave the order to move out. The Horde was on its way.

The Final Launch of Lieutenant Steffens

Lieutenant Steffens had already gone through his pre-flight checklist, and the Super Ag Cat was now roaring down the field beside his house. He'd begun his take-off run up in his driveway to allow him extra speed. With the added weight of his new spray tanks, he'd need every ounce of energy just to make it in the air.

Halfway down the runway, Harold got a sinking feeling in the pit of his stomach. He thought to himself, *I'm not going to make it.* But he pushed ahead anyway. He had to make it off the ground. Lives depended on it. Three-quarters of the way to the trees he began to pray. "Please God. Help me get in the air. I have to get in the air." Just as he reached the end of the field his wheels lifted off the ground, but the trees were looming ahead, getting bigger with each passing second. Harold prayed under his breath. *Please God.* Just before he reached the trees a gust of headwind pushed under his wings and lifted him above the woods. Harold started breathing again. "Thank you God."

The plane was sluggish with the extra weight, but Harold built up more airspeed and was soon gaining altitude. He looked back at the home he'd built with Myra, where they'd raised their children, where they'd lived their lives and made their mark, and he couldn't help but think, *It's hard to believe it was all but a vapor.*

He banked the plane and headed for The Horde gaining more altitude as he went.

The Deadly March to Town

Major Dan Branch had organized his new Rangers into four-person fire teams, and they began attacking The Horde five miles outside of town. This time The Horde was without quads and was unable to pursue them, so each fire team lay down in the open fields about one hundred yards north of the road and fired until The Horde had passed them by or until they ran out of ammo. But that wasn't a problem since the ammo was quickly replaced using stockpiles Dan and his Rangers had hidden along the route.

When cover was available they took advantage of it, but it hardly seemed necessary against a mass of two thousand people moving at two miles per hour. The trucks in the back of the column were carrying all the ammo, and they were quickly rendered useless with well-placed shots to the tires. Manny ordered his troops to carry the ammo by hand and this slowed them down even more. Dan had also placed hundreds of booby traps along the road in the early hours of the morning in the form of toe-popping mines, punji sticks and even a few claymore mines his uncle had given him. The claymores were the worst, going off and shredding dozens of people in the tightly packed column. Three miles from town only fifteen hundred Horde remained. As Dan watched from a hill above the road, he ordered his Rangers to intensify their fire. If even five-hundred of the Horde made it to town the city would be over run.

Sergeant Donny Brewster, Lisa Vanderboeg and Staff Sergeant Adam Cervantes were waiting in the Bradley Fighting Vehicle about two miles outside of town. They had it warmed up and ready to roll in defense of Iroquois. Lisa was manning the 25 mm cannon while Donny stood ready on the 7.62 mm machine gun.

Adam had parked the Bradley behind a berm which hid them completely about five hundred yards to the south of the road. Because there were Apache Attack helicopters in the area, behind them they'd dug small trenches to dive into just in case they were attacked from the air. Donny knew their Bradley was capable of killing everyone in the column and halting the advance, but, nonetheless, he felt uneasy. This was just too simple. And Donny Brewster had lived neither a simple nor a lucky life.

"Wait for me to open fire, Lisa."

Lisa nodded. Her stomach felt queasy, and she fought back the urge to vomit. When Donny's machine gun went off it startled her so much that it took several seconds for her to join in. But when her cannon opened up it deafened her ears completely. Donny, more practiced at shooting automatic weapons was dead on almost immediately. His bullets chewed up the column as he raked back and forth. People went down in blood and bone while others dove for nonexistent cover. Once Lisa's 25 mm cannon found the range bodies were blown in half and all hell broke loose. Donny concentrated on the left, while Lisa fired to the right.

Manny was near the front of the column when the machine guns opened up, tearing the center of his march to shreds. He dove for cover as did everyone around him. He immediately reached for his radio and tried calling Major Danskill again. But Danskill hadn't answered him in almost twenty-four hours now. He suspected the Major had captured Albert and his raiding party and was holding it against him.

From one mile east of the road, Major Danskill watched from the safety of the Abrams tank. Immediately he knew what had happened, indeed, had expected it. Because that's what he would do in that situation. Without bringing the Bradley's big guns to bear, Manny's column would undoubtedly roll through the town and remain a viable fighting force. And Danskill just couldn't have that, so he allowed Donny's machine guns a full minute before ordering the Apache to attack the entrenched Bradley. He laughed as Manny's men were torn to pieces.

"Reloading!"

The fire from the 7.62 mm machine gun silenced as Donny took time to arm up. Lisa slowed her rate of fire as targets were now on the ground and harder to find. Adam was atop the vehicle with binoculars searching the air.

Donny had just finished reloading and was about to fire again when Adam yelled. "Cease fire! Cease fire! Air attack!"

Donny swung the machine gun around and began firing on the approaching Apache Attack helicopter, but before it got close enough for accurate hits, Adam saw the Hellfire missile separate from the approaching aircraft.

"Jump! Get out!"

Donny saw Adam spring off the Bradley, so he jumped off himself. Lisa was the last to leave just before the Hellfire exploded into their fighting vehicle.

The helicopter hovered over the smoking Bradley. "Eagle Leader, this is Sparrowhawk. Enemy Bradley is destroyed. There are no survivors, over."

From over a mile away Major Danskill smiled. His plan was falling into place nicely. The lone Bradley Fighting Vehicle was the only weapon the town had capable of destroying an Abrams tank. Now his armor could roll in through the rear flank unopposed followed up by two-hundred well-trained infantry. He would rout the townspeople, and then kill Manny. Then he'd take command of the remainder of The Horde and march in to Traverse City where he would enjoy some R&R while waiting for further instructions.

"Sparrowhawk, this is Eagle Leader. Good job. Take up aerial recon above the city, over."

"Roger that, Eagle Leader. This is Sparrowhawk, out."

With that the Apache attack helicopter raced away in preparation for the next battle.

CHAPTER 24

Death from Above

THE ENGINE ON HAROLD'S SUPER AG CAT SPUTTERED A BIT, so he quickly adjusted the fuel mix to even out the engine. He could see The Horde column about a mile ahead. They were on the road and marching, but in less force than he'd seen last night on his final recon patrol. He passed the abandoned trucks, sitting there, dead and motionless on the road to town. He let them be. His primary objective was to kill as many people as possible before they reached the town. As the Horde moved away, he saw hundreds of dead bodies in front of him, but almost a thousand strong still marched on toward Iroquois City.

Harold looked down at the flare gun in his lap and smiled. The plan had been his all along, and he was oddly proud of it. He laughed out loud at the irony, but his laughter was lost to the sound of the plane's engine. The plan he'd devised and worked so desperately to bring to fruition would undoubtedly also bring about his own demise. But it was a death he could live with. It had honor, and how many people these days could hope for such an outcome.

Harold lined up on The Horde and began his final approach.

General Branch at HQ

It was the thing Rodney Branch hated the most about being a general; he couldn't stand the waiting while others were out fighting, killing and dying. The map was spread out in front of him on the table, and every time the radio reported a change, he'd reach down and move some of the plastic toys from one place to another. He reached down now and turned the Bradley Fighting Vehicle onto its side. Thank God Donny and his crew were okay. And thank God they'd taken out five hundred of The Horde before being knocked out. But it was a major loss ... one that Rodney had anticipated. The loss of the Bradley's TOW missile launcher was irreplaceable ... unless ... you happened to have several cases of them in your bomb shelter, which of course Rodney did. Several days ago he'd had his Ford F250 truck converted into a mobile TOW launcher. It was parked on the courthouse steps waiting deployment.

Over the decades General Branch had studied his Sun Tzu religiously.

"Appear weak when you are strong, and strong when you are weak."

The latest battle outside town had raised several questions for him. Mainly, why had they taken out the Bradley only after Donny had destroyed half the attacking infantry? Why hadn't the Apaches been flying cover for the ground units? Why were there no strafing runs on Dan's Rangers? Why was there no bombardment of the town by the Abrams tanks? This was not a traditional battle plan, and it led Rodney to believe he was dealing with two separate forces instead of one coordinated unit.

He thought about it and shook his head. He yearned to know the answers to those questions. He needed to know who he was fighting. For Sun Tzu had also said:

"If you know the enemy and know yourself, you need not fear the result of a hundred battles. If you know yourself but not the enemy, for every victory gained you will also suffer a defeat. If you know neither the enemy nor yourself, you will succumb in every battle"

General Branch knew himself, and he knew one of his two enemies but … it would have to do. Besides, he still had some surprises, and he was pretty certain neither of his enemies knew he existed.

Three Miles east of town

Major Danskill put the radio down and thought for a moment. Traditional rules of warfare demanded a softening-up barrage by the Abrams tanks before moving in, but that was unnecessary now that the Bradley was destroyed. If the enemy had mortars or artillery they certainly would have used them by now. Manny's approaching Horde would have definitely flushed them out. Everything the enemy had done so far suggested they were an organized resistance but possessed only small arms. With the best intel he had, Major Danskill concluded he was up against a force of about five-hundred well organized and determined fighters. They were probably all townspeople who were being lead by a combat veteran who just happened to live in this town. It made sense, and there was no reason for him to deviate from his original attack plan, He would send the armor in the back door as soon as Manny's Horde breached the town. Manny would then do most of the fighting and take the lion's share of the casualties. And that suited Major Danskill just fine.

And then he heard the sound of an engine approaching from the east. He turned and looked to the sky.

"What the hell?"

☆ ☆ ☆ ☆

Lieutenant Steffens opened the spray nozzles and hundreds of gallons of one-hundred octane gasoline sprayed down on the advancing Horde below.

Manny looked up at the approaching bi-plane and snarled. "What the hell?" Then he smelled the gas and watched as the deadly mist rained down on the remnant of his army. Manny flew into an uncontrollable rage, raised up his M16 and fired at the crop duster as it flew toward the head of the column. It was the last thing Manny ever did.

Major Danskill looked on in shock and disbelief as the remainder of The Horde was incinerated. His eyes followed the trail of fire as it blossomed in orange fury all the way up into the sky as if chasing the plane.

"Wow. That's impressive."

Then he angrily slammed his fist down on the metal armor of the Abrams and screamed out in pain.

"Who are you?"

Harold Steffens heard the unexpected concussion below him and glanced over his shoulder. Upon seeing the flames racing up through the sky toward his plane, he quickly fumbled to turn off the sprayer. The fire stopped climbing toward him. As he flew into the east side of town, Harold looked down at the useless flare gun on his lap. His original plan had been to make a second pass to ignite the gas, but he hadn't foreseen the fact that enemy small arms fire would do the job for him.

As Manny and his Horde burned all the way to hell, it finally occurred to Lieutenant Steffens that he was still alive. While flying over the old, red, brick courthouse, Harold rocked the bi-plane's wings. He'd always wanted to do that.

That's when he heard the voice of General Branch over his radio. "Great job, Lieutenant! You got them all!"

Harold smiled as he replied to his commanding general. "Roger that, sir. What are your orders?"

There was silence. Then a reply. "Stand by for further orders, Lieutenant."

General Branch put down his radio and smiled. He looked up at the bi-plane as it flew overhead. On the underside of the wings, written in hunter-orange paint were the words "Molon Labe." Rodney snickered to himself and thought, *That's a nice touch.* Then he turned back triumphantly to the task at hand. "One army down and one more to go."

But quickly his face grew stern. Four Bradleys, four Abrams and two Apaches plus two hundred infantry. The math didn't add up. He needed a plan. The General reached down and picked up his radio again. "Ranger One this is Iroquois Leader, come in, over." A few seconds elapsed before his nephew answered.

"This is Ranger One. Go ahead, Iroquois Leader."

"This is Iroquois Leader. All units return to base. Out."

Dan Branch looked down at the radio as if confused by the abruptness of the command. Then he looked out at the long trail of fire and smoke. There was no movement out on the road, but the smell of gas and burning flesh was causing some of his people to vomit. He thought to himself. *Okay, I guess he knows more than I do. Besides, no point in sticking around here.*

"Captain Jackson! Get everyone saddled up. We're heading back to HQ!"

The Captain smiled and yelled for the nearest sergeant. Soon, they were all on their way back into town.

✯ ✯ ✯ ✯

Two miles away Major Danskill looked down at the burning Horde. The flames were starting to die down now, but the smoke and the smell would linger on for some time to come. Captain Foster looked over at him before speaking in a tentative voice.

"What are your orders, sir."

His commanding officer didn't speak for almost a full minute.

"Sir? Your orders?"

Danskill looked up from his thoughts. Then he formed his words with a sneer.

"Tell the Apaches to find that bi-plane and shoot it down." He hesitated. "Tell the Bradleys and the Abrams to proceed to the rally point as planned. The Abrams will bombard the city and then the Bradleys and infantry will move in to mop up."

Captain Foster nodded his approval, confident that his boss was in full control of the situation. He scurried away to carry out his orders.

Several miles away Harold Steffens landed in an open field and taxied to a stop beneath the trees. According to his general's orders he was out of sight from the air. And now he waited.

CHAPTER 25

The Final Battle

"IT'S THE ONLY HOPE WE HAVE." GENERAL BRANCH LOOKED across the room at everyone present. Donny Brewster looked excited while Lisa and Adam seemed unsure. His nephew, Major Dan Branch, was wearing his best poker face. Colonel MacPherson was stoic as always. Rodney looked over at Sheriff Leif and was surprised to see him smiling.

General Branch raised one eyebrow before addressing him. "Care to speak your mind, Sheriff?"

Joe Leif looked down at the table and then back up again. Then he glanced around the room at each person present before speaking. "Every single time I've doubted you over the past six months you've proved me wrong, so I think I've learned my lesson. Last night I was arguing for an evacuation of the whole city, because I just didn't have enough faith in you or my fellow citizens. I was still seeing them as Bill the Pharmacist and Jim the factory worker and Louise the stay-at-home mom." He placed his folded hands up on the table top. "Well, I was wrong. I underestimated my town. We're not civilians anymore. We're fighters. We're warriors. I can't believe it, Rodney. I just watched an eighty-four-year-old man use a crop duster to destroy an entire army."

Colonel MacPherson shrugged. "Well, technically it was just a battalion."

Joe kept smiling. "Doesn't matter when it's the only battalion in town, and it's advancing to kill you."

Lisa piped up. "That's a good point." Then she turned to the Sheriff. "Sheriff I've seen things the past few weeks I thought I'd never see. I'm a Registered Nurse and I just killed a few hundred Horde with a 25mm cannon." She grew quiet and her eyes misted over for just a moment before drying up again. "Granted, they all needed killing, but ... the point is we've all changed. And if we surrender now, then it's only a temporary fix. There will be other Hordes, other rogue armies that will want to kill us ... or worse."

She looked past General Branch to the wall behind him. "I say we fight now while we can. I like the plan, and it has a chance of success."

General Branch looked over at Dan as if asking the question without speaking. Lisa noticed it and was amazed they seemed to know what the other was thinking. Major Branch simply nodded.

The General looked back to the group grimly and began issuing a string of orders. As each person was directed, they got up and left the room to carry out their part of the plan. If it was to succeed; if they were to survive; if the approaching armored units were to be defeated; they would have to work together; they'd have to be brave.

There was no room for error. And a little bit of luck would not go unwelcomed.

☆ ☆ ☆ ☆

By the time the bombardment of Iroquois City began, most of the inhabitants had already been moved into basements and to the outer edges of the town thereby minimizing casualties. Nonetheless, dozens of men, women and children died in the five-minute barrage. Half the buildings were fully or partially destroyed while many of the remaining houses were damaged.

Major Branch and Captain Jackson were in a foxhole on the western edge of town. They could plainly see the lone Bradley Fighting Vehicle drive down the road and stop just fifty yards from their position. Sheriff Leif was in another foxhole just thirty yards to their left. In his left hand he held the remote detonator. It was charged; it was ready to go, but he waited.

The Bradley's hatches opened up as both the machine gun and the 25mm cannon began firing on the nearest buildings. But no one moved. Everyone maintained their fire discipline.

Up on the ridge, standing beside the row of four Abrams tanks, Major Danskill peered down on the town with binoculars. He saw the foxholes and guessed they were manned. The fact his lone Bradley had not been attacked was suggestive of one of two reasons: they had no arms to destroy a Bradley, or, they were waiting for bigger prey.

Danskill had sent in the lone Bradley to verify the road wasn't mined and to get the defenders to tip their hand. Truth is he could no longer afford to underestimate his adversary. They probably had nothing to counter the Bradleys and certainly had nothing to destroy the Abrams, but there was no hurry. He could afford to feel them out. He looked over at Captain Foster who was standing beside him.

"Send in the other Bradleys but hold back the infantry."

Captain Foster nodded and passed on the order. A few minutes later the three remaining Bradleys moved down the road in standard formation, being careful to maintain a distance of thirty meters from nose to tail.

Back in the foxhole, Sheriff Leif watched as the Bradleys came closer. He waited.

He wanted the Abrams. He waited. But the Abrams didn't come. He waited. Eventually all three came to a stop behind the leader. Their hatches popped open and the guns were manned. Joe took one last look down the road to make sure the Abrams weren't coming and pressed the plunger.

The men jutting out the hatches were cut in half instantly. Everyone inside the armored cavalry were crushed like Jello as the concussion turned their insides to mush. Two of the Bradleys flipped over several times before landing off the road. The other two miraculously remained upright, but came to rest in a deep hole where the road used to be. There were no survivors.

Sheriff Leif looked on in awe. Jeremy poked him in the shoulder, but Joe hadn't plugged his ears and couldn't hear what the boy was saying to him.

Major Danskill's face flushed white in horror. He'd never seen a blast like that before. But his horror was quickly replaced with rage. *His Bradleys! They were gone! His cavalry was gone!*

Just then he heard the sound of a small-engine plane coming from west of his position. He looked over and saw the small crop duster coming toward him. It was but a speck in the sky, but it kept growing as it came closer. A queasy feeling grew in the pit of his stomach.

"Prepare for air attack! Where are my Apaches? Where is my air cover! I told them to shoot it down!"

As if in answer to his question, the Apache appeared on the horizon and began to close on the Super Ag Cat.

Lieutenant Steffens had flown the long way around town far to the south and taken up position to the west as General Branch had instructed him. And there he had waited until he received the call just a few minutes ago.

He looked ahead and saw his primary objective, then he saw the huge trench where the highway coming into town used to be. He thought to himself, *Nice job, boys. I'm not the only one fighting today.*

Then he looked to his six and saw the Apache closing in on him. He'd never make it to the ridge and the four Abrams tanks. He had to make a decision. That was when he saw two-hundred soldiers in a ravine to his left waiting to attack the town.

He laid the stick full over to the left and kicked full left rudder. As he turned he switched on the sprayers and dumped the fuel onto the enemy troops below. Harold looked ahead and saw the Stinger missile coming toward him. Harold smiled and dove for the ground, feeling more alive than ever before.

The ensuing fireball lit up the sky and quickly sucked all oxygen from the ravine. Most of the enemy died from collapsed lungs. Some inhaled fire while others were simply incinerated. The luckiest died instantly from the concussion. The remnants of Lieutenant Steffen's plane showered down hundreds of yards away, while the attacking Apache was caught in the blast and lost control. It crashed on the edge of the ravine. The remaining Apache, a mile behind, saw the danger, turned around and raced away to the west.

Major Danskill and Captain Foster looked on from half a mile away. At first they said nothing. Then the XO looked at his Commander. His face was white as a sheet. "What are your orders, sir?"

But his commanding officer said nothing. The warning of Sun Tzu kept running through Major Danskill's head like a broken record threatening to explode his brain.

> *"If you know the enemy and know yourself, you need not fear the result of a hundred battles. If you know yourself but not the enemy, for every victory gained you will also suffer a defeat. If you know neither the enemy nor yourself, you will succumb in every battle"*

Major Danskill turned and walked up to the nearest Abrams. He hopped on top, but not near as nimbly as he had a few minutes before. The Captain looked after him. "Are we attacking, sir?"

In answer to the Captain's question, Danskill turned his back on his XO and climbed down into the Commander's hatch. Captain Foster looked around, and suddenly noticed he was the only one outside. The turret moved to the left and then opened fire, the concussion knocking the XO to the ground.

Soon all four Abrams were once again bombarding the town, but this time they wouldn't stop until the town was destroyed.

CHAPTER 26

Kill or Die

"**H**E'S GOING TO DESTROY THE TOWN! WE HAVE TO GET them first!" General Branch ran out of the red brick courthouse as quickly as he could just as shards of brick and clumps of mortar rained down all around him. They were targeting the courthouse with its big clock tower first.

Rodney reached his pick-up truck and jumped inside. Soon he was rolling down Main Street headed for the north side of town. He picked up his radio and began barking out orders.

✮ ✮ ✮ ✮

Down inside the bunker, baby Donna was crying, so Jackie quickly made a bottle and shoved it into her daughter's mouth. She couldn't believe all that was happening. Five hundred of The Horde killed by her husband and his Rangers; another fifteen-hundred killed by an old man with a crop duster. She felt a sense of pride that she'd been part of that by helping Sergeant Steffens repair his plane. Four Bradley Fighting Vehicles killed by fertilizer. And now, another two hundred infantry and an Apache Attack Helicopter destroyed by Harold Steffens. Her heart went out to him as she realized he certainly must have died in the attack.

But her husband and her son were safe so far as she knew. She looked down at baby

Donna and smiled. The town was saved!

But wait! More radio traffic was coming.

☆ ☆ ☆ ☆

"Mac, I need you to lead the four mobiles up that slope and get them as close to the Abrams as you can. Then park them and get the hell out of there!"

Rodney thought for a moment. "Sergeant Brewster, meet me at the library. I need your help with the TOW." He waited for both men to reply, then continued his orders. "Dan, take charge of all ground units. Converge on the ridge from both left and right flanks. Draw their fire. Keep them as distracted as you can. You have to give Colonel MacPherson enough time to drive the mobiles up that slope."

Major Branch yelled some orders into his radio while Captain Jackson readied the men for attack. Two minutes later one-hundred men jumped out of their foxholes and ran thirty yards to the long trench caused by the fertilizer bomb. They jumped down inside and made their way to the end which brought them over one-hundred-twenty yards closer to the Abrams. On the east side of town two-hundred more of the Home Guard were readying for a similar flanking maneuver.

"Get everybody with a Molotov up near the front. And we have two LAWS. I want them up here too! The rest of you, get ready to move out. As fast as you can, follow me to that ditch line about one-hundred yards further down the road."

He looked over at Captain Jackson. Both men seemed wild-eyed with adrenaline. "Larry, I want you to direct the two LAWS. As soon as they bring their fire to bear on us, I want you to hit them as hard as you can."

Larry Jackson gave him a look of skepticism before speaking. "What if they don't fire, Dan? These things are probably left over from the Vietnam War."

Dan just slapped his friend on the back. "Well, if they don't go off, then we're all dead. Just make them work, Larry."

And with that Major Branch screamed out a command and climbed up the side of the trench. His men followed him like a trail of tireless ants.

Major Danskill laughed inside the tank as he watched the gunners fire the big 120 mm guns into the town. From only five hundred yards away pieces of the town came back at them crashing into the side of the hill. It was a joy to watch the town disintegrate in front of him. He wondered if the Militia Commander was already dead. He hoped not because he wanted the man, whoever he was, to suffer as long as possible.

"Major Danskill! Look at our right flank!" The Major looked through the periscope and saw several dozen men, scurrying like insects up the hill a few hundred yards away. They were currently buttoned down, so he barked out an order to his machine gunner. "Get up there and hit them with the fifty cal!"

A few seconds later he was relieved to hear the barking staccato of the fifty caliber machine gun. He looked into the periscope again just in time to see several of the men fall down in pieces. The others made it to a ditch and were pinned down there. Major Danskill smiled. They weren't going anywhere.

Captain Jackson looked over at Ed Brown, who had been the elementary school janitor prior to The Day. "Have you ever fired one of these before?"

Ed shook his head. "No, but I've read the directions five times. I think I can do it." Jackson let out a nervous laugh. "Okay then. We'll do it by the numbers in unison. Follow my lead!" A few seconds later Captain Jackson fired his LAW, and the 3.5 inch rocket plumed its way up the hill and slammed into the side of the nearest Abrams tank. The machine gunner was thrown backwards and his gun went silent. The janitor's rocket hit low and exploded in the ground below a second tank. The Abrams rocked slightly but remained undamaged. Captain Jackson and the janitor shrieked with glee from inside the trench. They looked up and saw Dan and his men rushing up the hill almost to safety.

"Major Danskill, look to our left flank. We've got about two-hundred infantry coming up the hill."

The Major brought his periscope to bear on the left flank and was surprised at what he saw. He couldn't believe that so many people were stupid enough to charge uphill into the teeth of four Abrams tanks. He thought to himself, *Stupid rednecks.*

"Man the fifties and the 7.62 mm machine guns and cut them down. But I want the big guns to keep chewing up the town." The machine gunners in three of the tanks moved out the hatches and began pouring lead into the advancing Home Guard. Dozens of them went down, but they kept advancing. Major Danskill watched from his periscope in awe of their courage or their stupidity or whatever the hell it was.

"Major! We have a frontal attack!"

Major Danskill couldn't believe his eyes. "Is that a Yugo?"

"Yes sir. And a Toyota Prius. And that one off to the left looks like a Dodge Charger. One of those old *Dukes of Hazard* cars."

As he looked on, another car pulled out of the town behind the others. It could barely run and was throwing black smoke out the back.

"Target them all with the main guns. I don't want them reaching us."

Dan and his twenty men had worked their way to the rear flank of the Abrams and were now only about ten yards away. Dan watched as the machine guns raked into the advancing townspeople. Something inside him snapped as he jumped up and began shooting into the side of the closest tank. His other men stood up as well and threw their Molotovs on the turrets. The gas erupted into flames and two of the machine gunners screamed as they burned. The remaining gunner turned his fifty cal around and two of Dan's men went down immediately. Dan ran forward and emptied his M16 into the machine gunner's body. Most of his rounds hit body armor, but several made it through to flesh. The fifty cal went silent. They threw their remaining Molotovs on the other tanks and rushed back into the brush behind them. All the machine guns remained silent, and the infantry on the left and right flanks advanced unopposed up the hill.

Major Danskill paid no attention to his machine gunner's dying screams. He was too focused on directing the fire of his main guns at the advancing automobiles.

"Get that Prius first!"

It took a few seconds, but the Toyota Prius was targeted and soon flew up in the air landing in fuel-efficient pieces.

"Now get on the Yugo!"

A few seconds later the Yugo was destroyed.

"Sir they're too close now, and they're zig-zagging up the hill. They're right on top of us sir! Sir, we're taking small arms fire from both flanks now. The machine gunners are all down."

Major Danskill swore as loud as he could through clenched teeth before issuing his next command.

"Take us down the hill as fast as you can. I'm going to run right over that hick town."

One of the tanks didn't move; it had been hit with almost a dozen Molotovs, but the other three started off down the hill. The lead tank hadn't gone far when it was rocked by a huge explosion as the Dodge Charger slammed into it. The remaining car bomb was too slow, and Major Danskill's tank raced past it unharmed. Finally, the old junker slowed to a halt unable to travel any farther. The engine sputtered and died.

Both tanks were halfway down the hill now and were firing their 120 mm guns as they raced toward the town. The infantry atop the hill was out of the fight now, and all they could do was watch from a distance as the two tanks destroyed their home.

Without warning, two hundred yards from the town, the aft tank blew up and rolled over on its side.

"What the hell was that?"

"We're the only ones left, sir." The gunner's voice sounded frantic as he struggled to maintain his military discipline. "What are your orders, sir?"

Major Danskill hesitated. *How had they done that? Who was he up against?* Danskill muttered under his breath. "I hate Sun Tzu!"

"Sir, what are your orders?"

The Major was visibly upset. He gritted his teeth in determination, but finally common sense overtook his emotions.

"Retreat! Full speed. Get us the hell out of here as fast as you can!"

On the outskirts of the town in front of the city library, Donny Brewster struggled to reload the TOW. General Branch moved away from the sight and stepped over to help him lift the missile and load it into the back of the tube for a second launch. It took the better part of two minutes to complete the reloading process. By the time the General returned to the sight, Major Danskill was out of range.

Sergeant Brewster threw his boonie hat down on the truck bed and stomped on it. General Branch keyed his radio mic. "All units report in."

"Major Branch reporting in, sir."

"Captain Jackson reporting in, sir."

"Captain Alvarez reporting in, sir."

Then silence. Rodney spoke again. "Colonel MacPherson, report in, over."

There was no answer. "Dan, did you see Mac. Where is he?" There was an uncharacteristic urgency in the General's voice. Dan's answer came back and crushed

Rodney like a hammer and anvil.

"I don't know. He was driving one of the car bombs."

There air waves were silent for several seconds.

"Find him!"

CHAPTER 27

The Price of Victory

"LET THE NAMES NOW BE READ. LET THE NAMES NOW BE honored. Let them be heralded and revered in story and song, passed down from one generation to the next. Let the names of all who fought and died in resistance to evil be remembered forever more."

General Branch, in his army dress uniform, stepped away from the pulpit. All the remaining townspeople were assembled inside the town's largest remaining church. There had been six churches before the attack. Only two had escaped the bombardment without damage.

It had been two days since the battle for Iroquois City, and the smoke had cleared. Most of the bodies had been removed. With the help of Mark Englerth's bulldozers and back hoes, The Horde had been buried in mass graves outside town. The ravine where Harold Steffens had incinerated the remaining two hundred enemy soldiers had been filled in. But every person, man, woman or child who had raised arms in defense of Iroquois County was now being given a funeral with full military honors.

Sheriff Joe Leif stood and walked toward the simple, wooden pulpit. He was also in his dress uniform, freshly shaved and as sharp as Marge could make him. When he reached the pulpit, he put the stack of papers on the wood in front of him. Behind him was a large, wooden cross. The piano was to his left, but it wasn't playing today.

"The following people died in defense of liberty:

Colonel Roger "Ranger" MacPherson - Shadow Militia
Lieutenant Harold Steffens - Honorary Shadow Militia
Lou Dobbins - Home Guard
Celeste Evans - Home Guard
Peter Smith - Militia Rangers
Larry Winkler - Home Guard
Connie Polowski - Militia Rangers
Robert Vanderveen - Home Guard
Richard Dyskstra - Militia Rangers
Henry Overbeek - Militia Rangers
Jonathon Janowski - Militia Rangers
Emily Duran - Militia Rangers

Stephen Frank - Home Guard

Jackie Branch sat in the front row with her husband and her son, holding her baby in her arms. Her family was alive. So many others were dead. So many lives had been shattered. In her heart, she knew - no matter what happened from this point on - life would never be the same again. She looked around to find Sergeant Donny Brewster, but he was strangely absent.

Up on the podium, Sheriff Leif continued to read the names of the fallen. Ten minutes later he finally finished.

Joe Leif looked up from the list he'd been reading and looked out into the church, filled to capacity and overflowing out into the lawn. They'd left the doors open so everyone could hear.

"Friends both old and new, citizens, all people of Iroquois. I am humbled by your spirits, your bravery, your focus and your sacrifice." Joe's voice started to waver, but he cleared his throat and pressed on. "Today we honor those who gave their lives so that we could live. Nothing we can do will ever outshine the way they fought and died in defense of our families and our homes." He cleared his throat again. "But there is one thing we can do to bring honor and give meaning to their sacrifice. We can rebuild." He paused to let the words sink in. "We can make Iroquois County a safe haven to all people in need, to all people who value freedom, who are willing to defend it with their lives as they did our friends on this list. We can and will rebuild our home and make it a bastion of liberty."

The Sheriff turned and faced General Branch. "But first, we continue to honor our fallen heroes." He snapped to attention and crisply saluted as best he could, copying what he'd seen from the Shadow Militia. The General seemed surprised, but he stepped forward, came to attention, and returned the Sheriff's salute.

After the salute, Rodney walked forward and placed his hand on Joe's shoulder. "Sheriff Leif, The Shadow Militia remains at your service. You are the leader of Iroquois County, and we are here in an advisory capacity, at your discretion. We hereby renew our pledge to give our lives, our fortunes, and our sacred honor."

General Branch turned to the citizens and proclaimed in a loud voice. "To all who would take our freedoms, we give warning; we challenge you; we chide you; we dare you with every wisp of our souls, Molon Labe. Come and get them. We wait for you."

The county of Iroquois stood to its feet, crying out in one voice:

"Molon Labe!"

"Molon Labe!"

"Molon Labe!"

"Molon Labe!"

All except one man, remaining small, almost invisible to the citizens. He pulled the hood to his coat down over his forehead and gritted his teeth in anger. Finally, now, only after defeat did he know his enemy. Major Danskill faded to the back of the crowd and then disappeared in the coming Iroquois spring.

As the Major walked away, seven independent blasts reached out into the sunshine of the fading northern winter and echoed into one. A few seconds elapsed and another volley was fired. And then another, as the twenty-one-gun salute was completed.

Behind him, fading as he walked toward the edge of town, the sound of bugles reached his ears. He sang the words to himself as he marched away.

Day is done, gone the sun
From the lakes, from the hills, from the sky
All is well, safely rest
God is nigh.
Fading light dims the sight
And a star gems the sky, gleaming bright
From afar, drawing near
Falls the night.
Thanks and praise for our days
Neath the sun, neath the stars, neath the sky
As we go, this we know
God is nigh.

☆ ☆ ☆ ☆

"What do you think, Colonel. Should we take him now?" Sergeant Donny Brewster looked through binoculars at Major Danskill as he marched out of town. The Colonel shook his head.

"Not yet. Let's see where he's going first. I want more intel."

EPILOGUE

THE BLIND MAN PUT THE SATELLITE PHONE BACK DOWN ON THE ebony coffee table. *The Shadow Militia.* He'd heard the name spoken in whispers, but had never believed it to be real.

Jared Thompson motioned with his right forefinger for his assistant to come closer. Sammy Thurmond obeyed him immediately.

"That was Major Danskill from Michigan. Send someone to bring him in for a meeting. I want to handle this personally. It could be important."

Sammy Thurmond moved out of the room, and the blind man was left to ponder. *A small army destroyed by mere peasants? Not likely.* He needed more information. Jared sat down on the couch and reached over to the coffee table for his glass of wine. It was so difficult to get good, French wine these days. The End of Days had played havoc on his wine cellar.

But now, what to do about the Islamic events now unfolding in Dearborn, just east of Detroit. While other states had already come under his control, Michigan was turning out to be a real pain in the butt. Jared picked up the file folder in front of him and pulled out the photo of Imam Abdul al'Kalwi. He was a ruthless man, a charismatic leader, unifying the huge Islamic population, and threatening to conquer all who stood in his way.

Jared took a small sip and placed the photo and the wine goblet back on the ebony coffee table. Yes, he contemplated the many problems he faced. Rednecks rising up in the South; mountain men holding out in the West; a small army of Muslim fanatics threatening to conquer the north, spreading over the land like a Saracen tide; and now, a new enemy came forth: The Shadow Militia.

The blind man took another sip of his wine, then leaned back on the couch and took a nap. Life was just getting interesting.

Book 3 in The God Virus Series

The Saracen Tide

Skip Coryell

PROLOGUE

I MAM ABDUL AL'KALWI HAD CONSIDERED KILLING HIS FRIEND quietly, without the shame of public humiliation, sparing him the suffering and pain of watching his life's work slip away only inches from the finish line. But, in the end, as much as he admired and loved his closest friend, he realized that Allah craved the blood of his mentor, and that he must die in a perfect and painless way. After all, it was the least he could do for his friend. In a way, he was doing him a favor. These were harsh and terrible times. In his heart, Abdul knew that his friend, Mohammed, was just not up to the challenge, even though his friend refused to see it for what it was. Mohammed was weak; therefore, it was time for his friend to enter into his paradise.

So he stood now beside Mohammed, their first in command, as he addressed the other Imams, laying out his plans for the future. The electricity had been out all across America for less than 48 hours, and already Mohammed was issuing orders of moderation, of love and charity and mercy. They were to reach out to the infidels, to offer them food and clothing and other forms of humanitarian aid, and in return the Christians would treat the Muslim community with tolerance and kindness.

That was the plan, and it left a sour taste of bile in Abdul's mouth. His throat tightened as his friend continued speaking. They were in a lower room of the mosque, separated and private. Abdul would have preferred a more public execution, but that just wasn't possible. Nonetheless, it would do. So long as the Imams feared him they would follow him. The Imams would follow Abdul, and the people would follow the Imams. In that way, there would be order and no doubt about who was in control.

The scimitar was hidden beneath his robe, and his right hand tightened on the hilt of it now. Abdul was not like the other Imams. They were men of peace, soft men, well versed in the Koran, but not in the ways of war. In preparation for this day, Abdul had studied the history of war as well as the skills of battle. He was an excellent swordsman, physically strong and fit in the prime of his life. He and he alone was best suited to lead in time of war.

And the war was about to begin.

In one fluid, practiced motion, Abdul drew his sword as he stepped behind his leader. The sword came out and rose head high and plunged forward into the right side of his friend's neck. He felt resistance as the blade came against the vertebrae, but he pushed on through it in accordance with his studies, and his friend's head flopped down onto the floor with a thud. The rest of the body hung there for a second, like a suspended rag doll puppet, as blood spurted up from the headless neck, then it collapsed to the rug beside the head. Lifeless eyes looking up at Abdul, his friend, as if asking ... *why, why, why?*

In reply, Abdul nodded to his loyal conspirators and three more Imams were struck down in unison. Their cuts were not as precise as Abdul's, and he enjoyed his superiority for a moment. Then he made a mental note to make them practice their cuts.

In the space of twenty seconds all power had changed. The world was now on a different course. Imam Abdul Al'Kalwi smiled as the blood of his friend bumped up against his sandals and slowly soaked into the carpet.

CHAPTER I

The Aftermath of War

DAN BRANCH SAT ON TOP OF THE ABRAMS TANK LOOKING down on the city. It had been three days since the end of battle, and he felt tired inside. There was an early spring rain filtering down now through a clouded sky, lending an eerie gloom to the town below. The tank's armor was wet and cold on his butt, and he shivered slightly as he watched the thin layer of snow melting on the ground all around him. It was a cleansing melt, and he welcomed it.

Most of the bodies were already buried, but it had been done in haste to prevent the spread of disease and to keep the smell down. In the mass graves they'd spread powdered lime on the bodies before covering them up to hasten the decomposition. With the rain and warmth of summer, the grass would grow and quickly wipe away most traces of death and battle. He glanced over at an oak tree just a few yards away. It was large, three feet in diameter, and had been burned and charred during his fire bomb attack on the very tank on which he was now perched. The tree would probably recover. Like the tree, Dan felt burned and charred, somehow fundamentally damaged inside. But ... he was alive, and so were his wife and children.

The town had been saved. But at what cost? Thousands of the enemy had been killed as well as hundreds of the townspeople and, because of the nature of the battle, only a few prisoners had been taken. His Uncle Rodney had wanted to execute them on the spot, but Sheriff Leif had intervened and banished them from Iroquois county. It seemed like such a small matter, after so much other killing, but Dan had been glad to watch the dozen or so prisoners run off into the woods unharmed. It seemed symbolic and somehow important, like they had made a decision to hold on to at least a small shred of their humanity.

Dan used his gloved hands to pull the collar of his wool coat up around his neck. The chill was getting to him. He got up off the dead and blackened tank, jumped to the ground and headed home to his family.

And now, it was time to rebuild.

****

"BUT UNCLE RODNEY, WHERE ARE YOU GOING? WE NEED YOU HERE!" Young Jeremy Branch stood in front of the door, blocking the path of his uncle who now stood poised to leave. The olive drab duffle bag was slung over his left shoulder, while his M4A1 carbine was clutched in his right hand. Uncle Rodney had become hard and tough over the last two months, but there was no longer a need for him here.

"I'm sorry, son. I'm needed elsewhere now."

Jackie stood off to one side looking on. She was smiling, not happy because he was leaving, rather privileged to have known him. She stepped forward now.

"Jeremy, it's okay. He'll be back if we're ever threatened. You can count on that."

Rodney looked into her eyes. They shared a moment of melding and trust. His eyes smiled and he found himself thinking. *She gets it. She really is a Branch.*

Jackie reached out and wrapped her arms around her uncle, pulling him close. He remained ramrod stiff for a moment, but then slowly softened his stance. The woman leaned in closer and put her mouth up to his ear before whispering softly.

"You made me a stronger person."

When Jackie pulled away she was smiling. Uncle Rodney's eyes moistened, but his face betrayed no hint of emotion.

"Make sure Daniel reads the letter."

General Branch pulled the M4 off his right shoulder and handed it to Jeremy. "Keep the family safe."

The young man reached out hesitantly before grasping it firmly in his hands. Without another word the general moved forward, skirting past his nephew and on out to the waiting helicopter. A few moments later it lifted off the ground and sped away into the rain-filled sky. Jackie and Jeremy watched from the porch until the tiny dot disappeared.

She went inside to tend to baby Donna, while Jeremy stood there in the drizzle, looking down at his new weapon. He moved his fingers over the collapsible stock and worked his way up to the rail system and barrel. It was getting wet, so he took one last look at the empty sky and then moved back inside to clean and oil his new carbine.

****

"HE JUST LEFT? HE DIDN'T EVEN TELL YOU GOOD BYE?" SHERIFF LEIF WAS looking down at the letter from General Branch. His fingers were trembling slightly. Dan Branch was sitting across from the Sheriff with his legs crossed one over the other, looking ahead blankly.

"I wasn't even there. He gave the letter to Jackie and then got in his chopper and flew away."

The sheriff lowered the letter and then looked up as he leaned back in his reclining office chair. "So when is he coming back?"

Dan folded his arms across his muscled torso. "Just read the letter. It says it all."

Joe Leif looked back down and read the letter aloud, pausing every so often to let it sink in.

To: Sheriff Joe Leif and Colonel Dan Branch.

From: Rodney Branch, Commanding General, Shadow Militia

Subject: Change of Command

The sheriff stopped reading and looked over at Dan. "Looks like you've been promoted to colonel." Dan Branch didn't answer. He just looked off toward the window with an unseeing gaze.

I, General Rodney Branch, do hereby relinquish command of all Iroquois county military forces to Colonel Daniel Branch. You have proven yourself in battle to be an honorable and formidable fighting commander. You are hereby charged with the defense of Iroquois county and the surrounding geography.

"The surrounding geography? What does that mean?"

Dan shrugged his shoulders and continued looking through the window. "I don't know. With Uncle Rodney that could mean the whole state of Michigan. Who knows?"

You will continue to report to Sheriff Joe Leif, the only remaining constitutionally elected civilian leader in your area. You will obey all orders given by him and support him as your resources allow, as I have done in the past.

Sheriff Leif laughed out loud. "Obey me as he has done in the past? That old man never obeyed me a day in his life!"

Dan smiled for the first time that morning. "Yes, my uncle never did take orders very well."

The sheriff thought back to the interrogation of the captured horde sniper, how Rodney had feigned compliance, only to torture the man as soon as Joe left the jail cell. Rodney Branch subordinated himself to no man.

"True. But when he disobeyed me, he did it with such flair and personality that a part of me enjoyed it, almost couldn't wait to see what the old man would do next."

Dan nodded his head in agreement. "I love the man. But he scares the hell out of me."

The sheriff chuckled before reading on.

Your command priorities shall be as follows:

1. Continue to train, organize and enhance the military forces of Iroquois county.

2. Enter into a mutual defense alliance with neighboring counties and assist them in training and organization.

3. Support Sheriff Leif and other civilian units under his command in rebuilding the town.

"That sounds like a full time job to me. How are you going to do all that, Dan?"

Dan Branch uncrossed his legs and leaned forward in the chair. "Beats the hell outta me." Then he looked Joe square in the eyes. "So how are you going to rebuild the town, feed us, clothe us, and ward off disease?"

The sheriff broke the stare and looked over at the blank wall. "I have no idea. I don't feel any more capable now than I did before The Day."

Dan nodded his agreement. "Neither do I. But … I have a notion that our feelings don't really matter much anymore. It doesn't matter what we *feel* we can do; it matters what we actually *can* do." He looked out the window again. "And you have to admit, Joe, we have some accomplishments under our belts. We fought off thousands of deadly cutthroats and won. Yeah, sure, we had some help from Uncle Rodney and the Shadow Militia, but, in the end, what *we* did … *we* did."

The sheriff let that sink in for a moment or two. Then he looked away from the wall and met Dan's gaze again. "I suppose you're right. Almost everything we did over the past few months went against our feelings but we did them anyways. Just a few days ago I felt like giving up. I did, in fact, give up. But Rodney picked me up, dusted me off and put me back in command."

Dan smiled. "Yeah, I know what you mean. Even when I was a kid, my uncle had this way of helping me believe I could do things I wasn't capable of. He always pushed me to my limit and then another ten percent."

Sheriff Leif looked back down at the letter and soberly read the valediction.

I write these instructions in my own hand, and they are to be carried out until further orders. It is with a heavy heart that I leave you to your own defense. But know this: if I can assist you in the future, I will. You are more than friends and conquerors. You have come through the fire, and you are as shining brass. You will do more than survive. With God's grace and strength, you will prevail and you will flourish.

Your brother in arms,

General Rodney T. Branch

Commanding General
The Shadow Militia

Sheriff Leif tossed the letter on his desk and shook his head from side to side. "Your uncle is the weirdest person I've ever known."

Dan Branch nodded his head and smiled. "You got that right." He hesitated a moment. "So what are we going to do?"

The sheriff swiveled nervously back and forth a few seconds in his office chair. Finally, he answered. "That old man knows more than he's saying. And it grinds me to admit that he's always been right in the past. The only sensible thing to do is follow his advice and just wait until whatever he knows is gonna happen, happens. At least then we'll be ready for it, or, as ready as we can be."

Dan Branch stood to his feet moved his palms over his shirt to straighten out the wrinkles. "I got some thinking to do and people to talk to. Shall we meet here tomorrow morning at zero eight hundred hours?"

Sheriff Leif laughed out loud, cognizant that Uncle Rodney lived on in his nephew. "Sure thing, Colonel. Eight o'clock sounds good to me. You bring the donuts."

CHAPTER 2

Major Danskill

IT WAS EARLY SPRING IN NORTHERN MICHIGAN, AND A TINY WISP of smoke curled up out of the wooded ravine. The rain had stopped, leaving Major Danskill soaking wet and shivering in his olive drab field jacket. His hands shook as he pulled the collar up over his bare neck. The major leaned forward and stirred the red coals of the fire with a stick, then he tossed the limb onto the coals and watched as the heat blackened the wood before bursting it into flames.

He mumbled to himself, "Know your enemy." He hated Sun Tzu more than ever now. Why hadn't he taken his time, gathered more intel? Instead, he'd blundered into a trap set by the leader of the Shadow Militia. He thought about General Rodney Branch, his adversary, his enemy, and then he thought of the Blind Man. They were two sides to the same coin. Both were powerful, determined and cunning, and Danskill knew in his heart that planet Earth wasn't big enough for the both of them. One of them had to die. But which one? That was the question. And which one was most likely to let him live? On the one hand he hated General Branch, because he'd been humiliated and defeated by him on the field of battle. Danskill had held all the cards, but Branch had bested him regardless. On the other hand, the Blind Man had the power to pick up the phone and have him eliminated. Or, he could capture him for interrogation. The major thought that was probably the most likely option of the two. The Blind Man would be desperate for intel. Like Sun Tzu he'd want to know his enemy. Danskill had information the Blind Man needed to know, and that could be the key to not only keeping him alive, but also to returning him to power.

They would be picking him up soon. In the quiet of the woods, Major Danskill made his decision. His best chance for glory was with the Blind Man. And then … there was always the matter of his unnatural appetites. The Blind Man would feed them so long as Danskill was a tool of value. But, in his heart, he knew that General Branch, a man of honor, could not and would not condone such practices.

COLONEL MACPHERSON LOWERED THE BINOCULARS FROM HIS EYES AND thought for a moment. "What's he doing down there, Donny?"

Sergeant Brewster shook his head back and forth. "I don't know, Colonel. He appears to be hugging himself and rocking back and forth."

Mac closed his eyes and listened, but no sounds save the wind in the trees came to him. "He's waiting, sergeant. They're coming for him." He looked down at the man beside the campfire, expecting the sound of an extraction helicopter at any moment. "We need to hurry. Get set up and take the shot."

Iroquois City HQ - 8AM

"SO WHAT IS YOUR FIRST MOVE, DAN?" SHERIFF LEIF LOOKED ACROSS THE conference room table at his military counterpart. Colonel Dan Branch, now dressed in pressed and starched military fatigues, stood up and walked over to the white board. The county courthouse had been cleared of rubble, and repairs were already underway. Structurally it was still sound.

"I've already assigned Major Jackson with the formidable task of reorganizing what's left of the Home Guard and the Militia Rangers. Captain Alvarez is in charge of logistics. He'll be collecting every weapon and ordinance he can find as well as developing new weapons systems. Captain Brown will head up training."

Dan wrote in block letters on the white board.

MAJOR JACKSON - REORGANIZATION

CAPTAIN ALVAREZ - LOGISTICS

CAPTAIN BROWN - TRAINING

"So what are *you* going to do, Dan?" Colonel Branch didn't say anything, he simply wrote on the white board in response to the sheriff's question.

COLONEL BRANCH - DEFENSE ALLIANCES

Sheriff Joe Leif nodded his head and folded his arms across his chest. "That means you'll have to travel." He hesitated. "Does Jackie know?"

Dan caught his drift and smiled to himself. It was no secret to the inner circle that his wife was very protective of him and hadn't appreciated his absence in the last battle. Even though she understood the extreme circumstances, a woman just didn't appreciate being away from her man. After all, technically, they were still newlyweds.

"No, not yet." He looked over at the sheriff, the only other man in the room. "Any ideas?"

Sheriff Leif thought for a moment. "She needs to feel important, and she's a very capable woman. I could use her in helping to rebuild the town. That wouldn't make her feel happy about you leaving, but it would give her something to do. And I need all the help I can get."

Dan nodded appreciatively. "Thanks Joe." He stepped away from the white board and back to his seat. "So what about you? What plans do you have?"

Joe Leif answered his question by sliding a sheet of yellow ruled paper across the table to him. Dan read the hand-scribbled notes silently.

Priorities

1. Food - gather food, plant crops, set up distribution system.

2. Organize medical personnel & supplies and schedule physical exam for all citizens.

3. Rebuild as time and supplies allow.

4. Set up system to handle refugees. Who goes - who stays.

5. Establish laws for births, marriages, deaths, transfer of property and commerce.

"I don't envy you, Sheriff."

Joe scoffed. "Hell, my job is easy compared to what you're going to be doing. I can't even imagine how you're going to convince people from other counties to train, prepare and equip for war when all they're worried about is feeding their families."

The sheriff paused and waited for an answer, but none came. He pushed it a bit further. "So, Dan, exactly how are you going to do it?"

Colonel Branch hesitated and gazed out the window at the brown grass on the courthouse lawn. It would be turning green soon. Finally, he answered.

"I'm going to offer them hope."

Sheriff Leif smiled. "And if that doesn't work?"

Dan laughed out loud. "Well ... then I'll have to just scare the hell out of 'em. I'll figure something out."

Joe smiled softly and looked down at the table in front of them. "Any word from your uncle yet?"

That was the unspoken question, the one all the townspeople had been asking. "Where is General Rodney T. Branch?" Dan thought it ironic that all his life the people of Iroquois had tolerated his uncle, viewed him as an oddity, wondered in hush tones about his very sanity. And now, they held him up as their hope, as their hero, as their savior. But what happens when your hero is gone? Who do you believe in then?

Somehow, Dan and Joe had to inspire them, give them hope, and a reason to fight and rebuild. Both men stood up and left the room, hurrying about to their appointed impossible tasks.

CHAPTER 3

Dearborn, Michigan

ON THE DAY THE LIGHTS WENT OUT, THE CITY OF DEARBORN, Michigan held the largest population of Muslims in the United States and the second densest Muslim population outside the Middle East, second only to Paris, France. Within days Sharia law had been firmly imposed in the city, and had already begun to spread to the outlying areas as the Muslim population branched out. As the events of The Day unfolded and Abdul Al'Kalwi quickly established unchallenged control of the region, he gave himself a new title, Supreme General Abdul Al'Kalwi. This coincided with his plan of conquest and eradication of all infidels first in Michigan and then the entire Midwest.

Within several months after The Day, Abdul had put to death all Jews and Christians refusing to convert to Islam. Thousands were publicly executed, as the streets ran red with kafir blood. The only infidels to survive were those who had recognized the threat early on and fled to the outlying rural areas. The Supreme General's plan was simple. Move west across the state like a Saracen tide, cleansing the land of all non-Islamic influence. In accordance with the Koran, the Hadith, and the Sura all kafirs who refused to convert would be put to death with the sword.

Now that thousands had already been beheaded, the other infidels would swear allegiance to Allah and to the Supreme General.

But before he could advance, he first needed to control two things: military hardware and the local food source. To do this he immediately seized control of all the local armories and food warehouses. Under normal circumstances this would have been difficult to near impossible, but after The Day most of the armories were lightly guarded and disorganized. Many military personnel had gone home to protect their families and would not be back. A few of the small arms had been pilfered, but Abdul found most weapons intact. He started out by taking the smallest armory first; that gave him the weapons he needed to move on to larger prey. Within a week's time, the Supreme General had gained control of hundreds of military trucks of all shapes and sizes: Humvees, light and medium military tactical vehicles, even some Heavy Expanded Mobility Tactical Trucks which were eight-wheel drive diesel-powered off-road capable vehicles. By the time he reached Selfridge Air National Guard base in Mt. Clemons just north of Detroit, Abdul felt unstoppable.

But what he found there was nothing but empty aircraft hangers and tarmac. The F-16 Fighter jets and the A10 Warthog ground support aircraft were nowhere to be seen.

In a fit of rage, Abdul had drawn his broadsword and decapitated the man closest to him. From his study of military history, he knew that airpower would make him invincible, especially in a world without electricity thrown back into the middle ages. But now, without military air support, his own vast army would be vulnerable from the air.

Despite the setback, Abdul had spent the first winter after The Day consolidating his hold on eastern Michigan all the way up to the thumb area. Where chaos once reigned, the Supreme General offered the people a system of order, food and purpose. Every day people lined up at designated distribution centers for their daily allotment of food. They never received more than one day's rations, which ensured they would always be forced to depend solely on him for the bread of life. In return, all he asked was submission to Allah and to himself. It was a fair trade … submission for life.

All through the winter months Abdul had organized and planned his spring offensive. By April the weather had cleared and he'd amassed twenty thousand troops: half conscripts and the other half loyal Muslims of Middle Eastern descent.

Finally, on a sunny day in mid-April, he stood at the top of one of the minarets at the Islamic Center of America looking out across the vast encampment. He liked coming up here to look at his army. It was huge and extended out as far as he could see. And he controlled it all. Abdul watched as the hundreds of trucks were loaded with supplies for their push west. They would move slowly, scavenging and raping the land as they went. There was no hurry. They would move straight down the US Highway 94 corridor all the way to Jackson. From there he'd divide his forces, half going north to Lansing to secure the capitol and the other half continuing on west to Kalamazoo.

Once both major cities were pacified, the two armies would move toward Grand Rapids in a double-pronged attack. He expected to subdue all of southwest Michigan in a few months. Then he would move south to northern Indiana and then west to winter in Chicago. Wherever they went, his plan was to clear a swath twenty miles on either side of his advancing army, gathering supplies, recruiting soldiers, and slaughtering all who resisted Islam.

The Supreme General looked out over his army and then up into the lightly clouded sky. It was a good day to follow the prophet.

The Blind Man

JARED THOMPSON SAT ALONE AT THE CONFERENCE TABLE IN HIS OWN, private situation room. When he was alone he didn't have to feign blindness, and that freed him up to get more work done. He read over the reports from the various regional commanders. They had pacified most of the cities on the west and east coasts. In fact, the eastern and western seaboards were his firmest strongholds. But the center of the country continued to elude him. The Rocky mountains were rife with rebels, while the Appalachians were still saturated with rednecks on the rise. It seemed like every rock had a freedom fighter hiding underneath it. *Why did they hang on to their liberty with such vehemence?* In his heart of hearts, Jared knew most of them would have to be killed. He threw up his hands and smiled. "Oh well. You can't make an omelet without breaking a few eggs."

Then he looked up at the large video screen on the wall. He pressed a few buttons, zooming in on Michigan. Here, he hadn't expected such resistance, such a concentration of unforeseen power. He needed more intel, and that's why he'd dispatched his right-hand man, Sammy Thurmond, to bring in Major Danskill. The National Guard commander would tell him everything he wanted to know, one way or another.

Escanaba, Michigan

GENERAL RODNEY BRANCH HAD JUST RETURNED FROM MONTANA, AND every muscle of his tired old body was sore and felt like giving up. For the past two weeks he'd been in nonstop travel mode, reviewing troops in Kentucky, advising resistance in Kansas, and meeting with rebels in Texas. Now, he sat on the edge of the cot in Colonel MacPherson's lavish mansion in the Upper Peninsula. Rodney had been overjoyed to learn that his best friend, Colonel Roger "Ranger" MacPherson had survived the battle for Iroquois County.

Rodney smiled when he recalled their first meeting decades ago in Vietnam. They'd both been young officers, just starting out on their journey to become master warriors. They had bonded the next few years, fighting a war neither understood nor enjoyed. Both men had learned much from the Vietcong, and Rodney suspected he'd need all his skill and cunning to defeat the enemy now trying to enslave America.

Mac had never understood why his commanding general always insisted on such common quarters. In fact, the room Rodney now slept in was nothing more than a walk-in closet with a cot, foot locker, nightstand and metal wall locker. Mac and Rodney had grown up in opposite worlds. Mac was the man of privilege, growing up with a silver spoon in his mouth, but on reaching adulthood, he'd rejected the plush lifestyle in favor of the ascetic warrior life. On his father's death, Mac had inherited a fortune composed mainly of research and development facilities and defense manufacturing plants scattered across the country. This had given the Shadow Militia their teeth in the form of all the arms and supplies they could ever use.

Mac and Rodney were the two founding members of the Shadow Militia, and over the course of thirty plus years they'd built the organization one recruit at a time. Mac, who had retired from the military after thirty years at the rank of Major General had hand-picked all the Shadow Militia personnel. Rodney had spent several years in the Marine Corps before transferring to the Army. When his brother died, he'd been forced to retire early to raise his nephew. Rodney had remained the strategic planner, because he could do that from the obscurity of Iroquois county. Mac, despite his superior rank and experience, had insisted Rodney command the group. They had turned out to be the perfect team to fight the second war for independence.

Just then, there was a knock on the closet door. Out of habit, Rodney placed his right hand on the 1911 pistol on his right hip. "Enter!" He relaxed when the door opened and Sergeant Donny Brewster walked in and stood at attention.

"The Colonel is waiting, sir."

General Branch smiled and nodded to the seasoned, young sniper. "Very well, Sergeant. Please inform the Colonel I'll be down in fifteen minutes." Rodney pulled on his olive drab fatigues and began buttoning up his shirt. He was surprised to see Donny still standing there.

"What's up, Sergeant?"

Donny hesitated before answering.

"Permission to speak candidly about a personal matter, sir?"

The General smiled for the first time since returning to Michigan. "Permission granted." He finished buttoning his shirt and moved to pulling on his pants.

"Sir, I would like to be temporarily assigned to Iroquois County."

Rodney thought for a moment. "And why is your duty station considered personal?"

The sergeant squirmed a bit, and Rodney found it amusing. Here was a highly trained, dedicated warrior with hundreds of kills to his credit, and he was nervous over a simple administrative request. It didn't make any sense. And then a light went on in the general's head.

"Ahh, I see now." Rodney laughed out loud. "This wouldn't happen to have anything to do with a certain young nurse, a very pretty and confident nurse?"

The young sniper lowered his head slightly and came close to blushing.

"Is it that obvious, sir?"

Rodney was standing now, buttoning his freshly starched olive-drab trousers. He took a half-step forward.

"At ease, Sergeant."

Donny's left foot stepped to the side and his hands moved behind his back. The grizzly old general looked his young charge directly in the eye.

"So, as long as we're speaking candidly, is it lust or love?"

A slight smile tweaked the corner of Donny's mouth. "Well, sir. I have vast experience with lust, but when it comes to love, I fear I'm just a lowly private." He hesitated as if forming his next words carefully. "However, in this case, I think it might be both, sir."

The General nodded. "I see. Well, you sure picked a hell of a time to fall in love, Sergeant."

Donny didn't know how to respond. "Yes sir. I understand, sir."

Rodney sat back down on the cot and pulled on first one black boot and then the other. He laced them up as Donny waited in suspense. The General seemed to enjoy his nervousness. When he was done, Rodney stood to his full height with a grim face.

"So what was her name again?"

"Lisa, sir."

General Branch nodded.

"And what color are her eyes?"

"Blue, sir. Aqua blue. Like Lake Michigan in mid-summer when it's really warm, and the sun is shining, and the birds are singing ..."

"Okay, okay! That's enough! I get the picture!" The General thought for a moment as if going over a million details in his mind. "Let me double-check with Mac, first. But I think we can swing some temporary duty to northern Lower Michigan. While you're down there you can assist Colonel Branch in training and reorganizing his forces. Understood?"

Sergeant Brewster snapped rigidly to attention.

"Sir, yes sir!"

Rodney turned away.

"Good, now let's go down and see what the Colonel has for us on this Major Danskill situation."

Rodney abruptly left the room, followed by Donny Brewster. General Branch paused long enough to place the padlock back on the door before striding briskly away with Donny in tow.

CHAPTER 4

Life in Iroquois County

AFTER THE BATTLE OF **I**ROQUOIS **C**OUNTY PEOPLE TRIED TO get back to the business of not only surviving, but also of improving their way of life. Because of the cosmos and stability put in place by Sheriff Leif, and defended by Colonel Branch, reconstruction work began on the city. It was slow going, because the daily lives of most people were occupied in growing and gathering food, bringing in firewood for the next winter, and in general, healing both physically and emotionally from the scars of war and the harshness of colonial-era life.

Sheriff Leif held a county-wide meeting in order to disseminate new laws and to gain consensus on a provision-sharing program. Joe felt uncomfortable with this, because to some it seemed like a forced tax. In the end the people agreed to give ten percent of their goods or labor to a county-wide reserve to be used during time of emergency. This was only possible due to the popularity and trust accrued by Sheriff Leif over a period of twenty years of living a life of integrity with the citizens of Iroquois.

Despite that, a small minority resisted and refused to sign on. Joe tried to bring them into the cooperative, but in the end, they'd refused. Joe publicly acknowledged their ability to choose their own destiny, which seemed to boost his popularity even higher. He confided with Dan that he just couldn't bring himself to force compliance on his friends and neighbors. The people of Northern Michigan had always been a tough and independent breed, and this had become even more the case after The Day.

The citizens rebuilt the churches and the school first, and by June they held a grand re-opening ceremony and feast. Pot-luck dinners used to be commonplace in frontier America, but had faded into disuse with the advent of modern entertainment, computers, sports bars and TV dinners. Now that electricity was all but extinct, the pot-luck dinner once again flourished. And although life was hard, there were unforeseen benefits. Prior to The Day, Iroquois suffered from a fifty percent divorce rate. In post-apocalypse Iroquois, that percentage dropped to almost zero. In fact, the only divorce request came from an older couple whom Joe had known his entire life. He tried to talk them out of it, but they'd insisted. Joe drew up divorce papers for them which they promptly signed. Then, to the Sheriff's chagrin, the old man and woman had kissed and went on home to live their lives as usual.

Drug and alcohol abuse had been prevalent in all of Northern Michigan, but since drugs and alcohol were in very short supply, those addicted quickly became unaddicted. One less thing.

After the Battle of Iroquois County crime dropped to almost nothing, and those crimes that were committed originated from outside the county, usually by drifters.

In accordance with his orders from General Branch, Dan worked with Joe to hunt down the criminals, which sometimes meant entering other counties to bring them to justice. Several times posses were formed just like in the Old West, thus, in doing so, the citizens were given an active hand in enforcing the laws they lived by. The laws and punishments were harsh but fair and necessary. After a fair and speedy trial, most evil-doers were given a brand on their right forearm of the letter "C", which meant criminal. They were then banished from Iroquois, and their return would result in immediate execution.

In post-apocalypse Iroquois, there was no such thing as rehabilitation. They didn't have the logistics to handle prisoners for more than a few weeks at a time. Serious crimes like attempted rape, rape, child molestation, attempted murder, murder and kidnapping held the death sentence and were carried out within twenty-four hours after trial with a single bullet to the head. But as of June only two executions had taken place, and those were former convicts from Jackson Prison who had wandered into the area. Sheriff Leif carried out the sentence personally in front of the courthouse for all citizens to see.

Before The Day Iroquois county had boasted a population of fifty-three thousand people. Almost all the casualties of war had been replaced, and now, they held steady at close to fifty thousand men, women and children. Throughout northern Michigan, Iroquois had gained the reputation of being a calm amidst the storm, a place to raise your family with the possibility of passing on that lifestyle to your children. Sheriff Leif had a backlog of residency applications, so he appointed a committee to winnow out the undesirables, thus making his job less time consuming. Of course certain people were highly sought after such as medical personnel, civil engineers, and Mennonites as well as Amish families, because of their extensive experience in frontier living. Almost on a daily basis either Colonel Branch or one of the other county leaders would come to Joe with a request for a certain skill. If that skill couldn't be met inside the county, then an applicant was offered Iroquois county citizenship. The offer was always accepted.

Colonel Branch used Militia forces to set up a series of listening posts all around the county border. All major roads were manned and guarded complete with radio communication. There was no longer any shortage of military manpower as most residents were now seasoned combat veterans. Anyone with sickness was not allowed to pass through as tens of thousands had died downstate from disease and malnutrition.

But the flood of refugees had slowed to a trickle by summer's start as most people hadn't prepared and had simply died of cold, starvation, disease or lawlessness during the first winter. So, because of their newfound reputation of fairness, strength and mild living conditions, Iroquois continued to grow and prosper while others suffered.

Indeed, several of the contiguous counties were in dire straits, so Colonel Branch traveled there first to offer them aid in return for joining a mutual defense pact with the strongest county of the region. Initially, Dan thought his job would be near to impossible, but he'd underestimated the power of legend and reputation. To those outside of Iroquois, the stories had spread of grand and glorious battle, how the Home Guard and Militia Rangers had stood up to a mighty horde of a million men and won using sheer courage and determination. Dan allowed them to believe what they wished, since it made his job so much easier.

And then ... there were always the stories of the ever elusive and powerful ... the Shadow Militia.

Dan made good use of Sergeant Donny Brewster in training the Home Guard and Military Rangers. The Guard received basic combat instruction, whereas the Rangers began intensive Special Forces training. They may never rival SEALS, but neither would they ever be mere farmers again.

Anyone with exceptional aptitude and ability in marksmanship was put into a special unit to undergo sniper training. Donny trained them personally, and, despite Dan's protests, Jeremy Branch had been one of his first recruits. Jeremy was now sixteen years old and a crack shot with any type of firearm. He had the gift.

But perhaps the biggest surprise of all was the contribution of Jackie Branch. She was appointed second in command of civilian forces by Sheriff Leif and served as a sworn Special Deputy, reporting directly to Joe. Her first project was to organize all the women of the county into a force capable of feeding and caring for its inhabitants. But to do that, first she had to educate them. Jackie formed a hard-working team (assisted by Marge Leif) and they began by interviewing every woman in the county, cataloging her strengths, weaknesses, her skills, and what training was necessary to better serve her own family as well as the community.

Every night a different community education class was held at the courthouse on such topics as home canning, food dehydration, family medicine, gardening, how to identify wild herbs, mushrooms and grasses, cooking with wood, doing laundry by hand and home sanitation methods. To accomplish this she drew on many older members of the county who had lived through the Great Depression and the Second World War. She also raided the local museums and auction houses for antiques which were promptly taken out of mothballs and put into service. Due to the hard work and innovative thinking of Jackie Branch, the abrupt move from computer age to frontier-era life became a much smoother transition.

Because of the harshness of life, people pulled together, not because they were superior in any way, but simply out of necessity and leadership by example.

CHAPTER 5

General Branch and the Big Decision

RODNEY BRANCH SAT AT THE CONFERENCE TABLE BESIDE HIS lifelong friend, Colonel Roger "Ranger" MacPherson. He squinted his eyes and furled his brow as he pondered the question before him: a question, whose answer could either save or doom the race of men in North America.

"I want your opinion, Mac. What do you think? Is this reliable?" He paused. "Or is this just wishful thinking of an old man and too good to be true?"

The colonel met his gaze head on. He knew what the general was thinking. *If I make the wrong decision, thousands will die, and it will be on my head.* Mac smiled inside. He had been here many times himself while still a general in the Army Rangers, and he didn't envy his friend one bit. Several times Mac had made the "wrong decision" and innocent and brave soldiers had died unnecessarily. It was inevitable. No one could be right all the time. The difference was when a sergeant made a bad call, perhaps ten men could die. When a general screwed up it could mean the lives of thousands.

But none of that mattered right now. Mac knew it and so did Rodney. But Colonel MacPherson took it by the numbers and slowly mapped it out for his friend.

"It's the best intelligence we have, General. We don't have eyes on The Blind Man, but the technology is sound and reliable. Right now, even as we speak, we believe The Blind Man to be interrogating Major Danskill deep inside a rock fortress in the mountains of Pennsylvania."

General Branch was deep in thought. He knew that Mac was simply stating the obvious, leading him to a decision pre-ordained by the facts and the desperate situation.

"We don't have a choice, do we Mac?"

The colonel didn't answer. He knew it wasn't really a question, just part of the decision-making process. The general would have to think it out, talk it out, and then go with his gut. That was Rodney's best trait as a commanding general. He had instincts that Mac did not.

"I understand that most commanders would jump at this chance but ... it just seems too easy to me. Something doesn't feel right, Mac. Something is giving me pause. On the one hand, we could move in with bunker busters and level the place. We could bury the guy beneath his own rubble, but then we'd never find him, wouldn't even know if he was dead or alive. And if we failed ... if the guy got away, then he would never underestimate us again. He would realize the Shadow Militia is the most real threat he faces. And isn't that why we refused to employ our forces in defense of Iroquois?"

Mac didn't answer. He simply waited for the general to talk himself out. General Branch looked over at his friend for help, knowing in advance that none would be there save the moral support and undying devotion of the strongest of men who would carry out his orders or die trying. General Branch sighed wearily and came to a decision.

"I want eyes-on surveillance from all four compass points over the next three days before we act. I want to know even the most mundane details of what goes on there. We can't underestimate The Blind Man. After that I want you to put together two plans: the first, an air strike using bunker busters, and the second, a conventional ground attack without air support. When it's all assembled and ready to launch, we'll talk again."

Colonel MacPherson stood up and swiftly strode out of the room. He was at his best when planning a mission. The only thing he enjoyed more than planning was leading the attack. Despite that, his general's orders confused him. *A ground attack without air support?* That was dangerous, risky and against all logic. But he didn't say anything, and he would carry out Rodney's orders to the letter. He had chosen his general, and everything in their life-long experience had taught him to trust Rodney's judgment and his instincts. He wouldn't change that now.

The Blind Man and Major Danskill

JARED THOMPSON WORE A TAILORED BLUE SUIT, SHINY, BLACK ARMANI shoes and dark sunglasses. He liked to cover his eyes during interrogations; it freed him up to look directly into his victim's eyes without their knowledge. He called them victims, simply because he seldom interrogated anyone and left them alive. On many occasions the illusion of his blindness had given him an edge, because people were more free with their facial expressions when they believed they were being interrogated by someone who couldn't see them.

"So, Major Danskill, that's a very interesting story." He hesitated for a moment to build the suspense. "But it fails to impress me. I elevated you to a position of power. I gave you all the right military toys to play with." He hesitated. "I even suffered and fed your somewhat unusual tastes in young boys, which, of course. I deplore, being a man of moral integrity myself." He paused before going on. "But, to each his own I suppose. Far be it from me to judge."

Major Danskill was duct-taped naked to the wooden chair. The rest of the room was empty, sterile and bright white. It had been scrubbed and bleached to a cleanliness that would make a hospital operating room blush.

"In short, Major Danskill, why did you fail me?"

The major raised his chin up off his chest and looked directly into The Blind Man's eyes before speaking.

"I failed because of my own arrogance. Arrogance is a weakness that was exploited by our enemy. I thought I was fighting an organized band of farmers, when in fact, they were trained and led by General Rodney T. Branch, commanding general of The Shadow Militia."

Jared Thompson's heart quickened. He already knew this, but there was something about the spoken word that gave the fact more power. On the one hand, he relished and welcomed the challenge of a worthy adversary; on the other, he was determined to move ahead flawlessly and without impulse. He had to be right. He had to move slowly.

"Tell me all you know about General Rodney T. Branch."

Major Danskill knew this was his one chance to make himself useful, and if he failed, well, he knew The Blind Man wasn't the sort of person to collect useless baggage. The problem was he knew very little of General Branch or The Shadow Militia. So, because he would be killed if The Blind Man had no use for him, then he had no other choice, but to lie.

"To meet a man on the field of combat is to learn of him in the most intimate of details. I didn't know him beforehand or I would have won the battle. But, with each defeat comes knowledge and power. I learned about my adversary as I grappled with him. Then, afterwards, I became a spy in the camp of my enemy and I ..."

But Jared Thompson was no longer listening to the man's fabrications. He'd already studied carefully the full biography of Rodney Branch. The general had an above-average IQ, but was by no means a genius. He had a college degree, but had graduated in the middle of his class. In fact, the only place Rodney Branch had ever excelled was on the field of battle. Somehow, some way, Rodney Branch always came out on top. He had a history of being put into hopeless situations and still winning. He was unpredictable, creative and he possessed courage, integrity and unequaled tenacity. And it was that last trait which impressed Jared the most. Sure, the courage and creativity made Rodney dangerous to him, and he would have recruited the general for his own purposes had he not possessed the flaw of integrity. But it was the tenacity that made him so deadly. Deep in his gut, Jared knew that tenacity never gave up; it just came after you over and over again until you killed it or it killed you.

Looking at Major Danskill ramble on about his qualities while he sat naked, duct-taped to a chair caused him to smile inside. This man would be of no use to him. He motioned for Sammy Thurmond, who had been at his right hand the entire time.

Sammy moved forward and pulled out a knife. Major Danskill stopped talking. The blade flicked open and cut the duct tape binding the major's hands. Danskill flexed his wrists to get the blood flowing again, and then he looked up and straight into The Blind Man's eyes.

Jared was seldom disconcerted, but this act more than anything else was uncomfortable to him. Somehow this man knew or sensed his sight. Jared wanted to know why, but his curiosity wasn't strong enough to spare the major's life.

Sammy Thurmond backed away, putting the knife into his pocket. Danskill couldn't stand as other tape still firmly affixed his butt to the chair. He could move his hands, but he wasn't going anywhere.

Jared Thompson then got up from his own chair and took a few steps forward. He took off his sunglasses and returned the major's gaze.

"How did you know?"

The major smiled. "Suffice it to say ... I knew."

Jared nodded and pulled the small caliber handgun out of his suit pocket.

"There's only one bullet. I'd like you to shoot yourself. I recommend a shot to the head to minimize your suffering. After all, you have been a faithful servant. However, you understand. I cannot allow you to live. It's nothing personal. You've always been very polite and congenial."

The major nodded once, his smile dissolving like late morning mist. He thought to himself, *I'm a warrior, and I won't go down without a fight. The Blind Man has to know this. He would never hand me a loaded gun.* Danskill reached out and accepted the pistol; it appeared to be a 32 caliber semiautomatic. Once he grasped the gun in his hands, he felt a wave of hope wash over him. *One bullet ... just one bullet. You'd best use it wisely.* A plan was already forming in his mind.

He moved the gun to his right hand and slowly slid back the slide just far enough to confirm a round was in the chamber. His heart skipped a beat when he saw the tail end of the shining brass. *One round, he had one round!*

Without hesitation he pulled the pistol up and placed the front sight between Sammy Thurmond's eyes. He quickly pulled the trigger.

Silence.

He pulled the trigger again. Nothing.

The major's heart sank, knowing he would soon be dead.

"Interesting. Very interesting. You had only one bullet, so you decided to kill the greatest threat first. Then you would no doubt have crushed the chair beneath you and killed me with your bare hands." Jared smiled. "I know all about you as well, Major Danskill. You are an expert in several martial art forms, are you not?"

Sammy Thurmond moved forward and took the pistol from Danskill's hand. There was no resistance. Then he stepped back and handed it to his boss. Jared hefted the gun back and forth in his hands, then he reached into his left coat pocket and took out a ring. He placed the ring on his right ring finger, and then pulled the gun up, pointing it directly at Major Danskill's head.

"You see, Major Danskill, this is a smart gun, and the ring sends out a signal to the chip in the pistol, thereby unlocking the firing mechanism. As long as I'm wearing the ring, and the gun is in my hand, the gun will fire, but minus the ring, this gun is simply a very expensive club, and a small club at that."

For a brief moment, Danskill thought of all the glory owed him that would never be paid. He thought of all the young boys he'd abused, and the ones who had gotten away.

Jared Thompson pressed the trigger, slowly and steadily to the rear. The shot rang out, and Major Danskill's head jerked back and then slumped forward onto his chest.

The Blind Man nonchalantly handed the gun over to Sammy Thurmond, who immediately put it into his pocket.

"Mr. Thurmond, after the autopsy, I would like you to take this body and cut it in half. Half the body will receive a proper funeral with full military honors. The other half will be taken to the woods nearby and tied to a tree, where wild animals will rip it to shreds and devour it."

He turned and looked into Sammy's eyes. He rarely did that. "Do you understand, Mr. Thurmond?"

Sammy quickly nodded. "Yes sir. It will be done as you command."

The Blind Man replaced his sunglasses, and put his left hand on Sammy's arm to be led from the room.

CHAPTER 6

Donny Brewster's Last Night Alive

"**Y**ES, I'M AFRAID IT'S TRUE. I SHIP OUT IN THE MORNING ON a very dangerous mission. I'll likely not survive. This will undoubtedly be the last time you see me."

Lisa Vanderboeg raised her left eyebrow, and the hint of a smile touched her lips. "Really? You must be terrified."

Donny Brewster shrugged his muscular shoulders nonchalantly. "No, not really. Us soldiers face death every day. We stare it in the eyes and we mock its existence." He looked out past her into the playground, feigning contemplation. "Yes, to a warrior, death is more of a release than a punishment."

Lisa's blonde hair had grown longer since her first meeting with General Branch, so she grabbed a lock of curls and flipped it back behind her. She spoke her mind as always.

"What a screwed-up world view you have, Donny. That is, if you really believe this cock-and-bull story you're feeding me."

She looked at him with more than a small measure of skepticism. Donny's gaze moved back to her face, then a hurt look came over him, which Lisa didn't know was real or contrived.

"What? You don't believe me?"

"Of course I believe you. I believe that you're shipping out in the morning and that it's probably a dangerous mission, but I don't for a moment believe you're terrified. On the contrary, I think you're excited about it; that you can't wait to get there and feel that adrenaline. I think you like killing people."

Something in Donny Brewster magically changed, and, this time, Lisa knew it was real. His face clouded over as his eyes moved off into the distance again.

"Is that why you don't like me, Lisa? Because I kill people?"

The young, blonde nurse squirmed on the park bench as her 5-year-old daughter played on the monkey bars with three other children her age.

"I didn't say I don't like you, Donny."

"But you didn't say you did either."

"It's complicated."

"How so?"

She looked off into the distance, trying to form her thoughts in a way that wouldn't hurt him any more than necessary.

"I'm not judging you. I've killed people too you know."

Donny turned back to her. "And what did it feel like for you?"

She shrugged her shoulders, not believing she was having this conversation. "Well, the first time my husband was in danger and I was in a fit of rage and terror. I didn't feel guilt. I just felt it was something that had to be done to protect the ones I love."

Donny turned back to face her. He looked into her deep, blue eyes.

"And the second time?"

"The second time I was with you at The Horde encampment. I was shooting a machine gun into the darkness. It wasn't so personal, and I just felt afraid and confused."

"Did you feel like you were doing the right thing?"

She thought about it a moment before answering.

"I suppose so. I mean The Horde was coming after us and would have killed my daughter if they'd made it here."

She made eye contact with Donny again.

"But it's different for you, because you enjoy it."

"And that's what you don't like about me?"

She nodded, almost ashamed of herself as she did so.

"I think so, yes. But the odd thing is, despite that, I still want you to exist. I want you to be there doing what you do best. I just don't want to be around it. I don't want to become like you. I don't want my little girl to grow up alongside a killer."

Donny flinched when he heard her say that as if she'd stabbed him with a knife. Then he looked out at little Samantha playing. All of a sudden he didn't want to be around Lisa anymore.

"I *am* a killer, Lisa. I was born and bred for it. I'm good at it, and I feel a sense of accomplishment when I kill bad people. The first few times it was a bit scary; then it was exciting; then it became a job."

Donny's eyes never left the four girl's playing on the monkey bars. His mind locked to them as if their presence and happiness gave him the strength to go on.

"But now, I feel damaged, Lisa. Like a part of my soul was wounded and had to be cauterized to reconcile and save my humanity. I don't enjoy killing, and I don't want to do it anymore. But the sad truth is this: it's what I do best and it's what the world needs most. Especially now."

Lisa let that sink in. She wanted to say something but everything crossing her mind rang hollow to her. All of a sudden she felt shallow and selfish.

"I'm sorry I feel this way, Donny. It's probably not fair to you but …" Donny interrupted her.

"I need to be around decent people like you and Samantha. I need to be reminded of why I'm doing this. I need to know that someday, when all this is over, I'll be able to put it aside and return to the rest of the human race, that I can be normal again. And maybe … just maybe … someone can love me and I can love them back. I don't want to kill. I want to create."

Lisa sat on the park bench dumbfounded. She'd always hated his arrogance and bravado, his smooth talk and cocky smile. But now, he seemed almost like a little boy who'd fallen and skinned his knee on the playground who needed holding. And she was a nurse.

She looked out at her daughter and tears welled up in her eyes. In her heart, Lisa knew that her daughter was allowed to play and laugh and run with other children, simply because of people like Donny Brewster who were willing to put their humanity on hold, to face their inner demons, to give up a piece of their soul in order for others to live and enjoy some measure of freedom and happiness. Before the Battle of Iroquois County, she'd always taken that for granted.

Lisa turned her blue eyes toward Donny, and their eyes locked together. She reached out and touched his hand. The feeling of electricity ebbed into his skin, and he tensed.

"I can't be what you want, Donny, but I can give you what you need."

Her eyes had softened, but Donny's took on a confused stare.

"Are you saying you want to have sex with me?"

Lisa's eyes turned to fire as she pulled her hand away from his.

"You idiot! Why do you always ruin moments like this!? Why do you always screw up these tender moments?"

Donny shrugged.

"I don't know. I'm a man."

Lisa jumped up off the bench and started to walk away. Donny just sat there, afraid to say anything else. He thought it odd that he found it easy to march into battle tomorrow, to face impossible odds, to attack superior forces, to shove a knife into a man's guts and hold onto him as the life drained away, to kill or be killed, but ... this five foot five blonde who couldn't beat him in arm wrestling just scared the hell out of him.

Lisa stopped and turned around abruptly.

"Listen, do you want me to be your friend or not!?"

Donny thought for a moment, then quickly nodded his head. "Yeah, sure."

"Good. Okay then. Go to war tomorrow. Kill lots of bad guys. And when you get back we can grill hamburgers at my place and talk about it. Okay?"

"Sure. Sounds good."

And then she picked up Samantha and walked away from the playground. Sergeant Donny Brewster, highly trained master sniper, killer of hundreds of men, softly smiled, all the while realizing that in head-to-head combat, he was no match for Lisa Vanderboeg and her five-year-old daughter.

Dan Branch Goes to War

"BUT WHY DO YOU HAVE TO GO WITH DONNY TO SOME SUPER-SECRET invasion just because Uncle Rodney wants you to?"

Dan knew it was a losing argument and one he'd best not perpetuate. "I don't know, honey. I just got this call from Colonel MacPherson, and he's sending down a helicopter for Donny and I."

There was a breeze on the porch this morning, and a lock of her coarse, black hair blew down into her eyes. Jackie brushed it away with more annoyance than the situation merited. She wasn't going to tell Dan this, but, if truth be told, she was upset because she didn't like being left behind. Baby Donna, now six months old was playing in a sand box just off the porch.

"What is this mission all about?"

"I don't know, honey. I'll be briefed when we get to where ever we're going."

Dan reached over and touched her shoulder, but she moved it away like his fingers were poison.

"Don't touch me, Dan Branch!"

It usually meant trouble when she used his full name. Dan wasn't a stupid man in most things, but when it came to a woman and her feelings, he felt no smarter than

Forrest Gump, just like the rest of the male race. A part of him wanted to throw up his hands and just give up, but the other part of him, the part that loved her and wanted a future, knew enough to hang in there until this storm blew over.

"Honey, why don't you just tell me what's wrong. I hate it when you try to make me guess. I'm not that smart. Just open up your mouth and tell me straight out why you're mad that I'm going on a top secret mission for Uncle Rodney."

And then it hit him.

"Oh my – oh my. I think I've got it."

She looked at him like he was crazy.

"You don't have anything. You're just talking."

Dan smiled.

"Yes I do. I know what's bothering you. You want to come with me, don't you?"

Jackie turned her gaze away to the west.

"No. You're a stupid man. Just go away."

Dan smiled and moved closer to her.

"I wish you could come with me. I really do, but I don't think we should be taking the baby into a dangerous situation like that. I have no idea what I'm heading off into. It could be a shooting war for all I know."

Dan placed his hand on her shoulder, and this time she didn't pull away.

"I just don't understand why the men get to have all the fun. You get to train and fight wars and go off on wild super-secret adventures while I'm stuck home breast feeding and cleaning dirty diapers. Why can't you stay home and take care of the baby while I go on the mission?"

A blank look came over Dan's face, then he reached down with his free hand and rubbed back and forth along his pectoral muscles as if looking for something.

"I don't know, honey. I keep waiting, but my milk hasn't come in yet."

Jackie tried to stifle a smile but couldn't hold it back. Dan turned her toward him and wrapped both his arms around her, bringing her in close.

"I love you, Jackie. Isn't that enough?"

She buried her face into his chest, was silent for a moment and then sobbed.

"I don't know what's wrong with me, Dan. I'm not like the other women. I work with them every day, and they just all seem to be content watching their men march off to war while they sit home taking care of kids."

She moved her head back and then looked up into his eyes imploringly.

"What's wrong with me, honey?"

Dan smiled and looked into her dark eyes sympathetically. He grabbed a handful of her black, Lebanese hair and let it run through his fingers like grains of sand dropping onto the beach.

"It's because you're special. You married into a strange family. Your father-in-law is the commanding general of the Shadow Militia; your husband is a colonel, and we're living in dangerous times, where any of us could die without a moment's notice."

He put his right hand on the back of her head and pulled it into his muscled chest. He gently stroked the back of her head as he spoke.

"You're special, honey. You're a Branch."

Jackie wrapped her arms around his waist and squeezed as hard as she could.

"I'm not going to let you go, Dan Branch."

Dan smiled and thought to himself. *I love this woman, but keeping her under control is like roping the wind.*

Baby Donna looked up at them and laughed as she shoved another handful of dirt into her mouth.

CHAPTER 7

The Blind Man's Bluff?

JARED THOMPSON LOOKED UP AT SAMMY THURMOND, WHO was standing beside the couch, waiting dutifully as his boss studied the autopsy report he'd just been handed. He always hated giving The Blind Man bad news, but, at the same time, it always interested him as to how his boss would handle it. In over fifteen years of crises, complications and complex plans gone awry, Sammy Thurmond had never seen his boss visibly upset. Jared Thompson was always in control of himself and the environment around him.

It took a full five minutes, but, eventually, Jared looked up from the paper and stared at the wall in front of him. Then he placed the report down on the coffee table and thought some more. Finally, he crossed his legs and leaned back as he spoke. His voice had the same edge of calm it always had.

"So there was a tracking device embedded in Major Danskill's right buttocks. Interesting. Very interesting."

He didn't know how it had happened, whether Danskill had known about it, or, had even collaborated in the venture, but, seeing as though Danskill was dead, it probably no longer mattered. Jared now realized he'd made a mistake in killing him so quickly. In retrospect, he should have first extracted as much information as possible. He would have to examine that further.

"We'll have to make it a matter of policy to scan everyone in the future before we bring them to the facility. However, that makes no difference now."

Sammy thought he sensed a violent edge to The Blind Man's voice.

"I want you to prepare for an attack. Triple the Combat Air Patrol and extend it out to a two hundred mile radius." Jared reached up and scratched his chin with his left hand, and then placed both hands in his lap.

"And reduce the ground-level perimeter security personnel by two-thirds. I want just a few armed security up top. Stage our special forces listening posts every five hundred yards out to five miles in all directions. They are to observe and report only. Do not engage.

"Place a combat-ready swift reactionary force of one thousand men on standby. Have twenty Apaches ready to fly at all times, but only two should be in the air until I give the command to do otherwise. Reroute the satellites so that I have real-time intelligence. I want to know the moment his troops enter the area."

The Blind Man hesitated, as if contemplating the seriousness of his next decision. He didn't want to admit it, but he was consumed with the idea of killing Rodney T Branch, not just killing him, but torturing him and destroying all he held dear. "And move all our infantry and armored reserves to within seven miles east of the compound. Tell them to prepare for counterattack. Divide them into three groups, and they should be ready to move at a moment's notice."

Jared was simultaneously angered and challenged by the fact his location had been compromised by the Shadow Militia. While the prospect of an attack excited him, he wanted to make sure he was ready for it and that he always maintained the edge. In the back of his mind, he kept reminding himself, *General Rodney T Branch has never lost a fight. Behave accordingly. Give him the respect he deserves – and then kill him. Never underestimate the Shadow Militia ever again.*

"And one other thing. Pack up my things and move them to the secondary headquarters. I don't want to take any unnecessary chances."

As usual, Sammy Thurmond showed no emotion, but, deep inside, hidden and protected, he began to harbor second thoughts.

Escanaba, Michigan

COLONEL MACPHERSON HAD JUST FINISHED LAYING OUT THE BATTLE plans for the coming attack on the hardened, underground facility in Pennsylvania. He walked back to his seat now. First, he'd gone over the ground assault which included ten thousand light infantry troops from Michigan, Pennsylvania, Ohio, West Virginia and New Hampshire. They would all converge simultaneously on the target and arrive mere hours before the attack launched. Second, had been the air attack. This included F-16 fighters for air cover as well as A-10 Warthogs and Apache helicopter gunships to ward off any counterattack.

General Branch stepped up to the podium and looked out at the fifty or so men and women seated before him. His nephew, Colonel Dan Branch was seated in the front row alongside Sergeant Donny Brewster, and Colonel MacPherson. General Masbruch, the commanding officer of Shadow Militia, Eastern Command, was also there with his Chief of Staff, Lieutenant Colonel Samuelson.

"Brothers and sisters in arms, friends, soldiers and patriots. I don't have to tell you what's riding on this one battle. Due to the ingenuity of Colonel MacPherson and a few high-tech toys, we've been handed the opportunity of a lifetime.

"We have the chance to end this war with one fierce, strong and vicious attack. Within forty-eight hours, if all goes well, this war will be over."

The dead silence was broken by people turning in their chairs to make eye contact with those sitting beside them. Some even spoke in hushed whispers. The excitement was obvious. General Branch waited a moment before raising his hand to restore military order. His officers immediately silenced.

"Because of this unique opportunity, I've decided to merge both of Colonel MacPherson's plans into one. We will launch a coordinated air and ground attack in less than forty-eight hours with everything we have. I hate to risk all our assets in one battle, but this is a formidable adversary and we'll need all our resources to accomplish the mission."

The silence in the room seemed to get louder. No one spoke or even moved. Finally, General Masbruch stood to his feet and began to clap. The other officers, one by one, stood up as well and joined in, and, within a few seconds, the entire room was on its feet and cheering.

General Branch smiled. For better or worse; they were ready for battle.

As EVERYONE FILED OUT OF THE BRIEFING ROOM, THE SENIOR OFFICER MADE his way out of the building and walked a full two blocks away before stopping in an alley. There was another meeting in thirty minutes, so he had to make this quick. He pulled out his cell phone, which, wasn't really a cell phone at all, but a high-tech satellite phone. He punched in the number and waited. Finally, a voice on the other end came on the line.

"What do you have for me?"

"I have to be brief. The attack is on. All Shadow Militia forces of both air and ground will converge on your location in forty-eight hours."

There were a few seconds of silence.

"Excellent. Thank you for your superior service, Colonel ..."

"No names. I told you no names!"

The Blind Man laughed softly to himself.

"Of course. I understand."

"It's risky for me to pass information on to you, so I'll only contact you again if there are any changes."

"As you wish, Mr. X. And once again, thank you."

Jared put the satphone down on the coffee table, carved from a rare jungle tree and stolen from a now-deceased Columbian drug lord. He took off his sun glasses and looked around at the sprawling bungalow. It was lavish and ornate with all the comforts of home. He was going to miss it.

Rodney Branch WAS SITTING IN THE HIGH-BACKED CHAIR, LOOKING across Mac's old, oak desk, wondering if he was doing the right thing. If he was correct, then the Shadow Militia would be saved, and the cause would survive, giving hope for freedom to the next generation. If he was wrong, then the enemy of freedom would be given a new lease on life, and this war would go on for years to come. The cost of human life would be great.

Sitting across from him were Colonel Dan Branch, Sergeant Donny Brewster and General Masbruch. Colonel MacPherson was standing up in the corner with his arms across his chest, his back ramrod stiff, peering out with eyes like blue granite.

General Branch was the first to speak. He decided to start out light, and then move into the difficult news.

"So, Sergeant Brewster, how are things going with that young nurse of yours? Any further news to report?"

The young sergeant seemed a bit taken aback, surrounded by colonels and generals, the lowly non-com felt out of place. Normally confident and sure, his voice wavered a bit as he answered his general.

"Well, sir, it's too soon to say. All I can report is initial resistance is strong, but that Marines don't surrender, and I will continue to press the attack."

Rodney nodded and smiled. He liked the boy.

"Rodney, did you actually call me in here to talk about this man's love life? Because I've got a mission to execute, probably the most important battle I'll ever fight."

Rodney looked over at the only other general in the room. This wasn't going to be easy.

"Actually, Dale, that's what I need to talk to you about." He hesitated as if choosing his words carefully. "I have a new mission for you."

General Dale Masbruch cocked his head to one side. "Excuse me?"

Rodney smiled, but then his face grew stern and deadly serious.

"The attack plans that Mac drew up are flawless and sheer genius. But there's a problem."

General Masbruch sighed but said nothing.

"We don't have the resources to execute it."

Dan Branch looked over at Donny, who returned his gaze. General Masbruch locked eyes with Rodney.

"Then why the hell are we doing this!?"

Rodney looked down at the desk, then brought up his hands and folded them atop the oak. He suddenly felt ten years older and very, very tired.

"Because we are weak, and we need to appear strong."

General Masbruch almost lifted himself off the chair, but forced himself to remain seated.

"For god's sake, Rodney, we're on the cusp of life or death of a culture and you're quoting me Sun Tzu? Just spit it out, man! What are we doing?"

Colonel MacPherson stepped forward. "General Branch, if I may?"

Rodney nodded and leaned back in his chair.

"We have a traitor in our senior command structure, and those of you in this room are the only ones to be trusted. When we reach the enemy headquarters in Pennsylvania every person we send will be attacked and annihilated, because our enemy has all the details of our battle plan. Aside from that, we don't possess a sufficient number of battle-ready F-16s and pilots or even A-10 Warthogs to successfully complete this mission. And we certainly don't have ten thousand troops to employ in battle."

He paused a moment before going on. He saw the large, green vein pulsing on General Masbruch's forehead and wondered if it was going to spring a leak.

"If The Blind Man knew exactly how weak we really are, then he would simply move in and crush us. We need to buy some time to build up and train an army. We need time to transform farmers and factory workers into battle-ready fighters. We need to create supply chains, and manufacture weaponry. We have to train and equip an army using nothing but the skeleton command of the Shadow Militia. That's our only chance. And, quite frankly, has been the plan from day one. 'Appear strong when you are weak, and weak when you are strong.'"

Colonel Dan Branch who had been silent up until now, finally broke in. "So who is

The Blind Man?"

Colonel MacPherson stepped back into the corner, and Rodney took over again. "The Blind Man is our enemy, and he has us outgunned, outmanned, and outsupplied. He has most of the technological capabilities of the former United States government. And here's how we're going to beat him."

Rodney talked on for a full half hour, outlining details and plans, all the while, General Masbruch's pulsing forehead began to subside.

CHAPTER 8

Attack of the Black Flies

"WHAT DO YOU THINK, MAC?" COLONEL MACPHERSON stared into the computer screen, watching the two lone guards pacing back and forth in front of the pole barn set into the side of the Pennsylvania mountain. They were in digital camo, with M4s hanging from one-point slings in front of them.

"I think you're right, sir. It's a trap."

General Branch reached up to stroke his chin with his left hand, and he continued to rub his thumb and forefinger along the sides of his cheeks in heavy contemplation.

"This guy's good, Mac. I'll give him that. He knows we have located his headquarters, and he also realizes how we found it. Which means he now knows something more about us and our capabilities. That's unfortunate. I liked it better when we were just a myth in the shadows."

Colonel MacPherson, who was seated beside the general picked up his coffee cup, blew away the steam and took a sip. "We could just back away, melt off into the shadows again, and live to fight another day."

Rodney got up and walked over to the coffee pot. He poured himself another cup before standing off to one side of the window and peering out into the Upper Peninsula June sky. The black flies would be out soon, and they'd be driving them all crazy with their terrible little bites. That's what they were to The Blind Man, just tiny little black flies, buzzing around his head, and making him mad. Rodney turned back to his colonel and smiled.

"We have to keep him guessing, Mac. We have to keep The Blind Man at an arm's length to give us more time to train and prepare for all-out war."

Rodney walked back to his chair and sat down again. He placed his coffee mug on the desk and began to trace circles with his forefinger around the rim of the cup. Colonel MacPherson tossed him a coaster and Rodney laughed out loud before placing the disk beneath his coffee cup.

"I think it's funny that you and I are planning the greatest war for freedom since the American revolution, and you still have time to worry about coffee stains on your desk."

Mac shrugged. "It's a nice desk."

"True. But it's still just a desk." He took a sip and burned his tongue. "I don't think he's going to underestimate us again, Mac. I think he's going to try and destroy us as soon as possible."

Mac looked over. "Meaning?"

"Meaning the time to look weak has come and gone. Now is the time to appear strong."

"Rodney, why do you talk in riddles so much and spend so much time thinking out loud. Just say what you mean."

Rodney liked it when Mac dropped the military formalities and addressed him more like a friend than a general.

"What is the heaviest, most powerful weapon we have in our arsenal?"

The colonel was taking a sip of his coffee, but he stopped and looked over at General Branch. "You can't be serious."

Rodney smiled. He put both elbows onto the desk and peered down into his coffee cup. "We have to do something, and the plan we've made is untenable. The worst thing we could do right now is to put forth an appearance of weakness. The Blind Man is beating us on all fronts. He's called in mercenaries from Europe and South America. We are running low on ammo and supplies all across America. We need to get his attention, to shake up the chess board a bit. Up until now he's felt invincible. I need The Blind Man to fear for his life."

Colonel MacPherson's military bearing returned as if it had never left. "But sir, we only have one."

General Branch nodded. "True, but The Blind Man doesn't know that. Besides, power is impotent without the resolve to use it." He took a sip of his coffee and placed the heavy mug back down. "And … once the internet is back up and running, I'll just log on to Ebay and buy us some more."

The colonel scoffed. "Right, Ebay. You don't even have a credit card, Rodney."

Rodney laughed. "True, but my best friend has American Express."

Mac smiled and shook his head from side to side. He turned and looked out the window at the Upper Peninsula sunshine. He had a feeling life was about to pick up the pace.

Ten Miles West of Blind Man HQ

"JACKIE WAS PRETTY UPSET WHEN SHE FOUND OUT I WAS LEAVING ON THIS mission."

Donny Brewster laughed out loud. "Of course she was upset! She's a woman! Women are crazy."

They were sitting on top of a mountain, on the edge of a rock cliff inside central Pennsylvania, looking out across a few lesser mountains to their objective. General Branch was conducting an air strike on The Blind Man's headquarters, and their orders were strictly to observe and report from due east of the target. Under no circumstances were they to approach within ten miles. Dan and Donny had both secretly wondered what they could possibly see from ten miles out, but both assumed they'd be told to move closer when the time was right. There was a small cave just a few yards to their right where they had stowed the quads. It was a sunny day and upwards of eighty degrees, and Donny and Dan, dressed in woodland camo, were already sweating profusely. If not for the strong wind coming out of the west, it would be a very uncomfortable day.

"So what do you know about women anyways. You've never been married have you?"

"Nope, never made that mistake."

Colonel Dan Branch smiled. "But I notice you've been spending a little time with Nurse Vanderboeg again. How is that going?"

Sergeant Brewster grunted. "Huh. It's going. I guess. I just don't understand women."

Dan took a drink from his olive drab canteen and put it on the ground beside him. "Well, she's a beautiful woman. So, whatever she's done, I suppose you'll have to forgive her."

Donny grinned at the colonel, showing a whole mouthful of teeth. "Why are us men such suckers for good looking women? They wiggle their butts, and we just follow them around like little, lost puppy dogs, no matter what kind of emotional hell they put us through."

Dan laughed. "I don't know. I imagine it has something to do with too much testosterone. Whatever it is, I hope I never outgrow it."

They were both lying on their stomachs in the dirt, and Donny rolled to one side to look Dan in the eyes. "Really? Do you think it's worth all the effort then?"

Without a moment's hesitation, Dan showed his own teeth and answered. "Absolutely, Marine. I would die for that woman, and I'm hoping you can find a lady of your own worth dying for."

Dan rolled over onto his back and looked up at the clear, blue sky. "Yup. Donny, I'll be honest with you. A good woman like Jackie is worth her weight in Mocha flavored Frappuccino."

Donny rolled over on his back and burst out laughing. "Wow! That good, huh?" A few seconds later he stopped and moved back onto his stomach before reaching over to his right. He started digging into his back pack for something.

"I almost forgot. I found this at that abandoned gas station a few miles back." He pulled out a clear glass bottle filled with dirty, brown liquid. Dan recognized it immediately.

"Holy cow! It's a Mocha Frappuccino! Is it mine?"

Donny tossed it down into the dirt like it meant nothing to him. "I wouldn't drink that stuff if my life depended on it. It's all yours, Colonel."

Dan held it in his left palm, and ran the fingers of his right hand over the plastic label. "I haven't had a Frappuccino since …" And then his voice stopped.

"What's wrong?"

Dan shrugged. "Nothing. I was just thinking of the last time I had one of these. It was the night I met Jackie."

Sergeant Brewster sat up and took a look around the perimeter. He wasn't usually so lax on a mission, but he had claymores set up all around them, with only one dirt road to access their position. Both men relaxed and lay flat on their backs, looking up into the blue sky of mid-day.

"So spill it, Marine. Talk to me."

A serious look came over Dan as he spoke. His voice had taken on a subdued tone. "It was the day after I'd killed my first man ... well, five men actually. Jeremy and I were camped in the woods by a stream in Northeast Wisconsin. I was reading the Bible and drinking Frappuccino cooled in the creek. Then Jeremy and I had a good talk, the first good one in a long time. We went to bed and woke up to a woman screaming. It was Jackie. She'd been kidnapped – her and her husband. I followed her, then killed the three men holding them." He stopped. Donny waited patiently.

"But I accidentally shot her husband as well. I wish I could take that shot back. But, if I did, well, then I wouldn't have her. It's a real cluster."

Donny was about to answer when he felt the ground shake beneath him. Almost immediately after the rumble they heard the explosion. Both men glanced up, almost at the same time, and took in the pillar of black and orange cloud rising up ten miles to their eastern flank.

"Holy shit!"

For a few seconds they stared in awe with mouths dropped wide open. Then Dan jumped up and ran to the cave where their quads were hidden. Donny was right behind him. Once inside they moved to the back wall, and huddled in the dark, waiting for the sound of the explosion to die away.

Over the fading sound of the detonation, Dan heard a tiny snap. The large glow stick lit up the small cave in a green iridescent glow. They were thirty feet back from the mouth of the cave with both quads behind them. Dan was the first to speak.

"Donny ... was that a nuke?"

Sergeant Brewster nodded his head in the dim light, all the while struggling to remember the details of his NBC training from the Marine Corps.

"Are we far enough away, Dan?"

"I think so. It depends on how many kilotons it was. If that was the objective, then we're ten miles from ground zero, and we've got about a fifteen-mile-an-hour wind blowing straight from the west. Plus, this cave should give us pretty good protection, provided it doesn't fall down on our heads."

Donny sat flat on his butt and leaned his back against the quad's rear tire. "That was different than all the nuclear blasts I've seen on television. It was a lot louder."

Dan nodded in the green light. "Yeah, and it was weird the way we felt the ground shake before we heard the blast."

"Colonel, I say we wait a bit and then get the hell outta Dodge."

Dan nodded. "I like the way you non-coms think. Let's see if the radio still works, then we can call this in, give our report and then put some clicks between us and Mr. Atom."

Donny glanced over at the quads. "What about them – the EMP – will they even start?"

Dan nodded. "I think so. They were inside the cave pretty far shielded by solid rock." He forced a smile on his face. "I guess we'll find out 'eh Marine?"

Donny smiled back nervously before answering. "Uh, yeah. I guess so." He looked around him for the radio, but it was nowhere to be found. "So, which one of us is going out there to get the radio?"

Dan's smile spread even larger. "Well, *Sergeant* Brewster. *Colonel* Branch thinks it should be you."

Donny's face clouded over. "You're going to pull rank on me after all we've been through? I thought we were friends."

"Of course we're friends. It's not my fault I have an uncle in high places."

All of a sudden Donny threw his head back and burst out laughing. Dan's face grew stern.

"What's so funny, Marine?"

After calming himself down, Donny said, "We left your Frappuccino outside, and it is now radioactive!"

Colonel Branch buried his head in his hands. "I don't believe this. The last Frappuccino on the planet was just destroyed by a nuclear bomb!"

The Blind Man - Alternate Headquarters

JARED THOMPSON WATCHED THE BIG SCREEN ROIL AND BOIL AS THE BLACK cloud mushroomed up into the air, atomizing and dispersing the now incinerated personnel and contents of his state-of-the art military headquarters. He guessed it to be a tactical nuke of about ten kilotons. For a brief moment he thought, *That could have been me*. But he quickly shook off the feeling of vulnerability.

Without thinking, The Blind Man slammed his wine goblet down on the beautiful coffee table, stolen from the now-deceased Columbian drug lord. The goblet shattered into a hundred pieces. Jared turned his back on the screen and rubbed his eyes with his left hand. He'd just lost his headquarters and thousands of soldiers, many of them irreplaceable Special Forces. Quickly, he regained his composure, and softly issued orders to his right-hand man.

"Mr. Thurmond, please gather as much intel as possible from the air and from any surviving forces on the ground. I would like to know what happened and how. Can you do that for me, please, Mr. Thurmond?"

Sammy Thurmond's stone-cold face betrayed no emotion, but inside he was secretly vexed. He doubted very much if anyone on the ground would survive the blast and ensuing radiation, which meant this was a major loss for The Blind Man.

He curtly nodded and bowed slightly before quickly exiting the room. It was a stunning revelation to see his boss was no longer in complete control.

Escanaba HQ

FORMER CIA AGENT JEFF ARNETT SAT ACROSS THE TABLE FROM HIS NEW boss, General Rodney Branch. Jeff had met many powerful men in his day, but none quite like Rodney. In Jeff's summation, most powerful men contained obvious flaws: either arrogance, selfishness or maybe greed or just plain brutality. But he still hadn't pinpointed the general's major flaw. The general was the first to speak.

"I need you to help me kill twenty-five-thousand Islamists."

Jeff was a tall man, and he made the chair he was sitting in appear smaller than it really was.

"Why?"

"Because they need killing, and I can't do it on my own. You know things I don't. You have the benefit of experience that I need to draw on. That's why we recruited you in the first place."

Jeff cocked his head to one side and smiled. "You recruited me? I thought I came to you."

General Branch shrugged. "Semantics. Who cares. You're here and I need your help."

Jeff watched as the general's right hand reached up to the left-breast pocket of his camo utility shirt. It stopped halfway and came back down. Special Agent Arnett immediately deduced the truth. Either the general had recently stopped smoking or just ran out of cigarettes. Jeff found that interesting and filed it away for future reference.

"Do you hate Muslims, General Branch?"

Rodney shrugged his shoulders and leaned back in his chair. "On a case-by-case basis, sure. For example, I hate the twenty-five-thousand of them who are marching this way and want to kill me." The general took a sip of his coffee and placed it firmly back down on the desk. "To be more precise about it, it's not that I hate them. I just don't trust them."

Jeff crossed his right leg over his left. "So why don't you trust them?"

Rodney looked at the man blankly. "I don't trust anyone who's trying to kill me."

Jeff smiled without thinking. That was unusual for him. "How about me? Do you trust me?"

"No."

"Why not?"

"Because you're asking me stupid questions and trying to psychoanalyze me and I don't like people getting into my head. It gives them power I don't want them to have. I am what I am and that's that. You can either like it or not like it. I really don't care. But right now I'd like you to stop wasting my time and help me figure out a way to kill these ragheads."

Jeff was amazed. He'd never met anyone so black and white. He thought for a moment. Rodney Branch intrigued him, and he liked that. He came to a decision and nodded.

"Sure. How can I help?"

Rodney leaned forward and placed his elbows on the desk. "I want you to tell me everything you know about Abdul Al'Kalwi. I want to know everything about Islam. I want to know the culture: what they eat, how they dress, how they think about everything. And, most importantly, I want to know how I can piss them off."

Jeff smiled again. He was really starting to like this man. By pre-The-Day standards, he was blunt to the point of rudeness, but he spoke his mind in a simple and matter-of-fact way.

"Okay then. Let's start by talking about the history of Islam, how it started, all about Mohammed. Then we'll move on to the culture of the Middle East and then Abdul

Al'Kalwi." He uncrossed his legs and sat up straight. "Can I get a more comfortable chair, though, because this is going to take a really long time."

Uncle Rodney laughed out loud, and Agent Arnett was taken aback by the suddenness of the outburst.

"Yeah, sure. Let's go into the other room." The two men got up and left Colonel MacPherson's office to begin the first of many multi-hour discussions on Islam and the Middle East culture.

CHAPTER 9

Iroquois City

"**T**HAT SON OF A BITCH REALLY DOES HAVE NUKES?! I DON'T believe it!"

Sheriff Joe Leif sat at the kitchen table of his house across from Colonel Dan Branch. Both were drinking coffee and eating corn bread made by Joe's wife, Marge.

"Joseph Grant Leif! Now you watch your language! I won't tolerate that in my house."

Marge Leif's fierce gray eyes glared down at her husband as she wiped her wet hands on a cotton apron tied to her front.

"Sorry honey. It just slipped out."

Marge turned back to her dishwater in the sink. "Seems like it's been slipping out more often than necessary these days." Her hands moved in the sink, and Dan Branch could hear the dishes clank together as she washed them.

"This is great corn bread, Marge. You should give the recipe to Jackie. I think she'd like it too."

Marge stopped washing and turned around to answer him. Her original sweet demeanor had returned. "Why thank you, Dan. I'll send it home with you." Then she turned back to her dishes as if the world depended on it. Joe and Dan continued their conversation.

"You should have seen it, Joe. Donny and I were only ten miles away and the ground shook before we even heard the explosion. I was surprised at that, but Rodney told me it's because shock waves travel through the ground faster than through the air."

Joe took a sip of his coffee. "I didn't know that."

"Neither did I. But we didn't know Uncle Rodney had nukes either."

"There's a lot we didn't know about your Uncle Rodney. Seems that old man just keeps on surprising us." Joe looked at the kitchen wall and stroked his chin. "I wonder where he got all that stuff. I know darn well it's wasn't from Ebay. So where's he at now?"

Dan finished swallowing his corn bread before answering. "I don't know for sure. I guess he's somewhere on the east coast, maybe New Hampshire. He's been traveling all over the country trying to rally the troops and get them better trained and equipped."

"Rally the troops? Rally them against who?"

"Some guy he calls The Blind Man."

"The Blind Man?"

Dan brushed crumbs off his lightly starched olive drab fatigues. "Yup. He seems to think he's public enemy number one. I guess this guy has usurped the lion's share of power on the East and West coasts, and now he's trying to pacify middle America."

"So what makes Rodney so sure this guy's the bad guy?"

Dan shrugged. "I don't know. I didn't ask. But have you ever known my uncle to be wrong in the past eight months, especially about military things?"

"Guess not." Joe sipped his coffee again. "Marge, honey, can I get a refill?"

Marge sighed and dried her hands before moving to the coffee pot. She refilled first her husband's cup and then Dan's. Dan had set the Leif family up with a limited number of car batteries and solar trickle chargers to give them certain luxuries like coffee pots and lamps. It was a pain in the butt to recharge and move them around, but it was better than living in the stone age.

"So, did the Doc check you out? You're not sterilized or anything from the radiation are you?"

Dan laughed out loud. "No. We were inside a cave and beat feet outta there pretty fast. We weren't there long enough to absorb a lot of radiation. It helps we were 10 miles upwind. Jackie was worried about the same thing. She's a bit mad at Rodney for sending me to watch a nuclear bomb go off."

Marge let the water out of the sink as she spoke. "Well, you can't really blame her for that." All the water for drinking, bathing and for cooking had to be hauled in from the creek a hundred yards from the house. The Leif's were on a waiting list to have a hand pump well driven to replace the useless electric well they now had.

"So what's going to happen now, Dan? Does Rodney know?"

Dan shook his head. "Maybe. Maybe not. You know my Uncle Rodney. Mr. Mysterious. He might know, but he sure as ..." And then he caught himself before swearing. He glanced at Marge, but she wasn't smiling. "I mean he probably knows but isn't telling me anything. That's just the way he is. He just keeps pushing me to strengthen the county alliances and expand them. We're training soldiers like I never thought possible. Just like Rodney's traveling around the country, I'm traveling around northern Michigan. We added three more counties just yesterday. They sent delegations to us, asking to be part of the mutual defense pact."

"Really?"

"Yup. Everyone wants to be allied with the biggest kid on the block, and, right now, that's Uncle Rodney."

Joe shifted in his chair to cross one leg over the other. "Well, that's true. He is the only nuclear power in northern Michigan that we know of."

Marge Leif abruptly changed the subject. "So, Dan, when are you and Jackie going to get pregnant?"

Dan turned to her and smiled. He liked her blunt, direct approach. People always knew what Marge Leif was thinking, whether they wanted to or not.

From there the conversation transitioned to the rigors of daily life. There was a market in town set up at the city park. Some people paid using silver, others paid in bullets, but most people used a system of barter. Some people had been concerned that Sheriff Leif would impose a consumption tax, but Joe had quickly squelched that rumor. "No sense in re-creating the mistakes of the past in rebuilding the new world," he'd said. "As long as I'm in charge, there will be no taxes, just mutual support and cooperation." The people had liked that and commerce began to flourish in Iroquois county, bringing in traders from across the north. Joe had a staff of ten deputies now who helped him keep the peace, but Dan Branch and his Home Guard bore the brunt of the county's border defense.

Dan and Donny continued to recruit and train soldiers. Beginners were taught basic skills, while veteran warriors continued on their journey to becoming snipers, recon scouts, demolition experts, guerilla warriors or whatever else was needed. Iroquois county, not through choice, but through necessity, had become the regional power of the North. And with power came a certain measure of stability.

The Blind Man's New HQ

Jared Thompson looked up at the big screen. He pushed a few buttons on the laptop and manipulated the maps a bit more until he had what he wanted. He had been thinking about only one man for the past two days now, and his obsession with General Rodney T Branch worried him. At first, he'd wanted to strike back immediately with overwhelming force. He'd considered turning Escanaba into a smoking pile of radioactive ash, but had caught himself. *What would that accomplish? It would merely reduce the size of my empire.* And what if General Branch traded him nuke for nuke? What then? Jared knew the answer was unacceptable. The crazy doctrine of Mutual Assured Destruction was as sane and pragmatic now as it had been during the Cold War. Unless he knew for sure how many nukes General Branch had and where they were deployed ... no, that was not the answer.

He knew he had to regain control of the situation and of his emotions. He'd learned from past mistakes that obsessions were a weakness and could prove his undoing. He'd have to kill General Branch, but his pride and his anger would have to take a back seat to rational, well thought out military strategy.

Every problem has a solution, and usually the solution is already embedded in the problem itself. He just had to analyze it and see it for what it was. Jared went back to the beginning and summarized his problem at a most basic level.

Pacification in the South was moving ahead, but behind schedule. Those damn rebel rednecks ... No! He caught himself and started over, this time without the emotion. He spoke out loud to lend a feeling of realness and accountability.

"I'm behind schedule in the South. I'm ahead of schedule on the east and west coasts. The Muslim horde is conquering lower Michigan and moving against Chicago. The Rocky Mountain rebels are still resisting fiercely. The Shadow Militia is the head of the snake. General Branch lives in northern Michigan. Conquer Michigan and you kill the snake, then all else will fall into place."

Good. So now I have a clear objective. But how to achieve it.

"I have no forces in Michigan now that Major Danskill is gone. I have assets in Ohio, but they are occupied. I could hire and ship in more mercenaries from Central and South America, but that takes time, and, quite frankly, they suck as soldiers."

He sat down on the plush, Corinthian leather couch and reached out for his wine goblet. Most of his best wine had been irradiated by General Branch. His emotions rose up again, but he closed his eyes and quickly beat them back down. *Control. I need control to maintain clarity of thought.*

"In Michigan I have two problems: The Shadow Militia and the Muslim horde." The Blind Man cocked his head to one side and repeated to himself. "In Michigan I have two problems: The Shadow Militia and the Muslim horde." He took a sip of his wine. "Interesting. The Muslim horde. The Shadow Militia."

Suddenly, Jared smiled. He lifted his hand in a beckoning manner toward Sammy Thurmond, who had been waiting quietly in the far corner, waiting to do the will of his master. Sammy moved closer and patiently hovered a few feet away.

"Mr. Thurmond. I want all the information we have on Supreme General Abdul Al'Kalwi within thirty minutes. I want satellite photos. I want history, childhood, everything. I want a personality profile, his strengths and weaknesses. I want it all."

Jared flicked his hand and Sammy scooted off through the door. The Blind Man's whole countenance suddenly changed. He took another sip of his wine. Yes, within every problem is embedded its own solution. Thoroughly understand the problem, and the solution reveals itself.

Jackson, Michigan

Supreme General Abdul Al'Kalwi looked out over the alfalfa field. It was already eighteen inches high, and, on any other year prior to The Day, it would have been through its first hay cutting already. But there was no gas to run the tractors, so the hay continued to grow unabated. Nature was reclaiming its hold, and people were starving everywhere; it's not that there was no food, just no way to run the equipment to grow, fertilize, spray, and harvest the crops. Most farmers still had their land, and their families were eating well, because they could grow and harvest enough for their own consumption, but, the days of mechanized farming and corporate agriculture were over and would not return for many years to come, if ever. That was why Abdul was making special deals with the farmers. He was allowing them to keep their land in return for sixty percent of their crops. Abdul knew that food was the key to life, and life was the key to control. If he threatened a starving man with death, then he would readily accept death, and Abdul gained nothing. However, offer a starving man food, and he would accept it and pledge his fealty in return. Abdul had thought all this out. He'd even gone out of his way to gain control of all the seeds he could find. And heirloom seeds had been given a priority, because they, unlike hybrid seeds, were capable of creating more seed for the next year. So, all of lower Michigan was becoming his food belt, and he planned on doing the same to Indiana and Illinois. Once he had enough food to sustain the nation, then the once proud American people would kneel at his feet in return for their daily allotment of bread.

"Make camp here, but do not destroy the field. Hurry! It is almost time for evening prayer."

The Supreme General waved his hand and his underlings moved off quickly to do his bidding. He walked out into the alfalfa, feeling the green grass tickle his bare ankles and toes through his sandals. He removed his footwear and sat down in the hay field. It was a beautiful June day, the beginning of summer, and life was very good for Abdul Al'Kalwi and his army.

Things were going wrong, and his progress had been slowed considerably by all the cars blocking the interstate, but his new arrangement would fix all that. Allah had provided a way beyond his wildest dreams. As Abdul sat in the field and felt the breeze on his face, he readied his heart for prayer.

The Alfalfa Field - The Next Day

SUPREME GENERAL ABDUL AL'KALWI LOOKED UP INTO THE SKY AT THE F-18 Hornet fighter jets racing above him. There were four of them, and they flew straight down in perfect wingtip-to-wingtip formation. They screamed down toward Abdul with deafening precision as he stood in the alfalfa field, once again in his bare feet. Thousands of his soldiers threw themselves to the ground in terror, but Abdul didn't move. He looked on in orgasmic anticipation as the jets made their pass, almost touching the earth before suddenly leveling out and beginning their near vertical climb back up into the sky.

That's when the Supreme General heard the helicopters coming in from the sunrise. He tried to count them, but there were too many. They were all gunships of some type, with machine guns and rockets beneath them. He smiled as the helicopters began to circle his encampment like angry wasps. Abdul had given orders that anyone firing at the aircraft would be tortured and executed. This turned out to be unnecessary as the sheer force of power had most of his men cowering in the dirt.

The larger helicopter moved in quickly and hovered over the alfalfa field. It slowly dropped down and cut its engine. Abdul watched as the rotors lost speed and eventually came to a stop. The door opened and the stairway dropped down. The Blind Man exited and walked slowly down the stairs followed closely by Sammy Thurmond. Sammy then moved to his master's side and led him toward the Supreme General who was meeting him halfway.

Jared was wearing his dark glasses and allowing himself to be led by his servant. When they merged in the field, Sammy Thurmond was the first to speak.

"The Supreme General is here, sir."

Jared smiled and offered a slight bow. Abdul didn't return it, but assumed a blind man wouldn't see it regardless. "Supreme General Al'Kalwi. It is a pleasure to meet such a fine military conqueror."

Abdul answered curtly. "Thank you."

For a clumsy moment there was silence, then the Supreme General motioned to his tent about thirty yards away beside the field. "We may speak privately inside my quarters."

Abdul turned and walked slowly away, assuming he was being followed. As they went, he couldn't help but glance up at the sky, filled with military attack helicopters and fighter jets. They were the one thing he needed to make his dream of conquests come true. And now he had them.

The agreement had been simple. Abdul would rule all of Michigan's upper and lower peninsulas, but his ambitions for Indiana and Illinois must be ended. Abdul would agree to the terms, but had no intention of limiting his ambitions. He just had to placate the blind man, tell him what he wanted to hear, and then he'd be free to do as he pleased until he had enough power to bite the hand extended to him in friendship.

Jared smiled inside, but kept his poker face. He could smell the man's arrogance and lust for power. He was the perfect tool to crush the Shadow Militia. And, even if he failed to kill General Branch, at least he'd be weakened. With a little luck and clever manipulation, General Branch and General Al'Kalwi would meet on the field of battle, and Jared would emerge the winner.

CHAPTER 10

June 15th, Lansing, Michigan

S UPREME GENERAL AL'KALWI STOOD BENEATH THE ROTUN-da of the State Capitol in Lansing and looked straight up one-hundred and sixty feet to the peak of the large, multi-colored cast iron dome.

Michigan's first capitol had been in Detroit back in 1837 when Michigan became a state. That first building had been much smaller and more humble. The granite cornerstone for this present building had been laid in 1873 and boasted four main entrances facing north, south, east and west. The architecture was termed neo-classical, because it incorporated motifs from both Greek and Roman architecture, including Doric, Ionic and Corinthian columns.

Abdul looked around him at the huge marble columns and nodded his head in satisfaction. Yes, this would suffice as an office until more suitable arrangements could be made when he eventually attacked Chicago and other larger cities to the south and east.

According to his original battle plans, he had split his forces in Jackson, sending half to Lansing in the north and half to Kalamazoo in the west. As of today, both objectives had been taken and pacified. His standing army now numbered twenty-five thousand able-bodied men. He did not allow women to fight, as Islam considered them the weaker sex, and used them only for domestic chores, child-rearing and the sexual pleasures of men.

Now it was time to move on to Grand Rapids, the largest city in western Michigan, or, at least it had been the largest prior to The Day. Over the past nine months many had died, buildings destroyed and ravaged by roving gangs and smaller armies. Some of the city had burned to the ground. But Abdul would rebuild all the cities, and make them great again. As Abdul's army conquered, he always left a small garrison behind to restore order and to impose and maintain Sharia Law. The larger the city, the larger the garrison.

In his heart, he knew that most people, once they'd experienced the stability and strength of Islam, would appreciate his conquest and rule. He was doing it for them and for their progeny.

The addition of airpower had been a great boost to his military campaign in two ways. One, instead of scouting ahead on foot, he could send Apache helicopters to gather intelligence from the air. This told him in advance what he was facing in each town and told him how to deploy his troops with minimal losses. Second, people who saw the Apaches associated them with the federal government, and, thereby assumed help was on the way, along with food, medicine and other much-needed supplies. Of course, technically, that was true, just not in the way they anticipated. In some towns, he was welcomed as a liberating hero, albeit, not the hero they'd expected.

Because of this, his campaign was ahead of schedule. His only drawback was the low number of conscripts and converts. Almost everyone he came into contact with was willing to join his ranks, but most people had already died or moved off into the countryside, typically north. Abdul learned that a smaller gang-led force called The Horde had moved through west Michigan a few months before and decimated the population without regard to their well-being. However, Abdul would not make that mistake. He wanted loyal subjects for Allah; therefore, he would be a "kinder and gentler" despot, giving food and comfort to all who would accept it. Of course, there were stipulations. As traditional Americans had so universally once agreed, "There is no such thing as a free lunch." Abdul made his requirements clear and simple: submit to Allah and follow Sharia Law as the Supreme General saw fit … or die. Abdul considered his terms both reasonable and compassionate. Submission had been a small price to pay to Allah for centuries, and Abdul saw no reason to change a business model that had worked so well in the past.

The Supreme General took one last look around him, and then lifted his right hand and made a beckoning motion with his forefinger to no one in particular. Immediately, a servant was there.

"I want the speakers to begin the regular call to prayer, just as we have in the other cities. I want it done by afternoon prayer, or your head will drop to this beautiful rotunda floor. Understood?"

The servant nodded and bowed as he backed away. *Good*, he thought. Abdul didn't like misunderstandings.

Ten Days Later - Uncle Rodney's House

THE APACHE HELICOPTER HOVERED GENTLY OVER UNCLE RODNEY'S HOUSE, whipping the newly leaf-covered trees into a frenzy. It descended slowly and touched down in his front yard. Dan, Sheriff Leif, Donny, Jeremy and Jackie and the baby stood clustered on the front deck watching. General Branch ducked his head down and stepped out onto the lawn. The grass was already a foot high. One of the benefits to the apocalypse was the absence of yard work, as no one was expected to mow their lawn anymore. Of course, Uncle Rodney had been one of the few nonconformists who hadn't mowed his lawn before The Day, so now his yard was considered normal for the first time.

Dan, Jeremy and Joe walked off the deck and moved out to meet the general. Jackie and the baby looked on. Normally, Jackie would be smiling, but she already knew that something was wrong, and that it would bode ill for herself and her family. Dan walked in the lead as Sergeant Brewster kept to the left and slightly abreast of his colonel. Jeremy just seemed to be tagging along to the right of his father.

Dan and Donny stopped at attention. As the ranking officer, Dan gave his uncle a snappy Marine Corps salute. "Good afternoon, General Branch." Uncle Rodney looked at his nephew and smiled before returning the salute. Then he reached out and shook first Dan's hand then Joe Leif's and then Donny's. Rodney stopped when he reached Jeremy. The sixteen-year-old boy was rendering his best, untutored military salute. Uncle Rodney looked Jeremy in the eyes, and they seemed to twinkle in the sunlight, before their hard, granite-like countenance softened.

"Colonel Branch, please wait for me inside with the others. I'd like a few minutes with this young soldier."

Colonel Branch saluted, and Rodney returned it with military precision. Once they were alone, Rodney reached out and touched Jeremy's right hand, moving it into the proper shape and position. Then he placed his left hand under the boy's elbow and moved it parallel to the deck.

"When you salute, always stand at position of attention. Bring your heels together sharply on line, with your toes pointing out equally, forming a 45-degree angle. The weight of your body should be evenly on the heels and balls of both feet. Keep your legs straight without locking your knees, and hold your body erect with level hips, chest lifted and arched, and your shoulders square. Keep your head erect with pride and face straight to the front with the chin drawn in so that the alignment of your head and neck is vertical. Let your arms hang straight without stiffness. Curl your fingers so that the tips of the thumbs are alongside and touching the first joint of your forefingers. Keep your thumbs straight along the seams of your trouser leg with the first joint of the fingers touching your trousers."

Uncle Rodney made several other adjustments to Jeremy's body. Then he snapped himself to attention and returned the young man's salute.

"As you were, soldier. You can relax now, Jeremy. It's just me."

Jeremy's mouth broke into a grin. "I knew you'd come back, Uncle Rodney!"

General Branch laughed out loud and slapped the boy on his shoulders as they walked toward the house. Jackie was still on the porch with baby Donna who was now nine months old and soon to be a toddler. Jackie spoke with a tiny edge in her voice as soon as Rodney's feet touched the top wooden step.

"You're going to be sorely disappointed if you expect me to salute you, Uncle Rodney."

General Branch smiled as he held out his arms and the two embraced. Baby Donna's face was pressed against Rodney's olive drab, starched shirt. She slobbered on the perfectly pressed collar before the two adults separated.

"Jackie, I would be disappointed if you did salute. You know you're special."

Jackie smiled. "I know."

The general glanced over at Jeremy. "Head inside and join the other men, Jeremy. Let them know I'll be inside in a minute. I need to talk to Jackie for a few."

Jeremy snapped to attention and saluted crisply.

"Yes sir, General Branch!"

Rodney chuckled before returning the salute. Once Jeremy was inside and they were alone, Rodney wasted no time getting straight to the point.

"They all think I came here to meet specifically with them, but you and I are the only ones who know the whole truth. Did you keep the secret?"

Rodney reached over to take the baby while they talked.

"Yes, of course. Dan suspects nothing."

Uncle Rodney nodded. The baby reached up and dug her fingernails into the old man's face.

"It has to stay that way until we execute the plan. In the meantime you have to keep getting ready. It's dangerous, but I don't know what else to do, and there's no one else I can turn to on this. You are uniquely qualified."

Rodney kissed baby Donna and handed the baby back to her and then reached into the cargo pants pocket of his trouser leg. He pulled out several sheets of folded paper and handed them to her.

"Here's the latest intel on the situation. You need to study it. I'll be giving the others an overview, but you'll need all the info you can get. I'll keep sending updates to you as I get them."

Jackie smiled and looked down at the papers. She then reached up and pecked the old man on the cheek.

"Sure thing, Uncle Rodney." And then she shifted the baby to her left arm and gave the general her best salute. He laughed out loud, gave her a brief hug and then walked past her into the house.

Inside the kitchen, seated at the dining room table, Dan Branch fidgeted nervously in the chair. The table had four chromed legs with a red Formica top flecked with tiny gray dots. It was the same table Dan remembered as a child growing up in this house.

"Relax, Dan. Your nerves are tighter than a gnat's ass stretched over a barrel." Donny smiled slightly as he talked. "She'll be okay. Just like always. You need to stop underestimating her. Jackie can handle herself. Besides, the old man likes her. I can tell."

Dan forced himself to unclench his hands and moved them onto his lap beneath table height. "I suppose so. I'm just responsible for her that's all. And I love her."

Jeremy laughed out loud. "Gnat's ass stretched over a barrel! I like that. Sounds cool."

Dan gave his son a condescending stare. Jeremy caught the hint and was silently reminded not to swear. "I mean … gnat's butt stretched over a barrel." He hesitated a moment. "Doesn't sound quite as cool though."

Joe Leif sat there quietly listening to the exchange. He had the luxury of under-standing everyone's perspective. He could relate to Dan's protective feelings towards his wife, Donny's carefree attitude, as well as the unsophisticated feelings of a young boy soon to be a man. It was a talent he'd developed over all his years in dealing with people as a cop.

At that moment the outside door opened and General Branch stepped inside the house. Dan Branch jumped to his feet and snapped to attention. "Officer on deck!" As a reflex action, Donny Brewster snapped up to attention as well. Jeremy, who thought it was cool, jumped up and saluted. Donny Brewster cringed inside. He was going to have to teach the boy the proper protocol for when to salute.

General Branch stopped at the door and looked around the room as if on an inspec-tion tour. Finally he nodded to Jackie who had followed in behind him. "Very good." She smiled. The old man walked over and sat down at the table. "Will you boys please sit down and relax. I've done enough saluting for one day. I just want to relax in the comfort of my own home for a little while."

The three men sat down. Joe Leif just crossed his arms and smiled. Rodney saw the look on his face and smiled back at him. "You must get a real kick out of all this, eh Sheriff?" The sheriff's grin broke out onto his face as he nodded.

"Do you remember the day I caught you stealing those solar panels, Rodney? Must've been just a few weeks after The Day."

Uncle Rodney nodded and the sheriff continued.

"You were still a chain smoker back then, and I was the sheriff and thought I was in charge. I gave you a lecture on stealing public property. And now look at you. You're the general of the whole darn world!"

Rodney looked him in the eye for a moment and then turned his gaze off into space as if imagining something no one else could see.

"Joe, there's a part of me that misses those days, the days of peace, the days of calm, the days of preparation for something greater and something turbulent." He chuckled and returned his gaze back to Joe's face. "But it's just a small part of me and getting smaller every day. We have so little time for reflection these days, but the time to re-flect isn't during the heat of battle, but after the smoke has settled, after the blood has seeped back into the ground, after the war is done." He hesitated. "And once again ... the heat of battle is upon us."

All three men and one boy looked Rodney in the face. He had their attention.

"Gentlemen ... there is a new threat."

CHAPTER 11

June 26th, Iroquois War Room

"**P**RESENTLY, WE ESTIMATE THEIR STRENGTH TO BE JUST over twenty-five thousand men along with several thousand women who render logistical support. Unlike The Horde, they are well supplied with military transport vehicles, such as Humvees, even some Heavy Expanded Mobility Tactical Trucks. They possess a large assortment of light and medium military tactical vehicles such as the M1126 Stryker armored fighting vehicles, along with Bradley fighting vehicles, which you are already familiar with. In addition to that they have access to F-18 fighter jets and an assortment of cargo and attack helicopters. They are here, just north of Grand Rapids in a small town named Rockford and heading north at the rate of ten miles per day."

Rodney Branch stood in the conference room of the old courthouse drawing on a chalkboard. Seated just a few feet away were Colonel Dan Branch, Sheriff Joe Leif, Sergeant Donny Brewster, Major Larry Jackson, Captain Ed Brown and Captain Danny Briel. Dan looked around the room and to the back. There was a man in civilian clothing sitting there whom he didn't know. His Uncle Rodney had shook his hand and spoken to him briefly before the meeting. He appeared to be in his mid-fifties, with graying blonde hair, cut short, and with eyes that could penetrate steel. His presence made Dan feel uneasy.

"At that rate, assuming they continue north up the US 131 corridor, they will reach Kalkaska in fifteen days. Just as before, if they turn west toward Traverse City, we will be in their direct path."

General Branch paused and looked around the room. "Are there any questions?"

At first, no one spoke. Sheriff Leif was surprised at the silence and even more surprised when he heard himself speaking.

"So how many Marine Corps snipers will it take to kill them all?"

The general smiled slightly. "More than we have." Joe Leif nodded his head but didn't follow up with another question. Dan Branch was the next to speak. "Why is everyone coming up here into the middle of nowhere? It doesn't make any sense. There's nothing up here but trees and cold weather most of the year. Why aren't they going south to the big cities and better climate?"

General Branch didn't answer right away. He had that thoughtful, contemplative look on his face like he always did when deciding how much to say of what he really knew. He looked around the room, making eye contact with each person one at a time. Finally, he spoke in one terse sentence.

"It's me ... they're coming after me."

There was silence in the room. Dan's brow furled. Joe Leif looked over at him, and Dan glanced back. Everyone seemed confused, but Joe was the first one to put the confusion into words.

"Listen, Rodney, I'm just a country cop who doesn't know much about global warfare, so I don't understand a lot of things that are going on right now. But I'm no idiot either. Will you please explain to all of us why twenty-five-thousand Islamic warriors are going two hundred miles out of their way to kill one man?"

Uncle Rodney didn't answer. He just stood there in front of them, not quite sure what to say. The sight of it made Dan sad. He'd never seen his uncle this way before. General Branch bowed his head, but didn't speak.

"General Branch, I'd like to answer that question if you don't mind." The stranger in the back stood to his feet and strode up to stand beside Uncle Rodney. The general smiled weakly, then squeezed the man's right shoulder before turning back to the room.

"Allow me to introduce Special Agent Jeff Arnett of the Central Intelligence Agency."

General Branch sat down in the front row and placed his hands on his thighs while the man readied himself to talk. Jeff Arnett was a tall man with a hawkish nose that dominated his face. He appeared to be around fifty-five years old with short hair, once blonde but now mostly gray. The man spread his feet shoulder width apart, square to his audience. Donny Brewster and General Branch seemed to be the only men in the room not intimidated by this new stranger.

"General Branch is correct. I am with the CIA, or, more correctly, I *was* with the CIA back before The Day. Shortly after the terrorist attack on the power grid, all elements of the federal government fell into disarray, and the CIA was not immune to this. One man came forth and offered each CIA agent an opportunity to be a part of the new government which he was already forming. He'd been planning it for years, and this one man, Jared Thompson, AKA The Blind Man, had amassed an ill-gotten fortune with which to buy loyalty and solidify logistics in preparation for the collapse. The CIA and FBI had been studying Thompson for years, trying to build a case against him, but he never did anything against the USA and operated mostly outside the country. So we left him alone for the most part. I realize now that was a mistake.

"I am one of the few people left alive to have had the opportunity to personally meet Mr. Thompson. Most people who see him in person happen upon mysterious deaths shortly thereafter. I was an exception because, quite frankly, he screwed up. He misjudged me, assuming I would join his cause. That is one of his flaws: he assumes that all people act selfishly, out of loyalty to themselves and no other, that every man has a price, and when offered that price, they will sell their very souls to achieve power and pleasure."

He looked down at the white tile floor, and paused for a moment before going on. "To be honest, I have to admit that I was tempted. I knew the world was going to hell in a hand basket, and was not likely to revive in my lifetime. I have no family to hold me accountable, so ... yes, I was sorely tempted."

He looked back up. "But, instead, I contacted Colonel MacPherson of the Shadow Militia and, after being thoroughly vetted," He turned to Rodney and smiled briefly "Vetted with extreme prejudice I might add ... I met with General Branch. Homeland security had been following the rumors of an underground militia for some time, but all leads came up empty. My contact with Colonel MacPherson was a last-chance shot in the dark which paid off.

"I am now a proud member of the Shadow Militia and work very hard to head up their clandestine intelligence service. I am qualified to do this based on twenty years in the field as an operative. My last ten years have been spent as a mid-level supervisor with an intelligence analyst group.

"And now, Sheriff Leif, with that background info out of the way, I'll answer your question." He looked Joe square in the face. "In the eyes of The Blind Man, General Branch and The Shadow Militia are public enemy number one. He believes them to be the greatest obstacle standing in his way of ruling North America." His gaze moved from Joe to General Branch before continuing. "And he is correct in that summation. There is no one person or organization on the entire planet better equipped to halt the evil now descending on America and then the entire world." He halted abruptly, took a deep breath and then continued on. "You see, Rodney Branch and the Shadow Militia are anathema to The Blind Man, simply because he cannot and will not ever understand them. In that one sense he truly is blind. He is blind to anyone with enough honor and integrity to sacrifice and die for his fellow man. And therein lies his major weakness. In order to *defeat* your enemy, you must *know* your enemy. And he can never truly know a man of honor. His only chance of victory is to corrupt enough pure hearts to overcome the Shadow Militia. He must erase all vestiges of hope and light from the land.

"But before he can do that he must first destroy the Shadow Militia. But the Shadow Militia cannot be destroyed without first killing this person you all call Uncle Rodney. You see, the Shadow Militia isn't just an army; it's a hope; it's a beacon of light, shining in the darkness for all to see. It gives all people everywhere a clear choice between good and evil. And Jared Thompson must eradicate that choice."

There was silence in the room.

No one moved. No one scratched their head or shifted nervously in their chairs. To any onlookers, they could have been mistaken for storefront mannequins on display.

Finally, Major Larry Jackson stood resolutely. "I say … we get ready to kick this Blind Man's ass clean on back to whatever rock he crawled out from under!"

Captain Briel stood beside him. "I'm with Larry. I say we kick his ass!"

Dan Branch and Donny Brewster both stood in unison and simply nodded to the general before coming to attention and saluting. Captain Brown stood to attention and saluted as well. Soon every person was on his feet, saluting General Branch.

Except for one man.

Sheriff Joe Leif shifted nervously in his chair. "What the hell have you gotten us into this time, Rodney? You are such a pain in the ass! I can understand why The Blind Man wants to kill you. You …" He let the words go un-uttered. Joe let out a huge sigh before slowly standing to his feet, like an old man doing work he once found easy, but was now beyond his years and his ability. Sheriff Leif snapped to attention and saluted Rodney Branch.

The old general doggedly moved to his feet, humbled by the show of fealty. Rodney stepped to the front of the room, faced them all and gave them his best Marine Corps salute. He held it for a full five seconds. Then he snapped his right arm down and said, "Please be seated."

Special Agent Jeff Arnett returned to the back of the room while the others sat back down. There were a few excited murmurs, but Rodney shushed them with a raise of his hand.

"I thank you for your commitment, but, quite frankly, that was the easy part. You have all proven yourselves in battle, proven to be worthy of my trust, my devotion and my very life. For that I thank you."

He stepped over to the chalk board, picked up the red rag beside it and wiped away the writing.

"I have a plan. It will take a lot of work and a lot of sacrifice. Many of us will die, but, if it works … it will leave the world with hope."

Sheriff Leif bowed his head and chuckled out loud. "Hell, Rodney. Sacrifice, hard work, lots of us dying … sounds like the same plan you had last time. What's not to love?"

In the back of the room, Special Agent Jeff Arnett smiled. He liked this group already.

CHAPTER 12

June 27th, A Spy is Born

U NCLE RODNEY STOOD JUST INSIDE THE POLE BARN DOOR with one shoulder propped against the door frame. This was Harold Steffen's old home, and Jeff Arnett was now setting up a computer network inside the very pole barn where Harold and Jackie had repaired the old crop duster used to save Iroquois from The Horde. Rodney had set up the location himself, citing its remoteness. On the outside it would continue to appear abandoned, but, on the inside, it would be a modern, pre-The-Day computer intelligence analysis center.

"Why do you want to do this, Jackie? Answer all my questions in Arabic, please."

The voice was that of Special Agent Jeff Arnett. He was standing before Jackie Branch, wearing blue jeans and a black t-shirt. She responded quickly in fluent Arabic.

"I don't want to do this. Only a crazy person would want to do this."

Jeff responded immediately.

"Then why are you doing it?"

"Because I want to help my family. I want to fight the evil that is coming to us. And because I appear to be the only one who can get the job done."

Jeff nodded.

"But aren't you afraid?"

Jackie smirked at him.

"Of course I'm afraid, you idiot! But no more afraid than my husband when he goes into battle and people are shooting at him."

Jeff folded his arms across his chest before going on.

"What is your biggest fear?"

"My biggest fear is that I fail and dishonor my family."

Jeff cocked his head to one side.

"Are you not afraid of dying?"

Her response was immediate.

"Of course not! I'm a Christian! To live is Christ and to die is gain."

"You really believe that?"

Jackie snapped back at him.

"Cut the foolishness and get to the heart of your testing! I don't have time for this. I want to get this done and get back to raising my family!"

Jeff looked over at Uncle Rodney and smiled.

"She's a feisty one."

Rodney nodded.

"I told you. She's a Branch through and through. She can do it."

"But Rodney, you don't understand. Her feistiness could get her killed. She's moving into a barbaric, male-dominated society and any hint of dominance could get her tortured and … well, tortured and many other unspeakable things. She speaks the language perfectly, like a native almost. She knows the culture, the religion, even how to cook the food, but, hey, let's face it, subservience is not her strong point, and Islam is all about submission."

Just then Jackie fell to her knees in tears. Her weeping appeared sincere as real tears fell from her eyes and onto her cheeks. She clutched desperately at Jeff's trouser leg and bowed her head low to the ground as she spoke.

"Please, master, please give me a chance to serve the Supreme General in the cause of Allah. Just give me some small token job to serve and support the warriors of Jihad!"

At first, Jeff Arnett looked surprised, then his face broke into a smile. "Now hey. That was good. Really good. You could have been a field agent in the CIA."

Jackie reverted back to English and to her cocky manner. She stood proudly to her feet and threw her shoulders back and raised her head. "I never trusted the CIA. But I can be a field agent for the Shadow Militia."

She looked over at Rodney, who was beaming proudly at her like a father watching his daughter at the altar.

"We have a few more details to work out. Then, right after Dan leaves for combat, I'll insert you into the Islamist army so you can strike a blow for freedom."

Jackie lowered her head. "I don't feel right about doing this behind Dan's back."

Rodney moved forward and put his right arm around her shoulder. "I know, Jackie. And I don't like it either. Normally I wouldn't do it. But … I just don't see an alternative. This is a chance to save thousands of lives and …"

Jackie interrupted him. "I know. And the needs of the many outweigh the needs of the few."

Jeff Arnett laughed out loud. "Oh my god, she's quoting Spock! She speaks fluent Arabic, is a fantastic actor, and on top of all that she's a Trekkie!"

Jackie nodded and raised her right hand into the air in front of her. She separated her ring finger from her middle finger in a perfect Vulcan salute.

"Live long and prosper."

General Branch tried to laugh with them, but the emotion wouldn't come. He was sending his loved one, the wife of his adopted son into almost-certain death. If it didn't go well … He let the thought slip away, cordoning it off with all the other partitioned emotions inside him. It was hard being a general, but even harder to command the ones you loved.

Jackie saw the look of concern on his face, and reached out with her right hand, placing it on the old man's grizzled cheeks. "It's okay, Uncle Rodney. Do you remember what I said when we first met? You asked me who taught me my sense of honor."

Rodney nodded. "Yes, I remember. That was the moment I started respecting you."

Jackie let her hand drop back down. " I developed my sense of honor after six months in the wilderness watching Dan and Jeremy risk their lives and shed their blood and sweat for the safety of my daughter, myself and my now-dead husband. We were strangers, but they took us in. They would have died for us. And now, if need be … I'll die for them."

Rodney lowered his head. Jeff Arnett tried to reassure him. "It's a good plan, General Branch. A damn good one. Just say the word and we go."

But Jackie answered first. "Of course we go! The issue was never in doubt. We are Shadow Militia. We are warriors, and this is the right thing to do so we do it no matter the risk or the cost!"

Rodney raised his head and smiled. He knew she was right. But it seemed the older he got the more difficult these decisions became, and the more he hated making them. He sighed and nodded resolutely.

"Yes, we go."

Off to Battle

COLONEL DAN BRANCH LOOKED OUT ACROSS THE NEAT FORMATION OF soldiers in front of him. To his left were several hundred of the Home Guard, most of them veterans of the last battle. To his right was the entirety of the newly formed and trained Iroquois Militia Rangers. They were five hundred strong and far superior in experience and training to the group he'd commanded in the last battle for Iroquois City. The Home Guard would be deployed to the South to await the Supreme General's arrival. The Militia Rangers would continue on south to meet the Supreme General. It would be a hit-and-run strategy, similar to before, but this time they'd be engaging close to thirty thousand troops instead of three thousand. The Horde had been an angry rabble without air support, whereas Supreme General Abdul Al'Kalwi was highly disciplined and motivated. Dan gave extra weight to their enemies air support. He still recalled with pain and sadness the day his previous command had almost been wiped out by one helicopter with infrared capabilities. This time, he would not make that same mistake. If they were to be killed, the enemy would work for it and be forced to hunt them down and kill them one soldier at a time.

Colonel MacPherson had been impressed with Dan's strategy saying it was the right plan for the right time. His uncle, however, had said nothing, and that worried Dan. As Dan stood at attention, looking out over his troops, he couldn't help but think to himself, *They outnumber us thirty to one. How can we possibly prevail?* But he was careful never to voice his fears, even to his wife … especially to his wife.

Jackie had been surprisingly supportive this morning when he'd left the house, and that worried him. Normally she would raise a fuss and try to talk him out of it, but her lack of resistance made him suspicious. He recalled the several times Uncle Rodney had sent her private messages via courier. The meetings she'd had with Special Agent

Arnett also came to mind. Jackie and Uncle Rodney were up to something. But it would have to wait until he got back home … if he got back home.

Major Jackson was beside him, flanked by Captain Briel. Captain Brown was heading up the detachment of Home Guard. Dan's own son, Jeremy, had left the night before with Sergeant Donny Brewster on special assignment with a unit of seventy-five snipers. Most of them were fully trained in the sniper's art, combat veterans of the last battle, but inexperienced in this new method of warfare. He expected that many would do well, while others would not. Dan thought of his own son and winced. There was something about Jeremy that made him nervous, almost afraid. Jeremy had already killed, but … still, somehow, he retained his youthful excitement and glorious vision of war. The boy thought himself to be ten feet tall and bullet proof. Donny had promised to take him under his wing and keep him protected, but that had been little comfort. Because Dan knew that if Jeremy was with Donny then he was sure to be in the thickest of the battle and therefore in extreme danger.

He pushed all these thoughts out of his mind for now. The time for reflection and regret would be days from now after the battle, and only if they were still alive. Dan watched as each Company Captain marched to the head of formation and posted in front of their unit and saluted. Colonel Branch returned the salute.

"Battalion! Parade rest!"

In unison, the boots of eight-hundred men moved to the right and slammed down on the hard-packed earth of the parade ground as their hands moved with precision behind their backs. If their enemy had been only three thousand of The Horde, he would have been impressed with more confidence, but that was not the case and he was not optimistic. He believed in his heart that most of them would die.

"We are about to embark on a mission of historical proportions." Dan paused. Why did that sound pompous and melodramatic to him. He started over, this time with less flare and with a colloquial tone of voice.

"Listen, men. Most of you have done this before. You're smart, so you know that some of us will die. All I can do is promise you I'll do my best to get as many of you home safely as I can. I'll make my best decisions. I'll push myself harder than I push you. I'll put my own life at risk as much as I risk the ones who serve under me. I'll ignore my fear and let my courage come to the forefront in battle. I won't surrender. I won't retreat. I will die alongside you if need be."

The men were all stone-cold silent as he spoke. "However, all of you know I have a wife and kids to protect as do most of you. And that's what we fight for. We fight for the ones we love, the ones too weak to fight for themselves. Duty, honor, sacrifice, they are more than just words. Because it's the shedding of our blood that give words meaning and purpose."

Dan hesitated. He saw Joe Leif and General Branch off in the distance to the west. They were listening silently. But what Dan didn't notice was the small drone circling overhead. It was small as a hawk, capturing his words and sending them back to his master a thousand or so miles away.

THE BLIND MAN PLAYED THE RECORDING OVER AND OVER AGAIN, HANGING on every word Colonel Branch spoke. He was impressed and filled with a sense of awe and confusion. While he was awed at the man's eloquence and courage, he was equally confused by the man's misguidance. They were determined to fight him to the death over a silly word called freedom. In reality he didn't want to dominate them, only to lead them, guide them in rebuilding America. Jared didn't see himself as a despot or a killer, but as a regal king with a royal destiny to any who would pledge their loyalty to him. Instead of fighting against him to the death, they would be better served to join him and aid in the re-unification of America. Only then would he be able to restore some vestige of freedom to the land.

Jared shook his head from side to side nonsensically. They were all brave fools, and they would all have to die. What a waste of incredible courage. It made him angry.

"Mr. Thurmond!"

Sammy moved up to his side immediately.

"Get me everything we have on this man. His name, birthplace, age, family, everything. He's a danger to us, and if he squats down to defecate then I want to know about it."

Jared made a clicking sound with his lips and teeth. "Yes, what a waste … a terrible waste."

Sammy nodded his head and left the room. A part of him couldn't help but admire the reckless abandon of a man fighting for his home. Sadly, he knew all men like Dan Branch would soon be dead.

CHAPTER 13

July 1st, The Big Slow-down

S UPREME GENERAL AL'KALWI LOOKED ON IN SHEER HORROR and rage as the man to his left exploded in a mist of red blood and white bone. It was as if the man's head had spontaneously disintegrated as he watched for no apparent reason. But Abdul knew the reason. It was the snipers. The Blind Man had warned him of this tactic, but he was amazed at its effectiveness. For the last three days the entire column of thirty-thousand strong marching down the US 131 corridor had ground to a crawl. Instead of ten miles a day, they were now lucky to make five.

The Apache helicopter was quick to react as it sped angrily over to the hilltop like a crazed hornet. The first day of the attack it had been easy to subdue the snipers. With the Apache's infrared and machine guns they'd quickly located the sniper and then blew him apart. But on the second day something changed. The sniper attacks were more coordinated. Instead of one rifle shot, there had been twenty, but all coming from different locations at the same time. The three Apache helicopters he had at his disposal were kept busy, but never seemed to make it to the target on time. Even with infrared capabilities, the snipers just seemed to vanish into thin air. He needed to know how they were doing it.

Abdul looked down at the body beside him. He'd forced the man to wear his own Muslim ceremonial garb as a test. Now he knew they were targeting him and this made it personal. He thought for a moment. He couldn't blame them. He could hate them, but not blame them. It's exactly what he would do in their position. In fact, this type of hit-and-run guerilla warfare is what his people and his ancestors had been doing for decades with great effectiveness. But The Blind Man had given him the name of his enemy, General Rodney T. Branch of the Shadow Militia. More importantly, he'd given Abdul the name of the town where the man lived: Iroquois City.

Even at their present rate of five miles per day they would reach Iroquois in thirty days. They were losing approximately one-hundred soldiers every day to snipers. Abdul quickly did the math. Thirty-thousand minus three-thousand is Twenty-seven thousand soldiers remaining. He smiled. Negligible. Not a factor. He thought to himself *You'll have to do better than that General Rodney T. Branch. Much better.*

The Supreme General raised his left forefinger and a man instantly moved to his side. "Give the command to all lieutenants, 'Shoot every man who takes cover from the snipers. Explain to them their chances of death by sniper fire are less than the surety of death at my hand should they flinch or feint in battle.'"

The man moved away and began to disseminate the order. Five hundred men died that day from friendly fire plus one-hundred by sniper fire. But an amazing thing happened. The next day instead of five miles, the Supreme General's army advanced twelve miles.

THE ALARM CLOCK WENT OFF AND JASON REACHED OVER AND SLAMMED THE button on top. The incessant buzzing sound stopped as quickly as it had started. He rolled over to kiss his wife good morning, but she was already gone. In fact, the kids must be gone as well, because their upscale ranch house in the suburbs of Grand Rapids was uncharacteristically silent. The big man just lay there in bed for a moment soaking in all the peace. Then his day started to get busier as he was reminded of all the meetings he had, the accounts he had to balance, and the facts and figures and graphs he'd need to remember in order to make it through the day's work.

Starbuck's. He needed hot, black coffee, maybe a double-shot espresso with a double-fudge chocolate brownie for breakfast. He thought about getting up but knew as soon as his feet hit the floor the day would change, mutate and spin out of control at an unbelievably fast pace, and he wanted so much for it to stay slow, like this, just laying here all alone with no responsibility nor care in the world.

As he lay there thinking about it between the clean, flannel sheets, soaking in the warmth and comfort, rain began to fall into his eyes again. His eyes fluttered open reluctantly, and he felt the rain wash down his neck and run lengthwise between his camo shirt and the water-soaked skin of his back.

"Lieutenant Little! Lieutenant Little! Wake up sir."

His eyes popped open for good now and he saw his sergeant looking down on him.

The sky above was clouded over but still some light filtered down to reach the wooded floor where he lay in a puddle of water and mud. Bracken ferns reached up around him, and their pungent aroma, mixed with black coffee reached his nostrils.

"Sir, the colonel has called a meeting for all officers. You meet in his HQ under the big oak in ten minutes, sir. Here's your coffee sir."

Jason Little sat up slowly and looked at the sergeant. He reached out for the coffee and was soon sipping the cold liquid. He remembered his dream and could almost feel the warmth of the flannel sheets, hear the silence of his beautiful home in Grand Rapids. It was burned to the ground now. His wife was dead, killed in the last battle for Iroquois City. Coffee grounds stuck in the spaces between his front teeth. But it was good and strong. It seemed to start his heart again and get him moving.

Jason took a few more sips and moved slowly to his feet. He picked up his AR-15 and walked slowly over to the big oak tree. "Thank you sergeant. Make sure the men keep their feet dry and their guns cleaned and oiled."

Jason thought to himself *Clean guns and dry feet. What a joke.* They'd been marching almost nonstop for three days and most of them would probably die with waterlogged feet and rusty weapons. When he reached the oak tree he sat down on the ground again and sipped his cold coffee while waiting for the other officers to arrive.

COLONEL DAN BRANCH STOOD UNDER THE TREES FACING AN ARRAY OF twenty or so officers and staff noncoms. The rain had stopped, and the sun was now trying to peek out through the clouds overhead. Eventually it would win the battle, but not before the wet and cold men began to shiver. It had been an unusually cold night for July, even in northern Michigan. Most of the men sipped canteen cups full of cold coffee. Dan had given strict orders that no one should build a fire of any kind as they were within ten miles of the advancing enemy army of almost thirty thousand troops.

"Sergeant Brewster and his Snipers have been successful in slowing the enemy advance for the last three days, but his tactics are no longer working, so we have to try something different."

There were no chalkboards, no flip charts, no computer screens to help Dan with the presentation; it was just one man talking to his comrades out in the boonies.

"So now it's up to us. Of course, the snipers will continue to kill as many as they can, but, truth is, we have only sixty-five snipers remaining, and the numbers just don't add up. They could shoot nonstop for days and still not be able to halt the enemy advance."

Dan looked at them all like dead men. He knew their chances of success this time around were slim, but still … they had to do their best, and just hope that Uncle Rodney had some plan up his sleeve.

"We're going to launch a coordinated attack on three fronts."

Jason Little's ears perked up. *Did the colonel just say five hundred men were going to attack thirty-thousand men?*

"All sixty-five snipers will begin shooting at exactly eighteen-hundred hours. They'll still have the setting sun at their backs and adequate light to make good shots.

They'll be transitioning from head shots to groin shots from here on out.

"As soon as the attack commences we expect the enemy to engage their light armor in a counterattack as quickly as possible. In fact, we're counting on it.

"As soon as the snipers begin shooting, a second force led by me will attack from the east at a range of fifteen hundred yards. This will undoubtedly result in an air strike by the three Apache attack helicopters. Normally this would result in a complete massacre of our troops as the Apaches have enough firepower with their M230 30-millimeter chain guns to kill us to the last man, however, we have a surprise for them, courtesy of General Branch."

Lieutenant Little smiled to himself thinking, *Okay, that's good, we won't be killed instantly then.* Jason quickly did the math in his head and raised his hand. Colonel Branch looked at him with an annoyed stare.

"Yes, Lieutenant?"

"Well, Colonel, I'm no accountant, well leastwise not anymore, but I just did the math and in order to win this battle each of us will have to kill sixty men."

Dan sighed to himself before answering. "No, lieutenant, not really. The mission isn't to kill all the enemy; our goal is to slow them down."

Jason Little squirmed in the mud, not really wanting to point out the obvious. "But, sir, and I mean no disrespect by this, but … if the enemy attacks with their light armor, and, we have no way to stop them, then … aren't we all going to die?"

Dan Branch couldn't help but smile. Jason Little was a smart-ass and a pain in the butt, nonetheless, he liked him.

"It would seem that way, lieutenant. However, if you'll allow me to finish detailing the plan, I think we might be able to give you all at least a moderate chance of survival."

Jason smiled. "Oh, by all means continue then. I'm all ears."

Dan nodded and outlined the plan in detail. Afterwards, he dismissed the men. In four hours they would launch … and, live or die.

CHAPTER 14

In Dire Need of Hope

A<small>T HIS HEADQUARTERS BACK IN</small> E<small>SCANABA</small>, G<small>ENERAL</small> Branch and Colonel MacPherson waited for reports to come in from the battle south of Big Rapids, Michigan. It would begin at any moment, and it affected him on a personal as well as a professional level. Dan was leading the attack, and his nephew, Jeremy, was now fighting in the sniper unit. Rodney understood the dangers of battle, of facing overwhelming odds, and he knew within a few hours both the men he loved could be dead.

"They'll be okay, Rodney."

General Branch turned around to look his friend in the eyes. Mac knew him too well. He always seemed to read his mind, even when he didn't want him to. "Maybe. It's a good plan, but … you know … things can go wrong, and nothing in war is a sure thing."

Mac nodded. "I know. But it had to be done. We needed to buy some time in order to figure out a way to stop them."

"I know, Mac. Just doesn't make it any easier. They were making ten miles a day and this attack, if it succeeds, will cut that distance in half."

They were both seated in Colonel MacPherson's office, Rodney behind the desk, and Mac in a padded chair off to one side. Mac picked up his coffee cup and took a sip.

"You still haven't told me how you plan to kill thirty thousand screaming Islamists without using air power and other classified Militia Ranger assets."

Rodney Branch took a sip of his coffee. Ever since he'd quit smoking, his coffee intake had dramatically increased. Eventually, when coffee was no longer available, he'd be forced to find some other emotional crutch.

"I just love the way you beat around the bush, Mac."

The colonel smiled and waited, but his general remained silent. Mac respected that and waited patiently, quietly sipping his hot coffee as Rodney leaned back in his chair and thought.

After five minutes, Rodney still hadn't said anything, so Mac left it alone. He would tell him when he was darn good and ready and not a moment before. It had never been Mac's job to pester his superior, but rather to support him using any means necessary. His role in this venture had always been one of support and encouragement.

And then it hit him. *What if Rodney didn't have a plan? What if there was no way out of this?* Mac didn't voice his doubts. It wasn't his place to doubt, but to believe, even when things looked hopeless … especially when things looked hopeless.

JEREMY BRANCH LAY IN THE DITCH WITH HIS HEAD FACING THE ENEMY encampment, shrouded in his Ghillie suit. It was open terrain, giving him a clear nine-hundred-yard shot. For the past three days Jeremy had been killing man after man after man with little time to reflect on his actions. But now, as he lay in his hole waiting for the alarm on his wristwatch to signal the attack, he had a few minutes to analyze the rightness and wrongness of what he was doing.

Donny Brewster had taught him the danger of thinking too much and of thinking too little. In order to become the best sniper possible, he had to believe in what he was doing without reservation, because even the slightest emotional or mental conflict could translate into a missed shot, either through unsteady nerves or irregular breathing. He'd learned in his training that everything had to come together perfectly to make those long-distance shots on man-sized targets.

That's why today, he was relieved his targets had been changed from men to vehicles … in particular, gasoline tankers. His job was to poke as many holes in the sides of as many fuel trucks as he possibly could in sixty seconds, then beat feet out to the rendezvous point.

He was shooting one of Donny's rifles, an M40A5 with an effective range of nine-hundred yards, but Jeremy had already made chest shots two hundred yards beyond that. Now, shooting at large tanker trucks, hitting them would be a breeze.

Donny had warned him not to be overconfident. Don't take the shot for granted and aim at the whole truck. Pick out a small point on the tanker and put the round exactly there. Jeremy guessed he could get off six good shots before bugging out.

It was odd. He'd been trained by a Marine sniper in personal one-on-one sessions, but he still felt like sixteen-year-old Jeremy Branch from Menomonie, Wisconsin who was sneaking out of the house at night to screw the neighbor girl. Had that life been less than a year in the past? It had. Though his whole life had changed, and he'd killed dozens of men since then, he still felt like the same kid inside. He thought to himself *God help me, I still have acne and I'm blowing people's heads off with little remorse.* Deep down inside he wondered *Will there be a price to pay for this? I'm doing the right thing. Everyone tells me I am. But it just doesn't feel natural.*

He still could remember the first man he'd killed just a few months prior to save his dad back in northwest Wisconsin. His father had been hanging by a rope, helpless to defend himself, while the man below him was about to shoot. Jeremy had killed the man without flinching, blown a big hole in his chest and then watched while the man had bled out. With horror, he still remembered the dying man's last words, "You're … a … boy?" He still remembered the crimson red spray landing out onto the snow. Even though he knew in his heart of hearts that he'd done the right thing and saved his father's life because of it, he still felt remorse. He'd confided this with Donny and immediately regretted his candor. "A good sniper feels regret and remorse after the shot. "A great sniper, the most effective at the art, feels only recoil."

Jeremy both feared and hoped that he would remain just a "good" sniper. The alarm on his watch vibrated on his wrist and he hunkered down to settle in for his first shot.

COLONEL DAN BRANCH HEARD THE FIRST SNIPER SHOT, THEN ANOTHER and another. Soon the little valley on the US 131 corridor was ringing out with dozens of shots. He pulled up his binoculars and watched as thousands of enemy soldiers scurried to their pre-arranged rally points in response to the attack. Donny Brewster's intel had told him this would happen, and much of the plan revolved around it.

Dan waited for just the right moment, then nodded to the two men kneeling on the ground a few feet in front of him. The Mark 19 grenade launcher opened up, spewing several hundred 40 millimeter grenades to just the right place in the center of the encampment. Two other Mark 19s started launching as well. In all eight-hundred of the small bombs were lobbed into the motor pool at the center of camp.

Suddenly, without warning, a huge series of explosions rocked the ground as tanker after tanker ignited and threw flames up and out, spreading all over camp.

Dan watched for a few seconds in awe at the fiery maelstrom below. The innate part of him that prodded all humans to chase fire trucks and ambulances beckoned him to stay and watch the fire and carnage, but he resisted the urge to gloat over his handiwork. Dan quickly ordered the three Mark 19 teams to pack up and move down the far side of the hill. Within seconds they were gone.

MAJOR LARRY JACKSON STOOD ON THE OPPOSITE SIDE OF THE HIGHWAY from Dan Branch. His job was perhaps the toughest and most dangerous of the three. Larry had deployed his men well; all five of the three-man teams were hidden inside the edge of the woods, but with a clear view of the sky. Major Jackson watched in awe as the flames below boiled up inside the center of the enemy encampment. He said aloud to no one in particular "Burn you raghead bastards!" The black smoke was rising higher now and blowing off to the east, leaving him in the clear. *Good. They'll still be able to find me.*

As he stood atop the hill in plain view, Larry hefted one of the smoke grenades back and forth in his hands. When he saw the first Apache helicopter rise up above the trees a mile away he pulled the pin, threw the grenade a few yards downhill and let the red smoke rise up. He did the same thing with a second and third grenade. Then he waited.

"Saracen Leader, this is Scimitar One. I have red smoke five hundred yards west of your location. Please advise if these are friendly or hostile, over."

There was a moment of silence as the Apache attack helicopter circled over the Supreme Leader's encampment.

"Scimitar One, this is Saracen Leader. We have no friendlies in that region. Engage and destroy enemy. Please acknowledge receipt, over."

Scimitar One continued to gain altitude as it switched to its infrared sensors. Scimitar Two and Scimitar Three rose up above the trees and took up position behind and to the left and right of Scimitar One.

"Saracen Leader, this is Scimitar One, we have infrared on sixteen targets. Beginning our attack now."

The pilot looked through the Integrated Helmet and Display Sighting System which was already slaved to the aircraft's 30 mm automatic M230 Chain Gun. Wherever he looked with his helmet, the chain gun followed. He smiled when he saw a lone man standing out in the open. He thought to himself, *Not the sharpest tool in the shed.*

Larry Jackson stood resolutely and alone on the hillside, watching the three Apache gunships come closer. They looked close enough to him, and he wondered why his teams hadn't engaged. *Has something gone wrong?* His eyeballs began to sweat as the gunships got bigger and bigger.

For a moment he thought about running, but then realized the futility of the notion. You can't outrun a Hellfire Missile or an M230 Chain Gun. He would either win … or he would die. In a moment of brave defiance, Larry raised his arm and waved his middle finger at the lead Apache. If he was going to die, at least he'd do it with some courage and style.

A moment later the first Stinger missile rose up from the hillside and streaked toward the lead Apache. The explosion raced across the sky as debris and flames scattered across the hill. A split second later four more Stingers groped up into the sky and soon the remaining Apaches were burning as they fell to the ground in smoking ruin.

Larry held his middle finger salute several seconds longer before dropping his arm. His heart was racing wildly, and then he saw the bullets tear up the ground around him from the small-arms fire below. They were already coming for him. He ran for the cover of the trees, glancing over his shoulder at the burning camp and the smoking aircraft.

"I never had a doubt."

Larry jumped on his quad and drove away with his five-man teams close behind him.

FIVE HOURS LATER, SUPREME GENERAL AL'KALWI SAT IN THE BRADLEY Fighting Vehicle he used as his mobile command post and ground his finger nails into his palms. His second in command sat before him, sweat pouring off his face, and it wasn't from the heat.

"We estimate seven thousand casualties, three thousand dead with another four thousand moderately or severely wounded. Many soldiers are suffering from headaches, concussions, smoke inhalation, second and third degree burns as well as shrapnel wounds."

"They are suffering for Allah. They should welcome the pain and thank him for it."

Abdul's eyes turned to fire as his right hand moved to grasp the hilt of his scimitar. He wanted so much to kill this man. Why hadn't he been warned against grouping all his vehicles in the center of camp beside the gasoline tankers? They should have foreseen this attack. By clustering their vehicles they had prevented sabotage but also unwittingly provided the enemy the means with which to destroy them in one fell swoop. Abdul spoke with a shake in his voice.

"And our vehicles?"

His lieutenant didn't answer right away. His eyes darted first to the left and then to the right as if looking for a means of escape. He started with the good news first.

"Most of the Abrams tanks were spared, protected by their thick armor, but a few were near the tankers and are still too hot to touch. Most of the Bradleys are okay, but the Strykers had their tires burned off and we have only a few spares. Their antennas were destroyed, so communication is limited as well. Again, we have few spare parts to fix them. Fifty percent of the HEMTT eight-wheel-drive heavy duty trucks are destroyed, most of the rest suffered minor damage. The Humvees are almost a total loss."

The Supreme General stood up as best he could and exited the Bradley. His underling reluctantly followed him. Once outside, Abdul drew his scimitar and turned to face his lieutenant. The smells of burning flesh, diesel fuel and rubber made it hard to breathe. He looked around him at the carnage as blood threatened to squirt out of his eyeballs.

With sword upraised, he asked his lieutenant a very important question. "How long until we can be moving again?"

The lieutenant swallowed ruggedly before answering. He moved his right hand up to wipe the sweat off his brow.

"Ten days, sir."

Abdul moved closer circling the man like a panther ready to attack.

"I'll ask you again. How long until we move out?"

The man reconsidered.

"Five days, sir."

"So, tell me, which hand would you like to keep ... your left or your right?"

He considered running, but knew he'd never make it. So he lied.

"We can move out day after tomorrow sir. I'll send teams to scavenge the area for petrol and we can work through the night on repairing the damaged vehicles. There are many repair facilities in nearby Big Rapids."

Abdul finally smiled.

"You are a good man, a good servant of Mohammed, peace be upon him. You have until morning to report back to me with your progress."

He sheathed his scimitar and waved his finger in dismissal. The man bowed low to the ground as he backed away, never taking his eyes off the Supreme General.

Once the servant was gone, Abdul looked again at the devastation around him. He sighed to himself. There was something The Blind Man hadn't told him, perhaps many things. And someday he would kill the Blind Man, perhaps torture the infidel first. He was sure of it. These were not mere farmers and peasants as the Blind Man had said. This attack hadn't come from farmers. It had been brilliantly conceived and carried out with flawless military precision.

The Blind Man had told him that a retired general by the name of Rodney T Branch lived in northern Michigan and had gathered up a small army of locals numbering about one thousand, composed primarily of farmers, factory workers and merchants. For some reason he'd failed to mention the Stinger missiles and the grenade launchers, not exactly standard issue to Michigan farmers.

He needed to find out more about General Rodney T Branch and this Shadow Militia. And, as an afterthought, *I'm going to need more helicopters.*

CHAPTER 15

July 3, The Saracen Encampment

JACKIE BRANCH HAD BEEN INSERTED INTO THE SARACEN camp three days ago and was now working as a scullery maid. The insertion had been easy as she'd simply walked into camp pulling a load of zucchini, summer squash and green beans in a small hand cart. She claimed in perfect Arabic that she worked in the kitchen and had been immediately let through the lines into the camp. Once inside she found her way to one of the many kitchen tents and began to work.

Jeff Arnett's instructions had been simple and precise. Blend in. Be plain. Don't be noticed. Look, feel and sound like everyone else and your chances of survival will go up exponentially. And that's exactly what Jackie did. Above all else, she was very careful to never make eye contact.

Her biggest challenge had been avoiding the "sex patrols". That's what she called them, because they were so loosely defined, but very precise in their purpose. They were unofficial, but prevalent, especially at night just before dark. Most women tried to stay out of the way so as not to be chosen, but it wasn't unusual for men to simply walk into the women's quarters and drag a victim out by the hair. Because of that, Jackie slept outside in the dark, usually in the cover of bushes or trees.

Jackie had been amazed at the carnage wrought by her husband's attack of three days earlier. The men were still burying bodies outside the camp and trying to get many of the vehicles running again. Seeing the widespread death caused by Dan and his men had helped her to better understand what her husband had been going through and why he didn't want her to be involved with it. He loved her and was protecting her.

Her second morning there she'd witnessed a public execution and seen the Supreme General for the first time. In full view of the entire camp, atop a building, Abdul Al'Kalwi, dressed in white, ceremonial robes had raised his sword and lopped off the head of his second in command. Jackie couldn't help but wonder why Donny Brewster didn't simply shoot the Supreme General from fifteen-hundred yards away. She knew he was out there and that he was fully capable of making the shot. But … for some reason unknown to her … this was not done.

Every day she watched as the Iroquois snipers shot armed men as they walked to and fro around the camp. On the first day alone she saw seven men die. The camp was huge and spread out for almost a mile going both north and south. She couldn't help but wonder how many of those men were killed by her son. It made her both sad and proud to know that Jeremy was out there, putting his cross-hairs on the people around her and pressing the trigger. She wondered if, perhaps, it was possible for her to be accidentally killed by her own son as she wandered around the enemy camp.

The vastness of the camp only made it easier for her to go undetected as she gathered information and watched under cover of anonymity. It was on the evening of the second day that Jackie executed the first part of Uncle Rodney's plan.

"WHAT DO YOU MEAN PEOPLE ARE NOT WAKING UP? I DON'T UNDERSTAND you."

The new second-in-command lowered his head and repeated the news to Supreme General Al'Kalwi. "There are five -hundred dead this morning and another two thousand who are not waking up. Some are awake, but cannot move. The doctor says that something is causing a paralysis of the respiratory muscles. People can't breathe so they die."

The Supreme General cursed aloud. "Bring me the physician!"

His lieutenant bowed as he left the tent and returned just a few moments later with the doctor in tow. The doctor bowed and stood in front of the Supreme General with his head politely lowered.

"Tell me what is happening!"

The doctor nodded and launched into the clinical explanation. "The victims appear to have ingested some sort of toxin. It appears to be a coniin alkaloid, derived from …"

"Toxin! You mean poison?"

"Yes, Supreme General."

"How did this happen?"

The doctor lowered his head further as he explained. "Through multiple patient interviews I've come to believe all the victims had been drinking the night before. Those who reportedly drank the most are already dead. Others who ..."

"How is that possible?" He kicked the chair he'd been sitting in over to one side and swore again. "The great prophet, Mohammed, peace be upon him, forbids us to consume alcohol!"

No one in the tent was naive enough to believe alcohol was not consumed in camp. In fact, even the Supreme General knew it was common practice, and he condoned it by turning a blind eye. Unofficially, there was a three-hundred gallon tank of wine transported on the back of a large pick-up truck, and, as they went from town to town, scavenging, anyone who found alcohol brought it to the tanker and dumped it in. In times when alcohol couldn't be found, the men in charge of the truck made their own. The doctor continued by holding up a small leaf and some waterlogged seeds.

"These were found inside the wine tank. They are from the plant called Conium maculatum."

Abdul was losing his patience with the man's medical gibberish. "Stop talking like a kafir and tell me what that is!"

The doctor lowered his head even further until his chin touched his pudgy chest. "It is from the poison Hemlock plant, sir."

Abdul turned to one side and stroked his beard, heavy in thought. He didn't understand what was going on. Everything had been so simple while attacking west. Jackson, Kalamazoo, Grand Rapids, even Lansing the State Capitol had been easy conquests, but ever since turning north ... Abdul was about to draw his sword and hack off the head of his new lieutenant, but something stopped him.

Ever since turning north ... It was the Shadow Militia!

He turned quickly to his lieutenant. "Ahmed! Get that Satellite phone we received from the blind infidel. We are talking to him immediately!"

And then as an afterthought. "The soldiers need to know what is going on. Proclaim to them that Allah is unhappy with their drinking and has passed judgment on those who disobey his laws and the edicts of the Supreme General. Anyone who continues to drink will be put to death. The laws of the Koran must be followed."

Ahmed scurried away to carry out his master's errands.

SAMMY THURMOND STEPPED OUT OF THE HELICOPTER AND WALKED TO-ward the Supreme General. Sammy knew there were several reasons why The Blind Man had not come himself to the camp. One, his boss wanted to send a message that he was displeased with the Supreme General. Two, he wanted to establish a hierarchy where he was on top. And if he came when summoned .... he would appear to be a servant instead of the master. Three, and most important, the Shadow Militia had nukes, and he had to assume the Saracen camp was being watched. One radio call and The Blind Man would be glowing in the dark for the next five hundred years. So he'd sent Sammy, his trusted servant. Sammy wasn't sure how he felt about that.

The F-18 fighters circled overhead running Combat Air Patrol while Apache gunships set up around the perimeter of the camp. Sammy was flanked by four men with

MP5 submachine guns in full body armor and tactical vests. Another Apache hovered overhead with its chain gun pointed at The Supreme General's tent, which, of course, was designed to make him feel a little less supreme.

When Sammy met Ahmed, The Supreme General's second in command in the middle of the field beside US 131, he smiled to himself. Sometimes he felt like he was on the playground again, surrounded by testosterone and ego.

"Where is your boss?"

The second in command responded as forcefully as he could. "The Supreme General awaits in his quarters for your arrival. Where is The Blind Man?"

Sammy looked around the encampment. They'd been watching the past six days or so. The Shadow Militia's attack on the camp had been incredible. Secretly, Sammy had watched in awe and respect at the precision and creativity of the attack. He was enjoying the ringside seat. But his boss was concerned, as well he should be, about the incompetence of The Supreme General. He was fine against peasants when he outnumbered them a hundred to one, but then, who wouldn't be. The Blind Man had quickly realized that Abdul would need extra help if he was going to prevail or, at least weaken, the Shadow Militia.

"The Blind Man is watching the submarine races."

Ahmed's brow furled. His English was good, but it wasn't perfect. He didn't understand how The Blind Man could be watching a submarine race when he lacked eyesight. He also had never heard of the sport of submarine racing, and assumed it to be exclusive to affluent America. Or, perhaps it was just one of those idiomatic expressions the English language was prone to and made no sense at all. He hated the language.

"I see. I hope his submarine wins."

Sammy smiled and nodded. "Please, Ahmed, take me to your leader."

As Ahmed led him to the large, grandiose tent, near the center of camp, he wondered to himself *How did the infidel know my name?* Of course, Sammy knew everything about him as he'd studied his file before leaving on the mission. He was aware of the man's four wives and twenty-two children; that he had been born in Yemen before moving to America back in ninety-seven. Sammy knew the man cheated on his four wives often and that he enjoyed cocaine while he cheated. He even had photos.

"Supreme General, the Blind Man's assistant has arrived to answer your call, sir."

Abdul had been standing with his back to the door on purpose. Indeed, he'd even heard them enter, but refused to acknowledge them right away in order to establish his self-importance. Sammy's guards remained outside the tent alongside those of the Supreme Guard.

Abdul raised his right hand moved his four fingers in a dismissive fashion. Ahmed immediately bowed and backed out of the room. The Supreme General turned to Sammy Thurmond. Clearly, he was not pleased.

"Where is The Blind Man?"

Sammy replied with zero hesitation. His voice had lowered to his foreboding Hannibal Lecter decibel, and it sent a chill down Abdul's spine.

"He's watching the submarine races."

The Supreme General frowned and turned his back on Sammy Thurmond.

"I will speak with The Blind Man only after he apologizes for this insult. Now, it is time for you …"

But Abdul's voice silenced when he felt the blade of Sammy's knife touch his throat. He reached slowly down to grasp his scimitar sword, but was surprised to feel Sammy's hand already there.

"Listen you ragheaded pig fucker. One move and I slit your worthless throat."

The Supreme General decided not to move.

"As a general you're anything but supreme. We've been watching you get your ass kicked by a bunch of farmers for the past week, and The Blind Man is losing confidence in your ability to conquer and rule Michigan."

Abdul's fear was turning to anger, but he dare not show it. "They are not farmers. They are experts in warfare and you chose to hide that fact from us."

"That's only because we know how cowardly you are, and we didn't want you to soil your holy robes and cry like a baby when you found out how worthy an adversary the Shadow Militia really is. Let's face it, Abdul, you don't even belong on the same battlefield with Rodney Branch. But my boss thinks you might be useful and could possibly even beat him, given the proper assistance. So here's what's going to happen."

Sammy pressed his knife just hard enough to draw blood as he talked. "I'm going to leave a file folder on that table over there and then walk away. You're going to read the contents of the file which contains everything you need to know and do in order to defeat General Branch. My F-18s and Apaches will stay in place over your encampment for the next hour. At the end of that time, if they've not seen a red flare go up over the camp, their orders are to attack and leave none alive. The red flare signifies your compliance with the contract. The contract simply states that if you destroy the Shadow Militia, then you will be allowed to live and rule all of Michigan. If you do not, then, well, then you will die a heinous death along with your entire army. Of course, your corpse will be given a proper burial in a nearby pig farm."

Abdul felt the knife move away from his throat. He pondered the deal for a moment. He could cry out and Sammy Thurmond and his men would be killed, but not before Sammy killed him. Then the F-18s would attack and all his power and army would be gone. All his work would be wasted.

"I need more air support. My Apaches have been shot down."

The Supreme General slowly turned to find himself alone in the tent. Sammy Thurmond, the man with Hannibal Lecter's voice … was gone.

Abdul's legs became weak and he collapsed on the grass of his tent floor. He felt the blood on his throat and tried not to cry. A few minutes later he struggled to his feet and moved to the table and the file folder. He opened and read. A smile came to his face. Perhaps … this arrangement could work.

"Ahmed! Get in here!"

Five minutes later a red flare arced up over the camp and The Blind Man's air force flew away.

CHAPTER 16

An Evil Trap

JACKIE WAS SURPRISED AT HER SUDDEN NAUSEA AS SHE spewed out the contents of her meager breakfast onto the grass behind the kitchen tent. Perhaps she'd contracted the flu or ... maybe ... perhaps she could have been exposed to the contents of the deadly plastic vial she carried in her pocket. But that didn't make sense. The doctor had inoculated her against it. She should be okay.

After wiping off her mouth and spitting several times on the grass, Jackie reached into her pocket and grasped the vial. This was her last mission, then she could head back to Iroquois and her daughter. The past five days had not been as glorious as she'd anticipated. Eating scraps, sleeping very little, always paranoid and on full alert had left her physically and emotionally exhausted.

Jackie moved around to the front of the tent where the large pot of stew simmered over an open fire on a tripod. Conditions in camp were a mix of twenty-first century technology and medieval culture. Five times a day the call to prayer sounded over loudspeakers, and, at the same time, people hauled water from the stream to the west and boiled it for drinking. The land had already been stripped nearly clean by The Horde and other looters, so provisions were scarce.

She waited until the woman turned away to get something, then she boldly walked up and poured the contents of the vial into the pot. Without stopping she quickly moved away from the tent and headed for the perimeter of the camp. She didn't want to be here when things started happening.

Escanaba HQ

J EFF ARNETT SAT ACROSS THE DESK FROM COLONEL MACPHERSON AND General Branch, briefing them on Jackie's progress.

"The message received last night said phase one had been completed successfully resulting in an estimated two thousand enemy deaths."

Rodney Branch nodded his head in approval. "I told you she was tough."

Special Agent Arnett continued his briefing. "This morning we received word she had initiated phase two."

Mac was the first to respond. "How long until we know whether or not it's going to work?"

Jeff leaned back in his chair, annoyed by its lack of comfort. "The doctor says this is an enhanced version of Typhoid and should spread quickly. It's not likely to kill more than half of the enemy, but it will certainly take out anyone already weakened by the journey along with the sick, old and ..." He hesitated. "The extremely young."

Rodney knew what that meant, and it was the reason he'd balked at employing biological warfare against the Saracen army. But, in the end, he'd relented to Mac's plan. Tactically it was sound and it was the right military response. For centuries collateral damage had always been exacted on the civilian populations. There was no way around it. And, in reality, it didn't matter what type of attack he made on the enemy, some civilians were guaranteed to die. War was dirty and not for the faint of heart. In the end … wars were only won by breaking things and killing people. Both Rodney and Mac understood that, however difficult it was now to carry out the plan. The important thing was this: it would give them more time to figure out a way to stop the Saracen tide from thoroughly overwhelming the state of Michigan.

"When will she be safely out of there?"

Jeff smiled. He'd grown fond of his pretty young protege over the days he'd spent training her for this mission. "She should be out by nightfall. Then she'll rendezvous with Colonel Branch and his Militia Rangers."

Rodney smiled. He knew Dan would be furious at him for putting her in danger, but those personal elements would have to take a back seat to the greater good. If Jackie could kill another ten-thousand enemy troops, then he'd have a fighting chance of stopping them. If not …

"I'm sure the colonel will be both surprised and pleased to see his bride so soon."

Jeff shook his head. "You sure you shouldn't let him know what's going on?"

Rodney pondered his question for a moment. "Yes, I'm sure. Dan can be a bit passionate at times. I don't want the knowledge to affect his combat decisions. As far as it goes, he has no need to know the identity of his pick-up. Besides, he'll find out soon enough and all's well that ends well."

Jeff Arnett wasn't sure he agreed, but decided to let it go, at least for now. Besides, time would tell. "So, you said you have another mission to discuss."

General Branch nodded and stood up. He walked to the window and looked out at the Escanaba summer. It was beautiful in the warm months, but the Upper Peninsula winters froze him to his core, and the older he got the worse it affected him.

"Yes, but only you and I and Mac can know about it."

Jeff glanced over at Colonel MacPherson, then back at General Branch. "Well, lucky for you the CIA is very good at keeping secrets. What do you need?"

Rodney turned back around. "It's simple. I need you to find out where I can get a freighter full of ammonium nitrate, 100,000 tons would be good. And I need to get it here within a week."

Special Agent Arnett cocked his head to one side. "Really? Just like that?"

Rodney nodded. "And I could use some nitromethane or maybe diesel or fuel oil if you can't find that."

Jeff smiled and shook his head from side to side. "What are you going to do … blow up the whole Upper Peninsula?"

Rodney laughed softly. "No, not the whole peninsula, just selected regions of strategic importance." And then he added as an afterthought. "Besides, it's good stuff to have around, and I'm running low."

The tall man stood up and sighed. "Well, I can't tell you where things are right now, but I can find out where they were the day the lights went out."

"That'll have to do then. Just give me some options. It's important."

Jeff Arnett turned and walked out the door, closing it behind him. Ranger MacPherson looked over at his boss and stared. Rodney avoided his friend's gaze.

"So, did you come up with a plan?"

Rodney turned back to the window and watched the ducks on the overgrown lawn. They were pooping on everything, and it was driving him crazy. Back home in Iroquois he would have shot them or sent his dog, Moses, after them. He missed Moses.

"It's still half-baked, Mac. But it seems so desperate and terrible to me that I don't want to say it out loud quite yet. It needs to stew a while."

Colonel MacPherson didn't answer him. He knew from experience that it would do no good. When Rodney was ready to bring him into the plan, he would be there.

Spy Hunting

"THIS IS THE WOMAN WE ARE LOOKING FOR." THE SUPREME GENERAL tossed the photograph onto the table and slid it over to his second in command. Ahmed picked it up and looked at it.

"She is Middle Eastern?"

Abdul nodded. "Yes, born in Lebanon. Then moved to America after her infidel father was killed by patriotic Muslims there. Her mother renounced the faith and turned to Christianity. The girl was raised in America and became a Christian missionary. She married the son of the Shadow Militia general, and now she is inside our camp as we speak. She is the reason our people are dying mysteriously. Catch her and bring her to me and you will be rewarded. Otherwise ..."

Abdul didn't finish the threat. There was no need as both understood the implications of failure.

"It will be done as you command Supreme General." Ahmed lowered his head and backed out of the room in holy submission.

The Supreme General looked down at the file folder in front of him. He wondered to himself ... *How had The Blind Man gotten all this information? He had to have been watching the Shadow Militia from the start.* He squirmed uncomfortably on the cushion beneath him. He thought to himself *It's not fair the infidels should have so much technology when the soldiers of Allah had little.* And then he heard a voice, or thought he heard a voice, whether it was coming from inside him or from without, he didn't know.

"The way of technology is the way of the kafir. But with you it is not so. The armies of Allah will succeed by virtue of strength and courage. You will triumph with the sword."

Abdul's smile spread across his face. He had just been visited by the great prophet, Mohammed, peace be upon him, and now all would be well. He was sure of it.

He placed his hand inside his robe and retrieved the plastic pill bottle. Inside was a fine, white powder which he spread onto the table in a line. Afterwards, he felt emboldened to carry out the will of Allah, confident he would win in battle, not just with General Branch, but also against The Blind Man and all his technology.

He stood to his feet and walked to the entrance of his tent. He moved the flap aside and looked out briefly up into the sky. Abdul wondered, *Can he see through the walls of my tent?*

IT WOULD BE DARK SOON, SO JACKIE HOVERED NEAR THE EDGE OF THE encampment. As soon as the last light began to fade, she would edge out into the darkness and be away from this God-forsaken place. She prayed quietly to herself for protection and for the night to come quickly. Her little girl must be missing her by now, and she wanted nothing more than to get back to her. Jackie vowed to herself, in the fading light as the campfires lit up one by one, *I will never do this again.*

A moment later there was a commotion from deep inside the camp. A part of her wanted to run, but she forced herself to be brave and patient, to stay with the plan. Running now would be suicide, and she knew her nerves were on edge. She just had to stay the course.

The camp seemed to come alive as more and more men picked up their arms in preparation of ... something. She waited inside the protection of her grey-hooded cotton top. *Was the bioweapon already working? Were people already getting sick?* She didn't think it was supposed to work that quickly. But, if so, then it was all the more reason to get out of camp.

Finally, Jackie lost her nerve and began to walk out the perimeter of the encampment. Just as she was about to enter the field between the camp and the woods, a loud voice boomed out behind her.

"Stop!"

As a reflex action, Jackie froze in her tracks and turned her head slightly to see what was going on. Four men were looking directly at her and all were armed with rifles. In retrospect, she should have run, but hindsight was not available to her. The men moved toward her and soon she was in custody.

Just West of the Enemy Camp

THE LAST RAYS OF GOOD DAYLIGHT WERE FADING DOWN ONTO THE HORIzon and in another thirty minutes it would be pitch black. Colonel Dan Branch lifted the binoculars to his eyes and peered down on the perimeter of the enemy encampment. The enemy camp hadn't moved since the last successful attack on the Saracen motor pool five days prior. They appeared to be focusing all their efforts on repairing as many vehicles as possible, an effort which Donny Brewster and his snipers had been exploiting as much as possible.

His orders had come directly from Uncle Rodney and they were very explicit that he should carry them out in person. He didn't understand it. A very important operative would be leaving the enemy camp at night fall. He was to meet him and take him back to safety where he would be extracted and flown back to Escanaba for debrief.

Dan assumed this person was a spy, and he wondered who it was and why he hadn't been told before now. He suspected this spy was somehow responsible for the mysterious deaths inside the camp which had been happening the past few days. Donny's snipers had been reporting more and more people being buried outside the camp to the east. If all went as planned, he'd be able to meet this man soon, and then he could hear the full story of what had been going on.

Whatever this spy had been doing, he just hoped it killed every last person inside that camp. There were still well over twenty-thousand enemy soldiers, and he knew in his heart there was no way the Shadow Militia could prevail against them. He suspected his Uncle Rodney knew that as well. Uncle Rodney would have a plan. He always had a plan.

Dan watched through his binoculars as the camp seemed to slowly come alive. Something was happening down there. He glanced over at Captain Danny Briel beside him.

"You see that Danny?"

The captain beside him, who was also peering through binoculars grunted before answering. "Yup. Something's starting to happen down there."

Dan Branch lowered his binoculars for a moment to rest his eyes, but the captain's voice interrupted him.

"Colonel! Look at that!"

Dan raised his binoculars again and quickly focused in on a cluster of men at the edge of camp. Four guards had detained a person and were in the process of taping his hands behind him. Dan thought to himself *I hope that's not our spy.* Then he watched as the prisoner's hood was lowered, revealing the face of a terrified woman. Dan's heart skipped a beat as adrenaline surged into his bloodstream.

"Oh my God! No!" Colonel Branch started to get up, but Danny Briel quickly pulled him back down to the earth.

"What are you doing?"

"I have to get her!"

Danny shook his head.

"No way! Are you crazy?!"

Dan Branch looked into his captain's eyes with determination made of fire, but Danny Briel met his stare with ice cold of his own.

"If you go down there right now she dies and so do you. You need a plan of action."

Dan glanced at the enemy camp and then back at Captain Briel. His head knew he was right, but his heart wanted to attack with all the unbridled ferocity he could muster. And then it came to him. He recalled Jackie's meetings with Special Agent Jeff Arnett, the courier messages from Uncle Rodney to Jackie. They all made sense now. *She was the spy!*

Dan pulled up his binoculars and scanned the edge of camp, but his wife was already gone.

CHAPTER 17

July 4th, The Game Gets Tough

"**B**Y NOW YOU MUST KNOW THAT YOUR SPY, YOUR DAUGH-ter-in-law is in my custody. You must also know that life is very precarious, and that I can do anything I want with her."

The Supreme General hesitated before going on. He looked over at Jackie, who was duct-taped to a chair in the middle of his tent. She was naked, her body covered in dried blood and bruises. They had tortured her to get the code to unlock the satphone. Above all else, Abdul wanted to speak in person with the man who'd been driving him crazy for the past week. He wanted the man to suffer, and he wanted to listen as General Branch, once proud, cocky and confident, was reduced to groveling in his proper place as a kafir.

"She is naked now, in her natural state. A very attractive woman, even covered in blood. I need you to know how serious I am, so I'm going to rape her now while you listen. If you hang up before I finish, then I will cut her throat."

Uncle Rodney's blood began to boil inside him. He wanted to kill this man. Mac stood beside him in his office with a restraining hand on Rodney's shoulder. The colonel sensed Rodney's anger and moved his finger up to his lips in a hushing motion, then he took the satphone from his general. In an excited and desperate mock voice, Mac spewed out a frantic reply.

"No! Please no! You've proved your point! I know you are serious. Just please, don't hurt her anymore and you'll be given free passage all the way to the bridge."

There was silence on the other end and Mac continued. "I will call back my snipers and my militia units, and you will not be bothered again by us. Just … please, don't hurt my daughter."

Abdul smiled. He was still going to rape her, just not over the phone.

"Agreed. But, if you break your word she will die a slow and painful death." Abdul lowered the phone to end the conversation, but hesitated, then brought it back up to his ear. "Oh, and one more thing. My doctor has confirmed that the woman is pregnant. If you cross me, then two lives will end."

Jackie watched in terror as Abdul lowered the phone and pressed the button ending the call. A few moments later he moved up to her and signaled his men to lay her on the table with arms bound behind her and legs spread out.

And then, he broke his promise.

But, through it all, Jackie did not scream. She cleared her mind, then filled it with her most happy thoughts, images of her baby Donna, of Dan lying on the floor beside her, the two playing and laughing as she looked on in better times. In her heart she resolved herself to live. The good times would come again, but first … she had to survive.

Escanaba HQ

"WHERE IS THAT SON OF A BITCH!?" COLONEL BRANCH HAD JUST STEPPED off the Huey helicopter and was already walking past Colonel MacPherson. He neglected to salute and continued hurriedly into the colonel's ancestral home, which was now the temporary Shadow Militia headquarters.

Colonel MacPherson didn't try to stop him. He simply followed behind, letting the scene play out. It was all foreseeable. The guards at the entrance raised their carbines in salute as Dan rushed through the door and up the stairs to Mac's office. The office door opened with a crash as Dan raced in with both fists raised. He saw his uncle standing tall in his olive drab fatigues and headed straight for him swinging.

With his arms still behind his back in an "at ease" position, Uncle Rodney stepped to one side and let Dan's momentum carry him on by. The general took a step back and aimed and fired, hitting Dan squarely in the back. Dan's body jerked and spasmed as twenty-thousand volts of electricity coursed through his frame.

"It's good to see you, Dan."

Dan Branch lay on the desk face first, wanting to move, but unable to fight off the after-effects of the electricity. Rodney pressed the trigger again sending another jolt into his loved one. Dan swore and tried to get up, but collapsed onto the hardwood floor. Uncle Rodney pressed the trigger one more time and then moved around to sit at the chair beside the desk.

"Son, as soon as you're ready, I think we need to talk."

The Saracen Encampment

THE TWO MEN STOOD ON EITHER SIDE OF JACKIE AS THEY LASHED HER TO the wooden cross with duct tape. Over her torso, she was wearing the tattered remains of her dirty t-shirt. Below her waist all she wore were the scant covering of her undergarment. First, her arms, then her waist, then her knees and ankles. By time they were done, she was affixed so securely they were able to hoist up the heavy cross and drop it down into the hole. There was a small wooden ledge for her feet, so she could stand on it and still bring in air to her lungs or else she would have suffocated.

When the cross hit the bottom of the hole her entire body shuddered at the sudden stop. But she felt no pain. She was beyond pain. Jackie didn't know how many times she'd been raped and beaten in the last twenty-four hours, but she did realize her body couldn't take a whole lot more. Oddly enough, despite the physical abuse, her mind was still clear and focused.

She tried to look around at the camp, but both her eyes were swollen nearly shut. The only thought in her mind was *Dan must be going crazy.* Jackie knew he must be close by, maybe even watching, because she'd been scheduled to rendezvous with him the night before outside the camp. She felt conflicted, wanting Dan to come in and rescue her, but also hoping he stayed away for his own safety. Jackie thought back to the first few months they'd shared together in that north woods cabin in Wisconsin. He was the bravest and most passionate man she'd ever known. She recalled their weird courtship, how he'd stood at the foot of her husband's grave and asked permission to marry her. What had seemed crazy then, seemed even more ludicrous now in retrospect.

But these were crazy times, so why shouldn't crazy things happen? Was crazy and bizarre the new normal? It appeared to be. How else could she have ended up duct taped to a cross in the midst of twenty-thousand Muslims? It was crazy, unthinkable, at least … in the old life before The Day. But now, almost anything bad could happen, and it usually did.

Jackie bowed her head and closed her eyes. She heard men jeering at her, but couldn't make out the words. She didn't want to.

The Blind Man

I ENJOYED READING YOUR REPORT, MR. THURMOND. YOU ARE ALWAYS SO precise and thorough. And I like your particular attention to detail. I find it refreshing in a time when so much anarchy threatens the world."

The Blind Man turned and paced slowly to one side, around the coffee table, to the wall, then back again. He bent down and picked up the crystal decanter and poured more brandy into his long-stemmed wine glass.

"But now I have more work for you, work that only you can do, work I can entrust solely to you, my right-hand man."

Sammy Thurmond stood almost at position of attention before his master, listening intently, but without emotion. He didn't answer, only because no answer was required; therefore any reply would be considered by The Blind Man to be a waste of words.

"I find the Saracen encampment to be insufficient. The "Supreme" General is anything but supreme. He lacks creativity, military experience, and is ruled by his emotions. He's already lost a third of his force, and, at this rate, will not have adequate manpower to weaken General Branch, much less defeat him."

He took a sip of his brandy.

"I want you to return immediately with a large force of security specialists. The man isn't even capable of protecting his own perimeter much less defeating a real general on the field of battle. Do what you have to do. Use whatever resources are necessary, but make sure the little toy general makes it all the way to the field of battle in sufficient numbers to draw out the bulk of the Shadow Militia."

He turned and faced Sammy.

"I need General Branch to commit the bulk of his airpower and armor. I want the bulk of the Saracen army to reach Iroquois City. That is where the battle will be fought. He will protect his home town. That is his weakness."

Sammy Thurmond said nothing. He knew the one-sided conversation was over, so he nodded his head and left the room.

Donny Brewster Stands Watch

IT WAS A GRUESOME SIGHT TO SEE THROUGH THE HIGH-POWERED SPOTTING scope, Jackie's body sagging in the heat of mid-afternoon sun. Donny noted the bruises, blood and the many swollen areas of her body. He doubted she would last much longer. Dan and Jeremy Branch had both been called back to HQ, and Donny guessed it was all about keeping him out of the area, so they wouldn't have to watch this. More importantly, so they wouldn't do anything rash that would get them killed.

Just then a ladder was placed against the cross, which was about twelve feet tall. A man climbed up with a cup and appeared to give her a drink of water. Jackie stirred momentarily, just long enough to take a few sips, before lapsing into unconsciousness again. Donny bowed his head down in despair. He had to figure out a way to get her back.

Just then, he heard the sound of fighter jets overhead, diving down toward the camp. The four F-18s pulled out of their dive and leveled off just in time to fly over the camp, leaving an army of terrorized Saracens in their wake. The man on the ladder fell off onto the ground.

Apache helicopters were coming in now, lots of them, so Donny packed up and headed further back away from the fringe of camp. With Apaches came infrared, and he was no match for that.

BY THE END OF THE DAY, SAMMY THURMOND HAD EXERTED COMPLETE control over all security aspects of the Saracen camp. He'd been careful only to insult The Supreme General privately, and then, just enough to force him into submission. Sammy knew that absent the overwhelming force of the Apaches and F-18s, Abdul Al'Kalwi would undoubtedly kill him in seconds. So Sammy was walking a fine line and he knew it.

Sammy didn't like change. It made him nervous. And he had noticed the change in his boss. The Blind Man was doing things he'd never done before, things like sending him into a camp of twenty-thousand people who wanted him dead. That was a big deal to him. Not that Sammy valued his life, or even had any aspirations toward retirement or any type of normal life. Normal had always bored him. Before, he'd never thought about the future; there was only the here and now, primarily because he'd enjoyed his job. It was exciting and it intrigued him. The Blind Man had intrigued him ... but not so much anymore. For the first time since taking employment with Jared Thompson, Sammy Thurmond was beginning to wonder what his next step would be. And he knew that was a very dangerous place to visit.

Sammy watched as his men installed security cameras around the center of camp. They were high atop a portable tower and faced all four directions, and powerful enough to scan the entire camp and on into the woods. His own men had taken control of the perimeter, assuming command of hundreds of Saracens to bear the brunt of the grunt work. But make no mistake about it ... Sammy Thurmond was in command.

Sammy looked over at the big wooden cross standing fifty yards to the east. He quickly barked out a command.

"I want her taken down and fed and exercised twice a day. She's no good to us dead." And then as an afterthought. "And no one is to hurt her. I want her strong and alert and obviously alive to the eyes of anyone watching."

Then he moved on to his new command post where he checked on the progress of launching the small drones. Sammy left nothing to chance when it came to security, especially his own security, and The Blind Man had rightly surmised that tying Sammy's fate to that of The Supreme General would be in his own best interest.

CHAPTER 18

**July 6th, Escanaba HQ**

DAN **B**RANCH WAS IN A HOLDING CELL AT THE **D**ELTA COUNTY jail, sitting on a bench attached to the concrete wall. His wife was, at this moment, undoubtedly being tortured … or maybe she was already dead. But Dan couldn't think that way. He had to stay positive or he'd never get out of here and never be able to save her.

He stood up and paced to the opposite wall, then he paced back to the bench. He'd already done it a thousand times, but he couldn't bring himself to stop. For some reason Dan had always thought better while walking. As he paced back and forth, Dan envisioned himself sneaking into the enemy camp in the dead of night and rescuing Jackie. He would need intel, but he could do the rest on his own.

Suddenly, he stopped in mid-pace. *Does Jeremy know?* He had to. He was there, and he was a sniper with a high-powered rifle and telescopic sight. And what about Donny? Would he help him? He thought so. He wondered about baby Donna. Was she okay? Was she crying right now? Was she being taken care of? Dan had been led to believe that Jackie was taking care of the baby while he was out fighting, and that was the only thing that had kept him going, knowing that his family was safe as he put his own life on the line. He could fight with vehemence and tenacity, but only when he knew they were safe. His focus was gone now and he cursed his own emotions for distracting him. Back to the task at hand.

How will I save her? Dan resumed his pacing. Back and forth, back and forth, back and forth … like a caged tiger. He moved with deliberation and passion, thinking, plotting, planning.

"I KNOW WHAT THE PURELY MILITARY DECISION IS. BUT I DON'T LIKE IT."

Colonel MacPherson stood mutely beside his general, watching as Rodney stared off into the wall beside him as if it wasn't there.

"I know I should kill her or at the least let them kill her. I should renew the sniper attacks and continue rallying the forces to make our final defense. That's what I should be doing, not sitting here with you trying to figure out a way to save her."

Rodney stood up from the desk chair and began to walk back and forth in the office. Each time he reached the far wall he did a perfectly executed about-face and walked one-hundred-and-eighty degrees in the opposite direction. Mac watched in fascination at Rodney's incessant pacing, which seemed to be identical to that of Dan's. He knew the two men were linked together by some bond, something unseen, some magical bond of unseen blood. Suddenly, Rodney stopped his pacing.

"What do you think I should do, Mac?"

But the colonel didn't answer, and Rodney resumed the pacing as if he'd never stopped or even asked the question.

"What are the ramifications of killing her or letting the Saracens keep her prisoner?" He answered his own question. "Colonel Branch will become ineffective as a fighting leader. The Militia Rangers will have no one to lead them and they will be demoralized to the point of ineffectiveness as they are forced to stand by leaderless, watching the Saracen Tide advance toward their homes and families."

He stopped pacing. "That is unacceptable." He paced again. "And if I mount a rescue attempt in a camp guarded by Apaches and F-18s, all who take part are likely to die and the rescue will probably fail. People will die in vain to save one woman."

The general looked over at Colonel MacPherson. "What am I missing, Mac?"

His friend shook his head from side to side. "You are seeing it clearly, General Branch."

Rodney resumed his pacing. The Shadow Militia had always been a lost cause. He knew that. In the old days, as a soldier for the United States military, he'd always had the upper hand, the advantage, the technology and superior numbers. But now … the shoe was on the other foot and he hated it.

"I'm missing something, Mac. I have to be. There's always a solution. Every problem contains its own solution. I just have to figure it out."

Mac still didn't talk. He had no answers and no way to help his friend. Finally, in desperation, he threw out a suggestion. "Perhaps we could call upon God?"

Rodney halted and snapped to attention. He did a left-face and stared into Mac's eyes. Mac had never said that before. It must mean something. He brought his left hand up to his mouth and rubbed his face several times in deep thought. *What could it hurt?*

"Colonel MacPherson! Send for Father Connors. I want him here five minutes ago!"

Mac smiled slightly and walked out of the room while Rodney resumed his pacing.

The Saracen Camp

PEOPLE WERE DYING EVERY DAY BY THE HUNDREDS, AND THE STENCH OF the camp was quickly becoming more than Sammy Thurmond could bear. Already three thousand people had died from the mysterious sickness. Sammy had called The Blind Man, who had immediately sent entire teams of doctors, scientists and medical personnel to protect his investment in the Saracen army. The doctors had quickly identified the sickness as a new strain of Typhoid, one not seen before.

Sammy couldn't help but frown when The Blind Man had cursed on the sat phone. He'd never heard him do that. Sammy Thurmond didn't like change; it was too precarious - too unpredictable, and he knew it was extremely hazardous to end up on the wrong side of change.

Already the weakest in the camp had died, but the doctors moved quickly to quarantine the sick and improve sanitary conditions. Sammy stood before the lead doctor now, questioning him on the prognosis.

"How many will die?"

"It's hard to say. No one can know for sure. We've never seen this strain before and it's quite hearty. Its high infectivity rate makes it difficult to contain. Fortunately, the lethality is only about forty percent."

Sammy Thurmond thought to himself. *Why do technical people talk like that, so fancy and formal?*

"How long until we can move again?"

The doctor seemed to be growing impatient. He wanted to get back to his work. He wanted to defeat this disease.

"These people can't be moved until they either die or until they beat the sickness.

Sixty percent of them will live, but they'll need at least four weeks to recover and regain their strength. That's assuming the quarantine works and the sickness burns itself out. That's difficult because of the close quarters and the primitive living conditions here in the camp."

Sammy looked out across the camp at the hundreds of tents and vehicles. Three thousand had already died and another three thousand had taken sick. He knew The Blind Man would not accept a four week delay. He did the math in his head and quickly made a decision.

"Kill the three thousand sick as quickly and quietly as you can. Anyone who comes down sick after that will be immediately shot. This sickness will end and it will end now. We move out as quickly as possible."

The doctor's lower jaw dropped open in disbelief. He turned to his colleague and said something in French that Sammy didn't understand. Then he turned back angrily.

"I will not kill anyone! I'm a healer, not a killer! And we will stay here and treat these people until every last one of them is well. We are doctors who've sworn a Hippocratic oath and ..."

But his sentence was interrupted by the knife blade against his throat. The steel severed the windpipe and carotid artery leaving nothing but a gurgling sound and a spatter of blood. The red liquid hit Sammy in the cheek and he put away the knife slowly and pulled out a clean, white handkerchief. He wiped away the blood on his cheek and dropped the soiled cloth to the ground. Then he turned to the remaining doctor and stared at him coldly.

The man stuttered in French, then quickly reverted to English. His hands and arms were shaking in fear as he looked down at his friend who was now bleeding out at his feet.

"I ... I, recommend cyanide. We have a healthy supply and can have it here by nightfall."

Sammy nodded his approval. "Good, I want it done by morning. No need to bury the dead. Just leave them." He turned to walk away and stopped. "Oh, one more thing. Don't speak that French crap to me anymore or I'll kill you. I don't like French."

The doctor nodded and spoke in perfect unbroken, English. "Yes, sir. I understand."

Sammy Thurmond, the man with Hannibal Lecter's voice walked away, all the while thinking, wondering *Am I on the winning side or the losing side?* He no longer knew for sure.

Sammy meets Jackie

SAMMY THURMOND HADN'T ALWAYS BEEN EVIL. IN FACT, THERE HAD BEEN a time, long, long ago when he'd been a good kid, some would say even exemplary. He'd gone to Sunday School, prayed to Jesus, and even been a boy scout for a time. Anamosa, Iowa had been a good place to raise a good kid. It was rural, conservative, a place where everyone knew everyone else and life was slow. Sammy had grown up playing on the banks of the Wapsipinicon River, a three-hundred-mile-long tributary of the Mississippi, full of catfish with a rocky bottom that always seemed to snag his lures and cost him plenty in fishing tackle.

Young Sammy could have been a preacher, or a school teacher, or maybe even a factory worker or farmhand on one of the nearby pig farms. But … that was not to be. As in so many other lives, the future of this small boy was altered by one event, one lone event, isolated from everything that had previously happened. Up until that one day, Sammy had been a good boy. But he'd been plagued with unacceptance. The other kids didn't like him and resisted his sincere and relentless overtures at friendship. They'd shunned him, not as a full-fledged pariah, but simply as someone a rung or two below them on the ladder of life. Sammy sensed this and would do anything to fit in. One day the other boys dared him to break the window of old man Garrison's garage. Sensing the opportunity for acceptance, Sammy hadn't hesitated.

After that one indiscretion, Sammy was no longer his own. He'd given up his freedom and his individuality for acceptance into the group. After that fateful day – they owned him. Breaking windows graduated to slashing tires, to setting fires, to reckless driving, to thievery. Finally, at age seventeen, Sammy was caught breaking into a convenience store. He'd stolen only a case of beer, but because of his past misadventures the judge came down hard, giving him the chance for prison time or enlisting in the military. He'd chosen the military and soon left Iowa behind forever.

One thing about Sammy Thurmond – he never looked back.

Sammy learned to kill in the army. In fact, he became very good at it. The act of killing fascinated him, so he practiced as often as he could and became proficient at its art. He was recruited by the CIA where he learned even more about killing and deviance and cunning. It was there, in the service of his country, where Sammy Thurmond's eyes turned cold-green and evil.

And by the time The Blind Man took notice of Sammy, he'd already killed hundreds of men, and any vestige of small-town Iowa had been rent from his soul. That had been ten years ago, and now Sammy was forty-five.

Sammy looked over at Jackie Branch now and smiled coldly. Now that she was cleaned up he could see how beautiful she was. They were inside his large tent. She was eating at the wooden picnic table while he looked on in a folding chair from ten feet away. She ate ravenously, like a wolf, and that only served to interest him all the more. Sammy listened intently to his self-talk and soon surmised his real interest in her was not her beauty, because he could have beautiful women at his beck and call. No, it wasn't that. He was surprised to learn that his interest in her was purely professional. Sammy was a cold-blooded killer by trade, but, sitting here in front of him, just a few feet away, was a woman who'd killed thousands in just a few day's time. And he respected that.

Jackie finished eating and looked over at him. "Do I have you to thank for the food and the clean clothes?"

Sammy didn't say anything. He simply nodded.

"Well then, thank you. I appreciate it."

Sammy nodded again. A year ago Jackie would have been terrified just being in the same room with this man, but so much had occurred to transform her, that she wasn't bothered by it. She could see the evil in his eyes, sense it more than see it. And it was obvious by his bearing and his demeanor that he was the most dangerous man in the room, wherever that room might be.

"Are you the one who ordered all the sick people to be killed?"

Sammy nodded and smiled.

"You realize you're doing my job for me?"

Sammy was wearing a black t-shirt with khaki tactical pants. There was a Glock model 22 strapped to his right hip with three extra mags on his left hip. His huge, muscular arms were wrapped around his massive chest tightly. But he didn't answer her.

"What's your name?"

Sammy narrowed his eyes slightly. "Names will not be necessary."

The coldness in his voice caused Jackie to shiver despite the stifling July heat and humidity. She forced a smile.

"I see. The strong, silent type."

Sammy felt amused and that fact surprised him, as he couldn't recall the last time he'd been amused. Jackie had been surprised to see the white, linen napkin beside the silver and china, but she picked up the linen now and lightly wiped her lips.

"What is going to happen to me?"

Sammy shrugged. "Life is precarious and unpredictable."

Jackie smiled at his remark. "Well, not as unpredictable as you might think." She forced herself to look into the man's cold, green eyes as she spoke. "I am going to die soon. It doesn't take a sage to figure that one out. The only question is 'Will I die with honor, as a tribute to my people?'"

She could tell her statement interested him.

Sammy uncrossed his arms. "Tell me please, what does it look like to die with honor?"

Jackie leaned forward and placed her elbows on the pine picnic table. "It means that I die for a purpose I believe worthy … a purpose of my own choosing. It means that my own death helps the ones I love to survive and to fight on against evil."

Sammy nodded. "Yes. Altruism. I recognize that. It's the practice of unselfish devotion to others. I've killed many altruistic people."

Jackie held his gaze. "I believe you." Then she hesitated. She knew in her heart that Dan was out there watching the camp, that he would undoubtedly try to rescue her and that he would certainly die in the attack. "I wonder … perhaps … if you might do me one more favor."

Jackie let the request linger in the humid air of the tent. The man didn't answer, but she could tell he was still interested, so she continued. "I respectfully request that you kill me as quickly as possible."

Sammy Thurmond leaned forward in his chair. The Blind Man would like this woman. She was so polite. "And why would you like that? Don't you have something or someone to live for?" Sammy threw the words out like a piece of cheese tossed with purpose to a helpless and hungry mouse.

Jackie's eyes misted over, but she willed the tears to dissipate. "Sometimes dying for the ones you love is more important than living for them."

"Really? How so?"

She folded her hands and placed them under her chin. "Because, as long as I'm alive the attacks on this camp will not reconvene. And if this army is not destroyed, then the ones I love will eventually be killed. Logic therefore dictates that I die in order for the ones I love to live."

Now Sammy truly was amused, perhaps more than he'd ever been amused in his adult life. "You have a husband. Colonel Dan Branch. A baby named Donna. A stepson named Jeremy. These are the ones you love. And these are the reasons you kill?"

Jackie nodded. "I kill for them. And I die for them."

Sammy Thurmond stood up to his full six-feet, two-inch frame and slowly walked over to where Jackie was sitting. He unholstered his Glock as he went. Jackie didn't move. Upon feeling the warm metal against her ear, she turned and faced him. "I want to look my killer in the eyes. And I want you to know that I bear you no ill will."

Jackie's dark eyes met Sammy's cold, green gaze. Neither moved for almost a minute. Then, slowly, Sammy's finger began to take up slack on the trigger. Jackie waited, knowing she would never see Dan Branch again, wondering what woman would raise her child, believing that someday another woman would share the bed of her husband. She regretted that it had come to this, but her soul was at peace. She would die with honor.

Sammy Thurmond smiled and reholstered his pistol. "I will consider your request." And then he walked out of the tent, leaving Jackie alone with her love and her logic.

CHAPTER 19

July 8th, Uncle Rodney's Reconciliation

"**S**O WHAT'S IT GOING TO TAKE, YOUNG DANIEL, TO MOVE you from the liability column back to the asset column?"

Dan Branch looked across the desk at his Uncle Rodney through bloodshot eyes. He hadn't slept in two days. "That's easy. Just take off these handcuffs. I'll do the rest."

Uncle Rodney looked over at the man he'd raised as his own son. He was proud of him, at his loyalty and bravery. But he was also disappointed at the boy's lack of logic and emotional self-control.

"Dan, you have to learn to control your emotions if you're going to have any hope of saving your wife."

Dan's eyes perked up. "You're going to save her?"

The old general looked tired and worn as he shifted in the plush, high-backed chair inside Colonel MacPherson's office.

"No, Daniel. I'm just a tired old man. I'm going to stay here in Escanaba. You're young and full of piss and vinegar. You're going to save her. After all, she's *your* wife."

Dan's shoulders slumped forward, letting his exhaustion show just a bit.

"Did you actually think I would let her die without even trying?"

The young man looked up into his general's eyes. Both men had suddenly softened their demeanor.

"I … I, just wasn't sure. I've been in that cell for two days, and … I know how you are."

Rodney's eyebrows lifted up. "Really? And how am I, young Daniel?"

Dan squirmed in the chair with handcuffed wrists on his lap. He hated it when he called him young Daniel. But he wanted to choose his words carefully. Angering the one man with the power to help him would do his wife no good.

"The mission is paramount. The mission is to defeat the Saracen army in battle and save Iroquois. You'll stop at nothing to achieve the mission ... even if it means sacrificing my wife to do it."

Uncle Rodney looked straight into his son's eyes. For a moment Dan thought he saw tears, but they quickly went away, immediately replaced with the hardness of granite and the heat of lightning.

"Anyone else's wife would already be dead, along with the rest of that Saracen rabble! I love Jackie, but she's alive because of you and only because of you."

Dan's eyes met his uncle's and they locked like the horns of a bull. "You would kill her yourself if it meant destroying the Saracens?"

Uncle Rodney nodded. "I certainly wouldn't ask someone else to do my own dirty work. Do you think she's the first casualty of war? Remember eighty-four-year-old Harold Steffens who died crashing his crop duster into two hundred enemy soldiers? Your wife helped him install the weapon's system on that plane. Harold died along with hundreds of others in the last battle. And Jackie knew going into this mission that is was a risk. She knew she could die, but she made that choice for herself, just like you make the choice every time you lead other men into battle. You're no different than I am and Jackie's no different than you and I. She risked her life to save her family. And why shouldn't she? She's as much a warrior as you and I."

Dan lowered his eyes. "I just ... it's just that ..." But he couldn't finish the sentence.

His Uncle Rodney stood up and walked around the desk. He went down to his knees and embraced his nephew. "I know. You don't have to say it."

Both men were quiet for a full minute. Then, Uncle Rodney stood back up and returned to his chair. "Here's the bottom line, Dan. I have a plan, but it requires no less than one-hundred percent of your cooperation and loyalty in order to succeed." He hesitated. "Are you willing to listen?"

Dan nodded. "Absolutely."

Rodney smiled softly. "Okay then. I need you to go to Ludington."

Dan's smile faded. "Ludington? How in God's name will that help Jackie?"

"Just hear me out, Dan."

General Branch filled him in on the details, and twenty minutes later Colonel Branch walked out of the office and boarded a helicopter headed for the Lake Michigan port city of Ludington in Mason county on the northwest coast of Michigan.

July 9, The Saracens on the Move

Eventually, the disease burned itself out, and the army was healthy once more and ready to move again toward Iroquois. Finally, the Saracen encampment packed up and moved forward once again, with Jackie Branch lashed tightly atop the wooden cross affixed to a Peterbilt semi-truck at the head of the column. Over three thousand of the sick had been executed and left to rot in the summer sun. The sound of buzzing insects feeding on the flesh could be heard even a hundred yards in the distance.

Supreme General Al'Kalwi stood atop his Bradley Fighting Vehicle and looked out across the expanse of his army and trembled with anger. He'd amassed thirty-thousand men, and they'd been reduced to only seventeen thousand in just a week's time. He was beginning to regret his agreement with The Blind Man. But … he looked up at the sky above him, filled with Apache attack helicopters and fighter jets. What choice did he have? He hated kafirs! And the Blind Man was the infidel he hated the most. Sammy Thurmond was a close second.

He tried to put that out of his mind now. Before he could kill The Blind Man, he first had to defeat this Shadow Militia. At least now he had massive air support and added protection in the form of Jackie Branch, displayed on a cross for all to see. They would not dare attack him so long as she was there. In practical terms that meant all seventeen thousand of his army would make it safely to Iroquois City for the big battle. Seventeen thousand, along with heavy armor and air support would be more than enough to destroy the Shadow Militia army.

Sammy Thurmond had over-viewed the plan to him. All his army had to do was show up to draw out the Shadow Militia's airpower and armored forces, then The Blind Man would swoop in to destroy them all and all of Michigan would be under the Supreme General's command. He let go of his anger for a moment. It was a good start.

He studied the caravan. No more Humvees. Only two of the Strykers could be salvaged, and they'd lost two of their Abrams tanks to heat damage. He counted seven, eight-wheeled drive heavy duty trucks still operable as well as several dozen deuce and a halves. His lieutenants were already scouring the nearby truck stops and rest stops for semi-truck and trailer replacements. But, in the end, they still wouldn't have enough vehicles to haul their men and their equipment.

Sammy Thurmond had recommended moving his army in two stages. They were still over 150 miles from Iroquois, and that normally could have been travelled in a single day, but aerial recon had reported several overpasses had collapsed onto the freeway, and that would dictate time-consuming detours.

By the end of the first day they made it to Big Rapids, a city of just over 10,000 people before the day. There was a small airport there about two miles northwest of the city, and that's where the Saracen army made camp. Abdul had argued against it, but Sammy Thurmond's insistence, backed up by fighter jets and attack helicopters had persuaded him to go along.

July 10, Big Rapids,

JACKIE BRANCH SAT AT THE FOLDING TABLE WITH THE WHITE PLASTIC TOP inside the office room at the Roben-Hood Airport in Big Rapids. Her hands were duct-taped behind her, but at least she was off the cross for now. It had been like this for the past two days. At sundown she was taken off the cross to a tent or another secluded room where she would dine with Sammy Thurmond. The table was always set with a white linen table cloth, linen napkins, china and silver. On this particular evening there was a lit candle and, beside it on the table, was a red rose. Jackie had no idea where he'd gotten the flower, but she could smell it, so she knew it was real.

While Jackie was deep in thought, she heard the door knob turn. She looked up to see Sammy Thurmond walk in alone and close the door behind him. Two of his guards stationed themselves outside the door. They held the same M4A1 automatic carbines she frequently saw with Uncle Rodney's Shadow Militia details.

The Blind Man's assistant sat down in the chair opposite her and watched her silently from across the table. Jackie met his gaze and once again felt the evil there, but it was somehow softer than two days ago. Inside she admitted, *Why not? Even sociopaths can be chivalrous if they want to be?* She waited for him to speak.

"Would you like to eat now?"

Jackie hadn't had anything except water and some bread all day long, and she was famished. But she refused him.

"Not right now. I was hoping we could talk first. I always like a little before-dinner conversation."

The big man in front of her nodded slightly. "As you wish. Begin."

"A few days ago you told me that names were not necessary. Is that still the case?"

Sammy nodded. "Yes. When it changes, I will notify you."

Jackie smiled slightly. "You remind me a little of my husband."

Sammy Thurmond moved a bit in his chair. Jackie noticed this right away. Normally he remained coiled with mannequin -like stillness.

"I remember when I first met Dan in that cabin up in Wisconsin. He was so stoic. He rarely talked to me." She glanced out the window at the setting sun. There was no air conditioning or ventilation of any kind with the power out, but she had long ago acclimated to the severe heat. "Are all strong men so quiet?"

Sammy answered curtly. "No, not all. Some men talk too much."

"Well, sir, no one will ever accuse you of being a chatterbox."

Jackie turned back and met his gaze. His evil green eyes were almost smiling as he spoke. "Was that humor?"

Jackie laughed out loud. "Why, yes, I believe it was. A subtle brand of humor I think, but, humor, nonetheless."

She rubbed her wrists back and forth to get more circulation in her hands. "General Branch is similar to you as well."

Sammy Thurmond's eyes perked up. "Talk about General Rodney T. Branch."

Jackie smiled and nodded in acquiescence. "I could do that. A little anyways." And then she grew silent as she decided what to say and, more importantly, what not to say. She contemplated lying to him, but somehow sensed he would know. The last thing she wanted to do was anger this man. Despite his kindness, she knew he was still an unpredictable sociopath ... and the enemy.

"Uncle Rodney is a gentleman, like yourself, but he's also very blunt, sometimes to the point of being rude. He tells the truth, even when I don't want to hear it. He is strong – very strong. And the only way to defeat him is to kill him." She paused a moment, contemplating the irony of her next comment. "I always get the impression he's the kind of man who opens the door for ladies with one hand while shooting his enemies with the other. He's an enigma I suppose."

Her captor lifted his right leg and crossed it over his left thigh. His arms were still folded across his muscled chest. Jackie waited, and finally he spoke. "I like him." There was silence. "And I respect him."

Jackie smiled. "Me too. Tell me why please."

Now it was Sammy Thurmond's turn to decide what to say and what not to say. If he killed her, then it wouldn't matter how much he told her. And, quite frankly, how could she possibly get away.

"If I was General Branch I would have used a sniper to shoot you while on the cross, then resumed killing the Saracen army. Why hasn't your general killed you?"

Jackie's eyes grew serious. She had wondered about it herself. In fact, she'd wished for death by sniper more than once while hanging helplessly on the wooden cross. She wouldn't have blamed Uncle Rodney for ordering her death, nor would she have thought less of Donny Brewster for carrying out the task, but ... she couldn't help but wonder *Is my son watching me through his spotting scope? Does he have the crosshairs on me throughout the day?* She would not want her own son to do the job. It would be too much for him to live with – too high a price to pay with little chance of long-term healing.

"I think ... because, Uncle Rodney is plagued by his own humanity. His job is to kill, and he's very good at it. But ... when he kills, he kills with remorse, and only when it's necessary to defend innocence."

Sammy Thurmond uncrossed his legs. "But are you not innocent?"

The question jolted Jackie like a shock wave, rocking her head slightly back, and Sammy knew he'd hit onto something important. It was several seconds before she finally answered.

"No. Sin is familiar to me."

The big man leaned slightly forward. "Tell me your sin. I want to know."

For the life of her, Jackie couldn't begin to understand why this man would want to hear her confession, but he did.

"I would rather not, sir."

"Tell me your sin, and I will grant your wish."

Jackie squirmed back and forth in her chair. She didn't want to confess to this man. It had been different with Dan and Jeremy. They were worthy; they cared about her. But that knowledge was not safe with this man. He spoke again, this time with more firmness.

"Tell me your sin, and I will release you from your pain."

It would save the lives of her son, her daughter and maybe even her husband. So she obliged him.

"I cheated on my husband. I slept with another man. My husband is white, but my baby is black."

Sammy Thurmond nodded slightly and briskly got up from his chair without hesitation. He walked behind Jackie and pulled out a quick-opening knife with a 4-inch razor sharp blade. He quickly flipped it open and Jackie shuddered to herself *No, not with a knife. Not that way.* But she said nothing.

Sammy reached down behind her and cut away the duct tape on her wrists. He then walked over and rapped on the thick glass. He nodded to one of the guards and soon food was brought in. Jackie couldn't believe her eyes when she saw no less than ten appetizers being brought in by servants. It was an authentic Lebanese mezze. an arrangement of flat bread, hummus, olives, tahini, salad and yogurt. Jackie quickly prayed and then dug into the food. Sammy Thurmond watched her with interest, but that didn't deter her. She only paused long enough to thank him. After she'd finished her plate, more servants entered bearing a variety of fresh vegetables and eggs, all prepared authentically Lebanese. Five minutes after that came several courses of spiced lamb, sausages and then some fish.

Jackie slowed down but continued eating for as long as she could. Finally, she placed the last bit of flatbread on her plate and nodded to her captor.

"Thank you. How did you do this?"

Sammy didn't answer her question. He just stood up and walked behind her. He put new duct tape on her wrists, and, as he was bent down beside her whispered quietly into her ear. "Life is extremely precarious and unpredictable."

And then he stood up and motioned for the guards to enter.

CHAPTER 20

July 11, Donny Brewster's Frustration

DONNY BREWSTER, MASTER SNIPER, FOUND IT DIFFICULT TO watch the Saracen army without shooting them, but that's exactly what he and his sixty-five other snipers had been doing ever since Jackie had been captured. He was watching Jackie now from over one thousand yards away in his hidey-hole. He studied her face, and couldn't help but note how healthy she appeared compared to just a few days ago. There had been a marked improvement ever since The Blind Man's assistant had arrived.

Several days ago General Branch had ordered him to lay out a rescue plan, but so far he'd come up with nothing. The enhanced security, complete with surveillance cameras, miniature drones and extra guards had made it all but impossible.

Donny hated the drones. They showed up at the most inopportune times, and they could get a man killed lickety split. He'd already shot down two of them himself, but more just kept coming. But, by far, the hardest task for Donny had been explaining the situation to Jeremy Branch. As predicted, the boy wanted to rush in with guns blazing on a rescue mission, but Donny had forbid it. It was a suicide mission, and Donny saw absolutely no hope, under the present circumstances, of mounting a rescue. Inside he feared that Jackie Branch was already marked for death. As soon as the Saracen army reached Iroquois city, Jackie would no longer be of any use, and they were but a day's ride away.

Major Jackson and the bulk of the harassing force had been called back to Iroquois the day before, so it was just Donny and a few of his snipers who were left here to observe and report. Down below the Saracens were packing up, getting ready for the final leg of their journey, and then they would be within striking distance of Iroquois. Dan knew that Sheriff Leif was coordinating the defenses, but had no idea about the details. Personally, unless the general had a trick up his sleeve, he didn't think the town could be held against these odds. If Jackie hadn't been captured, it would've been a different story, but ... she had. And that was a game changer. And, Donny Brewster, the Shadow Militia's most potent soldier was impotent. His hands were tied.

Iroquois City

"GET THAT TRUCK LOADED UP! EVERYTHING HAS TO BE READY BY NIGHT-fall!" Sheriff Leif couldn't believe they were evacuating the town, that it had come to this. But, he'd agreed with General Branch, that it was the best they could do, and that no reasonable hope existed of successfully defending Iroquois City. Joe didn't like it, but they appeared to have no choice. As soon as nightfall set in they would sneak out of town and head north to rally with the other fighters from the surrounding counties of the North. Marge and his son had already left along with the rest of the outlying countryside.

For the past week Sheriff Leif had been traveling across the contiguous counties to call up their allies. To his surprise, most of them had agreed to rendezvous and stand with The Shadow Militia. Joe thought they were all crazy, but he kept his lack of faith to himself. In all, they would be able to assemble perhaps four thousand troops against the Saracen army of seventeen thousand, but they would not be able to prevail. In his God's-honest heart, Joe knew that.

Deep inside, he secretly hoped that Rodney Branch had a plan. In the last battle, he'd bet against Rodney and lost, but now ... it just seemed so hopeless. Even with the Abrams tank and Bradley fighting vehicles they'd salvaged from the last battle they were still outnumbered seventeen to one.

"Hey! Hurry it up there. Bobby, get those crates loaded up!"

And then he moved to the next truck and the next one after that. But he did so with a resolute doggedness, understanding that he'd placed his life and the entire town in the hands of a mad man. His only reassurance was the fact that he had no choice. His list of options was growing mightily thin. A sigh passed by his lips uncensored and he thought to himself, *Yes, Uncle Rodney was a mad man, but he was his mad man.*

Precarious and Unpredictable

THAT EVENING AFTER HER LUXURIOUS DINNER WITH SAMMY THURMOND, Jackie Branch was placed back upon the cross. Her new captor had been more kind to her than the supreme general, had given her good food, medical attention, a new set of clothes, and had even given her hard-soled hiking shoes to wear while on the cross. But, unfortunately, he had not yet made good on his promise to kill her so that Dan and his Militia Rangers and Donny Brewster and his snip-ers would be free to attack the Saracen army.

Jackie's arms were duct-taped to the wooden crossbeams in such a manner that allowed her to move them just enough to stimulate circulation. The Supreme General had simply lashed her on with rough hemp rope causing abrasions to her skin which had become infected and swollen. They were almost healed now thanks to the medical attention authorized by Sammy Thurmond.

Jackie listened now to the sounds of the Saracen encampment as they set up and dug in for the night on the eve of battle. They had just finished the call to prayer over the loudspeakers, and men were moving again, going about their ways with various tasks. As far as Jackie could tell, the Saracens were nothing more than an organized rabble, held together by the consistent cruelty of one man: Supreme General Abdul Al'Kalwi.

But there were unexpected benefits to hanging on the cross surrounded by seventeen thousand people who hated you. Jackie was ready to die, was, indeed, at peace with it, and just waiting for it to happen. She felt a bit like the tribulation saints in the book of Revelation. She was dying for a cause and dying with honor in a way that would make her family proud of her. In that she had no regret.

Simply to be on this cross, two large barn beams dove-tailed and spiked together, helped her to empathize with her own Lord, the one called Jesus Christ. It had forced her to take stock of her life, to get serious about her beliefs and to get her soul in order before her death. How many other people could say that? Most people in these violent and dangerous times died in a flash without the opportunity to clean up their spiritual house before they died. In that, she was lucky. Oddly enough, even though she hung on a cross, sure to die, surrounded by hate and rage, Jackie Branch was more at peace than at any other time in her life.

More importantly, Jackie, for the first time since cheating on her husband, felt forgiven. Not just forgiven by God, but forgiven by herself.

Jackie looked over at the surveillance camera staring down at her from the truck off to the left. She looked into it and smiled warmly.

A hundred yards away, sitting comfortably inside his command tent, Sammy Thurmond saw her smile and chuckled for the first time in decades. This woman, with her courage and forgiveness and peace, had opened a door inside him. It swung open on rusty hinges with a loud clank, and would never close again. It was, at the moment of her smile, when he decided to keep his promise. He would do it tonight while the rest of the camp slept in preparation for battle.

Yes, tonight he would set this brave woman's soul free.

CHAPTER 21

__Ludington Harbor__

CAPTAIN JOHN DARKFOOTE SAT IN HIS USUAL ROYAL BLUE nylon stadium chair on the foredeck of the SS Badger as he watched the sun rise to its peak in the eastern sky over the small city of Ludington. There was a Beretta 92FS strapped to his hip and a 308 caliber hunting rifle leaning against the bulkhead just a few feet away. From the outset of The Collapse, most of the locals had respected his self-proclaimed lordship of the Badger, but for those who had not ... he was a pretty good shot with the 308.

Every once in a while some wayward soul would wander into the parking lot of the terminal and make his way toward the Badger. Usually, one or two warning shots would change their mind. The third shot was always center of exposed mass. In the ten months since The Collapse, John had allowed only one person to come aboard.

A sudden sharp pain hit him in the chest like a knife and he doubled over in the chair. He kept his head down, clutching his ribs with his right hand until the pain subsided. It was coming more frequently now, and he had no idea why it was happening. Whatever it was, it couldn't be good. After a few seconds the pain subsided, and he sat back up straight in his chair.

The harbor in Ludington was located inland on the Pere Marquette Lake at the mouth of a river bearing the same name. The lake itself was over 500 acres, with a channel that ran past the city marina on the right and the Harbor View marina just beyond it. After that it was a straight shot past the lighthouse and into lake Michigan.

John Darkfoote wasn't the real captain of the SS Badger. That man had left his post within twenty-four hours of The Collapse along with the rest of the crew. The others had family, so they'd hurried home, and John hadn't seen them since. John was the maintenance man, and he'd secured the stern gate and hoisted the gangway on the ship two weeks after all hell broke loose. It had been a necessary task, and one that undoubtedly saved his life.

Those first few months had been extremely dangerous. On the day of The Collapse, the harbor had been a peaceful playland for the rich and famous, filled with yachts, parties and a congeniality where everyone knew it was safe to rest or play. John recalled that on the day after The Collapse many of the boats had left the harbor. The stupid ones, not willing or able to fathom the scope and terribleness of a world without electricity, returned to their homes in large cities like Chicago, Milwaukee and Detroit, only to fall prey to a brave new world void of police and public services. They quickly died. Others stayed in port and died of cold and starvation over the winter. Several had tried to storm the SS Badger late in the fall, desperate, cold, but well armed. John had shot them dead and left the bodies in the gravel parking lot as a welcome mat to anyone else with similar designs.

John wasn't an ordinary maintenance man. He'd served first in the army as a ground pounder, then sailed in the engineering department on ocean-going freighters in the merchant marine for twenty years. Then he'd taken the job on the Badger thinking he'd put down some roots, maybe raise a family, perpetuate his lineage. He'd thought wrong. There was no family. No woman. No kids. Not a single friend. Sure, there had been work friends on board, but ... that was different.

During his past ten years on the ship. he'd learned everything he could about the

Badger. He'd read all the manuals, watched the rest of the crew and asked incessant questions about the many mundane details of their job. He could fire up the Four Foster-Wheeler "D - type" coal-fired boilers, he could even start the engines. Each of the two Skinner Unaflow four-cylinder steam engines were rated at 3,500 horsepower at 125 RPMs. At the time of The Collapse, the SS Badger had been the only coal-fired steamship in operation in the United States. The SS Badger was a car ferry over four hundred feet long and almost sixty feet wide. Before The Collapse it ferried people, cars, trucks, motorcycles and RVs back and forth from Ludington, Michigan to Manitowoc, Wisconsin. The trip was sixty miles and took four hours each way.

"Here's your coffee, John."

The woman handed him the steaming glass mug and John accepted it readily. He blew off the steam and took a sip.

"You make good coffee, kid."

The woman was beautiful, in her late twenties, with long, auburn hair with natural waves that draped lazily over her bare shoulders. Her legs were long, slender and tan. She was wearing shorts and a sleeveless flowered-print blouse. If there had been anyone else on board, they'd have noticed how much younger she was than John. They'd notice her beauty and juxtaposed it to the plain, weathered face of her sixty-year-old partner. But they'd also have picked up on the chemistry and natural connection that seemed to flow between the two.

John had saved her life, and, despite the age difference and the disparity in attractiveness, she'd fallen in love with him. She hadn't meant to; it had just ... happened ... in the most natural way with no pomp or lead-up, not even the hint of romance. One minute they'd been friends, and in the next heartbeat they'd become lovers. And for the first time in his life, John Darkfoote had someone to talk to.

"We're running out of coffee, John."

John nodded. "I know. Coffee, sugar, rice, flour. We're running out of everything I suppose." He hesitated. "Well, we still have plenty of fish." He chuckled to himself.

She sat down in the wooden deck chair beside him. She lifted up her left leg and draped it over his right thigh. The softness of her skin made his thigh tingle.

"I suppose you want me to rub your feet again."

Eileen smiled. "You don't think I keep you around simply for your good looks and charming personality do you?"

John chuckled out loud.

"I suppose not." He took off her lime-green flip-flop and began to run his hand up and down her arch the way she liked it.

"So what are we going to do when we run out of food, John? I'm starting to get worried."

John didn't answer right away. In reality, he had no plan, no answer, but he didn't want to tell her that. In truth, John loved her too, and didn't want her to worry.

"I have a plan. We have forty state rooms that aren't being used. We could rent them out to summer tourists. We could advertise online, and we'll be rich in no time. Don't worry your pretty little head about it."

Eileen smiled at his humor. There was no such thing as tourism anymore. People didn't take vacations. There was no rest from work as work was the only buffer between starvation and the wolves at the door. She recalled the night most of the condos surrounding the harbor had burned down. It had been in December when people had started heating with wood. But the condos weren't designed for that. Without proper chimneys and ventilation and a fire department the condos had burned to the ground in one night. John and Eileen had watched all through the night as the heat from one condo ignited the roof and walls of the building beside it. Like dominoes they had all fallen as the strong wind fanned the flames of cold winter destruction. John and Eileen had the harbor pretty much to themselves now.

"Why did you save me, John? You could have let that man kill me, and no one would have known. I simply would have died and faded away."

John remembered the evening last fall when he'd heard the woman's scream. He'd watched as Eileen had run from the city marina to the parking lot beside the SS Badger. Then the man had knocked her to the ground unconscious and began to remove her clothing.

Usually John took the more forgiving center-of-mass shot, but this time, for some reason, he placed the crosshairs on the back of the man's head, level with the brain stem and slowly pressed the trigger to the rear. By the time Eileen had awakened, she'd been redressed, cleaned up and her head wound attended to.

John Darkfoote knew nothing of Eileen's past. He just assumed she had something shameful she wished to hide or something very painful she didn't want to discuss. If the former, then they were kindred spirits, because John had plenty of shame and had no right to judge. If the latter, then it was none of his business unless she volunteered it, and he wished her no pain in the recollection.

From a practical standpoint none of it mattered. She was a beautiful, young, intelligent woman who was healthy to boot who enjoyed his company and loved him. Before The Collapse society would have frowned on their union, but now ... all bets were off. Society was destroyed, so people were left with two things: things that worked and things that didn't.

John and Eileen worked.

John Darkfoote leaned his head back, closed his eyes and took in the full force of the sun. "I know. You're a nuisance and a pain in the butt. I should have let you die, but... I don't know. I've always been a sucker for redheads, so I decided not to hold your youth, beauty and lack of experience against you."

The young woman placed her hand on his thigh and smiled through perfect white teeth. She squeezed and John immediately came alive below decks.

"Do you have any regrets, John."

He turned his head and looked her in the eyes. They were bright green and deep, like the waters of Lake Michigan.

"I regret we didn't meet sooner."

The woman let her leg drop down to the deck and moved to her knees between John's legs. She reached up with her slender fingers and cradled his weathered face while moving her lips up to his own.

"In all honesty, John. If we'd met much sooner, what I'm about to do to you right now would have been a felony."

John and Eileen slid down to the deck, basking in the July sunshine, oblivious their tenuous paradise was about to be shattered.

"WHAT ARE THEY DOING DOWN THERE, SIR?"

Colonel Dan Branch looked away and laughed out loud. "What does it look like they're doing! Move us away for a minute and give them a little privacy. Land us over there in that gravel parking lot."

Five minutes later the Huey's rotors had stopped spinning and all six of Dan's security detail had set up defensive positions around the parking lot in front of the SS Badger. Both the man and the woman were dressed and armed now, but neither pointed a weapon in their direction. Dan Branch, standing just outside the Huey, keyed the microphone before speaking. "Attention SS Badger, this is Colonel Dan Branch of the Michigan Shadow Militia, requesting permission to come aboard."

Five minutes later Dan stood in the sunlit passenger lounge beside Eileen and Captain John Darkfoote.

North of Iroquois City

RODNEY BRANCH LOOKED OUT AT THE RAG-TAG COLLECTION OF HUMANIty spread out before him in the state forest. Just a year ago they'd all been farmers, factory workers, school bus drivers, stay-at-home moms, with maybe a few small businessmen, doctors, lawyers and accountants thrown in just for good measure. Even at four thousand strong, they were no match for the seventeen thousand Saracens headed their way.

But it wasn't the army of Christian-hating Saracens that bothered Rodney the most; it was the fighter jets and attack helicopters flying combat air patrol overhead that seemed to seal their fate. Sheriff Leif was a good man, but he still didn't grasp the full scope of what was going on here. Rodney knew that Joe Leif resented the fact that he wouldn't throw all the Shadow Militia's forces, including airpower, into this one fight, but … if he did that … it would be over. He'd be playing into the Blind Man's hands, effectively giving him control of all North America.

And Rodney couldn't do that. This battle they were about to fight was just the beginning, just the precursor, the warm-up to an entire war that had to happen before all this madness and death would end. Rodney, sitting alone inside the cab of his F-250 pickup truck, sagged his head. But, in his heart, he knew that madness never ended, that senseless death never ceased. Any student of human history could see that. Because life was a constant struggle of good fighting evil, and that's where Rodney came in. He liked to think he was the good guy, but … sometimes he wondered. Sometimes he doubted his abilities and his motives and his … his own goodness.

So far very little had gone right in their battle against the Supreme General. Jackie Branch had killed thousands, but then … if only she hadn't been caught. But it was senseless to regret the fate of things, actions of others, events outside his control. And right now so much seemed beyond Rodney's influence.

He knew what the Blind Man was doing, and he both hated and respected him for it. The Blind Man, however evil and twisted, was a worthy opponent. And he seemed to hold most of the cards. Jared Thompson's forces were stretched thin by all the guerilla fighting going on in the South, the West, and the Midwest, so he'd recruited the Saracens to do his dirty work.

Rodney was well aware of his own weaknesses, and, apparently, so was the Blind Man. Jared Thompson knew that Rodney would stand and protect his home, even if it meant defeat and certain death. But Rodney knew his own heart, knew that he could never abandon his friends and his neighbors, just as knew that he couldn't allow Jackie to die all alone on that wooden cross.

Tactically speaking, he should have kept attacking the Saracens even though it would have resulted in her death. If he had, they undoubtedly could have killed thousands more of the approaching army. Strictly from a tactical standpoint, he should have moved ahead of the Saracens as they pressed north. He should have burned every town along the US 131 corridor, thereby denying them the ability to scavenge for food and supplies. That would have been the sound, military decision.

As with all men, Uncle Rodney's greatest strength was also his greatest weakness.

Rodney recalled his decision to seek out help from God and winced. Prayer was something people did when all hope was gone, when their plans failed; it was an act of desperation. But, truth be known, Rodney was indeed desperate.

General Branch looked at the setting sun through his windshield. In the next few days people were going to die. He knew that. But, what he didn't know was that Dan Branch was now in Ludington, and that he'd secured the SS Badger.

A Soul Set Free

It was night in the Saracen encampment. Tomorrow was the battle, so Supreme General Abdul Al'Kalwi had ordered sleep for his rowdy warriors. As Jackie hung on the cross from her arms, fading in and out of restless sleep, she could sense the difference. She didn't know the area south of Iroquois simply because she had never been here before. But she sensed they were getting closer. All day long, last-minute preparations had been made all around her. People scurried like mice, loading trucks, cleaning rifles, packing bags, all the things that happened before men went into battle.

Jackie raised her head with a great deal of effort and looked up into the darkened sky. Ever since The Day when the power had gone out, the nights had seemed so much darker. She could see the stars with more clarity. There was the Big Dipper straight ahead of her. She followed the two pointer stars in the end of the cup until she found Polaris, the North Star. She stared into it and smiled. She thought about baby Donna, pictured her beautiful face, then regretted that she'd left her for the glories of war, which had turned out to be so incredibly inglorious after all was said and done.

If only she'd run for the woods on the day she'd been caught and placed on this cross. They might have shot her in the back; but she might have made it to the tree line. She could have been with her daughter right now, with her husband.

Jackie looked back down at the ground below her. Regrets were so … unproductive.

Lost in her own thoughts, Jackie didn't notice the man climbing up the side of the semi-trailer to where her cross was lashed. But she heard the soft footsteps behind her, and a wave of adrenaline surged through every inch of her body. When she felt the man's breath on her neck, her muscles tightened. Then he reached around and placed the steel blade against her throat. Her first thought was *No! Not the knife. I wanted a bullet to the brain. So much easier, so much quicker.*

"Good evening, Ms. Branch."

The voice was a deadly whisper, a guttural spew. She shivered in the July heat and humidity, taking a few seconds to master her fear before answering.

"Good evening, sir."

She knew who it was, who it could only be.

"Do you know why I'm here?"

Jackie looked back up at the stars. She followed the line formed by joining the pointer stars with Polaris and found Cassiopeia and thought *How beautiful. There are worse ways to die.* At least here she had the backdrop of God and all His creation.

"You are a man of honor. You've come to fulfill your promise."

Sammy Thurmond laughed softly.

"Yes. You know me better than The Blind Man."

And then he paused. "I'm going to miss you Jackie." The knife pressed a little harder against her throat. "I so much enjoyed our dinners and our talks."

Jackie, looking up at the Big Dipper, forced herself to answer softly. "Yes, you made an otherwise terrifying experience, memorable and thought-provoking."

For a moment Sammy was silent, then she felt the sharp blade move away from her throat and then down her shoulder and the length of her arm.

"There is a small group of your snipers to your immediate left just inside the tree line about five hundred yards. I don't know where your husband is."

The knife blade cut easily through the duct tape on her right arm. It immediately fell to her side limp. It took a few seconds for the blood to return. Within just a few moments the blade had also freed her left arm and then her waist followed quickly by her feet.

"You may turn around now."

Slowly, Jackie turned. Sammy's face was hidden in the shadows of a hooded Islamic robe. He placed the knife back in its sheath on his waist. Even in the starlight his eyes looked cold and green.

"You're letting me go?"

Sammy's face remained stone-cold as he spoke. "Take this back to General Branch. Do not open it. Place it only in his hands."

Jackie reached out her right hand. Sammy Thurmond placed a plastic tube in her palm. It was about six inches long and an inch in diameter, and made of white, PVC pipe.

Jackie's fingers wrapped around the pipe. When she touched Sammy's skin, she was surprised to feel warmth emanating from his hand. She lingered there for a moment.

"I owe you my life."

"You owe me nothing. I make my own choices."

Jackie seemed confused by the coldness in his voice. It was out of place. This was a tender, intimate moment, but then she realized … it was the tenderness of assassins.

"Thank you, sir."

He then handed her a hooded sweatshirt and a small knapsack. She quickly put on the shirt and donned the pack.

"You have to hurry."

Jackie started to walk past him, but then stopped. She slowly reached out and embraced him. She felt his body tense and knew that the knife was already back in his hand on instinct alone. It was the reflex action of a highly trained killer.

She was reminded of the first time she'd hugged Uncle Rodney, and suddenly realized the two men were cut from the same basic cloth, however, different they'd turned out to be.

She moved back to arm's length, gave him one last look and turned to leave. But she was stopped dead in her tracks with his words.

"My name is Sammy."

From six feet away, Jackie turned and smiled.

"Thank you … Sammy."

Then she turned, made her way down the semi-trailer and filtered out into the camp before making her way to the tree line.

Sammy Thurmond reached up with both hands and moved the hood back to reveal his face. Then he watched until she was out of sight.

CHAPTER 22

July 12, Ludington Harbor

"I CAN'T BELIEVE I'M LETTING YOU DO THIS TO MY SHIP."
Dan Branch smiled at Captain John Darkfoote as the two men walked along the pier toward the lighthouse. As always, Dan's security detail was spread out all around him, some in plain view while others were hidden. They could hear the sound of semi-trucks backing into the cargo deck under the recently raised stern gate of the SS Badger off in the distance. So far ten trucks had arrived with more on the way. The Badger was being loaded for war.

"The plan has better than a fifty-fifty chance of success. These days those are pretty good odds." He hesitated for just a moment. "Besides, I'm sure Uncle Rodney has a back-up plan in case this doesn't work."

John Darkfoote ran his fingers through his thinning gray hair from front to back before answering. "Actually, I was kind of hoping for better odds than that."

Dan shrugged. "This is war, captain. Odds are we'll all be dead by this time next week anyway. The best we can hope for is to die with honor." Dan hesitated, looked down for a moment and then back up again.

"What's wrong, Dan?"

"Nothing. I was just thinking about my wife."

John looked off the pier into the lake. The water was dark blue today. "Where is she? Home?"

Dan looked out at the water now too, but his gaze was different than John's. It seemed to reach out further, all the way to the Wisconsin shoreline.

"Last I knew she was tied to a wooden cross being paraded in front of seventeen thousand blood-thirsty jihadis."

Captain Darkfoote didn't know how to respond. Normally he would assume the statement was some kind of sick joke, but Colonel Branch didn't seem like a joker, and his somber tone and sad eyes spoke louder than his words.

"You're serious. I can see that." He stopped walking for a moment. Dan followed suit, then started up again as soon as John moved forward. "That has got to be the first time in human history anyone has made that exact comment."

A flock of sea gulls flew overhead. Back before The Day birds like this would flutter over the hundreds of tourists, looking for free hand-outs. But those days were past, and now even the birds had to work for a living.

"Not really. Humanity has always been a cruel story. Good always fighting against evil. When evil wins then innocent people suffer and die. When good wins, there's a short-lived respite and a few days of peace. But the one constant has always been that evil never gives up, and it just keeps coming back at you generation after generation. No rest. Peace is a fleeting illusion – like smoke that rises up and is quickly blown out of reach."

John felt the wind on his face. It was hot but felt good nonetheless. "Well, Colonel, it was peaceful before you got here."

Dan forced a brief smile. He recalled the sight of two people making love on the foredeck of the Badger upon their arrival. "Yeah. Sorry about that." Dan looked out to the lake and then back to watch his feet as they fell to the cement … heel, toe … heel, toe … heel, toe – over and over again like some ghastly military machine that never gave in. "How long does it take to steam from here to St. Ignace?"

John Darkfoote thought for a moment. "Maybe twelve hours, give or take."

Dan stopped walking. He turned and faced John. "I need precision. You have to arrive at exactly the right moment or a lot of the wrong people will die."

Captain Darkfoote met Dan's stare. He reached up and stroked his chin nervously. "If that's the case then I recommend we make the trip in two stages. We could do the lion's share of the trip over night, maybe anchor at Beaver Island and then do a quick run in from the west. It's a lot more predictable that way, and less things can go wrong."

Dan thought a moment and then nodded his agreement. "That's a good plan. Thanks."

They both stood there on the pier, clumsily waiting for the other to speak again. Finally, Captain Darkfoote gave in. "So, Colonel, when are you going to tell me what's in all those trucks we're loading onto the Badger?"

Dan smiled and looked down at the cement. "It's a surprise captain – a really big surprise, and I don't want to spoil it for you."

John's eyes narrowed. "And you say I'll be handsomely compensated for my efforts?"

John nodded. "I'll work it out with the general. If we pull this off you'll be a hero and you can pretty much write your own ticket." Dan paused. "Of course, there is a risk – maybe a big risk. It all depends on how our enemies respond. I have to be honest with you, John. This isn't a milk run. You're not moving cars from Ludington to Manitowoc anymore."

They both turned and started walking back to the SS Badger. "All right then. As soon as you're loaded, then we can get underway. I'll need six of your men to help me sail though, and a few mechanics to help me get her ready. You promised me that."

Dan nodded. "Of course. Not a problem."

When the two men reached the parking lot, they shook hands and parted. Dan boarded the Huey, and John went back to his ship to prepare for departure. The captain felt uneasy about the lack of details to this plan, but it also excited him. Finally, after ten months of sitting around, he was doing something useful. But he couldn't help but wonder about the danger. In the end he concluded it was better to die in glorious battle in a just cause than to starve to death in port.

Seven Miles South of Iroquois City

A YEAR AGO JEREMY BRANCH WOULD BE CRYING, BUT NOW … HE COULDN'T bring himself to do it. He had killed so many people. True, they were bad people, and, as Uncle Rodney was quick to remind him "They needed killing." But, still … he was just a boy of sixteen. And now, they had his mother captive. He knew they were torturing her and … God knows what else. He'd seen her several times through his scope. He wanted to rescue her, but he didn't know how. He had the courage, but not the know-how. He'd spoken to Donny about it, and was not encouraged. Not even Donny knew how to save her.

So they waited and they watched … helplessly from the trees.

Jeremy was alone right now, taking a break from his listening post position. He was allowed a fifteen-minute break every four hours and his shift was twelve hours long. Every day he watched. Every day he did nothing to help his mother. The inactivity was killing him inside. He hadn't seen his father in days now. Donny said he was on a special mission for General Branch, but didn't know the details. Jeremy just wanted to go back home to Wisconsin, to the way things used to be before he'd killed those men. But … deep in his heart … he knew that was impossible. Even if God turned back the hands of time, Jeremy Branch had been changed forever. He was a man now, forever longing to return to boyhood.

He looked up and stared at the tree in front of him. It was an oak, solid, unmovable, unrelenting to all but the very strongest of winds. It was one of the hardest woods in the forest, never bending and seldom breaking. Somehow, over time and action, Jeremy Branch had transformed from a willow to an oak. And he didn't entirely like it.

A twig snapped fifty yards into the woods and Jeremy jumped up, raising his M4 to his shoulder facing the threat. It was the same carbine his Uncle Rodney had given him. The sound was between his location and the camp. He peered through the night vision scope and saw nothing but trees. The sound was still coming though, so he followed it with the scope. Finally, a human form stepped out from behind a tree and Jeremy rested the crosshairs onto the center of the intruder's body. Jeremy moved his finger down until it rested lightly on the trigger. The form was now only twenty yards away and moving toward him. Following protocol, Jeremy issued the challenge. "Halt!" The form stopped immediately. Jeremy issued the password challenge. "Orion's belt!"

There was a short silence. Jeremy's finger took up slack in the trigger.

"Jeremy? Honey, is that you?"

Upon hearing Jackie's voice, Jeremy lowered his carbine.

"Mom?"

The two rushed forward and embraced. All the tears the young man had been holding back now rushed out. His M4 rested lightly on the one-point sling between them as Jackie caressed his head. It was dirty, filled with black dirt and crushed pieces of dead bark, but she didn't care.

"It's okay, son. I'm fine. You'll be okay too. Go ahead and let it out."

And Jackie cried too, both of them together on the outskirts of the Saracen encampment. For a full five minutes they hugged quietly except for their tender whimpers. Then the silence was suddenly broken by a man working his way toward them in the darkness. Jackie and Jeremy quickly separated. Jeremy crouched down behind an oak tree in a defensive posture and issued the challenge. "Orion's Belt!"

Donny Brewster stopped walking and confirmed the challenge. "Maple tree."

When Donny stepped out into the small clearing, he saw the two and sucked in a surprised gasp of air.

"What?"

He rushed forward and gave Jackie a brief hug.

"Hurry! Follow me. We have to get out the word!"

All three of them moved quickly and quietly through the woods. In a matter of minutes General Branch was given the good news, and a new plan was formed.

July 13,the Saracen Camp

"DO YOU DENY IT WAS YOU WHO FREED THE PRISONER?"

"Yes, Supreme General! Of course I do. It was not me. And I have witnesses to prove it!"

Abdul's second in command was barely standing in front of him, quivering in fear before the power of his master, the Supreme General.

"Where were you last night?"

The lieutenant answered quickly and with forced and mock confidence. "I was with my women, sir. I was honoring them with my pleasure."

Abdul smiled inside, but remained stern. They were both standing in front of the white, plastic folding table with the laptop computer sitting on top of it. Sammy Thurmond stood quietly off to the side in a parade-rest stance of non-interference. The Supreme General reached down and pressed a button. The surveillance video began to play silently. The video was a little grainy, but clear enough for some measure of detail.

The lieutenant watched silently as a man walked up behind the infidel woman on the cross and whispered to her. Then he watched as she was set free with a knife. The man's face was shrouded in the shadows of a hooded robe. The woman turned around to face the man who had freed her. She was handed a small piece of white plastic pipe followed by a sweatshirt and a knapsack. The woman quickly donned first the shirt, and then the pack. She started to walk away but then stopped and hugged the man who had just cut her loose. She turned and walked away again, then stopped once more to turn around. The camera angle was from the back. Then she walked out of the picture. The man in the hooded robe stood there watching after her. And then, the lieutenant's pulse quickened in his chest as the man in the video reached up and pulled the hood back revealing his face.

The second in command gasped out loud as he saw a perfect replication of his own face. All the strength in his legs left him as he fell down to his knees before the Supreme General.

Abdul reached down and pressed a button to pause the video.

"Do you still deny the evidence?"

The man on his knees started to cry and saliva ran freely from his mouth and onto the bare ground. He tried to talk, but could manage only a series of blubbers.

The Supreme General unsheathed his curved sword, and, with one swift, perfect stroke, the man's head flopped off and onto the ground. Blood gushed up for a few seconds, then lessened and stopped as the man's body collapsed beside the head.

"You were a good man, a good servant of Mohammed, peace be upon him. So I grant you mercy."

Then he motioned with his hand to the soldiers standing around him. "Take his body and bury it along with all those living in his household. Spare none."

Sammy Thurmond watched without passion as the man's body was dragged away. But he was smiling inside, lauding the praises of Jackie's escape, and the miracle of Photoshop.

July 13, Boyne City, Michigan

GENERAL RODNEY BRANCH STOOD IN THE CENTER OF THE BARN SUR-rounded by thirty men. Some were standing, but the ones near the front were seated in the straw on the barn floor. Despite the heat and humidity, the barn doors were closed and guarded. When Rodney spoke, he did so in hushed tones, as if reading aloud from some top secret document.

"The Saracens have entered Iroquois City, and are presently camped there. We await their next move."

Rodney's words hung in the thickness of the July humidity for all to see and hear. They were solemn words. Sheriff Leif held his breath without realizing it. It was anticipated, as it turns out, even necessary, but …

"From this point out, our main mission is to lead the Saracen army up from Iroquois all the way to Mackinaw City. While we lead them, the snipers and the Militia Rangers will operate in small independent groups of no more than four-man fire teams. Under no circumstances are you to form up into a cohesive force. The Saracens enjoy total air superiority which includes infrared imaging technology. If you bunch up they'll kill you in a heartbeat. The F-18s and the Apache gunships now flying air cover are capable of destroying our entire force in a matter of minutes."

General Branch paused to let it sink in. "Our force of four thousand soldiers is all that stands between the Saracens and the straits of Mackinaw. Over the next few days we'll be attacking them with a series of uncoordinated hit-and-run movements." He looked out at the thirty or so leaders. He knew what they were thinking. *This is crazy. This is hopeless. We're all going to die.*

He needed them to be brave. He needed them to instill boldness in the ones they commanded. That had always been the job of the best field commanders. He needed to give them hope and blind courage.

"The Shadow Militia will destroy the F-18s as well as every last Apache attack helicopter. But first, you must lead them to Mackinaw City. If you get them there, we can do the rest." He paused trying to make eye contact with as many as possible. "You have to kill as many of them as you can, while keeping your own casualties to a minimum."

General Branch paced a few steps to his right, turned and then moved back to the left. "Are there any questions?"

Rodney watched as a few men looked at each other with uncertainty. Then he saw a hand rise near the back.

"Yes, you in the back."

General Branch was surprised to see Sergeant Donny Brewster step out from behind a group of three lieutenants. Last he knew the sergeant was still watching the Saracen army at Iroquois City.

"General, I'm just a non-com, so I want to make sure I got this right."

The general smiled.

"You want small groups of four people to attack a superior force of seventeen thousand soldiers while they're being protected by F-18 fighter jets and Apache attack helicopters, and we're not allowed to die in the process?"

General Branch nodded.

"And that's what I like about you, general. You keep things simple."

There was a chorus of hushed laughter as Donny sat back down and the general smiled again.

"I would think, Sergeant Brewster, that a Marine Corps sniper, backed up by flank protection on three sides is more than a match for seventeen thousand Saracens."

Donny Brewster jumped up and yelled as loud as he could "Oorah! You got that right, general! When do we start!?"

Up near the front of the crowd, Sheriff Leif shook his head in disbelief. Rodney Branch was a megalomaniac. Donny Brewster was crazy. And they were all going to die.

CHAPTER 23

July 13, Iroquois City

S UPREME GENERAL ABDUL AL'KALWI STOOD AT THE TOP OF
the old red brick courthouse inside the clock tower looking out across the
town of Iroquois City. He'd won the battle without firing a shot, and his enemies
had fled before him. They were terrified of him and his army, and wisely so. The
men beside him were setting up the speakers just in time to broadcast the next
call to prayer.

But Abdul was not happy with the easy victory. Earlier in the campaign he'd welcomed the addition of airpower to his army, but now ... the F-18s and Apache helicopters flying overhead had become less of a comfort and more of a thorn in his side. The
Supreme General now understood that he was but a tool, a detail in the larger plan of
the Blind Man, who was simply an infidel with more powerful toys than Abdul.

Supreme General Abdul Al'Kalwi was being used. And he didn't like it.
Unfortunately, he had no idea how to fix it. The F-18s and the attack helicopters had
the ability to kill everyone in his army with but a nod from his adversary, the Blind
Man. And now, he'd been forced to kill yet another of his lieutenants. That may have
been a mistake. He couldn't get the nagging question out of his mind: *Why had his
trusted lieutenant betrayed him? Why had someone so smart pulled back the hood and
shown his face to the surveillance camera when he knew full well it was there?* But
Abdul had been given no choice. The others had seen the video, and if he hadn't killed
him the word of his weakness would have spread across the camp.

Yes, he'd done the right thing, but ... he'd had no choice. And that's what he didn't
like. Everything was being forced upon him by the Blind Man and his sociopathic
pet, who was even now looking at him from the courtyard. More than anything Abdul
wanted to kill the Blind Man. But ... *you can't kill what you can't see.*

That thought lingered and the irony was not lost on him. But there was no denying
the fact of how he felt. He felt cornered, trapped and used. *Yes,* he thought to himself
*,The first chance I get I will kill the Blind Man and his crazy assistant. By myself it is
impossible, but with the help of Allah it can be done.*

But first ... the Shadow Militia. He must catch them and kill them ... to the last man,
woman and child.

Reunited

"YOU SHOULD HAVE LET THEM KILL ME, UNCLE RODNEY, OR MAYBE EVEN
killed me yourself. Now, they have overrun the town and they're still coming.
You could have been killing them all this time but ..."

General Branch raised his hand to silence her and baby Donna reached out and
grabbed his finger. She placed the big callused digit in her mouth and began to bite
down. She'd been teething in a major way.

"No, Jackie. I made a mistake and you almost paid for it with your life. And the rest
of us ... well, we could all die because of that one mistake. Such is the way of war.
When generals err – people die."

"You put too much on yourself, Uncle Rodney. I insisted, and wouldn't have accepted a 'no' answer from you. Don't forget that I was a very eager volunteer."

Jackie was wearing blue jeans and a gray t-shirt and they both were sitting on the ground with their backs against the same huge oak tree in the small township park. Baby Donna struggled to get loose now, and Uncle Rodney set her down on the bare ground.

"Perhaps. But the truth is I made a mistake. I didn't know myself as well as I thought I did. I thought I could allow you to die but I could not. The Blind Man knew that. He knows me better than I know myself."

Rodney lowered his head and sighed. "I have to do better or we're all dead and the world is enslaved."

Jackie laughed out loud. She covered her mouth with her hand in an effort to stifle herself, but couldn't manage it. "You men are all alike! Dan is the same way, putting the weight of the whole world on his shoulders, pretending that everything rises and falls on the actions of one man." She paused. "It's absurd! You realize that don't you?"

Uncle Rodney leaned his head back against the solidity of the giant oak tree, gaining strength and resolve from its ancient bark. The tree had seen Ottawa Indians and a world without telephones and computers, and in its wood lingered a wisdom and a point of view that had wrongly passed from all knowledge.

"I'm not responsible for what other men do. I'm only responsible for what I do. You're right. I should have killed you, but I didn't. The Blind Man saw the weakest part of my character and he used it for his own nefarious gain."

Jackie laughed out loud again. "Did you just say 'nefarious?' I can't believe you said that. It sounds like something from a cheap detective novel."

She reached over and gave him a hug. Rodney accepted it but still looked around to make sure no one was looking. Immediately, Jackie was reminded of Sammy. She reached into the knapsack beside her and pulled out the white plastic pipe that she'd been given on her release.

"This is for you." And then she told him the whole story of her escape. Uncle Rodney questioned her relentlessly about Sammy Thurmond, and then she was questioned again and again by Special Agent Jeff Arnett until she could no longer stand it. All the while, she just wanted to be reunited with her husband. But … at least she was alive and baby Donna was in her arms.

The SS Badger Leaves Port

Captain John Darkfoote stood on the bridge of the SS Badger. They had just left Ludington Harbor and were now making their way up Lake Michigan. After seeing all the cargo inside the big trucks, he now understood what was expected of him … and it chilled his soul.

He had a skeleton crew of eight people on board, and they were dead reckoning without GPS or radar or any other modern navigational aids. He was reminded of the mariners of old who'd sailed these waters a hundred and fifty years before his birth. At least they'd had help from the many lighthouses that dotted the western coastline of Michigan. But those were dark now, extinguished, perhaps for all time.

He would reach Beaver Island before dawn with just enough time to anchor and spend the day making preparations for his final run into the Mackinaw straits.

John's mind was lost now in thought and introspection. He had so many regrets, but at least now, at the very end of his life, he was willing to admit it. His few months with Eileen, his ecstasy with her, the extreme happiness of opening up to a woman and joining souls had helped him realize how foolish he'd been to choose a life of loneliness.

If he had the chance …

But he didn't. His was a life heralded with waypoints of regret and nothing could change that now. John Darkfoote had missed the important things in life, traded them all away for a life of stoic sadness.

Just then Eileen entered the dimly lit wheelhouse, and shuffled over to John in the near dark. She liked it up here at night, with only the green glow of the instruments. She hugged him from behind. "It's so beautiful out there in the darkness, isn't it, John."

John smiled and turned to take her in his arms. This young, beautiful woman was the pinnacle of his life, the one waypoint without regret. And he was about to set another.

"Would you like to steer the boat, my dear?"

Eileen smiled and they both looked out into the darkness, facing it head on together.

Cicadas in the Trees

IT WAS DARK NOW, AND JACKIE LAY PEACEFULLY IN HER HUSBAND'S ARMS on the eve of battle. How many more times would she be forced to contemplate his death? Once again she was reminded of Sammy Thurmond … of his ominous words "Life is extremely precarious and unpredictable."

But tonight it was a little different because she understood how Dan felt. She knew it wasn't all glory now, that it wasn't fun, that he was going out there and fighting not for his own glory, but for the lives and freedom of his family. She would do her part, but never again would she long for the glory of battle. That was an illusion that most people discovered only at the time of their passing.

"Dan? Are you asleep?"

She spoke softly so as not to disturb him if he was sleeping. She heard him chuckle softly. "Not anymore, dear."

She sighed. "Sorry honey."

"That's okay. They'll be plenty of time to sleep after I die."

She squeezed the hair on his chest and he winced. "Don't say that, Dan! Not to-night!"

"No problem. Just ease up on the chest hair will you?"

Jackie smiled in the darkness.

"So what were you thinking about, Dan?"

"I was asleep. I wasn't thinking about anything."

"So you have a flat brain wave? You can't do that, Dan. I'm your wife. I own you. Anything you think and anything you feel belongs to me."

Dan smiled. "And I feel lucky to be owned by such a benevolent master." He paused. "I just wish she'd let me get some more sleep. Especially on the eve of the battle of all time."

Jackie's fingers interlaced with his chest hair and squeezed again. He grimaced but remained silent.

"There is no such thing as the battle of all time, because there will always be another battle. The next battle will always be bigger, more paramount, more pressing than the previous." She hesitated. "Does it ever end, Dan?"

For a few seconds there was no answer. Dan listened to the cicadas high in the trees; their constant buzzing was the backdrop for all of northern Michigan during the month of July.

"No, honey. It never ends." He hesitated before going on. "But … it does pause, and we live for those pauses, those brief respites from pain and suffering. And, it's during the pause that we live most of our lives. During the pause we meet a woman we love. We marry. During the pause we have children and we love them." Jackie listened intently. She'd never heard him talk like this before." It's the pause that we live for, and the pause that we … die for."

Jackie hadn't told him all that had gone on during her capture, but … Dan knew. He sensed the change in her. The pain. She chose to leave it behind her in the past, and Dan was wise enough and compassionate enough to allow her that luxury. In his mind, Jackie, his wife, was a hero.

"Will Uncle Rodney's plan work?"

Dan sighed and pulled her closer. "I don't know. It's too complicated for my tastes. His too I think. If one thing goes wrong then …" He stopped in mid-sentence. "It doesn't matter. I'm with you right now. Let's just enjoy the pause and contemplate our new baby. What are we going to name him?"

Jackie raised her head up off his shoulder. Her black hair cascaded down onto his chest. "Him?"

Dan smiled. "Of course. You're going to give me a son. Didn't I mention that?"

"But what if it's a girl?"

Dan reached over with his right hand and tenderly stroked her long, black hair. "If she's a girl, well, then let's just hope she's not as flat-out, butt-ugly as you are."

Immediately she rolled over on top of him and started pounding his chest with her fists. Dan laughed and grabbed her by the arms and reversed positions until he was on top of her, his body between her legs. And then … he came down on her. She stopped struggling, grabbed the short blonde hair on the back of his head and moved up to kiss him with all the force of passion she could muster.

And, in that pause, with life growing inside her, on the eve of battle, while the cicadas buzzed their incessant backdrop, the two of them made wild, passionate love.

CHAPTER 24

July 14, The Deadly Prelude

THE SNIPERS FIRED THEIR FIRST VOLLEYS AT DAWN OF THE next day. Sergeant Donny Brewster took his mission seriously like no other, and hundreds were killed by his marksmen just north of Iroquois City. Then in the afternoon, further down the road, Major Larry Jackson attacked with more grenade launchers killing several hundred more. Undoubtedly he could have inflicted more damage if he hadn't run out of grenades.

That first day was a lot like the battle for Lexington-Concord on April 19th, 1775 when the British regulars were cut to ribbons on the road back to Boston. This time the airpower did little to stop the Militia Rangers as they seldom traveled in groups larger than two. They had taken General Branch's orders seriously, and this rendered the Supreme General's airpower almost useless to counterattack.

The Blind Man realized that every ounce of fuel burned, every missile launched and every bullet fired, was irreplaceable, at least for the next couple years until he could pacify and restore order to the country. Only then would he be able to build the country's manufacturing capability back to some semblance of its original power.

So the Supreme General was forced to endure the lone wolf attacks and suffer losses. On the second day, just north of Mancelona, the Saracen army discovered that small sections of the road north had been removed by diggers during the night, forcing the Saracen army to make costly detours. Many times those detours funneled the army into natural killing zones in the form of cedar swamps from which the snipers and rangers could pick a target at their leisure and shoot for much longer periods of time before moving on. The Supreme General learned quickly that sending his soldiers into the cedar swamp was a sure ticket to death. Another thousand Saracen soldiers died on the second day.

But that still left an army of almost fifteen thousand strong, and, at the present rate, well over ten thousand would reach the straits of Mackinaw, and that was more than enough to defeat the Shadow Militia in open combat.

On the third day, the Saracen army unexpectedly cut east over to the I 75 corridor, which was a larger highway with two lanes going south and two lanes going north. The Supreme General transported his men using all four lanes and made it all the way north of Indian River by nightfall. They were now only fifteen miles from the Mackinaw Bridge. The Supreme General sent two of the F-18s to monitor the bridge and cut off any mass escape from the lower peninsula to the Upper Peninsula. Because of this, the Shadow Militia and all four thousand soldiers were trapped at Mackinaw City.

It suddenly appeared to everyone that the Shadow Militia had been beaten and would soon make their last stand with their backs to the Straits of Mackinaw.

July 17, Shadow Militia Air Force

COLONEL MACPHERSON STOOD ON THE PAVED RUNWAY IN NORTHEASTERN Michigan and took stock of the Shadow Militia Air Force.

"How many aircraft in total?"

Major Fannemere was following to the left and slightly abreast of the colonel as he moved down the runway from plane to plane in their last-minute inspection.

"We have twenty-six planes and twenty-six pilots, sir."

Each pilot was standing in front of his aircraft at the position of attention. Colonel

MacPherson had spent the better part of the past week traveling across the state and enlisting as many pilots as possible. It had been difficult to recruit volunteers when he had to tell them they'd be flying against F-18 fighters and Apache attack helicopters.

Colonel MacPherson stopped in front of a pilot, and stood at attention as the man looked straight ahead and rendered his best salute. Mac returned the salute with dignity and grace.

"At ease, lieutenant. What's your name?"

All the volunteers had been given temporary commissions in the Shadow Militia Air Force and had some type of gold or silver bars on their collars. This man was old, and Mac was immediately reminded of Lieutenant Harold Steffens who'd fought and died so valiantly in the Battle for Iroquois just a few months earlier.

"Lieutenant Chet Hanson, sir."

"I appreciate your willingness to fly against such heavy odds. You do realize what you'll be up against, don't you?"

The old man looked the colonel square in the eyes before replying. "Yer damn right I do."

Colonel MacPherson smiled slightly. "And you're not afraid?"

The grisly old pilot turned his head and spit off to one side. "Are you kiddin' me, Colonel? When I flew in Nam I was too young-n-dumb to be afraid. But by time my third marriage rolled around I'd learned a lot about fear." He thought a moment. "Hell yes I'm afraid! I'm skeered shitless!"

The colonel laughed softly to himself. He had to remember to tell that one to General Branch, provided they were both still alive twenty-four hours from now.

"Me too, lieutenant. Me too. But I know you'll fight with honor up there tomorrow, and there's a slight chance you might even live to brag about it."

The old lieutenant snapped to attention before responding. "I'll take those odds, sir." Then he saluted crisply and Colonel MacPherson moved on down the runway. For just a moment he allowed himself to believe these men had a fighting chance. They had the heart; they had the attitude; they just didn't have the right planes and training.

After the full inspection, Mac sauntered off the field and into the metal-roofed Quonset hut to radio the general. For better or for worse, tomorrow they would fly – they would fly and they would die.

The Blind Man

THE BLIND MAN STARED UP AT THE SCREEN ON THE WALL OF HIS PRIVATE quarters. There were problems all over the country: they'd just been attacked in the mountains of Idaho and Boise was surrounded. It would fall by this time tomorrow provided he didn't send much-needed airpower and reinforcements. In the South it was even worse. Guerilla fighters from the Smoky Mountains were coming down almost every night and wreaking havoc on his supply chain. That was fairly common, but something had changed in the last twenty-four hours. Everything had intensified as if someone had thrown a switch. And then it occurred to him. General Branch and the Shadow Militia really were in control of all the rebel forces nation-wide, and they were using these coordinated attacks to prevent him from sending reinforcements to the Saracen army in Northern Michigan.

Jared swore under his breath. He'd always wanted a worthy adversary, but … this was becoming a bit too much of a challenge. All along he'd been careful not to underestimate General Branch, but, despite that, the old man had still managed to out-maneuver him at nearly every turn. On the one hand, he didn't want to give up. He wanted to defeat Rodney T. Branch in battle. On the other hand, he wanted to survive as well.

Jared put his dark sunglasses back on and reached down to press the intercom button. "Michael, get in here right now!"

A few seconds later a man opened the door and walked in carrying a clipboard. "Yes, sir."

Jared hated the clipboard and the little man. He didn't like things written down, and Sammy Thurmond had always been able to memorize everything. He hated pretending to be blind. In a moment of fury he threw his sun glasses down onto the desk and yelled at the man. "Get me General Holland on the line from Southern Command!"

The man just stood there in shock, not moving, not saying anything. Jared walked up to him to within ten inches of his face. He looked straight into the man's blue eyes and snarled. "Didn't you hear me? I said get General Holland on the video screen now!"

The man finally moved. "Yes, sir. Right away, sir." And then he backed toward the door, still struggling to understand what had just happened. He thought to himself *He was blind, but now he can see?* It was more than he could wrap his mind around, so he just backed out of the room as quickly as possible.

Once the other man was gone, Jared picked up his Sat phone and was soon talking to Sammy Thurmond.

"Mr. Thurmond, what is the situation there?"

As always, his assistant was brief and precise. "The Shadow Militia has retreated to Mackinaw City and by morning they will be totally surrounded. The Supreme General is attacking at dawn. The Shadow Militia is outnumbered four to one."

Jared nodded, happy that at least one area of the country was going well. "Is there any sign of the Shadow Militia Air Force?"

"No, sir."

Jared thought for a moment. There had been no sign of them in the South or in the West either. They had to be in the North. "Stay in direct contact with our air base in Ohio. Make sure the Shadow Militia's airpower is completely destroyed as soon as they enter the field of battle."

There was an uncharacteristic moment of silence, and Jared noticed it. But it was just a fleeting moment. "Yes, sir. It will be done."

And then Jared added. "And Mr. Thurmond, as soon as this is accomplished, I'd like you to return to me as quickly as possible. Keep me updated."

"Yes, sir."

The line went dead, and Sammy Thurmond stared down at the sat phone. Something was different. Did The Blind Man know about Jackie? Then he answered his own question. No, he did not. Why? Because he was still alive. But the phone call had left him more uneasy than before. He'd never sensed so much tension and uncertainty in The Blind man's voice. Something was different, and … different was always dangerous.

The Saracen Camp Prepares

THE SUPREME GENERAL LOOKED OUT OVER THE THOUSANDS OF CAMP FIRES in the darkness. They had finally arrived at Mackinaw City and had set up a perimeter just a mile outside the city limits. Before darkness had set in Abdul had seen the splendor of the Mackinaw Bridge. The locals called it Mighty Mac, and it was huge with its two towers rising up over five hundred feet as it separated Lake Huron from Lake Michigan. It was the third largest suspension bridge in North America, spanning five miles from shore to shore and joining Michigan's upper and lower peninsulas.

Abdul had fallen in love with the engineering marvel as soon as he'd seen it, and had vowed to make Mackinaw City the capitol of his new empire. He would live in the shadow of this giant, and it would allow him to travel to the northern half of his kingdom with ease.

His commanders had just left his quarters, and were busily preparing for the final battle in the morning. It would be an all-out attack from three sides, driving the infidels into the lake. Abdul wondered why they called it a lake. It was so huge. He would rename it the Sea of the Great Prophet, and he would drive General Branch and his army into the Straits of Mackinaw.

And then, he would turn his sights on The Blind Man.

Mackinaw Bridge, Setting the Charges

STAFF SERGEANT ADAM CERVANTES WATCHED AS HIS DETAIL RAN THE DET cord connecting each satchel of C4 together in a series. Adam had always been a bit of a pyromaniac and det cord fascinated him. Det cord was simply a high-speed fuse that exploded, rather than burned, The cord was suitable for detonating high explosives, and the velocity of detonation was sufficient to use it for synchronizing multiple charges to detonate almost simultaneously. The cord exploded at the velocity of four miles per second, and one of Adam's favorite things to do was use it to take down trees for firewood back on the farm. Of course, that had been illegal, but … well … he didn't live on the farm anymore, and the ATF was defunct, so … no blood – no foul. It was military-grade explosive and he'd been assured the C4 would do the job, provided he set it up in the proper configuration. But then again, he'd never blown up the Mackinaw Bridge before, so, it was all theory to him.

He stepped out from under the southern end of the bridge and looked up at the huge suspension cables and towers. The bridge was huge, and he wasn't so sure he could do it. Despite his pyromaniacal tendencies, he felt ambivalent about blowing it up. It was so beautiful; it had been here for so many years, decades, in fact, since 1957. It would be a shame to watch it crash down into the water. But ... it was better than having to fight fifteen-thousand psychotic Saracens to the death.

Adam had been fighting alongside the Militia Rangers in the last battle, and before that he'd been helping Donny Brewster train the new soldiers. They were a good force, as good as they could be in so short a time, but ... still ... fifteen thousand Saracens backed up by F-18s and Apaches was a big bite to swallow, and he hoped they didn't choke on it. He looked up into the sky. Sometimes he could hear the F-18s and the Apaches up there. They stayed up high, letting their radar and their thermal imaging capabilities do the surveillance job for them. If they came down low, they'd be vulnerable to Stinger missiles or other MANPAD-launched rockets, which the general seemed to have an ample supply of, but, so long as they stayed up high, their electronic countermeasures would be able to defeat the Stingers with ease. Adam knew that each of the four Hornets flying CAP above them carried one-hundred flares, rendering the Stinger missiles useless.

But, in the end, Adam knew it would all come down to General Rodney T. Branch. What did the old man have up his sleeve this time? It seemed hopeless.

But the thing that bothered Adam the most was the pilots flying CAP above them. He just didn't understand how so many American military pilots could turn traitor. It bothered him to his core. How was The Blind Man able to recruit once-patriotic Americans to slaughter fellow citizens? He would probably never know the answer to that question. He took one last look up into the star-studded summer night and then walked back underneath the bridge to continue his work of destruction.

CHAPTER 25

July 18, The Final Battle Begins

THE SUPREME GENERAL STOOD ATOP HIS BRADLEY FIGHTING vehicle surveying the expanse of his army. The sun was just rising over the Lake Huron shoreline as he looked on. He knew in his heart that by sundown it would be over, and General Rodney Branch would be dead. He was about to launch the advance into town when his aid yelled up to him.

" Sir! There is urgent news from the advance scouts!"

Abdul made his way down off the Bradley and was soon standing beside the man. "What is it?"

The man looked fearful. He always hated approaching the Supreme General as people sometimes lost their heads when giving him bad news. "They have spotted twelve tanks just inside the city limits, sir. They are cleverly hidden, and could not be seen from the air."

Abdul thought for a moment before issuing orders. *Where had they come from? They weren't there last night.* It didn't matter when he had the means to destroy them.

"Order the Apaches to attack. Then report back to me."

CAPTAIN VAN KRAI HAD LEFT THE AIR FORCE OF THE NETHERLANDS shortly after The Collapse to join The Blind Man here in America. Almost all the pilots in The Blind Man's air force were non-American, but all spoke English. In the case of the Apaches flying ground support over Mackinaw City, four were from the Netherlands, three from the United Kingdom, three from Japan and two from Egypt.

Captain Van Krai was a dedicated pilot who loved the Apache, and The Blind Man was the only opportunity he'd been offered to fly, so he'd seized it as soon as it was made to him. Besides, he had no other skills, no family, and no prospects and no other realistic means of survival.

The AH-64 he flew today could support numerous roles, but today he was loaded with sixteen Hellfire missiles, whose primary mission was to attack and destroy enemy tanks and armor. He quickly confirmed receipt of target coordinates and led his six Apaches down to attack while the other six were held in reserve at a higher altitude.

"Saracen Command, this is Apache One. We are commencing our run."

They attacked in parallel, firing at all twelve tanks almost simultaneously. He was surprised to see his tank seem to vaporize when hit by the Hellfire missile. This wasn't typical hit results.

"Apache One reports direct hit. All units report in."

Captain Van Krai listened as all units reported direct hits.

"Apache Two direct hit, target destroyed."

"Apache Three direct hit, target destroyed."

"Apache Four direct hit, target destroyed."

"Apache Five direct hit, target destroyed."

"Apache Six direct hit. But ... Captain. It didn't look right."

Captain Van Krai had the same nagging feeling that something wasn't right. "Apaches four, five and six go in low to assess damage. Apaches Two and Three switch to infrared imaging and circle for human threats."

The three Apache helicopters banked down and toward the town while the other three posted slightly higher to perform an overwatch function.

"Apache One, this is Apache Four. All traces of enemy armor gone. It's like they were never there."

That's when the first of six Stinger missiles were launched from hidden ground positions. Captain Van Krai watched in horror as three of his attack helicopters were struck and crashed in smoke and flames to the ground.

"Break off! Break off!"

But the warning came too late, and soon all six Apaches were gushing smoke and losing altitude.

"What the hell is going on?!"

"Evasive action!"

"More missiles incoming!"

Suddenly, the once-disciplined and professional radio commands were reduced to a barrage of frenzied chatter.

"I'm hit!"

"Bank left!"

"Damn! Damn!"

Three more of the Apaches went down in flames, as the other two picked up speed and fled the field of battle toward the south of Mackinaw City.

Down below, Supreme General Abdul Al'Kalwi looked on in horror as nine of his twelve Apaches crashed to the ground and continued to burn.

BACK IN THE CITY, HIDDEN INSIDE ONE-HUNDRED AND FIFTY-YEAR-OLD concrete and brick buildings, all nine of the two-man Stinger teams took advantage of the confusion and packed up and hurriedly bugged out back to the waterfront. The twelve tanks they'd built the day before out of two-by-fours and thin plywood had been destroyed. Once there, they boarded the rubber rafts and floated out to the Straits of Mackinaw headed for their next attack points.

IN AN OLD LIGHTHOUSE, JUST WEST OF ST. IGNACE OFF HIGHWAY US 2, General Branch and Colonel MacPherson looked to the south-east with smiles. Mac was the first to speak.

"Now that's a sight for sore eyes."

Rodney smiled. "Yep. Don't ya just love it when a plan comes together?"

Colonel MacPherson laughed out loud. "General, I just love it when you talk country and western."

Rodney looked over at him. "Well, my refined old friend, you can take the boy out of the country, but you can't take the country out of the boy."

Mac nodded. "How many more Stingers do we have here?"

Rodney watched as the smoke filtered up from across the straits. "Ebay had them a special, and we bought us a whole shit-load."

Colonel MacPherson knew the truth. The vast majority of Shadow Militia supplies had come from the US military or through foreign sources on the black market. The average citizen would be surprised to learn that every time weapons systems like the Stinger were upgraded, the older platforms had to be disposed of. With the right connections, a fair amount of money, and the proper paperwork, just about anything was possible.

Colonel MacPherson looked up high in the sky in search of the F-18s. They were mere dots above the straits, dispersed and flying a standard air patrol pattern.

"But what about the Hornets?"

Rodney took a sip of his cold coffee from the plastic, olive drab canteen he was holding. He reached up to his breast pocket for the cigarette that wasn't there.

"We have to deal with them, but … we don't have to shoot them down, at least not all of them." He was silent a moment and Mac just waited. "I have a plan."

Saracen HQ

THE SUPREME GENERAL WAS SCREAMING INTO THE SATPHONE AT THE Blind Man. "I need more helicopters. He shot them all down!"

The Blind Man was also furious, but he controlled his voice. It emitted a deadly calm that caused Abdul to stop talking. "That's right, Supreme General." He spat the words out like bile. "I gave you twelve state-of-the-art attack helicopters, and you promptly crashed nine of them to the ground through your own lack of military prowess." There was a pause. "I will not waste any more of my irreplaceable military hardware on the likes of you."

Abdul was so filled with rage that he could do nothing but sputter incoherently. The Blind Man waited for him to silence before going on. "General Holland will now be taking over tactical control of the battle. He will issue commands to you through Mr. Thurmond."

There was an indecisive silence.

"But what if I kill Mr. Thurmond and proceed on my own?"

Jared laughed softly into the satphone. "Then I will send my bombers to Mackinaw City and reduce your army to blood, bones, and rubble."

A chill ran through Abdul's bones. "It, it was just … a hypothetical question." Oh, how he hated The Blind Man.

Jared Thompson disconnected the call, then made another to General Holland who then conferred with Sammy Thurmond. An hour later a full barrage of artillery, armor and mortar fire opened up on Mackinaw City. By noon the once beautiful, historic town had been reduced to smoke and rubble. Not a single stone was left upon another.

The Supreme General looked on in disgust. His new capitol city of Mackinaw was now a tomb. An hour later his entire army marched through the rubble-strewn streets in unopposed conquest. Not a single person, alive or dead, could be found. Only then did the Supreme General realize the Shadow Militia had left the night before, abandoning the town and assuring their survival to fight another day. *How had they done it without the Hornets detecting it?*

The SS Badger

"IF YOU CAN DROP US OFF NEAR WILDERNESS STATE PARK NEAR THE south-western entrance to the straits, then we can move to our assigned locations in the dinghies before setting up our strike teams." Dan Branch had flown to Beaver Island in his Huey to meet up with the SS Badger before she left her anchorage for the final run through the Mackinaw Straits.

Captain John Darkfoote looked out into the early afternoon sky. It was clear now, but a bank of rain clouds was moving in from the northwest. These storms could move in fast off the Great Lakes.

"No problem. Just make sure you leave that Zodiac behind for me and the crew. When it all hits the fan I don't want to be standing in front of it. I want a fast ride out of harm's way."

Colonel Dan Branch smiled, then quickly frowned again as the Badger rolled gently on the small swells of Lake Michigan. "Roger that, Captain. I want the same thing."

The two of them had become friends in the past few days of loading and outfitting the Badger for this mission.

"You going to be okay, Dan? You look a little green around the gills."

Dan smiled weakly. "Let's just say I haven't quite got my sea legs yet."

John laughed. "No kidding. I didn't realize you were such a landlubber."

Dan rushed over to the metal trash can and heaved into it. He waited a second for the nausea to pass, then wiped his mouth with a rag he had stuffed in his waistband for just such a purpose. Captain Darkfoote laughed out loud this time, but Dan was quick to snarl back at him.

They had already moved fifteen hundred troops from Sturgeon Bay up to Brevort in the Upper Peninsula during the night. Most of them hadn't enjoyed the Great Lake's swells either and had puked for half the ride. John had found it amusing. Apparently another fifteen hundred soldiers had been moved on the Lake Huron side using the Mackinaw Island Ferries. One thousand had remained in the lower peninsula, spread out strategically dispersed to be used during another phase of the plan. But General Branch had moved them all from Mackinaw City, thus denying the Supreme General his coveted final battle where all the odds were in his favor.

"You're really enjoying this, aren't you, Captain."

John took his hands off the wheel long enough to shrug his shoulders and lift his hands up. "Not really. Can't say I enjoy the smell of your vomit all that much."

Dan followed the edge of the bridge bulkhead over to the door. "I think I'll go out on deck and check on the last-minute preparations for departure."

The captain smiled and turned back to face the east as Dan exited the bridge. Soon he was alone again. The ship felt good beneath his feet, and he quickly realized he'd missed his calling. He spoke out loud to the emptiness. "Better late than never I suppose."

And then his thoughts turned to the attack plan that Colonel Branch had laid out for him. It was a good plan, but... he wasn't fond of the outcome, plus, it had some weaknesses. It was just too complicated with plenty of room for error. And the whole idea of just 'trusting' General Branch to take the F-18s and Apache helicopters out of the equation seemed like a large leap of faith to him.

He knew a way to eliminate the weakness, but it came with a sacrifice. And then there was the question of Eileen. How would he get her to cooperate? At any rate, he had a few more hours to think about it before making a final decision. He continued his coastwise run off the lower Peninsula shoreline on his way north to Wilderness State Park near the south-western entrance to the straits.

A half hour later ten dinghies shoved away from the Badger and headed for their predetermined strike points. On their way east from Beaver Island, they'd already dropped off ten other dinghies, each with two-man strike teams on St Helena Island. They would fan out along the southern shore of the straits as well as set up on some of the tiny islands off the coastline.

He saw Eileen making her way up to the foredeck on her way to the bridge. He'd tried to persuade her to leave with Dan, but had come up short on that one The woman was as stubborn as a mule, and, since she was incredibly young, strong and beautiful, she usually got her way.

Without warning, the pain in his chest struck again, this time with the force of a knife-edged sledgehammer. His body doubled over, and he stayed there, hoping she wouldn't see him this way. Just as the bridge door opened be straightened up with a frown on his face.

She moved toward him with concern.

"You okay, honey?"

John forced a smile. "Of course I am." And then he added. "Now that my favorite person in the world is here. Eileen blushed. She lowered her eyes and reached out for an embrace. "Thanks honey."

John hugged her back and the pain subsided.

"Honey, would you like to steer the ship? I have something I have to take care of." Eileen's face lit up. "Sure honey!"

"Just keep steering the present heading of 350. But let me know if you see an iceberg." She raised her eyebrows at his last remark and smiled. She loved this old man and his wry and unpredictable humor.

"Icebergs. Right. I will."

John had only one preparation left to make. He gave her one last squeeze before moving from the bridge to the foredeck. He took the can of red paint and brush as he lowered himself over the bow in a bosun's chair. This was to be the crowning achievement of his life.

CHAPTER 26

The Mighty Mac

THE SUPREME GENERAL STOOD ATOP HIS BRADLEY LOOKING out at the five-mile expanse of the Mackinaw Bridge. There were whitecaps on both the Lake Michigan and Lake Huron sides of the straits and a storm was definitely coming in from the west.

He still had no idea how General Branch had moved four thousand troops to the opposite shore without using the bridge and being spotted by the F-18s on CAP above them. Once he captured the general, that was the first of many questions he would ask the man. This arrogant infidel had been tormenting him from just out of arm's reach for weeks now, striking at him from hidden positions, never coming out to fight fair, and Abdul was thirsting for General Branch's blood. In the end he would get his satisfaction and his pound of flesh.

"This end of the bridge is wired with explosives, sir. They were getting ready to blow it but the bombardment must have interrupted their work."

Abdul thought for a moment. It angered him. He already considered the magnificent bridge to be his property, part of his new kingdom, and General Branch had tried to destroy it. It also angered him that The Blind Man had been right about bombarding the town prior to attack.

"Dismantle the explosives and make it safe for us to cross the bridge. I want to be on the other side and killing kafirs before dark."

Sammy Thurmond stood about twenty feet off to the left. listening, taking it all in.

He looked across the straits of Mackinaw to the Upper Peninsula. *Something didn't feel right. why hadn't General Branch blown the bridge?*

His self-preservation instincts kicked in, and he determined himself to tread carefully from here on out.

MANPADS on Parade

CAPTAIN DANNY BRIEL WAS SITTING IN THE BUSHES AT THE BASE OF THE lighthouse off Round Island just south of Mackinaw Island. His rowboat with a small outboard motor was beached just a few yards away and covered with brush. He didn't know how much those F-18s could see, but he wasn't about to take any chances either.

He looked down at the metal case which housed the Stinger missile. He'd been told this was the latest Stinger configuration, and would be able to better penetrate the electronic counter-warfare flares of the F-18 Hornets. Not all the MANPAD teams had this latest version, but all were capable of taking down a Hornet, provided the jet was low and occupied on something else and not able to adequately respond to multiple threats.

In their briefing, he'd been told these Hornet pilots were from other countries, primarily Kuwait, Malaysia and Spain. That relieved Captain Briel to his core, as he had no desire to fire upon an American military pilot.

At last night's briefing, he learned all about the Hornet he was now trying to shoot down. Developed by McDonnell Douglas the F/A-18 Hornet is a twin-engine supersonic, all-weather carrier-capable multirole combat jet, designed as both a fighter and attack aircraft. It was designed primarily for use by the United States Navy and Marine Corps.

The F/A-18 has a top speed of 1,190 mph, and can carry a wide variety of bombs and missiles, including air-to-air and air-to-ground, supplemented by the 20 mm M61 Vulcan cannon. As a general rule, Danny tried to avoid being hit by missiles and cannons.

The F-18s rely on electronics countermeasures in the form of flare dispensers which, either manually or automatically shoot out flares of magnesium which burn hotter than the afterburners of a jet engine. These decoy the missile away from the jet. But Danny had the newest generation of the FIM-92 Stinger which utilized a dual infrared and ultraviolet seeker head, which allows for a redundant tracking solution, effectively negating the impact of modern decoy flares. That's what Danny had been told, and, although he didn't understand all the technical jargon, he did know how to aim and fire the Stinger missile, and that was good enough for his purposes.

Danny unpacked the Stinger and began to prepare for launch. And then … he waited and watched.

The Bait

LIEUTENANT CHET HANSON FLEW AS CLOSE TO THE DECK AS HE COULD get without crashing. His single-engine Cessna wasn't exactly state of the art, well, actually, it barely flew. Before every launch he prayed for an updraft, and at every landing he prayed for no cross winds. Chet knew he was flying today on little more than a wing and a prayer.

Engine problems had delayed him, and the other twenty-five planes had already launched so he was now struggling to catch up to the formation. His engine sputtered, forcing him to throttle back and reduce airspeed. Better not push it. He continued to fall behind the other planes, but still he pressed on.

At the final briefing they were told the truth of the situation and the unlikelihood of their survival. Despite that, all twenty-six pilots had chosen to fly into battle. Chet was old, and his wife had died over the winter, so he had little to live for. The decision had been easy for him. But he wondered about the others. So many of them were young, yet ... they were flying and fighting, knowing their young lives could be cut short.

He found himself wondering about their motives. Was it misguided glory? Was it bravery? He didn't know but expected each man flew for his own private purpose. But one thing he did know: save himself, each pilot was a hero, sacrificing himself for strangers, giving their lives so that others could live on and fight for freedom. For him, he wasn't brave. He knew that. He just wanted to end a life not worth living and be rejoined with his wife in the hereafter. There was no bravery in that. And that's when Chet realized he was a true romantic. And it made him feel good. Would his wife be proud of him, or would she scold him for his stupidity?

He shrugged in the tiny cockpit. "In a few hours, I'll be able to ask her myself."

Crossing the Rubicon

THE SUPREME GENERAL WATCHED PROUDLY AS HIS ARMY OF SARACEN SOL-diers lined up at the southern approaches to the Mighty Mac. The explosives had been removed, and several thousand of his men were already on the bridge and moving slowly to the north. The F-18 Hornet fighter-attack aircraft were high overhead. Yesterday there were only two Hornets, but today their number had increased to four. The Hornets overhead would notify them of any danger, while the remaining Apache attack helicopters stayed over Mackinaw City ready to attack any threat to the crossing army. Abdul had already prayed to Allah and his great prophet, peace be upon him, for a safe passage to the Upper Peninsula.

The joy in his heart threatened to spill out, but he determined to control himself for just a while longer. He couldn't wait to get to the other side and destroy the Shadow Militia.

A Yooper Lighthouse

"HERE THEY COME, GENERAL."

Rodney smiled as Colonel MacPherson relinquished use of the telescope inside the lighthouse. Almost six miles off he could see the army of Saracens marching onto the bridge like lemmings. In better times he would have called in an airstrike, but ...all he had right now was a force of twenty-six prop planes of dubious abilities. He had a nagging sense of guilt about his own plan. It called for too much potential sacrifice, with none of it his own. But ... if the Saracen army made it to the other side, much innocent blood would be shed, and many lives would be lost.

All through his military career he'd learned the importance of keeping his battle plan simple. The more complex the plan, the more things could go wrong. But now ... his options and equipment were severely limited, so he was forced to patch together forces from all over the chess board. And now ... the pieces were lined up like dominoes, but if one failed to fall, the others would not follow.

Rodney had taken much of his battle plan straight from history. The harassing of the Saracen forces from mid-Michigan all the way to Mackinaw City had been the classic guerilla warfare tactic used by the colonial militias on April 19th, 1775 on the road back to Boston right after the slaughter on the green at Lexington.

Then, he'd withdrawn his forces in the night, saving them from certain destruction, similar to what General Washington had done against the British General Howe in the Battle of Long Island. It was also reminiscent of the British miracle at Dunkirk.

Most painful of all to Rodney were the planes attacking from the east. This tactic came straight from the annals of the Battle of Midway. It could potentially end in great loss of life. And he'd ordered it.

The Stinger missile attacks were derived from the Afghan freedom fighters in the war to repel the Soviet Union from Afghanistan.

But the SS Badger ... that was new. And now, as all generals throughout time are forced to do, all General Branch could do was wait.

When Hornets Attack

"SARACEN HQ THIS HORNET LEADER, OVER." THE PILOT SPOKE WITH A Spanish accent and then waited for confirmation.

"This is Saracen HQ, go ahead, Hornet Leader."

"Saracen HQ we have radar contact twenty-five miles due east of your location. Large formation following the nap of the earth. Approximately fifteen aircraft, moving 255 miles per hour. What are your orders?"

"This is Saracen HQ, Wait one, over."

Commander Rubio Gonzales waited impatiently overhead as the radio operator consulted with command. He'd seen the nine Apaches go down in flames just a few hours ago, and his fighter pilot instincts were on full alert but also itching for a fight. Nonetheless, he wasn't anxious to go down on the deck with short-range surface to air missiles known to be operating in the area.

"Hornet Leader, this is Saracen HQ. You are ordered to send two Hornets to engage and destroy enemy aircraft. The remaining two will stay on CAP over the straits. More planes will join you shortly, over."

"Roger that, Saracen HQ."

He thought for a moment. He enjoyed flying the Hornet, but he was not a hero. He decided to send the other flight of two Hornets to the deck, keeping his wingman close in high cover. He would wait for reinforcements before entering the fray. Commander Gonzales preferred overwhelming odds and sure victory to going down in flames by a missile fired by a mere Michigan farmer.

Blind Man HQ

Jared Thompson listened to the radio chatter from the Hornets flying over the Straits of Mackinaw with delight. General Branch had finally committed his air power to the fight, and now he could utterly destroy them. It would be a severe blow to the rebel forces, and without the constant threat of retaliation by air, Jared would be free to operate more aggressively throughout the continental US.

He listened intently as General Holland ordered twelve F-16 Fighter aircraft to scramble from the airfield in Ohio to intercept and destroy the Shadow Militia Air Force. At this point he was near giddy, and had abandoned all pretense of blindness. Those around him still hadn't adapted to it, but he didn't care. The ruse of blindness had given him an edge for many years, but now, it was no longer needed. It felt good to throw off the nuisance and use his eyesight with wild abandon. Jared had wanted to send more fighters, but General Holland had advised him not to do so. There were other attacks still raging in the South where they would be needed, and the general assured him twelve F-16s along with the four Hornets would be more than a match to ambush and destroy the approaching Shadow Militia.

Jared forced himself to sit down in the recliner in front of the big screen before him. He picked up the decanter of brandy and poured a small amount. The alcohol burned all the way down. And now, all he had to do was watch and listen to the destruction of the Shadow Militia and his arch nemesis, General Rodney T. Branch.

Jared took another small sip. He so much hoped the general could be taken alive. He wanted to meet the man.

Outnumbered

"Hornet Leader we are closing on formation. We should have visual contact momentarily."

The lead F-18 and his wingman were at four thousand feet and closing. They would attack out of the setting sun from a superior altitude. They would undoubtedly fire the first shots and score overwhelming hits. The enemy formation would break apart and a dogfight would ensue. This would slow down the enemy planes long enough for the F-16s to attack from the South. Then the most unexpected thing happened.

"Hornet Leader this is Hornet Three. Radar now shows twenty-five enemy aircraft, over."

Commander Rubio Gonzales, still flying CAP high above the Straits of Mackinaw didn't respond immediately.

"Hornet Leader, this is Hornet Three. We are outnumbered twelve to one. We could use a little help down here, over."

"Hornet Leader, this is Saracen HQ. You are ordered to remain above the bridge in CAP. Hornet Three and Four proceed to attack the enemy formation, over."

Commander Gonzales looked around him and spoke on his intercom to his Weapons Systems Officer. "Keep your eyes peeled. We don't want to be caught off guard."

His WSO responded immediately. "We should go down and help them. They need us."

Rubio hesitated. He had to follow orders. Then it occurred to him. He'd been ordered to stay over the straits. No one said he couldn't circle back to the east and be closer to the fight. He slowly banked to the south and then east. His wingman stayed tight on his tail.

The SS Badger

"I WILL NOT LEAVE YOU!"

Eileen looked at him with imploring eyes. John Darkfoote was both incensed at her stubbornness and touched by her loyalty.

"You have to go now, Eileen! I don't know what's going to happen up there. I could die!"

She grabbed onto him and refused to let go. "And that's exactly why I'm not leaving this ship! If you die then I'll die right there beside you."

John Darkfoote suddenly felt ten years older, knowing that he could be responsible for her death. The others had left five minutes ago in the ship's rigid hull inflatable, and there was but one boat left, a small Zodiac.

"Eileen. I love you. You know I do. But I want you to live. This isn't some movie. It's not Romeo and Juliet, all filled with romance and excitement." He pointed up into the sky. "Those are F-18 fighter jets up there, and they're going to try and sink this boat. I have to make sure it gets to the bridge before that happens."

She grabbed his face in her hands. "So you admit it! You're going to die!"

John rolled his eyes up toward the bridge and tried to push her away as he spoke. "No, no! You stubborn woman! I'm going to put it on autopilot as soon as we get close enough, and then I'll jump overboard and swim back to shore. I'm a very good swimmer."

"But what about the fighter jets?"

John grabbed her by the shoulders and turned her to face him. "The general has promised to take them out. I'll be safe. I promise you."

Up ahead John could see the twin towers of the Mackinaw Bridge looming up into the sky. In a few minutes they'd be there, and it would be too late for her.

"Listen sweetheart, I'm an old man and you're young. You need to live a long time yet and have babies and raise a family."

Eileen started to cry, but he didn't stop talking. "Look at me, honey. I'm sick. Very sick. I haven't told you this, but I think I'm dying. Even if I survive I won't be alive for long."

She stopped crying and looked up at him. "Weren't you going to tell me?"

John threw up his hands in despair, suddenly understanding why he'd never married. This woman just would not give up.

"You were dying and you weren't going to share it with me! I thought we didn't have any secrets from each other!"

John grabbed his face with both hands and shook from side to side. "Oh, for the love of God!"

And that's when he heard the engines of the three Apache attack helicopters. Eileen heard them too, and they both looked out to the starboard bow and saw black shapes above the horizon between them and the bridge. Steadily they came closer. John looked back at her one last time. "Last chance, kid. Please leave the ship."

Her response was to shake her head from side to side and then kiss him full on the lips. "What can I do to help?"

Stinger Alley

HORNET THREE LOOKED DOWN AT HIS RADAR SCREEN AND WATCHED THE large group of green blips as they moved closer and closer. There was more than a little fear in his guts as his imagination wondered what kind of aircraft they were up against. He thought to himself, *how bad could it be?* He'd been told they were likely to be inferior to his Hornet.

That's when the blips disappeared. One by one they simply dropped off his screen and were gone from all reality. The voice of his WSO spoke his next thoughts verbatim. "What the hell?" Hornet Three waited a few seconds longer before reporting in.

"Hornet Leader, this is Hornet Three. The enemy planes appear to be gone now." He leveled out and continued to cruise past an island with a lighthouse a few thousand feet below.

"Hornet Three, this is Hornet Leader, say again your last, over."

"Hornet Leader, I can say it a hundred times more if you like, but that won't change the reality. Those planes are gone. Our radar shows no enemy planes, sir."

THE BLIND MAN COULD SCARCELY BELIEVE HIS EARS. HE LOWERED THE brandy from his lips without taking a drink. He was alone in the room, but he spoke aloud "What the ..."

And then it got worse.

DANNY BRIEL WAITED UNTIL THE F-18 PASSED HIS LOCATION AT THE lighthouse before firing the Stinger. The five-foot long missile was pushed out of the launcher by a small ejection motor to a safe distance before engaging the two-stage solid-fuel sustainer. The missile accelerated to the speed of Mach 2 as it headed for the tail of the Hornet. He watched the trail of smoke as it streaked away from him. Then it occurred to him, *I should get the hell outta here.*

"HORNET LEADER, THIS IS HORNET THREE. I'VE JUST LOST MY WINGMAN! I say again. My wingman is down."

That's when he heard his Weapons Systems Officer scream into his ear. "We've got multiple missiles headed our way. Releasing countermeasures now!"

Hornet Three moved to full throttle and began its near-vertical climb off the deck. The first three Stinger missiles followed the countermeasure flares, but the next one was not fooled. It streaked up and flew to within just a few yards of the huge exhaust nozzles of the Hornet before detonating.

"Hornet Three, this is Hornet Leader, over."

There was no answer.

"Hornet Three, this is Hornet Leader, over."

Rubio's heart sank in his chest when he realized he should have come sooner. By now they were well east of the straits and outside their patrol zone.

"Hornet Two, stay on my six and follow me up. Let's get away from those missiles."

They began to climb, which took them even further from the Mackinaw Bridge. His radio crackled to life, and Commander Gonzales listened to HQ while the feeling of dread filled him to his core.

"Hornet Leader, this is Saracen HQ, over."

He waited a few seconds before responding, focusing on his climb away from danger. "Saracen HQ this is Hornet Leader, go ahead, over."

"Hornet Leader, we have a large boat approaching from due west of the bridge. You are to attack and sink."

Rubio let the words hover in his mind for a moment. A large boat? How large? He didn't have any armaments on board that were designed to take out a ship! During the briefing they'd told everyone to be prepared for air-to-air combat, and that's how the Hornets had been armed, strictly with guns and air-to-air missiles. If only he had a Harpoon, but … he didn't. But Rubio acknowledged. "Saracen HQ, this is Hornet Leader. Roger that we will comply." Upon reaching altitude, he leveled out and banked to the west, knowing full well he might not make it in time.

SS Badger, 2 Miles from Mighty Mac

THE FIRST ROCKET HIT THEM JUST AFT OF THE BRIDGE, OPENING UP BULK-heads and overheads all around. John and Eileen were knocked to the deck. Eileen didn't get back up, but John forced himself to crawl over to her. The second rocket hit below them and he felt both their bodies being lifted off the deck before slamming back down. John heard an explosion and then another and another as he waited for the next rocket to kill them both. The overhead of the wheelhouse was ripped open by the collapsing foremast stack, letting a ten-mile-an-hour wind push in and blow on his back. The air brought him around and he groggily pulled himself up to his feet just in time to see all three Apache helicopters plummeting to the water in smoke and flames. He could still see the contrails of the Stinger missiles fading from view.

The wind was in his face now, and it seemed to bring him back to his senses. There was a piece of jagged wood sticking out of his left arm with blood flowing freely. Eileen still wasn't moving. He went to her rolled her over and saw the shrapnel lodged in her right temple. Her dead eyes stared up at him like a ghost. Anger surged through his body as he pushed himself back to his feet and moved to the damaged bulkhead. He saw the binoculars still hanging beside the wheel by the leather strap and picked them up. He focused on the bridge and saw thousands of soldiers with tanks and trucks and Bradley Fighting Vehicles across the entire span. Some of them had already reached the Upper Peninsula and were pouring out into the paved parking lot beside the toll booths.

Eileen was dead. They'd killed her! Only then did he realize how much he loved her. Fueled by rage, he moved to the wheel and made a slight correction. He tried to engage the autopilot, but it no longer worked. The old engines were fine, and he was still making eighteen miles per hour. He would be there in just a few short minutes. He looked down onto the deck and saw the Satellite Phone he'd been given to use as a detonator. It was still intact. He looked down at Eileen's body. All he had to do was make the call. All his pain would end, and the people who did this …

He quickly retrieved the satphone. He only had about thirty more seconds.

THE BLIND MAN STOOD TO HIS FEET AS HIS APACHES EXPLODED AND crashed to the water below. Two of his Hornets were gone along with all his Apaches in the region. It was a devastating loss. He took another drink, this time guzzling directly from the crystal decanter. But he could still salvage it all if the Saracens made it to the other side. And then he wondered out loud. "What is on that damn ship?"

TEN MILES EAST OF THE BRIDGE, LIEUTENANT CHET HANSON LOOKED down and saw twenty-some planes ditched in the waters of Lake Huron. Some of them had already sunk out of sight, but the pilots were bobbing up and down in orange life preservers. Chet breathed a sigh of relief, knowing that at least this part of the attack had gone as planned. He pondered whether to turn back or to ditch himself with the others. He looked to the west and saw small pillars of smoke rising from just west of the bridge's twin towers. A rush of adrenaline surged through him and he decided to check it out.

THE SUPREME GENERAL HALTED HIS BRADLEY IN THE MIDDLE OF THE Mackinaw Bridge and gazed at the SS Badger as it continued toward him. The topside decks were blown off, and smoke rose from a few fires from the passenger lounges and crew deck and storerooms as the boilers continued to churn energy. Abdul got a bad feeling in the pit of his stomach, and then the eerie sound of music came to him from the direction of the ghostly ship. He looked down at the bow where the name "SS Badger" had been crossed out and replaced with "Edmund Fitzgerald." The black clouds coming in from the west were over them now, as slashing sheets of rain cascaded down.

CAPTAIN JOHN DARKFOOTE HAD WRAPPED A RAG AROUND HIS ARM TO stem the bleeding, but he was already weak from loss of blood. He was still at the wheel and they were almost upon Mighty Mac. People were shooting at him now, but he no longer cared. He was determined to die. He looked down at Eileen's body and softly said, "This one's for you, kid."

And then he pressed a button on the CD Player. The eerie music rang out and upward toward the bridge through the speakers on the SS Badger. The dark clouds enveloped the ghostly ship as it plowed through the storm.

The voice of Gordon Lightfoot could be heard clearly by every Saracen as they stared out through the storm at the spectre moving toward them.

"The legend lives on from the Chippewa on down
of the big lake they called "Gitche Gumee."
The lake, it is said, never gives up her dead
when the skies of November turn gloomy."

EVEN SUPREME GENERAL ABDUL AL'KALWI, DEVOTED MUSLIM, RAISED IN the Middle East, even Abdul knew about this song. And he knew the Edmund Fitzgerald was a ship of death.

"Sink that boat! Sink it! Sink it now! Get off the bridge!"

The sound of terror in their fearless leader's voice caused a panic, and hundreds of soldiers began to run toward both ends of the bridge back toward shore. People were trampled in the confusion, slipped off the bridge in the rain and plunged to the waves below.

"Sink that boat!" Finally, one soldier manned the 7.62 mm machine gun and swung it around to open fire on the ship.

CHET HANSON SAW WHAT WAS LEFT OF THE BADGER JUST PULLING UP TO the center of the bridge. He saw the machine gun on the Bradley open up and struggle to put bullets on target. Plumes of water shot up in front of its bow.

Then he saw the most heartbreaking and inspiring sight of his life. A man was standing at the helm of the ship, holding onto the wheel as bullets flew all around him. It was only a matter of time before he would be killed and the plan would end in failure.

Without thinking, Lieutenant Hanson kicked the rudder hard to the left and then banked down out of the sky straight toward the center of the bridge.

THE SUPREME GENERAL HEARD THE SCREAM OF THE CESSNA AS IT PLUMMET-ed toward him. He quickly ascertained the danger to himself and pointed up into the rain. "Shoot that plane! Shoot the plane!" Then he looked down at the Badger again and yelled "Shoot that boat!"

All the while Gordon Lightfoot kept singing through the storm.

Lake Huron rolls, Superior sings
in the rooms of her ice-water mansion.

"Shoot that boat!"

Old Michigan steams like a young man's dreams;
the islands and bays are for sportsmen.

"Shoot the plane!"

And farther below Lake Ontario
takes in what Lake Erie can send her,

Chet Hanson gritted his teeth as the machine gun swung up to meet him and the bullets tore into the cockpit. He smiled and then crashed into the Bradley Fighting vehicle.

Captain John Darkfoote held the satphone in his hand. He looked down at Eileen, punched in a few numbers.

The legend lives on from the Chippewa on down
of the big lake they call "Gitche Gumee."

John's thumb hovered over the 'send' button And then he heard the mighty scream of two F-18 Hornet attack jets as they came down low on the water behind him.

Hornet Three and Hornet Four fired all their ordinance in a last-ditch effort to stop the boat. John's thumb came down on the satphone's 'send' button.

"Superior," they said, "never gives up her dead when the gales of
November come early!"

The Sidewinder missiles hit the boilers, causing an explosion below decks which quickly spread to the cargo deck. The first thing to ignite was a propane tank truck.

The Badger disintegrated as the entire load of nitromethane, diesel fuel and Ammonium Nitrate combusted. The center of the Mighty Mac ceased to exist. Five thousand men were immediately turned to jelly and thrown into the big lakes. With the center of the bridge gone, each of the twin towers fell, one to the north and the other to the south. They collapsed onto the remaining Saracens, killing them outright or drowning them in the deep waters.

CAPTAIN DANNY BRIEL THROTTLED BACK THE MOTOR ON HIS SMALL BOAT when he saw the Mighty Mac fall into the deep. He saw the large wave coming toward him and struggled to turn the little boat around and head back to the lighthouse. He didn't make it. His boat was lifted up and hurled onto the beach as water broke over him. He clung to the trunk of a small tree as the water subsided back into the straits. After several seconds of choking, he sucked air into his lungs. Danny sat up and looked out into the straits. Mighty Mac had fallen. But so had the Saracen Army. The straits were once again empty as they had been since the dawn of creation. Danny lay back down on the wet sand and stared straight up into the rain. And then, just as quickly as it had started, the storm subsided, the sun came out, and a flock of sea gulls landed down on the beach beside him. Profound as ever, Danny's only words were, "Holy shit-n-shinola!"

ON THE SOUTHERN SHORE, HIGH ATOP AN OLD CHURCH BELL TOWER, SAMMY Thurmond looked on and smiled in awe and respect.

CHAPTER 27

The Clean Up

IT TOOK THE BETTER OF TWO WEEKS TO HUNT DOWN THE RE-
maining Saracens. Those who resisted were killed. Those who surrendered
were sent back to Detroit. When it was all over, everyone returned to their homes.

Jackie, Dan, Jeremy and baby Donna travelled back to Iroquois along with the other
Militia Rangers. Sheriff Leif returned to his wife and child and set to work picking up
the tattered pieces of war.

Sergeant Donny Brewster had dinner with Lisa Vanderbogh and continued his attempt to win her heart. He was successful ... eventually.

In a special ceremony, the second in just a few months' time, the dead were honored
at the church in Iroquois City. Captain John Darkfoote was memorialized and a granite
monument was erected in his honor. Lieutenant Chet Hanson received a posthumous
medal for his bravery and sacrifice. The names were read and the bugles sounded.

August 1, The Courthouse

"WHAT IS THE BLIND MAN GOING TO DO NOW, UNCLE RODNEY?"

His uncle didn't say anything at first. He just picked up his coffee cup and took a sip.
Dan waited patiently beside Sheriff Leif. He took the moment to sip his coffee as well.

"War is a series of moves and counter moves."

He took the six-inch length of white PVC pipe out of the cargo pocket of his pants
and rolled it back and forth in his palms. He still hadn't opened it. For all he knew it
was a bomb, or a tracking device, but ... he didn't think so. He would give it to Agent
Jeff Arnett for analysis and scanning.

He looked up at Dan and Joe and smiled.

"It's his move. Now we wait."

EPILOGUE

THE BLIND MAN SAT IN HIS RECLINER, SIPPING TWELVE-YEAR-old scotch. His anger had subsided, but he wouldn't be entirely rational for some time. Calmly, he picked up his satphone. and punched a few buttons.

"General Holland. I have a mission for you of extreme importance." He paused. "I would like you to deliver a message to one General Rodney T. Branch." He took a sip of his scotch. "Yes, that's right. Make it one of our bigger tactical nukes. Make it your top priority. I want it done by tomorrow, and I want it videotaped for my collection. Better yet, I'd like to watch it in real time."

He placed the phone back down on the South American coffee table and leaned back in his chair to relax.

Then he said out loud to himself.

"Okay, General Branch. You have my undivided attention now."

Book 4 - The God Virus Series

The Conclusion

THE
BLIND MAN'S
RAGE

Skip Coryell

PROLOGUE

July 19th, the Blind Man's Lair

JARED THOMPSON SAT ANXIOUSLY ON THE COUCH INSIDE HIS spacious office deep in the underground complex somewhere near Spruce Mountain, West Virginia. This bunker was not quite as deep as his previous complex in western Pennsylvania, but that complex had been destroyed by ... The Blind Man didn't even want to think about the man's name right now. He couldn't recall a time in his life when he'd been this furious. Try as he might, he couldn't shake the anger and hatred he felt for General Rodney T. Branch of the Shadow Militia.

Spruce Mountain was nice, but much smaller and less technologically advanced than his previous headquarters. But, thanks to Rodney Branch, his underground Pennsylvania palace was now glowing in the dark for the next five thousand years.

Jared's back sank into the plushness of the corinthian leather couch as he gazed up, transfixed on the large video screen in his office. He propped up his feet onto the mahogany coffee table as the white-hot vortex of the nuclear explosion over Escanaba raced upward. Then, as it reached higher altitudes, it began to cool, to billow outward, and then the mushroom cloud was formed.

The Blind Man loved a good mushroom cloud.

Strictly, from a tactical perspective, even as he was giving the order to vaporize the small city in Michigan's Upper Peninsula, Jared knew it wasn't the best use of his limited nuclear arsenal. But, for the first time in his life, he couldn't help himself. He had to do something. He demanded satisfaction. His usual patience was gone, and, in the aftermath and fury of his most recent defeat, Jared felt an uncontrollable urge to strike back at his enemy.

As he watched the mushroom cloud, race upward, billow, form and then spread out across the horizon, he achieved a perverse satisfaction, knowing that General Branch was watching it too, or, better yet ... maybe he was even dead, burned to death inside the heat of a thousand suns.

But, there was something that Jared did not know ...

St. Ignace, Upper Peninsula

Sᴇᴠᴇɴ ʜᴜɴᴅʀᴇᴅ ᴍɪʟᴇѕ ᴀᴡᴀʏ ꜰʀᴏᴍ Sᴘʀᴜᴄᴇ Mᴏᴜɴᴛᴀɪɴ, Gᴇɴᴇʀᴀʟ Rᴏᴅɴᴇʏ T. Branch watched the same mushroom cloud form over the now irradiated city of Escanaba. A soft smile touched his lips as he looked over at his friend Colonel MacPherson.

"Sorry Mac."

Colonel MacPherson, standing at attention as always, looked on and nodded. "You were right, general. He did exactly as you said he would. Thank God we were able to evacuate in time."

Uncle Rodney moved his hands behind his back and clasped them together as if in parade rest position. "The wind is from the southwest. We should be okay for now."

Mac relaxed his stance and turned his head to look at Rodney. "How did you know he would do this?"

The other man turned and met Mac's gaze. "I didn't. It was just a hunch. Just human nature. We rattled him, thus forcing him to flex his muscles and reassert dominance."

The colonel's eyes narrowed. "But what if he'd chosen to flex his muscles here, in the Mackinaw straits?"

Uncle Rodney smiled. "Oops. I didn't think of that."

Mac looked at his friend in disbelief. "Oops? What do you mean oops? We could have all been melted where we stand."

The general put his hand on Mac's back and chuckled to himself. "Have I ever told you that you worry too much?"

Uncle Rodney turned to walk away and the colonel followed him. "Besides, now he feels vulnerable. He knows he's not 10 feet tall and bulletproof anymore."

Mac shook his head in disgust. "I think we just made him mad. Besides, he blew up my mansion. Where am I going to live now?"

Rodney laughed out loud. "I have an extra room in my basement. You're welcome to it."

Colonel MacPherson didn't answer his general. He just stoically trudged on behind his leader, all the while wondering ... where is he taking us now?

CHAPTER I

August 1, Sammy Thurmond

Iᴛ ʜᴀᴅ ʙᴇᴇɴ ᴀʟᴍᴏѕᴛ ᴛᴡᴏ ᴡᴇᴇᴋѕ ѕɪɴᴄᴇ Sᴀᴍᴍʏ Tʜᴜʀᴍᴏɴᴅ had watched in awe as the mighty Mackinaw bridge had collapsed into the deep waters of the Great Lakes. Now, he huddled beside the campfire overlooking the still-smoking rubble of Mackinaw City below. Every morning for the past two weeks he'd watched the sun rise over Lake Huron, and then each night he'd again watch as the sun slowly slipped down into Lake Michigan, all the while, the landscape around him soundless, except for the birds and the rustling of the leaves on the breeze. On rough days the white caps would kick up and lend beautiful contrast to the blue of the straits, but Sammy didn't notice the beauty. He had ceased to recognize natural beauty decades ago. His one exception to that was the woman with the long, black hair ... Jackie Branch.

The day of the great battle for the straits of Mackinaw, Sammy had called in on his satphone to report the results to Jared Thompson, AKA, the Blind Man. His boss had been stunned into silence for several seconds. Sammy had simply waited through the silence, had, in fact even looked down at his watch to time it. It had been fourteen seconds. And then the swearing had unleashed itself. Sammy had listened dispassionately to his boss, almost amused at the childish lack of self-control. Then he'd looked down at the waters of the Great Lakes, still churning after the collapse of Mighty Mac, and, it was at that moment, on the fifteenth second after the great battle, that he'd decided to leave the Blind Man.

Sammy Thurmond had put the satphone down and climbed from his perch inside the bell tower of the church in Mackinaw City. Within a few hours he'd used his switchblade knife to cut open his right thigh and remove the tracking transponder inside the muscle.

That same evening he'd watched the night sky light up to the west and slightly north. It had been the unnatural light of the Blind Man's rage and had lasted for several minutes, illuminating the woods around him. Aside from a few isolated campfires of Shadow Militia soldiers, Sammy Thurmond was engulfed in darkness, and, that darkness, had brought light and clarity to his thinking. It was at that exact moment when Sammy Thurmond began contemplating his new life ... a life, without the Blind Man.

Iroquois City Rubble

Normally, Sheriff Leif would call a meeting at the courthouse, but that building, along with every other building in Iroquois had been razed to the ground. The sheriff wanted to blame Uncle Rodney, but he knew better. The town of Iroquois wasn't made of brick and stone; it was composed of flesh, blood, bone and spirit, and, because of General Rodney T. Branch, most of the people had been saved. Therefore, the town had been saved, despite its obvious lack of a skyline.

But his thoughts quickly moved to Escanaba and the brilliant flash of light they'd seen on the night of the great battle for the straits. It had been the final shot of the day, and everyone recognized that the fate of Iroquois could have been much worse.

The sheriff's thoughts were suddenly interrupted by the words of Dan Branch.

"What are we gonna do now, Joe?"

The sheriff had been in such deep thought that Dan's voice startled him. He looked over at his friend, Colonel Dan Branch, nephew to General Rodney T. Branch, commanding general of the Shadow Militia and shook his head back and forth. He answered Dan's question with one of his own.

"Where's your Uncle Rodney? Shouldn't we be asking him that question?"

Dan looked across the table at the sheriff, almost apologetically. "I think so. But he took Jackie and the baby fishing down at the Mill Pond."

The sheriff couldn't believe his ears. His head jerked up involuntarily as he spewed out a venomous response. "He's gone fishing! How is that possible? Why would he do that?"

Dan stood up and walked over to the Formica-topped counter of his Uncle Rodney's kitchen and poured himself another cup of coffee. "You want another cup?" The sheriff held his palm over the mouth of his coffee cup and shook his head. "Better not today. Cup's still half full. Besides, the caffeine gets me riled."

Dan smiled as he poured the black liquid into his cup. He was pretty sure there wasn't any caffeine in this coffee. "I think my uncle gets you riled more than anything else."

The muscles in Joe's face relaxed a bit before answering. "You got that right. I love that man like a brother, always have, but I swear to god some days ..." But Joe Leif bit his lip in restraint. "That man could make a nun swear like a drunken sailor."

Dan sat back down at the table and moved his chair forward. It scraped across the bare, wooden plank floor. Uncle Rodney didn't believe in anything fancy like carpeting or linoleum, so every room in his very modest home was bare wood. It was the same with the walls and ceiling ... just bare planking or plywood or OSB, depending on what was on sale at the lumber yard or which decade he'd added that particular room. Uncle Rodney was a great general and warrior, but he'd never make a living as a carpenter.

"Escanaba is gone, Joe."

The sheriff nodded. "I know."

"Did you know that was Colonel MacPherson's home town? He grew up there and now his mansion is gone. He won't be able to replace that anytime soon."

Joe moved his hands up to the sides of his face and held them there. He massaged his temples trying to relieve the aching in his skull. "I don't understand how Rodney can go through all of this, two major battles in the matter of two months, watching thousands of people die, all the planning, the marching, all that stress and ... it's like he doesn't even feel it."

Dan smiled. He lifted the steaming cup of coffee to his lips and blew softly across the dark surface before taking a tiny sip. But Dan didn't say anything. In fact, many of the questions Joe was now asking he'd wondered about himself. How could Uncle Rodney do it all and make it look so easy, like it didn't even affect him.

"It's like the guy's a machine or something, Dan. Nothing gets to him. He just keeps right on a going like he's some deadly, nuclear-powered Everready battery or something. How does he do it? I don't get it."

Dan nodded. "I've been watching him around the baby. I think that's how he gets his batteries recharged. By playing with baby Donna. He's not nuclear charged. He's baby charged."

Joe dropped his hands to the table and met Dan's gaze. "He's baby charged? Did you just say that out loud?"

Dan laughed softly. "Yeah, it sounds stupid doesn't it. But I think it's true. I think it reminds him of why he's doing all this fighting. There are two sides to life, and baby Donna is the flip side of the coin. On one side is death and killing, misery, starvation and radiation poisoning. But, on the other, is a little baby who doesn't notice the suffering going on around her. All little children see are the good things in life. Like, playing with a stick on the ground, or eating dirt and then spitting it out cuz it doesn't taste so good."

Joe Leif turned away from the table and looked blankly at the wall. "Are all you Branch men crazy as loons?" Joe picked up his coffee mug and took a sip, but it was already cold. They called it coffee, but it was really chickory roots and a few other weeds that Joe didn't know the name of.

"Well ... I just hope he's having a good time fishing while we sit here worrying about the fate of the world." And then the eyes of the two men met again. Dan raised his coffee mug as if in toast. Joe lifted his as well and smiled sheepishly.

"To Uncle Rodney. May he catch a huge bass and figure out how to conquer the evil forces of the Blind Man in the process."

Joe nodded his head and both men took a sip of coffee in agreement. And then they talked about how much they missed real coffee, the kind from Columbia that used to be packed out on the mule of Juan Valdez. And they knew that real coffee would never come again, at least not in their lifetime.

But both men agreed that it could be worse. At least they were still alive and not glowing in the dark.

The Mill Pond

JACKIE BRANCH WATCHED FROM ACROSS THE POND AS UNCLE RODNEY held baby Donna on his lap with one hand and onto the old-fashioned cane fishing pole with the other. The old general was smiling as he looked down at the baby, and then Jackie saw him lightly kiss the top of her daughter's head. She had never seen him do that before. But then, this was really the first time since she'd known Uncle Rodney that she'd seen him in this type of relaxed and recreational setting.

Jackie looked out at the Mill Pond, at the shimmering sun on the surface of the calm water. It was a small body of water, and Dan had told her the history of it.

Iroquois City was first settled in 1867 by Major Jonathon Dremel who had served honorably for the Union Army during the Civil War between the states. He'd purchased a thousand acres of land, mostly virgin white pine forests, much of it with creeks and rivers running through the heart. Major Dremel had founded the town on his own property and built a sawmill on the Manistee River. The sawmill was the heart blood of the town, and it continued to grow and prosper all the way through the logging boom of the 1890s on up to the roaring twenties. Once the virgin pine forests were gone, the land lay desolate and exhausted of all its natural resources. Many people moved away, but some stayed on and Iroquois continued to limp along. Eventually the forests were replanted and harvested more responsibly.

At the time of the Fall just last year, the town had boasted 2,700 citizens and there was talk of putting in a WalMart. Of course, that would never happen now. This tiny

Mill Pond and its mill race was the last remaining vestige of Major Jonathon Dremel and his grand vision of Iroquois City. Now, the city was in ruins, almost totally destroyed by the saracen army ... but the Mill Pond remained.

Dan had recounted beautiful stories to her about how he'd fished and swam in it as a boy, and how every generation of boy and girl had grown up around the banks of the Manistee River, swam there, fished trout, and grown to adulthood.

Jackie looked out at the peace and serenity of the pond and couldn't believe how it defied the onslaught and power of geopolitical dominance and tyranny. No matter what happened in the outside world, it remained unaffected.

She saw movement to her right and noticed Uncle Rodney and baby Donna moving toward her. Rodney sat down beside her, and the baby reached out to her. Jackie accepted her daughter readily and held the baby close, pressing her face against the top of her head, taking in the smells and feel of the child she loved the most.

"So, what do you think?"

Jackie nodded her head and smiled.

"It's beautiful, Uncle Rodney. I see why Dan was so keen on moving back here."

Uncle Rodney unfastened the top two buttons of his red flannel shirt and wiped his brow. "It's really hot today."

Jackie laughed. "Well, you are wearing a heavy, flannel shirt. Why do you do that so much?"

Rodney smiled. "Because I'm a man who knows what he likes and I'm set in my ways."

Jackie shook her head and let Donna grab onto her thumbs to play with. She took on a somber look.

"What's going to happen now, Uncle Rodney?"

But Rodney was silent. Jackie turned her head to face him.

"You already know what's going to happen to us don't you." She said it as a statement of fact and not a question at all. Rodney nodded slightly.

"I suppose I do."

"And I'm not going to like it, am I."

"Nope. I reckon you won't."

Jackie pulled her baby in tighter.

"Are we going to die?"

Uncle Rodney smiled and ran his right hand across the top of his head from front to back, wiping the sweat away from his short crew-cut hair.

"I heard an interesting statistic the other day. According to a recent study done by the federal government, one out of every one person is going to die at one time in their life."

Jackie looked over at him and shook her head.

"That's stupid."

Uncle Rodney looked off to one side at the grass and then back at the pond. "No, seriously, it was a very important study funded by the government. I guess it cost the tax payers pretty near a hundred million dollars to figure that out."

Jackie responded softly. "Well, at least they won't be wasting any more of our tax dollars for a very long time."

Uncle Rodney looked down at the ground between his legs. He was sitting with his butt planted firmly on the grassy, moist bank of the pond. "Well, truth is Jackie, we all know we're going to die. That's a given. We don't know when or where and we don't know how. But ... maybe the more important thing is to pick a cause worth dying for." And then he glanced down at Donna. "Like that little baby there."

Rodney reached up and stroked his chin and the left side of his face with his right hand. "I spent my whole life getting ready for this final moment in the world's history." He paused a few seconds. "Most people have the luxury of growing up and falling in love, getting married and then they spend the rest of their lives creating beautiful memories for their kids and grand kids."

He looked over at Jackie and their eyes locked.

"That didn't happen to us, Jackie. For whatever reason, it just didn't happen to us."

Jackie shrugged her shoulders lightly and looked back out at the water. "That sucks."

"It would appear that our job is to reset society to its place of normalcy. Our job is to win this war, defeat the tyrant, and rebuild."

Jackie nodded. "I suppose so." She waited a moment as if contemplating a higher question. "And what happens after that?"

Rodney's eyes took on a faraway gaze as he answered. "I don't know, Jackie. By then I'll be dead and you'll be an old woman. I guess the only one who can answer that question is the baby in your arms and the one still growing in your womb. After all, they can only build on what we leave them."

He waited a moment. "So ... let's leave them both the ability to choose a good life and the freedom to start all over again."

Jackie kissed the top of baby Donna's head and looked out at the water. "I wish I had a boring life ... that all this conflict had never come to me."

She looked over to see Rodney smiling from ear to ear. "What? What did I say?"

He shook his head before speaking. "Look at what you've done in the past ten months little lady. You've lived a lifetime of adventure that few people in history ever experience. Some day, if humanity survives, future generations will be reading about you and Dan and I and everything we've done."

The old general looked down at the water ten feet in front of him. "That excites the hell outta me!"

And, it was at that moment, that very exact moment in time when Jackie finally understood her Uncle Rodney. She knew that he would never give up, that he would sooner die than give in to the Blind Man. It was as if Rodney had been preprogrammed before the dawn of time, before his birth, before the very foundations of the world to be exactly what and who he was at that very moment. And, if that were true, then she too, was destined to be sitting on the banks of the Mill Pond at this very moment, waiting patiently for the next battle, for the next round of killing and dying and overthrowing of tyranny.

She looked over at her uncle. "I suppose you're right."

Rodney smiled. "Jackie, when you get as old as I am, you realize that you're no longer fighting for your own future, but for the future of the ones you love, and, maybe, even for the future of strangers. Truth is I've got more life behind me than in front of me. I've lived a good life and it's been long. My only reason for existing right now is to kill the Blind Man."

That last sentence made Jackie want to cry; but she held it in, knowing instinctively that it wouldn't be appreciated. Jackie held baby Donna up to her face and kissed her on the forehead. Then, she girded up the loins of her heart to begin the next fight. She prayed to God she'd be equal to the challenge. She didn't want to let Uncle Rodney down. And she knew, in her heart of hearts, no matter what the task demanded of her, she knew that he was worthy of her devotion and sacrifice.

And through all these thoughts of profundity, the Mill Pond didn't care. It shimmered on, oblivious to the Blind Man and his evil, oblivious to the nobility and courage of Uncle Rodney.

CHAPTER 2

August 2 - Spruce Mountain

THE BLIND MAN WAS SITTING ON HIS COUCH, MADE OF CO-rinthian leather staring into the fireplace. It was a fake fire with just an electric log that glowed and dimmed in a preprogrammed sequence. If not for the Shadow Militia, he would already have the country pacified and he'd be living in the mansion of his choice by the seashore. He'd been looking at the map and plenty of photos, and had decided on somewhere in Florida. Problem was there was just too much resistance down south yet, and up north for that matter.

Things were definitely not going as planned. And now ... he'd lost his best and most trusted servant. Sammy Thurmond hadn't been heard from for over two weeks now, and that worried him. He looked down at the coffee table, and his eyes rested on the satellite phone. One of his Special Forces Teams had found it in a bell tower of a church overlooking Mackinaw City. He'd read the report a dozen times and even personally questioned the team leader. There were no signs of struggle, no blood, no notes, no clues of any kind as to the whereabouts of Sammy Thurmond. Even his tracking chip had stopped functioning.

Jared was a distrusting man by nature, that's how he'd managed to stay alive for so long in so dangerous a business, but ... he just couldn't imagine ... he let the thought pass him by in disbelief. Not Sammy. Not Sammy Thurmond. No ... never. He wouldn't do that. Perhaps he'd been captured by the Shadow Militia.

But the uneasy feeling in the pit of his stomach wouldn't go away. If the Shadow Militia had captured him ... the possibilities made him shiver. He reached down and picked up the decanter to pour himself another scotch. It would be so much better if Sammy was dead.

Yes, if General Branch had Sammy Thurmond ... it was a whole new ball game. He sipped the scotch, let it burn his throat and slip on down.

Shadow Militia Intelligence

SPECIAL AGENT JEFF ARNETT WAS A TALL MAN, WELL OVER SIX FEET, WITH a hawkish nose and eyes that could penetrate steel. He sat in the pole barn surrounded by desks and computers. There was a naked light bulb over his own desk that hurt his eyes, but was necessary if he was going to light up the darkness of the big room. He looked down at the thumb drive on the desk, as well as the rolled-up papers laid out before him. The container this information had been housed in was off to his left. It was a length of white, PVC pipe, about six inches long and an inch in diameter.

General Branch had given it to him shortly after returning from the Straits of Mackinaw. When he'd been told about how Sammy Thurmond had given it to Jackie with orders to give it directly to General Branch, he'd been miffed. *How could they have been so stupid?* It could have been a bomb, or a tracking device ... or both. But, luckily, it had been just a thumb drive with data. He picked up the stack of photographs. They were all pictures of Jared Thompson, AKA, the Blind Man. They appeared to be surveillance photos, all taken from different cameras and angles. In every picture but one, Jared was wearing dark sunglasses. And that's the picture that enthralled him the most. The man's eyes ... they were scary, deep and mystifying. He'd never seen Jared's eyes before. After all, they were always covered with dark glasses. But ... there was something spooky about this picture. The eyes ... the eyes ... what was it about those eyes. And then it hit him.

These eyes were not blind.

Jeff reached down and picked up a can of Mountain Dew soda. It was warm, and it was, so far as he knew, the last can of Dew in the county, or maybe even the state. Mountain Dew had always been his vice, but ... it just didn't taste so good when it was room temperature. He thought to himself, *probably just as well. If you can't pronounce the ingredients, it can't be good for you.*

But his dilemma remained. What to do about this thumb drive. He had to find out what was on it, but, ... it came from a hostile and unreliable source. For god's sake this man was Sammy Thurmond, the Blind Man's right-hand man, the only person in the world who had his trust. His imagination began to run wild. There could be all manner of malicious software on that drive. He couldn't very well open it with any of the machines connected to a network. He had to isolate it and then study it.

But one thing was certain. He had to find out what was on that drive. The Shadow Militia, if they were to defeat Jared Thompson, would need an edge they didn't presently have ... maybe ... even a miracle.

Marine in Love

THERE WAS AN INCREDIBLE SHORTAGE OF FAT PEOPLE IN THE WORLD THESE days. Sergeant Donny Brewster looked out across the encampment at the hundred or so Home Guard soldiers and couldn't help but notice how gaunt they all looked. He didn't think there was a fat body within five-hundred miles of here. Come to think of it, most of the people who were left, were all pretty lean and healthy. The diabetics were all dead. Anyone with heart disease or who depended on medication for survival had died long ago. Without the benefits of modern medicine, nature and law of the jungle had pretty much taken control and thinned the herd. Donny wondered if that was a good or a bad thing. He pretty much thought in black and white. On the one hand, it was good that people were strong, spirited and on their feet working again. Society before the Fall had become nothing but a culture of slackers and snowflakes ... weak, unmotivated ... a culture of selfish consumers and worthless eaters. But now ... now they were lean and strong and perhaps more alive than at any other time in their lives.

But ... at what cost?

So many millions had died. More than millions, hundreds of millions, maybe even billions across the globe. All because of what? Selfish men and their quests for power?

But society had always been like that, all throughout human history. There had always been one man who wanted to dominate another, the strong who controlled the weak and who were willing to kill and enslave to get and maintain that power.

And that's where Donny Brewster came in. He was strong, but he was different. He was willing to kill to protect the weak. He thought about it for a moment. No, he was more than willing. In times like these ... he was eager to kill.

"A penny for your thoughts, Marine."

Donny looked up and saw Lisa Vanderboeg, the woman of his dreams. And he thought to himself *What a terrible time to fall in love.* He stood up quickly, straight as an iron rod, to his full six feet of height and muscle, almost at position of attention. He saw her smile and the gleam in her eyes and began to relax. She put her arms around him and bent her head up to kiss him on the cheek.

"Nurse Vanderboeg. It's good to see you again."

The pretty, young woman, in her late twenties, kicked him in the left shin and squeezed him tighter.

"Don't be stoic with me, Donny! You know you love me and I own you now. So tell me ..." She pulled him closer. "What were you thinking about?"

Donny smiled and looked down at the beautiful woman. Her blonde hair had lengthened since their first meeting, and it fell down onto her shoulders again. The Marine sniper reached up and touched her face with his left hand. A month ago she'd acted like she hated him, and now ... it was like she'd always loved him, like she'd been born and bred for him specifically. He didn't understand women.

"And why should I tell you what I'm thinking? I'm a Marine. I'm stoic, remember?"

Lisa's smile broadened. "It's because I'll kick you in the shin again if you don't do as I say."

Donny laughed out loud for the first time since the Battle of Mackinaw. "That tells me that you trust me."

The petite blonde pushed away just far enough to look him in the eyes, but still held on to his waist.

"How so, Marine?"

Donny's handsome face and white teeth shone in the mid-day summer sunlight.

"Because I'm bigger and stronger than you. I could crush the life out of you with my bare hands, but still ... you trust me enough to kick me in the shins. You know I won't hurt you and I respect that."

Lisa cocked her head slightly to one side as if perplexed. "You are in dire need of therapy, young man." And then without warning, she kicked him again.

This time it hurt, but Donny didn't show it. "Wow! You must really be stuck on me!" And then he put his arms around her and pulled her closer. "Tell me you love me."

Donny felt her body tense up and pull away. Without warning or hesitation, she turned and walked back the same way she had come, leaving him alone with this awkward moment. Just then Jason Little walked up. Jason was six and a half feet tall, an accountant before the Fall, but now cross-trained into something useful, an infantry officer.

"What was that all about?"

Donny shrugged, still looking after her as she stomped away from them. "She just loves me, that's all."

"Oh." Jason looked confused. "It looked to me like she got mad at you, kicked you and walked away."

Donny turned and strode over to teach his class on close quarters combat. "I know. Ain't love grand?"

Jason followed him, all the while shaking his head more confused than ever.

August 3 - Near Pellston, Michigan

SAMMY THURMOND HAD BEEN ON THE ROAD FOR TWO WEEKS NOW. AFTER ditching his satphone and digging the tracker out of his leg, he'd wasted no time in traveling west down Wilderness Park Drive and then to the south. He'd stayed east of the Lake Michigan shoreline, traveling only at night and sleeping during the day. He ate mostly roots, berries and edible plants. At first he'd tried to forage from nearby houses, but there was just no food to be found. When he got really hungry, he shot a rabbit or squirrel and ate that. He didn't take a chance on building a fire - he just ate the meat raw. It felt good to be out on his own again, not beholden to the Blind Man or the government or anyone else.

Sammy was in no hurry. He just took his time, taking in the water of the many lakes and ponds and streams along the way, the sunrise, the sunset, the smells of the woods and the darkness of the night. It gave him time to think and time to plan. But most of all - he thought of her. That woman. The special one. She intrigued him, enthralled him, consumed his every waking moment. And he knew where she would be, where she must be.

For the very first time in his life, Sammy had no detailed plans. All he knew was that he wanted to see Jackie Branch again, and that he wanted to meet Rodney T. Branch, commanding general of the Shadow Militia.

Iroquois County

"WOMEN AREN'T LIKE THAT, DONNY! YOU CAN'T TELL THEM YOU CAN

crush the life out of them and expect a good response!"

Dan Branch and Donny Brewster were practicing hand-to-hand combat in a small clearing behind Uncle Rodney's house. It was early afternoon, and the sun was beating down hard on them both, causing sweat to bead up and quickly run off their faces and backs in tiny rivers. Dan faked with a left jab and came across hard with his right fist. The padded glove struck Donny on the left side of his face sending him crashing to the ground.

"Come on, Donny. You're not even trying today! Will you please try to focus."

The marine sniper shook his head from side to side. He got up doggedly to his feet and held up his gloves again.

"I can't help it, Dan. I just keep thinking about her. I want to fix it, but I don't know how. It's like if things aren't right with her then nothing else in my life is right either."

Dan lowered his gloves. "Really? It's that bad?"

His friend nodded and then walked over to the old oak stump ten feet away and sat down. Dan walked over too, rolled an oak log about 24 inches long onto its end and sat down beside him.

"It sounds like you're in love, Donny. That's the only thing that can mess up a man that much."

"Well, I don't much like it, Dan." Then he thought for a moment and shook his head as if trying to clear away the cobwebs in his mind. "Actually, I am in love with her. I want to marry her. And I'd be happy about it if she wanted to marry me too. But ... something's holding her back. It's like she loves me and hates me at the same time. It's confusing."

Dan Branch laughed out loud. "So she hates you one day and loves you the next. That sounds pretty normal to me."

Donny shook his head from side to side and then spit some phlegm off to his right. "No. That's not it. She doesn't hate me one day and love me the next, it's like she hates me and loves me simultaneously. It's like she's two women trapped in the same body."

Dan thought for a moment. "Didn't her husband die just a few days after the Fall?"

The birds were singing in the trees about fifty yards to the left. They sounded beautiful, and Donny wanted to shoot them all.

"Yeah, something like that. He was killed by some neanderthal thugs in Grand Rapids. I guess it was pretty hard on her and it took a while to get over it."

Dan glanced up and over at his friend. "Donny that was less than a year ago. She's not over it yet - not by a long shot."

Donny raised his head and looked over at Dan. "Really?"

Dan nodded. "Yup."

"So how long does it take? It won't be too long will it?"

Dan Branch smiled sympathetically and looked back down at the grass in front of them."It might take the rest of her life, Donny. People just don't get over things like that."

Donny bent his neck down and held his head between his hands. He rubbed his temples as if he had a migraine.

"I don't think I can wait that long, Dan."

Dan reached over and placed his hand on Donny's back and patted it firmly.

"You won't have to Donny boy. But you will have to be patient and try to understand her point of view."

Donny grunted. "So what's her point of view?"

With his free hand, Dan rubbed his aching knee from front to back while gathering his thoughts. His knee had been bothering him ever since the march back from Mackinaw City.

"My first wife killed herself right after the Fall."

Donny's back stiffened. "Really?"

Dan nodded. "She was cheating on me again, and Jeremy and I were coming to get her on our way to Iroquois. We found her in bed with her lover. He was already dead and she tried to shoot me with a shotgun when I came to rescue her."

Donny looked on in disbelief.

"An hour later she died of an overdose."

All of a sudden Donny felt very clumsy and needed to get away, but he forced himself to engage at least on a surface level for his friend.

"Sorry, man. I don't know what to say about that."

"You don't have to say anything, Donny. You just have to listen and try to understand." Dan rubbed his chin a moment before moving on. "Lisa still loves her husband just the same way that I still love Debbie."

Donny interrupted him. "You still love Debbie ... even after she cheated on you?"

Dan nodded. "So imagine how much Lisa still loves her husband after having a child with her. They had a happy family. She was forced to watch him die and there was nothing she could do to save him, even though she was a nurse."

Donny looked out into the woods and sighed. "She must feel terrible."

"It's worse than that, Donny. She feels terrible about losing the love of her life. She lost her home. Her daughter lost her daddy. She's been forced to kill to stay alive. That doesn't come natural to her. And some goon like you comes along and she falls in love again before she's ready. And that makes her feel guilty, because she knows she should still be grieving for the loss of her husband."

Donny felt blown away. "How do women feel so many things at the same time? I think my head would explode."

Dan shook his head in frustration. "I don't know. It boggles the mind."

"So what should I do?"

For the longest while Dan didn't answer him, and, when he did, it was in a hushed voice, forcing Donny to perk up and listen to every word.

"Don't talk so much. Just listen to her. Be patient. Don't talk about love. Let her have control of the relationship. Just take your cues from her and everything will be alright."

Donny stood up abruptly. "I guess I should go talk to her now."

"No! That's exactly what you shouldn't do." Dan motioned with his hand for him to sit back down. "You need to think about this for a while first. Give it a day or two. Go slow. Slow is good - fast is bad. That's your new mantra."

Donny nodded his head up and down. "Something tells me this is going to be tougher than a fifteen-hundred yard head shot."

Dan agreed in silence. They both stood up now and began walking back to the house.

"You might talk to Jackie about it too. She seems to understand women better than I do, and she's been through the same things as Lisa."

Donny nodded. "Yeah. Kind of like being on an intelligence-gathering operation."

Dan reached over and slapped the other man on the left shoulder. "Donny, welcome to the female world."

And then to himself he added, *This woman has you, and you don't stand a chance.*

CHAPTER 3

August 4 - the Blind Man's Lair

❝I WANT YOU TO HUNT HIM DOWN AND BRING HIM BACK TO me!" Jared Thompson looked dispassionately into the face of the man before him. Jared waited only briefly for a response before lashing out.

"Do you understand!?"

The young lieutenant, a former Special Ops soldier from France, nodded his head, snapped to attention and rendered his best salute.

"Yes, sir! It will be done, sir!"

Jared didn't return the salute. He never did. That was beneath him. "Do you have any questions?"

The lieutenant hesitated but then finally spit it out. "What should we do, sir, if ... Mr. Thurmond resists us?"

A smile moved over Jared's face like plastic melting in the hot July sun. When he answered, it was a venomous spewing. "I never said he had to be alive. I just want him back."

The young officer nodded before executing a perfect about-face and exiting the room. Once the door to the Blind Man's lair closed shut behind him, he stopped and looked down at the floor. *Why was the Blind Man doing this?* But he quickly shook the thought out of his mind before striding away in a military fashion.

"It's none of my business. Just do your job. Follow orders. Do your job and don't ask questions."

The young officer wiped the ambivalence from his mind, already starting to plan the details of the coming rescue operation, or assassination, or ... whatever it turned out to be.

The French lieutenant had always been a practical man, bent on success and a rapid rise in the ranks. His home country was in chaos, as was the rest of Europe. When he'd gotten this opportunity in America, he'd jumped at the chance. But ... he was slowly figuring out that America wasn't much better off than the rest of the world.

But ... at least here he had creature comforts and he could practice his trade. That was something to build on ... at least for now.

Young Sniper's Remorse

JEREMY BRANCH SAT ON THE HARD, WOODEN BENCH BESIDE THE GRAVE OF his grandfather. This was his father's father, a man he'd never met and knew very little about. But today, the relative stranger would be his closest friend.

"You've never met me, but I'm Jeremy Branch, Dan's boy. I guess I'm your grandson, technically I'm not cuz your son isn't really my dad, but ..." Jeremy looked off across the spattering of granite and marble headstones to make sure no one was listening or watching.

"Family life today is pretty complicated. Your son married my mom, and I was already born at the time. So I guess technically I'm your step-grandson and you're my step-grandad."

Jeremy was wearing faded, blue, cut-off shorts, with the hem of the pant legs frayed and blowing slightly in the gentle, July breeze.

"My dad still loves you. I thought you might want to know that. He didn't always understand you, but ... I think that's pretty normal in the whole father-son thing."

Jeremy looked down at an ant crawling up his ankle. He moved his hand down to squash it, but then stopped. He looked at the ant, moved his left hand up to it, and the tiny ant crawled on top of his hand and across his palm without so much as a hesitation. Jeremy watched the tiny bug for a few seconds and then gently laid him back on the grass beside his feet.

"I needed someone to talk to, someone I didn't know and who could keep a confidence. I figure since you're dead that wouldn't be a problem for you." Jeremy smiled sadly. "After all, you've got plenty of time and it's not like you're going anywhere real soon." The noon sun was high in the sky, and Jeremy was grateful for the relative cool of the shade. "And it's not likely you'll gossip to anyone about this - at least not with anyone I know."

There was a white pine tree off to his left about twenty-four inches in diameter, then an oak tree straight behind him about ten feet away.

"I like to come here. It's peaceful and no one interrupts my thoughts." Jeremy ran his left hand through his scalp from front to back. A residue of grease and sweat was left on his hand, so he wiped it off on his t-shirt. "I'm only sixteen years old, but I've learned that the dead can be very polite and accommodating. And ..." He hesitated before coming to the crux of the matter. "... very non judgmental."

"I've done a lot of bad things in my life. I took advantage of Tonya, our neighbor girl from Wisconsin. At the time I thought it was okay - that I deserved to make myself happy. But ... since then I've learned that it's not okay to be selfish if it hurts other people."

Jeremy wrung his hands together nervously. "I've killed a lot of people. If my count is correct, about 47 so far." He looked up at the sky. "I want you to know that I didn't enjoy it, that it's killing a part of me to do it, and that I'll probably have to do it again."

Jeremy looked down at the granite head stone, then back up at the sky, as if suddenly realizing he was talking to a dead person when he should be talking to the living God. He glanced back up into the sky and thought a moment.

"What should I do?"

There was no answer.

"Can you tell me what to do?"

There was a loud buzzing noise of a cicada coming from way up in the oak tree behind him. The breeze suddenly picked up, and it caressed his face softly, easing his tension, encouraging him and causing him to open up and talk more about his heart.

"I felt terrible when I shot that first man, but ..." Tears welled up into his eyes. "But if I hadn't, then, my dad would probably be dead right now. I felt like I didn't have a choice."

The cicada stopped buzzing, and another ant crawled up his ankle, the right one this time. He looked down and watched it. The ant's tiny legs tickled his skin.

"I don't think I'm a very good soldier. I'm not like Donny, or my dad or my Uncle Rodney." He paused. "They seem to do it so gracefully, like it's second nature to them, like it doesn't bother them at all."

Jeremy propped his right ankle atop his left knee and watched the ant's progress from a closer vantage point. He was amazed at how resilient the little insect was. It just kept crawling over one obstacle after another, never giving up, never hesitating, almost as if every time it faced a challenge, it became stronger and more determined to move forward.

And then it hit him. He was describing his Uncle Rodney. General Rodney T. Branch was like the ant. Always slugging along, never stopping, never pausing, never hesitating to mourn. He simply, in machine-like fashion, overcame the next challenge and then moved on.

"I just have to get through this next battle don't I. I just have to keep fighting until the bad guys are all dead, and then I can rest and maybe get back to normal." But, in his heart, Jeremy knew there was no normal - not anymore. But he needed to believe that it could happen again, that he could regain his innocence, that some day he could go back on the playground and take up where he left off before the Fall and finish recess.

He glanced over at his M4 carbine leaning against the bench beside him. Just a few months ago he would have been honored and yearning to carry that gun. But now ... it was a curse to him, a burden that weighed a million pounds.

He looked back up at God. "Lord, if you're up there, if you really do care about me, then please help me get through this last battle. I need to stay human, and I need a reason to live."

The cicada started buzzing again, so Jeremy stood resolutely to his feet, leaned over and picked up his carbine. With one fluid movement, the action of a seasoned warrior, Jeremy slung it on his back and marched away. Almost casually, he turned his head and called out behind him.

"Nice meeting you, Gramps."

And then the boy, now a man unaware, trudged off through the cemetery, down the hill and back to Uncle Rodney's house.

The cicada looked down at the grave and wondered if God would answer the boy's prayer. But it was just a cicada, just a bug, and in a bug's life things like that were unimportant. The cicada ceased its buzzing. The ant looked up and the breeze became silent again.

Uncle Rodney HQ

"So why do you want me to locate this man? I don't get it. Why is he so important?"

Special Agent, Jeff Arnett, head of the Shadow Militia intelligence gathering unit, bore his hawk-like eyes into the hard skull of General Rodney T. Branch. Rodney met the tall man's gaze with a casual air that he wasn't used to. Most people were intimidated by his demeanor and presence, but not Uncle Rodney. He just soaked it all in as if amused.

"That's a good question, Jeff." The general was dressed in a red flannel shirt and faded, dirty blue jeans. He'd just been hoeing the tomatoes in his small garden on the south side of his house and hadn't cleaned up yet.

"I strongly believe this man is the key to final victory in our fight against the Blind Man."

Jeff Arnett's staunch eyes perked up and he leaned in closer. "I'm listening."

Uncle Rodney leaned over in his chair to the left so he could remove a knife from his right pocket. Jeff saw the knife come out and instinctively moved back a hair. Uncle Rodney pretended not to notice.

"He's a weapons designer that Mac used to know 20 years ago." With a flick of his right wrist, the knife blade came out, and Rodney began to clean the black dirt of his garden out from under his finger nails.

"Okay. I can see where that would be helpful. But, we already have tons of weapon's designs, but they're useless without the industrial capacity to manufacture them."

Rodney nodded. "Correct. And that's what makes this man so important. He specializes in nineteenth-century weapons manufacture. He can design weapons that can be mass produced and built without electricity."

Jeff was interested now. "What kind of weapons systems?"

Rodney reached down to pick up his mug of tea. He took a sip and placed the mug back onto the table. It really wasn't tea in the traditional sense. It was made from the red berries of staghorn sumac, and had a distinct lemony flavor to it. Rodney had shown Jackie how to find and harvest the berries. At first he hadn't liked the beverage, but had eventually gotten used to it. It was true, he still had a few hundred pounds of coffee and black tea in storage, but he wanted to live like everyone else, lest jealousy set in and become a wedge to weaken his leadership.

"Mortars, rockets, cannons ..." then he hesitated before continuing. "Atomic bombs."

Jeff Arnett's eyes jerked up and met Rodney's gaze.

"Did you say atomic bombs?"

Rodney nodded. Jeff Arnett leaned forward and placed both elbows on the Formica top of Uncle Rodney's kitchen table.

"Since when are atomic bombs nineteenth-century weapons?"

Uncle Rodney smiled. "Well, atoms have been around a long time, Mr. Arnett. And this guy is a man of many talents."

The tall man, suddenly grasping the importance, placed his chin atop his fists as he spoke.

"So what's this guy's name?"

Rodney took another sip from his mug before answering him. "His name is Justice ... Justice Reed."

August 4, Coker Creek, Tennessee

JUSTICE REED LIVED A FEW MILES UP THE MOUNTAIN IN THE HEART OF THE Chippewa National Forest near a tiny town called Coker Creek. He lived there by design, to get away from people and all things modern. Tellico Mountain was just to the north, and Farner Mountain was to the south. He was at a place near where Georgia, Tennessee and North Carolina all converged in the southeast corner of the state. The trout fishing was good, and no one bothered him here. Justice planned on dying here on his porch, whenever God saw fit to take him. If he became sick, he wouldn't fight the inevitable, he'd just let life take its natural course, and one-hundred years from now he imagined some weary traveler would find his dried-out body still attached to this very porch swing.

Right now Justice Reed's only goal in life was to drink himself into a belated grave. He took a drink of his dandelion wine and placed the Mason jar back on his lap. Then he began to rock slowly back and forth in the shade of his porch swing. No one knew he was up here. He closed his eyes and listened to the birds. It was hot on the mountain, but a little cooler in the shade of his cabin. Justice Reed was seventy-six years old, and he hadn't ventured down the mountain in over seven years. He didn't have to. Everything he needed was right here at his homestead.

Every night he listened to his solar-powered radio for the news. Well, every night until over a year ago when everything suddenly went silent. He knew what had happened, and he was probably the only person on the planet who wasn't adversely affected by it. He grew his own food, had running water, minimal power requirements, and had neither need nor desire for human companionship.

The old man looked ancient and frail, not an ounce over one-hundred and thirty-five pounds soaking wet. The skin on his face appeared to be draped over his skull and then pasted down with Elmer's glue and then stapled on the very edges. He looked out at the kudzu vines growing anywhere they could find sunlight and couldn't help but wonder, *can I make wine out of that?*

Justice Reed was a certified genius. A nuclear physicist with advanced degrees in Chemical Engineering, Electrical Engineering, Aerospace Technology, Military History and Mechanical Engineering. It had always been his goal to be a well-rounded scientist, but to also be practical. That's why he'd diversified his education more than others. Over the years, before his failed life-long experiment with inebriation, Justice had worked at a lot of different jobs: Chief Engineer of a nuclear power plant, advanced weapons designer for the Department of Defense, as well as a short stint as an illegal arms dealer.

It was that last one which had caused him most of his grief. In fact, he'd spent several years in a federal prison before being pardoned by the last president, in return for a five-year commitment to help design a miniaturized atomic weapons system. That had been fifteen years ago, and he hadn't enjoyed it at all, aside from the challenge of it and the unlimited budget.

The problem was this: Justice Reed liked to work alone, and he just didn't work and play well with others. That, and his addictive personality. He took another drink of the wine, this time letting it linger at the back of his throat before swallowing.

There was movement to his right, down at floor level, and Justice looked down to see a small mouse scamper across the broken-down porch floor of his house. He didn't like mice; they carried too many diseases and they pooped all over everything. They bred like rabbits, and if he didn't do anything about it, they'd soon over-run him from his own home.

He made a mental note to build a better mouse trap.

There was a book beside him, a hardback, and he picked it up and opened it to his bookmark. He read it out loud to himself.

1 Peter 4:2-3
New International Version (NIV)

2 As a result, they do not live the rest of their earthly lives for evil human desires, but rather for the will of God.
3 For you have spent enough time in the past doing what pagans choose to do—living in debauchery, lust, drunkenness, orgies, carousing and detestable idolatry.

Justice put the Bible back down on the bench and looked out at the woods around him. And then he said out loud, "That about sums it up for me."

Indeed, he had spent enough time on drunkenness and debauchery, that was true enough and he couldn't deny it. He wondered what would have happened with his life if he'd not given himself over to the bottle, had not dived headlong into immorality for all those years. And now ... now he was old and all used up. And he wondered ... was the part in the Bible about grace and forgiveness really true? He understood the law and justice and wrath, but ... Justice did not fully understand Jesus. And, most of all, he wondered if it was too late for him to change course.

He decided that he regretted his youthful indiscretions, and would try to do it different in another life, if it was given to him.

Then he thought about verse 2, about doing the will of God, and he wondered, how does anyone know the will of God. Does He tell them in dreams or visions? He just didn't know these things, but had a desire to find out. He made a mental note to himself: *After I finish that mouse trap I'll find out what is the will of God.*

He thought about the state of the world, the anarchy, the chaos, the violence and the mayhem ... about what he would cook for dinner tonight. And then it occurred to him that none of these things really mattered ... except for the dinner.

Justice picked up the Mason jar and drank until it consumed him. He fell asleep on the porch swing, and slept right on through dinner, unaware that the mouse had gone inside his home and had eaten his fill with impunity.

**Lake Michigan - 50 miles offshore**

Jᴇꜰꜰ Aʀɴᴇᴛᴛ sᴀᴛ ɪɴ ᴛʜᴇ ᴄᴀᴘᴛᴀɪɴ's ᴄʜᴀɪʀ ᴏɴ ᴛʜᴇ sᴍᴀʟʟ ᴄʜᴀʀᴛᴇʀ ꜰɪsʜɪɴɢ boat with the laptop on his thighs. The thumb drive from Sammy Thurmond was in his right hand, poised over the USB port on the side.

He wanted to put it in the computer. The curiosity was driving him crazy, and General Branch had ordered him in the most clear terms to do so, but ... it just didn't make any sense to him. Why would the Blind Man's right-hand man give them anything of value? The spook part of him distrusted ... but the human part of him hoped.

In the end, he inserted the thumb drive into the USB port and waited for the hard drive to be erased or for a cruise missile to come crashing down on him. If he was the Blind Man, that's what he'd have done ... given them a carrot of hope, a deadly carrot to annihilate them once and for all.

But there was no virus - no sirens, no bells or whistles, not even a cruise missile. Just a prompt that said:

"Enter Code Key."

The sun was shining down on him, making it hard to see past the glare of the laptop screen. He typed in a few random keys and pressed enter. Almost immediately the screen shot back:

"Incorrect Code Key."

He tried another with the same results.

Then, he entered a third sequence and the response surprised him.

"Patience is a virtue."

Jeff Arnett swore under his breath. He didn't have time for patience or virtues or some smart-aleck software programmer with a perverse sense of humor. He didn't have time for anything except quick and easy success. He thought for a moment, and finally closed the laptop and stood to his feet. He would need his lab to break the code, but at least he knew it was safe to work with back at Iroquois.

Jeff motioned for his bodyguard to tell the captain they were heading back to land. He looked over the side of the boat and felt a sudden queasiness. The motion of the boat, rocking up and down on the swells caused the bile to rise in his throat. He leaned over the railing and emptied the contents of his stomach into the water. He suddenly felt very, very poorly. And then he thought to himself ... *What hope do we have of winning? We don't have a chance.*

CHAPTER 4

August 5, The State of the Disunion
South of the Mason-Dixon Line

Gᴇɴᴇʀᴀʟ Rᴏᴅɴᴇʏ T. Bʀᴀɴᴄʜ, ꜰʟᴀɴᴋᴇᴅ ᴏɴ ᴛʜᴇ ʟᴇꜰᴛ ʙʏ Colonel MacPherson, moved on down the line from one soldier to the next. If the Blind Man knew the condition of the men opposing him, he would laugh out loud and be renewed with confidence.

"What's your name corporal?"

The man in front of him was about sixty-five years old, but, based on the way he looked, Rodney guessed he didn't have too many more winters in front of him.

"Eric Olsen, suh." The man's voice was raspy and old, like worn out sandpaper. Most of his teeth were rotting or missing completely.

Rodney nodded. "What's your job, soldier?"

The old man's eyes darted back and forth for just a second, then fixed back down on the general's collar button. Rodney noticed the nervousness.

"My job's ta try'n stay alive 'n send my men back ta the ones that love 'em."

The general smiled and then nodded. The man was a soldier, but he had no uniform - none of them did. They were dressed in various shades and designs of camouflage, denim and canvas. Most of them had been farmers and blue-collar workers before the Fall.

"Sounds like we got the same job, corporal." He thought he saw the corporal's weary eyes almost smile.

Then he paused. "So, corporal, do you have any advice for the general?"

The old soldier wasn't sure he was hearing correctly, so he paused for a full ten seconds before answering.

"Well, suh, the way I see it we got two choices. We kin kick this Blind Dude's ass or he kin kick ours. I perfer we kick his. I just wanna gitter dun so's I kin get back home 'n pick my corn."

The general nodded his head in thanks and then moved on down the line with the colonel in tow closely behind him. Every so often he would stop and converse briefly. His intent was to assess the individual character of the men which always gave him a good assessment of the fighting capability of the unit as a whole.

When they were done, the troops were dismissed and Rodney and Mac returned to the command tent. Major General Masbruch was already there waiting for them.

Rodney returned his salute sharply, and then the two men hesitated briefly before sitting down at the folding table in front of them.

"It's good to see you again, Dale. You've done a great job building up this army down here and to the east."

General Masbruch's hard, green eyes looked first at Colonel MacPherson and then back at his commanding general. "Well, Rodney, it's not like I had much of a choice. We didn't have squat six months ago. We had to do something."

Uncle Rodney nodded and smiled. "And now, thanks to you and your staff, we have twenty-thousand men, all trained and battle-ready."

Mac chimed in from the left side of the table. "You did a hell of a job, General Masbruch."

At first, General Masbruch smiled, but then the smile slowly faded as he began to slowly sense they were about to tell him things he didn't already know.

"Why are you two being so nice to me? And since when does Mac address me as "general?" What's going on that I don't know about?"

And then he rose to his feet, the chair almost falling down behind him. "What the hell are you two up to now?"

Rodney looked up at him and his eyes squinted tensely. "Just calm down, Dale, and sit back at the table."

Colonel MacPherson smiled and then looked down at the white, plastic folding table. "There's just a few logistical and strategic details we need to fill you in on."

Dale's green eyes narrowed fiercely, then he broke eye contact and looked out at the training camp around him. Many of his amateur soldiers were sleeping under lean-to's made of sticks, branches and moss. They couldn't even afford tents. Suddenly, General Masbruch began to understand George Washington's predicament at Valley Forge.

"All right, Rodney, give it to me straight. What are we in for?"

As General Branch spoke softly and methodically, Dale's old face sagged, then his head hung down almost until his chin touched his chest. His bald head was tanned and glistening with sweat from the severe heat and humidity of the southern summer.

Rodney pulled out some intelligence papers and maps and showed him the plan, but it did little to ease the old soldier's pain. If anything, he became even more skeptical and distraught.

Finally, General Masbruch lifted his head back up and looked Rodney square in the eyes.

"Have you completed a risk assessment of this plan, Rodney?"

Rodney said nothing.

"Hell, Rodney, you got more holes in this plan than you've got plan. It's too complicated, and there's just way too many things that can go wrong!" He was raising his voice now without even knowing it. All three men were silent for a full minute. Then General Masbruch regained his composure and looked off in the distance.

"Dale, you've got good men here. They've got spirit and they'll fight for you."

Dale looked him in the eye again. "I know that." And then he paused before getting to the heart of the matter. "They are good men. Excellent men, the best I've ever trained or served with. I know they don't look like much, but they've got more piss and vinegar than any army on this planet." He paused, looked over at Mac and then back at Rodney.

"Rodney, I want you to give me your word that my men won't die in vain. This plan of yours doesn't have much more than a snowball's chance in hell of success, so I want your very best promise that you'll do everything you can to keep my men from dying without purpose."

General Branch looked down and then over at Mac before speaking out loud. The two seemed to read each other's thoughts, and that had always bothered Masbruch. It felt like they were speaking a foreign language right there in front of him and he felt left out of the conversation. General Branch finally looked back over at him.

"You have my word of honor that your men will have a fighting chance of success, and, even if they die, it will not be in vain."

General Masbruch lowered his head again, then came back up, drew a handkerchief out of his pocket and then wiped his brow with it.

"Rodney, you are one crazy son of a bitch, but ..."

And then, it was as if a switch tripped on deep inside him and he remembered who he was. "If it can be humanly done, then we will accomplish the mission, general."

And then he stood to his feet and rendered his best military salute. Colonel MacPherson rose to his feet and saluted as well. Rodney stood slowly, as if he held the weight of the world on his shoulders, and then he summoned all his energy and saluted sharply and crisply.

After formal good byes, Rodney and Mac got in their helicopter and flew away.

General Masbruch, old, tired, worn down to the bone, sagged back down into his chair. After a few moments of rest he yelled for his aid and summoned a staff meeting. With renewed energy, he kicked himself into high gear, and it was as if he'd never been discouraged.

CHAPTER 5

Coker Creek Tennessee

THE UH60 HELICOPTER HOVERED TWO HUNDRED FEET ABOVE the clearing on the side of the mountain. The pilot had told them to accelerate their descent because of dangerous and shifting thermal currents, so Dan Branch hesitated for just a moment before rappeling down. He glanced over at Sergeant Donny Brewster who was grinning from ear to ear at his longer than normal pause. Donny lived for the excitement of danger, but Dan had been out of the Marine Corps for many years and, to be quite frank, never had relished jumping out of aircraft.

"Do you want me to go first and show you how it's done old man?"

Dan grimaced and pushed himself out the door and down the rope. It's not like he hadn't done this before; it's just that he'd only done it a few times and he didn't enjoy heights. About half way down the rope Donny Brewster passed him. Dan thought to himself, *why is everything a competition to him?* But that thought quickly left him as he looked down and watched Donny disappear into the brush below. Dan was surprised when his legs crashed into mountain laurel and he was turned upside down before landing on his head. Fortunately, thick kudzu vines softened his fall, and his neck didn't break. He felt Donny Brewster's strong hand lift him up and set him back on his feet.

The two men quickly unhooked from the rope and the helicopter raced away to the rendezvous point several miles away.

"This stuff is so thick I can't even see through it!"

Donny nodded in agreement and quickly pulled out his machete. "It's that way, to the east." And then he began swinging his blade with enthusiasm. Dan Branch backed away just in time to keep from getting hit with it.

"Careful marine!"

But Donny just laughed and kept swinging. "Lead, follow or get out of the way, colonel."

Dan shook his head from side to side, adjusted his M4 to ride better on his front and then tightened the straps on his light pack. "Good thinking, sergeant. I think I'll just get out of the way and follow."

Donny hacked through the kudzu vines and laurel for about fifty yards before it finally gave way to pine trees and a more open terrain. They both sat down on a log to rest.

"How much further, Donny?"

The sergeant looked over at his friend with his young, green eyes and smiled. "What's the problem old man? Tired already?"

Dan frowned. He hated it when Donny made cracks about his age. "I'm not old! I'm only thirty five!"

Donny laughed out loud. "Sorry colonel. Didn't realize you were getting so cranky."

Dan took off his olive drab boonie hat and used it to wipe the sweat off his brow. The summer heat and humidity were nearly unbearable here in the mountains of Tennessee. Dan took a moment to regain his self-control.

"Stop calling me colonel when we're alone. You know I don't like that." Then he looked over at the kudzu they'd just hacked through. "So how old are you, Donny?"

Donny's green eyes seemed to sparkle in the mid-day sun. "I'm old enough to know better."

Dan looked over at his friend and gave him a quizzical smile. "What kind of answer is that?"

Donny fished his compass out of a cargo pocket and took a compass reading. "We need to go that way, about another mile."

Donny stood up to march away, but Dan reached out and grabbed his arm. "Hold on there, sergeant. Just exactly how old are you?"

Donny smiled. "Are you pulling rank on me over a silly, little thing like my age?"

But then it was Dan's turn to laugh and he let Donny's arm go. "If it's such a silly, little thing then you certainly won't mind telling me."

"Do you really want to know?"

"Yer darn right I want to know."

Donny hesitated before answering.

"I'm thirty-five years old."

Dan's eyes opened wide with surprise. "You're the same age as me?"

Donny shook his head back and forth. "No way. You're two months older than me. I checked your records."

Dan threw his hat down on the ground before raising his voice. "For the past three months you've been calling me an old man and you're the same age as me!"

"But we're not the same age. You've got two months on me." His green eyes glanced over into the woods ahead, looking for danger. "Besides, look at you and then look at me. I'm obviously the younger, finer masculine specimen."

Dan couldn't believe he was hearing these words. "A finer, masculine specimen?" He turned his head and spit onto the ground a few feet away. "I can't believe you said that."

Donny laughed, but then his eyes narrowed and he grew strangely quiet. Dan looked at him, trying to figure out what was wrong.

"What are you thinking now?"

Donny shrugged. "Nothing."

"Nothing? You're thinking nothing?"

Donny turned to walk away and this time Dan picked up his hat, put it back on his head and followed him. They walked another half mile before Dan spoke again.

"You don't look thirty-five years old. You could pass for twenty-five with no problem."

Donny stopped walking and turned to meet his friend. "Why thank you, colonel. If it's any consolation to you, you don't look your age either."

Dan smiled. "Thanks."

"Right. You could pass for forty-five in a heartbeat."

Dan reared his right hand back to slap his friend on the head, but then quickly stopped.

"Do you hear that?"

Donny turned his head toward the sound and nodded. "Yeah. We must be closer than I thought."

"What is it?"

They crept forward through the pine needles another hundred yards. The pines gave way to laurel and kudzu, forcing them to pick their way carefully and quietly through the dense underbrush. It took them another thirty minutes to make their way through the dense undergrowth. Finally, they peered out into the clearing up ahead to a small cabin with a back porch and a rocking chair.

Justice Reed was stark naked, drinking wine and singing at the top of his voice.

"Swing low ... sweet chariot."

He took another drink of dandelion wine.

"A comin' for ta carry me ... home."

Dan Branch reached into his left, breast pocket and pulled out the plastic bag containing the picture. He looked at it briefly and then handed it to Donny.

"Hmm, he looks different without clothes."

Dan nodded. "Uncle Rodney says our fate lies in this man's hands."

His voice boomed out louder. His voice cracked and he went suddenly way off key. "Swing low ... sweet chariot. A comin' for ta carry me home."

Justice looked out and saw both soldiers stand up and step away from the cover of the brush into his back yard. He took another long drink and didn't stop until the bottle was drained. He passed out and the Mason jar slipped out of his hand and hit the wooden planking with a crash and a shatter of glass.

His last thoughts before fading off to sleep were, *They've found me and I'm going back to prison.*

Dan crept up to the back porch while Donny circled the house on a quick perimeter check. Donny came through the front door, which was unlocked and then cleared each room. When he reached the back porch, he saw Dan still staring down at the naked old man. Donny broke the silence first.

"Why does your Uncle Rodney want this guy so much?"

Dan shook his head from side to side. "I don't know. But if this guy is our last hope then ..."

Donny finished the sentence for him. "Then we're in a world of shit."

Dan didn't disagree with him. The two men wrapped Justice in an old blanket, then searched the house and gathered up anything they thought would be of interest to General Branch and Jeff Arnett.

Three hours later they were on board the Blackhawk and on their way back to Iroquois.

Justice Reed and his needs

Rodney Branch looked over at Justice Reed and smiled. The man was sitting in a straight-backed folding chair in his kitchen, drinking staghorn sumac tea that Jackie had given him. Jackie sat off to the side now, fascinated by the frail, old man. He couldn't be more than five feet four inches tall, skinny as a rail, with the malnourishment typical of many alcoholics. His hair, what was left of it, was disheveled and silver, sticking up at odd angles all around the sides of his head. And, quite possibly, the most unusual thing about him was his obvious lack of clothing.

"Why is this man naked, Sergeant Brewster?"

Donny, who was off to the side, up against the wall answered abruptly. "We gave him clothes, sir, but he refused to wear them."

Colonel Branch had a fly swatter in his hand as he walked around the room, sneaking up on house flies and then dispatching them with a quick flick of his wrist. Justice Reed appeared to be watching Dan with interest. And then he spoke for the first time since being in the room.

"It's very important to kill the flies as early in the day as possible, because they tend to gather in groups. I studied flies every day for several months before coming to that conclusion. They really bother me when they land on me. Very dirty animals they are. Yes, very dirty. It gives me the heebies when they get on my skin."

Dan Branch smiled and killed another fly. "I hate them too. Nasty little buggers. Drive me crazy as a loon."

Justice smiled as if he'd just found a new friend. And then he nodded and turned back to looking at the table in front of him. Uncle Rodney hesitated and then spoke softly.

"Do you know why we brought you here, Dr. Reed?"

The frail, old man looked up from the table and then out the window, watching a robin on the ground in the front yard, as it hopped from one stick to another. Then it pecked the ground.

"You want me to build killing machines."

Uncle Rodney, dressed in olive drab utilities, with three stars on his collar, nodded his head. "Yes, that is correct."

Justice looked Rodney in the eye and held his gaze. Rodney returned it and his own eyes softened. He saw the pain, the brokenness, the despair, and then ... just a tiny spark of life. And that tiny spark caused him to have a glimmer of hope.

"I don't like to kill people, General Branch. I don't like it at all."

Rodney nodded. "Neither do I." He looked down, breaking the man's gaze, but then quickly back up again. "But ... I don't see a way out of this one. We have to kill to survive. Kill to maintain our freedom."

Justice laughed out loud, a boisterous, full-bodied roar that originated in his gut and was forced out his throat by his diaphragm. Rodney raised one eyebrow, but didn't say anything.

"Freedom. That's funny. You kidnapped me from my home. Stuck me in a helicopter and flew me hundreds of miles away against my will ... and you dare talk about freedom?"

A smile touched Rodney's lips. "You make a good point. I guess that gets us off on the wrong foot, doesn't it. I guess that makes us hypocrites."

The smile on Justice' face hardened, then dropped off like a dead bird falling from the sky. "Yes, I suppose it does. But, you see, I'm a hypocrite too, so I don't judge you. I am not righteous. There is none righteous, no not even one."

Rodney nodded. "Romans chapter three."

Justice Reed smiled again. "Yes. You are a follower of The Way, general?"

The general shrugged. "I am a man of war. I study a bit of everything. It helps me know myself, helps me know my enemy ... It gives me the edge."

Justice crossed his arms and seemed intrigued. Then he put his right forefinger to his lips and held it there. "If you know the enemy and know yourself, you need not fear the result of a hundred battles. If you know yourself but not the enemy, for every victory gained you will also suffer a defeat. If you know neither the enemy nor yourself, you will succumb in every battle."

Justice and Rodney locked eyes, like two sumo wrestlers engaged in combat, neither one giving an inch to the other.

"I see you know your Sun Tzu, Dr. Reed."

The naked professor nodded before continuing.

"And who is your enemy, General Branch?"

"My enemy is the Blind Man and his rage."

Justice shook his head from side to side. "Yes, to be sure, the Blind Man is your enemy, but his rage is your friend. His anger will aid you in his own demise."

Rodney thought about it a moment before answering. Dan Branch stopped pacing back and forth looking for flies to kill. Jackie held baby Donna close to her breast for all she was worth, while Donny Brewster looked on at the intellectual duel in fascination.

"Point well taken, Dr Reed. Do you know the Blind Man?"

Justice nodded.

"How?"

The old man hesitated, as if counting the personal cost of his reply; it was the hesitation of a man about to lose his life, but couldn't decide whether to fight or surrender. Finally, he spoke softly, barely a whisper, and every other voice in the room silenced as every ear strained to hear.

"Jared Thompson once owned me."

CHAPTER 6

August 7, A Tough Nut to Crack

J EFF SHOOK HIS HEAD FROM SIDE TO SIDE. **"I'M SORRY, GEN-**
eral. Not at this time. We're still trying to decipher the data on the thumb
drive given to us from Sammy Thurmond, but ... let's just say that it's slow
going."

Rodney looked Jeff in the eyes before replying. "How slow?"

A slight hint of a smile toyed with the corners of Jeff's mouth. "You've heard the
phrase 'slower than molasses in January?' Well, we're just a little bit faster than that.
But we'll break it eventually ... just a matter of time."

General Branch leaned back in his chair, then placed his hands behind his head,
interlaced. "Forgive me, Jeff, but it seems like it's taking a long time. What exactly is
the hold-up?"

Jeff Arnett didn't like the general's tone, but ...it was understandable, given the
gravity of the situation. He placed his hands up on the table and leaned in before
answering. "It's not like I'm back at Langley, general. I've got a bunch of laptops and
desktop PCs networked together. What I'm used to working with, what I really need to
do this job efficiently, is a supercomputer the size of a warehouse where I have nearly
unlimited speed and processing power."

Jeff leaned forward even farther. "This is not the easiest task, general, and my people are working on it twenty-four seven."

Uncle Rodney smiled and then nodded his head. "I'm sure you are Agent Arnett.
Forgive my impatience." Then he stood up slowly, stretched his arms and then his
legs. Lastly, he arched his back to take out a few of the kinks. He hated getting old,
but he just needed to last a little bit longer ... just this one, last mission, and then he
could rest.

Jeff Arnett jumped up quickly for a man of his size, nodded his head and quickly
walked away without speaking again. Uncle Rodney watched him leave, staring after
him, wondering ... can this man do the job I need him to do? But he filed the question
away for another time. Jeff Arnett would just have to crack the code and access the
files as best he could. And the sooner - the better.

In the meantime, Rodney's job was to try and come up with an alternative plan, just
in case Jeff Arnett failed. But how could he do that? How could he defeat a man who
held all the cards, who had all the power, and who seemed to have all the time in the
world? Offhand he didn't know. But he would think on it, and, rest assured, Uncle
Rodney would come up with a workable alternative to help them all defeat the Blind
Man, come hell or high water. After all, what choice did he have?

August 7, What Women Want

"I HAVE NO IDEA, DONNY. I REALLY DON'T KNOW HER THAT WELL." JACKIE
Branch looked over at Donny Brewster, but his muscular, shoulders sagged at
her reply.

"But ... you're a woman, you have to know what's going on with her! She's just not making any sense. One minute she's kissing me and the next she's slapping me across the face. Just tell me what I'm supposed to do!"

Deep inside Jackie felt sad for the poor man. And then she thought to herself, *Why is it men can do so many great and wonderful things, Edison invented the light bulb, Einstein the theory of relativity, but when it comes to understanding women ... they were all morons.* She smiled sympathetically, wondering how she could put it into terms he could understand.

"Donny, have you studied Sun Tzu and *The Art of War*?"

Donny looked up and scoffed. "Of course I have. Hasn't everyone?"

Jackie thought to herself but said nothing out loud. *The man is so clueless about normal people.*

"Donny, perhaps you need to work on your timing a little bit. I think she loves you and that you love her, but ... maybe this just isn't the right time for her to make a commitment."

Donny nodded. "Okay, Dan said something like that too. Something about her feelings I think. But what does that have to do with Sun Tzu?"

Jackie looked off into the distance. They were on Uncle Rodney's small front porch. The baby was playing down on the ground below them. "Donny, sometimes the direct frontal attack isn't the best option."

Donny nodded. "Sure, I know that." But he said nothing more. Jackie tried to coax him along.

"So what do you do when your frontal attack is repelled? Do you just give up or do you try a different tactic?"

The marine shrugged his shoulders. "You back off, gather more intelligence, and then try things from a different angle. Maybe probe the flanks a bit and test for weakness."

Jackie nodded. "Yes, and then?"

"Well, when you find a weakness in the line, you plan a coordinated attack, amass your forces and attack the weakness and continue to hammer it until you break through. After that it's just a matter of mopping up resistance. You know, taking prisoners, rendering aid to the wounded, interrogating their officers, setting up a defensive perimeter, you know ... stuff like that."

Jackie smiled softly. "That's right. And capturing a woman's heart is a little like a military campaign. It could take many battles to win her over, but you never should keep doing things that aren't working for you. After all, you have plenty of options, right?"

Donny hacked up some phlegm and spit off to the side. It made her think *I hope he isn't doing that in front of Lisa and her daughter.*

"Yeah, Sun Tzu says, 'In military strategy, there is only the direct and the oblique, but between them they offer an inexhaustible range of tactics.'"

Jackie smiled again. "That's right, and what does Sun Tzu say about timing?"

Donny thought for a moment. He looked out across the yard, now grown over with weeds, waist high of every kind. "He says there are roads that should not be followed and there are enemies that should not be attacked."

Jackie glanced down at her baby who was putting sticks in her mouth and chewing with delight. "And what else?"

"Well, Sun Tzu says you should only attack when you are sure of your direction, that you should be patient, that you should wait for exactly the right moment when success is assured."

Jackie's face beamed. "That's right. I think you've figured it out now."

Donny turned his head to one side in confusion. "I have?" He reached up his left hand to stroke his cleanly shaven face. "So what should I do?"

The woman felt like reaching over and slapping him up side the head. But she took a deep breath and remained calm. "The timing isn't right, Donny. You have to wait for her. Don't talk so much. Let her talk about her feelings. Let her laugh and let her cry. Don't try to understand her, because it's way above your pay grade." She paused a moment, searching his face to see if any of it was sinking in.

Donny had a blank look on his face. "So what should I say to her to get her to fall in love with me?"

Jackie thought about that for a moment, and then she replied. "Well, Donny, I think ... in your case perhaps less is more."

He cocked his head to the right and raised an eyebrow. "Excuse me?"

Jackie sighed. "Just say things like, 'Oh, I see.' Or maybe 'So how did that make you feel?' or maybe 'That must have been terrible for you.' or something like 'Well, you're going to be okay' or 'These things just take time.' You know, simple little things like that."

Donny quickly reached up into his left breast pocket of his camo shirt and pulled out a small, green spiral notebook and a blank ink pen. He began to write furiously.

"This is good stuff, Jackie! What was that last one again?"

Jackie took a deep breath and repeated all of them over again as he wrote. And then she thought to herself, *This is amazing, so truly amazing.* Here before her was a powerful man, a great leader, a highly skilled military fighter, but he was intimidated and reduced to blubbering incoherence by a woman half his size and strength. Donny Brewster could reach over and snap her neck with one twist. He could shoot an adversary in the head at one thousand yards. He could hike nonstop for days and knife a man in the liver, slicing all the way around his rib cage. But, despite all that, he trembled beside the woman of his dreams ... all one-hundred-and-ten pounds of her.

JUSTICE REED LOOKED GENERAL BRANCH STRAIGHT IN THE EYES AND RE-fused him point blank. "I won't do it!"

Rodney glanced over at Colonel MacPherson and then quickly back at the frail scientist sitting before him. He'd expected some resistance, but not the massive vehemence being exhibited by the man before him. Rodney stared over at Justice from the other side of his kitchen table. Roger MacPherson stood to his left and slightly abreast with his hands folded behind him. A tired sigh escaped Rodney's mouth and his head sagged just a little.

"Please tell me why, Dr. Reed."

The old man was wearing clothes now, a pair of faded blue jeans, white t-shirt with a brown flannel shirt over it. Justice glanced off to his left, looking over the sink and through the window that was now open. A tiny breeze came in, caressing his face before fading into calm.

"I'm retired."

Rodney broke into a sudden laugh. His left hand moved up to his clean-shaven face where he rubbed it harshly before suppressing his smile. "Dr. Reed, you aren't retired, you are in hiding. There's a difference."

Justice smiled softly. He was more interested in the two black squirrels scampering about on the lawn than he was the battle plans of General Branch. "I have no desire to help you recommission twelve tactical nuclear devices."

"And why not?"

"Because I'm obstinate, Mr. Branch! Because I don't like being kidnapped at gunpoint and taken from my home."

That was the first time the doctor had raised his voice, and Rodney took careful note of it. Apparently this wasn't going to be as easy as he'd originally hoped.

The two squirrels disappeared around the oak tree and then spiraled back around and on up into the canopy out of sight. Justice looked back into the room. "I was happy, Mr. Branch. I was about to begin work on a very important project when you invaded my life and took me captive."

Ranger MacPherson spoke for the first time in the conversation, his voice low and without a lot of feeling. "And what project was that, Dr. Reed?"

Justice looked back out the window, but he could no longer find the squirrels and that perturbed him to no end. *Where did the squirrels go? I want the squirrels to come back so I can watch them!* He looked up at the colonel. "I was about to devise a new type of mouse trap. I've always wanted to do that."

Uncle Rodney smiled again. He placed his hands up on the Formica table top and joined them with his fingers interlaced. He looked down at his joined hands and then back up. He searched the bloodshot eyes of Justice Reed before speaking.

"So how do you know this new mousetrap will work?"

It was Justice Reed's turn to smile now. "I don't." He looked down at the red Formica, connecting the silver specks with his eyes in a geometrical pattern. "And that's half the fun, general. I never know what will work and what will not. And that's the fun of it all." He paused. "It's the journey, General Branch ... not the destination."

Rodney Branch nodded his head. He was finally beginning to understand the old scientist. He turned slightly in his chair and spoke directly to Colonel MacPherson.

"Mac, I want you to provide Dr. Reed with everything he needs to build a better mouse trap. Make sure he has decent quarters, plenty of food, supplies, whatever he wants we give it to him, provided we have the power to do so."

Rodney paused. "And make sure he has adequate protection. Even if he won't work for us ... we can't have him falling into the hands of Jared Thompson. That would be most unfortunate."

Justice looked up from the Formica and stared into Rodney's eyes. Rodney held his gaze and gave it back to him double. Finally, Justice nodded.

"Thank you, General Branch."

Rodney stood up and reached across the kitchen table, extending his right hand to Justice as he did so. The old scientist hesitated, but then reached out his own right hand and grasped the olive branch extended to him. They locked eyes for just a tiny moment and then Justice smiled and turned away to leave the room.

Colonel MacPherson turned to follow, but then hesitated and turned back toward his general. "What the hell are you doing, Rodney?"

General Branch was surprised by the colonel's question. Mac hadn't spoken to him that way in many years. He was usually all polish, military precision and bourgeois refinement. Rodney hesitated before answering, looking Mac straight in the eyes, assessing the man's question.

"Colonel MacPherson, you are to follow through with my orders in all haste and without question. It is extremely important that Dr. Reed complete his mousetrap as quickly as possible."

The colonel nodded and then snapped to attention before turning to leave the room.

"Oh, and one more thing, colonel." Colonel MacPherson stopped near the door but didn't turn his body toward the general. "You are to compose a memo to the general staff, informing them of this Top Secret project, which shall be called Project White Horseman."

Mac raised his brow and then turned his head back to General Branch. "You'd like me to help Dr. Reed, a devout, possibly insane scientist, some would call him a mad scientist ... you'd like me to help him build a better mousetrap?"

General Branch nodded. "And then you'd like me to distribute a memo detailing this Top Secret project to the general staff, and it is to be named Project White Horseman? Is that correct, sir?"

Rodney smiled and nodded his head. "That is correct, colonel. But under no circumstances are the details of this project to be revealed to anyone. Only say that the project will be the culmination of many centuries of scientific venture, that it will result in the loss of many lives, vermin who have plagued mankind, and it will bring a quick end to the Blind Man and his diabolical plans."

Colonel MacPherson smiled and shook his head from side to side. He didn't speak for a moment, then he turned, snapped to attention and saluted.

"It shall be done, sir, exactly as you ordered."

General Branch returned the colonel's crisp salute with one of his own. Ranger MacPherson strode quickly out of the room, on his way to building a better mousetrap, leaving General Branch to his own thoughts.

CHAPTER 7

__August 8, The Prophet__

SPARKY FILLMORE WAS A VERY NONDESCRIPT MAN. HE'D never done anything great, at least not by the world's standards, but one thing he'd always done consistently, was to obey the Lord and all His commands. But when God came to him on that particular day, after the apocalypse, while he was milking the cow, Sparky had questioned the Lord.

"Are you sure this is what you want me to do? You want me to leave my wife and all I've built up here, in a hometown my family has lived in for generations, and you'd like me to walk halfway across the country just to give some stranger a message?"

God had never spoken to Sparky before ... well, at least not in this way; the Lord's voice was almost audible, and the feeling he got was like he was standing on holy ground, like the very air around him had suddenly been transformed into something other-worldly, like a spiritual electricity had been infused into the space around him. When the message came to him he half expected to see a burning bush, or, in this case, a burning bale of hay or straw.

Sparky had been a deacon in the local church for much of his adult life. He'd even done a bit of preaching from time to time, especially when the little congregation was between pastors, as happened occasionally with many small country churches. He read his Bible everyday, even studied it with his wife, Edna. She was his childhood sweetheart, and they'd been married for fifty-three years. Their three children had been successful as adults, two of them moving across the country, one as a doctor and the other as an engineer. The third owned a farm just a few miles from Sparky's own home in western Kansas.

A million questions and thoughts and concerns all competed for voice as the old man contemplated his answer to the Lord. He knew that God loved him, but he also knew, from his immense study of the scripture that to question God rarely ended well. One man in particular came to his mind as God waited for Sparky to give account. It was the story of Zechariah. The angel Gabriel had gone to him and told him his wife would give birth in her old age. But Zechariah, had doubted the angel and been struck mute until after the birth of his son, who was later known as "John the Baptist."

And Moses had also questioned God but to no avail. The Bible was filled with stories of people questioning the commission of God, so, no matter how crazy it might sound, Sparky uttered his reply.

"Command me Lord and I shall go."

So the Lord commanded Sparky Fillmore, a man of little consequence to travel to Michigan in search of a man named General Rodney T. Branch. God didn't give him the message, but simply demanded that Sparky trust Him in all things. And so, Sparky believed and obeyed the Lord, and it was credited to him as righteousness.

And Sparky left that very same day, with nothing but the clothes on his back and a lunch of raspberry jam and peanut butter sandwiches that his wife had fixed for him. He also brought one can of Spam, just in case, and hoped that God wouldn't see that as a lack of faith on his part. And Sparky wondered, in his heart of hearts. *Will I surely die?*

But the Lord was with him in all that he did.

August 8, The Woods of Iroquois County

SAMMY THURMOND HAD BEEN WATCHING THE REMAINS OF IROQUOIS CITY for the past two days, but had seen nothing to impress him. In fact, he'd seen very little of anything. The town per se had been almost totally destroyed by the saracen army weeks before on their march to Mackinaw City. He sat perched atop the burnt-out shell of an Abrams tank on the hill overlooking the town. An oak tree was off to his left; it was a full three feet in diameter, and the bark about head high was charred from the same battle that had killed the tank. Despite the damage, the tree was doing its best to recover and live. Its leaves were green and hardy, and Sammy respected the tree for fighting so hard to stay alive.

Sammy had read all the reports of the first battle for Iroquois City, as it had come to be called, and he was in awe of the incredible leadership skills and military tactics of General Branch. He'd even seen the video footage from the drones as the three cars had raced up the hill to try and destroy the tanks, and he wondered to himself, *how do you convince people to give up their lives in a battle that can't possibly be won*? Because Rodney Branch should not have won that battle. He'd been outgunned, outnumbered and outmaneuvered. The Shadow Militia and the Iroquois County Home Guard should have been soundly defeated and every last man, woman and child killed. But they weren't. They had won ... not only won, but gloriously and soundly they had destroyed every last attacker, almost to the man. Sammy wanted to meet the person who'd conceived of that victory, the man who'd inspired these farmers and shopkeepers and factory workers to rise up and fight against hopeless odds.

So Sammy watched now, trying to figure out a way to find the general. A year ago he could have simply done an internet records search and gotten his home address through the county clerk's records, but that was no longer possible. For all intents and purposes, the internet was dead, and would not be resurrected for many years to come, maybe even decades.

And then there was the question of Jackie Branch, the woman he'd become enamored with. Women had always been mere objects to him, things to be possessed, to be exploited, mere toys he could play with for his own amusement and distraction. But Jackie ... Jackie Branch had been different. He'd tried to play with her, but had been flummoxed. There was some inner strength she possessed that made her unconquerable, indomitable and unyielding. She had a quality that intrigued Sammy Thurmond. And it was that undefinable quality that had caused him to set her free, had indeed inspired him to leave the Blind Man and come to Iroquois, what was left of it.

It was odd for Sammy to contemplate what he was doing, because it defied logic. The Blind Man held all the cards, all the power, all the means to come out on top in this fight. But still ... Sammy had left him, had deserted the obvious winner, and with it, fortune and power and a sure future. But still ... there was a muse drawing him here, the muse of a strong, beautiful woman, and the sirens of General Rodney T. Branch. General Branch, who was not supposed to win, indeed it had been impossible for him to win, against the cutthroat murderer named Manny with his three thousand barbarians, and then again against the saracen tide of tens of thousands, backed up with military armor and F18 fighter jets. Still, the general had won.

So Sammy Thurmond waited now for what he knew not, for whatever would happen next. He simply released his grip on the bank of life and let the river take him, and suddenly, he believed in fate, and maybe ... even a higher power.

August 9, Five Miles East of Hays, Kansas 8AM

Sᴘᴀʀᴋʏ Fɪʟʟᴍᴏʀᴇ ᴅɪᴅɴ'ᴛ ꜰᴇᴇʟ ʟɪᴋᴇ ᴀ ᴘʀᴏᴘʜᴇᴛ, ʙᴜᴛ ᴡʜᴇɴ ʜᴇ ᴇxᴀᴍɪɴᴇᴅ it closely, which, he had plenty of time to do while walking down the incredibly hot West Kansas pavement, he couldn't help but see some similarities. Throughout the Bible, prophets had been simply ordinary people whom God had called to give messages to people or to nations, sometimes messages that were not well received, and could even cause the death of the messenger. Sparky couldn't help but be mindful of the words of Jesus Christ when talking about the prophets of old.

"Jerusalem, Jerusalem, you who kill the prophets and stone those sent to you, how often I have longed to gather your children together, as a hen gathers her chicks under her wings, and you were not willing."

Luke 13:34 (NIV)

Sparky desperately wanted to be well received by who ever God was sending him to meet. And he hoped above all else that he was giving them good news. He hated so much to be a bearer of ill omen. With feet hurting, hot and sweaty, with a lower back that cried out for him to collapse on the side of the road, Sparky plodded on. The heat in Western Kansas this time of year was oppressive, but the old man had grown up here and was used to it, as much as anyone could be. But still ... walking almost a thousand miles in the scorching heat was different than working for a few hours at his son's farm or hoeing the vegetable garden.

Funny, but it hadn't occurred to Sparky to question whether or not he'd actually be able to walk that far at his age. Sure, he'd wondered about a violent death, being robbed, beaten and left to die on the side of the road, because Sparky was not a violent man. He didn't even own a gun. Other than a few years in the army back during the Vietnam War, Sparky had never taken up arms. What would happen to him if someone attacked? Would God protect him or would he be killed? In his mind's eye, Sparky saw his body lying motionless on the side of the road, bloated in the intense heat of the day, as a turkey vulture circled overhead.

But Sparky knew this mission, or quest, or whatever it was had come from God, not just because God had spoken to him, because something like that had never happened before, but because of the way his wife had responded to him. When Sparky had told Edna that he was going to walk from Kansas to Michigan to give a message from God to a man that he hadn't met, and that he had no idea what the message was, she had simply said, "I know." And then she'd packed him the lunch and sent him on his way the very same hour. Sparky hadn't even said good bye to his children. He'd thought about it, but then asked the question "why?" After all, they would just call him crazy and try to talk him out of it, and, to be honest with himself, he didn't think he'd be able to withstand any kind of peer pressure, that he could have been very easily persuaded to stay home, that this venture was ludicrous and dangerous and the ravings of a crazy man. So, Sparky had left his home and the wife he loved that very hour.

And now, alone with nothing but his own thoughts ... he wondered about his own sanity. But, regardless of whether he was sane or stark, raving mad, there was nothing left for him to do but to walk on. After all, what else could he do? Could he turn around and go back to his wife and home? What would he tell her; that he'd been afraid, or foolish, or that his feet hurt?

And then he was reminded of the story of Christian, in the book *Pilgrim's Progress*, written by John Bunyan, and of the many hardships that had been encountered. He kind of felt like Christian in that story, like he was going against the grain of everything that made sense. So, renewed in his purpose, the old man kept going. And then, way up ahead, shimmering off the waves of heat coming up off the hot asphalt, Sparky saw something and quickened his pace.

Uncle Rodney's kitchen

"GENTLEMEN, WE ARE HERE THIS MORNING TO TALK ABOUT WHO IS GOING to lead the new America once we've defeated the Blind Man." Uncle Rodney was standing before them at the head of the red, Formica-topped table in his kitchen. Seated around it were Colonel MacPherson, Jeff Arnett, Dan Branch, and Sheriff Joe Leif, while Jackie Branch and baby Donna were seated off to the side.

The intense and sad irony of the situation didn't escape Dan, nor did it elude anyone else around the table. Just over a year ago this type of high-level meeting wouldn't be held in a run-down kitchen of a private home, but in the halls of congress or in the White House itself. But now ... so much had changed. Here they were, just a ragtag group of citizens, deciding who the next leader of the free world would be.

Just a year ago Dan had been in a failed marriage, awaiting his inevitable divorce, working in a factory for a mere penance as a wage. But now, he was a colonel in the Shadow Militia, commanding thousands of seasoned combat veterans and presiding over the only force on the planet capable of defeating the next tyrant, Jared Thompson, also known as the Blind Man, the person who had orchestrated the demise of the United States, and, for that matter, the entire world. His plan had proceeded almost flawlessly, and half of America had already been pacified, but there was only one thing standing in his way of continental domination, and that was ... Rodney T. Branch and the handful of people sitting around the table.

As Dan looked back on the past year, he recalled the horrors of battle and the butchery he'd witnessed; it was more than any one man could ever want, but still ... if he had to do it all over again, he would act with even less hesitation than before. Dan had gained confidence as a military leader, even though he'd been a mere sergeant in the Marine corps in what seemed like a distant life. But still ... one thing was there that he could not deny ... what they had done ... they had done. It was there, staring him and all the others in the face as they presided over what might become the most important meeting they'd ever had. And it was all being decided over a red, Formica table top dating back to the nineteen-fifties, and they were sipping casually on sumac-berry tea and chickory-based coffee. All this ... and there was no ice to cool their tea.

"Uncle Rodney." Dan placed his tea down on the table in front of him before continuing. "I just assumed that you'd be leading America once the Blind Man was out of the picture."

General Branch was already shaking his head from side to side before Dan could even finish his statement. "No. It can't be that way. Though I appreciate your vote of confidence. The succession of power has to be as outlined in the US constitution. That's the way the Founding Fathers wanted it, and nothing has changed in that regard."

Joe Leif chimed in. "That's right. The country may be down and out right now, but we still have to maintain the rule of law, and the constitution is the supreme law of the land."

Colonel MacPherson and Jeff Arnett nodded their heads in approval before Uncle Rodney continued. "We will be proceeding with the continuity of government plan that was in place at the time of the Fall, over a year ago. Agent Jeff Arnett will brief us on the details." Rodney nodded to Jeff, who then stood and moved to the kitchen wall behind him. A large chalkboard, taken from the debris of a local elementary school had been nailed there. Uncle Rodney took his seat.

Jeff Arnett picked up a piece of white chalk and wrote the letters C - O - G in big letters near the top of the old-fashioned chalkboard. "Continuity of Government, gentlemen, that's what we are here to decide." He looked around the room, meeting each person's gaze one at a time before going on. "First, a little background information. Continuity of government establishes defined procedures which allow a government to continue its essential operations in case of a catastrophic event such as nuclear war, or, in our case, a widespread and open-ended long-term power loss."

Dan Branch had always been impressed by the professional bearing of Agent Jeff Arnett. He was always prepared, always formal, and seemed to radiate confidence whenever he spoke to a group.

"COG was first created by the British government before and throughout World War II to meet certain threats, for example, the Luftwaffe bombing during the Battle of Britain. After that, the necessity for continuity of government gained new expediency with nuclear proliferation following World War Two.

"During and after the Cold War many countries developed contingency plans to minimize chaos and disorder during a power vacuum in the event of a nuclear attack.

"Here in America, COG is no longer limited to nuclear emergencies, as it was activated following the September 11 attacks on New York City."

Jeff scanned the room to see if there were any questions. Seeing no quizzical looks, he pressed on.

"The US plan sets up a line of succession that allows for certain elected officials, and, some appointed officials to be included in the presidential line of succession. And they are as follows:" Jeff moved closer to the chalkboard.

"If the president is no longer able to perform his duties, the vice president will be sworn in as president. If the VP and president are deemed unable to lead, then the following offices will be named as acting president of the United States. Number three in the line of succession is the Speaker of the House, Number four is the president pro tempore of the Senate, followed by cabinet positions in the following order: the Secretary of State, then by Secretary of the Treasury, Secretary of Defense, Attorney General, Secretary of the Interior, Secretary of Agriculture, Secretary of Commerce, Secretary of Labor, Secretary of Health and Human Services, Secretary of Housing and Urban Development, Secretary of Transportation, Secretary of Energy, Secretary of Education, Secretary of Veterans Affairs, and then Secretary of Homeland Security."

Jeff looked up from the list he was reading and quickly scanned the room. He had everyone's attention, and no one seemed to have any questions at this point, so he quickly moved on. "Our best intelligence tells us that the president, vice president, speaker of the house along with the president pro tempore of the senate are no longer alive. Also, the following people in this line of succession have met with an untimely demise:

Secretary of State

Secretary of the Treasury

Secretary of Defense

Attorney General

Secretary of the Interior

Secretary of Agriculture

Secretary of Commerce

Secretary of Labor

Secretary of Health and Human Services

Secretary of Transportation

Secretary of Energy

Secretary of Education

Secretary of Veterans Affairs

Secretary of Homeland Security"

Jeff Arnett paused to let the message sink in. Sheriff Joe Leif was the first to ask the obvious question. "So ... how did all these people die?"

Jeff answered the question promptly and without emotion. "The majority were killed when the Blind Man attacked the designated underground strongholds of Cheyenne Mountain, Mount Weather and Raven Rock. These underground facilities were hardened against nuclear attack and highly fortified, and previously considered impregnable to nuclear attack. However, the Blind Man somehow pumped vast amounts of deadly nerve agents into the ventilating systems of these complexes and killed every last inhabitant.

"That occurred just a few days after the nationwide power loss. There were only four people in the presidential line of succession to survive after that. The secretary of state, secretary of education, secretary of transportation and the secretary of veterans affairs."

Joe Leif followed up with another question. "So where are these people now? Why didn't they assume command?"

Jeff Arnett paused a moment, as if girding up the loins of his mental strength to continue on. "The secretary of state was shot in the head with a pistol at close range. The secretary of education died of food poisoning, and the secretary of transportation was attacked via a predator drone attack. That last one wasn't confirmed visually, but we assume he is dead, since no one has seen or heard from him since."

There was a deathly silence in the room. Dan looked over at Joe. Colonel MacPherson didn't move, standing ramrod straight and at the position of attention behind General Branch. Joe Leif was the first to talk.

"I don't understand what the big deal is, Rodney. There's only one of these guys left, the Secretary of the Department of Veteran Affairs. It sounds like the Blind Man is way ahead of us on this one. He probably already knows where this person is, because he's systematically exterminated anyone who could possibly lead the United States out of this mess."

Dan Branch nodded his head in agreement. "He's right, Uncle Rodney. The Blind Man has effectively eliminated all the competition. Besides, even if we could locate the secretary, what would that gain us? The Blind Man has taken control of what's left of the US military. The secretary of Veteran's Affairs would just be a symbol without any real power."

General Branch stood to his feet and glanced around the room before speaking. Then he nodded to Colonel MacPherson, who immediately stepped forward. "That's not entirely true, Colonel Branch. There are still many isolated pockets of Army, Navy, Marine and Air Force resistance who are holding out against the Blind Man. However, they are not actively fighting against him, because no one is holding legitimate consti-tutional power who can order them to attack."

Uncle Rodney interrupted. "It's not like the Shadow Militia can take control of US Military bases. We can't do that. It would be wrong and we'd have to kill American military warriors to do that." There was a momentary silence before Rodney contin-ued. "However, if we can find the secretary of Veteran Affairs before the Blind Man, then we can link him up to military bases across the country, re-establish command and control and we will unite beside them. Our combined forces might be enough to win the day."

Dan Branch took a sip of his tea before speaking. "So who exactly is the Blind Man getting to fight for him, if not the US military?"

Colonel MacPherson nodded to Jeff Arnett, who began speaking immediately. "Some of the American forces lined up behind him, but he also has a combination of Caribbean, Central and South American, as well as western and eastern European military personnel. Most of them came on board shortly after the collapse. But it was orchestrated from the beginning. The Blind Man had his military forces organized on paper before the attack, then he simply mobilized them in the ensuing chaos and after-math. The bulk of their equipment and arsenal was captured within a few days of the collapse from existing armories across the country. One weakness the Blind Man has is airpower. He has a limited number of trained pilots and operational planes. That's how we've been able to stay in the fight as long as we have. He is hesitant to commit his airpower because it is irreplaceable. His nuclear arsenal is also limited."

Sheriff Joe Leif mumbled under his breath. "Tell that to the residents of Escanaba."

Dan ignored Joe's comment. "So, do we know where this guy is?"

Jeff moved to the chalkboard and wrote the name 'Joseph Donnelly.' Dan's hand moved up to his chin and stroked it thoughtfully. "That name sounds familiar to me."

Jeff Arnett nodded his head. "Yes, you probably heard his name in the news. Just a few weeks before the collapse it was announced that the FBI was investigating him on possible misuse of government funds."

Jeff let the indictment hang in the air, like the smell of burning rubber in a closed room. Joe Leif moved both his hands up to the sides of his head and sighed. "So he's a crook?"

General Branch took a step closer. "He's a politician, Joe. But he's the only politician who can legally take control of what's left of the US government."

The baby began to cry, and Jackie hushed her, picked her up and rocked her back and forth. "So, General Branch, where is the secretary now? Do we even know where he might be?"

Turning to the chalkboard, Jeff Arnett wrote in big letters.

"HAITI"

Jackie's heart leaped into her throat. She looked down at her baby girl, with black skin and black, kinky hair. She'd spent a lot of time in Haiti with her first husband on mission trips. They'd also spent time in neighboring Dominican Republic. She knew the island well. But ... there was a darkness in her past, and it centered on an island just 800 miles from Miami, Florida.

She looked over at Dan. His head was down, and there was a sadness about him. She looked up at General Branch, and he was looking directly at her. Jackie looked down at her baby, then back up to Dan, who refused to make eye contact with her. She let out a deep breath, then sucked it back in, establishing eye contact with her Uncle Rodney.

It was at that moment in time she began to understand the bond between Uncle Rodney and Ranger MacPherson, the way they could talk with each other without speaking, the way they always seemed to know what the other was thinking. She took one last look at her husband, begging for help, but none was forthcoming. Resolved, she glanced back at General Branch and nodded her head slightly.

Jackie Branch would leave her baby and travel across the country, back in time to the land of her nightmares. It was a decision that broke her heart.

CHAPTER 8

August 10, Jackie Prepares to Leave

DAN BRANCH WAS NOT A HAPPY CAMPER. THE LAST TIME HIS Uncle Rodney had sent his wife on a secret mission she'd been raped, tortured and hung on a cross to die. And to be quite honest, Jackie was not happy either. She was now three months pregnant with Dan's baby, and she wanted so much to give birth, and raise their child, to love and cuddle, and watch both her babies grow up. Jackie reached down and felt the bump on her stomach.

She so much wanted the chance to grow old.

Of all the places to be sent, this was the last place on earth she wanted to go. It felt to her like returning to the scene of the crime, like a constant reminder of her life's greatest sin, like a reminder of the evil she'd perpetrated against a good and godly man.

And then there was her baby, little baby Donna, almost a year old now, but still a baby to her mother. It pained her to leave the little girl she loved. Against the saracen tide, Jackie had been eager to get into the fight, to be a spy in their camp, and she had indeed killed thousands of the enemy, but ... her eagerness to battle had turned to sand in her mouth as the reality and horror of war had taken hold. She had been content to sit this one out, to simply stay home with her baby and let the men go off and do all the fighting this time around, but ... that was not in the cards, and she couldn't argue with Uncle Rodney. This mission was crucial to the cause, and it stood a higher chance for success with her as its leader.

Baby Donna was already with Marge Leif for the next few days; they'd said their good byes, and, of course the baby had no idea what was going on, that her mother may never return, that she could be an orphan soon. Jackie thought about that for a moment. *But wasn't that always true, especially these days?* Even before the collapse, life had been precarious, but now ... the Blind Man could find them and kill them at any moment, and they wouldn't even know it was coming. And then she silently rebuked herself. She should have more faith in Uncle Rodney ... and in God. Both had never let her down.

She looked over at her husband sitting on the edge of the bed as she finished filling her backpack.

"I don't like this, Jackie. Last time you almost died."

Jackie paused a moment, but then forced her hands to keep working. "I don't like it either. But the logic is sound."

Dan wanted to argue, but he couldn't in any reasonable way. The mission was sound, and it was necessary. And then Dan surprised her. "I want you to know how proud I am of you for doing this."

Jackie stopped and turned to face him. Tears ran down her cheeks as she moved across the bed to embrace him. "Thank you, honey. I really don't want to go this time. I just want to stay home and take care of the baby and let other people do the work. I'm not ashamed of thinking that way either."

This seemed to surprise Dan, but he let it go. "You need to be careful, Jackie. You need to come home to me and Jeremy and Donna." He reached down and rubbed the small bump on her stomach. "We need you here."

Jackie reached up and touched Dan's cheek. She ran her thumb across his face from up to down and then back to his ear. Then she pressed her own lips against his in a passionate embrace. Jackie pushed him down on his back and made love to him like it was going to be the very last time.

An hour later Dan drove her to the rally point, where they said goodbye. Dan waved as the helicopter faded into the night sky. It would be days, perhaps weeks before they saw each other again.

August 11, A Bicycle Built for One

THE KANSAS PROPHET PEDALED AS FAST AS HIS 72-YEAR-OLD LEGS WOULD carry him, though that wasn't really all that fast. He should have been singing a great hymn of the faith, like *How Great thou Art* or perhaps *A Mighty Fortress is Our God*, but no, Sparky Fillmore was singing a Toby Keith song as he sped down the flat, smooth road of Interstate 70 as he headed east.

> *I said Dave!*
> *I ain't as good as I once was,*
> *My how the years have flown,*
> *But there was a time,*
> *Back in my prime,*
> *When I could really hold my own,*
> *But if you want a fight tonight,*
> *Guess those boys don't look all that tough,*
> *I ain't as good as I once was,*
> *But I'm as good once, as I ever was.*

He remembered when that song had come out a long time ago, and he'd liked it then, but only sang it when Edna wasn't around. His wife didn't approve of secular music,and she certainly didn't want him singing a bar-room brawl song. She said it was from the devil. And, maybe it was, Sparky didn't know for sure. But what he did know is that it took his mind off the pain in his lower back and the cramping in his ankles. He hadn't ridden a bike since he was a teenager, but there it was, leaning against the road sign with a note on it that said: "Take me - I'm yours!"

And so he had. For the past three days he'd pedaled the bicycle across Kansas from west to east, watching the sunrise every morning, being scorched in the noontime heat, only to have the sun at his back in the afternoon. With the help of the bicycle, he was making amazingly good time. Already he could feel his old muscles beginning to tighten up and get back into shape. True, like the Toby Keith song said, he'd never be as good as he once was, but, still, perhaps he could be good enough just this one, last time. It certainly helped that he'd found some ibuprofen in an abandoned house the day before yesterday.

He had a two-quart milk jug that he filled with water on every occasion possible, which wasn't very often. Every time he passed an abandoned home or business, he went inside, found the hot water heater, and filled up his container to the top. Sometimes he'd find food as well. Yesterday he'd eaten a dead rabbit lying by the side of the highway. It wasn't roadkill, because there were no cars. He didn't know how it had died, but simply assumed it was from God. His new rule was: If it doesn't smell too bad, then go ahead and eat it.

And that's how Sparky survived on his way to testify God's Truth to General Rodney T. Branch.

August 11, Mission to Montana

"HAVE YOU HEARD ANYTHING FROM JACKIE AND HER TEAM?" DAN BRANCH sat across the table from his Uncle Rodney. Jeremy was seated to the left of his Uncle.

"Nothing since last night. They reached Port-au-Prince okay and have started searching the resorts and hotels. We think he may be holed up there or in the surrounding countryside on a small ranch. I guess they call them plantations down there."

Rodney watched Dan's reaction for signs of stress and saw plenty. "But we don't expect to hear from her again until tonight."

Dan looked out the window, at a loss to say anything. Jeremy spoke next. "It's okay, Dad. Donny is with her, and you know how good he is. He won't let anything happen to her. Donny is the best."

Uncle Rodney smiled sadly. "And don't underestimate her, son. You know how tough and smart that woman is."

Jeremy laughed out loud. "That's right, Dad. She can beat you in a game of Risk almost every time!"

Dan looked over the table to his son and couldn't help but smile weakly. "You still remember that night?"

Jeremy nodded. "Yup. And I'll cherish that moment for the rest of my life."

Dan laughed softly. "I think that's the night I began to fall in love with her."

"I think that's a story I need to hear, but not right now. We have something very urgent that needs my two best men. And it has to be done right away."

Dan forced himself back into military mode, and his face changed back to its prior sternness. Then he nodded to his uncle. "I'm listening."

Uncle Rodney leaned forward in the rickety, wooden chair as he spoke. "I need the two of you to lead a team out west, to Montana. There's something that has to be picked up and brought safely back to Iroquois."

When Uncle Rodney reached to his left, breast pocket for a nonexistent cigarette, Dan knew this was something big. He hadn't seen his uncle do that in weeks. Something about this made the general nervous, and that was saying something, because his Uncle Rodney seemed to always be in such firm control.

"What is it?"

Rodney paused, but then shifted in his chair to gaze out the window at the gray squirrel scampering about on the lawn. He didn't see a lot of gray squirrels in Iroquois. Most of them were the tan-shaded fox squirrels or the black squirrels. That's why he hadn't yet eaten this particular squirrel, though, sooner or later, if things got bad enough, he'd have to shoot this one as well. He turned back to his nephew.

"Twelve nuclear warheads."

August 12, Sammy Thurmond's Calling Card

Staff Sergeant Adam Cervantes stood at attention in front of General Branch. Colonel MacPherson was off to one side. standing at ease, but still rigid and alert. Mac was the first to speak.

"We found the staff sergeant duct taped to a tree about fifty yards inside the trees and just outside the perimeter. He had this sheet of paper taped to his chest." The colonel handed the note to General Branch who read it quietly to himself.

"I respectfully request to meet with you at a time and place of your choosing. We have much to discuss. As a token of good faith, I have chosen not to kill your staff sergeant.

Respectfully, Samuel Thurmond

Uncle Rodney smiled, and then lowered his head, shaking it from side to side. "Staff Sergeant Cervantes. Will you please explain to me how this man was able to duct tape you to a tree within one-hundred yards of my command post?"

Adam nervously bit his lower lip before answering. "I, I'm not sure, sir. Actually, sir, I have no idea."

Uncle Rodney cocked his head to the right just slightly and took an intimidating step forward.

"You have no idea?"

Adam did his best to maintain a position of attention, but it was a losing battle. He'd been thoroughly humiliated.

"That is correct, sir. I never saw him. I never heard him. The man was a ghost, sir."

The general nodded his head and then glanced over at Colonel MacPherson. Then he turned back to the staff sergeant before continuing. "I see. Well, staff sergeant, I don't believe in ghosts ... however, this man is probably about as close to that as they come." Then he glanced back over at the colonel. "Colonel MacPherson, this man is not to be punished. There is no shame in what happened to him. It could have happened to any of us." Then he paused, glancing back over to the colonel. "However, we cannot be caught unaware again. Please spread the word that the staff sergeant was subdued and duct-taped to a tree by a lone man. Everyone must be on high alert. and we can't afford for this to happen again."

The shoulders of Staff Sergeant Cervantes slumped involuntarily. He thought to himself, *I'll be the laughing stock of the unit.* And then an even more painful realization occurred to him: *What if Donny Brewster finds out? I'll never hear the end of it.*

And, unknown to Adam Cervantes, that is exactly what the general was counting on.

"That is all, staff sergeant. You are dismissed."

"Sir, yes sir!"

Adam did a perfect about face and strode out of the room. Once he was gone, Rodney turned to his friend.

"There's a storm comin' Mac. Can you feel it?"

The colonel let out a deep sigh, one filled with age and weariness. He nodded his head. "I suppose I do. For good or ill."

Rodney looked out the open window. It was hot, but a sudden breeze came into the room as if on cue. "Yes, for good or for ill." And then he turned to leave the room.

"Make the arrangements, colonel. It's time to meet Sammy Thurmond."

August 13, Sammy and Uncle Rodney

UNCLE RODNEY SAT ON THE GROUND FACING THE GRANITE HEADSTONE, listening to the birds in the white pine tree off to his left, watching the black squirrels scamper beneath the oak tree off in the distance. He heard another squirrel chatter in the big oak about ten feet behind him. His butt always got numb if he didn't shift back and forth from one cheek to the other, so he made the transition now to ward off the inevitable.

Rodney's eyes rested lightly on the granite rock in front of him, the words before him, etched in stone, left a permanence and a feeling of mortality that was disconcerting. You'd think Rodney would understand life and death by now, having witnessed so much of it over the last seventy years, but ... it was still largely a mystery to him. But seeing his last name on the headstone always seemed to unsettle him, to make him think twice, to question even the most basic ideas and the bedrock of his beliefs.

Six feet below him lie his brother, the little boy he'd grown up with, played with in the woods around him, splashed with in the Manistee river; they'd even played on many of these very headstones here in the cemetery a full sixty years prior.

It seemed like a lifetime ago.

And then Rodney laughed out loud at his silly thought, because, after all, it really had been a lifetime ago. His life was mostly gone now, all used up, with more thoughts behind him than in front, more deeds done than not. In many regards he felt like he was coasting now, just playing out the hand dealt to him, the last hand, but maybe the most important hand he'd ever played.

A cardinal, bright red in color landed on the tombstone in front of him. It always amazed him how quickly they could move. The cardinal was one of his favorite birds, perhaps because of their resilience. They stayed here in the winter, lending their bright red to the white snow, always staying, never giving up, always bright, lending color and contrast to the cold death of the north woods winter.

But now it was summer, and summer was the time for action. Rodney read the name in front of him "Ronald T. Branch." He'd been close to his brother, a twin in every regard, and that's why he'd retired early from the military to care for Dan when Ronny had died. There was a bond inside him that went deeper then mere blood. It was spiritual. A bond of the strongest kind - a bond of unseen blood. Yes, he and Ronny had always been close. and, indeed, always would be close, even in death.

But he hadn't come to his brother's grave to visit, at least not today. No, today was all business. He had come to meet his enemy, and, perhaps, just perhaps, the enemy of his enemy.

"You can come out now, Mr. Thurmond. I've been waiting for you."

The bushes on the west edge of the cemetery rustled just a bit, and then Sammy Thurmond stepped out, revealing himself for the first time. Rodney waited patiently as the man walked over. General Branch analyzed the man's walk; it was a gait of confidence with just a hint of military precision.

As he approached, General Branch moved doggedly to his feet and extended his right hand. Three feet away Sammy stopped and looked Rodney in the eyes. He hesitated, as if looking for something in particular. Then, appearing to find it, he reached out his right hand and clasped Rodney's in his own.

"Thank you for meeting with me, general."

For now, Rodney kept a stone face and simply nodded slightly. Sammy glanced down at the granite headstone in front of them. "Your twin brother. Died of an unfortunate accident at age 35. His wife had died a few years prior to that. You retired from the military, even though you had a great career ahead of you and you came home to Iroquois to finish raising your nephew, Dan, as your own son."

Uncle Rodney nodded and then motioned to the west. "Shall we walk, Mr.

Thurmond?" Sammy didn't answer, but began slowly walking. Both men walked past one headstone after another. Rodney took note that Sammy fell in to his left and slightly abreast.

"You are a military man, Mr. Thurmond." It wasn't a question, and wasn't taken as such, so Sammy simply nodded. "The Blind Man is a civilian. I see nothing in him so far to indicate otherwise." Sammy nodded again before speaking.

"Yes, that is true. But he makes up for that lacking with an unusual understanding of human nature."

Rodney thought about this for a moment before continuing. "But the Blind Man has a weakness."

Sammy suddenly stopped. They were standing in front of a gravestone now in the older part of the cemetery. It was a larger stone, jutting up in a slab, with letters and numbers that were extremely worn and covered over with some moss. Rodney's old eyes could barely make out the words.

Pvt Jeremiah A. Cole
Born 1845 - Died 1864
13th Michigan Artillery

Sammy looked down at the head stone as well. "Apparently 13 wasn't his lucky number."And then he paused before continuing. "Yes, of course he does. Everyone has a weakness, General Branch." Sammy looked over at a grey squirrel ten yards in the distance. Rodney couldn't help but notice Sammy's fascination with the animal, as if it was the first time he'd ever seen one. There was a sudden childlike aura to the man that undergirded the extreme evil that showed on the surface.

"The Blind Man has many weaknesses. But ... he also has many strengths."

Rodney looked over at Sammy and began to walk again. The man quickly took his place to the left and slightly abreast. "Talk about the Blind Man."

Sammy wasted no time in answering him. "The Blind Man is highly organized. He likes everything just so, with nothing out of place, no loose ends, nothing that can come back on him. He is tidy and neat. He is a very polite man, and insists that others be courteous in his presence, even if they are about to die at his hand."

Rodney smiled. "That might be a bit too much to ask from a man."

Sammy's stone face hardened even more. "I never said he was reasonable. He is a hard man, unrelenting, inflexible, and pays great attention to detail. Much of his success is attributed to ruthlessness. He also prides himself on the amount of information he is able to gather on his enemies. He considers information to be power."

Rodney nodded. "So he knows his enemy well. How well does he know me?"

Sammy Thurmond stopped walking and turned to look at the general. Rodney also halted and turned. Both men locked eyes. "He knows every public detail about you plus many things private and considered unknown. He knows all save the most private thoughts of your heart that you have locked away for only yourself."

Rodney examined the man before him. He was a fascinating person, able to kill at a moment's notice, able to turn his emotions on and off as if flicking a switch inside him. Despite that, Rodney felt safe beside him, if, for no other reason than this: if

Sammy wanted him dead, the deed would already be done, and they would not be talking right now.

"Mr. Thurmond, I assume, by virtue of our meeting, that there is something you wish to tell me, and that there is also something you wish to receive from me."

Uncle Rodney glanced around him at the head stones and chose the grave of Mary A. Redmond, born 1875, died 1917, the year Vladimir Lenin led the Bolsheviks in a successful revolution against the provisional government of Russia. He sat down atop the marble. He imagined the poor woman dying of influenza, reluctantly leaving her husband without a wife and her children without a mother.

Sammy Thurmond kneeled down beside a large, granite stone about five feet away. "What I want is quite simple, and, just by speaking with me you've already satisfied half my desires." He paused to let this sink in.

Rodney smiled. "So that tells me your weakness is curiosity?"

Sammy's face remained like a stone, but his eyes seemed to twinkle just a speck. Rodney noticed.

"But, General Branch, there is also something very important to me that I wish." Rodney waited patiently. "I would like to have dinner with your daughter-in-law."

Uncle Rodney was surprised, but he forced himself to remain unmoving. He simply nodded his head in understanding. He thought about it for a moment and then met Sammy's gaze once more. "Jackie is on assignment right now, and won't be back for a few days." Uncle Rodney hesitated a moment before going on. "Can you wait that long?"

"Yes."

Uncle Rodney was deep in thought, but he forced himself to focus on the hardened killer in front of him. "I will speak with her as soon as she returns, but I will not force her to comply."

Sammy answered right away. "If she was a woman who could be ordered, then she would be of no interest to me."

Uncle Rodney laughed spontaneously and honestly. "Yes, that's our Jackie. You know her well." And then he waited, but Sammy remained silent."So, Mr. Thurmond, what is it you'd like me to know?"

Sammy looked over to find the squirrel again, but he was already gone, probably high atop the maple tree. "I would like you to give this message to Special Agent Arnett."

The general gazed into Sammy's cold, green eyes and waited. *How did he know about Jeff Arnett?* But he didn't press it.

Sammy Thurmond leaned forward and extended his hand, palm down, and held it there, waiting for Rodney to meet him in the middle. General Branch leaned forward and placed his own palm below Sammy's. A small aluminum tube about an inch long and a half inch in diameter dropped down into Rodney's hand. Rodney withdrew his hand, as did Sammy. The general rolled the simple metal tube between his fingers and examined it closely. It seemed to have a seam in the center, but Rodney did not attempt to open it. He simply placed it in the left breast pocket of his red, flannel shirt.

Both men, sensing that the meeting was over, stood simultaneously, and took one last look at each other.

"This has been ... interesting, General Branch."

Rodney smiled softly. "Same here, Mr. Thurmond. As soon as I talk to Jackie, I'll leave a note for you on my brother's gravestone with instructions on how to proceed."

Rodney turned to leave, but Sammy remained riveted in place. The general saw this and hesitated. "Was there something else, Mr. Thurmond?"

Sammy looked around, his eyes resting on several of the trees off in the distance on the edge of the cemetery. And then he asked an unusual question. "How many guns are trained on me right now?"

Rodney smiled and answered briefly. "Seven."

Sammy nodded. "Hmmm, I counted only six." And then he looked straight into Rodney's eyes. "It's always the one thing closest to you, the obvious thing, the thing that you don't see that gets you killed. Take a step back, general, and look for the obvious."

And then Sammy turned and walked away. Rodney watched after him, memorizing his gait, and every other detail he could find. Seven tiny, green laser dots licked hungrily across Sammy Thurmond's back, each dot wanting to reach out and touch him in a more intimate way. But Rodney didn't give the signal, and soon Sammy had escaped inside the trees.

A female cardinal, not near so brilliant as her mate, landed on a small bush ten feet away. Rodney looked over at it and smiled. Trusting an enemy had never been his strong suit. And then he walked away as well, leaving the dead to their own devices.

CHAPTER 9

August 14, Port-au-Prince, Haiti

"**W**HAT DO YOU THINK, DONNY?"

Donny Brewster took a step back and looked at the disheveled hotel room. At one time it had been a five-star resort, but now, without power for almost a year, it had fallen into intense disrepair, but that wasn't what bothered Jackie the most. Most disconcerting of all was the pool of blood on the floor, and the spray of dark red up onto the once-white drywall. It had been four days since Jackie had left Iroquois, but still, she was no closer to finding Joseph Donnelly, the Secretary of Veterans Affairs.

And now ... it looked as though he might be dead, indeed, may have been murdered in this very room. The country of Haiti had a lot of people in it, approximately ten million at the time of the collapse, though over half of those people had died due to starvation, waterborne illnesses and dysentery since then. The people who remained lived primarily in the surrounding rural countryside, somewhat insulated from the disease and violence so rampant in the city now. The upper class here in Haiti spoke French, while the commoners spoke Haitian Creole. The two were similar, and Jackie had a working grasp of both. That had made it possible for them to get around, but, still ... it was tough to communicate to the average Haitian as they were now very suspicious of foreigners, especially foreigners toting M4s and Squad Automatic Weapons.

Jackie looked out the window of the hotel suite. It stunk inside now, but just a year ago she wouldn't have been able to afford even one night in this once-elegant room. But this was definitely the type of hotel that Joseph Donnelly would have stayed in, and that's what had drawn Jackie and her team to this building. She looked down at the pool. There were still plush lawn chairs lined around the edge, but they were now tattered and rotted. The pool itself was filled with green algae, and she thought she even saw a rotting arm jutting up through the sludge.

She turned to Donny. "We have one more place we can go. I don't want to, but ... it seems we have no choice."

Donny cocked his head to one side, a bit puzzled. "Why not? What's wrong?"

Jackie shook her head back and forth, dismissing his question. "It doesn't matter. We just have to go there. This woman has been here a long time and knows a lot of people." She turned and strode out of the room. Donny, still puzzled, followed her. He activated his comm gear and ordered all to converge on the pick-up truck in front of the hotel.

Fifteen minutes later they were heading out of Port-au-Prince and into the surrounding villages.

Kenscoff, Haiti

It took Donny and Jackie almost ninety minutes to travel all the way up to Kenscoff. The road was still in place, but with lots of potholes, and a few places that had washed out recently. But, because they had four-wheel drive, they were able to make the trip without incident. When they got there, Donny was awestruck by the view.

"I can't believe this. We're looking down at the clouds."

Jackie nodded her head. She remembered the incredible sight from two years ago when her and her first husband had been missionaries here. Looking now across the beautiful landscape and down the mountains, it was hard to believe that half the population had died and that the entire world had been thrown into chaos and darkness.

"The orphanage is just up ahead. Be careful not to scare the children with all the guns."

Donny nodded and issued orders to the four Shadow Militia soldiers in the bed of the pick-up truck. They quickly jumped out of the truck bed and formed a defensive perimeter around Jackie and Donny as they made their way down the hill.

A few minutes later they stood in the center of a worn-down playground. The swings were broken, and the merry-go-round remained deathly still. There was a silence about the place that chilled even Donny Brewster. Suddenly, a white woman stepped out from the door of the closest building with a shotgun leveled in their direction. She yelled out firmly in French.

"Pourquoi êtes-vous ici ?"

Jackie saw the woman and smiled. "Gena, it's me, Jackie."

The woman looked over and squinted her eyes, then she slowly lowered her shotgun and smiled weakly. "Lord God, Jackie, how can you be here?"

Jackie ran to the woman who lay down her gun and both embraced. Donny nodded to the four soldiers who quickly set up a defensive perimeter around the building.

Five minutes later they were inside, sitting around a bare, wooden table. The room looked like it used to be a cafeteria for the children.

"Gena, where are all the kids?"

The orphanage director looked down at the scarred, wooden table and cried un-ashamedly. "They are all gone. Taken."

Donny sat off to one side. watching the two women. They seemed as close as sisters. "Who took them, Gena?"

Gena paused long enough to wipe the tears from her eyes before speaking. "There is a white man who seized control of the city just a few months ago. He appears to lead the local gangs from Port-au-Prince. I guess they had to move out of there because of all the diseases. They moved up here and came to get the children last week."

Jackie interrupted her. "But why would they want the children? All those mouths to feed."

Gena's eyes welled up again. "They are not good men, Jackie. Use your imagina-tion."

Jackie remembered many of the children she used to love and play with here during her time with her first husband. She had fallen in love with them, and had been sad-dened when they'd left to return to the states.

Jackie lowered her head. "Oh, I see."

But then a fierceness came over her, filled her body like an adrenaline surge and heat emanated from her skin. "Where are they now, Gena?"

The missionary started to speak, but Jackie quickly shushed her. "Donny, get over here and take notes. I want those children back, and I want all the men who hurt them dead."

Sergeant Brewster looked at her strangely and then over at Gena. The woman was about five feet two inches tall, with unkempt, brunette hair. Her skin was a milky white, and her figure slim. It looked like she hadn't properly eaten in several days. Donny sat down at the table directly across from the two women. He took out a small, green, spiral notebook and black ink pen. As Gena talked, he listened and wrote down every pertinent detail.

Orders from Headquarters

JACKIE LISTENED INTENTLY AS GENERAL BRANCH SPOKE TO HER REGARD-ing the situation there in Haiti.

"How many children are there?"

"Twenty-seven were kidnapped. But we don't know how many are still ... well ..., you know."

She paused and held the handset pressed tightly against her right ear.

"You understand, Jackie, that this isn't part of your mission, that getting involved in a bloody fight in a foreign country with a street gang could well get all of you killed?"

Jackie bit down lightly on her lower lip. "Yes, sir, I know."

Uncle Rodney took note of her use of the word 'sir.' He knew in his heart that what she wanted to do was the moral thing, but ... it could also jeopardize not just her mission, but also the entire future and stability of the United States. But he also knew that Jackie had the stubbornness of a Branch, and that, despite the fact she was asking permission, she might also disregard his orders should he refuse her. He sighed deeply, and Jackie could hear his struggle even across the thousands of miles. She played one last card.

"Uncle Rodney, we have no place else to look. And for all we know the Secretary of the VA could also be a prisoner along with the children." She paused, and when the general didn't answer right away, she spoke again. "It may lead us to another clue, general."

Uncle Rodney smiled but maintained a firm voice.

"Please put Sergeant Brewster on the line."

Jackie smiled and handed the handset to the sergeant who was standing beside her. Donny took the handset and pressed it to his right ear.

"Yes sir."

"Sergeant Brewster, I'd like you to reconnoiter the situation and get back to me as soon as possible. I want to know the feasibility of rescuing the children and preventing the hostiles from hurting any other innocent civilians. But it must be clean, and you are not to do anything that would risk the failure of your primary objective, which is to bring Joseph Donnelly back to CONUS. Do you understand, sergeant?"

Donny smiled slightly and then glanced over at Jackie. "Roger that, general. I will proceed immediately."

General Branch put down the handset to the SINCGARS radio. He shook his head from side to side and glanced over at Colonel MacPherson.

"She wants to rescue twenty-seven orphans from the evil clutches of a gang of monstrous killers."

Mac nodded his head. "That's not exactly mission-critical is it?"

Rodney didn't answer.

"Would you like some coffee, general?"

Rodney looked his friend in the eye. "You read my mind, Mac. Better make it black and extra strong. And the real stuff this time. Not those chickory weeds we've been drinking lately."

Colonel MacPherson nodded and went to the next room to make a cup of coffee. Uncle Rodney shook his head slowly from side to side. This was definitely not like the real army. But then ... he thought to himself. *That's what happens when you let the women do the fighting.*

Donny on Recon

THIS WAS NOT DONNY BREWSTER'S FIRST TIME IN A JUNGLE. IN FACT, HE'D seen lots of jungle during his time in the Corps, starting out with the army Jungle Operations Training Course in Hawaii. Since then he'd been deployed on covert operations all through Central America and the Caribbean, though this was his first time in Haiti and the Dominican Republic. But as far as Donny was concerned, jungle was jungle; they looked pretty on a post card but when you dropped down through the canopy you could pretty much plan on sweating, getting muddy, and getting rained on a lot.

This particular jungle was mountainous with one ravine and ridge leading to another. There was a lot of limestone and sandstone, which meant the ground beneath his feet could give way if he didn't watch where he was going.

At the moment he was seated on a piece of limestone, overlooking a cluster of large homes about two hundred feet below him. A large fern-type plant was growing right out of dirt lodged in a crack in the limestone, but it gave Donny ample concealment to watch the people below without being discovered. There was a small river beyond the houses, and this was obviously the rich part of town. The hostiles had set up house below him, apparent by the many trucks parked in a cluttered array across the lawn.

He slowly raised his binoculars up to his eyes and scanned the site below him. There were six men out front as well as roving patrols, seemingly without any hint of military precision or discipline. It reminded Donny of the horde of cut throats that had attacked Iroquois City just a few months ago. These men below were obviously experienced killers, but without military training, his men would have the edge in an all-out fight.

Donny made a sketch of the area on his notepad, then took several pictures on his cell phone. Most of the men walked with AK47s slung on their backs, but a few had only pistols, either in drop-leg holsters or simply shoved in the small of their backs.

Three hours later it was dark, and Donny took note of the changing of the guard. The foot traffic became much lighter, but the noise inside got much louder. Apparently, this gang had nothing to fear, because they partied with impunity, taking advantage of all the local residents, stealing their food, their property and also their women and children.

He made his way down off the ledge, traversing down the cliff from left to right, going slowly so as to not raise suspicion. The exterior was dimly lit with torches, and Donny was grateful that the power was out here as well. After reaching the bottom, Donny stayed off to one side of the dirt road, hidden in the bushes. He took out his night vision monocular and used it to scan the shadows in front of him. He saw no one and quickly scooted across the narrow road to the cover of an outbuilding.

There were three outbuildings that Donny was interested in, and he checked out the one he was leaning against first. He peered through the window screen but saw only darkness. It was then he heard the clucking of hens and realized it was just a chicken coop. He moved around to the door and stepped inside just to be sure. Donny thought to himself *Nothing but us chickens in here.*

He stepped back out and moved to the next building. It was further back into the shadows, making it easier for him to move around unseen. It appeared to be a garage with a cement floor. It was barren inside except for a folding chair in the middle. Tied to the chair was a naked man. Donny moved closer. Blood dripped down the man's bare back, and his head slumped down onto his chest.

The man appeared to be unconscious, so Donny moved in closer. Something about the man seemed familiar, but he couldn't quite place it. And then the man's eyes opened wide and he spoke.

"You're an American!"

Donny quickly hushed him. "Shh! Be quiet!"

Donny reached into his left, breast pocket and pulled out a picture wrapped in plastic. He looked at the man in front of him and then back down at the picture. And then Donny asked him. "What is your name?"

The man's voice was weak and raspy.

"My name is Joseph Donnelly. Please help me."

Donny stared back at him in disbelief. And then he thought to himself. *Jackie was right. Sometimes doing the right thing pays off even when it doesn't make sense.*

"How did you get here, Mr. Donnelly?"

The man lifted his chin off his chest. It seemed to take a lot of effort.

"They kidnapped me from my hotel in Port-au-Prince. They were under the notion that I could be ransomed back to someone in the states."

Donny looked at the man in the darkness of the room. He was struggling with a moment of indecision. Normally, Donny knew exactly what to do, but this case presented special conditions. This man was his primary objective. He could take him now and declare his mission a success, but that would jeopardize the rescue of the twenty-seven children. Frankly, if the gang inside discovered Joseph Donnelly was missing, they would be alerted, then it might make a second rescue attempt impossible for the children.

The look of hesitancy in Donny's eyes caused a rush of fear to run through Joseph Donnelly's body. And then he said something that Donny hadn't expected.

"Aren't you going to save me?"

Donny smiled, showing his white, perfect teeth, then he pulled out a small k-bar knife and held it in front of the man's face. The fear on his face was quickly replaced with terror.

"Are you from the Blind Man?"

Donny moved his knife down to the man's bindings and quickly cut them away, causing the man to go limp and fall to the floor.

"Well, Mr. Donnelly. This is your lucky day. Now tell me. Where are they keeping the children?"

The Rescue

"This third building is where they are keeping the children. I saw only one guard and he is posted at the front door. It's a small building down by the river, maybe a boathouse or something, but it should be fairly easy to get them out. Then we'll float them down the river out of harm's way while we launch the assault on the compound."

Donny looked into the eyes of each of his four soldiers. "None are to be left alive. Do you understand?" The four men nodded and Donny jumped to his feet. "Okay then. Let's go kick some bad-guy ass!"

The Secretary of Veterans Affairs

"WHY ARE YOU LOOKING AT ME AS THOUGH YOU HATE ME?"

Jackie Branch was staring at Joseph Donnelly without even realizing it. They had blundered into the completion of their mission not through skill or tact or even a well-thought-out plan. They had found the heir-apparent to the United States of America either by providence or by sheer, dumb luck. She was relieved by that, but right now she was more concerned with the pending rescue of the orphans more than Joseph Donnelly and his curiosity.

"Sorry, I don't hate you. Just worried about the children, that's all. I have a lot on my mind."

The man sitting across the table from her nodded slightly. He was about fifty years old, with black hair, and gray moving up from his temples toward the top of his head. "I understand. It's very noble of you and your friends to risk your lives for the orphans. Those men down there are animals and they need to be stopped."

Jackie didn't say anything. She didn't really feel like talking right now. The VA Secretary was quiet for a moment, until he could hold it in no longer. "Did the Blind Man send you?"

Jackie looked up in disbelief. "No. Of course not. We're fighting against the Blind Man. He's trying to take over America. We're fighting him to keep our lives and our freedom."

The man looked relieved. "But who are you? Forgive me, but ... you look like military, but not quite like conventional US military forces."

And then Jackie smiled. "We are the Shadow Militia."

The VA Secretary looked confused. "I've never heard of that one before. Please explain."

Jackie took a sip of the cup of water before her. "The Shadow Militia is a group of highly trained US military veterans, mostly special forces types who were prepared for the collapse. We stood in the gap and prevented the Blind Man from taking total control."

The man reached down and took a drink of his water as well. "So, Jackie. May I call you Jackie?"

She nodded. "Jackie, what has become of the conventional US military? Where are they?"

Jackie hesitated, wondering how much she was authorized to tell him, but, in the end, decided that he'd have to be told sooner or later or all their effort was wasted.

"The Blind Man has some of it, but the bulk of Army, Navy, Air Force and Marines are holding out. Unfortunately, they are not unified. There is no one with constitutional authority left to command them."

Joseph nodded his head in understanding. "Yes, I know things are in a state of disarray. The president and vice president were killed along with most of Congress and part of the cabinet, but there must be someone who stood up and was sworn in to take over."

Jackie didn't say anything. She simply thought to herself. *He doesn't know.*

"That's the reason I fled the states. I have no security detail. They broke into my house and killed my whole family."

He stopped talking for a moment, and Jackie thought he might burst into tears, but he managed to choke them back.

"They were trying to kill me, but I got out before they succeeded." He lowered his head, as if in shame. "I should have died too." When he looked back up at Jackie, tears were in his eyes. "But I ran."

Jackie didn't say anything. She didn't know what to say that would make him feel any better. Nothing could bring back his family, nothing could turn the power back on or make all the death and destruction go away or give it any worthwhile meaning.

"I came down here because I thought it was the last place they'd look for me. My wife and I used to come down to the Dominican Republic on short-term mission trips with our church to help build houses. I thought they'd never find me, but they did and I was forced to flee Santo Domingo, and I've been running for months now."

That information got Jackie's attention. "Who did you work with in the DR for your mission trip?"

The man hesitated. Then he softly smiled before continuing on.

"Praying Pelican Missions out of Minnesota. Do you know of them?"

Jackie's mood softened just a tad. "So you know John and Karen Stratten then."

"Absolutely. My wife and I have been to their house several times." And then the sadness returned to his eyes. "We had some good times with John and Karen."

Jackie suddenly had to admit she'd been judging the man, because he'd been investigated for possible fraud charges by the FBI way back prior to the collapse. And then she thought to herself *Who am I to judge? I cheated on my husband.*

But despite that, she still harbored an ill suspicion of the man. She didn't know exactly why, but for some reason she just didn't like this man, even though he appeared to be on the up-and-up.

"It's a shame when their son died last year. He was so young to have a heart attack."

VA Secretary Donnelly didn't hesitate to answer. "Yes, it was. A shame, a terrible shame."

Jackie nodded her head knowingly, but then the tone of her voice began to soften now. "Listen, Joseph. There's something you need to know." But then she hesitated before going on. "We are here to rescue you, but we have ulterior motives."

Joseph leaned involuntarily back just a bit. "Go on."

"Mr. Donnelly, you are the last remaining person who is authorized by the US constitution who can take over command of the country and its remaining military forces."

Jackie thought he was going to fall off his chair and onto the floor, but he managed to catch himself on the edge of the table with both hands. He sat back up straight and appeared to will himself back into control.

"I'm sorry. I guess I'm still weak from the torture."

And then he lowered his head again. "So ... my friends, my colleagues ... they are all dead?"

Jackie nodded. "Yes. You are the last one."

All Hell Breaks Loose, 4AM

DONNY BREWSTER WAS POSITIONED IN OVERWATCH HIGH ABOVE ON THE same limestone ledge he'd used to do the recon earlier in the day. His four men were deployed all around the house, waiting for the go sign. Donny tapped his comm button. "Go! Go! Go!" And then all hell broke loose. Simultaneously, four white phosphorous grenades were tossed into the windows of the house and immediately began to burn anything within reach. The Willie Peter was followed closely by smoke grenades and flash bangs to create chaos. After that it was just a matter of shooting the rats as they abandoned the ship. First, Donny dropped the guard in front of the house with his .308 via a perfect head shot. Then two more ran out and paused on the porch. He dispatched them quickly with single shots to the sternum. Donny did his work quickly and methodically, void of all emotion, aside from a bit of excitement, but nothing that impeded his ability to kill.

He heard shots ring out at the back and sides of the house. hundreds of them. About two minutes into the fight, Donny heard the whine of a truck engine as it climbed up the driveway to the big home. Donny yelled into his microphone. "Get the SAW up front. I've got reinforcements coming in!"

When the truck arrived, Donny opened up with his .308 and managed to kill two men before the truck rolled to a stop. The other six men began to pile over the side, but didn't make it far before the SAW chimed in and cut them down like cordwood. Donny quickly dispatched the driver as he tried to escape on foot.

Donny heard a large explosion to the rear of the house."What was that? Somebody talk to me!"

"It was the propane tank cooking off. Not a problem."

"Angel Four, do you have the kids?"

There was no answer.

"All angels check in with sit rep."

"Angel one, all quiet on the west."

"Angel two, all quiet on the south."

"Angel three, still mopping up."

Donny was frustrated at Angel Four's silence.

"Angel Four, this is Archangel. Sit rep now!"

Nothing but silence.

"Angel one check out Angel Four and report back to me."

"Roger that, Archangel."

"Angel Two, slip over and help Angel Three with the cleanup."

"Roger that Archangel. Moving now."

Donny looked down, staring into the growing flames of the mansion below. It would no doubt destroy anyone inside, and soon leap to the houses closest to it. This whole block of rich people's homes would be black ash by morning, but Donny felt no remorse. The home owners were probably already dead anyway. Even so, this was Donny's purpose in life ... to kill people and break things. And Donny was very good at his job.

"Archangel, this is Angel One, over."

"Go with sit rep, Angel One."

"Angel Four's comm is down, but all children are secure, and floating down river."

Donny smiled. Gena had volunteered to extract the children. It was the obvious choice since she knew the river and would be able to calm the children and organize them quickly.

Donny and his men stayed another fifteen minutes just to make sure all hostiles were down. Three more were killed as they came in on a truck, but, after that, all was silent save for the crackling of the flames. Donny could feel the heat of the burning homes even two hundred feet above.

With great satisfaction, he withdrew his men, picked up the kids and beat feet back to the orphanage. With any luck, they'd be back in the states tomorrow night, and he couldn't wait to see his favorite nurse.

CHAPTER 10

August 16, I Smell a Rat!

RODNEY BRANCH SAT WITH HIS BACK TO THE MAPLE TREE about fifty yards from his home. He knew that he should be happy right now, that he should be celebrating with the others back at his house. The VA Secretary was recovered and safe, and, if all worked out, they would soon have a nuclear arsenal with which to battle the Blind Man, as well as portions of US air and naval forces. But ... something wasn't right, and he needed some distance, some time alone to think. It wasn't that his plan wasn't sound, because it was; it was a very good plan. At least as good as any he'd come up with and certainly the best he could hope for when his back was against the wall. The Blind Man had him outmanned, outgunned and, at least for right now, he was calling all the shots.

But things were going well. Jackie had found Joseph Donnelly, the VA Secretary, and he was in a secure location while he decided whether or not he'd like to be sworn in as the president. Even now they were busy trying to locate a federal judge in case they needed a swearing-in ceremony.

Justice Reed was working away at his better mousetrap, but Rodney suspected the old scientist was starting to get bored with the prospect, and that he might soon be ready to move on to something more potent. Of course, Justice Reed was just a back-up at this point. If the VA Secretary was sworn into office, then it would no longer be necessary for Dr. Reed to recommission the nukes.

Rodney looked up at the sky. It was a pretty blue up there today. A few wispy cirrus clouds were blowing by way up in the jet stream, so he watched them for a moment. Rodney thought out loud. "What are you doing Mr. Blind Man? What are you up to, and what are you going to do next?"

Jeff Arnett was furiously trying to decipher the password to open the files given to him by Sammy Thurmond, and that could be a game changer, depending on what was inside them.

Rodney thought about Sammy again. That man was an enigma. Strange. Very Strange. A deer fly buzzed around his head for a while, and Rodney kept swatting at it, trying to kill it, but it was just too fast. Every time he swatted, the fly buzzed away, and it was driving him crazy. If the fly would just sit still long enough, then he could kill it.

And then it occurred to him. The Shadow Militia was the deer fly, and they were driving the Blind Man out of his mind with frustration. But if they weren't fast enough, if they made even one tiny mistake, if they lingered in one place too long ... they'd get swatted and the game would be over.

Rodney took one last swat at the deer fly, pinning it to his scalp, where he rolled its body into death before flicking it off into the weeds. He looked after it and sighed.

"Let's not make any mistakes, general."

And then he thought long and hard about Sammy Thurmond's parting words to him.

"It's always the one thing closest to you, the obvious thing, the thing that you don't see that gets you killed. Take a step back, general, and look for the obvious."

Rodney couldn't help but think that there was something he wasn't seeing, something obvious, but camouflaged so well, that it eluded him. He felt like he was walking into a trap.

And then there was the cryptic information on the tiny slip of paper. inside the small aluminum tube given to Uncle Rodney by Sammy Thurmond back in the cemetery. He'd chosen to read it first before passing it on to Jeff Arnett as Sammy had instructed. Reading the contents of the capsule had rattled him to his core. At first he hadn't understood the clue, but after some research it had all come clear.

Uncle Rodney had been shocked and saddened, almost to the point of despair when he'd discovered the name of the traitor. When he'd realized his friend was the traitor, a wave of coldness and nausea had overcome him. There are some things a man never recovers from, like the horrors of war, but the loss of a lifelong friend, that you've trusted with your very life was even worse than that. When he'd first discovered the name, he'd wanted to disbelieve it, but ... he knew in his heart of hearts that the accusation was true. It made things clear.

But before jumping to conclusions, he first had to confirm the information from Sammy Thurmond. He needed proof. After that, the only practical question remaining was *How do I turn this to a tactical advantage?*

And then another question popped into his mind that saddened and terrified him even more. *What if he's not the only traitor among us? Who can I trust?*

But the answer to his question was not forthcoming. Uncle Rodney felt an extreme need for a cigarette right now as the weight of responsibility and his age beared down on him like gravity. And gravity always seemed to win. She was a tough taskmaster who never quit. And time was on her side.

The Blind Man's Lair

JARED HELD THE LONG-STEMMED GLASS OF PORT IN HIS LEFT HAND AND swirled it just for fun before taking another sip. If this war didn't end soon, then his wine cellar would start to run low, and he certainly couldn't have that. In his right hand he held the handset close to his ear as he listened intently to all his operative had to say. Once the man on the other end stopped talking, Jared answered him politely but succinctly.

"Excellent. I appreciate the information. You will be handsomely rewarded of course."

The man started to answer Jared, but the Blind Man quickly hung up, not out of rudeness, but more out of excitement than anything else. Jared suddenly lost his appetite for wine, and set the glass down on the table in front of him. His mind was busy trying to sort out all the details of what he'd just learned. This had real ramifications, and some heavy consequences if General Branch was able to pull it off.

"So ... you now have Joseph Donnelly. And you plan to swear him in as acting president of the United States?" Jared turned and walked toward the door.

"You are in for a big surprise, General Branch."

And then he focused his mind on the other important piece of information. "And you are trying to recover twelve nukes."

That little bit of information was most reassuring to Jared, as it confirmed that the Shadow Militia no longer had a nuclear capability. And then he smiled and chuckled to himself.

"Sorry, general. No nukes for you!"

Pole Barn Headquarters

Jeff Arnett sat at his desk, contemplating everything that had been happening just in the past two months. Life was so unpredictable, so unpredictable and oh so fleeting.

General Branch sat down across from him in the simple. metal folding chair. He just didn't look like a general that Jeff had ever seen before, but still ... he commanded so much respect. It was as if all his people were lining up to die for him. Jeff didn't understand that fierceness of loyalty, at least not on an experiential level.

"We have a traitor in our midst, Mr. Arnett."

Jeff's hawkish nose tilted down, and his eyes narrowed their gaze. He hesitated for a moment and then leaned back in his chair before answering. "How do you know?"

Rodney leaned back in his chair as well. Then he reached into the left, breast pocket of his flannel shirt, where he used to keep his cigarettes and pulled out the aluminum tube that Sammy Thurmond had given him. "This was given to me by Sammy Thurmond along with a warning that someone in our inner circle is passing information on to Jared Thompson."

Jeff reached out to take the tube, opened it by twisting both ends. He looked inside and read the contents.

"This seems confusing. I don't know who any of these people are. Should I?"

Uncle Rodney smiled. "I didn't know at first either until I did some research, but then it all came clear to me."

So Uncle Rodney explained everything to him, and both reluctantly agreed they had a traitor in their midst. Jeff Arnett had an immediate plan to verify the identity of the culprit and General Branch instructed him to put it into action.

Rodney looked out the window of the pole barn. It was a small window, but he could still see outside, and it let in just enough light to see. "I hope that somehow, that we're wrong but ...."

Jeff Arnett frowned, trying to imagine how the general might feel right now."

"I'm sorry, general."

Rodney shrugged. "Thanks." And then he got up from his chair, a little more tired than he was before and turned to walk away.

"I'll let you know as soon as I get anything, general."

And then he called after Rodney.

"Wait, there's one more thing."

The general stopped and turned back around, waiting for Jeff to speak.

Jeff picked up a pen from his desk. It was blue, with a removable cap. He began to nervously pull off the cap and then replace it over and over as he talked. "

"I haven't been able to even make a dent in cracking the password for the files Sammy Thurmond gave us." He paused, but General Branch didn't speak. The news had silenced him.

Jeff let his word trail off into the pole barn. It still smelled a bit like horses in here. He couldn't believe that he'd fallen so far, that he was now working in a pole barn that used to house horses and cattle.

"So what seems to be the hold-up? What can I do to help?"

After several seconds of quiet, Jeff Arnett finally spoke.

"A supercomputer would be nice. Do you have one?"

Uncle Rodney tried to smile, but it just wasn't in him today. "Sorry, Mr. Arnett. I was always more interested in tanks and grenade launchers than computers. Lack of foresight on my part, I suppose."

Jeff nodded and let out a sigh. "I just don't have the resources to do it here. Breaking a code like that usually takes a ton of processing power, and all we have here are laptops and desktop PCs with very limited software. It could take weeks to find the password, and even then ..." Jeff let his words trail off before continuing. "Even then we may not be able to crack it. I just wanted you to know that at this point in time, unless something changes, it's a long shot." He hesitated. "I just wanted you to know so you weren't planning on it."

Uncle Rodney's face grew stern and hard, then it seemed to relax into a thousand natural frowns, like leaves turning brown in the fall, just before they died and floated down to the earth. Gravity was a law that could not be denied.

"So, we can't open the files from Sammy Thurmond, the VA Secretary solution is a bit shaky, and we have a traitor in our midst. Any other good news, Mr. Arnett?"

Jeff Arnett lowered his head. "No, I think that about covers it, general. I'm sorry."

Uncle Rodney fumbled furiously for his left, breast pocket, but was quickly disappointed when no cigarettes were found.

"But what about the twelve nukes? Any problems there?"

Jeff nodded. "No problems there, sir. That option is still in play, and plans are already underway to take delivery." He didn't take his eyes off Uncle Rodney as he spoke. It was like he was analyzing every action, even the most minute. "But those will be useless to us unless Justice Reed comes through." He paused a moment. "Is he still trying to build that stupid mouse trap?"

Rodney smiled nervously. "Yes, I'm afraid so." And then he looked off into the distance. "We may have to find another way to recommission them."

There was silence between the two men for almost a full minute. Finally, Jeff Arnett broke the silent stasis.

"General? Are you ... okay?"

Rodney let out a sigh, and then moved slowly and wearily to his feet. "Don't worry, Mr. Arnett. It's always darkest before the dawn." And then he cocked his head to one side as if in deep contemplation. "I wonder who said that?"

Jeff smiled slightly. "I think it was Thomas Fuller, sir."

Rodney hesitated. "Who?"

Jeff pushed his chair back and stood as well. "Thomas Fuller, back in 1650 or so. He was an English Theologian and historian."

Uncle Rodney laughed softly. "Of all the things to know." He turned to leave but mumbled back over his shoulder. "Well, let's hope the man knew what he was talking about."

The two men parted, unbeknownst to one another that both were beginning to doubt the other.

One Hour Later

THE BLIND MAN LOOKED OVER AT THE FRENCH LIEUTENANT STANDING before him at the position of attention. "It has been eleven days, lieutenant, and you still have yet to find Mr. Thurmond?"

The young lieutenant fought to maintain his military bearing, but the urge to squirm nervously was overwhelming him.

"That is correct, sir."

There was another man in the room beside them. This man was wearing a white lab coat and stood stock still, as if he didn't want to be noticed by the Blind Man. When the Blind Man glanced over at the scientist he didn't move or say anything. The scientist had learned long ago that if the Blind Man wasn't thinking about him, then he would probably live out the day.

The Blind Man turned his back on the lieutenant long enough to reach inside his front, right pocket and retrieve his pearl-handled .32 caliber handgun. He brought it up in one smooth motion and fired a round into the lieutenant's face. The shot was a bit to the left, and the French lieutenant went down but did not die. It was at that moment that Jared Thompson realized just how much he missed the efficiency of his former assistant, Sammy Thurmond. Sammy would have made a perfect shot to the ocular cavity, and the lieutenant would have died instantly with minimal mess. As it was, the lieutenant thrashed on the ground wildly, like an animal in his death throes. The scientist stepped back, but Jared heaved a deep sigh and moved in closer for the kill. He raised his gun and tried to aim at the man's head, but it was moving back and forth too quickly. Finally, because he couldn't get a good shot to the head, Jared aimed at the man's chest cavity and emptied the remaining five rounds into his body. He bled some more, spattering his blood on the floor and onto Jared's pant legs. The Blind Man looked on with disgust. The lieutenant's thrashing slowed before he quietly expired.

The scientist tried not to stare. He'd seen the Blind Man's barbarism before, but never by his own hand. Usually Sammy Thurmond would do his bidding. The Blind Man looked up from the dead body and made eye contact with the scientist. His eyes were ice blue, boring into him like cold death. The scientist tried to look away, but he couldn't.

"And now ... Dr. VanFleet ... let's talk about plan B."

Plan B, the Blind Man

WITH THE FRENCH LIEUTENANT'S BODY STILL BLEEDING ONTO THE FLOOR just a few feet away, Dr. VanFleet tried to compose himself long enough to give Jared an explanation.

"Well, you see, sir." He paused, sucked in some more air and tried to continue again. "It's not based on traditional RFID technology, but, rather on an advanced prototype of human-injectable tracking chip. The tracking is done via satellite, so we will know the subject's heading, course, and speed. It is accurate up to two meters."

The Blind Man turned away from the dead body and stepped over a widening pool of blood as he strode casually over to the couch. He sat down on the corinthian leather and leaned back as if fatigued. The unloaded gun was still in his hand. "And what will happen to Mr. Thurmond once you have activated this device which is already deep inside his body?"

The scientist glanced down at the dead body of the lieutenant before answering. "Well, the subject will begin to feel nausea and perhaps even experience a sense of disorientation. It will be mild at first, but eventually will increase, and within a few days will become debilitating."

The Blind Man frowned. "You are not to call him a subject. His name is Mr. Thurmond. He is twice the man you are." Jared reached down and picked up his wine glass from the mahogany table in front of him. "And how long will he live?"

Dr. VanFleet folded his hands together in front of his stomach. "A few days, sir. Perhaps as long as a week, but I doubt it. But the death will be very painful and discomfiting."

He took a small sip as if contemplating something deep. "What a shame. He was such a useful man." Then his blue eyes looked over at the scientist and made eye contact with him. "And he was so polite. So very polite. And incredibly efficient." He glanced down at the dead body on the floor. "Not at all like the French. I despise the French. They have no soul - so arrogant."

Dr. VanFleet took extra notice of the comment, and couldn't help but wonder *How does he feel about ... the Dutch?*`

August 17, A Dangerous Pick-up

"WHY ARE WE DOING THIS, DAD?"

Dan Branch looked over at his son just long enough to make brief eye contact.

"Because Uncle Rodney asked us to."

Jeremy nodded his head. He glanced down at his M4 carbine and double-checked to make sure the selector switch was on safe. "Well, I know that, but ... what are we going to do with twelve nuclear bombs?"

Jeremy tipped his head back as if pointing with his eyes to the semi-trailer they were hauling. "I'm not sure I like being in the same truck with that much firepower. How do we know it's safe?"

Dan nodded his head as he drove down I-80 just west of Davenport, Iowa. They were over halfway home. "They're not activated, son. They are perfectly safe. In fact, it would be impossible for them to go off even if we were to shoot them."

Jeremy glanced out the window to his right. There was an incredible lack of corn in Iowa these days. Normally the fields would be a sea of green stalks reaching up ten to fourteen feet in the air. Some people joked that the corn grew so tall in Iowa that you could hang a treestand on a stalk to hunt deer. But that was before the collapse. Now there was very little diesel fuel available for the farm machinery, so the fields had not been planted this year. In fact, most of America, the bread basket for the world, was now lying impotent and fallow.

"Still makes me nervous, Dad. Can the radiation leak out and kill us?"

"Probably not."

Jeremy's head jerked back to his left. "Probably not!" His eyes got big with fear. "Are you telling me we could die hauling these things halfway across the country?"

Dan smiled lightly. "Don't overreact, son. When we took the radiation readings back in Montana, everything checked out fine. And the soldiers in back are all wearing dosimeters, so if it starts leaking then we'll know about it."

Jeremy rubbed the top of his head with his left hand before answering. "Okay, yeah, but ... doesn't radiation make men sterile?"

Dan Branch laughed out loud. "You mean to tell me, son, that we're carrying twelve nuclear warheads just a few yards behind us, and your biggest fear is future sterility?"

Jeremy suppressed a smile of his own. "I know, Dad. That probably sounds weird, but I'm still young, ya know. I mean, There could be a woman and kids in my future still."

The father reached over with his right hand and patted his son's knee. "Don't worry, son. I would never jeopardize the existence of my future grandkids. I plan on living to a ripe, old age myself."

"You've already lived to a ripe, old age."

Dan's face took on a mock sternness. "Hey! Watch yer mouth, son."

Jeremy laughed again. "Don't get mad at me. It's not my fault yer so old!"

And then Jeremy took on a serious air. He leaned his head over and pressed the right side of his forehead against the window glass. "Dad ... it occurred to me the other day, that ... well ... maybe I've already lived to a ripe, old age. Ya know what I mean?"

Dan let out a sigh as he pondered his son's statement. "Yeah, I know what you mean. The average life expectancy of a man these days doesn't seem to be as long as it used to be. Life is pretty tenuous when you stop to think about it. It always was. We just didn't realize it while life was so easy back before the Fall."

Jeremy looked out the window again. The fields were full of weeds taller than a man. The farms were already returning to prairie. "What do you think Tonya is doing right now?"

Dan squinted with his eyes at the question. "Our old neighbor back in Menomonie?"

"She wasn't that old ... younger than me."

Dan smiled. "So you still think about her huh?"

Jeremy got a faraway look in his eyes. "She's the only woman I ever ... well ... you know." He paused. "And it's not like I didn't have any feelings for her ya know."

Dan didn't answer. He didn't quite know what to say. "Dad, do you think she's still alive? I mean ... it was getting pretty rough there when we left."

Dan nodded. "It's possible, son. I think for most people, if they survived the first winter, then they'll be okay."

His son stared up ahead at the almost-empty interstate. "I suppose I'll never see her again though. Things are so screwed up out there."

The two men were suddenly silent together. Dan changed the subject. "What mile marker is that truck stop at again?"

Jeremy snapped back to reality and took the folded map off the console between them. He opened it up and looked for the spot.

"It's the Flying J, just two exits down on the right I think."

Dan nodded and they rode the next few miles in silence. When they reached the exit ramp, Dan pulled off the highway and drove into the parking lot. There were several other semi trucks there, but they appeared to be abandoned, and one had been set on fire.

"Keep a sharp eye out, Jeremy. It's a bit risky pulling over here."

"Then why are we doing it, Dad?"

Dan looked around cautiously while the Shadow Militia soldiers piled out the back and set up a defensive perimeter around them.

"Because I need to go to the bathroom really bad, and it's the kind I can't do while driving. I recommend you do the same thing."

Jeremy smiled and looked around for a place to go. They'd already learned that every truck stop or gas station had already been looted, and sometimes had someone living in the abandoned buildings. The toilets didn't work, but that hadn't stopped people from using them; they were always clogged to the brim and incredibly stinky. Dan had learned to just find a bush with some cover and let nature take its course.

After both men had gone, they sat off to one side of the truck under a tree. Dan fired up the radio and contacted his Uncle Rodney. He'd been ordered to phone in his progress every four hours.

"Dad? Do you hear that sound?"

Dan dropped the handset. "Yeah. I think it's a helicopter."

Dan yelled over to the Shadow Militia team, but they were already deploying behind cement embankments and any other cover they could find.

"Get down inside that drainage ditch, Jeremy!"

His son followed him down the ditch and into the concrete tunnel about three feet high. It was dry now, but in the spring and fall it would funnel water under the drive and away from the parking lot.

The Apache attack helicopter came in low from the south, just above the buildings and treetops. It took only one pass to blow the semi-trailer to pieces and set it on fire. Dan and Jeremy cringed under the safety of concrete and dirt as they listened to the thirty millimeter M230 chain gun rip their ride to shreds. Then they heard the Hydra 70 rockets firing and reaching out to the semi-truck just a hundred yards away. There were several explosions as the two point seven five inch rockets found their mark. Dan involuntarily covered his head with his hands and waited for the radiation to consume him.

CHAPTER 11

August 17 - Sparky Sees Action

"HOLY MOLEY LORD GOD ALMIGHTY! WOULD YOU LOOK AT that!"

Sparky let his bike coast slowly to a stop as the explosions to the east of him rocked the Flying J parking lot. He'd been dutifully pedalling his bicycle every day now since leaving Western Kansas without so much as a single day off. Every morning he woke up at daybreak and had a meager breakfast, and would peddle from sunrise to sunset. Sometimes he would eat something he'd scavenged from an abandoned house. There were many of them around as so many people had died, either from disease or a myriad of unnatural causes. Once he'd found a box of Twinkies and was amazed at their freshness. They still tasted just like they had before the collapse.

At other times he met good, Christian people who were willing to feed him a meal, plus give him something to take with him. Whenever he ran across an empty vehicle, he always stopped and searched it thoroughly. It was amazing what one could find in glove boxes and beneath the seats of old cars. Half-eaten granola bars, chewed-up teething biscuits stuffed down under a child car seat, even a few packets of melted gummy bears. Sparky didn't complain, simply because he had come to the realization that he was on a mission from God. He just wished he knew more of what the mission was and why he was doing it.

But at times when he started to doubt, the old man simply quoted one of his favorite Bible verses.

Romans 1:17 King James Version (KJV)

17 For therein is the righteousness of God revealed from faith to faith: as it is written, The just shall live by faith.

So many stories in the Bible were becoming more than just stories, because he was living them out in his daily life. He found himself understanding in an experiential way how the Israelites may have felt as they followed Moses across the desert for forty years. So the Jews had manna from heaven, and Sparky had Twinkies from Hostess.

Sparky looked at the growing plume of black smoke rising up above the truck stop as he decided what to do. This was indeed unusual as he hadn't seen anything like this on his trip. In his experience most of these truckstops were abandoned, and he'd avoided the ones that weren't.

He hopped up onto the seat of his bike again and began to pedal toward the smoke, singing all the way, sure in every way that God would protect him against any danger that might be out there. After all - why not? He had so far.

I ain't as good as I once was,
But I'm as good once, as I ever was.

Dan Calls Home

"THAT'S AFFIRMATIVE STONEPIT. WE ARE WITHOUT A RIDE AND OUR PAY-load has been destroyed by hostile fire."

Colonel Branch stood beside the pavement on interstate 80 and waited for Colonel MacPherson's reply. As he listened he glanced down to the west and watched a tiny speck moving on the horizon. It was moving slowly but steadily in their direction. Dan pointed it out to Jeremy and the other Shadow Militia soldiers who quickly redeployed to meet the potential threat. Dan moved a few feet to the south down into the ditch where he couldn't be seen.

"Yes, sir. That is correct."

Jeremy looked over at his father, wondering what was going on. *Why had they been attacked? How were they going to get home. and. foremost on his mind, were they going to die of radiation poisoning?* Jeremy looked back to the west at the approaching person. He appeared to be on a bicycle.

"We sustained zero casualties, sir." A pause. "Yes, sir we remain battle ready."

When the bike rider was within fifty yards of Dan, the Shadow Militia soldiers moved out of cover and quickly apprehended the rider. Dan watched with interest as they quickly and efficiently frisked the old man, spoke to him briefly and then brought him forward to Dan.

"Yes, sir. We will head east and await further orders."

Dan replaced the handset in the SINCGARS radio pack, and then turned to his soldiers under his immediate command.

"What's going on, sergeant?"

The sergeant moved forward with the old man while the others deployed back into their defensive perimeter.

"He's unarmed, sir."

Dan reached his right hand forward to shake the old man's hand.

"Sorry about the rough greeting. We were just attacked and can't be too careful. I hope you understand."

The old man nodded. "Sure. No problem. My name is Sparky Fillmore." He accepted Dan's grasp.

"Colonel Dan Branch, Shadow Militia."

Sparky retrieved his hand and let it drop at his side.

"Really?"

Dan smiled. "Yes."

Sparky laughed out loud and Dan's smile faded.

"Why is that so funny?"

The old man turned his head as his laughter faded before answering. "I'm on my way to Michigan to meet with General Rodney T. Branch, commanding general of the Shadow Militia. You wouldn't by any chance know him would you?"

Dan's face grew stern. "I see. That seems like quite a coincidence."

Sparky turned to watch the smoke, still rising up from the Flying J. "There are no coincidences in the Lord's work, Colonel Branch."

Dan scrutinized the old man closely, looking deep into his eyes, but he saw nothing but peace and kindness, certainly nothing his men should fear.

"So, tell me, Sparky, is the general expecting you?"

The old man smiled and shook his head from side to side. "Well, I would hope not. We've never met before. Although I wouldn't put it past the Almighty to give him forewarning."

Colonel Branch cocked his head to one side before answering. By now Jeremy had moved up and was standing beside Sparky and his dad. But Jeremy stayed quiet in deference to his father and his rank.

"Where are you coming from?"

"West of Hays, Kansas."

Dan folded his arms across his chest. Jeremy lowered his M4. "You rode on a bike all the way from west Kansas?"

Sparky shook his head and smiled yet again. Sparky loved to smile, and, when he did, it seemed to magically take ten years off his age. "No, not all the way. I started out walking, but God provided me this nice bicycle before I'd gone too far. The Lord always provides - does he not?"

Dan reached up with his right hand to stroke his bare chin. He'd just shaved before leaving Montana.

"In answer to your first question, we know the general."

Sparky smiled again. "Well, okay then." And then he raised his hands up as if in mock surrender. "Take me to your leader!"

Jeremy laughed out loud. "This guy's cool, dad. I like him."

Dan's face grew serious again. He yelled to the Shadow Militia soldiers. "Let's go men! We need to put some distance between us and that burning radiation pile. Form up and double time."

The men formed up on either side of the highway and jogged to the east. Sparky Fillmore fell in to the west of them and followed casually behind on his bike. And he couldn't help but wonder *What does God have in store for me now.* And also *I wonder what my wife, Edna, is having for dinner tonight. Probably not Twinkies.*

A Cryptic Message

SPECIAL AGENT JEFF ARNETT LEANED BACK IN HIS OFFICE CHAIR. THERE were three other people around him working at computers, trying desperately to hack into the Blind Man's network and to discover the ever-elusive password they needed to open the files given to them by Sammy Thurmond. But so far they'd been unsuccessful. Try as they might, they could not break into the Blind Man's system or open the files they so desperately needed to defeat the Blind Man. Jeff was starting to wonder if he'd signed up with the wrong team.

Jeff pulled open the pencil drawer in front of him and looked down at the jumble of pens, pencils and paper clips. There, nestled among them all was a small aluminum tube about an inch long and a half inch in diameter. The tall man looked cautiously around him, making sure that no one was looking. Finally, he reached down and lifted the silver capsule out of the drawer and held it in his right hand above his lap. He rolled it back and forth in his fingers.

Why had Sammy Thurmond given this to General Branch to deliver to him? Why was the former right-hand man to the Blind Man now trying to help them, if indeed he was. For all Jeff knew, this could be part of the Blind Man's plan. In Jeff's line of work, trust was a rare commodity.

The Blind Man was a formidable adversary and not one to be trifled with, and Sammy Thurmond was his right-hand man, or at least he had been until recently. Jeff pondered it for a moment. Had Sammy Thurmond really abandoned his old boss? And if so ... why? In Jeff's mind, the best course of action was to just kill Thurmond at the first opportunity, just to be safe. He doubted they'd get anything useful out of him. The man was crazy, a total lunatic, but General Branch seemed to believe there was something useful about him. His mind drifted off to a list of possible outcomes, none of them desirable to him. Sammy Thurmond was an impossible mystery with no resolution in sight.

Jeff moved the aluminum capsule to the thumb and forefinger of his right hand. He placed his left thumb and forefinger on the left side of the capsule and twisted. It turned with moderate pressure and Jeff pulled it apart. The tiny slip of paper dropped out onto his lap. Jeff picked it up and held it out to the light before reading it again for the umpteenth time:

Keith Allen
Roger Rees
Alan Wheatley

At first he'd thought the names were a list of people who were disloyal to the Shadow Militia, but it hadn't been that easy. General Branch had told him that Roger Rees had been a British actor that had been in the movie *Robin Hood Men in Tights.*

Apparently all these men had something very important and unusual in common. They were all actors, and they had all played characters in some production of *Robin Hood.* They had all played the part of the Sheriff of Nottingham. And that had troubled Special Agent Arnett. Suddenly, he began to wonder if Rodney Branch was still able to lead the fight. He'd seemed discouraged lately, and many of his plans were coming unraveled.

Jeff put the paper back inside the capsule and tightened it down again. He slipped it into his left, breast pocket and leaned forward, resting his elbows on the desk in front of him. Jeff folded his hands together and placed them under his chin as he contemplated the far-reaching ramifications of having a spy in their inner circle. *The Blind Man could know everything.* And, if he did, then none of them were safe and it was only a matter of time before they were all killed and the Blind Man won.

Jeff thought back onto his last meeting with General Branch. Rodney had seemed so sad, so ... discouraged, maybe even resigned. That had to mean something. But despite that, Jeff determined that the old man wasn't about to give up. Or was he? And then another thought occurred to him. *Why was Uncle Rodney always one step ahead of him?*

Special Agent Arnett had enacted his plan to confirm the identity of the spy, and soon, very soon they would be able to flush him out, but, in the meantime, they would use the spy to their advantage.

The Inner Circle

"Who do I trust, Jackie? Who?"

Jackie Branch leaned back in the folding chair and sighed. Baby Donna was on her lap, reaching up with her soft, baby hands and trying to grab onto her mother's lips as she spoke.

"I don't know Uncle Rodney. Why are you asking me?"

Uncle Rodney smiled softly, almost humbly. "I ask you because you're a woman."

Jackie looked up from her baby and laughed. "Uncle Rodney, I'm pregnant, full of unstable, racing hormones, and you're asking me for advice on life-and-death issues? I'm not sure that's wise. Besides, you've known me less than a year. For all you know I could be on the Blind Man's payroll."

Rodney lifted his right hand to stroke his chin. "Hmmm, I see your point." And then he laughed again, but quickly grew serious. "Jackie, I need your help. I need a woman's intuition. That's one thing I've always trusted is that magical, unseen insight that only women seem to possess."

Jackie reached down and held her baby with both arms. "Uncle Rodney, you're starting to scare me. Why are you talking like this?"

Rodney picked up his chickory drink and took a sip. "What do you mean?"

Suddenly baby Donna let out a loud, unabashed baby fart, and it seemed to break the tension in the room. "I mean where is your confidence? You always seem so sure of yourself. You exude confidence, so much so that it infects everyone around you and makes them believe in you as well. Uncle Rodney you have the unique, almost mysterious ability to lead nervous people in a crisis, to give them hope and help them believe that they can win even when there appears to be no rational reason to have faith."

Jackie held her baby closer. "Uncle Rodney, you can't start to doubt yourself, because if you do then everyone around you will begin to doubt as well. And then ... the Blind Man will win."

Rodney set his coffee mug down on the desk in front of him. "I know you're right. But here's the deal, Jackie." And then he hesitated as if girding up his loins before battle. "One of us inside our circle of trust is a spy. Someone is feeding information to the Blind Man. That's how he knew exactly where Dan and Jeremy would be with the nuclear warheads. We lost all the nukes, Jackie. We lost them all, and we almost lost Dan and Jeremy."

Jackie frowned and nodded in agreement. "I know. Would you mind holding baby Donna for a minute?"

Rodney seemed put out by the request, but he reached his arms out and scooped up the baby, before setting her on his lap. Baby Donna immediately reached over her head and grabbed onto Rodney's cheeks and squeezed as hard as she could. Rodney bent his head down and kissed the baby on top of her head. Jackie smiled and leaned back in her chair.

Uncle Rodney, there's something I haven't told you yet, something that might be important, but which I don't have any proof. But, if I'm right, and this is just a hunch, women's intuition as you say, then it could mean the death of us all."

Rodney cocked his head to one side and then held the baby closer to his chest. "So why didn't you tell me this sooner?"

Jackie shrugged. "I needed to think about it first, get it straight in my own mind before I passed it on to someone else. But, after thinking about it for a few days, I still can't shake the feeling that I don't trust him, even though I have no tangible proof to the contrary."

Uncle Rodney moved baby Donna over to his left knee and held her there so he could get a better look at Jackie's face. The question kept lingering in his mind, like a splinter that had festered and swollen. "Okay then. let's have it. Who is this person you don't trust?"

"It's Joseph Donnelly."

Uncle Rodney didn't say anything at first. He just sat there as if not wanting to hear what she was saying.

"And what lead you to distrust him?"

Jackie told him of her conversation with the VA Secretary in as much detail as possible. Uncle Rodney took it all in, storing it away and comparing it with information he'd already received from other people. In the end, he agreed that Jackie was right to distrust him. But that didn't soften the emotional blow. If she was right about this one thing, then they were in worse shape than they were before they found Joseph Donnelly, and he didn't see much hope on the horizon.

Jackie saw the despair sinking in, threatening to destroy her general, so she quickly changed the subject, lest he give in to the gravity of the situation.

"I think we should make a list of everyone close to us, everyone who had knowledge of the nuke delivery, then and only then will we be able to have a chance at knowing for sure who the bad guy is."

Jackie reached past Uncle Rodney and scooped up a notebook and pen from his desk. Then she sat back down and began to write.

"What about baby Donna. Do we trust her?"

Rodney and Jackie laughed out loud, and baby Donna quickly followed suit. Thirty minutes later, they felt more positive and light-hearted about the whole situation. Rodney left the room feeling more confident than he had in days, and Jackie's faith in Rodney was bolstered as well.

Sparky Meets the General

"COLONEL BRANCH, WILL YOU PLEASE TELL ME HOW IN GOD'S NAME THE Blind Man knew exactly where and when you would be in Davenport, Iowa?"

Even though he knew it was just his Uncle Rodney, still, being chewed out by the old man was definitely a sight to behold, but not one to be desired.

"I don't know, sir."

General Branch cocked his head to one side and looked at his nephew with shock in his eyes. Everything inside him wanted to yell and scream, but he knew that it would accomplish nothing, that it would simply demoralize his colonel and damage their personal relationship. Besides, he knew in his heart of hearts that Dan was not to blame. It's just ... he was counting on those nukes to defeat the Blind Man.

"May I remind the general that patience is indeed a virtue and one of the sought-after fruits of the spirit as outlined in the book of Galatians, chapter 5 and verses 22 and 23."

General Rodney T. Branch looked over at Sparky Fillmore, a man he'd never met before today, and when he looked at him, he couldn't believe his ears. He'd just lost eight nukes, and now a total stranger was quoting scripture and rebuking him for his lack of self control. Rodney fought for patience.

"And who the hell is this man?"

Dan started to speak, but Sparky beat him to it. He moved forward quickly and thrust his right hand out to shake the general's hand. "My name is Sparky Fillmore, from western Kansas and I was sent here by God to give you a message."

Uncle Rodney put his fists on his hips and looked incredulously at the man before him. He started to talk, but slowly regained control of his anger. Finally, he reached out and shook Sparky's hand. "There now, General Branch, now doesn't that feel so much better to be in control of yourself? I can already feel the tension lifting."

Sparky looked over at Jeff Arnett, then at Colonel MacPherson, then to his nephew Dan. Jeremy Branch was the only one smiling in the room. He alone appeared to be having a good time. Finally, after mastering his emotions, the general spoke.

"Okay, Mr. Fillmore, I'm not above help from God, so why don't you go ahead and give me the message. What exactly does God want you to tell me?"

Sparky laughed out loud and starting shaking his head from side to side. "I have no idea, general! And isn't that just like God to do something like that? All I know is that God came to me while I was milking my cow one morning and told me to travel to Michigan in search of Rodney T. Branch, the commanding general of the Shadow Militia. He didn't tell me why or what message to give you. I'm still waiting for that part."

Uncle Rodney's head sagged down, almost far enough to rest on his chest. He was discouraged. After several seconds, he looked over at the maple tree to his left and saw the bright, red cardinal perched there on a small branch. Rodney watched the bird for several seconds, until it flew away into the woods. Before speaking, he let out a huge, audible sigh.

"Well, in that case, Mr. Fillmore, I'd like to thank you for traveling so far at your own expense and inconvenience to give me this message that hasn't quite come to you yet." He looked into Sparky's face and tried to smile. "Welcome to Michigan, Mr. Fillmore."

Jeremy Branch moved forward and slapped the old man from Kansas on the back. "He can bunk in my room. I'll sleep on the floor. I like this little guy."

Sparky smiled and turned toward his new, young friend. "Why thank you, young man. I really appreciate that. But I can sleep on the floor. Not a problem."

General Branch ignored the rest of their conversation as he turned back to his nephew. "Dan, I need to speak to you about a very important matter. Meet me in my kitchen at twenty-two hundred hours."

Colonel Branch snapped to attention and saluted. Rodney returned the gesture and strode away into the woods to finish cooling off. He needed some time to think and sort things out. So much was happening, so quickly.

CHAPTER 12

August 17, The Great Debate

"**A**BSOLUTELY NOT! THERE'S NO WAY IN HELL I'M LETTING you have dinner with that man!"

Dan Branch was fit to be tied as he paced back and forth in Uncle Rodney's dining room. Colonel MacPherson and General Branch were seated at the kitchen table, both with their hands folded atop the Formica. Jeremy and Donny were off to one side, leaning against the wall. Jeremy seemed entertained. Joe Leif stood beside the kitchen sink with a cup of coffee in his hand and had a concerned look on his face.

"Why not, Dad. It sounds like fun to me."

Dan Branch shot a piercing stare into his son, quickly silencing him for the duration of the conversation. Jackie was seated at the table across from Uncle Rodney.

"Now Dan, just calm down. I didn't say I was going to do it."

Dan walked to the far wall, turned around and came back again. "I can't believe he's even asking you to do it. First he sends you into a saracen camp of twenty-thousand men, and then he flies you down to Haiti, and now he wants you to have dinner with the most dangerous killer on the planet!"

Dan stopped and pointed his finger out at his uncle. "This is too much! You've just crossed the line! I will not allow this to happen."

Baby Donna curled her lower lip and began to whimper in Jackie's arms. "Please, Dan. You're scaring the baby."

Dan saw his daughter's fear and tried to calm himself down. He took a deep breath and tried to maintain more control as he addressed his uncle.

"Why are we doing this?"

Uncle Rodney sighed and looked up at his nephew. He thought about it for a moment before speaking. "Well, Dan. We're doing it because this man has information we need to defeat the Blind Man. In fact, he has intimate knowledge of every aspect of Jared Thompson's capabilities and I believe a small part of him wants to help us."

Dan crossed his arms over his chest and stood defiantly. "And just what makes you think he wants to help us?"

General Branch remained calm and stone-faced. "Because he abandoned the Blind Man at risk of his own life. He came to us and has already given us valuable information. And now that he's committed himself he has nowhere else to go. If he returns to the Blind Man he'll be tortured and killed."

Dan, normally a calm and rational man, was anything but rational when it came to the safety of the woman he loved. He turned to stare out the kitchen window, trying desperately to make this topic go away. Then he looked back at Uncle Rodney with pleading eyes. "But what if he kills her?"

General Branch opened his mouth to answer, but Jackie cut him off. "Dan, please. Calm down. You don't know this guy like I do. He could kill any of us at any time he pleases. He doesn't need to set up a time and place where we have control in order to do it." She stood up and handed the baby to Jeremy before turning toward her husband. "Besides, if he was going to kill me he would have done it when I was in the saracen army camp." She moved to Dan and placed her hands on each side of his face. "But he didn't do that. Instead, he let me go and gave me information that might defeat the Blind Man to boot."

Dan saw an opening and interrupted. "None of that information has helped because we haven't been able to access the files. He's given us nothing!"

Uncle Rodney stood to his feet, followed by Colonel MacPherson. Joe Leif was still sipping his coffee and trying to stay out of the line of fire.

"Jackie, why don't you and Dan take a walk and try to figure it out as a couple. All I can tell you is I won't order you to do it, and whatever you two decide is what we'll live with."

Dan looked over to his uncle, but then returned his gaze to his wife. He looked into her dark eyes. "Honey, do you have any idea how many people this man has killed?"

Jackie lay her head on his chest, her long, black Lebanese hair cascading down around her. Then she looked up into Dan's face and smiled. "Honey, I hear what you're saying, and I love you for it. But ..." She hesitated. "But honey, I doubt very much this terrible man has killed any more men than I have."

Dan's face tightened. She'd just said something that he'd never considered before. And it was true. In the last battle alone before being captured in the saracen camp, she'd killed over eight thousand people using poison hemlock and then a biological agent. His wife, however sweet and loving to her family, was a seasoned and proficient killer. He opened his mouth to speak, but all that came out was empty air.

August 18, A Touch Under the Weather

SAMMY THURMOND WAS NOT FEELING WELL THESE DAYS. IN FACT, HE hadn't been feeling well for almost a week now. He looked around the abandoned house he'd been staying in and felt a bit of a chill, despite the eighty-two degrees all around him.

Sammy slowly rolled off the bed, and his shaky legs hit the floor with a thud. A sudden wave of nausea spread over him, but he choked it down and stood upright. He was a little dizzy, but it seemed to pass as he walked out of the bedroom, down the stairway and into the bright sunshine. The strength returned to his legs and he made it the rest of the way to the cemetery with no more ill effects.

The nausea had begun a few days ago, and now he was feeling disoriented, and finding it very difficult to focus on things he needed to do. This was a disconcerting feeling to Sammy, as he'd always been in full control of his faculties as well as his body. It was frustrating to lose control of himself when he was accustomed to controlling not only himself but most others around him. Something was wrong, but he didn't know what it was.

Pausing at the edge of the cemetery, Sammy watched the trees at the far edge of the cemetery. After fifteen minutes, he caught the movement, however slight, and then brought his binoculars up to his eyes to focus in. They were cheap binoculars, a pair he'd found in the garage in a chest full of old bowhunting gear at the house where he was staying, but they were enough for him to identify the man in the ghillie suit keeping watch over the grave of Ronald T. Branch.

Sammy watched for another half hour, seeking out any other soldiers, but saw none. In Sammy's mind, one soldier would be there simply to observe and report, but a squad of soldiers would be a kill team. Not that it mattered. If General Branch wanted him dead, he could certainly have killed him on their last meeting. But he hadn't done so. Sammy and the general had achieved a delicate detente of sorts which allowed them both to live and breathe and meet. Sammy knew that it was temporary, that it had to be, and that it was based solely on a personal one-on-one principle of mutual assured destruction. They both had something the other wanted, and, as long as that situation existed, as long as both believed the other could kill on demand, then both men could rest easy. But for now, the tenuous truce was in force and Sammy had nothing to fear. Despite that, he approached from the east side of the cemetery instead of the west as he'd done before. Sammy would never be good at trust.

He stood up and walked briskly toward the granite headstone. When he got closer, he saw the piece of white paper sitting atop the stone inside a plastic bag. He looked at it for a moment as if searching for some form of treachery. At last, he reached down and picked it up. As he was opening the bag, Sammy sat down on the headstone across from Rodney's brother. He read the note and almost smiled inside ... but not quite.

"Tomorrow, 6PM, this location. Bring an appetite. It will be good to see you again, Mr. Thurmond.

Respectfully,
Jackie Branch

Before he realized his actions, Sammy lifted the paper to his nose and sniffed it. He could still smell her.

Then he folded the paper back up and placed it neatly inside the plastic before putting it inside his front jeans pocket. He would need to take a bath and comb his hair.

DONNY BREWSTER WATCHED IN HIS RIFLE SCOPE AS SAMMY THURMOND walked toward the woods as he departed the cemetery. It would take but a pound of trigger pull to kill this man, but his orders had been specific: do not engage under any circumstances. Simply observe and report. And that's exactly what he'd done. Donny was confident that he hadn't been seen, so now he watched just long enough to seal the deal and complete the mission.

But then the man hesitated and slowly turned back toward the cemetery. Donny was a hundred yards away, but the man looked up, into Donny's tree, and seemed to be looking directly at him. Donny frowned and zeroed in on the man's head via the scope. He could see the man's face perfectly now, his cold, green eyes, the chiseled, stone-like features of his jaw and face. And then the man smiled slightly and turned to walk away.

Donny was dumbfounded. And then he whispered out loud. "Well I'll be buggered." And then he couldn't help but smile respectfully. "Amazing."

August 19, Dinner Date with Death

THE NEXT DAY, JACKIE BRANCH STOOD BESIDE THE PLASTIC FOLDING TABLE at the grave of Ronald T. Branch. The table was eight feet long and there were two comfortable folding chairs set up across from one another. At the center of the table was a candle. Jackie struck a wooden match and lit the wick. The candle burned, flickered, and then burned brighter. The air was a dead calm, the sun leaning down toward the treeline which lengthened the shadows and lent a coolness to the late summer air.

Sensing movement to her right, she glanced over and saw Sammy Thurmond walking toward her across the grass. Normally, the grass of any cemetery was short, thick and well kempt, but now the grass was almost knee high and already starting to turn brown from the unrelenting heat of an entire summer. She was nervous inside, but kept her jitters hidden as she forced a smile onto her face. She bowed her head slightly as Sammy stopped at the table across from her.

"Good evening, Mr. Thurmond. I'm glad you could make it."

Sammy nodded his head and stood in front of the chair for several seconds with an awkwardness uncharacteristic of his usual demeanor. Finally, he bowed his head slightly and then walked around and held the chair back so Jackie could sit down.

"Thank you, sir."

He then moved back around and seated himself. At first he said nothing, but Jackie didn't rush him. A tiny breeze kicked up and the candle flickered slightly, but then burned bright again as the air died down.

"I am happy to see that you are still pregnant, Mrs. Branch."

Jackie smiled softly and answered politely. "Why thank you Sammy. I've just started my second trimester, and it's starting to get a bit uncomfortable with all this heat." She hesitated, but he didn't join in, so she continued on. "But in another month it will cool off again and things will get better."

Sammy looked across the table past the candle and deeply into her eyes. Two months ago the intensity of his gaze would have rattled her to her core, but now ... it was different. She was different. She met his stare and returned it.

"General Branch says you just returned from an assignment." He paused. "I hope it went well."

Jackie nodded. "Yes, it did. It went very well." She couldn't help but be reminded of a husband and wife, talking about their day at the office over a romantic dinner. Oddly enough, she found it intriguing, two deadly assassins, both having killed thousands of people, talking over dinner as if they were normal.

"I was in Haiti on a special assignment."

Sammy broke eye contact and looked away. When he turned back, Jackie thought she saw a bit of compassion in his eyes. "Was it hard for you to go back there?"

She kept the smile pasted on her face, but her eyes were frowning now. She simply said "Yes. Hard. Very hard."

"And did you find what you were looking for?"

Jackie hesitated, wondering how much he already knew and how much she should tell him. Then she recalled the last dinner she'd had with him and how well it had gone. She had been very open and candid with him, so she decided to do the same today. Instinctively she knew that any information she withheld would carry the same weight as a lie.

"Yes, we rescued the Secretary of Veteran Affairs from a gang. He'd been kidnapped."

Sammy nodded with renewed interest. "We had located him in the Dominican, but he slipped through our grasp several times. The Blind Man was very disappointed."

And then Sammy looked away from the table and scanned the trees and the edges of the cemetery. "How many people are watching us right now?"

Jackie didn't hesitate. She was totally committed to her role. "I'm not sure. I didn't count them. But at least twelve I think."

Sammy's face brightened a bit. "That's good. I like to be taken seriously, anything less than ten would have been an insult."

Jackie laughed softly. "Mr. Thurmond, is that humor?"

Sammy nodded. "I hope so. It's been a long time though, so please do me the honor of chuckling regardless."

She laughed again, this time with a more genuine tone. "A sense of humor is like riding a bike I suppose."

"So, General Branch is going to place Joseph Donnelly as the acting president, take control of the remaining US military forces and attempt to defeat the Blind Man?"

Jackie paused and then nodded. "Yes, I believe that is the plan. At least most of it. Uncle Rodney would never usurp power though. Once the Blind Man is defeated and constitutional control is once again secure, then all of us will quietly bow out and return to our normal lives."

Sammy cocked his head to one side and looked at her as if she'd just said something very surprising. "General Branch is going to willingly give up power?"

Jackie nodded. "Yes, of course. Anything less would be dishonorable."

And then Sammy looked off over Jackie's shoulder, as if remembering a Truth that had somehow been forgotten long, long ago. "Hmmm, that is highly irregular, to give up power I mean." Jackie said nothing in response.

"The Blind Man will not see that coming."

He turned his head back to Jackie and stared into her eyes. "But you must understand that he will not allow the general to follow through with his plan. He will have to counter."

Jackie moved her hands up on the table top and clasped them together lightly. "By that you mean he will try to kill Mr. Donnelly?"

He looked into the flame of the candle burning on the table. The flame flickered in the center of his eyes. "Be careful with him, Jackie Branch. Skim milk masquerades as cream."

Sammy smiled, and his icy green eyes made the hairs on Jackie's neck stand up. "I doubt you'll anticipate what the Blind Man has already planned." He looked at the dishes on the table. "If The Blind Man wishes the secretary to be dead, then he will soon be dead. If he wishes to use him in some other way, then ..." Sammy let his last statement trail off into the woods beyond the cemetery. Jackie took note of it and stored that information away for later analysis.

"Enough shop talk for now, Mr. Thurmond." Jackie lifted the cover off the cast iron kettle to her right as she changed the subject. "I hope you are a meat and potatoes man. I made beef pot roast. It's one of my specialties."

The man moved his hands back down to the table top and his smile softened. She seldom knew when he was playing games and when he was deadly serious.

"Mrs. Branch, I'm guessing that you already know how much I love pot roast. If you don't, then it would be impossible for me to respect General Branch if his intelligence gathering were so shoddy."

"You grew up in Iowa, Sammy. I would be very surprised if you didn't appreciate a good roast served with corn on the cob, butter and mashed potatoes and gravy."

Sammy laughed out loud, but this time it didn't sound creepy. Jackie asked for his plate and quickly cut him a generous slab of pot roast, then some corn on the cob and mashed potatoes. Last, she ladled on some beef gravy.

"I hope you brought your Iowa farm-boy appetite with you today."

Sammy didn't say anything. The smell of the roast wafted up and into his nostrils, causing the nausea to rise up as bile in his throat. It came over him quickly, but he mastered it almost immediately. Jackie noticed a slight change in his face, but then it was gone, almost as quickly as it had come.

"Are you alright, Mr. Thurmond?"

Sammy nodded and smiled slightly. He reached over to accept the full plate from her. Then he slowly picked up his fork to eat, but Jackie quickly admonished him.

"Not yet, Sammy. First we give thanks."

The stone-cold killer across from her hesitated, as if making a decision that didn't quickly compute, and then he closed his eyes and folded his hands on the table in front of him. Jackie did the same and then began to pray.

"Dear Lord, we thank you for this food. We thank you for this wonderful day and for all the ones who love us. Amen."

While Sammy ate, Jackie made a plate for herself.

"So, Sammy, what do you think?"

Sammy waited to finish the bite in his mouth before answering. "It's absolutely wonderful, Mrs. Branch. I expected no less."

Both of them ate in silence for the next ten minutes. Jackie pondered the craziness of the situation she was in, eating a civilized dinner with a pathological murderer, a man who could kill on command without batting an eye or feeling an emotion. It was a job to him. And then she wondered ... how much of a difference was there between Sammy and Uncle Rodney, or Sammy and Donny Brewster? All three of those men could kill, in great numbers, skillfully, had indeed studied the art and science of killing and had mastered it like a craft, like a painter or a concert pianist.

And then she wondered ... *how many people have I killed?* And, more importantly, *am I any different than Sammy? If I continue killing, will I become unrecognizable, like the creature, Gollum, in Lord of the Rings? What would distinguish me from the man sitting across the table?*

Sammy finished his food and gently dabbed his mouth with the white, linen napkin. Jackie quickly finished her last few bites and did the same.

"Well, Mrs. Branch, I want to thank you most profusely for the conversation and the meal. It was most enjoyable."

Sensing that he was about to leave, Jackie was tempted to ask him questions, to get information that would help them defeat the Blind Man. She knew that's what Uncle Rodney would want, but ... somehow, she sensed that pushing him would be the wrong move. But if he told them nothing, then why was she going through all this trouble? Jackie bit her tongue and responded politely.

"It was no trouble at all, Sammy. I'm glad we had our talk. It's my way of returning the favor you gave to me." She looked him directly in the eyes now, and what she said next was neither forced nor contrived. "You saved my life, Sammy. I know that, and I'm grateful."

Sammy smiled so genuinely, that Jackie found it hard to remember that he was a heinous killer. He could be very charming when he wanted to. He slid his chair back roughly in the grass and then stood to his feet. Jackie saw him hesitate halfway up, and Jackie wondered what that was all about, but he straightened and then nodded politely to her.

Jackie extended her hand, and Sammy reached down and gently touched her, lifted her hand to his lips and pressed them together in gentlemanly fashion.

"Chivalry is not dead, madame, especially in Iowa. I want to thank you for this warm and wonderful down-home, Iowa dinner. As always, you've been a splendid hostess, and I want you to know that this one meeting, coupled with my conversation with General Branch, made all the sacrifice worthwhile. Thank you so much."

Jackie smiled and nodded as he released her hand. She was confused by his warmth and gentleness, and by his words. *Sacrifice? What did he mean by that.* As she looked into his stone-green eyes, she thought she saw a hint of compassion, but it was fleeting, there for just a moment, like a vapor, and then it rose up and was gone. In her heart of hearts, she knew that Sammy Thurmond was a huge tome of secrets, that it might take a lifetime to figure him out, but still ... she forced herself not to push him. He would share when he was ready, and, somehow, she sensed that they would be having dinner again soon.

And then Sammy Thurmond turned and walked away, slowly at first, with the subtle hint of a military stride, and then he gradually slowed. Jackie watched as he walked, not knowing what to expect, thinking, *is this all there is?*

And that's when Sammy Thurmond fell to the ground and ceased to move.

CHAPTER 13

Life and Death

"SAMMY THURMOND! SAMMY! WAKE UP!" JACKIE BRANCH kneeled down on the cemetery grass beside her dinner partner. There was a sudsy, white foam coming from his mouth now, and Jackie wiped it away with her linen napkin. There was a chalky pallor to his face that seemed eerie in the failing light of the graveyard. And then he began to shake. At first, Jackie grabbed his arms and tried to hold him still, but he was much too strong for that.

"Sammy! Are you okay?"

But Sammy didn't answer. His body continued to convulse, and then his eyelids snapped open wide. Just for a moment, Jackie looked into the icy, green stare, but slowly, ever so slowly, the green of his irises rolled up into his head and only the whites showed. The shaking continued for almost a minute, and then it stopped as quickly as it had started. Sammy lay there in Jackie's arms, exhausted and motionless on the ground, with the tall, brown sedge grass rising up around his head.

He opened his eyes and looked up at Jackie. Then he spoke weakly. "You are such a beautiful woman."

Jackie laughed out loud nervously, but relieved that he was still alive. She could hear people running up behind her and knew her protection detail would be there soon. She sensed that things were coming to a climax, or perhaps even a hasty close. She didn't know what to say, so she just spoke from her heart.

"Why thank you, Mr. Thurmond. I hope my pot roast had nothing to do with your present condition."

Sammy chuckled softly with all the energy he could muster. "No, my lady." Sammy looked up at Jackie's face, a silhouette against the darkening sky. He smelled the dead and dying sedge grass around him and knew he was standing on a new precipice. "This one is courtesy of the Blind Man." His words were becoming forced now. "Not altogether unexpected. I wondered what surprise he had for me." Sammy's eyes looked up into the sky beyond Jackie's head. "The Blind Man seldom disappoints."

Jackie smiled down compassionately. "Is there anything we can do to stop it?"

Sammy tried to shake his head from side to side, but the motion served only to heighten his vertigo. "No. The Blind Man has always been ... thorough. Do not under estimate him or you'll suffer my fate."

The whites of Sammy's eyes started to pool up with blood at the corners, and then worked its way into the irises toward his pupils. The mixture of red and icy green was horrifying to Jackie, but she pretended not to notice. And then Sammy's skin took on a flushed, pink color, and his very blood began to seep gently out through the skin of his face and arms.

Jackie steeled her will and continued to make eye contact with him. Right now she was feeling so many conflicting emotions for this man, this cold-blooded killer, this chivalrous hero who'd saved her life and treated her with kindness as he'd murdered so many others. "What can I do for you, Sammy?"

Just then Donny Brewster arrived. Jackie held him back with a wave of her uplifted hand, causing him to just hover in the background and Sammy whispered his last.

"Come close, my lady."

Jackie hesitated just a second, but then moved her face down closer to his own. "I have a message for General Branch."

She was confused, but nodded her head.

"Remember."

Jackie moved just a bit closer.

"h, 4, 8, b, 5, a, t, plus, k, w, l, s, minus, 8, y, h, 4, g, u, q."

Sammy closed his eyes for a few seconds, then opened them back up again. The edges of his eyesight were failing now, and he knew the end was near. He thought back to so many other countless men that he'd killed. At the time he'd given no thought to his own death, but ... he wondered. *Had it been like this for them as well?*

Jackie looked up at Donny. "I need a paper and pen! Quickly!" But she saw that Donny was already writing down the characters in his sniper notebook.

Sammy repeated the sequence again, this time softer and harder to hear. And then he was quiet for a few seconds before looking back up into Jackie's face. So many he'd killed ... with knives up close, cold and impersonal at one-thousand yards, bullets in the ear, the back of the head, sometimes in the guts just to watch them suffer.

So many of the deaths did not bother him, but he still remembered his first. It had been the hardest, and it weighed on him now, like an anchor that threatened to drown his soul in a sea of lifelessness. And then the name Steven Maxwell came to his mind ... the man who had unwittingly started it all, the man who'd injected the god virus into the heart of America. He still remembered Steven by name, as a pitiful man, a geek with no future outside a computer screen. If memory served him correctly, he'd shot that man in the eye, the left eye. And then he thought out loud, his words confusing Jackie. "It wasn't such a bad death."

Sammy Thurmond came out of his musings and tried to reach up to Jackie, but he didn't have the strength. Jackie reached over and grabbed onto his right hand with her left. She felt the wet, slippery blood, seeping through his skin, but felt no compunction to pull away from him. No man, even a killer, deserved to die alone.

"I'm here, Sammy. I'm here for you."

The sight around the edges of his vision began to close in on his pupils even more, like a tunnel of light, surrounded by an ever-growing and unstoppable darkness.

"Sammy! Stay with me! What can I do?"

The man's voice opened and a small puff of air came out, trying to form words. Jackie didn't understand, so she moved down closer to just a few inches away from his mouth.

"Pur ... pose."

There were tears flowing down Jackie's cheeks now.

"Get ... him."

The last thing Sammy Thurmond saw was Jackie's black hair covering his face. The last he felt was her tears falling lightly on his cheek. The last he heard was the whimper of a woman who cared about him. And then his senses failed him, all save one ... the light smell of olive oil, scented with lilac. And then his final thought on earth ...

It's more than I deserve.

Jackie felt his hand go slack, and she collapsed onto his chest and wept.

GENERAL BRANCH STOOD OVER THE GRAVE OF SAMMY THURMOND, A hardened criminal, a killer, and only God and the Blind Man knew what else. But Jackie had insisted on a proper burial, and Uncle Rodney had agreed with her. Whatever else Sammy Thurmond had been at his death, it had not always been so. At one time he'd served his country with distinction and honor. And it could be argued that his country had used him and helped to make him what he was at his death. Regardless, Rodney gave him a military funeral with full honors and a military honor guard. Their new and mysterious friend from Kansas, being a religious man, had presided in the burial service. Now, Sparky Fillmore had moved to the back to give Uncle Rodney center stage.

General Branch stepped forward and rendered one, final salute. The others in the group, Colonel Ranger MacPherson, Colonel Dan Branch, Sergeant Donny Brewster, and Corporal Jeremy Branch, along with the honor guard, all saluted as well, then cut away when Uncle Rodney lowered his hand.

Jackie cried off to one side until Dan pulled her in close and held her tight. He didn't fully understand the bond between her and the killer, but ... he forced himself to accept it and not ask questions. Four soldiers lowered the pine box down into the ground with ropes. They buried him pretty much where he and Jackie had enjoyed their dinner the day before. Uncle Rodney owned several plots near his brother, and determined it was only fitting.

Jeremy and Dan stepped forward with shovels and began to throw dirt into the hole. The others filtered off into the distance, some talking softly to one another, but, eventually, it was just Jeremy and Dan, alone in the cemetery. Jeremy was the first to speak.

"This brings back old memories."

His father thought about that a moment or two before making the connection.

"Yeah. It's amazing isn't it. A year ago I'd never dug a grave, but since then I've been digging a lot of them, sometimes for people I had to kill myself. It's amazing what a year of time and life can do to a man."

Jeremy's upper body had filled out since digging his first grave back in Wisconsin. The first had been for his own mother who'd committed suicide the day after the great fall. Both men thought quietly as they shoveled.

"Dad, do you still think about Mom sometimes?"

Dan stopped in mid-shovel and looked over at his son. Sometimes he forgot he was still a bit of a boy inside, in light of all the living, fighting and killing they'd both been forced to do in the past year.

"Yeah, sometimes. Though, I have to admit that with so much going on and so much we have to do just to survive, I don't have as much time for introspection as I would like."

Jeremy shrugged. "I suppose so. But ... ya know, Dad, us snipers have a lot of time to think. That's mostly what we do, just sit around making plans for the next battle or laying in a hidey hole just waiting for the next person we have to kill."

The words of his son spoke volumes, and Dan moved closer, dropped his shovel and embraced Jeremy. The boy had grown tall and strong and was physically now Dan's equal. Jeremy returned the embrace.

"I'm sorry I haven't been as accessible to you as I should be. There's just so much to do, son."

Dan had been surprised to hear his son identify himself as a sniper, as a killer, and it saddened him to his core. Jeremy moved back away from him and sat down on the edge of the hole. There was still about two feet of dirt that needed to be filled in.

"Do you remember what you told me last year when we were burying those three guys who attacked Jackie at her cabin in Wisconsin?"

Dan thought for a moment. "No, not really. What did I say?"

Dan then sat down on the edge of the hole across from his son.

"You told me that we bury good guys in single graves, and we pray over them, but the bad guys get one hole and no prayer?"

Dan looked over at his son, not really sure how to respond. "I really said that?"

"Yep."

"That sounds kind of callus doesn't it?"

Jeremy had the shovel in front of him, so he grasped the wooden handle tightly in both hands.

"Yeah, I suppose. But Dad, in your defense, those were some pretty tough times. I mean ... think about it. We were burying guys left and right back then and it was still pretty new to us." And then he paused and leaned a bit forward until the left side of his face made contact with the wooden handle. He paused just long enough to form his thoughts. "I think it was pretty good advice, considering the circumstances."

Both men were silent for almost thirty seconds. "So why did this guy get prayed over and a salute and the whole honor guard thing? He was a pretty bad guy, right? He worked for the Blind Man and he must've killed a lot of innocent people."

Dan leaned forward on his shovel handle as well, thinking about the best way to answer his son. "Well, yeah, you can look at it that way I suppose, but ... I don't know, everything isn't as black and white as we'd like it to be, ya know. Talking about good guys and bad guys and like everything is black and white and easy to figure out." A bird flew over to a nearby headstone and landed lightly atop it. "People aren't all good or all bad. We're all a mix. Sammy did mostly bad things in his life, but ... at the end, maybe when it mattered the most, he did some pretty good things." The bird flew away, and Jeremy agreed with him.

"Yeah, I can see that. First he saved Mom's life. Then he gave us all those files, and then some kind of code to try and help us get back at the Blind Man."

Dan nodded. "Yeah, he did some good things at the end."

The two men stood back up and started filling in the hole again. Jeremy spoke again. "So, is this guy going to hell or to heaven?"

Dan dug his shovel into the sand pile and threw another heap into the hole. "I don't know, son. But the way I figure it, questions like that are way above my paygrade."

The two men smiled gently at one another as they shoveled. "Good point, Dad. So should I ask Uncle Rodney or Mom?"

Dan finally laughed out loud as he continued to shovel, and then he said. "Yes! Absolutely!"

When they were done, a small mound of sand lay before them. In another few weeks the fall rains would come, the days would shorten, and grass would start to grow up, as well as various kinds of weeds. And by this time next year, there would be no trace of the man buried below ground. His life, the sum total of his good and bad, would live on, but only in the lives of those he'd impacted, for good or for ill.

They both stood there, leaning against their shovels, wiping sweat from their brows in the early afternoon heat of August. By now everyone else had gone. Dan turned to Jeremy, put his right arm around his shoulder and they both walked away without looking back.

CHAPTER 14

August 20, H4!b5at+kWls-8yh4Guq

JEFF ARNETT HAD BEEN UP ALL NIGHT LONG, STRUGGLING with the password given to Jackie by Sammy Thurmond. It looked like a twenty-character alphanumeric string, randomly generated by a computer. As such, that made it nearly unbreakable with just the laptops they had at their disposal. If he'd still been in Langley, then yes, by all means. He could put a supercomputer on it along with a full team of cryptologists, and they'd have it cracked in a matter of days. But now ... now he had what appeared to be the majority of the character string in tact. But when he typed it in, it didn't work.

In order to solve the mystery, he went on the assumption that Sammy Thurmond really did want them to access these files, so that meant that it was indeed possible. Jeff closed his eyes and tried to put himself in Sammy's shoes. He was in pain, semi-conscious and convinced that he had but a few seconds to live. He would have to abbreviate, saying things as concisely as possible, even if they weren't one-hundred percent precise. On top of that, he would either be convinced that he'd just been poisoned by Jackie, or that the Blind Man was somehow killing him. Jeff guessed the latter simply because the Shadow Militia had no reason to kill him; it would be in their best interest to keep him alive for the information he might give them. Besides, Uncle Rodney could have had him killed after their first meeting, but he had not. On top of that, the Blind Man had motive. He certainly could not allow Sammy to live, because he possessed a mountain of information that could possibly bring the Blind Man to his knees. Certainly, it was in the Blind Man's best interest to kill Sammy Thurmond, and

Sammy would definitely decipher that. After all, he knew Jared Thompson better than anyone else in the world.

Jeff studied the character-string again. *What was missing?*

There are no upper-case characters. A computer program designed to create a random, twenty-character password would definitely use at least two upper-case letters. What else? And then he smiled. Yes, the words 'plus' and 'minus' had to go. They should be replaced with mathematical characters. And then he looked at the '8' character just following the minus. A dying man, in Sammy Thurmond's condition, would find it very difficult to say the word 'asterisk.'

Jeff pulled up the software program he was using to try and crack the password. He opened the code and made a few changes, saved and then executed the program again. After two more hours of trial and error, Jeff got the message 'password accepted."

What Jeff saw in the directory amazed him. There were hundreds, maybe thousands of files at his disposal. He double-clicked on one and opened it up. Agent Arnett nearly fell off his chair. He had to call the general at once.

August 21, Pole Barn HQ

"So HERE IS THE RAW ALPHANUMERIC SEQUENCE THAT WE WERE GIVEN BY Sammy Thurmond as he lay dying." Special Agent Jeff Arnett wrote the following characters on the whiteboard in front of him. They were in the pole barn he used as an operations center. They had minimal power, so the room was dimly lit, but they could still see just fine, especially dark characters on a white board.

h, 4, 8, b, 5, a, t, plus, k, w, l, s, minus, 8, y, h, 4, g, u, q

"So we go ahead and change the words 'plus' and 'minus' to numeric characters, then we change the first occurrence of '8' to an asterisk symbol, and then we have this:

h, 4, *, b, 5, a, t, +, k, w, l, s, -, 8, y, h, 4, g, u, q

"Any decent hacker knows that to make a near unbreakable password, you need twenty characters using a mixture of upper case and lower case with numbers and special characters as well. So I ran it through our code-breaking program, which took almost 25 hours, and came up with this password:

H4*b5at+kWls-8yh4Guq

Under normal circumstances, we could have eventually broken the password without his help, but things being as they are, with limited power and working without super computers, it's safe to say that we never would have broken the password without Mr. Thurmond's help."

Jeff Arnett turned away from the board and back to his audience. General Branch and Colonel MacPherson were seated in folding chairs while Dan, Jeremy and Jackie stood off to one side.

General Branch interrupted him impatiently. "So, are you saying that you broke the password, and you can now access the files he gave us?"

Jeff nodded his head. "Yes, General Branch, that's exactly what I'm telling you."

Uncle Rodney smiled widely. "Good job! Did you find any actionable intel?"

Jeff smiled uncharacteristically. "Only the location of the Blind Man's alternate headquarters as well as a list of his military assets and where they can be found, along with security details that will make it possible for us to launch a surprise attack on his forces and his supplies."

Uncle Rodney stood to his feet, the chair pushing back behind him, scraping loudly against the cement floor before falling over with a crash. "Thank God! Now we have a fighting chance!"

The general walked around the table and shook Jeff's hand, pumping it up and down vigorously. Colonel MacPherson breathed a sigh of relief and then folded his arms across his chest. Dan Branch looked nervously around at the others, wondering if anyone else was thinking what he was thinking. Jackie reached over and hugged her son with her left arm. After several seconds of congratulatory celebration, Dan spoke out loud.

"Mr. Arnett, how do we know this information is accurate?"

"Excuse me?" Jeff turned toward Dan Branch. "What do you mean?"

Dan took a deep breath. "Listen, I don't want to rain on anyone's parade here, but ... has it occurred to anyone that maybe Sammy is feeding us this information on purpose, and that maybe this is part of the Blind Man's plan? If we act on this intelligence without confirmation, we could be walking into a trap."

The room suddenly turned quiet. No one moved. The smiles faded and eventually disappeared altogether. Jeremy was the first to speak. "So, dad, why would he lie to us?"

Dan pivoted to face him. "Oh, I don't know. Maybe because he's a sociopath and he likes to play games with people's heads even if it is from beyond the grave."

"Dan has a point." Colonel MacPherson moved up to the white board and stood beside Uncle Rodney and Jeff. "The man is a lunatic, and we have to be very discriminatory about how we use any information from him."

Jeff Arnett nodded his head in agreement. "Absolutely. Every bit of information we get from these files should be verified before putting people in danger."

Uncle Rodney took a step back and leaned against the hot steel of the pole barn walls. The humidity was blistering hot today. It was almost like a steaming jungle both inside and out.

"Dan's right. We need to send people out to confirm every scrap of data we get from Sammy Thurmond. That just makes sense." And then he paused before looking over and making eye contact with Dan. "My gut tells me that we'll find everything Sammy gives us to be accurate."

Dan met his gaze, all the while knowing in his heart of hearts that what Uncle Rodney was saying was most likely true. He nodded without saying anything and Rodney smiled. Jeremy quickly broke into the conversation. "What makes you so sure that his intel is reliable?"

Rodney took a step forward again, and, as he did so, the sheet metal of the pole barn snapped back in with a small pop. "It's obviously a matter of the heart, Jeremy." But his grandson looked confused. "Sammy's personality and actions are always consistent. When he was loyal to the Blind Man, then he was fiercely, loyal, even unto death." And then he paused. "But then he met Jackie and transferred his loyalty to her ... and everything changed."

Jackie's face flushed red and she looked down to hide her eyes. Dan looked over at her, but she refused to meet his gaze.

When she finally looked back up, there was hair in her eyes, so she brushed it back away with her long, slender fingers. "I ... I think he was ... in love with me."

All the color drained from Dan's face, but he said nothing. He was in a state of shock. Jeremy spoke first. "That does make a little bit of sense. After all, he did help her escape from the saracen army. And then he put his own life on the line when he abandoned the Blind Man and walked for weeks to get here to Iroquois. That sounds like the kind of thing a man will do when he's in love."

Dan lowered his head as Jeremy continued, not really knowing what to think. "And then when he arrived, he wanted to have a candlelight dinner with that same woman." Jeremy nodded his head up and down. "Yep, That makes sense to me."

Uncle Rodney nodded in agreement. "Sammy Thurmond didn't give us the information so that we could save ourselves or because he believed in our cause. He did it to save the woman he was in love with."

There was emotional tension in the room, and it made Ranger MacPherson uncomfortable. He looked down and then quickly back up again. "General, with your permission I'd like to get a copy of this data and begin examining it, assuming that it's verifiable, and then draw up plans for possible attacks."

"Absolutely. And Dan, I want you to make a plan for sending out recon teams to verify all this information. We need to know for sure that it can be trusted before we put people in harm's way, and we need it done as soon as possible."

Dan looked up and nodded, still wrestling with the concept of another man being in love with his wife. "Right away, sir."

General Branch, in a loud command voice started issuing orders, but Jeff Arnett quickly interrupted him.

"General Branch, there's something else you need to know."

Uncle Rodney stopped in mid-sentence, and everyone else turned to stare in his direction. "You mean there's more?"

Jeff nodded. "Yes, I'm afraid so, sir."

But Jeff didn't continue. He simply looked down at the bare concrete floor as if waiting for permission to continue.

"Okay, Mr. Arnett. What do I need to know?"

Jeff moved over to his desk off to the right. "Perhaps it's better if I show you, sir."

Jeff moved his mouse to awaken his screen, then he quickly clicked and launched a jpeg file. All the others in the room began to gather around Jeff's desk to get a closer look. After several seconds, the photo began to load from the top, until, finally, two men could be seen shaking hands. They appeared to be at a gas station after the collapse as the pumps were plainly visible. A handwritten sign was taped over the face of the pump saying 'NO GAS."

Jackie Branch sucked in her breath and placed her hand over her mouth. Dan gasped out loud but said nothing. Ranger MacPherson stiffened to attention, but also remained quiet. Jeremy started to say something, but his father raised his hand to stifle him.

Uncle Rodney's darkest and most frightening suspicions had just been confirmed. He stepped closer to the screen, placing both hands on the desk top as if needing the support to keep from falling.

The man on the right was Sammy Thurmond, but the man on the left was the one commanding all the attention. Uncle Rodney looked into the man's eyes, as his own face seemed to harden, taking on a stone-like visage.

Uncle Rodney began to shake his head involuntarily back and forth. "I ...was hoping it wasn't so."

Jeff Arnett took a step back from the screen before answering. "I'm sorry sir, but it's confirmed. The man we were counting on to save us ... is a traitor."

God Finally Speaks

"UNCLE RODNEY? SPARKY WANTS TO TALK TO YOU, AND I THINK IT'S IM-portant." Sparky and Jeremy had become quite good friends in the past few days of bunking together. Sparky served as a grandfather figure to the young man, and also had helped Jeremy to work through his feelings of guilt at having to kill so many people in the past year.

General Branch was looking at a laptop computer screen with Jeff Arnett inside his kitchen at the table. Uncle Rodney looked over at Jeff Arnett who seemed to smirk, just a bit. Jeff had already run as complete a background check as he could under the present grid-down scenario, and had found nothing to suggest that Sparky Fillmore was anything other than what he claimed to be: and old man from west Kansas who'd been sent by God to deliver a message. But Jeff didn't fully believe it.

"Hold on a second, Jeff." Then he turned to Jeremy. "Show Mr. Fillmore in, please."

Jeremy left the room and Sparky walked in shortly after, with Jeremy close on his heels. "Thank you for seeing me, General Branch."

Uncle Rodney sat down in his chair and motioned for Sparky to do the same. "Would you like some tea or lemonade, Mr. Fillmore?"

Sparky's smile brightened even more. "You have lemonade? Really?"

The general laughed out loud. "Well, Mr. Fillmore, it's what we call lemonade, but it's really made out of staghorn sumac berries and sweetened up a bit with honey. And, of course, there are no ice cubes."

"I'd like to try that, general. It sounds very interesting to me."

Rodney motioned to Jeff. "Do you mind, Jeff?"

"Not at all, general." And then Jeff moved over to the sink and began pouring four cups of sumac lemonade into coffee mugs. He then brought them over two at a time and placed them on the table. Jeremy sat down to the right of Sparky.

"Okay, Mr. Fillmore. How can I help you?"

Sparky took a sip of his lemonade and his face seemed to glow with happiness. He'd been spending most of his time alone in his room the past few days, just fasting and praying, reading his Bible and seeking out any word from God.

"Oh my! This drink is delightful!" And then he looked up. "There's no alcohol in it, is there? Because I don't think Edna would approve of that. She's a bit of a teetotaler you know."

Rodney smiled patiently. "No alcohol, Mr. Fillmore. Now what is it you want to tell me?"

Sparky glanced over at Jeremy and smiled. Then he looked back over at Jeff who was now sitting down with the rest of them.

"Well, general, God spoke to me last night, and here is his message." Sparky paused, took a drink of his lemonade and then continued on. "First, God wants to encourage you and commend you for all your work. He thinks you're a lot like his servant Joshua." He chuckled to himself. "I think so too."

Rodney smiled slightly. "Go on, please."

"Also, he'd like you to know that your pending trip to Texas is a good idea, and that you will succeed, provided you rely on his strength instead of your own, and that you keep faith in Him."

Uncle Rodney almost dropped his coffee mug. He glanced over at Jeff Arnett, then back to Sparky. "And how did you know about our trip to Texas?"

Sparky ran his right forefinger around the rim of his coffee mug, trying to make it squeak, but it wouldn't work for him. "Well ... general, I just told you. God came to me and gave me the message."

Rodney looked over at Jeremy. "Son, did you tell Mr. Fillmore about this?"

But the young man shook his head from side to side. "I didn't know about it until just now. When are you going to Texas?"

Then Jeff Arnett spoke up. "General, only you and I and Colonel MacPherson knew of this plan. I've told no one else."

The general nodded. "I didn't even tell Dan about it. I haven't seen him since we made the plans to go." Then he looked over at Jeff. "I'll double-check with Mac to make sure he held confidence as well, but ... it would be unprecedented for him to break mission secrecy."

"Oh, and there's one more thing."

Rodney turned his head back to Sparky. "And that is?"

Sparky smiled eagerly. "God says I'm supposed to go with you."

The general's face screwed into a frown. "Excuse me?"

"God says the mission will fail if I don't go along. I don't know why."

Jeff interrupted. "General, that would be totally foolish. He's completely untrained. We don't know him. We don't trust him, and he certainly is not mission critical. He would be nothing more than an unknown liability."

Sparky laughed out loud. "Yes, I know. Isn't it the craziest thing you've ever heard?" And then his face got more serious. "But God has a history of picking people to serve him who are ungifted, who have little to offer, at least by the world's standards. David was a mere shepherd boy. Moses had a speech impediment. Gideon was a farmer." And then he looked deeply into the eyes of General Branch. "But despite their lack of talent and training, these men led God's people to victory."

General Branch pushed his coffee mug forward and stood to his feet. "Well, Mr. Fillmore, I want to thank you for delivering the message. I'll confer with my Chief of Intelligence before getting back to you on a final decision." And he quickly added. "And, of course, I'll be sure to consult the Lord about it as well."

Sparky's entire face beamed. "Now that's always a good idea, General Branch!" Sparky pushed his chair back and then quickly left the room, followed closely by his young protege.

Once they were gone, Jeff and Rodney looked at each other dumbly. Finally, Jeff broke the silence. "Okay then, general, do you want to pray first or should I?"

Uncle Rodney shook his head from side to side as he spoke. "This is the damnedest thing, Jeff. The damnedest thing I ever saw."

Secret Location - VA Secretary

JOSEPH DONNELLY LOOKED DOWN AT THE FOOD IN FRONT OF HIM. IT WAS in a sealed, light-brown, waterproof, plastic bag, and he was seriously perturbed at the prospect of eating these things the military called food even one more time. He couldn't wait to get out of this hole and back into some semblance of civilization.

He was living temporarily in what appeared to be an old wooden barn. There was old straw on the floor, and a few animal stalls off to his left. The place smelled musty, like dried manure that had been reconstituted. Joseph picked the survival food pack off his lap and read the contents.

```
Menu 23, Pizza Slice, Pepperoni
MRE, Meal, Ready-to-eat, Individual
Warfighter Recommended
Warfighter Tested,
Warfighter Approved
```

Joseph threw the food down on the barn floor in disgust. He was not a warfighter! The first thing he was going to do when sworn in as president of the United States was to outlaw MREs and hire himself a decent French Chef. Then he thought to himself *How did I get into this mess? I should have told them no when they'd first approached me.* Then he laughed softly. The truth is he hadn't had much of a choice. At least he was alive and was just waiting to be sworn in and take command of what used to be the most powerful country on the planet. Who knows, maybe it still was, but ... it didn't matter now. Even if America was still the most powerful country on earth, which he'd find out later after being sworn in, it still was only a shadow of its former self.

Hunger pangs growled up from the pit of his stomach, so he reluctantly swallowed his pride and reached down to the floor for the MRE packet. He tried to open the plastic, but the seal was too strong for him. He yelled over to one of the Shadow Militia soldiers in his protection detail.

"Hey soldier! Can you help me open this damn thing up, please?"

Sergeant Donny Brewster slung his M4 onto his back and walked over to where Joseph was sitting on an old, wooden potato crate. Donny stopped beside him and reached down to take the bag. Joseph was disgusted, and maybe even a little ashamed of himself when Donny opened the bag with ease and handed it back to him. Joseph grunted out loud.

"Okay, so I need to work out a bit. I'll do that later."

Donny smiled and returned to his post, watching the yard through the spaces between the wooden slats of the barn. He didn't like this assignment any more than Joseph Donnelly, and he found it disconcerting that the fate and freedom of the entire free world depended on the backbone of this weak and sniveling shell of a man. Donny didn't like him, but ... what could he do? Orders are orders, and he'd fight to the death to keep this man alive, at least until orders to the contrary came down the pike.

His mind drifted off to more desirable thoughts, more memories of a certain beautiful, blonde nurse, and he composed a list of things that he'd say to her, of chivalrous deeds, and gifts he'd present to her that no woman could resist. He was determined to win over the love of his life, but first ... they must defeat the Blind Man. And then he looked over at Joseph Donnelly, who was having trouble opening the interior plastic bag of his MRE, and he couldn't help but doubt the plan from General Branch. And then he thought to himself, *Maybe we're putting too much hope and stock into one man ... a man who can't even feed himself?*

But Donny Brewster was just a sergeant, and noncoms don't get paid to think; they get paid to obey orders, so that's what he would do. Donny Brewster would hurry up and wait, and then he would carry out his orders unflinchingly and to the letter. And, after that, when all the fighting was done. he'd head back home to win the girl of his dreams.

The Shadow Militia - out of the Shadows

"IT'S A PLEASURE TO MEET YOU, GENERAL MACDERMID. THIS IS MY EXEC, Colonel MacPherson, and my Chief Intelligence Officer, Jeff Arnett."

Sparky Fillmore stood behind them, but Uncle Rodney didn't mention him. The commanding general of Dyess Air Force Base in Texas looked skeptically at the man in front of him, claiming to be the military leader of some outfit called the Shadow Militia. General MacDermid had heard of the Shadow Militia, but only knew what his intel people were telling him: That they had engaged the Blind Man and were fighting to defeat him. He'd even heard intel suggesting that General Branch had a nuclear arsenal.

General MacDermid appeared to be about fifty-five years old with a cleanly shaven head. His most distinguishing characteristic was a large, bulbous nose. His eyes were set closely to one another, and were an intense brown color. General MacDermid had been the commanding general of Dyess Air Force Base in Texas for over a year now.

"Well, General Branch, or whoever the hell you think you are. The question foremost on my mind is how in god's name did four unauthorized civilians get past my security and into my office? For that matter, how did you even get through the front gate?"

General Branch glanced over at Jeff Arnett who immediately launched into an explanation. "Well, sir, we simply accessed government Top Secret files to learn everything possible about your installation's security measures. Then we created our own security badges, giving us access to everything at your command. It was quite simple, really."

The general was visibly perturbed and made no attempt to hide it. "And how the hell did you do that? You make it sound easier than ordering chinese take-out. Is my security that lax?"

Jeff smiled. "Everything's easy if you know how to do it, general. But you have nothing to be embarrassed of. I doubt anyone else would be able to do it, especially in this climate."

The general was standing now with his fists on his hips, taking turns glaring at each man in turn. "Mr. Branch, give me one good reason why I shouldn't yell to my sergeant out there and have you all arrested!"

"Because we have the president of the United States, and we'd like to turn him over to you."

General MacDermid cocked his head to one side and lifted his left eyebrow. "What the ..."

And then he walked from the other side of the desk and stood before them. "The president, his staff, the VP and all the cabinet and most of congress are all dead. As far as we know, no one is in charge of the government right now."

Uncle Rodney started shaking his head from side to side and smiling. "No, that's not true. We've located the last remaining person in the presidential line of succession, then we found a federal judge and we are about to swear him in as president."

The general yelled to the aid outside his office, sitting at a desk. "Jenkins! Get in here!"

A man in a blue uniform rushed in and stood at position of attention. "Yes, sir."

"Call security and have an armed squad come to my office immediately!" He looked at General Branch and then over to Jeff Arnett. "Tell me how you learned to break into my system and forge security badges like that."

"I served for twenty-five years in the CIA, right up until the lights went out last year. The CIA was basically inoperative, so I offered my services to General Branch until the government got back up and running."

He turned to Ranger MacPherson. "And you? What's your story?"

The colonel remained stoic at the position of parade rest. "Forty years in the army, retired at the rank of Major General. Four tours in Vietnam and plenty of time playing in the sandbox earned me three purple hearts, the Distinguished Service Cross, two silver stars, two bronze stars, a bunch of other hardware, and, last but certainly not least, my Ranger tab."

And then Ranger MacPherson snapped to attention and crisply saluted before saying, "Rangers lead the way, sir, but it sure is nice of you fly boys to give us rides and air support from time to time."

The general didn't return the salute, so Colonel Macpherson cut his own salute and returned to parade rest. Uncle Rodney looked over at Mac and smiled. "Mac, is that a sense of humor you're growing? Hell, I've known you for over fifty years and I had no idea you could make jokes like that."

Mac smiled right back at him. "I've been waiting for the right moment, sir. Timing is everything in comedy."

Then General Branch looked back at General MacDermid. "So why don't you just call up Military Intelligence? MI can confirm all our stories. In fifteen minutes you can have our service records printed out and on your desk."

Just then a much older man in uniform walked through the door. He glanced over at the three strangers and then at his commanding general. He seemed to have a million stripes on his sleeve.

"I'm sorry, sir, I didn't realize you had visitors. I can come back another time." He turned to leave, but General MacDermid stopped him.

"Chief Master Sergeant McHenry!"

The man turned and faced his superior. "Yes, sir?"

"Before you transferred out of the army and into the air force, you served two tours in Vietnam did you not?"

"Yes, sir."

Then he pointed to Colonel MacPherson. "I'd like you to ask this gentleman some questions about that little ruckus that only a man with extensive combat experience would know about."

The Chief Master Sergeant looked over at Colonel MacPherson and the two men held eye contact for several seconds. And then his response shocked General MacDermid as well as the others in the room. He pushed past Colonel MacPherson and thrust his hand out to Sparky Fillmore.

"Sparky, is that you?"

Sparky smiled and took a step forward, shoving out his right hand. "It's good to see you again, Danny. It's been a long time."

And then the air force sergeant grabbed Sparky's hand and pumped it up and down happily. "My god, I haven't seen you since 1972! It's so good to see you again!"

General MacDermid looked over at his Chief Master Sergeant totally dumbfounded. "You know this man?"

Chief Master Sergeant McHenry forced himself to turn back to his commanding general. "Yes, sir. We served together in a grunt unit on my last tour in Vietnam."

As they were talking, a squad of uniformed military police stormed into the outer office. A lieutenant rushed in and stopped at position of attention in front of his general.

"Sir, you sent for a squad?"

The general looked over at his Chief Master Sergeant, then over to Rodney Branch who was trying not to smile.

"Damn it I hate surprises!"

Then he turned back to the lieutenant.

"Lieutenant, I'd like you to run an extensive background check on these four men, and then report back to me. I want it done within the hour. In the meantime, post two armed guards in the outer office here."

And then he turned back to General Branch. "Okay Mr. Branch. Have a seat and let's talk. I want to know everything, starting from the moment you popped yer ugly head out of yer momma's womb."

Rodney nodded and both he and Jeff Arnett moved to sit down on the couch up against the wall. The Chief Master Sergeant took Sparky Fillmore to the outer office where they got caught up on old times. General MacDermid yelled for an airman to bring them all coffee. And then Rodney Branch told the general everything he knew about the Blind Man, how the fall had happened, and how he'd located the presidential successor. After that he answered all the general's questions about the Shadow Militia.

Two hours later they shook hands.

CHAPTER 15

August 23, There is Another

JEFF ARNETT SAT ALONE AT HIS DESK. EVERYONE ELSE WAS taking a break, but Jeff, who refused to stop working, even for a moment, continued munching on the jalapeno cheese spread and crackers from inside his MRE. He knew it probably wasn't real cheese, just some hydrogenated soybean oil or some such thing, but he knew what he liked, and he loved this cheese spread. Sometimes, he even ate it without crackers, just sucked it right out of the foil package.

The door to his right opened and General Branch walked in with Jackie not far behind him. Uncle Rodney was wearing a red, flannel shirt, long-sleeved of course, and blue, denim jeans. Jackie held baby Donna on her right hip as she walked in. They both walked directly to Jeff's workstation.

Jeff smiled when he saw them, and leaned back in his chair with his hands interlaced behind his head. "Thanks for coming so quickly, general." Then he nodded at Jackie. "And it's always good to see you, my young, clandestine protege."

Jackie smiled back at him, but said nothing. Jeff had been the man who'd taught her how to spy prior to being inserted into the saracen camp. She couldn't help but notice that Special Agent Arnett was in an unusually good mood today. Uncle Rodney was the first to speak. "I hope you have some good news for us today."

Jeff nodded before picking up a file folder and placing it into Rodney's hands. "Read this. I think you'll like it."

Uncle Rodney sat down in the chair beside Jeff's desk, opened the folder and began reading. Every so often he looked up and over at Jeff, but quickly went back to reading the contents of the file without saying anything. Jackie sat down on the concrete floor and took some toys out of her diaper bag for Donna to play with. She wanted so much to know what was in the file folder, but she knew enough to let Uncle Rodney read in peace.

Finally, a half hour later, Uncle Rodney sighed and leaned back in the chair. "Holy mackerel!"

And then he gave the file over to Jackie, who immediately began to read to herself. "Did you verify any of this, Jeff?"

Jeff nodded curtly. "I did. Well, as much as anyone can in a grid-down scenario. But, I can safely say that I'm eighty percent certain that the US Secretary of Transportation is still alive and hiding out in an extremely well concealed location."

General Branch looked out through the closest window, staring out, deep in thought, analyzing the ramifications of what this new information meant to their cause. "This changes everything, Mr. Arnett. Where did you find it?"

The tall man with the hawkish nose looked over and nodded as he smiled. "I found it in one of the files that Sammy Thurmond provided to us. It's actionable intel, and I think we should get on with it." He paused. "Apparently, not even the Blind Man knows that he's still alive."

The general stood to his feet. "What is the Secretary of Transportation's name?"

"His name is Michael Townsend."

General Branch mulled this new information over in his mind before speaking. "I agree with you, Agent Arnett. We need to act decisively, but I want it done in a certain way. I'll coordinate it with Mac. If we do this right, it exponentially increases our chances of victory."

Baby Donna was on Jackie's lap, and now eating away at the corner of the file folder in her hands. As Jackie pulled the cardboard corner out of her daughter's mouth, she looked up. "I want to help, and please don't tell me he's in Haiti."

Jeff smiled and shook his head from side to side. "Not this time, Jackie. Think closer to home. Because the Secretary of Transportation has relatives right here in Michigan."

Uncle Rodney tore his gaze away from the window and looked Jeff full in the eyes. "Okay, I'm listening."

So Jeff Arnett then gave the outline of a plan he'd been forming over the last few days.

August 24, The Master Plan

ALL THE INNER CIRCLE OF GENERAL RODNEY T. BRANCH SAT AROUND THE dining room table, listening to every word as if their very lives depended on it, because, of course, they did. Seated from left to right were: Colonel Ranger MacPherson, Colonel Dan Branch, Chief of Intelligence Jeff Arnett, Jackie Branch, Sheriff Joe Leif, and Jeremy Branch.

"Here's the situation." General Branch stood before them, the white board moved off to one side as he spoke to them earnestly and candidly.

"This has been kept secret and should not leave this room. Justice Reed, the scientist Sergeant Brewster and Colonel Branch recovered a short time ago, has agreed to recommission eight more nuclear devices for us. As you recall, the first arsenal of twelve were destroyed by the Blind Man. For the past two weeks Professor Reed has been working feverishly on making these eight nukes battle ready." He looked around the room solemnly. "I've just been informed that all eight nukes will be ready for deployment in just two days time."

Dan looked over at Jackie and smiled. Jeremy let out an adolescent shout, but the general quickly admonished them.

"Calm down everyone."

Dan Branch lifted a finger and the general acknowledged him. "General, exactly where are these nukes being kept? Are you sure they're safe? We lost them once and I don't want it to happen again."

Rodney smiled and nodded. Then he looked over at Sheriff Leif. "I think you'll appreciate this one, Sheriff. Do you recall our little run-in with the Chief of Police at a town in Wisconsin?"

The sheriff looked up and squinted his eyes. ""You're kidding me. Eagle River? You're keeping eight nukes at Eagle River? How are you doing that? The last time we went there we were both almost killed by that maniac!"

Uncle Rodney's smile got even bigger. "Well, let's just say that there's been a major realignment of power in that city and that the good chief is no longer serving in a law enforcement capacity."

Sheriff Leif bowed his head and wagged it from side to side. "Rodney did you kill that man?"

The general raised his hands as if in mock surrender. "Of course not, Joe. Let's just call it an early retirement and leave it at that. We were able to make an agreement with the mayor and city council. In exchange for safety, we are now using the city and its small airport as a refueling base for our choppers. All we have to do is keep out the riffraff, and, in this case, that included the former Chief of Police. I insisted on that one personally."

The sheriff glanced over at Dan who was sitting beside him. "Can you believe this guy, Dan. He just took over a whole city in Wisconsin."

Dan smiled and looked down at the table. "Quite frankly, Joe, I like the idea of a little payback. If you'll recall one of his deputies beat me almost to death." And then he added as if in passing. "Besides, it's just a small city. Not a big deal."

Then General Branch interrupted them. "Let's move on, gentlemen. There's more." Uncle Rodney glanced over at Jackie for this one. "Jackie, after you rescued the VA Secretary from Haiti, we moved him to a small military base in Denver. The VA Secretary will be sworn in as president at noon day after tomorrow at that same base. Once that is done, we'll be flying the acting president to the USS Ronald Reagan, an aircraft carrier off the Gulf coast. At that time, the new president will commence consolidation of the remaining US armed forces and commence the destruction of the Blind Man and his military forces."

Everyone around the table began to chatter back and forth excitedly. Only General Branch and Colonel MacPherson maintained their silent military bearing. The two men made eye contact for a moment. then glanced around the room at the happy and long overdue celebration.

Fifteen minutes later, after a short question-and-answer period, all attendees were dismissed, leaving Mac and Rodney alone in his dining room.

"Well Mac, what do you think?" Colonel MacPherson shrugged and shook his head from side to side. Finally he answered curtly. "I don't know, general. Ask me again in two days and I'll tell you. Right now, I'm not sure I even know what to think. So many of our plans this time around have fallen apart."

Blind Man HQ, August 25

JARED THOMPSON LISTENED ASTUTELY TO THE VOICE ON THE OTHER END of the line, analyzing every detail and committing it to memory. He paced back and forth as he held the handset to his right ear, every once in a while taking a tiny sip of wine from the goblet in his left hand.

Another thirty seconds passed before he finally spoke to the other man. "Very good. But you are certain of the accuracy of this intelligence?" He listened to the other man's response and smiled as he nodded his head.

"Why do you want to be extracted at this point? You are worth more to me embedded in your present location."

The Blind Man nodded. "I see. Yes, they will definitely know it was you. Your cover is blown. Meet us at midnight tonight at the predetermined extraction point. Don't be late."

Jared sipped his wine again. "Yes, correct. You and your family. You will never know strife or discomfort again. Get ready for a life of luxury and warm winters."

The Blind Man pressed a button and ended the conversation before calling for his aid. The man had learned long ago to be ready at Jared's beck and call. He immediately popped his head through the open doorway and Jared waved him in before seating himself in the recliner in front of the mahogany end table. He propped his Italian, leather shoes onto the glass top and took a tiny sip of his wine, savoring it in his mouth before swallowing. The aid waited patiently and nervously. He never knew what to expect from his boss. Finally, Jared looked up as if suddenly becoming aware of the other man's existence.

"Have you confirmed that Sammy Thurmond is no longer with us?"

The man nodded as he spoke. "Yes, sir. Dr. Van Fleet confirmed it. He is certain, sir."

Jared looked up at the oversized TV screen on the wall before him. "Hand me the satphone then."

Deep inside, the aid muttered in disgust. On the inside he wailed with protest and called the Blind Man a lazy beast! But on the outside, he complied as a dutiful and grateful servant, walking over and picking up the satphone, which was already within the Blind Man's easy reach and respectfully handed it to him.

"You may go."

While his aid left the room, Jared punched in the number and then placed the phone beside his right ear. As he waited for the connection to complete, he mulled over his predicament.

"Yes, General Holland. I have a fire mission for you."

He waited a few more moments before continuing.

"General, I'd like you to obliterate Eagle River, Wisconsin."

He nodded. "Yes, that's correct. I want it done at midnight tonight, and I'd like to watch it on the big screen as always."

Jared disconnected the call and tossed the satphone down onto the couch. He put his wine down on the table and then leaned back to savor the moment. General Branch just didn't know when to give up, but Jared found the challenge worthy and exciting, so long as he had the upper hand. And, so far, he definitely had the Shadow Militia outgunned and outmanned. They continued to give him problems in the south and in the east, but that would soon end. He had a surprise for the general, and his only regret was that he wouldn't be able to see the look on his enemy's face the moment he found out.

But, alas, we all had to make sacrifices in time of war. He yelled for his aid to bring him another bottle of port.

Justice Reed's Change of Heart.

"DOCTOR REED. IT'S GOOD TO SEE YOU AGAIN. I'VE BEEN TOLD YOU'D LIKE to talk to me."

Justice Reed was sitting about ten feet away from his workbench on a wooden stool, and he had the look of a man who'd been humbled, but was not happy about it. His silver hair, what was left of it, stuck up at odd angles all around the circumference of his head. As usual, he was stark naked. Justice nodded. "Yes, general. I have some issues with the accommodations here. They are totally inadequate."

General Branch smiled slightly and nodded. "Yes, I can see that, professor. I'll talk to my men immediately about getting you some clothes. I apologize that it hasn't been done yet. We would never willingly make a man walk around without clothing."

But the old man waved him off impatiently. "No, no, no, general; that's not what I'm talking about. You already gave me clothes, but I don't wear them. They're over there on my workbench."

Uncle Rodney tilted his head to one side. "Okay. So, what exactly is it I can do for you, Doctor Reed?"

Justice crossed his left leg over his right and put his left hand to his whiskered chin while leaning his left elbow to his left knee. "It's my mousetrap, general. I just can't seem to get it to work."

Uncle Rodney was amused, but tried not to show it. He was having trouble focusing on the face of a totally naked old man, with legs like a chicken. "And what seems to be the problem, Doctor Reed. I thought you would have completed it by now. Are you not getting the supplies you need. I can help with that if it's the problem."

"No, that's not it. Your men have been great. It's just ... well ... my hypothesis didn't pan out the way I'd hoped and I fear I'm getting bored with it."

General Branch nodded slightly. "I see. So what's the problem?"

Justice threw up his hands and waved them about excitedly. "It's the damn gravity, general! It always seems to work down, and I can't get the trap to function properly. You see, general, my mousetrap is revolutionary. There's never been anything like it, but it seems to only work in a gravity-free environment."

Justice Reed looked at the general as if the problem was easily understood and elementary to even the most basic of unscientific minds. Rodney tried not to disappoint him with more questions. "I understand and I share your disappointment, Doctor Reed. It's truly a loss to all of humanity as there is a terrible shortage of mice in space." And then he paused. "I don't suppose I could tempt you with a project of my own ... one that might keep you occupied, at least until you solve the gravity problem ..."

General Branch waited for what seemed like hours, but in reality was only about ten seconds. Justice Reed brought his frail hands up to his chin and sighed thoughtfully. "Perhaps. Do you still need those twelve nuclear devices recommissioned? I could do that for you."

General Branch thought it was odd, that a man was referring to activating nuclear devices as if it was as simple as making toast or boiling an egg. "Well, doctor, that job is no longer available."

Justice looked offended. "You got someone else to do it? Who was it?"

Rodney threw up his hands and then let them fall back down to his sides. "It's not like that, Doctor Reed. You see ... it was the Blind Man. He destroyed them while in transit, and, as you know, nuclear explosive devices are not that easy to come by."

Doctor Reed looked crestfallen, downright shattered. But then a glint came to his eyes. "Well, okay. But do you still need them or not?"

Uncle Rodney nodded without speaking.

"Well okay then. I'll tell you where to get more, and then you can run out and pick them up for me. Sound good?"

The general raised one hand to his chin and held it there as he thought. Finally, he couldn't hold back his amusement any longer. "Doctor Reed, you make it sound as easy as sending me out to pick you up a pizza!" The general's eyes danced happily in their sockets. "But hey! What's your plan?"

The doctor smiled openly. "Let's just steal some from Jared. He's got lots of them, and I know where they all are."

Not wanting to sound too anxious, General Branch waited for a full five seconds before responding. "Okay, so let's say I'm open to the idea. Where are these nukes and how do we get them?"

The old scientist jumped nimbly off the stool as excited as ever. "It's easy, general! I used to be the Blind Man's weapons designer. Most of what he has, I built for him." And then Justice Reed squinted his brow as if confused. "Are we still in Michigan?"

Rodney tried not to let the eccentricity of the doctor discourage him as he thought to himself. *Okay, so he doesn't know where he is half the time and he refuses to wear clothes, but ... that doesn't mean he can't recommission a nuclear bomb. Right?*

"Doctor Reed, let me get Colonel MacPherson over here on the double, and we'll get this whole thing worked out."

The nuclear scientist sat back down on the stool and clapped his hands together excitedly. "Great! There's one more thing, general."

Uncle Rodney furled his brow and waited.

"Do you have any bourbon?"

The general cocked his head to one side reluctantly, but the old scientist pressed him further. "It's medicinal bourbon. You know, for my aching joints. It helps keep me limber while I work."

Rodney smiled and shook his head from side to side. "I'll see what I can do, Doctor Reed."

And the old scientist smiled from ear to ear.

August 25, Uncle Rodney Goes Shopping

"Mac, I want you to lead this team personally." General Branch looked intently at his second in command. "Make sure you take Sergeant Brewster as an overwatch. That man is a helluva force multiplier. Doctor Reed obviously has to go, but our recon team suggests you'll need at least a platoon to breach the complex and still have enough time to recover the nukes and get out before the Blind Man can react."

Uncle Rodney looked at the men around him. There was Major Larry Jackson and Captain Danny Briel, both leaning against the wall of the pole barn. Lieutenant Jason Little was seated at the table beside Colonel Dan Branch and his son, Jeremy. One of the Apache attack helicopter pilots was seated beside Dan along with one of the Blackhawk pilots. General Branch had insisted that Dr. Reed at least wear boxer shorts for the meeting, and he sat to the left of the Blackhawk pilot. He was sipping away at a decanter filled with scotch. The general had quickly learned that Justice Reed worked much better when he was properly medicated, as partial inebriation steadied his nerves and even his hands and concentration. Jeff Arnett stood near the back of the room thinking about the oddity of taking a naked, drunk man on a military operation where heavy fighting was likely to occur. But, then again, if he'd been in charge instead of General Branch, they wouldn't be mounting a major operation based on unreliable intel from a hopeless drunk. However ... he had to admit, General Branch did it all the time, and, so far, he'd been right. The man seemed to have a very accurate gut-check.

"According to our best intel, there is a minimal defensive force at this storage facility. It seems General Masbruch and our forces in the south and east are keeping the Blind Man very busy these days, using hit-and-run guerilla tactics. General Masbruch has played hell with the enemy's supply lines, and they've had to spread themselves more and more thin in order to protect their supply convoys."

The general pressed a button on the remote control he held and the laptop projector displayed a picture of the facility. "This particular facility is located in Grand Rapids, Michigan to our south. It will be easy to get to and is located outside the most dangerous parts of the city. The area around the grounds is relatively rural, primarily corn and fruit orchards as well as some urban sprawl. There could be significant resistance from criminal gangs in the city."

He clicked the remote several times and went through a series of aerial photos of the buildings on the complex. General Branch continued another five minutes and then asked for questions. Dan Branch was the first to raise his hand.

"General Branch, why would this facility be so lightly guarded. I mean, after all, if there really are nukes there ... that doesn't make any sense."

General Branch pointed to the only half-naked scientist in the room. "I'll let Dr. Reed field that question."

Justice Reed stood to his feet and turned to face the majority in the room. "Well, that's easy. Those nukes have been there for over fifteen years. You know. Just sitting there in cases, waiting for Jared to use them for whatever he wants." He started to sit down again, but then stopped. "Besides, why guard something that is best hidden in plain sight? As soon as you put a bunch of soldiers on the ground in a populated area then you draw attention. Those nukes have been safe there for almost two decades, so I doubt Jared would be worrying about them now. He didn't even bother guarding them until after the collapse."

Rodney then called on Major Jackson. "So what kind of nukes are we talking about here?"

The general nodded again to Dr. Reed, who was already starting to answer the question. "Oh hell, we got quite an assortment down there. A few of the bigger ones I made myself, but most are small, tactical nukes of five to twenty-kilotons each. But the big ones are about five megatons a piece. They're not real big by modern standards but certainly enough to get a man's attention."

Rodney gave the nod to Captain Briel.

"Dr. Reed, since they've been down there so long, how do we know they still work, or, for that matter, if they're even safe to transport?"

Dr. Reed laughed at him. "Of course they're not safe! They might even be leaking. These are nuclear weapons we're talking about here." And then he turned further around to look the captain square in the eyes. "Why do you think I drink so much? This is a dangerous job!"

General Branch broke in quickly. "The doctor has assured me that he can repair any damage and bring the nuclear devices to full operational capability, provided we can safely transport them to a secure location."

Jeremy Branch raised his hand high in the air, and the way he did it reminded Dan of a young schoolboy. "So, where are we going to take them?"

The scientist looked over to the general and smiled, waiting for him to give them the good news. But the general hesitated, so Dr. Reed blurted it out. "We're taking them to the Palisades Nuclear power plant near Covert, Michigan. It's about sixty miles southwest of Grand Rapids, just off the lakeshore." He waited for a positive response, but the soldiers in the room didn't seem to share his enthusiasm. "What's wrong? It's a perfect place for this. It'll have all the labs and equipment I'll need to recommission the nukes."

Major Jackson looked first at Captain Briel, and then over at the general before he addressed the elephant in the room. "So, General Branch, at the risk of seeming undedicated, is this nuclear power plant safe? I mean ... it's been unattended for over a year now."

The general smiled softly and pointed back at Dr. Reed, who immediately launched into a technical explanation. "Oh, heck yeah! It's really safe, well, as far as nuclear power plants go. I mean ..." He stopped long enough to take a drink of his scotch. "Sure, there is some minor leakage from the reactor and a little from the spent fuel rods, but you have to expect that kind of thing when you just let a nuclear power plant go uncared for." He took another drink. "We flew over it just yesterday, and, based on our measurements, we project it to be much safer than Fukushima and a whole lot safer than Chernobyl." Dr. Reed looked around the room, just now figuring out that people were uncomfortable being exposed to large doses of nuclear radiation. "Oh, guys it's nothing, really. I've had a lot more radiation than that, and look at me!" No one said anything. Colonel Branch looked down and held his head in his hands. But the doctor wasn't finished reassuring them yet.

"Just think of it in terms of having a CT scan every day for a year, only you're doing it all in one day." And then he smiled before sitting down and drinking some more scotch.

Rodney looked around the room and then shook his head. "Please forgive our eccentric friend. Let me fill in the blanks in layman's terms."

And then he turned back to the projector screen and advanced through the presentation. "We'll be wearing full radiation protection suits while on site. It will be clumsy and hot, but it's better to be uncomfortable than sterile or dying of cancer ten years from now."

Young Jeremy Branch looked at his father and reached down to cover his groin region. "I'm going to be sterile?"

Uncle Rodney looked at his relative impatiently. "No, son. You're not going to be sterile. You'll only be there for a few hours while you get the doctor set up in his lab and the nukes are unloaded. Almost all the risk will be taken by Doctor Reed."

Colonel Branch looked around the room and then rose to his feet. "Well, then, general, I have only two questions left. When do we leave, and how much of that scotch can you give us. Cuz I think we're going to need a drink."

Doctor Reed smiled and raised his decanter in salute. "General Branch, I've always liked that man."

CHAPTER 16

August 26, Money fer Nothin' and yer Nukes fer Free!

COLONEL MACPHERSON PEERED OUT TO THE GYPSUM MINING complex in Grand Rapids, Michigan, through his binoculars, looking for any sign of military security. He quickly noted the four men bunched together at the foot of the loading dock on the east side. They could easily get to the tree line and neutralize all of them in a matter of seconds with a coordinated sniper attack with suppressed rifles.

That particular fire team had been there since seven AM once they'd relieved the night watch. They appeared to have four men on the surface at all times, which meant three shifts of four, and there were at least twelve soldiers assigned to guard the complex. Mac guessed another ten or so below ground in support.

He looked over his shoulder at Sergeant Donny Brewster and Major Jackson. "Sergeant, I want you and your snipers to take out all four simultaneously. I want all four to go down and make it sound like one gunshot. Got it?"

Donny nodded. "Not a problem, sir. We'll suppress our rifles just in case."

"Major, you can take your platoon in through the main entrance there while Captain Briel takes his platoon down the freight elevator in back. That should give you overwhelming firepower to get the job done. You'll have Dr. Reed with you, and that should enable you to locate the devices fairly quickly. He claims to know where they are. There are a lot of shafts and tunnels down there, so we can't afford to get lost."

Major Jackson nodded. "Not a problem. Then as soon as we find the nukes we radio out for the transport team?"

"Affirmative, major. But, above all else, this has to be done quickly, before anyone inside can report the activity to the Blind Man. Eventually, he'll discover what we've done, but we'd like it to be later rather than sooner. Understood?"

Larry Jackson paused before answering. "Yes, sir. It'll be done. Should only take a few minutes to get down and take control. I'll radio up as soon as I'm ready."

The colonel looked out again at the facility, at the parking lot, the loading dock and then again at the four enemy soldiers shooting the breeze in the hot, August sun. They were probably happy to have such a low-risk job, but ... today that would end.

"Sergeant, we launch in fifteen minutes." He turned to Major Jackson and Captain Briel. "Get your men in place. You go as soon as you see the sentries go down."

Ranger MacPherson radioed to General Branch that all was well. Then he waited for everyone to get staged. At exactly fifteen minutes after eight AM, all four sentries crumpled down in a heap. One was inhaling a cigarette, another was urinating on a wall, while the other two were just talking together. All four shots to the cranium ensured that none of them had time to cry out for help. In fact, none of them saw the other fall; it happened that fast.

Mac watched as Major Jackson and his men entered through the loading dock door. So far there were no other gunshots.

Captain Briel radioed in his progress. "Cave Leader this is Caveman two, we are on our way down. No contact so far."

Larry Jackson called in as well.

"Cave Leader this is Caveman One. No resistance. We are on our way down to lower levels."

Colonel MacPherson smiled to himself. There was no one with him except his protective detail of eight men who had formed a protective perimeter around him. So far no resistance. That was good, Surprising ... but good.

"Cave Leader, this is Caveman One. We are at the lower level, on our way to the target. Have linked up with Caveman Two and he has our back."

CAPTAIN BRIEL DEPLOYED HIS TWENTY-FIVE MEN AROUND HIM AND AT each tunnel entrance. He was surprised to encounter no resistance. So far not a single shot had been fired by his men. He looked around at the tunnels branching off in four different directions. They appeared to be used as storage for computer media and even some paper files. Apparently the gypsum mine hadn't been producing product for many years now, and had simply rented out the storage space to local corporations. The tunnels were no longer dirty and filled with loose rock. The floors had been cemented over and load-bearing columns had been added to shore up the ceilings.

Captain Briel began to get nervous. He always worried when things went too smoothly. He made the rounds, checking in with his sergeants, but everything appeared secure. So now all he could do was wait for Major Jackson to find the nukes.

MAJOR JACKSON LOOKED AROUND AT THE TUNNELS SURROUNDING THEM. Justice Reed seemed to be confused.

"Come on, Doc. We don't have all day. Let's just find these nukes and get the hell outta here!"

Dr. Reed stopped walking and pointed down the tunnel to the left. "I think it's down there."

Major Jackson sent a fire team down the tunnel with a wave of his hand. They quickly ran down the tunnel, with flashlights groping out like long, shiny talons. But Five minutes later they came back. "Sorry, major. Nothing down there but old mushroom-growing pallets. Just a bunch of old compost and dirt down there."

Larry looked back at the doctor. "Come on, Doc. Now's the time when you come through. You can either be the hero or the goat. And if you're the goat, then I'm gonna shoot yer sorry ass! Got it?"

Justice Reed nodded and started to sweat. "I need a drink."

Larry laughed out loud. "You can have a drink as soon as you find the nukes we need, and not a moment sooner!"

This seemed to motivate Justice Reed even more. He stopped to think, as if remembering something he'd forgotten all along. "Oh, I remember now! We're not supposed to go east. We need to go south!" And then he started running off ahead of Major Jackson. Larry looked on and shook his head from side to side. He thought to himself, *This is ridiculous, following a drunk down into a mushroom cave in search of nuclear bombs.* He reported in to the colonel.

"Cave Leader this is Caveman One. We've got nothing so far. We may need Caveman Two to assist in a random search of all tunnels."

"This is Cave Leader. What is the hold-up?"

"Our bird dog seems to be inebriated, sir."

Ranger MacPherson turned his head to one side and spit on the wooded floor beside him. *Damn that old man! He was drunk more often than not.*

"Caveman Two, this is Cave Leader. Leave a few men for flank security and begin a systematic search of all tunnels."

"This is Caveman Two, roger that. Commencing search pattern now."

Blind Man HQ

AT THE SAME TIME MAJOR JACKSON AND CAPTAIN BRIEL WERE SEARCHING for the nuclear devices hundreds of feet underground, Jared Thompson was watching them on camera in his office. He sipped a crystal glass of cognac as he flipped from one camera angle to another. He watched the teams searching underground for several minutes until he caught sight of Justice Reed. Then he said out loud. "You should have stayed in your mountain cabin, Dr. Reed. I was content to leave you there until I needed you. But now ..." He shook his head from side to side and switched the camera feed to the drone circling high over the gypsum facility.

He picked up his satphone and was soon talking to General Holland. "General, you will proceed on my command. I'll count down from five." He took another sip of his cognac and then placed it on the glass table in front of him.

"Five, four, three, two ..."

He looked up and focused on the television screen on the wall, smiling with all his heart.

"One."

COLONEL MACPHERSON NOT ONLY HEARD THE BLAST, BUT HE FELT IT AS he was lifted off the ground and thrown twenty feet in the air. He landed against the trunk of a sapling. It bent and cushioned his fall. Dust and sand rained down around him along with pieces of rock, cement and wood. He lowered his head and covered it with his hands until the debris shower subsided.

Mac raised his head and then crawled over to the edge of the embankment. When he looked at the facility, his heart sank. A tremendous cloud of gypsum dust had billowed up from the ground and was now settling back down into a giant crater.

He crawled over to his radio and keyed the microphone. "Caveman One, this is Cave Leader. Come in, over." But there was nothing but silence except for the sound of falling dust on the August leaves around him.

"Caveman Two, this is Cave Leader. Come in, over."

Mac wiped the gypsum dust from his eyes before trying once more. "Overwatch, this is Cave Leader. Come in, over."

Donny Brewster responded at once. "Cave Leader, this is Overwatch."

"Overwatch, do you see any survivors?"

There was silence for almost a minute. Colonel MacPherson forced himself to wait patiently. Finally, Sergeant Brewster responded. "Cave Leader, this is Overwatch ..." And then a pause. "I see no signs of life."

Mac dropped the handset and rested his head in his hands. Part of his protection detail tugged on his sleeve. "Sir, are you alright?"

Mac turned around but didn't answer right away. "Sir, what are your orders?"

Colonel MacPherson looked around him, then off into the settling cloud of dust and the massive crater in front of him. Finally he responded.

"Prepare to move out, sergeant."

August 26, 11:30PM - Catching a Rat

SHERIFF JOE LEIF AND HIS WIFE AND SON BUILT A LARGE BONFIRE IN THE clearing below the ridge. The sheriff was waiting for a helicopter from the Blind Man to come and take him to a retirement home in Florida. Joe loved this town, but his wife, Marge, did not. She never had, though she'd always put up a good front in public. And then so much had happened after the lights had gone out, so much that had made living here for her even more unbearable. But he'd been told that there were parts of the country with power and near-modern living conditions, and, quite frankly, he and Uncle Rodney had never quite seen eye to eye on how many things should be run.

Even with all that, it had been a difficult decision for Joe to make when the Blind Man had contacted him. In his own way, he loved Uncle Rodney and the town of Iroquois, though not much was left of it anymore. The sheriff had wrestled with the problem for days, but finally capitulated when it had been made clear that he really had no alternative. Either throw in his lot with the Blind Man, or his wife and child would suffer in darkness and possibly even death at the hands of Jared Thompson and his forces. He knew, indeed, had always known, that General Rodney T. Branch didn't stand a chance against the Blind Man, but the sheriff had kept his silence.

That, and he just didn't like Rodney's methods. He'd tortured a prisoner in his own jail by stabbing him with a knife, and even before the collapse he'd purchased illegal guns and all manner of military weaponry against state and federal laws.

No, Joe couldn't live like that. He needed the rule of law. He needed a sense of purpose and a hope that things would return to the way they were. The sheriff wouldn't admit this to himself, but, perhaps even more than anything else ... he needed electricity and refrigeration; he needed clean clothes and a shower everyday and a hot cup of coffee ... not that artificial stuff Uncle Rodney made out of chickory and lawn clippings, but the real stuff - with real caffeine!

The fire was blazing high now, and they had to back up a few feet to keep the heat from hurting their faces. Marge moved in closer to Joe while his son picked up a long stick to stab into the fire.

"We're doing the right thing, Joe." His wife put her arm around him in an attempt to console him, but it did no good. "We have no future here. With Jared we'll be in warmer weather during the winter. We'll have electricity again. Someday the country will rebuild, and, when it does, our son can have a real place in it." She squeezed Joe tighter. "Things can go back to normal for us."

Sheriff Leif just looked out into the night without saying anything. He wasn't sure of that, but ... none of that mattered anymore. He'd done the deed. He'd betrayed his friends, and now ... now he'd have to live with that ... for the rest of his life.

Suddenly, they heard the sound of a helicopter off in the distance, the thrumming of the rotors, slowly getting closer and closer. They were early. In a few minutes they would be off and away, never to return, beginning a new and exciting life. Joe Leif allowed the guilt he felt to slowly wash away. He was doing this for his family. Joe stepped away from the fire and out into the clearing. He raised the flare gun and fired it over his head high and into the air, according to the instructions he'd been given.

He could see the aircraft now and it adjusted its course and was soon hovering overhead. Joe watched the helicopter land in the clearing, the adrenaline rushing through his body as he felt the wind from the rotors push against his face.

A man stepped out of the Blackhawk helicopter and walked over to the sheriff and his family.

"Sheriff Leif?"

Joe thought he heard a foreign accent in the man's voice, and this surprised him.

"Yes. I'm Joe Leif, this is my wife, Marge, and my son."

Just then, Joe was surprised to see three soldiers in digital camo jump out of the chopper and rush over, quickly surrounding Joe and his family on three sides. The officer who'd first approached him took a few steps back, and then raised his right arm high over his head.

"I have a message from the Blind Man. He wishes to thank you for your service, but regrets to inform you that your request for political asylum has been denied."

Marge moved closer to Joe, grabbing her son as she did and pulling him up against her. The little boy shook with fear. Joe could hardly speak, knowing that he would soon die, that his family would die, and that ... he was the one who'd killed them. He was to blame.

"But ... but ... that wasn't the deal. I ..."

And then the gun shots rang out into the night. They fired again and again until all three figures fell to the ground. When it was finished, the officer, with his right arm still raised over his head looked bewildered over at Joe Leif and his wife and son. And then he stared down at the bodies of his bullet-ridden soldiers on the ground around him. He heard the sound of the Blackhawk engine gain RPMs as it began to inch off the ground. But then two final shots rang out and the engine slowed, whined down, and then settled slowly back to the earth unharmed. The pilot and co-pilot both slumped over, dead.

The officer then looked down at his chest and saw the green dot of light dancing slightly from left to right. He decided not to move. Joe saw the green dot on the man's chest, so he quickly looked down at his own chest. There was a green dot there as well. He quickly looked over at Marge and his son, and was quickly relieved to discover that they were not being targeted.

And then the bushes behind them exploded with white light as a dozen Shadow Militia soldiers came out from behind cover, their SureFire flashlights, mounted on the rails of their M4s seeking out and lighting up the night. Soon, all four prisoners were surrounded. Joe Leif and the officer were disarmed and proned out on the ground, and then their hands were zip-tied behind them before they were hauled to their feet again. In the background, Marge could be heard crying as she hugged her son closely.

When all was secure, General Rodney T. Branch strode crisply out of the brush and walked up to his friend.

"Hello Joe." And then he looked Sheriff Leif straight in the eyes. "You look surprised to see me."

Joe turned his face away, then back again. He tried to hold Rodney's stone-cold gaze but could not. In the end, he looked down at the ground and his zip-tied hands in disgrace. He said nothing.

General Branch turned to the soldier beside him. "Lieutenant Little, take this enemy officer back to camp for interrogation. Special Agent Arnett is waiting for him there. I will be along shortly."

The Blind Man's officer was lead away in silence. He didn't resist. Uncle Rodney turned back to his friend.

"Fifty of my men were killed by the Blind Man today, Joe. Along with Larry Jackson and Danny Briel." Joe turned his face away, looking out into the darkness.

"I've known about you for a while, Joe. But ... I just had to see it for myself before I did anything about it. You need to know that I used you for military gain. Normally I wouldn't do that to a lifelong friend, but ... under the present circumstances, you didn't leave me much of a choice. Besides, I'm in a real nasty mood tonight."

And then Uncle Rodney's voice softened. "I'm sorry it came to this, Joe. I know you never totally subscribed to my role as commanding general of the Shadow Militia, but ... that doesn't change the truth of it all." He hesitated. "You got a lot of good men killed today, and you're gonna have to pay for that."

General Branch looked Joe Leif square in the eyes as he talked, even though Joe was trying to avoid his gaze. "I am the general. And I am in charge. Soon, the Blind Man will realize that as well."

Joe Leif looked straight down and mumbled to himself. "I'm sorry Rodney. I ... guess I lost faith."

Rodney nodded. "I suppose that's one way of looking at it."

Just then two more men stepped out of the nearby woods and walked over. It was Colonel Ranger MacPherson, walking ram-rod stiff, followed by a more laid back Colonel Dan Branch. They both stopped to the left of General Branch and remained slightly abreast as both colonels snapped to attention and saluted. General Branch returned the salute.

"At ease, gentlemen. Let's get this over with." He looked over at another nearby soldier. "Staff Sergeant Cervantes. Take the woman and her son away for a short time. I don't want them to witness this."

The staff sergeant led them away at gun point with another soldier, and, when they were gone, General Branch turned back to his two colonels. "Let's get this over with."

Two soldiers brought out three folding chairs and set them up behind a portable, white plastic table. Sheriff Leif looked on, confused. A few seconds later, the general and the two colonels sat down in front of him.

"Bring the prisoner forward."

Joe Leif was led up to the table. He stood before them, head and eyes bent down. The flames of the bonfire still danced away, throwing shadows into the grass around them.

"Read the charges please, Colonel MacPherson."

Ranger MacPherson pulled up a sheet of paper and clicked on his flashlight before he began reading.

"The accused, Joseph R. Leaf, Sheriff of Iroquois county, is hereby charged with high treason, that he did willfully and purposely conspire with the enemy of Iroquois county, that he did willingly and knowingly enter into contract with one Jared Thompson, to give away military secrets and the transfer of those secrets to the enemy, and that these secrets jeopardized the safety and well-being of Iroquois county and its residents. Said actions were in violation of the oath of his office of sheriff and the executive order signed by Sheriff Joseph R. Leif, governing these criminal acts."

"Thank you, colonel." General Branch looked over to his left. "Colonel Branch, what evidence does this tribunal have in support of this charge?"

Dan Branch picked up a manila folder and opened it. "Sir, we have transcripts of these intercepted communiques between the defendant and the leader of the enemy forces, one Jared Thompson. We also have recordings between the defendant and his wife, Marge Leif, as they discussed the crime and their subsequent escape. We also have eyewitnesses of Mr. Leif and his wife as they rendezvoused with a known officer combatant of the enemy, this last evidence witnessed by everyone here tonight."

Dan laid down the folder and remained silent. General Branch moved his hands to the table top and folded them there. "How does the defendant plead? Guilty or not guilty?"

Joe Leif looked up for the first time. He tried to talk but was having trouble finding the right words. "I ... just ..." and then he managed a quick flurry of a response. "I request legal counsel."

General Branch looked over at Colonel MacPherson and nodded. Colonel MacPherson shook his head from side to side. Rodney looked over to his nephew, Dan, who also shook his head from side to side. General Branch looked back at the defendant before speaking.

"Request denied."

"But ... how can you do that? I'm a citizen! I have constitutional rights! You can't do this to me!"

Uncle Rodney sighed and looked down at his folded hands. "Listen Joe. I know this seems harsh, but ... you put all of us in danger, and you did it for financial gain. You betrayed us all, and, if we hadn't found out about it in time, all of us would have died because of your actions. As it is, two of my best officers and fifty of my men are now dead and buried in a sink hole. At least you're getting a military trial. They got nothing."

Joe Leif didn't say anything.

"Sheriff, you've disgraced yourself, this county and your office. The evidence against you is overwhelming, and, quite frankly, we don't have time to give you a trial that lasts six months. All that bullshit went out the window a year ago when the lights went out and martial law was declared. You have a right to a speedy and public trial. We've given you those rights. Is this not speedy enough for you? And you certainly can't get any more public than this."

General Branch leaned back in his chair. "Under martial law and the terms of your own executive order, your right to an attorney is waived. We have a war to fight, Mr. Leif." The general leaned forward again. "Now, this is the last time I'm going to ask you. Do you plead guilty or not guilty?"

Joe Leif didn't answer right away. He was still looking for a way out of this mess, but the general would not be denied.

"Joe, listen to me. This isn't just about you. Your wife is also guilty of conspiracy to commit treason, and we have plenty of proof to that as well. Conspiring with the enemy during time of war is punishable by death by firing squad." Rodney locked eyes with Joe. "Don't make me kill your wife too, Joe. Not in front of your boy. At least let him grow up with one parent."

Joe Leif finally nodded his head slightly, and then he spoke. "The defendant pleads ... guilty."

General Branch didn't waste a moment. "Let the record show that the defendant has pleaded guilty to the capital crime of treason. The tribunal hereby accepts that plea." General Branch stood and Colonel Branch and Colonel MacPherson followed him to their feet.

"This tribunal hereby sentences Joseph R. Branch to death by firing squad, a sentence to be carried out immediately."

Sheriff Leif's mouth dropped open in surprise. "But ... but ..."

General Branch immediately drew the Colt 45 caliber pistol from his holster and walked around the table until he was standing in front of the convicted. Rodney raised the pistol to his friend's head. "Sergeant remove the prisoner's badge of office."

The soldier closeby stepped forward and removed Joe's sheriff's badge, then stepped back again out of the line of fire. Uncle Rodney's right thumb moved to the safety release and clicked it off. Dan Branch looked down and then away. He was struggling, trying not to show any emotion. Colonel MacPherson looked dutifully on as General Branch moved his right forefinger to the trigger of the pistol.

"Does the prisoner have any final words?"

Joe Leif struggled with his mouth, and finally managed to open it and speak. "I ... I want to apologize to my community for the wrongs I've done. I let them down. I lost faith, and ... I'm very sorry." He looked down and then quickly back up again before

Rodney could shoot him. "And I think most of all, I apologize for making my friend shoot me. I know you don't do this lightly, Rodney, and that it will affect you greatly for a long time to come."

Uncle Rodney pressed the trigger on his pistol and a loud boom rang out across the clearing. But the shot went over Joe's head and he didn't fall to the ground as expected. Joe began to cry and he suddenly fell to his knees, his ears ringing and his head hurting from the noise and the concussion.

"Joe, on behalf of Iroquois county, I accept your apology." And then he holstered his pistol. "In lieu of death, I hereby commute your sentence and replace it with banishment. You and your family will leave Iroquois county and never return."

Joe looked up and into Rodney's eyes. "If the convicted does return, then he will be shot on sight." Uncle Rodney bent down to eye level and looked straight into Joe's eyes. "Do you understand, Joe?"

Just then, there was a tiny flash of light just off the western horizon. It lit up that part of the sky for a few seconds and then began to fade.

Joe Leif looked out at the flash of light as did everyone around the bonfire, which was now beginning to fade into embers.

"What was that?"

Rodney lifted Joe to his feet, pulled out his knife and quickly cut the restraints from Joe's wrists. Rodney looked over to the west with the others. "I'd say that's probably Eagle River, Wisconsin being vaporized by the Blind Man."

And then he turned over to Mac. "I'll say one thing for the man, he doesn't waste any time and he always goes strong."

He quickly turned back to Joe Leif. "There were no nukes in Eagle River. That was disinformation designed to confirm your guilt, and you fell right into it."

He turned to Dan. "Colonel Branch, get Marge and the boy up here and let's get them on their way. We have a lot of work to do. I have a sudden urge to kick Mr. Thompson's not-so-blind ass!" And then he turned back to Joe Leif. "Up on the logging trail you'll find a cart filled with enough supplies to last a week. You'll also find an M4 for protection, a thousand rounds of ammo, ten ounces of silver, and we'll also return your sidearm to you."

He turned to walk away but then stopped halfway. He turned and made eye contact with the former sheriff. "Joe, you need to understand that I'm serious about this. If you come back before this war is over, then I'll put you down personally."

Joe Leif nodded. "I know, Rodney. This is all on me. I won't be back." And then he reached out to shake his hand. Joe's lone hand hovered there between them for several seconds. Finally, Uncle Rodney stepped forward, grabbed his hand and pulled him in close. After a brief embrace, General Branch turned and walked away into the treeline without looking back. Colonel MacPherson followed his general.

Dan Branch stepped forward and held his hand out to his friend. Tears welled up in Joe's eyes as he accepted it. The two embraced, and then Dan held out a small piece of paper.

"This is the name and address of a family with an extra house two counties over. They've agreed to rent it to you until this is all over. They know nothing of your crimes, so you can live with some measure of respect."

Joe took the paper and nodded. "Dan, will he ever forgive me?"

Dan smiled. "Hell, Joe, he's already spared your life twice tonight. If that's not forgiveness, then I don't know what is."

He turned and barked out orders to the sergeant and his soldiers. "Escort this man and his family safely to the county line, point them in the right direction and then return to base."

Without another word, Dan Branch turned and walked away from the clearing. Joe Leif looked after him until he disappeared into the trees. Then his wife and son arrived and were escorted to the logging trail and their supplies.

An hour later their escort peeled away and returned to base, leaving Joe and his wife to face the night, their shame, and a lifetime of regret.

CHAPTER 17

August 26, Swearing in the New President

GENERAL BRANCH STOOD BEFORE VA SECRETARY JOSEPH Donnelly in a pasture just outside the wooden barn, surrounded by Shadow Militia soldiers, all bearing M4s and facing outward as if to ward off any physical threats.

"Let's get you back inside Mr. Secretary. I don't want to take any unnecessary chances in the home stretch."

Joseph Donnelly was dressed in a black suit that hung a little too loosely off his now slender frame. His hair was combed back neatly and greased into place with the only thing the soldiers had been able to find: a jar of Vaseline petroleum jelly. The two men walked back inside the barn, followed by several of the soldiers.

"The federal judge should be here momentarily. We played hell finding him. That's why it's taken so long before swearing you in."

Joe nodded impatiently. "Let's just get it done so we can get down to business."

General Branch smiled. "This has been a long time coming, and I'm just as anxious as you are. The sooner we get you sworn in, the sooner you can take charge of the military and get this country back on course."

The VA Secretary smiled. "To tell you the truth, general, I'd settle for a hot bath, a shave and a haircut."

General Branch laughed out loud. "Well, Mr. Secretary, I would think that the United States of America, even in its present diminished capacity, should be able to accommodate that request."

Joe Donnelly thought to himself. *The president of the United States doesn't make requests ... he issues orders!* But what he spoke aloud was something completely different. "I just want you to know, general, that I'm eternally indebted to you and your group for getting me out of Haiti." He hesitated, looking briefly into the general's eyes. "The country will be needing men like you to help us lead our way back to world dominance."

Colonel MacPherson stepped up behind General Branch and whispered into his ear. The general nodded and turned back to Joe Donnelly. "Mr. Secretary, the judge has arrived. Are you ready to become the President of the United States of America?"

Joe smiled broadly. He couldn't believe this was finally happening. He was going to be president of the United States, the leader of the free world! He smirked deep inside. And to think that just a year ago he was being investigated by the FBI for possible fraud charges. Of course, he'd been guilty, but ... it no longer mattered. Any evidence of his guilt was probably no longer available since the collapse. He was now free and clear. And then he thought to himself *America truly is the land of opportunity.*

They milled around for a few minutes and then US District Court Judge Edmond Roloefs walked through the barn door. He wore his black robes, but they were clearly in need of a good dry cleaning. He was carrying a large, black Bible in his left hand.

"Good afternoon, Mr. President."

Joe beamed inside, his emotions almost out of control. This was the first time anyone had used his new title. "Well, your honor, let's not get hasty. I'm not the president yet."

Judge Roloefs smiled as he replied. "Well, that's a technicality I plan on resolving right away. Are you ready to take the oath?"

Joe nodded, barely able to control his excitement. General Branch and Colonel MacPherson moved back a few paces, taking their rightful places in the background. Sergeant Donny Brewster moved up closer to his commanding officer, to the left and slightly abreast, his M4 on a one-point sling against his lean stomach. He didn't like the new president, but there was nothing he could do about it.

"Please raise your right hand and repeat after me."

Joe Donnelly placed his left hand on the Bible and then raised his right hand. His lips were dry, so he licked at them nervously.

"I do solemnly swear."

"I, Joseph Donnelly, do solemnly swear."

"That I will faithfully execute the office of president of the United States."

Joe's hands were sweating now. It was finally happening.

"That I will faithfully execute the office of president of the United States."

"And will to the best of my ability."

Joe could hardly speak. His throat constricted and his voice became suddenly very weak. But he pressed on.

"And will to the best of my ability."

"Preserve, protect and defend the Constitution of the United States."

Judge Roloefs waited for the VA Secretary's response, but it didn't come. He leaned in closer to Joe Donnelly and whispered. "Are you okay, Mr. President?"

Joe pointed to his throat and tried to speak, but nothing came out. Judge Roloefs turned to the small crowd. "General Branch, can we get some water for the president?"

General Branch motioned to Donny Brewster, who quickly walked forward, and handed his canteen to Joseph Donnelly. The VA Secretary looked at it sceptically, wondering ... *did this sergeant put his dirty lips on this canteen?* But, despite his petty reservations, he reached down to unscrew the cap. He turned as hard as he could, but the cap wouldn't budge. Donny Brewster saw his problem and shook his head in disgust. He reached out and grabbed the canteen, unscrewed the cap before handing it back to the soon-to-be president of the United States. Joe grudgingly took a small swallow of the warm water. It was disgusting to him, but at least it moistened his throat enough so he could talk.

"Thank you sergeant."

Donny returned to his place beside his officers. Judge Roloefs turned back to the VA Secretary and gave him time to put his hand back on the Bible and to raise his right hand again.

"Just say the last phrase and we'll call it good, Mr. President."

Joseph Donnelly uttered the final words which made him the official president of the United States of America.

"Preserve, protect and defend the Constitution of the United States."

Judge Roloefs reached out to shake the president's hand. "Congratulations, Mr. President."

Joe smiled and shook the man's hand. Then he was congratulated by everyone there, going around the room, shaking hands and accepting praise and congratulations. After fifteen minutes the new president turned to General Branch.

"So what happens now, general?"

In response, General Branch turned to Colonel MacPherson and issued commands. "Colonel, you are to take the president to Dyess Air Force Base in Texas so he can better carry out the duties of his office." The colonel stood to attention and saluted sharply. The general returned the salute and then pivoted back toward the president. "Mr. President, that particular base has complete power and facilities to help you regain command and control of all military forces. This base is home to the Seventh Bomber Wing, composed of two squadrons of B1b Lancer Stealth bombers as well as the 317th Airlift Wing which is the largest force of C-130J Super Hercules remaining in the world. The base is over six thousand acres and should be able to serve you well until you can choose a more suitable command post. The commanding general of the base has been apprised of your situation and is eagerly awaiting your arrival."

The president nodded. "Very good, general." And then he hesitated. "One other thing, general. I require a satphone so I can begin my work right away."

"Absolutely, sir. The colonel will provide you with one immediately. And, Mr. President, with your permission, I'd like to return to my home. I believe the Shadow Militia has completed its mission and can be of no further use to you."

The president smiled and extended his hand to General Branch. "On behalf of a grateful nation, I thank you." The two men shook hands and Uncle Rodney turned and left the barn. Colonel MacPherson handed his satphone to the president.

"We'll be outside when you're ready to depart, Mr. President."

When he was alone in the barn, Joe Donnelly punched in the number and held the phone up to his right ear. When the call connected, he spoke in hushed tones.

"It's done. I am now the president of the United States." And then he paused. "What are your orders?"

On the other end of the line, Jared Thompson smiled. *He had won. He had beaten*

General Branch without firing a shot.

Dyess Air Force Base - Texas

THE BLACKHAWK HELICOPTER CIRCLED ONCE OVERHEAD, THEN CAME down softly on the runway, followed closely by the two Apache gunships that were providing escort. According to the terms agreed upon by General Branch and General MacDermid, newly sworn-in President Donnelly exited the Blackhawk as the base band played hail to the chief. Colonel MacPherson exited after him but stayed in the background in case he was needed. General MacDermid strode proudly up to the new president and crisply saluted him. Colonel MacPherson had given the president a quick private lesson on rendering salutes, and the president did a passable job his first time around.

"It's good to welcome you to Fort Dyess, Mr. President." There were several hangers closeby, but the president couldn't see the B1 bombers from this part of the base. There were about a thousand airmen standing at attention on the tarmac, and President Donnelly was visibly impressed.

"It's good to be here, general. So what happens now?" General MacDermid pointed toward the assembled airmen and the small stage at the head of the group. "Would the Commander-in-Chief care to address his troops, sir?"

Joseph Donnelly thought to himself. *Commander-in-Chief, I like the sound of that.* "Absolutely, general. Please lead the way."

General MacDermid walked briskly toward the small, portable stage and then up the steps where he approached the podium and spoke into the microphone. When the music stopped he addressed the troops.

"Thank you for coming today. It is with great pleasure and relief, that I introduce to you, the president of the United States of America!"

The general backed away and waited for the president to reach the podium. He saluted again and then Joe reached out to shake his hand. The thousand or so men roared with enthusiasm, but when the new president stood behind the podium and raised his hands, they gradually quieted down.

"Thank you so much General MacDermid, and thank you to all airmen and officers of Fort Dyess. It's truly an honor to serve as your Commander-in-Chief, and I will do my utmost to lead you with the dignity and honor that you are all accustomed to." And then he paused. "Now, it's been over a year since I've been on a US military base, and I can tell you I've never been happier, or felt more secure. All of you have sworn an oath to protect and defend the country, and your diligence is needed now more than ever as we seek to rebuild our great nation and continue to protect against all who would seek to destroy us.

"Over the ensuing weeks, I will work to form a new working government and to restore America to its former greatness."

The crowd erupted in applause and President Donnelly raised his hand and waved to them as he turned to leave the stage. Several other high-ranking officers lined up to shake the new president's hand and he accommodated them dutifully.

After several minutes, President Donnelly was led away from the blazing hot tarmac and into a waiting limousine. The limo was flanked on both ends by HumVees, armed with 50 caliber machine guns. President Donnelly could barely contain his delight as he drove away to begin reforming the United States federal government.

Colonel MacPherson looked after the motorcade as it pulled away from the stage. He nodded in satisfaction before getting back into the Blackhawk helicopter and flying away.

August 27 - Somewhere South of the Mason-Dixon Line

GENERAL MASBRUCH LOOKED DOWN AT THE MAP SPREAD OUT ON THE table in front of them. "Where did you get all this information, General Branch?"

Rodney looked down at the map as well and smiled. "The Blind Man had a spy in his midst, and he didn't even know it. His name was Sammy Thurmond."

General Masbruch's tan face was lined with wrinkles, especially at the corners of his eyes. His bald head was shiny, but his green eyes seemed to glow with appreciation as he looked down at the plans that Colonel MacPherson and General Branch had explained to him in great detail. "Isn't he the one they called "the Blind Man's pet?"

Rodney shrugged. "I think so."

"What caused him to betray his boss?"

Rodney smiled. "He appeared to fall in love with my daughter-in-law."

General Masbruch looked up and out through the door of his tent. "So where is he now? I'd like to talk to this guy, especially if we're going to be risking everything based on information he's given us."

Colonel MacPHerson fielded the question. "I'm afraid that's impossible, General Masbruch. He's dead. Killed by the Blind Man."

The general sighed. "Most unfortunate. You say you confirmed all this information with boots on the ground?"

Mac nodded. "That's right."

Masbruch reached up with his left hand and wiped the sweat away from his bald head. "This damned heat and humidity is oppressing." And then he looked up and smiled at Mac and Rodney. "General Branch, I'll start positioning my people right away. We'll time everything and coordinate the attacks perfectly." And then he reached over to shake Rodney's hand. "Thanks Rodney. The Blind Man will never see it coming."

Rodney looked over at Mac. "Did you just hear what he said, Mac?" And then he looked over at General Masbruch. "General Masbruch, are you developing a sense of humor in your old age? The same thing happened to Mac just a few days ago."

For a moment the general looked confused, then a light seemed to go on in is head and he laughed out loud. "The pun was not intended, general. Though it does seem appropriate."

"We have to get going now, general. But we'll leave this part of the campaign in your capable hands. Please let me know if you need anything or get in trouble."

General Masbruch took a step back and snapped to attention. Then he saluted sharply as Rodney did the same. Mac and Rodney turned and strode out of the command tent and walked to their waiting Blackhawk. They had work to do.

The New Administration

"GENTLEMEN. I HAVE SOME PLANS ALREADY LAID OUT, AND I'M GOING TO need some support from the military to make it happen."

The conference room at Dyess Air Force Base was large and immaculate. The table was rectangular, and every seat was filled, bringing the total in the room to about fifteen. "My new Chief of Staff will be flying in tomorrow, and I need him to report to me as soon as he lands. I also need some office space as I plan on appointing cabinet members soon."

General MacDermid was seated to the president's right. He turned to his exec. "Make a note of it, John."

The colonel nodded and was already writing it down. "It'll be done, sir."

"The next order of business is appointing my vice-president. He'll be flying in from West Virginia at fourteen-hundred hours tomorrow. He'll be flying a Lear business jet with two F18s as escort. Please see that he's given immediate clearance as well as quarters appropriate with his office."

General MacDermid raised his eyebrows just a bit. "Is it someone we know, Mr. President?"

Joe Donnelly shook his head from side to side. "I doubt it. Most of the people we all knew a year ago are either missing or dead. But I've known this man for a long time, and he'll do a great job until we can get the country back on its feet and hold regular elections."

"I understand, sir. What is his name, Mr. President?"

Joe Donnelly hesitated for just a moment. "His name is Jared Thompson."

The general nodded to the colonel. "Did you get that, Colonel Frank?"

The colonel nodded. "Yes, sir. We'll see that he's given a proper greeting in accordance with his high office. Then we'll take him immediately to the conference room where the president can confer with him. If that's what you want, sir."

The president smiled. "That'll be fine, colonel. I'll be waiting for him. Please make sure there's a hot meal with the proper wine."

The colonel glanced over at his general and then back at the president. "The proper wine, sir?"

The president seemed perturbed by the question. "Yes, you do know what wine is don't you?"

The colonel nodded in military fashion. "Absolutely, sir. It'll be done, Mr. President!"

Joe Donnelly was enjoying the office of president, and he was just getting started. "See to it that you do, colonel."

And then the president stood to his feet, the chair scraping against the tile floor. "This meeting is over gentlemen. I'm off to take a nap before dinner is served. See that I'm not disturbed."

The rest of the people in the room rose up and stood at attention as the president walked out of the room. When the door closed behind him, General MacDermid turned and looked at his exec. "Well, Colonel Frank, I'm convinced. What about you?"

The colonel smiled. "I was hoping you'd say that, sir. I'll get General Branch on the horn and start the ball rolling." The two officers walked out of the room, each with their own missions to accomplish.

CHAPTER 18

The New Vice President Arrives!

"THE LEAR JET IS LANDING NOW, SIR. WE'LL BE WITH YOU in just a few minutes." Colonel Frank was about fifty years old. His hair was half-gray, but it made him look distinguished. He replaced the handset to the radio back in its place. Then he watched as the two F18s circled overhead on CAP and the Lear jet descended down into the glide slope. Five minutes later the door to the jet opened and the new VP walked out and into the blazing hot Texas sun. The vice president wore an immaculate grey suit with a red power tie. There were dark sunglasses on his head and he carried a cane in his right hand. He was helped down the steps by an aid. The colonel met him at the foot of the stairway. He saluted sharply, but the Blind Man didn't return it.

"Welcome to Dyess Air Force Base, Mr. Vice President! The president is waiting for you." The Vice President didn't say anything. He just turned toward the voice and his aid led him after the colonel. They got into the same limo that had transported the president the day before and drove to the conference room. The president was already there and seated at the head of the table. He stood to his feet when the VP walked into the room.

"Jared, it's so good to see you. I hope your flight was good."

The Blind Man nodded. "It was well ... all things considered."

The president hesitated and looked at his new VP with a questioning stare. Jared Thompson leaned in close as they shook hands and whispered something into the president's ear. The president pasted on a smile.

"Won't you sit down beside me here, Mr. Vice President?"

The Blind Man sat down with the help of his aid, and then everyone else sat down as well. There was a dignified and official air to the room, and all fifteen chairs were once again filled with high-ranking officers from the air force, army, marines and the navy. They had flown in from existing bases and ships from all over the country for this very meeting.

"Well now. I'd like to introduce all of you to my new vice president, as soon as we get him sworn in. This is Jared Thompson."

General MacDermid stood and began to clap. The other generals, admirals and their aids rose and clapped as well. Finally, the president motioned for all of them to be seated.

"Let's get on with it, gentlemen. We have a country to run."

But before he could get started, the door opened and five men walked in. They wore dark suits with radio earpieces and took up flanking positions around the room. One of them spoke into his wrist. "Position is secured. Eagle One may enter."

President Donnelly rose to his feet. "What is going on here, general? Who are these men?"

General MacDermid smiled and rose to answer. "They are part of the president's secret service detail, Mr. Donnelly."

The president turned and looked over at the general. The look on his face was one of total befuddlement. But after a short moment it was replaced with anger. "You will address me as Mr. President! Is that clear, general!"

But the general just laughed, and this infuriated the president even more. He stomped his foot down hard and reasserted his dominance. "I said, general, you will call me Mr. President right now, or I will have you relieved of your command!"

Just then newly sworn-in President Townsend walked proudly into the conference room. At once, everyone inside rose and stood at the position of attention.

General MacDermid snapped to attention and turned to face Michael Townsend. "Good afternoon, Mr. President. We've been waiting for you."

Right behind President Townsend, General Rodney T. Branch strutted in, followed closely by Colonel MacPherson. Both wore full, army-dress uniforms. There were four stars on Uncle Rodney's collar.

"What the hell is going on here? Who is this man?"

Michael Townsend looked at Joe Donnelly and smiled. "You don't mean to tell me you don't recognize me, Joe? I guess it's been a few years since we've talked, but ... still. I'd think you'd remember a fellow cabinet member."

And then the color drained from Joseph Donnelly's face as he recognized the Secretary of Transportation. "But ... but ... you're dead."

President Townsend laughed out loud, followed by most people in the room. The Blind Man turned and looked at President Townsend and General Branch. An evil sneer formed on his lips.

"But, I was sworn into office first! It's too late! I'm already the president! You can't be president after I'm already president!"

President Townsend smiled and shook his head from side to side. "You were always such an ambitious and cowardly man, Joe." And then he looked over at General Branch. "Rodney, did you have this man sworn in as president of the United States?"

General Branch stepped forward. "I did, Mr. President."

"And who was the man who administered to Joe the oath of office? Was he a federal court judge?"

"No, Mr. President. The man who administered the oath was the president of the Iroquois county drama club." Uncle Rodney smiled. "But he was very convincing, sir. We all thought it was his best performance ever."

The president slapped Rodney on the back with glee. "And who was given the oath first, Joe Donnelly or myself?"

"You were, Mr. President. The swearing-in ceremony of Joseph Donnelly was just a sham. He was never the president, sir."

Then Uncle Rodney looked closer at the Blind Man and frowned. He suddenly went on full alert and lowered his center of gravity. The Blind Man reached his right hand into his pocket and ran toward President Townsend. The secret service detail was caught off guard, seeing a blind man run as though he could see. Jared Thompson pulled out the pearl-handled thirty-two caliber pistol and raised it to fire.

A loud boom rang out and then another and another. The secret service men cleared their coats and drew their pistols, but it was too late. By the time they were ready to shoot, the Blind Man's body was already bleeding on the floor and Uncle Rodney was holstering his forty-five. The new Chairman of the Joint Chiefs had just administered two to the chest and one to the head.

President Townsend was being ushered quickly out of the room by his secret service detail, but he violently shrugged them off. "Stand down, you fools, Can't you see the danger's gone now!" The president looked down at the body, bleeding on the floor in front of him. Then he looked back up at Uncle Rodney. And then he laughed nervously. "Well, hell, Rodney, looks like I made the right choice for my new Chairman of the Joint Chiefs."

Joseph Donnelly's legs gave out and he sank back down into his overstuffed chair. And then he lowered his head down into his hands and cried. "I'm not the president."

President Townsend smiled, but he couldn't totally conceal his sympathy. He turned to General MacDermid. "General, will you please place the VA Secretary under arrest, pending formal charges of treason? I'll let the military handle the tribunal."

Joseph Donnelly was taken into custody. His hands were cuffed behind his back and then he was led away, still crying as he walked. The president started to walk to the conference table, but General Branch stopped him.

"Mr. President. We have a big problem."

President Townsend stopped and turned. "What is it, Rodney?"

Rodney bent down to the floor and rolled over the dead man on the tile floor.

"This man is not Jared Thompson."

The Blind Man's Lair

JARED THOMPSON HAD WATCHED THE LEAR JET LAND ON THE TARMAC AT Dyess Air Force Base and watched as his double was led away, seeming with all the honor and pomp ascribed to a man of his high office. It was possible that his extra caution had been unnecessary. But still ... extra caution and even paranoia had kept Jared alive for most of his life. He should be getting a call from the new president any moment now. He would wait to make sure.

Preparing for War!

"WE NEED TO GET THE PRESIDENT OUT OF HERE AS SOON AS POSSIBLE! WE also need to scramble every jet you've got and prepare for attack!"

General Rodney T. Branch continued to bark out orders and all the generals and admirals around him rushed to carry them out as quickly as possible.

General MacDermid turned to Colonel Frank. "Get it done, colonel!"

Colonel Frank turned and rushed out of the room. Rodney called out to Admiral Fletcher who was standing nearby. "Admiral, how many planes can we get airborne in the next two hours?"

The admiral met his gaze and thought for a moment. "I'm not sure what you need. We can get everything in the air, but that doesn't mean they'll have the range you need. I need more details."

Both Admiral Fletcher and General MacDermid sat down at the conference table with the Chairman of the Joint Chiefs. "I need to know what our assets are and where they're located and I need to know right away."

The general nodded. "Sure, we can do that for you, but it'll take about fifteen minutes. We'll write it up and have it on your desk. But, General Branch, there is one problem."

Rodney looked over at General MacDermid and frowned. "What is it?"

The general looked down at the table and fidgeted with his hands. "We don't have much in the line of ground troops these days. Most of them are still overseas, and many of the ones that are left here in the states went home to help protect their families after the power went out."

General Branch nodded. "That's okay. Just include what you have in the asset list. I already have enough foot soldiers to do the job. But what we really need is air support."

Both the admiral and the general smiled broadly. "Now that, General Branch, isn't a problem. Between the air force and the navy, we can give you plenty of airpower, sir."

Just then a siren started to sound all across the base. General Branch looked at General MacDermid with questions in his eyes.

"It's an air raid siren, sir. We're about to be attacked."

Rodney clenched his teeth grimly. "Did you get the president out in time?"

The admiral nodded. "Yes, sir. He should be landing on the aircraft carrier in the gulf any minute now."

Then he turned back to the air force general. "General MacDermid. Did you get everything scrambled?"

"We're doing it now, sir. Everything will shortly be in the air that can be in the air."

Rodney smiled grimly. "Okay then. Let's get farther underground to the Combat Information Center and see how the battle is going."

General Masbruch Attacks

COLONEL MACPHERSON STOOD BESIDE GENERAL MASBRUCH INSIDE THE mobile command post. It was just a big semi trailer filled with comm gear with soldiers running back and forth, delivering messages and sending their radio traffic. It was far from state of the art, but it got the job done.

"We're attacking on three fronts right now general. We are looking good in Georgia and in Montana, but the attack on the West Virginia complex is not going well. There were more forces there than we'd been led to believe, and we're being pounded by F16s and Apache attack helicopters."

The general rubbed his temples with the first two fingers of both hands. "What about our air support?"

"Nothing yet, sir."

The general looked at him in disbelief. "Nothing? Are you sure?"

Mac nodded. "Yes, general. I just got off the line with Colonel Branch, who is leading the ground assault. They're bogged down a mile from the complex and taking heavy losses from the air."

General Masbruch slammed his fist down on the table. A few soldiers looked up, but then quickly went back to work. "Get General Branch on the phone right now!"

Mac nodded and pulled out his satphone. "I'll do my best, general."

Colonel Branch - Spruce Mountain, West Virginia

"JEREMY, GET YOUR HEAD DOWN! DON'T TAKE SO MANY CHANCES, SON!"

Corporal Jeremy Branch looked over at his father and tried to smile. "That's a little bit like the pot calling the kettle black isn't it? I mean look at you, Dad. You keep running back and forth out in the open. There's a bullet hole in your boonie hat and another on your sleeve."

Dan Branch hunkered down behind an oak tree as more bullets ripped the ground around them. They were taking intense sniper fire, not to mention the fire from the air was beginning to intensify.

"I thought Uncle Rodney was going to send us some air support, Dad. But I don't see any planes up there except the ones shooting at us."

Dan nodded in agreement. They were being systematically exterminated on this ridge, and if they didn't take control of the air soon, they'd all be dead.

"Get General Masbruch on the line. We're going to have to pull back and regroup or else none of us will be left alive for the final assault on the complex."

Jeremy nodded and pulled out the handset to relay the information.

"Jason! Prepare the men to pull back. Pass it on down the line! Every other man will pull back one hundred yards at exactly 0937 hours. Then at 0945 the remainder of our forces will pull back. Make sure no one is left behind."

Jeremy looked over at his dad frantically. "Dad, I can't get through on the radio. I think we're being jammed or something."

Colonel Branch watched as another of his men went down as an Apache gunship made another pass with his M230 chain gun. Four more men were cut to pieces, their bodies shredded and their blood splattered against the trees around them. He yelled at the others out of desperation. "I said stay down! Get behind a big tree until we move out!"

Lieutenant Jason Little moved away quickly down the line, passing the word to everyone. But unknown to Colonel Branch, he would never make it all the way and many of his men would be left behind to die on the ridge. The .308 sniper bullet reached out and found its mark in the center of Jason's forehead, ripping away the top half of his skull. It was a painless end to an otherwise honorable and successful life. His big body went down hard onto the broken shale of the West Virginia mountain-side, his blood seeping out into the rich, dark humus and brown leaves of the woods.

Donny's Last Charge

A HALF A MILE AWAY, ON THE NEXT RIDGE OVER, SERGEANT DONNY

Brewster and his breaching force of 75 men didn't get the order to retreat. Some of his men carried M4s with plenty of grenades, while others had some variation of the older M16s. A few had simple AR15s, but none of them were prepared to take out Apache attack helicopters. The master plan put forth by General Branch had counted on overwhelming air superiority, so they hadn't bothered with carrying many heavy Stinger missiles with them. Their mission depended on speed, but they weren't going anywhere until their air support arrived.

"Get Colonel Branch on the line. We need to find out what's going on!" Donny could barely hear individual voices with all the sounds of gun fire and rockets going off all around him. He looked over at the radio man and saw the gaping hole on the left side of his chest. He was just now in the final stages of bleeding out. Donny grabbed the handset but the cord was no longer attached and half the radio had been blown away.

"Damn!" He looked around him and saw that a third of his men were dead or wounded. They would not survive if he didn't do something and fast. He grabbed the nearest living corporal and yelled at him.

"We're going to attack!"

Corporal Eric Olsen looked at him like he was crazy. "Are ya outta yer cotton-pickin' mind! Were gonna be kilt!"

Donny grabbed him by the shirt and pulled him in closer."You're already being killed! Besides, you're already ugly as a fish and half your teeth are gone. Do you wanna live forever that way? I said we're going to attack and we're going to do it right away. These are snipers and plenty of them. The longer we stay here the more of us will die." He looked out at the ones closest to him. "Everyone! Fix bayonets! We need to get in as close as we can as fast as we can. They'll have flank security with automatic weapons and claymore mines, so we're going to head straight down the gullet into the center of their line. We're going downhill, so we'll have the benefit of speed. Once we get inside their line we kill them all!"

He pushed Corporal Olson away, picked up a handful of mud and blood and smeared it on his cheeks. "Corporal Olson, you lead them down the left and I'll take the right. We don't stop until they're all dead!"

Corporal Olson looked down the hillside at the scattered dead and dying. He suddenly thought of his corn crop back in Georgia and wondered if it would ever get picked. And then he thought *What the hell. I'm already 55 years old. Do I want to live forever? Besides, if ya gotta go; this isn't such a bad death.* He took out a tub of Redman and quickly stuffed a pinch into his left cheek. And then he screamed and raised his carbine up over his head.

Donny laughed out loud and screamed as well. Soon all his men were screaming and shaking their weapons over their heads. Two more men went down from sniper fire, and then Donny headed down the hill, screaming like a maniac, thinking of Nurse Vanderboeg and her beautiful blonde hair, locks that he would never again touch.

CHAPTER 19

Inside the Blind Man's Lair

JARED THOMPSON LOOKED OUT AT THE SCREEN IN FRONT OF him. It was all state of the art. He knew exactly who was dying and who was living, and, so far, he was winning this battle. His air force had already destroyed the runways at Dyess air base in a surprise attack along with half the buildings. He'd wanted to send another sortie to finish them off, but had been surprised to learn that the Shadow Militia ground forces were attacking all three of his major bases in Georgia and Montana and here in West Virginia. This had forced him to conserve his airpower and pull it back to protect his own position as well.

But now he was making General Branch pay for his arrogance. Unfortunately, he didn't even know where the general was right now. If he had known, he would have sent one of his precious nukes to take him out, just out of spite. His original plan had been to meet the general face to face, to talk to him first, and then put a bullet in his head so he could watch the look of despair on his face and then to slowly savor the flow of his blood into the ground. But ... to the general's credit, he'd been a worthy adversary, and so, Jared would just have to kill him at a distance, in a more impersonal way. So be it. Wasn't it General Eisenhower who'd said that even the best war plans only survived the first shot. He would have to improvise and adapt.

By now the new president, Michael Townsend, would already be dead, killed by Jared's own stunt-double, assassin. He was proud of that one. As soon as he'd found out about the general's plans to reinstate the presidency, he'd been one step ahead of General Branch all the way. Jared liked dangling carrots in front of his adversaries, making them think they were winning, when, in reality, they'd never had much hope, even from the beginning.

No, this rebellion that the Shadow Militia had formed was now being systematically destroyed. They were leaderless and in disarray. He'd always wanted to bring the Shadow Militia out of hiding, knowing intuitively that he had them outmanned and outgunned. The only chink in his armor had been the sudden alliance with Dyess Air Force Base in Texas. He hated Texas. But now that he'd destroyed their airpower while still in their hangers, it was all done except the mopping up.

Jared looked back up on the TV screen above him. Now, it was time to shift some of his airpower to Montana and Georgia to finish destroying the attacking ground forces of the Shadow Militia. He reached down to move the mouse and press a button, but a sudden jolt threw him off his feet and he landed onto the couch several feet away. The explosion had rocked his facility even two-hundred feet down inside the earth. The wine glass on the mahogany table top spilled onto the floor and shattered.

He yelled at the top of his lungs. "What is going on out there?"

His assistant rushed into the room. "I don't know, sir."

"Well ... find out and find out now!"

Another explosion rocked the room and Jared was thrown to his knees. He got up slowly and leaned against the corinthian leather of the couch. He looked up at the state of the art computer screen and watched it flicker off and on several times. It no longer seemed to be updating in real time.

Another explosion, this one bigger than the first two rocked the room and Jared Thompson stayed on his knees. All he could think of was *Damn you Rodney Branch! I'm going to kill you if it's the last thing I do!*

Dyess Air Force Base, Texas

GENERAL MACDERMID RELAYED THE NEW INFORMATION QUICKLY TO HIS new Chairman of the Joint Chiefs, who was personally coordinating every detail of this attack. "We have direct hits with all the cruise missiles, General Branch. Their command and control is now severely damaged."

Uncle Rodney nodded his head in satisfaction. "Good. Now release the heavy bombers. I want Spruce Mountain leveled. Bury the Blind Man in his own personal tomb!"

General MacDermid passed down the orders and reported back. "The B1s and B52s are almost there, sir. The B52s will carpet the surrounding area with conventional 500-pound bombs. Each B52 has a payload of up to 70,000 pounds. They're flying out of Barksdale in Louisiana, sir. The BONEs are from here. The BONEs will drop GBU-37 laser-guided, bunker-busting bombs that can possibly collapse the concrete down on their heads. "

General Branch frowned. "What do you mean, possibly?"

"Well, sir, they are 4,700 pound bombs that are designed to break through hardened targets. They're pretty standard so far as bunker busters go."

Uncle Rodney reached up to stroke his chin. "So, how do we know for sure they'll reach down into the Blind Man's operations center?"

General MacDermid looked over at Colonel Frank and hesitated. "Well, sir, I guess we don't really know for sure. We don't have the specs on his facility. We don't know for sure the thickness of the concrete or even how far down it's buried in the earth."

Rodney Branch walked over to the general and looked him square in the face. "This man has a knack for surviving. I want Jared Thompson's guts blown all over West Virginia. Ya got anything for the occasion? Something bigger?"

Colonel Frank tried to stifle a grin, but couldn't quite do it. General MacDermid still wasn't used to Rodney's methods or demeanor. When he spoke it was slowly and with proper enunciation.

"Well, sir ..." But he hesitated. Rodney gave him an impatient look.

"Yes, general? You were saying?"

"Well, we do have Big BLU."

Rodney nodded. "And what is that exactly?"

"Big BLU is, more specifically, the GBU-57A/B Massive Ordnance Penetrator bomb, sir. They're 30,000 pounds a piece and can penetrate up to 200 feet of dirt and 20 feet of concrete."

Rodney smiled like a kid in a candy shop. "So, how many do you think we'll need?"

This was the first time General MacDermid laughed today. "Well, general, I think one should do it. We certainly don't want to blast clean on through to China."

General Branch nodded. "Ya know boys, what good are toys if you can't take 'em out and play with 'em once in a while."

He turned away and then back again. "Let's do it."

"Are you sure, sir?"

Now it was Rodney's turn to laugh. "Yer damn right I'm sure. Never underestimate the Blind Man, general. Today ... it's time to go strong or stay home!"

Rodney's smile was bigger than ever. "Give the order, General MacDermid."

DONNY BREWSTER WAS STILL SCREAMING WHEN HE REACHED THE FIRST sniper,who was proned out in a slit trench with rocks mounded up in front of him. The man tried to get up and turn his rifle toward Donny, but was quickly cut down with two, three-round bursts from Donny's M4 carbine. Donny ran to the next trench, firing his carbine as he moved, killing another and then another. By now other Shadow Militia soldiers had caught up with him and were killing enemy snipers of their own. Donny couldn't believe how many there were, but he just kept killing as quickly and efficiently as he could.

A sniper came up behind him and leveled his rifle before firing. The .308 round tore into Donny's left arm, spinning him around and throwing him to the ground. The enemy soldier rushed forward and lined up for the killing shot. Corporal Olson came out of nowhere, thrusting his bayonet into the man's back with a loud scream. He jerked back hard and pulled out the knife before thrusting it in again and again and again, until the man finally dropped to the ground, squirming just for a few seconds before bleeding out on the dirt and shale.

Donny jumped to his feet, blood dripping from the wound in his arm, but he kept moving forward. "Go men! Go! Kill them all!"

Two minutes later, totally spent, like a fired cartridge, Donny collapsed onto the leaves and stopped moving. The shooting had died down now, but Donny Brewster no longer had the strength to keep going. Corporal Olson hurried up close and plopped himself down on the ground beside him. He looked at the bleeding arm and then at Donny's pale skin and swore out loud to himself.

"Ya done got shot, Donny. Ya crazy son of a bitch!"

Sergeant Brewster lay back on the leaves, his mind floating in and out of consciousness. Corporal Olson worked quickly to apply the tourniquet, hoping above hope that he was in time. Donny reached up with his right hand and stroked Eric's dirty, greasy hair softly and tenderly.

"Thank you, Nurse Vanderboeg. I love you. I will never leave you again."

Eric threw back his head and laughed out loud. "Crazy bastard. I love ya too, sergeant, but don't be expectin' a wet, sloppy kiss from me!"

Suddenly, he heard the heavy bombers overhead, and the sound of bombs falling. The massive explosions began to erupt close to the underground complex. Corporal Olson yelled as loud as he could. "Take cova' men!"

And then he drug Donny's body down into a slit trench to wait out the pounding.

CHAPTER 20

The Blind Man's Concern

TWO HUNDRED FEET BELOW THE SURFACE OF THE MOUNTAIN, Jared Thompson began to realize that everything wasn't going exactly as he'd planned. Where was all this firepower coming from? He'd neutralized the air base at Dyess. He'd assassinated the new president. This should not be happening! But it was. The computer screen on the wall flickered off and on again. He cursed below his breath. Then he felt the concussion of 500-pound bombs as they detonated on the surface above. There were dozens of them going off every few seconds or so. And then the bunker busters began to hit, maybe a dozen in all. Suddenly, he started to doubt the impregnability of his underground fortress.

After a few, quick moments of reflection, in the mindless dizziness of the Blind Man's rage, Jared Thompson started to understand. He had not beaten General Rodney T. Branch. He had, indeed, underestimated his enemy again. He had killed Sammy Thurmond ... his right-hand man. Sammy Thurmond was dead and could not save him. But, more importantly, General Branch was alive! The Shadow Militia was now attacking all his installations and in great force, backed up by massive airpower, and he had no idea where it was coming from. All his intel, from day one, had told him that the Shadow Militia had very little airpower. That was their weakness, and, therefore, that was Jared's big advantage.

The Blind Man swore out loud over and over again. He'd been planning this attack his whole adult life. He was born to rule! His mind and will were superior to any other. It would be a travesty if he could not rule unopposed. Another bunker buster went off and shook the room around him. Pieces of drywall dust fell down upon the Blind Man, and he tried to brush it off his Armani suit, but to no avail. And then he thought to himself, *My wine cellar. What is happening to my wine cellar?* He called out to his assistant over and over again, but the man was already lying on the floor, dead and motionless in the next room.

And then, after all these years of success, of winning every battle, after all these years of scheming, killing and controlling those around him ... it suddenly occurred to Jared that ... control was an illusion.

Colonel Branch Gets Through

"COLONEL BRANCH! THE RADIOS ARE WORKING AGAIN! I HAVE GENERAL Masbruch on the line, sir. He wants to talk to you."

Dan walked over and grabbed the handset. He could hear the pounding of the 500-pound bombs falling onto the Blind Man's underground complex. "Yes, general."

"Dan, I need you and your men to fall back. Fall back as quickly as you can!"

Dan shook his head back and forth without thinking. "I don't understand, sir. Why should we fall back? As soon as these bombs let up we're going in for the final ground assault as planned. We need to get into position."

But General Masbruch laughed nervously on the other end of the line. "No, colonel.

I am ordering you to retreat several hundred yards and stand by for further orders. Get up high where you can see, and then observe and report back to me."

Dan hesitated, He looked over at his son, Jeremy, just a few feet away. "Yes, sir. We are to fall back and watch. Anything else, sir?"

There was a moment of silence. "Well, Dan, you might want to tell all your men to plug their ears. Just watch the show, Dan. You're going to love it. Courtesy of General Rodney T. Branch."

"Yes, sir. We will comply immediately." And then he turned to his right and looked over at his son, Jeremy.

"What's wrong, dad?"

Dan Branch smiled. "He says Uncle Rodney has a surprise for us, and that we should plug our ears."

Jeremy looked out past the ridge, then back at his father nervously. "Dad, is he going to nuke them?"

Dan shook his head, "I don't know, son. But let's get back as far as we can just in case. You know your Uncle Rodney. He tends to get a little excited sometimes."

Colonel Branch turned to his men and began barking out orders, and soon they were all retreating off the ridge.

Desperation Sets In

JARED THOMPSON WAS NOT A GOOD LOSER, BUT THAT WASN'T TOTALLY his fault. After all, he'd had very little practice at losing, and it was not something he'd set out to excel at in the first place. So, it was no surprise that, when the Blind Man realized he'd been beaten, that he would take it poorly.

Jared looked up at the computer screen hanging by its wires on one end, protruding out the wall. He looked around him at his corinthian leather couch, covered in plaster and debris from the ceiling, and he wondered to himself *How did this happen?* But, to be quite frank; it really didn't matter anymore. It wasn't like a football game where you could blame the referees, especially not when you ran a totalitarian organization.

The bombs had appeared to stop falling up top, but that gave him little consolation. Most of his people had deserted him or been killed, and it was then, that Jared realized that he was almost useless without other people to do his bidding. He wanted to escape from this mess, but, he didn't know how to do it. Normally he would just order someone to take him away, but ... there was no one left to order around.

Jared looked at the empty bottle of wine on the carpeted floor beneath his feet. He bent down to pick it up. He read the label out loud. Domaine Leflaive Bâtard-Montrachet Grand Cru Chardonnay. It had been bottled in 2015. That had been a very good year for wine and for him personally. It was a white chardonnay out of Burgundy, France. It certainly wasn't the best of wines, but it was good for everyday. If memory served him correctly he'd bought several cases at an auction for only five-hundred dollars per bottle. He tossed the bottle back onto the dirty carpet.

First, General Branch had destroyed his palatial bunker in Pennsylvania, and now ... this.

Jared Thompson had no way to escape, no place to go if he did escape, and ... quite frankly ... not a whole lot left to live for. He'd wanted to meet Rodney Branch, but ... not as a vanquished foe, but, rather, as the glorious victor. But now ... what would happen to him? They wouldn't let him go, probably wouldn't even let him live, and, if they did ... he would be in prison, surrounded by common criminals. That was beneath him.

To go on living in a world that he did not control was ... unsupportable. He'd made his decision.

Jared moved over to what was left of his control station. Auxiliary power had kicked in shortly after the second wave of attacks, and the emergency klaxon was blaring away with the most annoying of sounds.

Thankfully, there were still lights on the control panel, which meant he could still do one more thing. He looked up at the dangling computer screen; it was dark and empty. He had no idea what was going on up at the surface, but this one thing he knew. They would be coming for him soon ... coming en masse, and ... there was one last gift he could give them. He just hoped that General Branch was up there, somewhere close enough to experience it. Jared had installed the twenty-kiloton atomic warhead device last year, just in case something like this happened. Jared prided himself in foresight, among other things.

The Blind Man punched several keys on the keyboard. The control panel screen hadn't broken, so it was easy enough to see what he was doing. The computer asked for his confirmation keycode. He took off his Rolex watch and smashed it on the table in front of him. The parts sprayed out into the room. Jared picked up the back plate; it was solid gold of course. He looked at the engraved numbers and smiled. Yes, there were always options to those who took the time to think ahead.

Quickly, he punched in the numbers and pressed "enter."

The countdown started.

Dyess Air Force Base, Texas

"So what's happening in Georgia?"

Colonel Frank smiled and gave General Branch the good news. "The fighters from the USS Ronald Reagan reached the battle and have turned the tide. We enjoy air superiority on that battlefield, and have commenced pounding the Blind Man's ground forces. It'll all be over in Georgia soon, sir."

Rodney nodded his head. "Okay then. What's happening in Montana?"

This time General MacDermid answered. "It's pretty much the same story there, sir. Carrier planes from the Nimitz and Enterprise have established dominance and the enemy is surrendering en masse."

General MacDermid waited for Rodney to say something, but nothing came out, so he went on. "For all practical purposes, sir, the war is over. The Blind Man's done ... he's finished. We beat him, general!"

But General Branch still remained silent. Even after all these years, after all this killing, especially after all these years and all this killing ... he found no glory in war. "Make sure the president is kept informed, General MacDermid."

The colonel nodded."He's listening to everything on board the USS Ronald Reagan in real-time, sir."

Rodney looked up at the bank of computer screens on the wall in front of him. The art of war had changed so much in the decades since he'd last fought in Vietnam, but ... one thing hadn't changed, indeed, never would change. When it all came down to it, no matter how advanced the technology, it was always one man against one man. And the wisdom of Sun Tzu would remain forever timeless.

> *"If you know the enemy and know yourself, you need not fear the result of a hundred battles. If you know yourself but not the enemy, for every victory gained you will also suffer a defeat. If you know neither the enemy nor yourself, you will succumb in every battle."*

200 Feet Below West Virginia

JARED LOOKED AT THE DIGITAL TIMER IN FRONT OF HIM. HE COULD LITER-ally count off the seconds of his life, watch them tick on by like individual leaves falling from a tree or blades of grass blowing in the wind. In the end it was always about control. Control and power. Money bought him power, and power got him control. But now ... money was worthless. But still ... he had control of his own destiny.

And then he thought the most profound thing. How many people actually know the moment of their death. Only God knew that, and so, he thought to himself. *I am a god. I hold the power of life and death in my hand.* He glanced down at the digital clock and smiled. Forty-nine seconds to live. Forty-nine seconds to immortality. He hoped the general was close enough to watch it happen. He would love to meet him in hell.

Dyess Air Force Base, Texas

"BIG BLU IS ALMOST OVER THE TARGET NOW, SIR. HE'LL BE LAUNCHING any second now."

General Branch nodded his head in acknowledgment, but didn't make a move. He would not rest until he knew for sure that the Blind Man was dead.

And then he couldn't help but wonder if Dan and Jeremy were okay. Last he knew they were alive, but ... he needed to find out, but ... first, he had to focus on this one final task.

"Big BLU is on the way down, sir."

General Branch stood motionless, waiting patiently.

200 Feet Below West Virginia

THE DIGITAL READOUT SAID TEN SECONDS. THEY COULDN'T STOP HIM NOW. He had no regrets. This was it. This was the end. The last glorious ... And then he heard the impact of something very large and heavy above his head. It seemed to be traveling toward him as fast as gravity could take it.

He looked one final time at the clock. Two seconds. And then ...

One Mile West of Spruce Mountain

THE FORCE OF THE BLAST THREW DAN BRANCH TO THE GROUND AS IT shook the earth like an earthquake. His son, Jeremy, reached out to grab a nearby tree and managed to stay on his feet.

"What was that, dad?"

Dan quickly got to his feet and looked to the east. There, rising above the treeline was a very large cloud of dust and debris.

"Holy crap that was loud!"

Jeremy looked at his dad with fear in his young eyes. "Dad, is that a nuke? Are we all going to die now?"

Dan searched back in time to Pennsylvania, to the day when he and Donny Brewster had watched the malevolent mushroom cloud form over the Blind Man's underground headquarters after Uncle Rodney has used his one and only nuke. He calmed his son's fears.

"No, I don't think, so son. This is different than the nuke I saw from ten miles out with Donny." And then he thought to himself before continuing. "It's big though. No doubt about that. I didn't know we had non-nuclear bombs that big."

Jeremy walked up and stood beside his dad. "Where do you think Uncle Rodney got that thing?"

Dan Branch smiled. "Well, I'm pretty sure we can rule out eBay this time around." And then he looked at his son's face and laughed out loud. "Can you imagine the shipping costs alone on something that big?"

Debris suddenly started to fall around them, so the two men quickly took cover under a shale outcropping. The rest of Dan's command covered their heads and sought what cover they could as sticks and rocks and other objects rained down on them. A few minutes later the debris stopped as quickly as it had started. Dan looked around them and then stood up. Jeremy soon joined him, and they both began to walk, scanning the ground to make sure the men were okay.

"Hey dad! Look at this!"

Jeremy reached down to the ground and picked up a bottle. "Is this wine?"

Dan walked up and stood beside his son. "Yeah, I think so. It has a foreign language on it. What, maybe French or Italian or something?"

Jeremy nodded and handed the bottle to his dad who read it out loud. "It says Grand Vin de Château Latour, 1961." He thought for a moment. "I think that's French."

A few other men began gathering around them, brushing the dirt and falling dust off one another.

"Should we open it up, dad?"

Dan shrugged his shoulders. "I don't know. I guess you're old enough to have a drink now." He looked up into the sky. The dust cloud was starting to settle back down now. "I'm glad this thing didn't hit us in the head. I think these bottles usually have corks in them don't they?"

Dan looked around at the men gathering behind him. "Any of you men got a corkscrew?" But no one answered. He turned to Jeremy. "You got a canteen, son?"

Jeremy nodded and took the small pack off his back. Soon he held out the plastic, military-style canteen. Dan unscrewed the cap and then rapped the neck of the wine bottle against the shale outcropping. It took two tries, but the bottle broke and he carefully poured the wine into the canteen before tossing the bottle back onto the ground beside them. Dan raised the canteen up high over his head and laughed out loud. "To victory!"

The men behind him cheered as Dan took the first drink. He lowered the canteen and smacked his lips together. Then he handed the canteen to his son. "Well, it's not as good as Mocha flavored Frappuccino, but ... it's better than water I guess."

Jeremy took a sip and made a face. "This stuff sucks, dad. I'd rather have a Mountain Dew."

Dan shrugged and passed the canteen back to his men who were waiting for their turn. Dan climbed up onto the rock outcropping and was soon joined by Jeremy.

"That's okay. There's no accounting for bad tastes, I suppose." And then he looked around at the wooded hillside and thought to himself. *I bet this place is awful pretty when people aren't blowing it all up.*

Just then a captain ran up to the rock. "Colonel Branch, my men need to know what to do. Are we going to attack now?"

Dan looked over at Jeremy and laughed. Then he looked down the mountainside at the giant crater left by Big BLU. "Captain, if you and your men want to attack, then go right ahead, but Jeremy and I are gonna have some lunch."

The captain looked confused, but didn't say anything right away. Then he looked at the giant hole in the ground and turned to walk away. "I guess we'll have lunch too, sir."

Dan reached over and put his right arm around his son. He squeezed it hard and then let up. "Well, son. What'd'ya say we pack things up here and head on back to Iroquois?"

Jeremy smiled and then wiped the dust away from his eyes so he could see better. "Yeah, that's a good idea." And then a thought came to him and he laughed.

"What's so funny?"

"I was just thinking, well, at least we won't have to bury the Blind Man. There's nothing left of him."

Dan nodded his head. "I suppose you're right, son."

And then a bright, red cardinal landed on a tree limb just a few yards away. Dan looked at it and smiled.

"Let's go home, son."

EPILOGUE

PRESIDENT **M**ICHAEL **T**OWNSEND STOOD BEHIND THE PODIUM on the flight deck of the aircraft carrier, USS Ronald Reagan. The USS Reagan was the ninth supercarrier of the Nimitz class to be built, and, prior to the fall, operated out of Japan. However, after the global collapse, all military personnel were eventually called home to defend America's own borders and to deter other nation's from attacking the crippled once-superpower.

The nuclear-powered aircraft carrier was a big ship by anyone's standards, almost 1,100 feet long, with 3,200 people on board to serve her. She was capable of launching ninety-plus aircraft from her decks, and remained one of the mightiest war machines ever built, especially now, in a world where most countries couldn't even power an electric light bulb.

"We are here today to honor both the living and the dead, the heroes of renown, those who fought and lived, as well as those who fought and made the supreme sacrifice to their nation.

"I feel it's only fitting to award that honor on the deck of the USS Reagan, on the deck of the ship which launched the final sortie of the last battle of that great war."

He paused long enough to look around. All the key players were there. General MacDermid and Admiral Fletcher were seated off to one side. The general was now the new Chairman of the Joint Chiefs, while the admiral had been promoted to the president's cabinet as the Secretary of Defense. The new head of the NSA, Jeff Arnett, sat beside them. He was much happier since moving out of Uncle Rodney's pole barn.

Seated to the left of the president in the front row were Jackie and Dan Branch. Jackie held the new baby, a healthy boy who rested happily against her chest as she listened. Dan had a harder time, holding down baby Donna who was now a toddler and always trying to get down to play on the flight deck. Jeremy sat beside Dan. He had joined the US Marines and was now in his dress blues. Jeremy had received a battlefield commission and was now the youngest lieutenant in the US military.

Seated next to Jeremy was General Masbruch, who had stayed in the regular army for another three months until moving back home, south of the Mason-Dixon line. He was retired now and in a hurry to get back home to his vegetable garden.

Sparky Fillmore, the old man who'd walked from western Kansas to Davenport, Iowa in response to God's call, was seated in the third row beside his wife, Edna. Sparky's wife still had trouble believing that he'd traveled all that way just to vouch for the Shadow Militia on that first day with General MacDermid, but ... without him there, the entire course of history would have changed, and Jared Thompson would now be in control of the entire United States.

Sergeant Donny Brewster had reluctantly accepted a commission as a Captain in the Marine Corps, heading up the newly reformed sniper training school. He'd been a sergeant for so long, that the idea of people saluting him seemed too bizarre. But he was adjusting to it. His left arm still gave him trouble when the weather changed, but it had healed up well under the tender loving care of Lisa Vanderboeg. They'd been married now for six months and she was pregnant with their first child, a child who would be born in a free America.

Colonel Roger "Ranger" MacPherson, the Executive Officer and co-creator of the Shadow Militia, now wore three stars on his collar and was helping to rebuild the army after so many in America had died. It was indeed a daunting task.

Seated beside Mac was Uncle Rodney. He now wore a pair of clean blue jeans and a red, flannel shirt. The president's staff had tried to get him to dress up in his uniform, but Rodney had told them in no uncertain terms to bugger off. General Branch had stayed in the army long enough to ensure the rebuilding of the military was on track, before finally bowing out and returning to Iroquois county. At first he'd declined the president's request to attend this ceremony, but President Townshend was every bit as bull-headed as Rodney. When Marine One had landed in Rodney's front yard yesterday, he just hadn't had the heart to tell the man no. After all, both of them respected each other, and, to some extent, had fought a war together.

"And now, let us get to the heart of the matter. America would not be free without the sacrifice of an outfit called The Shadow Militia. Prior to the collapse, the FBI would have arrested this man." He nodded over at Uncle Rodney, who just smiled. "However, fate, it seems, is not without a sense of irony, because today, I am here to bestow honor on the very outfit that, in a more civilized time, would have been considered an enemy of the state." He paused and looked again over at Rodney.

"Rodney T. Branch, commanding general of the Shadow Militia. Will you please step forward."

Rodney stood to attention, did a perfect left face and marched to the podium. He stood in front of his president quietly. And President Townsend surprised the old man by snapping to attention and rendering him a perfect, military salute. Tears welled in Rodney's eyes, but he held them at bay behind dams of stoicism. Rodney returned the salute and the president quickly cut away as did Rodney.

"Thank you so much, my friend. America can never repay you enough."

Rodney said nothing. He just nodded in reply.

President Townsend turned slightly and spoke into the microphone. "It is with great honor and humility that I do hereby award to the commanding general of the Shadow Militia, this Presidential Unit Citation for displaying overwhelming gallantry, determination, and esprit de corps in accomplishing its mission under extremely difficult and hazardous conditions. When America was down, the Shadow Militia was at its best, and you defended us all when we could not."

President Townsend shook Rodney's hand and then pinned the ribbon to his chest. Afterwards, he gave him an engraved plaque. Rodney accepted it, noting that it felt heavy in his hand.

And then the president moved back to the microphone and spoke again.

"Now, this next award is one that I didn't tell General Branch about, simply because I feared he wouldn't show up to accept it. However, I would be derelict as president if I did not recognize the general for his extreme sacrifice both in and out of uniform, because without him, we wouldn't be standing here today."

The president reached under the podium and pulled out a wooden box, ornately carved and inlaid with gold. He set the box on top of the podium and opened it up. Ceremoniously, he lifted the blue ribbon out of the box, a metal star hung from it with an eagle just above the star. Uncle Rodney saw it and his knees suddenly went weak, but he quickly steeled himself and remained at attention.

"For conspicuous gallantry and intrepidity at the risk of life above and beyond the call of duty, I award General Rodney T. Branch the Medal of Honor."

He stepped forward and draped the ribbon over Rodney's neck. Rodney didn't move. He didn't say anything.

"Would you like to say a few words, Rodney?"

Uncle Rodney looked down for a moment and then back up again. Finally, he nodded and stepped up to the microphone. He looked out at the thousand or so sailors, marines and soldiers before him and cleared his throat.

"Thank you. Normally I don't tolerate this kind of showboating, but ... since the president is ordering me, I suppose I should put up with it." There was a ripple of laughter through the crowd, and the president himself couldn't help but smile.

"Listen folks ... I'm not a hero. I'm just someone who saw a need and filled the gap. That's all. The Shadow Militia was made up of Americans, just like you and me, and America has always been filled with heroes, so, it's no surprise that this unit is being honored today."

He looked down again at the plaque in his hand. "Some people would say that I was the leader of the Shadow Militia, but ... the truth is, when I thought I was leading them ... they were really leading me. In all, just over the past year alone, ten-thousand Shadow Militia soldiers died in defense of our country. But it wasn't me who died. It wasn't me who marched in the mud, killed the enemy, and stood neck-deep in blood, watching my fellow soldiers die around me." He looked out at his fellow warriors and his face grew stern.

"I was just the general."

And then a tear finally escaped the dam and trickled down his cheek. "I accept these awards, but only in the name of the people who really earned them. Men like Lieutenant Harold Steffens, who, at the Battle of Iroquois, dove his plane into two-hundred enemy soldiers, thereby sacrificing himself but winning the battle. Harold was 82 years old at the time. He didn't have to fight, but he wanted to, was eager to. And it was bravery from men like him that won this war. A general can only issue orders, but ... it's the officers and noncoms under him that carry them out, and it's the privates and lance corporals and airmen and sailors who do most of the fighting and dying."

He looked out over the crowd and then over at President Townsend. "Mr. President, I accept this honor on behalf of all the men and women who died under my command in service to our country. God bless their souls ... and God bless America."

With that, the soldiers and sailors stood to their feet and began clapping and cheering as loudly as they could. The applause lasted for five minutes until, finally, the president led Rodney back to his seat of honor and then closed out the ceremony.

THAT WAS THE LAST TIME RODNEY BRANCH SPOKE IN PUBLIC. HE RETURNED to private life in what was left of Iroquois county and started to rebuild. Uncle

Rodney lived another fifteen years after that, adapting to civilian life as best he could. His friends visited him often, and he enjoyed their company, but he was always equally glad to see them go, so he could get back to his privacy.

Dan and Jackie, along with baby Donna and their three children that followed, built a house closeby. Rodney worked hard at being a good grandfather, just like he'd promised he would. But most of the time, he took walks in the woods, went fishing at the Mill Pond, or just sat on his porch watching his bird feeder.

And when he died, it was with the smell of sulphur on his breath, and the roar of battle in his ears. He was a warrior until the end.

Twenty Years Later

JACKIE BRANCH STOOD OVER UNCLE RODNEY'S GRAVE. IT HAD BEEN TWEN-ty years since his death, but she missed him now more than ever. She was now an old woman, and not a day went by when she didn't recall the words of Uncle Rodney when she'd first moved to Iroquois before the war.

He'd seen her as a potential threat and had asked her: "So, young lady. What's it going to take to move you from the liability column to the asset column?" In retrospect, she had been a liability, but he'd given her the benefit of the doubt and the respect she hadn't yet earned. In the end, she had become the warrior he'd always wanted her to be, and, in the process, they'd earned each other's undying respect and love.

She remembered their fishing trip and the little talk at the Mill Pond just after the battle for the Mackinaw Straits. She had asked him if they were all going to die, and his answer intrigued her to this day.

> _"Well, truth is Jackie, we all know we're going to die. That's a given. We don't know when and we don't know how. But ... maybe the more important thing is to pick a cause worth dying for._

> _"I spent my whole life getting ready for this final moment in the world's history. Most people have the luxury of growing up and falling in love, getting married and then they spend the rest of their lives creating beautiful memories for their kids and grand kids._

> _"That didn't happen to us, Jackie. For whatever reason, it just didn't happen to us._

> _"It would appear that our job is to reset society to its place of normalcy. Our job is to win this war, defeat the tyrant, and rebuild."_

And then Jackie had asked him what comes after that. His reply had been profound.

> _"I don't know, Jackie. By then I'll be dead and you'll be an old woman. I guess the only one who can answer that question is the baby in your arms and the one still growing in your womb. After all, they can only build on what we leave them. So ... let's leave them both the ability to choose a good life and the freedom to start over again."_

Jackie looked down at the granite headstone in front of her. There was a US flag stuck in the ground beside it. There were four stars on the stone with an engraving of the Medal of Honor.

And underneath the name 'General Rodney T. Branch" were the words:

God ... Family ... Country

Jackie turned to walk away, but she would be back tomorrow. This time Dan would come with her ... the walk would do him good.

Skip Coryell lives with his wife and children in Michigan. He works full time as a professional writer, and *The Blind Man's Rage* is his twelfth published book. He is an avid hunter and sportsman, a Marine Corps veteran, and a graduate of Cornerstone University. You can listen to Skip as he co-hosts the syndicated military talk radio show *Frontlines of Freedom* on www.frontlinesoffreedom.com. You can also hear his weekly podcast *The Home Defense Show* at www.homedefenseshow.com

For more details on Skip Coryell, or to contact him personally, go to his website at www.skipcoryell.com

Books by Skip Coryell

We Hold These Truths
Bond of Unseen Blood
Church and State
Blood in the Streets
Laughter and Tears
RKBA: Defending the Right to Keep and Bear Arms
Stalking Natalie
The God Virus
The Shadow Militia
The Saracen Tide
The Blind Man's Rage
Civilian Combat - The Concealed Carry Book